POPPY DAY
AND
BIRMINGHAM ROSE

Annie Murray comes originally from Berkshire, where she grew up over an antique shop. She studied at Oxford University and has had a variety of jobs, including in factories, on an Indian railway tour, and as a journalist and a nurse. Above all, she has always written. She lived for many years in Birmingham, where all her four children were born. She now lives with her family in Reading.

D1102537

Also by Annie Murray

Birmingham Friends
Birmingham Blitz
Orphan on Angel Street

Annie Murray

Poppy Day

and

Birmingham Rose

PAN BOOKS

Poppy Day first published 2000 by Macmillan and
simultaneously in paperback by Pan Books
Birmingham Rose first published 1995 by Pan Books

This omnibus edition published 2003 by Pan Books
an imprint of Pan Macmillan Ltd
Pan Macmillan, 20 New Wharf Road, London N1 9RR
Basingstoke and Oxford
Associated companies throughout the world
www.panmacmillan.com

ISBN 0 330 42093 3

A CIP catalogue record for this book is available from
the British Library.

Printed and bound in Great Britain by
Mackays of Chatham plc, Chatham, Kent

POPPY DAY

For Sam, my son.

Acknowledgements

My thanks to Colin Fox at Reading University who taught me far more about the First World War than could ever be encompassed by this book; to some of the many historians who have written on this period, especially Jay Winter, Denis Winter, Lyn MacDonald and to Terry Carter for his chronicling of the experiences of the Birmingham 'Pals' Battalions, the 14th, 15th and 16th Royal Warwickshire Battalions; as ever to Dr Carl Chinn at Birmingham University; to the Birmingham City Sound Archive and the Imperial War Museum; to my agent Darley Anderson and editor Suzanne Baboneau for their help in every way – I couldn't ask for better; to Marsha Hamilton for just being Marsha and putting up with me turning up now and then.

A special thank you and lots of love to my husband John, technical expert, cell mate and tolerant fellow traveller. xxx

Part I

One

On a freezing evening in March 1914, a young woman was walking through Deritend, the old iron and tin-smiths' district of Birmingham. Jessica Hart was dressed in the serviceable clothes and sturdy boots of a country girl and the bundle she carried, wrapped in a bright patchwork quilt, was hugged close to her as if for comfort. She was looking fearfully about her, longing to see a friendly face, but no one among the drab crowds trudging home from factories and shops even troubled to look at her.

Evening seemed to come too early to these dark streets. At home, dusk would only just be edging across the fields, now green with spring shoots, whereas here, whichever way she looked the light was obscured by buildings, their smoking chimneys pouring out filth which begrimed every roof, every wall and window. A hard lump rose in Jess's throat. The city was a noisy, stinking place.

''Scuse me!' She hurried towards a bobby, strolling his beat along the main road, known as Digbeth. 'Can yer direct me? I want to go to Allison Street.'

The policeman saw a pretty face looking out from under a snug black hat with a white band, wisps of brown hair visible round it. Even in the murky light he could see her rosy complexion which confirmed her as a stranger to the city as much as the desperate look in her eyes. And she was so sweet he'd have liked to kiss her.

'You've passed it already. Tell yer what – where is it yer want exactly? I'll take yer along.'

Soon they turned off the main road and Jess was relieved to be away from the clashing of hooves and loud rattle of the trams, but the sight of this mean-looking side street made her heart sink even further. Is this really where they live? she thought. But what shall I do if they've moved on and no one knows where they've gone? Her mind played with every possibility of disaster. The thought of spending the night wandering these terrifying streets and alleys was more than she could stand.

'Fifty-three, did yer say?' Sensing her agitation he led her along the regiment of blackened dwellings, speaking to her as if she were a child. 'Not far – see – yer was nearly there . . .'

The houses all opened directly on to the pavement. Jess saw someone watching her from behind one of the windows opposite, their breath misting the pane.

'I'll just see yer awright.' The policeman stood back as Jess put her bundle on the step and raised a trembling arm to knock.

In a moment the door opened a little way and the scrawny face and shoulders of a young woman about the same age as herself appeared.

'Yes? What d'yer want?'

'I—' Jess's throat was dry. She could manage barely more than a whisper. 'Are you Polly?'

The girl scowled, pulling the door even closer to her chest as if prepared to slam it shut.

'Why? Who're you then? – Mom!' she called over her shoulder. 'There's some wench 'ere . . .'

'Is your mother Olive?'

This provoked a look of even greater suspicion from the girl, but the door was yanked out of her hand and an older woman pushed herself into view. Her hair was scraped severely back from a tough, worn-looking face and there was a large mole at the top of her right cheek, close to the outer corner of her eye.

'What's going on?'

Jess felt herself recoil. It was as she most feared. They'd gone. This hard-faced woman couldn't be her! And yet that mark on her cheek, the voice ... 'Olive? Olive Beeston?'

The woman's eyes jerked back and forth between her and the young policeman. 'Who are you?'

'I'm Jess Hart – Louisa's girl.' As she spoke her voice cracked under the pressure of suppressed tears. 'Only, if the Beestons don't live 'ere any more can yer tell me where they went? I must find them 'cause I've nowhere else to go! Olive Beeston's my auntie.'

'Jess! Mom, it's little Jess!' the girl shrieked.

Her mother stared, taking in the dark eyes, the curvaceous shape of the young woman in front of her, then sunk down on the step, leaning limply against the door jamb, her face drained of colour.

For a few moments Olive Beeston could only manage a series of groggy sounds. She sat forward, head down between her knees. Another girl appeared at the door and stood staring.

'She get like this often, does she?' the policeman said.

'No – never!' Polly was biting at the end of her thumb as she stared at her mother.

After a moment Olive began to straighten up again, taking deep breaths.

'She looks better,' Jess said. 'She is my auntie then?'

Polly nodded.

Jess thanked the policeman and when he'd gone, Olive Beeston managed to sit up properly and look at her.

'What's going on, Mom?' Polly's voice was gentler now. She looked up at her sister's frightened face. 'I don't know what's come over 'er, Sis. Look – 'er's shaking like a leaf!'

'I'll be awright, stop mithering.' Olive tried to stand up but failed, and sank back on to the step. Glancing across the road she said, 'I'm giving that nosey old bag o'bones over there summat to chew on awright.' She looked up into Jess's face and after a moment the tension in it was replaced by a poignant kind of pleasure.

'So – Louisa's Jessica. God in 'eaven – I never thought you'd grace us with a visit, wench. What're yer doing 'ere?'

'I need somewhere to . . . I've . . .' Jess had held on to her emotions all day, but now she burst into desolate sobs. 'Oh Auntie Olive, please, please say you'll help me!'

Two

Olive poured dark, frothing tea into thick cups and sawed at a loaf of bread. There was silence now that Jess had sobbed out the long and short of her story.

She felt them all staring at her: Polly, Bert and Sis – her cousins, who she wouldn't have recognized if she'd met them on the street, and the babby, Ronny, who couldn't have been more than two or three and could barely see over the table. Jess hadn't known about him.

The room was small and cramped, the table squeezed in close to the range. The mantel was covered by a length of plum-coloured cloth with a pattern of white flowers, a pewter candlestick holding it down at each end and a clock ticking loudly in the middle. On the wall above hung an oval mirror. Olive had lit the gas, trying to control the shaking in her hands, and the room was warm and cosy from the fire.

Jess took a slice of bread and margarine and chewed ravenously on it. She was light-headed from hunger, having had nothing all day but a cup of tea at Leamington station, and her head was aching violently.

Olive didn't join them in sitting down. She took a long, considering slurp of tea and clinked the cup back down hard on its saucer.

'So she wanted yer wed and out from under 'er feet, is that it?'

Jess nodded, tears welling in her eyes again. Her

7

stepmother Sarah had forced her into a loathsome betrothal to a man called Philip Gill, her father's assistant in the forge. Jess's father had raised no objection, however hard she begged him. He took Sarah's side in everything, and it was this lack of care for her, his rejection of her true feelings that hurt most.

She looked across at her aunt, her one hope, and was chilled by the bitterness on Olive's face. She folded her arms tightly and her voice was as grim as her expression.

'And you just took off, without a word or a thought for anyone, is that it?'

'I didn't . . .' More tears escaped down Jess's cheeks and her head throbbed harder. All this way she'd come, terrified and worried sick, and now her aunt was turning against her as well. '. . . didn't know where else to go, what to do!'

Olive leaned towards her with such ferocity that Jess began to tremble. 'And what d'yer think I'm s'posed to do about it, wench, eh? Don't yer think I've got enough on my plate already?' She straightened up again, glaring at her.

'Mom,' Polly protested. 'Our Jess's come a long way – don't go on at 'er.'

Jess was momentarily encouraged by the kindness in Polly's voice. And she saw Bert winking at her across the table, which also restored her courage.

'Jess can stop 'ere for a bit, can't she? She could bunk up with me and Sis.'

'She can 'ave my bed if she wants!' Sis, sixteen and hungry for anything new to happen, was all for it.

'Please,' Jess implored. She could see her aunt eyeing her little bundle and her hat on the chair by the door. 'I've nowhere else to go. I'm not going back there, not for nothing. I'll walk the streets or sleep in a doorway, but I won't go back and marry 'im – I might just as well kill meself!'

'Oh what are yer canting about, yer daft wench.' Olive stood, glowering at her and Polly. Jess waited, face so full of pleading emotion that no one with a heart could have resisted.

'Ah Mom,' Bert said. 'Yer can't turn 'er away, can yer? She's family.'

'Will yer stop carryin' on?' Olive dismissed him. 'I'm trying to think.' She came at Jess again, forefinger wagging.

'Teking off and leaving everyone else to face the music's in the blood in this family . . .' she was shouting.

Jess glanced desperately at Polly. She hadn't a notion of what her aunt was raging about. Polly's expression indicated that neither had she.

Olive brought her face up so close to her that Jess could smell tea and bad teeth on her breath. 'D'you 'ear me?'

'Yes,' Jess whispered. 'Yes, Auntie.'

Olive straightened up abruptly. 'Poll, Bert—' She jerked her head towards the ceiling and the two of them left the table without a word and disappeared upstairs, Olive following them.

Jess put her head in her hands, tears running out between her fingers. 'Where'm I going to go? It's nearly dark, and I'm so scared! What's happened to Auntie? I thought she'd be good to me!'

''Ere—' Sis put a skinny arm round Jess's shoulders. 'What yer carrying on like that for? She said yer could stop 'ere for a bit, daint she?'

Jess looked round, bewildered, her eyelashes wet. 'Did she? When?'

Sis giggled. 'Don't yer speak the King's English?

Course our Mom'd never turn yer away – 'owever 'ard she might be on yer.'

The house, back-to-back with another, had a living room and tiny scullery downstairs with two bedrooms above. Bert slept downstairs on the sofa, Olive had Ronny in with her in one bedroom and the sisters shared the other. In the candlelight Jess saw a tiny room with the girls' iron bedsteads crammed into it, leaving barely enough room to squeeze a straw mattress in between them on the bare floorboards. Olive had no other spare bedding to speak of except an old grey bolster.

'If yer want any more you'll 'ave to put yer coat over yer,' she said.

'I've got the quilt.' Jess showed her.

Olive stared at it. 'Did *she* make that?'

'Yes – it's the only thing of Mom's I've got.'

However poor and spartan the room, Jess felt light-hearted with relief at the sight of her place for the night under a roof with this long-lost part of her family.

Sis, snub-nosed, freckled and cheerful, was full of excitement at having a guest.

'It's gunna be a laugh 'aving you sleeping with us, cousin Jess. I 'ope yer can stop for a long time.'

'Let's just worry about tonight for now, shall we?' Jess smiled. She liked the look of Sis, with her cheeky expression. Polly's face was more severe.

The three of them bedded down together, Polly and Sis's bedsprings screeching noisily as they settled in. Jess lay smelling the fusty smell of the room mixed with camphor and sweat and a faint trace of urine. This last smell was coming from somewhere close by and Jess turned and made out the white shape of a chamber pot near her head.

'Can I move the po' a bit? Could do without it under my nose.'

'Sorry,' Polly chuckled from the bed above her. 'Shove it down the end there.'

Jess's headache had eased a little, and she was exhausted, longing for sleep, but her cousins, agog for details, weren't having that.

'Come on then, Jess,' Polly commanded. 'Tell us all about 'im – this husband-to-be of yours.'

Jess could just make out Polly's angular shape, lying on her side, leaning over her.

'The wedding's s'posed to be Sat'dy.'

'What – *this* Sat'dy!' Polly's tone was awed. 'You really 'ave taken off at the last minute – 'ere, d'you know, you've jilted 'im, 'ain't yer! You know 'ow they say that ... "She was jilted at the altar!" And now you've gone and done it! Ooh, but they'll be livid with yer!'

'I'm scared stiff they'll come looking for me.' Jess could feel her cousins listening in the dark. She felt ashamed, a failure, not brave and colourful as Polly was making out.

'Who is 'e?' Sis asked shyly.

'Yes – what's so terrible about 'im then?'

'His name's Philip Gill. I've known 'im nearly all my life because 'e worked for my dad at the forge. He's much older than me – thirty already ...'

'*Thirty*!'

'She – Sarah, my stepmother – decided it. She never said a word to me 'til she'd already asked him, and then 'owever much I argued and begged them it were too late. I was already promised. They 'ad the banns read so

11

quick, people were looking me up and down to see if I was – you know – in trouble.'

She heard Sis give a little snickering laugh in the dark.

'That was after she made me walk out with 'im. 'E just started turning up, Sundays. I was working up the farm and Sunday was the only time I had off. I opened the door and there 'e was, said e'd come to take me out. And I never knew a thing about it before then.'

'And is 'e really ugly and horrible?' Polly was enthralled, as if hearing about the giant in a fairy story.

'Well,' Jess said. ''E's awright really. Kind enough. But 'e makes my flesh creep.'

That Sunday last winter, she'd opened the cottage door to find him on the step, scrubbed up in his Sunday best, hands stiffly clasped in front of him, feet positioned just too far apart to look normal. He'd grown a beard in the last couple of years, which made him appear even older.

'You and I are to go walking,' was all he said.

Jess laid one hand on her chest. 'Me – go walking with you?' she repeated like an idiot.

Philip beamed at her. In the winter sunshine his ears were the dull, thin-skinned red of newborn mice.

Without asking him in, Jess went next door to where Sarah was darning, her two children, Jess's half-sister and -brother, Liza, eleven, and Billy, nine, sitting beside her.

'It's Philip,' Jess whispered, pulling the edges of her cardigan together in agitation. 'Says he wants me to walk out with 'im.'

'Oh—' Sarah looked up with a wide smile. 'Didn't I say he'd asked? That'll be lovely for yer! You run along and 'ave a nice time.'

She spoke loudly, making sure Philip could hear.

12

'*But I don't want to go,*' Jess hissed urgently. 'Why do I have to?'

Sarah's expression darkened. She stood up, a wool sock in one hand, gripping Jess's arm with the other.

'Now you listen to me, miss. Philip's keen on yer and he's a good lad and 'e wants to make you 'is wife. You take yer chances where you can in this life. Now you'll go, and you'll be nice to him, d'you hear?' Her neck was doing its chicken movement, as it did when she was irritated.

Polly was eager for details. 'So you walked out with 'im?'

'For two months.'

'And – what did 'e do – what's 'e like?'

Jess shuddered. ''E's just – 'orrible. I mean 'e wouldn't hurt a fly. It ain't that. 'E lives with 'is Mom and sister still and the house was damp and it smelt horrible – of dogs . . .'

'I'd've thought there's worse things to stink of!'

'Ooh no, it was horrible, Polly – and 'e was like a dog with fleas 'imself whenever I was about. Couldn't keep still. And we'd not a word to say to each other . . .' Jess looked up into the gloom, the lump coming up in her throat again. There were those horrible walks, Philip all nods and twitches and hissing intakes of breath through his teeth, looking at her sideways all the time. Their silence. Jess rooting round for conversation.

'Bit warmer today,' she said, as the winter shrank back.

'Ar, it is,' Philip nodded enthusiastically. 'Warmer now, oh yes . . .' pressing down on his cap, as he often did, as if afraid it was about to jump off his head. 'Spring coming, that'll be.'

More silence. Jess had rolled her eyes impatiently.

13

Now it's your turn to say summat, she thought. But not much ever came from him.

He grew bolder, taking her hand in his huge, rough one. One day he stopped her, at the edge of the estate belonging to the Big House. The field beside them was fuzzed with green, like threadbare corduroy. His big, wet lips fastened on hers. Jess felt a disgusted pressure mounting inside her, as if her blood was trying to force its way out of her veins.

'I just couldn't,' she told Polly and Sis. 'Ooh no, never. Not 'im.' She couldn't put into words the revulsion she felt at the idea of marrying Philip. It was just wrong: it seemed to go against nature.

'Dad would've made me. He never 'ad time for me after Mom died. He just went along with anything *she* said. You can't just be *made* to want someone. Your Mom'd never force yer on someone yer didn't want, would she?' Jess looked up at Polly in the dark. She needed reassurance that she was not wrong and wicked like they'd made her feel.

'Yer an ungrateful little madam!' Sarah had shrieked at her. 'You should take what yer offered and feel lucky like other folk!'

'No,' Polly said. 'Course not.'

'She don't need to – our Poll's courting!' Sis said.

'Oi you – shurrup!'

'Are yer?' Jess asked, finding herself surprised at the fact.

'Well . . . sort of . . .' Her voice came coyly through the darkness. ''E's nice, Ernie is.'

'I think you're brave, Jess, I do,' Sis interrupted. Maybe she'd already heard quite enough about Ernie. 'Leaving like that and coming all the way over 'ere.'

'All that woman wanted was to get me out,' Jess said

14

fiercely. 'Ever since she come to live with us. Well she's got what she wanted now all right. But at least she ain't buried me alive with Philip!'

'I couldn't just go off like that,' Polly said. 'I'd be frightened to death.'

'It wasn't brave. I just 'ad to, that's all. And anyway, I cut up my wedding dress.'

Polly gasped, then Jess heard her loud laugh. 'My God, Jess – you're a one, ain't yer!'

Sarah had become almost motherly once the banns were being read. She'd explained to Jess about the physical side of marriage. It wasn't too big a surprise: there were too many animals about for that. But the thought of the bits of Philip she'd seen, let alone those she hadn't, and the smell of him – was enough to make her sick. And Sarah made Jess's dress.

'Was it really pretty?' Sis whispered.

'Nice enough, I s'pose. Cream with pink flowers.'

It had been hanging on the back of the door when she woke early that morning, caught in the light of sunrise through the window, its frill round the neck fashioned from the same material. She'd had to hurry – to act as if it was a normal day and she had to be out early to work. Downstairs she'd crept, scared rigid that she'd wake one of Sarah's two young children, looked round for Sarah's scissors ... When she snipped across the waist the skirt crumpled to the floor like a wind-swept bird.

'If I went back I should think she'd kill me.'

'We'll help yer, Jess,' Sis said. She sounded, finally, as if she was drifting into sleep.

And Polly added, 'Course we will. Don't worry about our mom.'

'I don't want to cause Auntie any trouble. She wasn't

all that pleased to see me, was she? Why did she go all funny? I thought she was 'aving a fit.'

'I don't know. It must've give 'er a shock seeing yer.' Polly sighed. 'She's 'ad a lot to put up with one way or another. But she'll come round. Just don't keep on at 'er. She 'ates people keeping on.' Polly reached over, took Jess's hand for a moment. 'I'm glad you're 'ere. I can remember coming out to see yer, when your mom passed on.'

Jess smiled in the darkness, wiping her eyes. 'D'you remember my mom?'

'A bit. She put my flowers in 'er hair.'

'I do that. Makes me feel like her.'

'Yer won't find many flowers round 'ere!'

''Ave to grow some then, won't I?'

When the others had fallen asleep, Jess still lay awake, hearing them breathing each side of her. One of the memories she held on to came to her: long ago, walking into the kitchen to find her father holding her mother close. Louisa's back was to her, a small crimson rose twisted into her skein of hair, her father's eyes were closed and he looked happy in a way she didn't normally see in him. Little as she was she took in that there could be passion tucked under the flat, practical things of every day, like currants inside a bread pudding. And she didn't see why she should settle for less.

Eyes open, she stared into the darkness, longing, feeling it as an ache inside her.

Three

Jess woke early the next morning and went down into the cramped little living room. She found it full of the irritable chaos of a family trying to get out in time for work.

Bert was at the table, peering into a small hand-mirror, scraping a cut-throat razor across his cheeks and attempting to whistle at the same time. Polly was by the window, cursing over a button missing from her blouse, and Sis, busy stuffing paper into one of her shoes to cover a hole, looked up and smiled. The kettle was boiling away unnoticed on the hob so the room was filling up with steam.

'Get a couple of fillets o' coley for tomorrer...' Olive was in the scullery, rattling something in the sink, shouting instructions to Polly.

Jess badly needed to relieve herself but didn't like to interrupt. Surely they didn't pee in a pot in the daytime here as well? She crept across and moved the kettle, then whispered to Polly who was pinning the front of her blouse together.

'Yer 'ave to go down the entry. Come on, I'll show yer.'

She took an old cotton reel with a bit of string on it from which dangled a key and led Jess out into the street and down an entry between two houses, its walls damp and covered in slimy green moss.

To Jess's surprise she found there was a little yard behind with more houses crammed in all round it, dingy, dark and in very poor repair, and the smell of the place was overpowering.

All round her Jess could hear the inhabitants of the houses going about their morning business – a door was open and a broom flicking out dust and bits. There was shouting, the splash of water, clink of plates, children squabbling. A mangle and a tin bath were pushed carelessly close together in one corner of the yard, and at the far end, a stinking heap of refuse, fresh ash steaming on it in the cold air.

'There yer go . . .' Polly opened the door of one of the three privies for her. Jess stepped inside full of dread and locked herself in. Through the badly fitting door she could still hear most of the racket from outside. At home, when she sat in the privy out at the side of the cottage, all she heard was birds in the trees, or the chickens.

She had no more time to wonder whether running away had been a dreadful mistake because someone was rattling at the door.

'Yer going to be all day on there, are yer?'

She pulled her bloomers up and skirt down and hurried out, red with embarrassment. A middle-aged man with a swarthy, unshaven face stood back to let her out, one hand on his fly, giving her a good look up and down. She could feel other eyes on her as she and Polly crossed the yard.

'No peace round 'ere, is there?' Polly grinned at her. 'Take a bit of getting used to.'

The family all downed their porridge at such a rate that Jess was left way behind. Even little Ronny had nearly finished before her. She looked round as she ate.

Bert, dark haired and stocky, ate fastest of all. When he saw her watching he winked at her.

'Awright this morning, Jess?'

'I remember you when yer was a babby – running round like 'im.' She nodded at Ronny.

Bert smiled back, winningly. 'Bet I was beautiful, wasn' I?'

Olive tutted. 'Don't give 'im any encouragement – 'e's full enough of 'isself as it is.'

'You weren't bad,' Jess said. She calculated – she was twenty and Polly nineteen, so Bert must be nigh on eighteen. He was nice looking – not handsome, but full of friendliness and cheek. He told her he worked in a metal rolling mills in Bordesley, and, moments later, was out of the door on his way, with a 'T'ra then,' over his shoulder.

Polly went to the scullery and came out cleaning her teeth with salt from the block Olive kept out there.

'I'll be off in a tick,' she said through the finger stuck in her mouth.

'Ar – and you will be an' all if yer thinking of stopping round 'ere,' Olive said to Jess. Having fed everyone else she'd finally sat down to eat.

'What – today?' Jess was full of alarm at the thought of wandering round trying to find work in this enormous, teeming place. But she felt a tingle of excitement too. She'd do it. By God she would. She'd prove she could find a job, and be allowed to stay!

'Why not today?' Olive said. 'Unless yer want to stand by me up to me elbows in the maiding tub. Though heaven knows, I could do with someone to keep an eye on 'im.' She smacked Ronny's hand as he'd started rubbing it round the inside of his bowl.

'Where d'you work?' Jess asked Polly who was gathering up a little cloth bag and her hat.

'Oh, not far...' She opened the front door. 'Off Bissell Street. Clark's Pens. Sis does an' all. You ready? T'ra Jess, Mom – see yer tonight!'

'See yer later—' Sis came and shyly kissed Jess's cheek. Jess was delighted.

And then they were all gone. The room went still, seemed to settle and expand. They could suddenly hear the fire in the range and voices from the house behind. Ronny had picked up his bowl and was licking round it.

Olive looked disparagingly at him then said, 'Oh well – keep 'im quiet for a bit.' She poured them each a cup of tea and sat down in her apron.

'What work was yer doing out there then?' she asked, as if Jess had arrived from the North Pole.

'I worked up at the farm – churning, collecting eggs – the lot really. I used to carry the milk up to the Big 'Ouse when I were younger, so in the end Mrs Hunter at the farm gave me a job. I thought – now I'm 'ere I could look for a job in service.'

'Oh – yer don't want to do that.' Olive sat straighter. 'Yer life's not yer own if yer do that. You can go and look for summat in a shop or a factory. I won't 'ave any of mine skivvying in service – oh no.'

Jess was encouraged by the way she said 'mine'. So her aunt wasn't planning to put her back on the next Leamington train.

There was silence for a time. Jess watched as Olive stared into her cup, trying to make out the face of the younger woman she remembered. In repose, Olive's expression was less harsh, but she looked tired through and through. The years had obviously taken their toll.

20

Jess was moved, watching her. She knew next to nothing about what had happened to her aunt though, except that she was widowed two years after Louisa died.

'I've not kept up with yer as much as I should – seen what was 'appening to yer.' Olive looked up at her. 'Things've been hard over the years, no two ways about it. She kept yer awright any'ow. Yer look healthy and you've got meat on yer bones.'

'I liked your letters. I've always kept 'em.'

There was a note every Christmas. In 1902, a black-edged card: 'I'm sorry to say that Charlie passed away in November.' They were always short, the barest snippets of news. Sometimes when she was sad Jess had taken out this pile of little notes and hugged them to her chest.

Olive shrugged. 'There should've been more of 'em.'

'Auntie—?'

'Ummm?' She was standing, stacking dishes tacky with porridge. Ronny solemnly passed his over.

'Come 'ere—' Olive wiped his face and hands on her apron and he squealed until she let him get down and he waddled over and sat on the stairs, bumping up and down the bottom two steps.

'Will yer tell me about Mom? And the family, and that?'

Olive looked up at her. After a long pause, she said, 'What's to tell?'

She took the dishes and Jess heard her put them with a clatter into the stone sink. Her voice came through from the scullery.

'I'm not one for canting, in the 'ouse or out of it. And I'm not about to ask yer any more about what 'appened out there. If it's bad enough to make yer come running to me after all these years, that's enough for me to know.' She came back into the room. 'But we're going to 'ave to let 'em know yer safe—'

'Oh no – not yet, Auntie, please!' In her urgency, Jess got to her feet. 'I'm due to be wed to 'im on Sat'dy! They might come and make me go back. At least wait 'til the day's gone by.'

'Ah well – awright then. We'll leave 'em to stew. At least for a week or two. So – now yer can go out and find yerself a job.'

Jess looked anxious. 'I do want to get a job, Auntie. I want to be able to pay my keep, like, since yer've taken me in. Only I don't know where anything is or what to do. I'll get lost straight away!'

'No yer won't. Wherever yer are, ask for Digbeth. Anyone'll direct yer. I'll give yer a piece to take for dinner, and sixpence for a cup of tea or two. All yer've to do is go round – look out for signs up, or ask.' Olive pulled sixpence out of a little cloth purse she kept tucked in her waistband. 'And Jess – you'll not be used to factory work. Why not try the shops round 'ere for a start – up Digbeth and the Bull Ring, see what's going?'

Jess got ready and picked up her hat, all nerves. She was off to take on the big city by herself!

'T'ra then, Auntie.' Her voice wavered. 'See yer later – when I've got a job!'

'Go easy.' Jess was touched that she showed her to the door. 'And mind the 'orse road. There'll be more going back and to than yer used to!'

Olive stood at the window watching her niece as she left. She knew Jess was in a bit of a state, despite her brave smile, head held high, her quick, bouncy walk as if she might break into a trot at any moment. Still, she was going to have to start somewhere if she wanted to make a go of it here.

The sight of her stirred up Olive's emotions again. She was so like Louisa as a young woman – especially from a distance. That dreamy, innocent look she had, while Olive knew that she herself had never looked pretty or innocent. Never felt it either, she thought bitterly.

Course, Jess looked healthy from the country air as Louisa had never done as a girl. But the way she walked, that beautiful hair ... The loss of her sister swept through Olive again. She ached with it, as she'd done so many times over the years. But it wasn't just Louisa. Jess was even more like ... like ... She could not let her mind pursue that. Get on now. Things to do.

She was about to move from the window when she glanced across the road and caught sight of a face, watching.

'Bugger me – just look at 'er!'

The front door of number fifty-seven was also open a bit – just enough for Bertha Hyde, the street's nosey parker, to peer out in the direction Jess had just taken. Olive felt a terrible, dizzying rage surge up in her.

'What're yer gawping at, yer nosey old bitch?' She was out the front door, striding across the street.

'If you're so keen to know my business why don't yer come and ask me, 'stead of poking and prying, eh?'

The door of fifty-seven slammed smartly in her face, leaving her staring at its flaking green paint. Olive felt herself boil over. She raised her hand and thundered on it with her fist.

'Everyone has to know, don't they? Has to meddle and spread lies!' Her voice shrieked high, verging on hysteria. 'Why can't yer leave us alone – all of yer?'

She marched back into her house, kicked the door shut and lowered herself unsteadily down at the table. She was panting, half sobbing, her full breasts forcing at the buttons on her dress. She put her face in her hands, overwhelmed with shame and misery, with fear at the unbalanced tone she'd heard in her voice. And last night – when Jess arrived, seeing her like that, unexpected, with that copper next to her . . .

'What's happening to me?' a frightened moan escaped her. How could she have lost her temper like that? As if a trigger had been pulled inside her, out of her control. She pulled the empty cup and saucer towards her on the table and gripped her hands round it until she thought she might crush it.

All these years she'd been all right – hadn't she? Life with Charlie, having the babbies, bringing them up . . . She'd made herself believe she'd forgotten. Past was past.

But now, suddenly – seeing Jess, then feeling the merest hint that she was being watched . . . It brought it all back with heightened, uncontrollable emotion. The persecuted years of her childhood. Tongues wagging, the insults, the horrified stares . . . She'd thought she was free of it.

Her legs felt unsteady as she got up and squeezed the last dregs out of the teapot, stewed dark as dubbing. She was shaking all over.

'Could do with a drop o' hard stuff if there was any . . .' Her hand rattled the cup on the saucer as she picked it up. She became aware of Ronny watching her, staring in the doorway.

'It's awright, son . . . just 'aving a last sup of tea.' To herself she whispered, 'Dear God, help me . . .'

Four

Jess set off in the weak sunshine that chilly morning, walking tall in her dark coat and hat, full of determination to make a success of her day and prove she could earn her keep and meet her aunt's approval. Although she was very nervous she felt strengthened and comforted by the friendliness the Beestons had shown her, especially Polly and Sis. She had been welcomed and taken in by the only people she could now call family, and she knew in her heart that they were kin and that she belonged to them. She had such strong memories of their place in her childhood, even though she had only met them twice before in her life.

The first time she had seen them was long ago in 1898 when she was a tiny girl, four years old. Olive had come out to Budderston to her sister Louisa's house, the old cottage next to the Forge.

They came on one of the trains that Jess could hear each day chugging across the far side of the farmland, stepping on to the platform, skirts catching the breeze, hands going up to hold their hats on. After a moment of looking, bewildered, round the country station, Olive was waving, other arm corkscrewing high in the air, her voice carrying right along the platform.

''Ello, Louisa – ooh, and look at little Jessica – ain't she got your hair!'

'Listen to that, Jess,' her mother had tugged at her

arm. 'Them Brummies are 'ere! That's your auntie, that is. Oh Olive!' Her voice was thick with emotion. It was the first time they had seen each other's children.

Jess felt herself caught up in Olive's sturdy arms, face pressed against the soft cotton of her frock. She smelt of smuts and lavender.

'She's beautiful, Louisa – a proper little pet. Ooh—' holding Jess away from her. 'Yer bonny, you are!' She studied Jess's face, and for a moment her eyes met her sister's.

Louisa was exclaiming over Bert, a stolid toddler with an expression of pure cheekiness, and skinny little Polly, socks a-dangle over the top of her boots.

'Oh Olive – it's lovely to see yer, it truly is!' The sisters linked arms and walked out of the station chattering about their husbands and their children, who trailed behind. Polly dragged Bert along by the hand. Jess was too young to notice, but as well as these two children who came with Olive, her aunt must have been expecting then, because later the child was born – the one before Sis – a boy who died very soon after. They learned this news by post. Jess's mother cried after she read the note in Olive's childish copperplate, and stood for a long time staring out of the back window over the yard.

That first time they came was during summer. In the hayfield over the wall, the seeded tips of grass reached higher than Jess's waist. Jess was several months older than Polly, and taller. The two of them stood apart, giving each other sidelong looks, each fishing for fistfuls of their mothers' skirts: Louisa's a buttercup cotton, Olive's a cream background with mauve swirls which cheap soap and wear had reduced almost to grey.

'Oh go on with yer, Poll,' Olive ordered her wearily.

'Look – 'ere's our Jess to play with. She won't bite yer!' She groaned, a long-suffering smile directed at her sister. 'Proper titty-babbies they can be when they want to, can't they?'

'She'll come round,' Louisa said. ''Ere, Jess – take our Poll 'ere and show 'er the pig.' Jess felt her mother unlock her fingers from the skirt. 'I'll get yer some scraps to give 'er. Off yer go – 'er Mom and I want to have a good natter!'

Jess sized Polly up without saying a word. The girl had pinched cheeks, a pasty face and squinty grey eyes. Her hair was brown rat's tails and she wore a tunic dress in a sludgy brown and sagging button up boots. To Jess she looked foreign and unwholesome. Jess with her plump, tanned arms, pink cheeks and her mop of thick curls, shiny as a newly polished saddle.

'Come with me,' she commanded. Polly followed, a finger in her mouth.

Carrying a paper bag of food scraps, Jess strode off, sturdy legs pushing through the grass at the edge of the cottage garden. Louisa was a townie, but she had taken to growing things as if born to it. Potato plants lay tilted over, arms open, rows of beetroot shoots, their spines river valleys of maroon: cabbages, leaves a silvered green. The air was heavy with risen dew, bees knocking against flower heads, tiny, tight apples on the orchard trees.

'What a stink!' Polly said in a reedy voice. You could smell the pig long before reaching the sty: urine and rancid food trampled to a mush on the brick floor.

''Ere y'are, Sylvia.' Jess ignored Polly and tipped in the bag of apple peelings.

Sylvia lurched to her feet grunting throatily and trotted over, pushing her wet, wiffling nose between the wooden bars of the gate. Polly squealed and stumbled backwards.

'Down there, yer dafty,' Jess addressed the pig. Polly was already well beneath her contempt.

Ecstatic snorting and squelching noises came from the pig. Jess reached through and scratched a bristly shoulder.

'Now—' she turned to Polly. 'What d'yer wanna do then?'

But Polly was kneeling in the orchard picking flowers, already grasping buttercups and a lacy head of cow-parsley in her fist.

Huh! Jess thought.

For most of the day, in rapt silence, the little Brummie girl gathered clumps of blossoms from the orchard, the lane, the hayfield. Buttercups, moon daisies, poppies, bunches which she presented to Olive and Louisa, flecked with blue viper's bugloss, shaggy with tough shreds of ragwort.

'Why don't yer play with Polly?' Louisa said to Jess now and then.

'She don't want to play,' Jess said sulkily.

The sisters agreed that the girls were both 'daft little nibs' and went back to their chatter, sitting out on the grass at the edge of the orchard. Louisa sat with her legs stretched out, arms behind her taking the weight, a gold seam through the orchard green in her buttery frock. Her hair was gathered up at the back, soft tendrils of it round her face. She liked to decorate it with flowers, or bright hips and haws, lustrous jewels, in season. Today she took three of the big field daisies from one of Polly's bunches and threaded them in so they rested over one ear. Olive was so much more sober, her bent knees pulled up to one side, skirt covering her feet, lank hair fastened in a bun with a straight fringe.

For some reason – Jess always connected it with the flowers, although that couldn't really have been it – Olive became suddenly furious, face screwing up with anger.

Their heads had been close together, faces long, talking in secret, grown-up whispers. Earlier on Jess had seen tears on Louisa's face. Olive reached over and clasped Louisa's hand, talking, talking, words a half-whispered jumble to Jess, but Jess thought it must be babbies they were talking about because her mom had lost two and that always made her cry. Then Polly sidled up and presented her aunt with a bunch of flowers from which she dressed her hair, and after, for no reason Jess could see, Olive's face was red and puffed up with anger as if she was going to burst, and they were arguing, straining to keep their voices lowered.

Snatches reached her like torn up notes – 'That's not how it was . . . I was the one always kept in the dark . . .' and, '. . . you should've put it behind yer . . .' from Louisa.

'Yes – you were always the one who . . .' and Olive's voice sank too low for Jess to hear, then rose, finishing, '. . . to be together. That's what I always wanted.'

But later, again, as if some solemn business was over, they relaxed, joking and giggling. Jess couldn't remember seeing her mother laugh like that before, and never saw her do so again, her head back, having to wipe tears from her eyes.

Nothing else they said stayed with Jess, and she was too young to understand how deeply troubled the two sisters were by their past. What she did keep, though, as a memory from the midst of that green orchard, along with Polly's dumb quest for flowers and Bert having to be retrieved sweaty and truculent from the hayfield, was a sense of rightness. That blood ties counted, no matter what. She had no memory of her father being there that day. He must have greeted Olive, shyly stroking his beard the way he did. Perhaps he ate with them too. But what she remembered was seeing Louisa as enlarged, strung as she had been in Jess's mind until then, between the cottage, forge and village, between her father and herself. There was more to her mom: a past, relatives, Birmingham, which as she grew up she heard spoken of as a huge manufacturing town, way over there, further than she could ever see, beyond the soft curves of Warwickshire.

It was winter the next time, 1900, icicles hanging from the eaves, tongues of ice between the furrows. That morning, which cruelly sliced one part of Jess's life away from the other, had begun full of excitement. The Shires were coming from the farm to be shod!

'If yer can walk without fidgeting about, you can help lead 'em down,' her father said. He was gentle then, although unsure how to talk to her even in those days, as if she was not his business. She was her mother's province and Louisa made sure it stayed that way. Jess was her one, precious child.

The farm boys helped walk the 'big girls', Myrtle and Maisie, the two black and white Shire horses, along from Lea End Farm, their fringed hooves striking on the frost hardened track, breath furling from their nostrils.

Jess tore along to meet them, hair a crazy bird's nest,

holding up her thick winter dress. The arrival of the Shires felt like a dignified royal occasion. Jess's father was ready for them, with Philip Gill. The forge was open on one side, facing the yard. Smoke curled out into the sharp air. The furnace was stoked high and it was dim inside even in the winter sunshine. Rows of tools hung on the main ceiling beam, and alongside the fire.

William Hart, clad in his working apron, tucked the end of his long beard between the buttons of his shirt to keep it out of the way.

'Can I hold Maisie while you shoe her – *please*? Dad, Philip, let me!'

Philip, eighteen then, stood rubbing one of his enormous ears, making hissing noises of amusement through his teeth. 'You know 'ow to keep on, don't yer?'

William Hart said nothing.

He prised the old shoes off, working his way round the horse, clicking at her and leaning against the hard flanks to make her lift her hooves. Jess talked to her, kissing her nose. Maisie tolerated this for a time, then lifted her head with an impatient jerk.

'Eh now,' Jess said, trying to sound grown up. 'There's a good girl.'

When it happened, she was standing with a hand on Maisie's neck, wrapped in the hot smell of horse. A shaft of sunlight cut into the dark forge, shot through with motes of smoke and dust. William, a shadowy silhouette in the firelight, hammered a glowing cresent of iron.

From the doorway of the cottage her scream broke along the yard.

'William! Help me – for God's sake!'

There was Louisa, doubled up, gasping on the step,

face contorted in agony, hands thickly smeared with blood, and William Hart was running, hammer slammed down, the air abruptly emptied of all other sounds but his boots along the yard. Even the horses stared, rock still.

Jess felt her mother's agony and fear pass into her and her limbs turned weak.

'Mom! Mom!' She was struggling, crying, everything else a fog around her. Strong arms caught her. Philip carried her into the forge, sat her on a stool.

'There now – there,' he said, mopping her cheeks. Jess screwed up her nose at the smell of him.

She was not allowed in the house all day, freezing as it was. The widow Mrs Guerney was sent for from the village, and the doctor. William stayed inside and Philip shod the horses. All day there was a dreadful quiet over the place which frightened her as much as her mother's screams. Left alone, wrapped in her old coat, Jess wandered to the back gate which led to the path, then the hayfield. Atop the wall, on that diamond-hard day, cobwebs had frozen, crystalline and perfect across clusters of blood-red berries. Jess whimpered, hugging herself. Nothing felt right or safe any more. She kept seeing Louisa's red hands, hearing that bloodcurdling cry, the last sound she would ever hear her mother utter.

Late that night she saw Louisa laid out. Her hair was arranged loose on the pillow. She was cold and there was no expression in her face.

Jess looked up accusingly at Mrs Guerney. 'That ain't Mom,' she whispered. Then screamed, 'What've yer done to my mom – that ain't 'er! Where've yer taken 'er?'

Sarah Guerney made clucking sounds with her

tongue, led Jess briskly downstairs again and fed her bread crusts dipped in sweet milk. Her father sat by the range, staring ahead of him. He didn't speak to her, didn't even seem to see her.

'Your mother's gone to Heaven to be with the angels,' Mrs Guerney told her. Jess thought she looked pleased about this, and hated her.

When they took Louisa to be buried, the dead child, a daughter, who had cost her her life, was laid to rest in the same coffin.

And Olive came. The only break between her black garments was her face, raw with grief, the mole on her cheek very dark against her pallor. Louisa was her younger sister by two years.

With her she brought Polly. The girl was still bone thin and pallid from city life, but she had more presence now, and a wry look in her eyes.

William Hart, Philip Gill and a group of neighbours carried the coffin from the curtain shrouded cottage, their feet moving to the toll of the church bell. William was dressed in his Sunday best, his beard brushed flat. He kept his gaze ahead, not looking at anyone. The love of his life was gone, a small daughter no substitute at all. That morning, when Jess tried to go to him, looking for comfort, he had pushed her away.

'Leave 'im be,' Mrs Guerney commanded her. 'He's in no fit state to talk to yer.'

Olive walked holding the girls' hands. Jess was dressed in navy, her thick hair gathered into two plaits. She insisted on picking up a brown, stiff leaf and holding it. She had to hold something or she would float away, lost. Her toes roared with the pain of chilblains. Now and then the stiff black stuff which swathed her aunt's arms brushed against her cheek. Olive squeezed Jess's hand with her own.

Friends and neighbours walked with them. At the church Olive waited with the girls at the end of the path as the coffin withdrew. The backs of the men carrying Louisa moved in a stately sway along the little path, and as they disappeared inside, Jess felt Olive's hand tighten convulsively and a strange shudder seemed to go through her. She drew herself up.

'Come on. That's men's work in there. Time to go 'ome.'

Jess sobbed, distraught as they turned from the church. Looking up she saw tears coursing down her aunt's face. Olive's hand kept clenching and unclenching on hers.

Olive could only stay one more day before going back to Birmingham. She organized for Sarah Guerney to help out in the house. And she tried to take William Hart to task.

'You'll 'ave to take a bit more notice of 'er,' she said, eyeing Jess. ''Er's only six and yer all 'er's got now.'

He was numb with grief, spoke like a winded man.

'I can't be a mother to her, now can I?' Jess heard him say. ''Er needs a mother.'

While Olive was there she seemed like part of Louisa, and was the woman of the house for now. That second day Jess was kept away from school, and played with Polly. Jess took her up the track to meet the farmer's boys, but they were wary, as if death followed you round like a smell. She and Polly went and cracked the ice at the edge of the pond on the green.

''Ave yer got nits?' Polly asked conversationally, shifting a brittle triangle of ice with the toe of her boot.

'No. Don't reckon so.'

'I wish I 'ad hair like yours. It's ever so nice, yours is.'

They were drawn to each other this time.

The night after Olive and Polly left, Jess lay in bed, cuddled in the deep dip of the mattress. The house was quiet and dark. After a time the stair treads creaked as her father came up, a candle stuck on a saucer. The door squeaked as he crept into her room, the flame wavering.

Jess pretended to be asleep. Through her lids she sensed the light thinning, bulbing outwards as he held the candle high over her. He looked down at her for a time, then sighed, a massive expulsion of breath from the depths of him. In a moment he went out again, crossing the landing to his cold, silent room. It was the closest he ever came to trying to comfort her.

Jess lay still, the blackness seeming to pulse round her. She thought about the dark yard below her window: outside it, black fields lit only by an ice-flake moon . . . And beyond them more darkness reaching on forever . . . She began trembling, sobbing, curling into a tiny, tight ball, crying out her distress into her pillow.

'Mom! Oh Mom . . . Mom . . .!'

Five

Sarah Guerney was in her late thirties when Louisa died, a lanky woman with black hair, rather hooded brown eyes and a surprisingly thin neck, giving her head an unbalanced, chicken-like appearance made more pronounced by the pecking little nods she gave when nervous or irritable. Jess had never taken to her, even at the beginning.

Sarah had married first at twenty and been left a widow two years later with a daughter to bring up and a grocer's shop to run. As time passed she took on an assistant in the shop and started to attend births in the village, supported the women until they were Churched, and laid out the dead. As well as gaining a certain status, she earned a small fee for each attendance, or a basket of eggs or fresh vegetables if money was short.

'I see 'em in and I see 'em out,' she would say, full of her own importance.

She set her sights on William Hart almost as his lovely young wife was breathing her last. She did not expect her objective to be achieved quickly, nor did she expect love. What Sarah saw before her was an opportunity for combining assets – she had the shop, he the forge.

So in the year after Louisa's death she left her daughter in charge among the tins, packets of Bird's Custard and motley array of local produce, and set out to make herself indispensable to the Hart household.

She worked for William Hart with the tireless commitment of someone who's after something. She carried water from the pump, cleaned, cooked and tended Louisa's kitchen garden (the spare produce from which she could sell in her shop). She took brisk – not unkind, at the start, but never tender – care of Jess. She scrubbed, washed and darned, her gaunt energy adding a domestic pace and wholesomeness to a house which would otherwise have been bereft. As the months passed, like sand trickling into a hole she began in some measure to fill the space Louisa had left.

Sarah was a practical woman who had always made her decisions on the basis of what she could get out of a thing. She was not prepared for the violence of feelings this situation would lead her to.

She fell devotedly, jealously in love with William Hart, only to inhabit a house haunted by the presence of the woman he had adored – and her daughter. Brooding Jess, whose eyes held only resentment towards her. Sarah was all sharp fingers and elbows, and a sharp tongue to match – no cuddles against a soft body, or feminine prettiness. With all of her being, Jess wanted her mother.

She was almost eight when she had to be Sarah's bridesmaid and followed her new stepmother up the aisle, face gaunt, giving off no joy at all. Once the ceremony was over, the neighbours departed, she went to the end of the garden with the bouquet of carnations she had been made to carry. She stood them in a jar on the wall of the sty and set fire to them. They didn't burn well, being fresh and moist. She lit more matches until the petals were wizened and black, and left them there, an offering of resentment and loathing. Sarah found them the next day.

'What's this?' She held out the jar, quivering with fury and upset.

Jess looked back at her. 'Wedding flowers.'

There was a terrible expression in Sarah's eyes. 'I've tried with you, my girl, by God I have. And this is how you repay me.'

'You're not my mom. You'll never be like her.'

The new Mrs Hart came closer, hand raised to strike the girl. Then she sank down at the table and burst into tears.

Sarah had her two children by William Hart, Liza and Billy, and they always came first. Jess was pushed aside, barely clinging on to the edge of this new family. Her father mostly ignored her. Chose not to see what was happening. Dealing with children, girl children especially, was 'woman's work'. Sarah made sure he was out of the way when she slapped Jess, or screamed at her with poison in her voice. Jess was a sad shadow of the child who had once been the centre of a mother's love, growing up now with only the most basic attention paid to her, and almost no loving care.

As she grew older Jess got a little job. Before and after school every day, she carried cans of milk from the farm to the Big House at the edge of the village, and earned half a crown a week, and Mrs Hunter at the farm was kind to her. There was one afternoon in particular which stuck in her mind. The day was much like any other except for the torrential rain outside, the clouds swirling like thick smoke, and Jess got caught out in it. When she trailed in from school late, clothes saturated with rain, the new Mrs Hart was storming round the kitchen of Forge Cottage in a furious temper.

'Where've yer been? Always in a flaming dream you are – no use to anyone!'

The sight of Jess only increased her fury. Beautiful in a way Sarah could never be, pensive, a sprig of blackthorn blossom twined in her wet hair, her large eyes looking back with a combination of loathing and fear. 'You've not even taken the milk up yet and there's no end to do 'ere! I s'pose yer've been hanging round the cemetery again? Talking to 'er grave ain't going to bring 'er back, yer know, so yer might as well get that into yer head once and for all. And get that muck out of yer hair!'

She went to pull at the flowers hanging on Jess's ponytail but Jess backed away, eyes narrowing.

'No! Why should I take it out? What harm's it doing yer?'

Sarah thought she would boil over. Lord, she had only to set eyes on the girl and she wanted to scream!

'Yer should do what I tell yer. Have a bit of respect.'

Jess's gaze burned into her. She didn't say a word. Didn't need to. Her eyes said it all. Why should I? You're not my mom. I hate you.

Their mutual loathing crackled round the kitchen. Jess moved away and put her cloth bag down wearily. Little Liza, five, was at the table toying with bread crusts on a blue and white plate. Jess looked longingly at them. She was frozen, soaked to the skin and ravenously hungry.

'You'll 'ave to wait,' Sarah said with harsh satisfaction. 'That's what happens to yer if you fiddle about and don't get on – yer go hungry.'

Billy, aged two, was on the floor, banging at the tiles with a child's rolling pin. Sarah suddenly whipped round from by the range and snatched it out of his hand. He started yelling.

'You'll drive me to distraction – all of yer. Now go on – clear off up the farm out of my sight, or they'll get someone else to do the job.'

Jess trudged along the muddy track as more clouds were piling up, swollen with unshed rain, and the wind swept across the fallow winter fields. She was a lonely, bedraggled figure, her clothes too small, hugging her wet coat round her, teeth chattering so much she had to clench her jaw to keep them still. Her boots kept slipping and sliding, wet rat's tails of hair lay plastered to her forehead, and under the weight of her cold and misery her heart was so heavy she thought it might fall out of her body. She was so wretched that afternoon that she started to cry, tears mingling with the rain as it began to fall again, sobbing out her longing to be loved by someone, to matter to anyone in the world. She cried with longing for her auntie Olive, for the feel of that sleeve of her black dress as it had brushed against her face. Olive who had been kind. Who felt like her only family in the world apart from Louisa's gravestone, the only place where she could go to pour out her feelings.

Jess remembered that afternoon as she set out from Olive's house along the strange city streets, still able to recall it so sharply that for a moment tears stung her eyes. After so many moments of doubt on her way to get here, after all her soul searching and worry, she knew at that moment with fierce certainty that coming to Birmingham had been the best decision she had ever made.

Six

May 1914

'Jess, what the hell are yer *doing*?'

Polly turned, lifting a pail of ash to take out, and stopped short at the sight of her cousin dreamily rubbing condensed milk all over her face.

Jess's mind was obviously miles away. She stared at her gooey fingers, then back at Polly.

'Yer a case, Jess – yer really are!' Polly burst into her loud laugh, and Sis started giggling too.

'S'good for yer skin, milk is. Mrs Hunter at the farm told me – top of the milk.'

The farmer's wife had dipped a spoon into the thick surface of the cream and rubbed it on Jess's cheeks with her rough index finger.

'Keep yer skin lovely, that will.' And Jess believed her. Mrs Hunter's eyes were sunken with exhaustion and her body sagged like an old mattress, but her cheeks were radiant as rose petals.

Polly was chortling away. 'But that ain't fresh, Jess – it's out of a tin!'

'I weren't thinking. It were just force of habit.' She laughed and laughed, then suddenly found she was in tears.

'We was only teasing, Jess!' Polly dropped the pail and slipped her arm round Jess's shoulders. 'This ain't like you.'

Jess was laughing and crying together.

41

'I'm awright,' she spluttered. 'Don't know what's come over me. I just feel a bit strung up, that's all – oh ta, Sis.' The girl had poured her a cup of tea. 'Better wash me hands and face first, hadn' I?'

She went into the scullery, bewildered at the odd mix of feelings inside her.

She'd been in Birmingham two months and it had been an emotional time. She'd caused the family a lot of laughs with her strange ways. Used to the freedom of her own room she stripped her clothes off with no hesitation, not mindful of who might be about, looking through windows. Polly and Sis who were more coy and easily embarrassed went into fits at the sight of her.

'Yer want to watch it, Jess – plenty of peeping Toms round 'ere!'

So Jess tried to be more modest. She learned lots of new things. That each family took turns cleaning out the stinking privies in the yard and she'd be no exception. That she'd be taking a bath in the tin tub by the fire once a week if she was lucky and sharing the water with her cousins. That if she wanted to grow flowers and herbs she was going to be hard pushed to find anywhere to do it. She spent a few pennies on seeds: chives, parsley, pansies and Sweet William and planted some pots, but she didn't trust the children in the yard not to knock the tops off. So she stood them out the front and they struggled to grow, poor, sickly looking offerings. Jess decided it was probably more effort than it was worth. She learned that if she suddenly felt like running and jumping in the street as she might have done on the farm track at home, everyone'd look at her as if she was stark staring bonkers and probably tell her so too. And she learned, for the first time in her life, what real family teasing was like, and that she had a sense of humour which had never found a proper outlet before. She loved her cousins and the longer she stayed the more she spoke like them and understood their teasing. She found Bert and Sis easygoing enough. Polly and Olive were more tricky. Polly could be moody and liked everything just so, although Jess found she could often tease her out of being crotchety. Olive was more of a puzzle. She could be warmth and kindness itself, then the next minute distant, angry. And though Jess kept trying to find different ways of asking about her family, all the relatives she'd never seen or known, she got nowhere.

'There's nowt to say. Stop keeping on,' was typical of the abrupt response she got. She found it odd and disappointing.

She had, though, found a job that first day, setting off past small workshops making screws, and copper piping, out into the wide main street which led uphill to the Bull Ring market and St Martin's Church. All the trams and carts and people seemed to be heading there. The street was busy, a bobbing mass of hats in front of her: caps and homburgs, straw hats and bonnets.

Away from the back streets, and the nearer she walked to the Bull Ring, a host of smells mingled together: roasting coffee, freshly baked bread, fresh horse manure and the rough smoke of cigarettes. There was so much to see, and smell and hear, the clatter of carts, the delivery men and market stallholders bustling about hollering at each other.

Jess felt her spirits soar. This is my new home, she thought. It's where Mom came from and I'm going to like it here, even if it is rough and ready. At least it's nice to see a place with a bit of life in it for a change!

The Bull Ring teemed with people moving round the

stalls which seemed to sell everything you could possibly imagine. Jess wove a path between piles of fruit and veg and crocks and rags, looking at everything. There were flowers and birds in cages, live chickens clucking, women with trays of lavender, sweets and cakes, a knife-grinder, sparks showering from his grindstone ... Tarpaulins over the stalls protected the holders from heat or rain and they stood behind their stalls waving and all trying to see who could yell the loudest.

'Get yer peaches 'ere – luvverly peaches!'

'Best spuds in town ...'

'Oranges over 'ere – sweet and juicy!'

In the background the shrill voices of lads selling the *Despatch* competed with them. Jess saw a man walking in small circles waving a Bible and shouting and the stout lady selling flowers was in full voice. She found herself grinning affectionately. Flipping noisy lot, these Brummies! And now she was going to be one of them.

The thought of getting a job almost slipped her mind for a time. She wandered on, up New Street, past the Great Western Railway Station at Snow Hill. Dinner-time came and went. She ate her piece of bread in a church yard and ambled on, until gradually it dawned on her she had no idea where she was.

On the corner of a main street she saw a policeman.

'Please – can yer tell me where Digbeth is?' she asked.

He stared stonily ahead and there was such a long silence she thought he wasn't going to answer. Then suddenly he said, 'Well unless you was thinking of going via Wolver'ampton, yer'd be best advised to turn round.'

Eventually, tired now, she found herself back in the Bull Ring again. In a side street the aroma of coffee made her mouth water. Perhaps she could afford a minute or two for a drink . . .

The little shop had a sign outside saying 'A.E. Mather – Coffee and Tea House'. In the window Jess could see plates with a few cakes still left on them. A little girl in filthy, ragged clothes was standing with her face pressed up against the window.

Poor little mite, Jess thought. I wonder when she last had a meal in her belly.

She was about to offer her a penny for a cake when the child scampered away and in the place where she'd stood Jess saw the little sign in the window. 'Help Required.'

It was gloomy inside, sawdust on the floor, a few plain wooden tables squeezed in round the room. At one sat two women with tall, thick glasses of tea in front of them. Jess felt them sizing her up.

'What can I get yer? Coffee or tea?' A thickset man with a moustache spoke to her from behind the narrow counter at the back. On it sat two or three plates draped with white cloths.

Jess went to him shyly. 'I've come about the sign.'

'Sign?' The man's eyes twinkled. 'A sign in the celestial 'eavens, would that be? A portent and wonder?'

'No,' Jess said earnestly. 'The one in the window.'

'Ah, go on with yer, wench – I were pulling yer leg.'

'Oh. I see.' She felt foolish, but the man was smiling at her.

'Why – you offering? Only we're short-'anded, see. The wife's just 'ad another babby and she ain't back on 'er feet yet. It might be only for a week or two, like, but I could use yer.'

Two little children with Mr Mather's slate-coloured

eyes were staring at her from the doorway behind him. She smiled at them and the older one smiled back.

'I'd like the job,' Jess said. 'I need to start somewhere.'

'Not yer first job, is it? Yer look more'n fourteen.'

'Oh no – but I've only just come to Birmingham. I don't 'ave any references to give yer.'

Mr Mather snorted. 'We take yer as we find yer, wench. References be damned. If yer don't come up to scratch yer'll be out and that's that. Awright?'

He explained that her job would be to wash up, keep the tables and floor clean and generally keep the place nice while he brewed coffee and tea and looked after the customers.

'Think yer can manage that? It'll be six shilling a week – I can't spare more.'

'That's awright,' Jess was pleased. She'd have that to give to Auntie Olive for her board and food. 'When do I start then?'

Mr Mather's eyes filled with mirth again, looking at the pretty, and somehow unworldly girl in front of him.

''Ow about this minute?'

'That's all very well,' Olive said when Jess proudly presented her with her first week's earnings. 'But yer've got to keep yerself clothed and shod as well.'

Jess's excitement subsided a little. 'Oh – I 'adn't thought of that. Sarah made a lot of our clothes, see . . .'

Olive perked up, hearing this. 'Did she teach yer? You any good at sewing?'

Jess absolutely loathed sewing, but she was anxious to please the hard-faced woman in front of her.

'I can sew a bit.'

'Well that's summat, 'cause we're a right cack-'anded lot 'ere, all of us. Why didn't yer say? You could get yerself a job as a seamstress.'

'I never thought,' Jess said, vowing silently that that was the last thing she'd ever do.

'Not to worry – yer can move on when yer've found yer feet a bit. Factory pay's better, no doubt about it. Tell yer what – you keep this family in darned stockings and yer can keep 'alf your wages every week. 'Ow about that?'

Over the first week as she settled in, they had a mattress stuffed for her and got some bedding from a pawn shop sale. She lay down to sleep between her cousins every night and it was cosy, chatting before they slept. That was, until Bert shouted up to them.

'Shurrup gassing, will yer, and let us get some kip!'

Sometimes they could hear him snoring, and Olive snored like a dormant volcano as well.

'It's a wonder the house can stand it!' Polly giggled sometimes, when they were both at it.

The weeks had passed and Jess hadn't reminded Olive about writing to Budderston. It was only now that Olive remembered.

'I reckon it's about time you let 'em know where yer've taken off to. Yer father wouldn't've kept a note of my address, would 'e?'

'No. It was only on your letters and I've got them.'

Olive painstakingly penned a note saying that Jess had come to live with them, had found work and was in good health. She wrote her address clearly at the top of the paper.

'Right – you go and post it.'

Jess felt churned up as she slipped the letter in the post. She walked back slowly down the road.

I miss 'em, she thought, in a funny way. Even though being ignored and used as the family drudge was what she had been used to. She longed to know whether her father would forgive her for taking off, even though she knew it was his fault she had had to go.

And as much as that she missed the beauty and familiarity of the countryside, the peace of it. Faces she recognized all round the village, when here she saw only strangers.

I wish I could just go for a visit and come away, she thought. See the house again, and my room and the apple trees. She imagined walking along the edge of the hayfield, the rustle of the dry grass which she'd heard every summer of her life, until now. At that moment the city felt such a big, noisy, squalid place. Jess felt suffocated by it, longed to breathe fresh country air, be away from the turmoil and human squalor.

I don't belong here, she thought, in this miserable mood, walking back along Allison Street. I don't really belong anywhere.

As the spring passed, along with the fun and warmth of living with the family, sitting round the table to eat, the jokes, there were other things Jess was starting to notice. Polly was worried about Olive.

'Mom—' she protested when Olive gave her another long list of shopping to fetch in after work. 'I can't carry all that back on me own – and I won't 'ave time! Why can't yer get it this morning?'

'I'll do some,' Jess was always glad to feel useful. 'If you go up Jamaica Row, I'll go in the Market Hall and we can do half each.'

Gradually the girls got into the habit of doing all the

shopping between them. If anything extra was needed Olive sent someone out – Sis, often, on an errand.

'I don't know what's got into our mom,' Polly said one night. 'She don't seem to want to go out the house nowadays. I think she'd get us to go to the lavvy for 'er if we could.'

'Yer'd think she'd want to get out and 'ave a bit of a gossip for a while,' Jess said, remembering that Sarah had usually come home in a marginally better temper from a walk to the village to fetch groceries and chat to anyone she met.

'She don't want to see anyone,' Sis's voice came softly through the darkness. 'It ain't like 'er.'

'She won't say why,' Polly said. 'I've asked 'er.'

Jess thought about the night she'd arrived, her aunt's reaction.

'It's not summat I've done, is it?'

'No – why should it be? I s'pect she'll get over it. P'raps she ain't feeling too good and don't want to make a fuss.'

When they'd lain quiet for a time, Jess asked, 'Poll – this is nosey to ask, but – Ronny. Who's 'is father?'

But there was no reply. Polly was either asleep, or pretending to be.

Jess also started to notice the way Olive quizzed Polly – not herself, just Polly – almost every time she came in from work or shopping.

'Seen anyone?' This was said in a casual way, but Jess could hear an edge of anxiety in her voice.

'No,' Polly would reply, puzzled. 'Who am I s'posed to 'ave seen?'

Jess wanted to say, 'But you must've seen *someone*. It was swarming with people out there!'

Once Olive asked, 'No one following yer, was there?'

'No!' Polly laughed, then looked solemn. 'Mom? Why d'yer keep asking all these funny questions?'

'Oh – no reason,' Olive said. 'Just wondered.'

Polly's worried eyes met Jess's for a second. They were coming to understand that 'anyone' meant 'someone' in particular, and that this 'someone' was someone who was preying on her mind, who she seemed afraid of seeing.

But they couldn't get any more out of her, could all feel the strength of emotion round the subject. And Olive continued to stay in. She was all right in the house with them, but she seemed scared to step outside her own front door.

Seven

'Shift yerselves, you lot, and see what's coming down the 'orse road!'

Everyone else was in a Sunday afternoon stupor: Bert sleeping off a few pints, Olive dozing. Ernie, Polly's beau who was round for the afternoon, was entertaining Ronny, tossing him about on his lap, a game Ronny never tired of. Jess watched them sleepily through half-closed eyes. She'd liked Ernie straight away, his chubby face and gingery beard, the way he was good with Ronny. It was Polly who'd got up to put the kettle on and looked out of the window.

'Come out quick and look!'

Jess, Ernie and Sis followed her. Olive stood in the doorway, craning her head round. Bertha Hyde opposite was at her window having a good nose. Sis took one look and started running down the road, laughing and calling out.

'Don't flap yer arms about and frighten it!' Polly shouted after her.

The grey mare came towards them along the road, hooves slowly clip-clopping. Her ears were swivelling back and forth in a startled sort of way, perhaps because her rider, with no saddle, and no shoes on, was standing up on her back, holding the reins high, his boots slung over the horse's withers with their laces tied together. He balanced, knees bent, concentrating hard, but as they came nearer he looked up, a smile spreading across his face.

'Well I'll be . . .' Olive gasped. 'It's our Ned!'

Jess remembered hearing his name mentioned, Ned Green, the lad Olive had known since he was knee-high. He was now a fireman and Olive obviously thought the world of him.

Bert came out yawning and stretching his arms. 'What's 'e playing at! Awright, Ned, yer silly bleeder!'

Ned loosed a hand for a moment to wave. Jess found herself grinning. The sight cheered her up no end. She'd seen pranks like this back in the village but she certainly hadn't expected anything of the kind in Allison Street. And what a lovely animal! Then she looked at its rider, drawn to him, curious, seeing a strong body, a face with a wide, smiling mouth and fair wavy hair.

'Whoa there now, Bonney – eh, stop, yer daft wench!'

Bonney, who seemed to be enjoying her stroll in the sunshine, stopped with reluctance and Ned slid down to the pavement. Sis pulled his boots from off the horse and handed them to him.

'Ta.' He gave her a wink.

'We thought yer was too good for us these days.'

Jess looked round, hearing the gruffness in Olive's voice. To her astonishment her aunt looked quite dewy-eyed.

''Ow are yer, Auntie?' He came over and kissed Olive's cheek.

'All the better for seeing you. Where've yer bin, yer bad lad?'

'Sorry, Auntie – been busy.'

Everyone was trying to talk to Ned.

''Ow d'yer stay up there without slipping off?' Polly

said. Jess noticed she looked flushed, and saw Ernie watching her. 'Whose 'orse is it?'

'She's from the fire station,' Ned patted her. 'I said I'd give 'er a bit of a walk.'

'Can I 'ave a ride?' Sis cried. 'I've never been on an 'orse!'

Jess went and took Bonney's reins since everyone else seemed to have forgotten that she could just walk off any time.

''Ello, gorgeous,' she stroked Bonney's nose. 'Oh I've missed the likes of you, I 'ave!'

She stood letting the horse fumble in her hand with its lips, but soon her gaze was drawn to Ned. His eyes as he looked round at them all were full of affection and fun. He was wearing a white shirt, the top couple of buttons undone, and a worn-looking pair of trousers. As he stood down to lace up his boots she saw a stripe of his neck, between his hair and collar. The skin looked soft, edged by the thin down of hairs at the margin of his hairline. She felt intensely conscious of his every movement. The hairs on her own skin stood up, making her shiver.

Sis was still clamouring for a ride. Ned stood up and turned, and his eyes met Jess's. To her embarrassment she found she was blushing until she turned hot all over. Her palms were turning clammy.

'Who's this then?'

'This is Jessica, my niece,' Olive said. 'Our Jess. She's come to stop with us.'

Her hand disappeared into his for a moment. His was very warm. 'How long yer staying?'

Jess shrugged, giving a wry smile. 'I don't know!'

'Nice to meet yer, Jess, anyway.'

''Ow d'yer get up 'ere?' Sis was throwing herself

excitedly at the horse's flank, and kept sliding down again.

They all watched, laughing. 'Give us a leg up, Ned!'

''Ere – I'll show yer!' On impulse, Jess, still holding the reins, led the mare alongside the front step, and from there she vaulted up on to Bonney, managing to fling one leg over, her dress riding up to show a length of bare thigh.

'Oh Lor'!' Olive laughed. 'She's a country wench this one, all right. Look at 'er go!'

Jess clicked her tongue, digging her heels into Bonney's sides. She quickly broke into a trot and Jess clung on, even though riding bareback was a slippery business.

'That's a girl!' They trotted off along the street and under the railway arch where the sound of Bonney's hooves echoed until they were out in the sun again, and round the corner. Jess didn't want to stop. She loved the feel and smell of being on a horse again. But she turned Bonney round and trotted back. Her cheeks were pink, hair fastened back haphazardly so some of it hung loose on her shoulders, and she looked the healthy, country girl she was, the joy of it shining out of her. As she drew closer to them all she felt Ned watching her and her smile grew wider.

'I wish I could go on all afternoon!'

'We can see that!' Polly laughed.

'Oh let us 'ave a go!' Sis was jumping up and down with impatience.

Jess swung her leg over, ready to slide off Bonney as if she was a helter-skelter.

'Can yer manage?' Ned came and took her hand.

Jess laughed. 'Been doing it all me life – but ta any'ow. There—' She pulled her skirt down. 'I'm decent now!'

As she reached the ground he caught her by the waist for a second to steady her. They held each other's gaze for a moment, then Sis was once more trying to scramble up on to Bonney. Ned let go Jess's hand, but Ernie had already taken pity on Sis and was hoisting her up.

'I'll help 'er!'

Jess was full of energy, as if she was on fire. She ran up and down, leading Sis as she bumped about on Bonney's back, shrieking that she was going to fall, giggling so much by the end that she did slither off the side. Bert had a go, clowning about, then Ronny was allowed to sit up on Bonney's back for a moment.

'Tek 'im off!' Olive protested. ''E looks worried to death! Yer coming in for a cuppa tea now yer 'ere?' She took Ned's arm.

'What'll I do about Bonney?'

'Oh I'll hold her,' Jess hooked the reins round her wrist and sat down on the step. The room was so small that she wasn't left out by sitting down there. Ned sat at the table with his back to the range, the others round him except Polly who was brewing the tea. Jess listened to them talking. She sat quietly, watching him until she felt his eyes on her, watching her curiously for a moment, then glancing away. She couldn't seem to stop looking at him.

But after a few moments she heard Olive say, 'So tell us all about it. Why daint yer bring Mary with yer? 'Ow long's she got to go now? She got over feeling poorly?'

Jess's heartbeat began to pick up speed. She found herself thinking, no – oh please, she can't mean . . .?

'Oh yes, she's got over that, but there's only a few weeks left. She's feeling it now, what with working and

55

that – it's taking it out of 'er. She's gone to bed this afternoon.'

Olive made sympathetic noises. 'She still at Coopers?'

'No – Griffiths. Been there a while she 'as now – over in Vittoria Street, making rings. Ain't I told yer that?'

'Not that I remember. Oh – so yer'll be staying over that side now.' She sounded disappointed. 'I'd 'oped yer'd come back over 'ere so we'd see a bit more of yer.'

'Oh, yer won't catch Mary moving away from 'er mom,' Ned said. ' 'Specially now, with the babby on the way.'

Jess listened with part of her mind, but a shrinking, disappointed feeling crept through her. So Ned was married. How daft could she be, never thinking for a moment that he might be! But he had affected her so strongly – and the way he had looked into her eyes when he helped her off Bonney ... But it must have been all in her silly, inexperienced imagination. She sat closed into her own thoughts, only half hearing now as Ned talked about the Fire Service, about Mary. Her earlier sense of excitement had melted away and suddenly all the joy had gone out of the afternoon. She sat feeling foolish and cross with herself.

She came to as Ned got up to leave and he took Bonney's reins from her.

'So – where did you spring from, Jess?'

'Budderston – Warwickshire.' She answered calmly, glancing at Olive. 'I wanted to come and see my auntie and find work 'ere for a bit.'

'Bit different 'ere in Brum, I'll bet. D'yer like it?'

'Mostly.'

Ned laughed. 'You don't sound all that sure!'

'She gets a bit 'omesick for the country now and then,' Polly said.

'Well, yer can visit, can't yer? The countryside ain't going to run away.'

'She can't.' Bert stated the facts with no malice intended. ''Cause they don't want 'er. Ain't that right, Jess?'

'Bert!' Polly protested. ''Ow could yer?'

Jess felt a blush of fury and mortification burn across her cheeks. This was the truth – of course it was. But it was terrible to hear it blurted out so baldly. Quietly, she said, 'Seems like they don't.'

Ned stopped attending to Bonney and looked round at her.

'How come? Why wouldn't they want yer?'

Jess felt them all staring at her. Olive started to say something, but Jess pulled her shoulders back.

'No, Auntie. There ain't no shame in the truth.' She looked at Ned. 'I ran away from home 'cause they were making me get wed and it weren't what I wanted. So they'd be none too pleased to see me at the moment.'

She felt Ned's interest. 'Why didn't yer want it?'

Jess was startled to be asked such a question. Wasn't it obvious what you should want? Everyone was waiting for her to speak.

'Well,' she said fiercely. 'It ain't no good marrying someone if yer don't love 'em, is it? I mean yer've got to love 'em so that nothing else matters – not just marry 'cause it suits.'

'Think yer might need to lower yer sights a bit,' Olive said. There was amusement in her eyes. 'She's a quaint one awright,' she told Ned. 'All sorts of odd notions 'er comes out with.'

Jess looked down, hands clenched into fists, fury swelling in her right up to the back of her throat. Why had she said what she really thought? Looking up, mutinously she said, 'Otherwise what's the point?'

'The point,' Olive said, 'is sticking together to keep bellies fed so yer don't 'ave the Workhouse hanging over yer. And you'll find that out, Ned my lad, soon as your family starts arriving.'

'Weren't just yer own family you was feeding either, Auntie, when yours were littl'uns. Yer'd even find a piece for me when I turned up like a bad penny.' Jess could tell he was trying to smooth things over. The affectionate cheekiness of his smile disarmed Olive in a second. Jess watched, aching inside. Not only was Ned married, but now she'd made a fool of herself in front of him as well.

As he left, Ned said, 'You are going to come over and see our place, aren't yer?'

Olive didn't promise. She gave him a non-committal nod, from the step. Ned leapt up on to Bonney's back, keeping his boots on this time.

'Bring Mary to see us, and don't leave it 'til I'm walking with a stick.'

Ned gave a salute, smiling round at them. His eyes met Jess's for a second. Then he winked at Sis.

'T'ra then!'

He turned Bonney and they watched him trot off down towards Digbeth, waving a hand.

The others started to go in.

'Come on, Jess,' Polly tried to take her arm.

Jess pulled away, shaking her head, eyes fixed on the horse and rider until they disappeared round the corner.

*

58

'Wasn't it lovely to see Ned?' Sis sat up in bed that night, yanking a comb through her hair. 'Seeing 'im on that 'orse – 'e was like summat out of a fairytale. And 'e's so handsome! Lucky Mary.'

'Why does 'e call yer mom Auntie?' Jess asked.

'Oh – she's known 'im all our lives.' Jess wasn't sure if she imagined a stiff tone in Polly's voice. 'Thinks the world of 'im, Mom does. 'E's like another son to 'er.'

'I can see why.'

Polly sat up. 'I know yer can – it was written all over yer. Yer could've lit a fire off your face this afternoon. But 'e's spoken for. Ned and Mary've known each other for years and now they're wed, so it's no good you coming 'ere getting any ideas in yer 'ead. 'E ain't free, so it's too late for you or anyone else!'

Eight

Ned stepped out of Albion Street fire station the next Sunday afternoon after work. The afternoon was warm and he took off the black uniform jacket and slung it over his shoulder as he automatically set off towards home. After a few yards he stopped and turned back towards town. Mary would be asleep, or round at her mom's so he might just as well go back over to Allison Street again for a bit. There was a warm welcome there all right.

'Making up for lost time, are yer?' Olive said seeing him turn up again. 'Talk about a bad flaming penny!'

'Thought I would. Mary's bad, at the moment.'

'Well yer've missed Bert, and Polly's out with Ernie . . .'

'I came to see *you*, auntie!' Ned said, throwing his jacket over a chair, eyes searching the room. I didn't come to see Polly, he thought, nor Bert, nor even Olive if he was honest with himself. *She* was here, the cousin, the pretty one, prettier even than he remembered. He was intrigued by her, by that smile that seemed to pass right into him. He nodded at her.

'Hello,' Jess said. She had a pink dress on with short sleeves and her arms were tanned, the hairs on them glowing gold. The dress showed off her curves. She's perfect, he thought. He'd never seen anyone like her before, never knew there could be anyone like her.

'Oh Ned,' Sis was saying. 'Daint yer bring Bonney with yer this time?'

He dragged his attention to her. 'Not today. I'll bring 'er again sometime if yer want.'

''Ere—' Olive put a cup of tea on the table. 'Get this down yer.'

He sat and drank his cuppa with them, listening to Sis's chatter, answering Olive's questions about the family. He could only hope he was saying the right things because his mind could only fasten on her, on Jess sitting opposite, close enough to touch, her strong fingers on the handle of her cup, drawing him with her eyes. There was a twist of excitement in his belly like none he'd ever had before, a married man who shouldn't be having thoughts like undoing the buttons down the back of the pink dress, seeing it fall softly from her with her naked under it . . .

'You awright, Ned?' Olive asked him as he sat moving his cup round on the table.

He looked up and smiled. 'Course – sorry. Miles away I was there, for a second.'

'Got a lot on yer mind, I should think, with the babby coming and that. Never mind – soon he'll be 'ere and you'll get used to it all.'

Reality chilled him like a bucket of ice water. I don't want to get used to it. I want another life. I want to start again.

He didn't stay long. Said he'd better be getting back, and stood up to slip the jacket back on. He looked broader, taller in his uniform than in the old clothes he'd been wearing before. As he left he spoke to all of them politely.

'Cheerio, Sis . . . Jess.'

'T'ra, Ned,' she said. Her soft voice vibrated through him. He looked away from her quickly.

His visit filled Jess with longing. However much she told herself she was being ridiculous, each brief look or exchange of words she had had with him seemed charged with significance. She relived his visit over and over that week, lying on the prickly mattress after Polly and Sis were asleep, or standing with her hands in tepid water, washing tea and coffee dregs out of thick glasses at the back of Mather's. She kept seeing his eyes turned to her, interested, in some way puzzled, it seemed, when he looked at her.

I've got to stop thinking of him, she thought. We barely know each other and he's married and I bet Mary's really beautiful . . . I'm nothing to him. She was ashamed at the extent of her feelings, her preoccupation with him, hour after hour which she could not seem to overcome by willpower.

Her need to think of Ned blocked out other feelings of longing. Neither her father nor Sarah had written back to answer Olive's letter.

So they don't want me, even enough to drop a line . . . But she no longer felt homesick. For what would life be, if *he* was not there? In two weeks Ned had invaded her thoughts until she could keep her mind on almost nothing else.

The next week he did come with Mary. Jess was in a state of nerves all morning, wondering if they'd come. When they arrived she backed into the scullery, peeping out to get a look at Ned's wife.

She heard Mary's high, slightly nasal voice first.

'Lovely to see yer, Mrs Beeston.' Jess thought she sounded nervous.

'Yer'll want to sit down,' Olive was saying. 'Ooh, yer carrying low awright! Never mind, bab, soon be over now. Come on in and take a pew.'

Trying hard to look casual, Jess stepped out of the scullery. The first thing that struck her was Mary's smallness beside Ned. She was a tiny, pale thing with freckles, auburn hair tied in a high ponytail and arms poking out of her loose stripey frock which were so white and skinny they looked as if they'd snap like kindling. She was carrying the child well out at the front and the burden of it looked enough to topple her over on her face.

Jess was rocked by the violent stab of jealousy that went through her. Savage thoughts ran through her mind. She's barely worth having, scrawny little thing! And look at that thin neck, and those arms! For a second she placed her hands on her own waist, feeling her strong, hourglass shape.

She was ashamed at her thoughts. What right did she have to be so horrible? Mary was bound to be very nice – she was Ned's wife, after all! She knew Polly didn't think much of Mary though. Was there a good reason for this?

She managed a smile at Mary. She had a sweet face, even Jess could see that, with high, arched eyebrows which made her look permanently surprised and interested.

'I'm Jess. Polly's cousin.'

'Oh—' Mary nodded. 'That's nice. Come to stay for a bit, 'ave yer?'

'Sit down and 'ave a cuppa tea – and I might rustle up a bit of cake if yer lucky.' Olive nodded over at

Mary. 'Look as if yer could do with feeding up, wench.'
It sounded like an accusation.

They stayed a couple of hours, Mary laughing and
joking, full of importance as a young wife who was
about to have her first baby. Jess did her best to smile
and laugh. She wanted to shine in front of Ned, for him
at least to notice her. She sat Ronny on her lap and fed
him mouthfuls of cake, kissing his cheeks. He'd get
down, play about for a bit, run to Ernie for a time, then
scramble up on her lap again.

'Come 'ere,' she said as he approached her again.
'Ooh, yer don't make up yer mind, do yer!'

She felt the strength in her arms, lifting him up, and
glanced across, longing to see Ned looking at her. For
all she attempted to pull herself together and be sensible,
she wanted to know he was watching. His being there
lit her up. She felt as if she was glowing in the room.
But he never seemed to see her. Was looking anywhere
but in her direction, it seemed, whenever she looked up
and tried to meet his eyes.

'You're settling over there then, are yer?' Olive
asked. 'I was hoping yer might move closer over 'ere.'

'Oh, I wouldn't want to leave me mom,' Mary said.
'She still needs me 'elp like – all me brothers and sisters.
I'm the eldest of ten,' she explained to Jess.

'She's got 'er 'ands full then,' Jess smiled.

'None too well either, is she?' Ned was sitting back,
legs stretched out. Still he didn't look at her.

'No – I don't know what our mom'd do without me
close by. And Ned's been ever so good – says 'e'd live
anywhere to be with me.' Mary smiled at him adoringly.

Polly got up and refilled the teapot. Jess watched,
saw Polly holding her shoulders stiffly. As she came

back to the table she looked directly at Jess. See? her expression said. No good you getting any thoughts in *that* direction. But then she noticed that Olive had suddenly closed her eyes and sat back as if overcome by dizziness. Jess saw Polly exchange a worried glance with Sis.

'You awright, Auntie?' Ned leaned towards her.

Olive opened her eyes, dazed for a second, then took a deep breath. 'Oh ar – I'll be awright. You carry on.' She held out her cup for tea, shaking her head to dislodge the flashes of memory which had appeared in there, unbidden.

Jess held Ronny tight with one arm, looking down and stroking his soft little legs. She felt as if she was in a dream, one in which she was in a familiar place but everything in it felt wrong.

You're so stupid! she raged at herself in her head. You can't work up any feelings for the man who was given you on a plate, and now you're all of a flutter over someone who's married to someone else! Just stop acting so daft and get 'im out of your head, for God's sake!

She looked up again, sensing a movement beside her. Ned was leaning forward, playing a game with Ronny.

'I'm gunna 'ave that!' He tweaked at Ronny's nose, then held his thumb trapped between two fingers. Jess saw that he had wide, flat nails. She could smell him, soap, leather, sweat, breathed him in. 'Look – 'ere it is. I've got it – want it back?'

Ronny looked at him open mouthed for a second, put his hand up to his nose, then gurgled with laughter.

'There yer go – back on!'

He pretended to give the little boy his nose back. As

he touched the child's face he looked at Jess for a second, laughing. She smiled back, but Ned turned, abruptly.

'We'd better be going, Auntie. You ready, Mary?'

As they left, Olive stood on the step waving them down the street. She turned to come inside, still smiling.

'Lovely couple, ain't they?' she said. ''E's done really nicely for 'imself there.'

A few days later, when everyone was out, except the babby, Ronny, Olive stood in her house, her thoughts agonized. It was getting worse. Some days she was all right. Normal. But days like today were terrible. Memories rushing back at her like a flock of ravens flying into her mind. Things she had avoided thinking about for years, as if some cavity in her had opened, spilling over.

'It's no good – I can't carry on like this . . .' Hearing her speak, Ronny looked up from his seat on the floor where he was playing with a handful of pegs.

For a moment she stared at him, distracted. So like his father he was! Her face contorted with bitterness. The child couldn't help it, but by God she would rue his existence to the end of her days. A few moments of weakness, of need. Carried away – her, Olive Beeston carried away by sweet talk and a man's fumblings! If she'd known anyone else be so bloody stupid she'd've soon told 'em . . .

With trembling, clammy hands she pulled open the little drawstring bag she kept tucked in her pocket and counted through her change. She turned over the coins, counting and recounting with the sense of wonder that came to her whenever she handled money. It still seemed a miracle when they brought their earnings home. Polly, Bert, Sis – and Jess was bringing in a small amount ... They had enough now with four earning! Not a princely amount, but enough.

Her days of bone freezing poverty never left her. Worrying about every farthing, not even having enough on many a day for a half pail of slack for the fire, Polly and Bert slinking down the canal to pinch it off the barges, begging outside pubs when ice shone like crystals on the cobbles with her babbies clinging round her skirts, so bad with fever she barely knew what she was doing. If it hadn't been for the charity of the church missions they'd have starved. These memories and many others forced themselves into her mind whenever she handled money.

But the things she most wanted to forget, to block right out of her mind, went further back. God knows she'd tried to force the memories away, but suddenly it wasn't working any more. It all seemed to be bearing down on her like a goods train, with her tied to the track, like those pretty wenches in the films, the hot breath of the train on her face.

'Today's the day,' she said to Ronny. 'I gotta do summat about meself. 'Ow can I go on like this? I can't even get to the shops!'

Polly or Jess were doing all the shopping. She could tell Jess was puzzled by this. After all, Olive was the one who was at home all day. She had the time. That morning as they set off to work Polly had said,

'What d'yer need bringing in tonight, Mom?'

'Don't bother. We'll get by on what we've got,' she said. Polly looked surprised but was in too much of a rush to argue.

It was no good – she'd have to go. They were out of

milk and tea, and there wasn't a heel of bread in the house.

She pulled her coat on like a suit of armour, although it was June now and warm, took her hessian bag from the hook where the coat had hung and picked Ronny up.

'Come on, son—' She was aflutter with nerves. 'You're going to Agatha's for a bit.' She forced herself to the front door and carried Ronny round into the yard and went to her neighbour's house.

Agatha's pinched face appeared at the door. She looked taken aback at the sight of Olive Beeston in her hat and coat. Word had got round that she'd 'turned a bit funny' and wouldn't go out of the house.

'Could yer take Ronny for me for an hour?' Olive said brusquely, trying not to turn her nose up at the dank, sweaty air that gusted out through the open door.

'You going out?' A nosey smile had begun at the corners of her mouth.

'Ar – I'm going out. That awright with you?'

'No trouble,' Agatha said, holding her arms out. Ronny's face screwed up and he started roaring. 'Oh come on, bab, don't start that. You go – 'e'll be awright wi' me.'

Olive left a beetroot-faced Ronny trying to hurl himself out of Agatha's arms. She made it out of the yard, but down the entry stopped and leaned against the wall, all the old fear flooding through her. She bowed her head, closing her eyes, sweating inside her thick coat. Her hands felt clammy, and for a few moments she was panting in panic.

Oh pull yerself together! she gasped to herself, scared stiff someone'd see her. She straightened herself up and walked on weak legs towards the street.

It had only got this bad since Jess arrived. She knew that was what it was. Seeing her that evening, that copper beside her. Gave her the shock of her life. All these years she'd kept it at bay. And borne so much alone. No old man to tek care of 'em. No Charlie. He kept her steady when he was alive, those years they had together.

Taking deep breaths she turned down Allison Street. Immediately she spotted Bertha Hyde at her window across the street, like a ghost between her twitching net curtains. Olive's fury at her restored her a little and she gave a mocking wave.

There's nowt to be afraid of. Nowt. Just keep walking. Down to the main road – morning, Mrs Eldon, awright? A smile, that's it. No, I don't see you out often either . . . that's it, round the corner.

Digbeth and the Bull Ring were packed with shoppers. Her fear began to subside a little in the anonymous bustle. She enjoyed the smells of the market, music from someone playing a French horn, felt the early summer sun on her face.

Ain't good to be cooped up inside all day long, she thought. I ought to do this all the time, silly old woman I am.

Stepping into the first shop was a relief though. As if she'd been washed up on a rock. She felt her body relax, and only realized then that she'd been clenching her teeth hard.

But then she saw one of her neighbours from down the road was just turning from buying her bread as Olive's turn came.

'Mrs Beeston, ain't it?' the woman said, not troubling to keep her voice down. 'Don't see yer about much – yer been bad or summat?'

Olive's jaw tightened again. Mind your own cowing business! a madwoman's voice shrieked in her head. Don't go nosing into my business, yer upstart busybody you!

She forced a tight smile. 'My daughter likes to do the shopping as a rule.' She turned away. 'I'll 'ave a large cottage and a bag o' cobs, ta.'

She moved carefully from shop to shop for what she wanted: tins of Handy Brand milk, a quarter of Typhoo Tipps, a pound of cheap mince, onions, spuds and carrots off the Bull Ring. They slung them straight into her carrier for her. Triumphant, she gathered up her purchases and headed across towards Digbeth. Straight home and get the kettle on. She could leave Ronny with Agatha a bit longer and have a morning's peace. She'd done it! It had only taken breaking the habit . . .

A tram was lumbering down the road and she glanced to one side, half looking at it. There was an advertisement for Hudson's Soap plastered along the side of it. She was none too keen on trams passing too close to her. All those faces behind the glass staring down at her. Made her prickle all over. She avoided looking at the windows, and the tram rattled past.

And then she saw it, across the street. Her insides gave a violent lurch of shock so that for a moment she thought she was going to be sick right there in the gutter. Among all those people milling along there, that face turned towards her. The face she lived her life in dread of seeing, eyes staring straight at her from under the brim of a black hat . . . It happened in a second and Olive spun round, pressing herself against the sooty wall of St Martin's. After a moment she turned back, searching the crowd, but there were so many hats, so many people in drab clothes, and her eyesight was not all it might be. She dropped her bag and onions rolled out across the pavement. A woman stooped and helped her pick them up.

She almost fell through her front door, her face wet with perspiration, hands trembling so that she could barely unbutton her coat. She put the kettle on the hob and sank down at the table, panting as if she'd run all the way home.

Everything led back to that house. That room where she'd been found. They'd come towards her, approaching her slowly as if she was diseased or dangerous, leading her away by the hand . . . away . . .

'Oh God in heaven,' she whimpered. 'Oh Louisa . . .'

She sat for a long time, staring across the room. Steam gushed unheeded from the kettle's spout.

'We've got to move on.'

Polly was greeted by these words as she got in from work that night. Olive was huddled up in the little room which seemed very dark after the light evening.

Polly put her bag down, looking round for Jess or Sis. 'Where are the others?'

'Jess ain't back. Sis's round at Enid's.'

Carefully, Polly said, 'What's 'appened, Mom?'

'I saw 'er.'

'Saw who?' Polly sat down at the table, rubbing her hands over her pale face. 'What're yer talking about?'

'I went up the Bull Ring. I 'ad to get . . .'

'You went up the shops?' Polly sat up, smiling. 'Did yer manage by yerself? That's really good, Mom, ain't it. Yer could get out more now . . .'

'But I saw – this woman. Lived round Saltley when Louisa and me lived with yer Dad . . .' Polly could hear the tightly strung emotion in her mother's voice. Olive couldn't seem to stop talking, thoughts which had been pressing in on her all day, rushing out, even though Polly didn't know, wouldn't understand. 'She's aged a bit of course, but it was 'er awright. Oh Poll, I thought my 'eart was going to stop she gave me such a shock. She's after me again, coming to find me . . .'

'Mom, stop it!' Polly shouted. She grabbed Olive by the shoulders, starting to shake her. 'I don't know what yer going on about. What woman? Why's anyone going to be after yer? Yer ain't done nothing, 'ave yer?'

Olive's face was crumpling like that of a terrified child.

'Don't!' Polly cried harshly. She released her mother, frightened by the look in her eyes. 'This's got to stop, Mom. I can't stand any more of it. Yer making a nervous wreck of me an' all. Yer not making any sense.'

'I'm sorry, Poll—' Olive started crying, sobs breaking out from her throat. 'I just can't go on living round 'ere if she knows we're 'ere. She's wicked – evil . . .'

Polly was close to tears herself. 'Mom, I don't know what all this is about. I'm worried about yer – yer don't seem yerself at all lately. Please don't talk like this. You're frightening the life out of me. There's no one after yer, is there? Why would there be?'

As she spoke, Ronny came bumping down on his bottom from upstairs, took one look at his mom and started wailing in alarm.

'Come up 'ere, bab.' With a huge effort Olive rallied herself, sat Ronny on a chair and wiped her eyes and nose on her apron. 'Don't cry, son. I was just telling Poll 'ere that we're going to move to a bigger 'ouse soon. Yer'd like that, eh?'

Polly was protesting that they didn't need to move

anywhere when the door opened, setting the coats on the back of it swinging. The two of them froze. Jess walked in, preoccupied until she saw her aunt's tearful face.

'What's going on?' she spoke cautiously.

Polly and Olive looked at one another. Olive stood up. 'Nothing for you to worry about.'

Jess felt about as welcome as a fox in a chicken run. She couldn't get another word out of them, so she asked Polly later, upstairs.

'She's been acting real funny lately.' Polly sat on her bed, twisting the sleeve of her cardigan round and round. 'I'm bothered about 'er, Jess. The last couple of months – not going out, and now she's on about seeing some woman who's scared 'er half to death and she wants to move 'ouse. She won't say why. I'm worried she's going a bit, well, you know . . .'

Jess sat beside her in the half-light. 'She seems awright in 'erself – you know, not sick or anything. But you're right – she does seem to be acting funny. I saw 'er the other morning looking out the window – up and down the road, worried like, as if she thought someone was coming. Who does she say this woman is?'

'She don't—' Polly looked round at her, wide-eyed. 'I've never heard 'er talk about this woman before. And the worst of it is, Jess – I'm not at all sure there is any woman!'

Nine

'Oh sod it!'

Jess caught the hem of her dress on her heel as she stood up from bending to wipe Ronny's face. She heard the waistline rip.

'Well it'll have to stay like that – I ain't got time to mend it now.' More sewing, she thought grumpily. On top of all the mending she was doing for the family.

No one took any notice. They were all rushing to get to work. Jess was in a bad mood because yesterday Mr Mather had announced Mrs Mather would be taking over again in the Coffee House and that she was no longer needed. Having seen Mrs Mather, a terribly thin, sallow woman, with a robust infant who looked as if he'd sucked the very life out of her, Jess had thought she'd be there for some time to come. But no. She'd have to look for a new job.

'Yer've been a good worker,' Mr Mather said. 'If yer do want any of them references anywhere like ... only yer'll 'ave to write 'em. I've never writ well meself.'

'I know where I'm going to look for a job,' Jess told them at home. 'The Jewellery Quarter.' If that Mary could get a job there, she thought, I don't see why I shouldn't. 'I like the sound of it.'

'Well there's always girls wanted,' Olive said. 'But you'll 'ave a walk – that's the other side of town.'

74

'It's not that far – I could walk it in a half hour if I hurry . . . I'm going early.'

She downed a cup of tea and a quick bite of breakfast. 'T'ra then!'

'Tara-abit,' Sis called to her.

Jess walked briskly but despondently through town, joining the early morning hurly-burly of people scurrying to work. It was an overcast morning, the ground wet. Soon she felt water seeping in through the sole of one of her shoes.

Darn it, she thought. I've not enough for another pair. I'll have to stick some paper in the bottom. The morning suited her mood. Here she was in this smoky grey place, away from home, no job and now to cap it all, she had holes in her shoes! She felt very glum, as if all the world was against her.

She didn't even see the horse bus coming until someone shouted. It was almost on top of her and she dashed to avoid it, tripping over a tram track and falling on her face in the road. She felt the cobbles scrape along her cheek, heard a horse screaming above her as the driver reined it in to avoid her, prone on the ground. Jess curled up, covering her head as the hooves clashed and scraped round her. All was confusion and the first thing she was properly aware of was a man's voice shouting,

'What in God's name d'yer think yer was doing! I could've bloody killed yer!'

Things gradually stilled. Slowly, dazed, Jess raised her head. Her hat was lying crushed in the road in front of her. She sat up and looked round. There was a crowd of murmuring faces round her, the bus stationary on her left, its horse still jumpy, the harness frothed up round its mouth.

'So – are yer awright or what?' The driver squatted in front of her. Jess stared at the buttons on his uniform.

'Yes. Think so.' She felt giddy, knocked out of shape. Her head was throbbing. 'Sorry. I never saw yer.'

'That's 'cause yer weren't even flaming looking!' He seemed to be calming down now, having seen there was little damage. 'If yer can get yerself up, all these good people and myself can get on.'

'It's all right. I'll take care of 'er.'

Blearily, Jess found herself looking at a pair of heavy black boots. She followed the line of them up, black uniform, brass buttons. He knelt beside her.

'Jess? You awright?'

'Ned?' For a crazed second she wondered if the tram had hit her and she'd died, and was this what heaven would be like.

'Let's get you off the road . . .' He helped her stand, taking her hand with a firm gentleness she noted, even in her stunned state, and led her through the staring people to the pavement and a little way up the sloping street opposite. Her left shoulder and her knees were hurting, and her right cheek stung, bringing tears to her eyes.

'Can yer make it up 'ere? There's a churchyard where yer can sit down.'

Jess nodded, and without a word he offered her his arm and they walked together until they reached the graveyard of a blackened church. Ned held on to her until they reached a bench and sat down. Jess rubbed her shoulder, trying to ease it.

'Is my face a mess?'

''Tis a bit, yes. Sorry – I've got no hanky, nothing like that.'

'Nor me.'

'Yer going to be awright?'

'There's not much wrong. I just feel all shaken up, that's all.'

'Couldn't believe my eyes when I saw yer. What're yer doing over this way? I thought you worked in town?'

She was touched that he remembered. 'I did. Lost me job yesterday. So I come over 'ere to find another one. Only I seem to be making a hash of it so far.' She started laughing until he laughed as well. 'Sometimes I don't think I'm cut out for living 'ere.'

'You'll get used to it. We're awright really, yer know, us Brummies.'

Jess smiled. 'I know. Didn't mean it like that. Shouldn't you be going to work?'

'Just finished. I was sent to run an errand to Newhall Street before going home. I work over in Albion Street.'

'Yer must be tired.'

'Not yet. Takes a while after a night like last night to unwind, like. There was a blaze over in Hockley – not far away.' Close to him now, she saw streaks of grime on his face. 'Listen – if yer want to find a job I'll 'elp yer. I know these streets like the back of my hand.'

'Would yer? I don't know where to go to start. Only – aren't I too much of a mess?'

'No, that don't matter. There's loads of jobs round 'ere. We'll find yer summat.'

He led her through the narrow streets of the Jewellery Quarter, lined with narrow old buildings which had once all been houses, but had gradually been taken over by many different little businesses. Graham Sreet, Vyse Street, Vittoria Street. They walked along, reading the signs over factory doorways. Ned pointed to one: 'Griffiths . . .'

'That's where Mary works.' Jess noticed he didn't suggest she work there, although there was a sign outside saying, 'Girls wanted'. 'Shall we walk on a bit, show yer the lay of the land?'

There was silence for a while as they walked along.

'Did yer really do what yer said?' he asked suddenly.

Jess frowned up at him. 'What?'

'Run away from 'ome – cut up yer wedding dress . . . Only it's not every day someone tells yer summat like that.'

'Who told yer that – about the dress?'

'Sis.'

Jess was silent.

''Ave I put my foot in it?'

'No – I don't mind yer asking.'

'So, why?'

'I told yer why. They wanted to marry me off to someone I couldn't stand for more than five minutes, let alone a lifetime.'

'Oh. I wasn't sure if you was 'aving me on, that's all.'

'Why would I be 'aving you on? 'S'not the sort of thing yer just make up off the top of yer head, is it?'

'I s'pose not. Sorry for asking.'

'S'awright.'

'Look—' He stopped. 'What about this? "Blake's Brooches and Badges."'

Jess looked at him, eyebrows raised.

'They might 'ave summat. Enamelling job. Let's go and ask.'

To get to the entrance they had to go down a narrow alley at the side. Jess followed Ned, feeling as if she was in a dream. With him, she thought, everything felt right. As if she'd come home. The realization was followed by the pain of reality. No! Of course not. She could not think like that. He could never be hers.

'What d'yer want?' a woman's voice said.

'You got any vacancies?'

'Depends what for.'

'My er . . . Miss Hart wants to learn a trade.'

'Miss Hart does, does she?'

'Jess,' Jess said.

The woman's shrewd eyes looked her up and down. 'Where've yow worked before?'

'On a farm and in Mather's Coffee Shop, in the Bull Ring,' Jess told her.

The woman rolled her eyes. 'Well that's gunna be a lot of use to us, ain't it? Yow can only come and start laying on if yer want. That's all I've got if yow've got nothing previous. What's amiss with yower face?'

'I fell over.' Jess looked at Ned. He gave a tiny nod. 'Yes – I'll come and do . . . laying on.' She hadn't the remotest idea what this meant, but if Ned thought it was right she'd do it.

'Yow can start tomorra. Can't be doing with it today. Get a note from yower doctor to say yer fit for work. Yow'll be on ten shilling a week minus stoppages.'

The door slammed shut.

Outside, Jess laughed with relief. 'Well – thanks a lot! I thought that was going to take me all day.'

'Oh you'll get on awright. Just need to learn yer way around a bit.' He smiled at her. Jess thought he looked exhausted.

'Yer can go and get some kip now, can't yer?'

Ned hesitated. 'D'yer fancy a walk?'

'A *walk*?'

'You know – yer keep sticking one foot in front of the other.'

Jess tutted, though her heart was going like a drum. Nothing could be nicer than the thought of spending some more time with Ned. 'What d'yer take me for? I just thought you'd want to get home.'

'Well – you've not got to be at work 'til tomorra and I've done for today. And yer look as if yer could do with cheering up. 'Ow about it?'

'Wouldn't Mary think it were a bit funny – you taking me out for a walk?'

'No – course not,' he said hastily. 'I'll show yer Handsworth Park. It's nice, this time of year. It's a couple of miles. D'yer want to catch a tram?'

'No! Oh no – I'll walk.' All her aches and pains were nothing compared to the thought of Ned asking her to go with him. No man had ever shown such kindness to her before.

'I'll stop yer throwing yerself under any more buses,' he smiled round at her as they started walking. Seeing his dark, mischievous eyes looking into hers, Jess panicked for a moment and she wished she'd said no. How could she enjoy this time with Ned without it being more agonizing knowing he felt nothing for her but sympathy?

They walked north, out of the city, to Soho Hill and the gracious suburb of Handsworth with its fine villas and wide roads. Ned led her to the gates of the park, where a nanny and two small children were climbing into a trap pulled by a skewbald pony.

'Oh – look at 'im!' Jess went up closer. 'Lovely, ain't 'e?'

Ned watched Jess as she shyly went up and asked if she could pet the pony. The nanny nodded, reluctantly, and Jess stroked his smooth neck and tickled his nose before saying goodbye. The woman in the trap stared

Ned up and down, surprised to see a fireman out strolling the park, helmet under one arm, but saw he was oblivious of her scrutiny. All his attention was taken by the sweet-faced young woman with him. He was so obviously captivated by the sight of her as she petted the pony.

'I'll 'ave to bring Bonney out to see yer again, if you like horses that much,' he said as they walked through the gates together.

'Oh would yer? I'd love another ride. I've always loved horses.'

She told him about the shire horses at the farm. The days they came for shoeing, and how that was what they were doing when her mom died.

'I can still remember that day – everything was covered in ice, like sugar. Beautiful. But it was the worst day of my life.'

They were walking round the big pond, brown water to their right, grass on the left. A watery sun forced a bright patch through the cloud.

'What 'appened to her?'

'She died in childbirth. I'd've had a sister. My stepmother – well, later she was my stepmother – told me after.'

'And you didn't like 'er – your stepmother?'

'No.'

'You don't look anything like yer auntie – or Polly.'

'I look like my Mom – Olive says any'ow. I do remember her, a bit, but I wish auntie'd talk to me more about 'er. I can't get a word out of 'er.' Jess looked up at him. 'She thinks the world of you though.'

'I know – she always has. She and Charlie ran their hucksters shop in Sparkbrook and our mom and dad lived just round the corner, off the Stratford Road. I was in and out of the shop for a penn'orth of rocks and she took a shine to me. Gave me 'em for nothing some of the time. She weren't so poor then as she was later. Course, I never knew 'ow bad things were for 'er after Charlie died. You don't see things as a kid, do yer? But she was still pleased when I used to go and see 'er when she lived up by St Alban's Church. Mom and Dad would've helped 'er out if they'd known, but I just said she was all right.'

They strolled slowly round the park talking. Ned told her his mom and dad lived in Selly Oak now: his dad worked for a small firm producing yeast and his elder brother Fred was married with two boys. Jess said she had no one. Told him about her father, and Sarah.

The morning went very fast. After a time they found they had stopped talking, as if something had stalled and they couldn't get it started again. Jess stopped by the boundary with a church yard and looked across the gravestones. A bird was singing.

'Peaceful in there,' she said, but felt desolate, couldn't bear another second in his company suddenly, because with every fibre of her being she wanted to reach out and touch him and knew she must not. As he stood close to her, the hairs rose on her neck and arms. 'We ought to go back,' she managed to say. 'We shouldn't be 'ere. Neither of us.'

He looked into her face and saw her eyes were full of tears.

'What's the matter?'

'Nothing. I just want to go home.' A tear rolled down her cheek. 'I want . . .' She turned away. 'I don't know what I want. Just leave me, Ned. I know the way 'ome. Please.' She put her hands over her face, wanting to pull them away again and find him gone, yet feeling she'd fall apart if he wasn't there. She was afraid of what he would think of her.

'It'll be the shock,' he started to say, but had to stop and swallow to clear the sudden tightness in his throat. 'From this morning. Look – I'll take yer back and make sure you're safe. You might faint or summat. We've had not a crust to eat.'

She'd given no thought to food, but knew it was nothing to do with that. I mustn't say a word, she thought. If I say anything, it'll be all wrong. Silently she wiped her cheeks.

'Jess—' There was a tone in his voice which made her raise her eyes to him, but he'd turned away abruptly, was staring across the park, his broad shoulders black against the green beyond.

After a moment he turned back to her, finding his resolve. 'We'd best catch a tram.'

All the way back, they were silent, sitting on the tram's hard seats, pressed together at the hip. Jess felt cold and desolate inside. Ned stared out of the window. He seemed hundreds of miles away to her. Of course he was, because that was right, he felt nothing for her and she was a fool.

'Will yer be all right walking from the Bull Ring?' he asked as they got off. The afternoon had darkened again.

'Yes, course,' she said flatly. 'And thanks, Ned. For 'elping me, and the walk and that. We'll be seeing yer sometime I s'pose, with Mary.' As Jess spoke her good-byes she was scarcely able to look at him. She crossed the road, not turning to glance back, so she was unaware of how long he stood watching her as she walked away.

He picked her out among the crowds, straight-backed, with a solitariness and proud dignity which made him clench his fists as he fought the desire to run after her. He walked exhaustedly back towards Hockley to meet Mary out of work. His mind was in a tired, feverish turmoil, a confused array of feelings strung between his fragile, trusting wife, and the lonely, bewitching girl with whom he was falling passionately in love.

Ten

'Oi – are yow listening to me or am I wasting me breath?'

Even as the grim-faced woman in charge of the workshop showed her how to lay the coloured enamel powders on small round sheets of metal ready for firing, it was Ned's face Jess could see before her. The way he'd said her name that day – what was he going to say that he never finished, didn't dare to say?

She shook her head to dislodge him from her mind.

'Yow awright?'

'Yes – course.' She tried to concentrate on what the woman was saying to her.

'After they've been fired, they're ready for filing and polishing – so they go to them lot over there ...'

Once she was left to do the job, arranging the blue and white powders on to make the badges, she quite enjoyed it. Care was needed and she became absorbed, hearing the chatter of the other workers. Eavesdropping was no problem as they worked in such a small, dark room. It might once have been someone's bedroom over the street. But at least there was the work to distract her. The ache in her heart let up a bit. She ate her dinner with a freckle-faced girl called Evie, who was chatty and cheerful. Afterwards she went back to work much less weighed down.

Put him out of your mind, she told herself. He's

someone else's. There's not a thing you can do about it now.

But the next week, one morning she started crying. She wet the enamel powder with her tears and had to start again.

''Ere – what yow playing at – it costs, that does!' the gaffer was on to her straight off, seeing her scraping the powder off the badge again. 'What's the matter with yow today?' She scowled at Jess's tearstained face. 'Look – go outside and pull yowrself together, and then get back in 'ere and make a proper job of it.'

Mortified, Jess went out of the workshop with everyone having a good nose round at her from their benches.

There was nowhere much to go. She sank down on the stairs, put her head in her hands and burst into tears again, sobs rising from somewhere deep within her.

'Oh Ned . . .' she cried. 'Oh God, Ned, please . . . please . . .'

Tears dripped through her fingers on to her work overall as the words poured out. In her state of turmoil she only knew that everything felt wrong. She would have to live with Ned calling on them in Allison Street with Mary and the baby when she had such overwhelming feelings for him as she'd had for no one else and she could not tell him or show him.

He was being kind to me, that's all, she told herself. He doesn't *need* anyone else. Of course he don't feel the same. Even if he did like me he couldn't say, could he?

She pressed the heels of her hands against her eyes.

I've got to stop this. To pull myself together, or I'll lose this job as well.

'Hope yer feel better tomorrer,' Evie said to her as they packed up work. Evie always tried to look on the bright side of everything. 'I feel a bit any'ow meself today. Let's 'ope the wind changes, eh? See yer then – I'm in a rush!'

Jess stepped out along Frederick Street. The evening was warm, the air seeming to stroke her skin. She always walked home instead of using up money on tram fares, and this evening she set off head down, not looking about her. Other people were coming out from the factories and workshops in the surrounding streets. She stopped for a moment as a crowd came out of the Griffiths Works, afraid that Mary might be among them.

Maybe I should move on somewhere bigger when I've done a bit of time at Blake's, she was thinking, when she felt herself gripped forcefully by the arm and pulled to one side against the railings. She let out a cry of alarm before she saw him.

'Ned! What . . .?'

'Can yer come with me – just for a minute?'

He led her quickly away from the factories, back down to St Paul's church yard where she had sat to recover from her run-in with the horse. There were other people about, but all of them on the move, in a hurry to get home and get their tea inside them.

They sat down on the same bench, gravestones behind them. A group of boys were throwing stones at a row of empty bottles. Jess didn't dare speak. She had to know what he wanted to say. She could feel an enormous tension coming from him. For a few moments he sat leaning forward, arms resting on his knees, looking at the ground.

He feels something for me, he does, she thought. But in her mind she was also prepared for the opposite, for this to be about something else completely. Eventually, the silence had gone on so long that she said,

'What d'yer want, Ned?'

He put his hands over his face. 'Don't yer know?'

'No. I can't say I do.'

There was another silence, then he said, 'This is terrible. I shouldn't be here. Neither of us ... I've got to go and meet Mary in a minute.' He sat up and turned to her.

She looked ahead of her.

'Jess—'

Slowly, frightened, she turned her head.

'Help me ...' He managed the words at last. 'What yer said about it not being worth it if yer don't feel more than just a bit of fondness ... I'd never, I mean I didn't know what it was, how I could feel ...' He looked fearfully at her, then plunged in. 'Ever since you've been 'ere I've thought about yer all the time. You've taken me over – I keep seeing you everywhere. I didn't know it could be like this. I mean me and Mary, we've always been good pals. She's a nice girl, a good girl, and I'm fond of 'er, but ...'

He waited for her reaction. Her face was solemn, not angry or laughing at him as he'd feared. The emotion in her eyes affected him so he could barely speak.

'Say summat to me. I don't know what yer thinking of me.'

Her voice came out barely more than a whisper. 'You're in my mind all the time as well, whether it's

88

right or not, Ned. I can't seem to help it. I feel as if I belong with yer and I can't make any sense of it.'

He opened his arms and after a second's hesitation she leaned into them, clasping him very tightly, raising her head to search for his lips. She felt them urgent, on hers. Then they sat holding each other, his chin resting on her head, both of them rocking together slightly, as if for comfort.

'You're so beautiful,' he said. 'I've never met anyone at all like you before. When I was at yer auntie's I 'ad to keep looking somewhere else, keep my eyes away, so I didn't just sit and stare at you all afternoon. It was like an ache in me—'

'You're married to someone else.'

Ned pulled away.

Jess was wide-eyed, stricken. 'That's the truth of it. You made vows in church. I'm frightened, Ned, by all I feel. I've been lonely all my life, wanting someone to love, and now I love you it's not right. I can't stop thinking about yer and wanting yer but I don't see how it can be anything but wrong...'

He gave a great anguished groan. 'Jess – I 'ad to tell yer – to see yer. It was wrong of me. She's going to 'ave my child any day now...'

Jess watched his face as he spoke, her eyes full of tears.

'I'm stuck with it – all those things Auntie Olive said, about sticking together and keeping bellies fed. That's what yer marry for, Jess... And there's my mom and dad to think of...'

'I know – I know, I know...' She was weeping. What she wanted, longed for, was an enormous, inconceivable thing.

'But I can't do it to Mary – and her mom. Yer should see 'em Jess. Her Mom's so thin and ill, and all them

89

children she's got. It'd kill 'er if I broke it off. And Mary ... I've 'ardly slept thinking of it. Not knowing what to do for the best. I 'ad to see yer, to know 'ow yer felt, but I can't just throw it all away ... I'm sorry, Jess.'

She pulled herself to her feet, hugging herself as if to nurse her aching heart, her face wet with tears.

'I don't know if I wish you hadn't come to me and told me. I couldn't stand loving you and thinking you had no feeling for me. But now I know ... what you've said ... us having to go on as we are ...'

Unable to bear seeing her in such distress he went to comfort her.

'Don't touch me!' She slapped his hands off her shoulders. She saw his look of pain and made as if to reach out and stroke his face, but she drew back, wiping her eyes. 'I want you to hold me in your arms forever, Ned, but I don't think I can stand it if you touch me now.'

'Please—' Again he tried to move close to her. 'I love you, Jess. Come 'ere, just for a minute, while we've got the chance.'

She backed away. 'No. No. I'm going now. You go and catch up with Mary. And don't come round to ours when I'm in. I don't want to see yer.'

She walked away, her arms still folded tightly.

'Jess!'

But she didn't turn. Ned stood watching helplessly. Her shoulders were hunched, head held at a dejected angle, her thick hair escaping in wisps from its pins. He felt as if she was taking a part of him with her as she left. His whole being ached for her.

He sank down again on the bench and stared desolately ahead of him. He couldn't stand the thought of going home.

Part II

Eleven

June 1914

Mary laboured long and hard to produce her child. When Ned got in from work that evening the next week, she was well underway. Her mom, Mrs Smith, was up there with her, and Mrs Martin, a local woman who came in to help with birthing. The fire was lit and they were up and down the stairs for water and cups of tea, stoking the range, looking knowingly at him.

'She's doing her best, poor lamb,' Mary's mom said. She was a thin and wrung-out looking woman, forty-five years of age but appearing sixty if a day, though with a genteel dignity about her. 'There's a stew on the fire, Ned. Will yer have 'taters with it?'

He nodded, accepting as graciously as he could. He'd known when he married Mary that they'd live close to her mother in her little terrace in Handsworth. He just hadn't bargained on it being next door. They were in and out of each other's houses, Mary's brothers and sisters too, as if they all lived together and there never seemed to be a moment's peace. He knew he should be grateful. It saved Mary worrying, and Mrs Smith was close by to see her through with the babby.

It was just that sometimes he felt he was married almost as much to Mrs Smith as to Mary.

'That all right for you now?' his mother-in-law laid a plate of scrag-end in front of him, edged with potato. The whole meal was the grey of an old floor cloth.

'Yes, ta.' He tried to tuck in, glad once she'd shuffled off upstairs again in her badly fitting shoes. From the room above his head, he could hear the leg of the bed banging on the uneven floorboards and the women walking about, exchanging a word or two in low voices. Now and then came a low, muffled moan.

Ned ate up his tea in large, hungry mouthfuls, then took his cap and went down to the corner for cigarettes. God knows, he was going to need summat to get him through the evening. He didn't want to think about what Mary was going through. It only stirred up the turmoil of emotion within him even further.

Once he'd bought ten Woodbines he still wanted to stay out. It was a still, summer evening and his pace slowed. The thought of going back to the cramped house full of all the disturbing, female things going on in it filled him with revulsion and guilt.

He passed a church and thought about going in to sit in the musty gloom to try and set his thoughts straight, but he could hear the chat and laughter coming from the pub so he went there instead, settled with his pint at a table awash with spilt drink, amid the smells of beer-soaked sawdust and smoke. He lit up a Woodbine, not wanting company. If he sat here for a bit, he might get home when it was all over. It was fuggy and comforting in there and his mind drifted. He couldn't bear to think about the future or what he was going to do.

It was getting on for ten when he walked in. Nothing seemed to have changed in the hour and a half he'd been out. The kettle was boiling. Mary's mom came down and brewed tea.

'Getting a bit closer,' she told him. 'It's not often very quick the first time you know, Ned. Nothing to worry yerself about.'

It only then occurred to Ned that he might worry. He thought of Mary upstairs, her scrawny body writhing on the bed. That was as far as his imagination went. He didn't know what was involved, not really. He sat by the fire drinking tea, a saucer between his feet on the peg rug Mary had made. Over the mantel, a picture of a puppy with bright eyes and a shiny nose stared down at him. Stew and beer formed an uneasy partnership in his belly. The noises from upstairs were growing louder, coming more often, although he could tell Mary was trying to stop herself crying out. Occasionally the cries crescendoed out of her control, like a lid lifted off something.

The clock ticked. The saucer at Ned's feet filled up with stubs. He sat in the murky light feeling like an old man. The path of his life seemed laid out straight in front of him. Get up, go to work, come home. Mary, babbies, young'uns tearing in and out, struggling to feed them, clothe them, until he dropped dead.

Mary was a good girl, a sweet wife. Cheerful, dutiful, bound up in family, as he'd known she would be. As he'd imagined he would be too, thought that was what he wanted. He'd chosen. But he'd chosen because she was always there, because his family liked her – because he'd barely thought of it as a choice. That was what you did.

He hadn't seen Jess since the day she'd run from him, crying. Memories, her shape, the way she moved, her eyes, came back to him with such force that he closed his eyes, letting her take him over. She moved before him like a cinematic show, her smile, her dark-eyed gaze burning into him, her lithe figure bounding on to Bonney and trotting off along the road. The feel of her lips on his, that once ... The thought made him long for her like a hunger. An agonized scream came from upstairs. He got up and paced the room. Lit another cigarette from the fire.

Upstairs, Mary lay limp as a rag between the bouts of pain, her hair soaked with sweat.

Mrs Smith sat on a chair beside the bed, holding her daughter's hand. Mary almost crushed the bones of it during each contraction, so that her mother barely managed not to cry out too. She was suffering through every pain with her daughter and her face was dragged down with exhaustion.

'Terrible, watching your own go through it,' she said to Mrs Martin.

Mary's teeth were clenching again. She cried out at the height of it, then sank down again, exhausted.

'Mom?' she murmured as Mrs Smith wiped her face.

'Yes, darlin'?'

'Is Ned here?'

'Oh yes – 'e's downstairs, waiting.' The corners of Mary's mouth turned up in a faint smile.

Finally, at three in the morning, when everyone concerned felt tested past endurance, Mary pushed out her baby, a girl, and a 'tiny snippet of a thing' as Mrs Martin called her. She coughed and squeaked and finally cried, gratingly, waking her father from his uneasy sleep in the chair downstairs.

Ned sat listening to the unfamiliar sounds round him. He heard the child and felt it was a dream. But he was excited. Was that sound part of him?

After a long time he heard the slow tread of his mother-in-law on the stairs.

'You've a lovely little daughter.' She smiled, revived by joy. 'Go up and see.'

The tiny face was just visible, a triangle of dark pink flesh between the tight swaddlings. She was lying in the crook of Mary's arm in the candlelit room.

'You'll all be right now,' Mrs Martin yawned. She stood by the door, waiting.

'Oh – 'ere,' Ned slipped coins into her hand. He was shy of her, of what had gone on in this room.

'Thank you,' Mary murmured. All her attention was on the baby.

But when they were alone, Ned knelt beside the bed, looking at the pair of them, awed, but distant from what had gone on.

'Ned?' Mary's eyes fluttered open.

'What, love?' He leaned closer to hear her.

'Can we call 'er Ruth?'

'Awright.' He would have agreed to anything at that moment. 'Ruth's a good name. In the Bible, Ruth is.' He took Mary's hand and kissed it.

'She's pretty, ain't she?' Her voice was fading.

'She's the prettiest girl in the world,' he whispered, gently stroking the infant's cheek with the side of his finger. ''Cept for you.' At that moment he meant it, was humbled and full of gratitude.

Mary barely managed to smile. She was falling asleep.

He stayed there in the deep quiet of the night, the creaks of the old house and their breathing the only sounds. He watched the child, her face twitching in sleep. He had not yet seen her with her eyes open. He felt his sense of himself expanding, taking in this new responsibility. New life. Family. This was where his duty lay. Eventually he climbed gently on to the bed beside them, and they all slept.

'We must take her and show her to Mrs Beeston,' Mary said.

It was Sunday morning. Little Ruth was ten days old, and though tired, Mary was well recovered from the birth. She sat holding the baby, suckling her, smiling down into her face. 'She'll be ever so annoyed with us if we don't pay a visit. We promised, daint we?'

Ned was in the scullery, bent over in his shirtsleeves, trying to unblock the sink. For a moment he froze. Mary didn't see him.

'No hurry. Why don't we leave it for a bit? You'll get tired traipsing all the way over there. It's even further now they moved.'

'Ned!' Mary laughed. 'I want to take 'er out and show 'er off a bit! She's starting to look quite bonny. And Mrs Beeston said she wanted to see the babby, soon as it arrived.'

Ned hesitated. 'We ought to give 'em a bit of warning – take a note to say we're coming . . .'

'Why? What the 'ell's got into yer? You always said she'd be pleased if you turned up anytime. She sent 'er new address, din't she? So she wants to see yer. We'll go after we've 'ad some dinner. 'Ow about that?'

'What's the matter with yer, Jess – yer poorly or summat?'

Jess was lying on her bed in their room in the new house in Oughton Place. Olive had insisted they move. Apart from the fact that the neighbours on one side, the

98

Bullivants, who had nine children, were a raucous and sometimes quarrelsome lot, they'd had a lucky find. The new house was on a terrace which backed on to the railway, close to Camp Hill Goods Yard. It was much more roomy than the back-to-back they'd been in before, with an extra bedroom, and although there were the usual problems of damp and bugs, the previous occupants had done their best to keep it nice. All the rooms were papered and the roof was sound. Olive kept saying they should have done it years ago.

'I'm awright.' Jess lay on her side. Bert had the smallest room, and there was just enough space to squeeze three proper beds into theirs. The wall in front of her eyes was covered with a cream paper patterned with trailing blue roses.

The house was quiet. Olive, feeling more herself since the move, was bolder about going out, and had gone with Sis up the road to the Baptist Church. She wasn't fussy about the denomination, but liked to go to church somewhere. She said she'd had help from all sorts and she'd pray with all sorts, and Sis liked a sing-song when it was on offer. Bert was outside, below their window, slopping whitewash on to the little wall of the yard.

Polly was, as usual, tidying up. They had a small chest of drawers between the three of them, and she was kneeling in front of it taking everything out, folding and refolding their few garments, even the stockings, which Jess had patched and darned until they were almost unrecognizable.

Jess wished she'd go down and leave her alone.

'What yer doing that for?' she snapped. 'Yer always fussing and fidgeting – yer've done that I don't know 'ow many times before and no one's touched it since.'

Polly sat back on her heels. Her mousy hair was scraped back and tied with a piece of string, her face pale and strained. She also looked annoyed at Jess's attack.

'It makes me feel better, that's all. Keeping the place a bit nice. What's wrong with that? If it was left to you we'd live in a right heap. When Ernie and I . . . when we 'ave our own 'ouse I'll keep it nice I can tell yer.' She got up and went to sit beside Jess on the bed. 'Look – you're not yerself. What's ailing yer, Jess? It can't be that bad yer can't tell me?'

This wasn't the first time they'd had a conversation like this. Jess's moods had been up and down for weeks, sometimes calm, sometimes silent and withdrawn, and at others viciously irritable.

How could she tell them about Ned? There was no one she could confide in. And all the time she was eaten up with sorrow, with longing.

If I can't have him, there'll be no one else, she vowed to herself. I won't be with anyone just for the look of it, or because that's what everyone else does. I won't have second best. Not like Sarah. My dad never loved her. He was scared stiff of the woman. It wasn't like that with Louisa, not with Mom. If I can't be with Ned, what's the point – of anything?

There were a couple of lads at the works who'd taken a shine to her and asked her out. They were all right, except she found nothing to interest her in their company. She wouldn't go again and they told everyone she was a bit hoity-toity.

'Cor – daint yer like Billy?' Evie goggled in amazement. 'I'll 'ave 'im off of yer!'

'Yer welcome to 'im.' Jess smiled at her eagerness. If only she could feel the same.

People were noticing she'd lost her vitality, Polly especially. She was always on at her, like now, trying to worm out of her what was wrong.

'Jess—' Polly touched her cousin's back which was turned away from her. 'Is it yer family – them not writing or nothing?'

Jess shook her head. 'No – I never really thought they would. I mean if they'd left it that long . . .'

'Is it – well, summat we've done to upset yer?'

Another shake of Jess's head.

'Yer can't go on like this – yer getting scrawny like me – 'ere, I can feel all yer bones! When yer came yer were all bonny and strong. I wish there was summat I could do to help yer. Yer acting as if yer pining for summat . . .'

There was a long silence, then Jess's broken voice suddenly burst out, 'Oh Polly!' She buried her face in the bed.

'What's up, eh?' Polly patted her agitatedly. 'You can tell Poll. Just get it out – you'll feel better.'

Eventually Jess spluttered out, 'It's Ned!'

'Ned?' Polly actually started laughing. 'Jess, yer not still hankering after 'im, surely to goodness? I knew yer 'ad a flame lit for 'im when yer first came. I mean everybody goes for our Ned – me included, once upon a time. I know Mary's the last sort of person yer'd think 'e'd go for, but 'e's married 'er and that's that! Yer can't go on like this over 'im. I mean you hardly know 'im, do yer?'

Jess rolled over and sat up, hair in a mess and her face wet.

'I do – more than you know. I've seen 'im – a few times. He said he couldn't stop thinking about me and he – kissed me.' She saw Polly's face sober up in shock.

'I love him, Poll, and I know he loves me! Babby or no babby, it's me 'e should be with. If you feel that way about someone, that's where yer belong, ain't it? I can't stand the thought 'e'll be with *her* for ever more. In the wrong place with the wrong wife!' She put her head down on her knees and started crying all over again. 'I feel as if I'm losing my mind over him!'

'Oh for pity's sake—' Polly took hold of her shoulders and shook her furiously. 'What the flaming 'ell're yer going on about? This ain't some threepenny romance – this is life going on 'ere, Jess – they're married with a babby . . .'

'Don't—' Jess shook her off. 'I know it's bad of me – that's the worst of it, but I can't get over it! I can't stop wanting 'im . . .'

Polly got up and stumped over to the pile of clothes on the floor. 'I've no sympathy with yer, that I ain't. Never 'eard such a load of clap-trap. Yer just want to pull yerself together. There'll be someone else. Plenty of men about. Too many if yer ask me. Yer can't go after someone else's, that yer can't. Yer've no right.'

They heard the door rattle open downstairs. Olive and Sis were back. Sis was singing a bit of a hymn with her sweet young voice.

'Don't let on to our mom about this,' Polly hissed. 'That's the last department you'll get any sympathy from!'

'Can't say I've 'ad a lot from you neither,' Jess sniffed.

'Well—' Polly turned, angrily. 'What the hell d'yer expect?

*

'Ooh – Mom, look who's paying us a visit. Oh, and the babby – 'ark at 'er blarting!'

The tiny hall was crammed full of people all of a sudden, vying for a space on the lino as Sis opened the door. Dinner was over and the house still smelt of tasty stew. They were all sitting having a cuppa to finish off the meal. Ernie was there, as usual now, on a Sunday.

Polly's eyes whipped round to meet Jess's, full of warning. Jess looked away. She could hear Ned's voice in the hall and she was paralysed. Her hands turned clammy, heart feeling as if it was hammering a path out the front of her. She put her cup down, clattering it on the saucer.

Somehow she managed to stand up and do the expected things that the others were doing.

''Ere she is then, after all the waiting!' Mary held her out to be admired as if everyone's lives had been spent in anticipation of this moment. She beamed round at them.

'You sit down, wench,' Olive said, guiding her to a chair.

Jess took in the sight of Ned as he came round the door. Had he changed? Thinner, a bit. Tired. But still the person she loved, and longed for.

'Poll. Jess.' He nodded at them. He didn't hold Jess's gaze. He looked quickly away, but so did she.

Everyone stood round Mary, cooing over Ruth, even Bert.

'She's a bonny one, Ned. Ain't yer?' He held Ruth up, making playful faces at her. ''Ere y'are, Poll – I can see you're dying for a hold.'

Polly was drawn to the child in spite of herself. She

smiled stiffly at Mary and said, 'She's a lovely babby,' and Mary beamed like a cat with the cream and said,

'She's the prettiest babby *I've* ever seen and I don't think it's just me being partial.'

Jess's thoughts raced elsewhere. She could read nothing in Ned's face. He was like a stranger, his expression closed. Had her lips touched this man's? Had he aroused such feelings in her? But her body remembered, making her flushed and unsteady, even if her mind had doubts. She prayed no one would notice, especially not him. Oh, but the effect he had on her. Even a look from him!

She had to go and admire the baby. In any case, she was curious to see what Ned's child would be like. Mary was chatting on, cheerful.

'She's a right greedy little thing,' she told Olive. 'On and off of me all day long. I never knew it'd be like that. Ooh, I was sore to start with ...'

'It'll settle down.' Olive couldn't take her eyes off the infant. She lifted Ronny up to look. 'See what our Mary's brought to show us – she's called Ruth, look, Ronny.'

'Babby!' Ronny shouted reaching out to her, hands smeary with gravy. 'Babby, babby!'

Jess watched quietly. She found she was standing next to Ned, although she was sure he hadn't intended to come close to her. She felt she must say something. 'She's a lovely babby, Ned. Congratulations to yer both.'

'She is.' He smiled faintly. 'Ta, Jess.' He looked round at her. Jess didn't know if her eyes held any of the hurt she felt. In his she saw ... something. Longing? Sorrow? Or did she imagine that? Then Olive was saying,

'We can't just stand about all afternoon – park yer-selves on a chair if yer can find one. There, Ned – pull up one of these from the table.'

'I like yer new house,' Mary said, eyes roving the room. This was one of the things that aggravated Polly about Mary, always poking round to see what you've got. Always after more. She had an eye for the main chance marrying Ned, Polly always said. Her family wasn't much, after all.

'It was time we 'ad a bigger place,' Olive said quickly. 'Now Jess's stopping with us, and Ronny getting bigger.'

'That Regency stripe in the front's lovely, ain't it, Ned? We could do with some of that in ours. This is pretty in 'ere, an' all . . . I like a pretty paper on the wall I do. Gives the whole place a clean look . . .'

She chattered on, Jess barely listening, until she realized Mary was talking to her.

'D'yer want to 'ave a hold?'

'Oh – yes. Awright then.'

Blushing, she took the little scrap on her lap, sup-porting her head. Ruth peered up at her with pebbly blue, still slightly crossed eyes. Her face was covered in pink blotches. A moment after Jess took her she screwed up her face and started crying.

''Ere—' Thankful, Jess held her out to Mary. 'It's you she wants, not me. I ain't no good to her.'

She's going to look like her mom, Jess thought. It was as if there was nothing of Ned in her. She glanced up at him, and he smiled for a moment, rather absently, then turned his eyes towards his wife. Jess saw him quickly look away again as Mary began to suckle the baby.

Jess found those two hours an agony. His being

there, so close to her, yet they couldn't talk and were afraid to look at each other. She wondered if his feelings for her had died, now he had a child.

She barely took any notice as talk turned to the assassination of Archduke Ferdinand in Sarajevo, to the threat of war. Outside was so warm, so breathlessly still that it seemed an impossibility on this summer day, a distant dream, despite all the sabre rattling.

'We must be going,' Mary said eventually. 'It's quite a walk and our mom's expecting us back. Said she'd cook us tea tonight.'

'That's very nice of 'er,' Olive said, a bit sarkily Jess thought, as if to say, it's all right for some. 'Sis – you get the pram outside for Mary, will yer? None of us'll get out the door else.'

Mary got Ruth bundled up in her blanket and they heard Sis struggling down the step with the pram.

They were going through the 'lovely to see yer's and 'come again soon's, Ned nodding round at Polly, and Jess – 'T'ra then' – when Olive shrieked,

'Ronny? Where is 'e? 'E's gone – oh my God 'e'll be in the 'orse road by now!'

'Oh Lor'!' Polly cried. ''E must've got past Sis when 'er opened the door!'

There was a rush to the front, Polly and Ernie, Mary holding Ruth, Olive yelling at Sis – 'Where's yer brother, yer idle wench?'

Jess was on the point of following, when she saw that she and Ned were the only ones left standing in the back room. She turned at the door. All the desperate emotion she had been holding back all afternoon flooded into her face.

'Ned—'

'Jess—' He quickly moved closer. 'I didn't want to come today. It was Mary – you know, the babby ... I ...'

'D'yer love me? Do yer? Say it, Ned. Or say yer don't and yer never did.' Her gaze burned into him. He could feel her trembling, but there were voices outside. He gripped her hand tightly for a moment.

'Meet me – Tuesday night. Snow Hill. Under the clock. Can yer do it?'

There were voices coming to the front door, Ronny's loud, indignant yells.

Jess nodded. 'Course I can do it.' How would she let anything stand in her way?

They loosed hands as the others came in, Olive with Ronny grasped under one arm.

'Oh stop yer blarting – yer lucky not to be under a tram, yer little bugger. Found 'im outside the Friends Meeting 'Ouse! Moves like a clockwork engine, when 'e gets going.'

'You awright, Ronny?' Jess turned and picked him up, kissing him. In a moment when Olive's eyes were turned away she looked at Ned and mouthed, 'Half past seven?' He acknowledged it with a tiny movement of his head.

'Lovely to see yer, Auntie.' He kissed Olive. Jess watched, full up with feeling. He was so handsome, so lovely, and above all, he loved her ... For the first time in ages, she found herself smiling, joy swelling in her.

'You look after 'em both, my lad.' Olive clapped him affectionately on the back. 'That's your job now.'

'I will – don't yer worry on that score.'

They all stood waving them down the road, Mary pushing the pram.

Polly turned to go inside.

'Never seen such a scrawny little scrap of a thing,' she said. 'I'd've fed that one to the cat.'

'Poll!' Ernie sounded disappointed in her. 'That ain't very nice.'

'Huh,' Polly said.

Twelve

'Evie's invited me back to meet 'er family,' Jess said on Tuesday morning. 'So I'll not be back for tea.'

'Where's she live then?' Olive grunted, bending to pick up a cloth from the floor.

'Off Constitution Hill somewhere.'

'She got any brothers?' Sis asked with a cheeky grin. 'Maybe she'll get yer set up, like.'

'As a matter of fact she has – she's got two. One's fifteen—'

Sis groaned.

'—and the other's twenty-one.'

''S'e married?'

'Not as I know of.'

'Oooh!'

'What's 'e do for a living?' Polly asked.

'I don't know, fer 'eaven's sake!' Jess laughed. 'I ain't set Evie up as an official matchmaker – for all I know 'e might look like Frankenstein's monster!'

'Good match for you then,' Bert said.

'Oi – watch it . . .' Jess grinned. She was aquiver with excitement, but was trying to act normally.

'It's put you in a better mood, any'ow,' Polly observed.

It felt terrible, lying to them the way she was. But what choice was there? All day long she was full of pent up nerves. She had difficulty keeping her mind on her work. Each hour seemed longer than the last. Every few minutes she looked up at the clock on the wall. Maybe it had stopped? It scarcely seemed to move.

When work was finally over she clocked off and stepped out into the hazy summer evening. Smells of cooking drifted from the back yards.

She got there five minutes early. Standing under the enormous clock in Snow Hill Station getting her breath back, she looked round at the other figures moving back and forth to the platforms. Every so often one of the trains gave a shrill whistle, and there came the powerful chuffing noise of it getting up a head of steam.

Two men were standing near her. She saw them greet the people they were waiting for one by one and she was left alone, pacing up and down, looking up every few seconds to see the big spider's leg of a clock hand edge past the six and up, up the other side. Twenty-five to eight, twenty to eight. The light outside began to dim as the sun went down. Jess looked round, straining her eyes to see who was coming into the station. Twice, unable to keep still, she went to the entrance and looked out, each way.

By a quarter to, her throat was aching with unshed tears. Stupid fool she was, rushing here to meet a married man who wasn't going to come. MARRIED. The word thundered in her head. She leaned back against a poster advertising Fry's Chocolate and closed her eyes, aware of her heart's painful hammering. All the tension she had felt these months, the waiting, this long, difficult day she had had, and now this. Tears began to well up under her eyelids.

'Everything awright, miss?' Jess jumped, heart pounding. A young man dressed in the Great Western uniform stood in front of her.

Jess stood up straight, tried to make her voice normal.

'Yes ta – er, thanks. I'm just waiting for someone.'

'Right. Only I kept seeing you there – thought you was looking poorly.'

Over his shoulder, in that moment, she saw Ned's face.

'Oh—' She burst into tears, unable to hold back her emotion. 'Oh my God – I thought you weren't coming!'

'Jess . . . love.' He wrapped his arms round her. 'I was worried yer'd have left. Only Ruth wouldn't settle and Mary'd got behind – there was no tea ready. I couldn't just go 'cause I said I was going to the pub and I never do that without 'aving tea first . . .'

Jess sobbed even harder. Ned's words about what he did or didn't do at home, habits, that married routine, made her feel even more wretched. Mary had so much of him, and what did she have?

She nestled into his arms, as he held her tightly, his coat rough against her wet face. She drank in the sensation of being held in his arms.

'Come on,' he said. 'Look – let's get out of 'ere. It feels as if everyone's watching. No one'll take any notice outside.'

Once out in the street, along the side of the Grand Hotel, they dared to hold hands in the dusk. A horse and carriage clattered past them on Livery Street, hooves sparking on the cobbles. Jess could smell smoke from the trains. Opposite the end of the station they crossed into Bread Street.

'No one'll bother us 'ere,' Ned said.

He turned, holding her again.

'Tell me you love me,' she said. 'Everything'll be all right just so long as I know you feel like I do.'

'Jess . . . Jess—' Ned gave a deep sigh, eyes fixed on

hers in the gloom. 'I wish I'd met you months before I did. As soon as I saw you it was summat else. Summat much – I don't know 'ow to say – bigger than what I feel for Mary. Beyond everything. It's made me feel, and do things I never thought I'd do in a thousand years. You're 'ere in my head and I can't get you out. I've tried.'

Jess was laughing and crying at once. She stood on tip-toe and they kissed. She felt the urgent force of his lips. When he released her she had to remind herself to breathe.

'What are we going to do?'

He leaned towards her again, not wanting to talk, only to fill himself with the sensation of her. He kissed her until he was drunk with it, his strong hands pressing her close, longing to touch every part of her lovely, curving body, knowing bitterly how wrong it would be, that it was forbidden him.

They stood for a moment, foreheads pressed together, both breathing fast. Then as if knowing a limit had been reached, they moved apart and walked on.

'I can't just leave 'er. Not with the babby. I owe 'er, Jess. And how would yer feel about me if you knew I'd just walk out on a woman and my own child?'

I don't know! she wanted to say. I just want you to be mine. To come with me and start again. But she knew he was right.

'So why're you here, Ned?'

'Because I can't keep away from yer.' He stopped again, taking her by the shoulders. 'She's the mother of my child, and you're the woman I love. I feel knocked to one side. As if I can't recognize myself. When I think of you it's as if nothing else matters. But I know it's wrong, like – to both of yer. We'll have to stop this, to keep apart. I can't expect to 'ave it both ways.'

For a moment neither of them spoke. A train came rumbling out of the station, making the ground shudder, smoke woomp-woomping out in hard-working bursts. The sound of it built, then died away.

'Yes, you can.' Her voice came out very strong, determined. 'If we can't do what's right to be together, we'll just have to live in the wrong. If it is wrong. I don't seem to know what's right and wrong any more.'

'God, Jess – what're yer saying to me?'

'Where did you say to Mary that you was going tonight?'

'Down the pub.'

'So you told 'er a fib. And I said to Auntie and the others I was going to Evie's – she's a girl at work. That makes both of us liars. But if I have to lie to see you, I will. Even though I know it's wrong . . .'

She felt his hand in the hair at the back of her neck, stroking her, saw him smile at her. 'How can this be wrong . . . Feeling like this?' But then he loosed her and turned away, towards the wall. 'How can we? We can't go on telling fibs, sneaking about, pretending to people . . .'

Jess put her hand out and touched his back, felt the tense hardness of it.

'So you'll not see me again? Is that it?'

He turned slowly, looking at her, helpless. Both of them tried to imagine going on now, without the other.

'No – that's not it. Come 'ere.'

His arms wrapped so tight around her he almost knocked the breath out of her. 'You're my woman. Deep down that's the truth of it, no matter what else. I can't change that even if I wanted to.'

'Do yer?'

'No, I don't. If doing the right thing means doing without you, Jess, I'm damned, that I am.'

'And me,' she nuzzled his neck. 'We'll both be damned together.'

Later, he walked her into town and they parted in New Street. On the corner of Corporation Street they stood in each other's arms for a long time.

'I can't let you go back to 'er,' Jess said. 'I can't stand it.'

'I've got to go – she'll wonder what's 'appened to me.'

After a last, long kiss, they parted. She began walking slowly along New Street, in a daze, still with the feel of his arms round her. Her lover, her man. And she his . . . his . . . She stopped abruptly.

'Oh!' she said, out loud. His mistress! That's what she was, however you dressed it up. It sounded bad that did. Terrible. But that was what she was. What she wanted. Because above everything else, she wanted Ned, whatever it involved, because nothing else mattered. She had never felt so loved or needed before, so safe and sure. She stood by the kerb, taking in deep breaths. What in heaven's name would Polly say if she knew?

''Ere – clear off out. Go on – shove it.'

Jess looked round, bewildered to hear a woman's voice, husky and low, directed menacingly close to her.

She was a tiny person, in a wide-brimmed hat with a strip of gold stuff tied round it making a huge bow. In the gloom, Jess could just make out a beauty spot on her cheek, and she smelt pungently of perfume.

'What?'

'I said clear out. Bugger off. This is my patch – yer can eff off and find yer own. Shouldn't try anything down this stretch if I was you – it's all spoke for.'

'What d'yer mean?' Jess protested. 'I was only . . .'

The woman laughed nastily. 'Just get 'ome – go on – get out of my sight before I decide to forget me manners.'

Jess raced the last mile home as fast as she could in the dark, unnerved by this strange woman. What the hell'd she been going on about? She slowed a little as she came closer to the house, panting hard. The ecstatic happiness she'd felt when she was with Ned seeped away and her mood became more sober. His loving her, knowing he felt as she did was the most wonderful thing that had ever happened. But the chill reality which had begun to impinge on her before she met the strange woman flooded through her again. Ned was going to stay with Mary, with his child. So when would there ever be a time, a place for her? When could the two of them ever belong together? By the time she got home she felt near to tears. But outside the house she met John, the eldest of the Bullivant sons from next door, a strong, handsome-looking man.

'Evening – awright, are yer?' he called out. Jess managed a reasonably cheerful reply and it helped her compose herself a bit by the time she walked into the house.

'Nice evening, was it?' Polly called to her.

Jess knew her face was flushed. She was too restless, too emotional. Would her guilt show in her face? She unbuttoned her coat and hung it in the hall with her hat, then forced a grin on to her face.

'It was awright,' she said, going through to the back. 'We had a bit of a laugh and they got some ale in from the Outdoor. Evie's mom's nice, and 'er brothers.'

Everyone was all ears.

'So – what's 'e like?' Sis was tilting her chair next to the table. Olive glowered at her and she lowered all four legs to the floor.

Jess frowned. 'Who?'

''Er brother of course – the one you thought she might set you up with!'

'Oh – well . . .' Jess made a face calculated to keep them all guessing. 'Not bad – not bad at all . . .'

'Better looking than me?' Bert asked.

'Miles better. Anyroad, it were a good evening. Only, on the way back I met this queer woman.'

She told them what had happened in New Street.

'She was ever so sharp with me,' she finished indignantly. 'And I was only getting my breath back! What's so funny, eh? Yer look like a barrowload of Cheshire cats.'

Olive's lips twitched and Polly and Bert were grinning from ear to ear.

'I told yer, didn' I – not to hang about in town of a night!' Olive chuckled, pressing a hand to her chest. 'That'll teach yer!'

'Well, who was she?'

'Yer lucky she daint scratch yer face off of yer,' Polly laughed. 'Ain't you ever heard of Ladies of the Night?'

The penny began to drop. Jess pressed her hands to her hot cheeks. 'Oh my . . . she was a . . .?'

Olive nodded, looking meaningfully at Sis.

'A what?' Sis said. 'Oh go on – a what? Why won't yer tell me?'

'What yer don't know won't hurt yer. And yer should be getting to bed this time of night. Go on – up yer go.'

Sis groaned and moaned her way to the stairs, but knew she could ask Polly later.

Jess looked round at them all. They hadn't guessed. And next week she could go again, pretend she was interested in Evie's brother. At least she could see him. Feel his love. That was all that mattered. She smiled.

'Anyone want a last cuppa tea?'

Thirteen

She met Ned the next week, but the third Tuesday he didn't turn up and Jess went home miserable. He managed to find her the next day, outside Blake's when she came off work.

'Sorry about last night.' He sounded very fed up. 'It's our Ruth – 'er's been bad with a fever. Up and down all night. I couldn't just leave Mary to cope all evening as well.'

'What a good father.' She'd felt horribly jealous and tense all day. But soon, out of relief at seeing him, she relented and smiled. She knew he was trying to do right by both of them. 'It's awright. Is she any better?'

'Not much. Look, I'm going to 'ave to go – I just wanted to see yer in case you was thinking – well, you know.'

Before he went he kissed her quickly on the cheek, looking round anxiously in case anyone he knew was about.

'Eh – who was that then? He's a looker!' Evie followed Jess's gaze as she watched Ned disappear.

Still straining to see him along the crowded street, Jess said, 'Evie – I need a favour off of yer.'

'What's that then?'

'Look – come with me. I'll treat yer to a cuppa and tell yer.'

They went to a coffee house nearby which reminded

Jess of Mather's, only it wasn't nearly as well kept. The sawdust looked as if it hadn't been swept up for days.

'Bit of an 'ole this,' she said, looking round.

When their tea arrived the glass felt grimy, a silt of sugar still stuck to the outside, but Jess was too preoccupied to complain.

'I've got to come clean with yer, Evie. I've been using you as an excuse to get out of an evening.'

Evie leaned closer, all agog. 'What – you seeing that good-looking fella?'

'That's it. I told my auntie I come over to see you and yer mom and brothers, Tuesd'y nights . . .'

Evie laughed. 'Jess, I ain't got no brothers! There's just me and Edith and Sal.'

'I know – any'ow, might as well be hanged for a sheep as a lamb. But they've sort of got the idea I'm keen on this brother o' yours. I'm just telling yer, 'cause I feel bad using yer like that and you not knowing.'

'Well I s'pose that's awright,' Evie didn't sound too sure.

'I won't get yer into any trouble.'

'I'm glad you told me any'ow, Jess. What about this feller of yours then . . . ain't they too keen on 'im?'

Jess didn't feel she could tell Evie quite all the truth. After all, she had to protect Ned as well. She looked down at the greyish tea in her glass. 'No. They ain't. My auntie's very strict – looks out for me like. But they've got 'im all wrong.'

Evie was full of curiosity. 'D'yer love 'im then?'

'Like mad. But I don't see 'ow we can ever be together. Not properly.'

''Cause of yer family?'

Jess nodded solemnly, appalled at the way she could lie so easily.

Evie reached across and touched her hand. 'If yer really love each other, you'll find a way. They can't stop yer forever, can they? You could go to Gretna Green. Ooh, it's just like in a story!'

''Cept in stories you know there'll be a happy ending,' Jess said tragically.

'Eh – cheer up. Tell yer what. As you're telling them yer coming over to see us, why don't you come for a visit. Our mom'd be ever so pleased to meet yer!'

'Awright,' Jess smiled. 'I'd like to. Just not on a Tuesd'y night, that's all!'

When Ned met her the next week he looked tired. They walked south, away from the Jewellery Quarter, through St Paul's churchyard. It felt safer, more anonymous to head for the middle of town.

'You awright?' she asked anxiously. 'You look all in. Been out on a blaze?'

'No – I just ain't getting much sleep. One minute Ruth's up wanting feeding and then I'm – well, I don't get to sleep easy. Listen, I've been thinking – whether there's a way we could spend longer together. Away somewhere. It's hopeless here – there's no privacy anywhere.'

Jess's eyes widened in hope. 'What – yer mean . . .?'

'I've been thinking how I could get a day out.'

'A whole day! Oh, that'd be – Oh Ned!' Her face fell. 'But how? I mean we're either at work, or there's no reason we can give for going out. Oh, but I'd do anything to spend a bit more time with yer, yer know that!'

'Could yer get away on Sunday?'

She didn't hesitate. 'Yes. I'll just go and answer questions later.'

'Mary's mom's often round ours of a Sunday. Can't get away from the woman. But if I say there's a reason I 'ave to be at the Fire Station, or summat like that . . . Giving it a special going over . . . I'll sort summat out. Oh God, more lies, Jess . . .'

'Where shall we go?' Jess asked. She was all but jumping up and down in his arms. 'Oh I can't believe it – just you and me!'

'Let's go as far away as we can get. On a train – eh?'

'Oh, I know!' Her face lit with excitement. 'I know exactly where we can go!'

It was a perfect, still, July dawn.

This can't be wrong, doing this, Jess thought as she crept out of bed, cringing as the bed creaked. Otherwise God would've made it rain and be miserable.

She dressed silently in the prettiest of her two summer frocks, white with blue checks. Over the top she wore a cardigan the colour of mulberries, and her old summer shoes with a strap and a button. All the time she watched Polly and Sis, on tenterhooks, but both of them stayed fast asleep. Jess felt even the sound of her heart thumping might wake them, she was so highly charged. She'd barely slept all night. She could hear muted snores coming from Bert's room.

She was too impatient and nervous to brew tea. Taking a slice of bread with a scraping of butter she let herself out, eating it as she hurried along the Moseley Road. It was too early, but she could not have kept still in the house any longer. A clanging sound came from the goods yard behind, but otherwise the road was quiet. The sky was clear, but hazy, and although it was still cool, it was obviously set to be a beautiful summer's day.

She tried to slow her pace and look around her. The Bull Ring was shut up and almost deserted as she walked through, and she was soon in New Street station waiting for Ned.

The station was anything but deserted. Over to one side of the area near the ticket office, a group was gathering. Jess stood, half her attention on them, the other on watching the entrance with impatient excitement. A few more joined the group. They were all women, most smartly dressed in calf length skirts, jackets and elegant hats. She saw that one of them was holding a placard with the initials 'WSPU' on it. Another was handing out sashes which they were all shouldering on over their clothes. Jess squinted to read them. '. . . s for Women' was all she could make out. She turned away as one of them glanced at her, and saw Ned coming. He kissed her briefly and took her arm, steering her to the ticket office.

'Come on – let's get right away from 'ere.' Excited, she clutched his arm.

The train ride was bliss. Away from the danger of meeting anyone they knew, they settled down together, Jess by the window, Ned's arm close round her. She laid her straw hat in her lap and leaned against him, resting her head on his shoulder, smelling the smoky upholstery. They had the carriage to themselves. The train rumbled out through Adderley Park, then Stechford. Jess let out a great sigh of contentment.

'The air feels clearer already.' She twisted her head, smiling up at him.

'Not in 'ere it don't.' He leaned down and kissed the tip of her nose. 'My country wench.'

'I miss it. I want to take you and show you.'

'You going to call on yer dad?'

She was silent for a moment, fear and uncertainty mixed with her excitement. 'I don't know. In a way I want to. But 'e's never writ me even so much as a word. I could be dead for all 'e knows. Or cares.'

'Maybe yer should. Yer might run into someone else who'll let on they've seen yer. And it might make yer feel better.'

'Yes, and it might not,' she retorted. 'I'll see 'ow I am when I get there. I just want to see the place – the fields and everything. That's what I've missed. And how'm I going to explain you away, sunshine?'

'I'll hide behind a wall 'til yer done! Anyroad – they don't know me, do they? We could be married.'

Jess twisted round in his arms. 'We should be married, Ned. We're married in our hearts, whatever else.'

Ned watched her face, the force of her feelings plain in it. Desire rose in him. What would she be like as a lover, this fierce, passionate girl? Mary was sweet and obliging. Didn't refuse him. But her response was nothing more than dutiful, friendly. Obedient even. But Jess – he could feel the taut arousal in her even when they kissed. The instinctive way she moved against him. She made the same sounds of need, of frustration as he did. Yet she was scared. And he knew how wrong it was even to be thinking of making love to another woman. But he hardly seemed to be able to think of anything else these days. His need of her was total, consuming him.

She was intent on the view from the window, hungry

for old, familiar sights. The city had faded away behind them.

'Oh look, Ned!' she cried. 'Look at the fields, the colours of everything. It's so beautiful. I want to get out – now!'

'I think yer'd better wait 'til the train stops in a station!' He laughed, ran his hand slowly down her back, feeling the warmth of her.

At last they stepped out on to the platform at Budderston. Jess immediately thought of her aunt, waving in this spot all those years ago, and told Ned.

'She looked like a fish out of water in the country. And as for Polly!'

'Well . . .' Ned was looking round. 'It's a bit quiet, ain't it?'

'It's Sunday – what d'yer expect!'

It was already well on in the morning and the sun was hot. Jess took off her cardigan and carried it over her arm. To her relief, no one was about. Only the station master's black dog snoozed in the shade at the front of the station.

'So – where're we off to then?' Ned asked, suddenly gruff. He was thrown a bit by the unfamiliar surroundings.

'I thought,' Jess turned, uncertain. 'Maybe we should go up to the Forge and get it over – see my dad.'

He saw how vulnerable she was, coming back, not knowing if she'd be wanted.

'It'll be awright,' he said, taking her arm.

'We'll go the back way. I don't want people staring and gossiping.'

Arm in arm, they walked along the back lane, across

the brook. Jess saw that the wood which made a bridge over it had been replaced. The pale, unfamiliar planks now laid there enforced her sense of separation. She'd known almost every grain in the old ones: they formed part of her memories.

'This is my favourite place,' she said, stopping, breathing in deeply. She could smell the long grass, the wheat ripening in the field behind, shifting in the breeze, flecked with red.

Ned put his arm round her shoulders. Gnawing at him constantly was the need to touch her. 'It's very nice. Lovely place to grow up. And you look right 'ere, Jess.'

'I used to play out 'ere for hours on end – and help with the haymaking and that. Our 'ouse is just down there.'

She stopped at the back gate. They looked over, seeing the orchard trees, the path to the house, startlingly familiar when she felt so changed. There was no one about, but a loud snuffling came from their right.

'That'll be Sylvia – the pig!' Jess found she was whispering. 'Oh Ned – d'yer think I should just stay away? Would that be the best thing? I feel sick at the thought of going in.' She laid her hand on her chest as if to slow her heart.

'Yer might as well – now yer 'ere. Yer might not get the chance again in a long while.'

She took several deep breaths, then nodded. 'Awright. With you.'

The first person she saw was little Liza, sitting on the cottage step shelling peas into a basin. The girl looked up. Without smiling, she stared for a moment, then called out,

'Mom. Jess's 'ere.'

In a second, Sarah appeared disbelievingly in the doorway. Jess saw she'd grown a little stouter. She stepped out, stared, seeming neither pleased nor hostile, only wary.

'I'm sorry I cut the dress,' Jess said, eventually. 'I couldn't marry Philip.'

Sarah swallowed. Nodded. She seemed unable to think of a word to say. Eventually she asked, 'Who's yer friend?'

'This is my . . .' she wanted to say 'husband'. Wanted to show she could choose for herself. But it was such a big lie. Bigger than all the others and she couldn't bring out the words. 'This is Ned.'

Sarah nodded at him, then looked back at Jess. 'Yer father's in the forge if yer want to see 'im.'

'Is Philip there?'

'No. Not today.'

As they went closer she could hear William pumping up the fire with the huge bellows, the crackle and spit of the flames. They stepped in, just able to feel the heat on their faces, eyes adjusting to the smoky gloom. She didn't say anything, just waited for him to see her.

When he did turn, he jumped, startled. He peered at her, eyes watering from the smoke.

'Louisa?' It was a whisper of hope, defying time.

'It's Jess. I've come back to see yer.'

'Jess.' The moment of wonder passed and his expression became more guarded. He came towards her, wiping his hands on his apron, beard tucked between the buttons of his shirt. His eyes, always childlike, seemed paler, his skin a little slacker. Jess was moved. Could it have been the shock of her going which had aged him in just a few months?

But then, with obvious disquiet, he said, 'Not come back for good, 'ave yer?'

'No!' Hurt and anger burned in her again. Why had she let herself think he might have missed her? 'Not likely. I just thought you might be pleased to see yer daughter once every blue moon, that's all. But I can see I got it wrong!'

'I am pleased to see yer. I just didn't expect yer.'

'Why didn't you answer Olive back when she writ yer? That wouldn't 've cost yer much, would it?' Ned could sense the anguish behind the aggression in her voice.

William shrugged. 'She said you was awright. Come to no harm. You wanted to go, and yer went.'

Jess turned away. What was the point? Nothing had changed. She'd got out of their way and that suited both of them.

She looked back at her father. 'To think I came back wanting forgiveness from you! It's you who should be on yer knees begging me for it. Come on, Ned – I'm not wanted 'ere. Never was.'

Sarah met them on their way back across the garden.

'We won't stop to get in yer way,' Jess said. 'I've done quite enough of that in my time already.'

'Yer upset 'im, going like that, yer know. Took 'im an age to get over it.'

'Well 'e seems to be over it now.'

Jess stood by the vegetable patch, arms tightly crossed. She was infuriated to find herself fighting back tears.

'Yer can come in and have a bite to eat if yer want,' Sarah said. 'I don't mind.'

'No,' Jess retorted. 'Maybe yer don't. But I do. I'm never sitting at a table again where I'm not welcome.'

Sarah took a step away, as if there was work she needed to get back to. 'Give us a bit of warning next time yer decide to come.'

'Oh – there won't be a next time. Goodbye, Sarah.'

They went down to the lane and shut the gate. Jess stopped, leaned against the back wall and put her hands over her face.

'Oh I wish my mom'd never died! God knows, all I wanted was to feel 'e might be pleased to see me.'

Ned's arms came round her, warm and comforting as the sobs broke from her. She had had no idea that coming back here would make her feel quite so desolate. She had done wrong running away, she knew, but could they not see the wrong they'd done her by trying to marry her off to Philip? She had still hoped deep down, that beneath her father's reserved ways he really loved her, that one day he'd be able to show her. But now she felt utterly cut off: more alone than ever. She clung with all her strength to Ned as he held her. He was her life now, her anchor.

'Never leave me, Ned. You won't, will yer, promise me?'

He held her while she cried like a little child.

In a while she wiped her face.

'Let's go over there.' She pointed beyond to where the hayfield met the wheat, the hedgerow a dark line between. 'No one ever goes there, not except at harvest or sowing time. We can just pretend there's no one else in the world but us.'

'That sounds my sort of place,' Ned said. Her tears had roused in him a powerful combination of tenderness and desire.

Jess looked anxiously at him. 'Are yer hungry? We could get summat in the village.'

'No—' He reached for her hand. 'That can wait.'

They walked hand in hand across the hayfield, swishing through the grass, hearing the wind moving through it. The feel and sound of it filled Jess with a wistful longing. It was the sound of her childhood, once happy, then so cruelly spoilt. She looked up at Ned beside her, white shirtsleeves rolled halfway up his arms, jacket slung over one shoulder. Just the sight of him made her want to hold him close: his wavy hair, shaped rather squarely round his forehead, darker eyebrows. She pressed his hand to her lips.

'You suit the country an' all,' she said. 'D'yer fancy being a farmer?'

He laughed. 'Not sure I'd know one end of a cow from another! I'd 'ave to leave that to you!'

Jess thought of Mrs Hunter, the farmer's wife, and her exhausted face. 'It's one of the hardest jobs there is, I reckon.'

There was a strip of unsown land where shorter, scrubbier grass was growing, but it was in the shade, so they walked to the gate and climbed through to the wheatfield.

'That's better,' Ned said. 'It feels even further away from everything.'

'Let's sit down.' Jess took Ned's coat and her cardigan and laid them together. She looked shyly at him. 'Half the day's gone already. I wish we could stop it going so fast.'

They lay resting back on their elbows, looking out across the corn, hearing the breeze, the occasional grating cry of a crow, and smaller birds darting between the heads of wheat. Between its tough stalks, the glowing petals of poppies blew on their curved stems, their blooms wide open to the sun. Jess rolled over and snuggled closer to Ned.

'It don't matter about them any more. I've got you. I mean I know I ain't really got yer – but I have for today, so I can pretend.'

'I wish you could meet my mom and dad. They'd like you.'

'They like Mary though. So they wouldn't, would they? Not as things are. If they knew they'd hate me!'

Ned was silent. He picked a stalk of grass with his free hand and nibbled the end. Suddenly he rolled on to his side and looked into her eyes. They seemed to hold a question, whether directed at him or within herself, he couldn't tell. For a moment she looked deeply serious, then a smile broke over her face.

'My Jess,' he said. 'My wench. Yer lovely, you are.' If only he could tell her properly what he felt! But words were no use. He kissed her mouth, slowly moving his hands over her body. Her dress was light cotton, only her bare flesh beneath. He worked his way, stroking until he reached her breasts and reached inside until he could move his hands over them and they were so firm and beautiful to touch. She didn't object, as she had sometimes in the park, thinking people could see. She arched her back, responding to his kisses, pressing against him until he was aroused past reason.

Jess's mind was awhirl. Here they were, for the first time ever in a place where they were truly alone. The one time where she could have with him what Mary had. She could have his whole body. She felt a throbbing between her legs at the thought. No one would know. No one except the two of them. The idea of this act with Philip had so repulsed her, but now, as

130

Ned touched her, it felt right, the only thing to do, inevitable.

Ned tried to hold on to his self-control. He mustn't go too far, it was wrong. For some time they lay together, wrapped in each other's arms, until he pulled away and knelt above her.

'Oh God, Jess—' he sounded desperate. 'I want you – let me have you . . .'

She gave a small, uncertain nod, then whispered, 'Yes.' She reached out and began to unbutton him, hearing him panting in surprise.

He unfastened her dress, looking around, afraid that despite what she'd said, someone was coming. But there was no one. She raised her arms and he pulled the dress over her head, then took off his own shirt.

They made love beside the rustling wall of wheat, her strong fingers pressing on his bare back, her legs locked round him, urging him closer and deeper to her.

Everything was quiet, then, except for the sound of their breathing, pressed close to one another, and the swish of the corn. She moved her hands over him, in wonder at what had just happened.

'What a woman you are, Jess,' Ned murmured. 'There's no one like you.'

She kissed his neck, holding him close looking up at the tiny puffs of cloud against the blue sky, and the brilliant red smile of the poppies.

Now he's mine, she thought, without shame. Really and truly mine.

Fourteen

Jess bought the *Gazette* that Bank Holiday Monday, a week after her day with Ned. She read it in Aston Reservoir Grounds, lolling on the grass with Olive, Polly and Sis, buying Scattoli's ice-creams as a treat, the tinkling music and roar of engines drifting to them from the Fun Park where they'd come for a day out. It was a hot, festive day, smelling of fried onions and engine oil. The idea of war seemed abstract and far away, despite the talk in the factory all week.

'D'yer think it'll 'appen, Mom?' Polly looked round at Olive who was sitting behind them, legs splayed, shoes off to air her bunions.

'Looks as if it might. They want to get it over with, that they do.'

The next day, 4 August, England declared war on Germany, and three days later, Bert came home jubilant.

'I've joined up!'

Jess had never seen him look so excited. He seemed taller suddenly, shoulders back, proud of himself. The women stood in a ring, giving him their absolute attention.

'Well,' Olive said. 'Yer father was an army man – in the early days.'

'I asked about joining his regiment, but they said I might as well be in the Warwicks – with Sid and Jem. They'll let us know, soon's they want us.' He pulled his

132

boots off, looking up at them from his seat by the cold hearth. 'Can't be worse than all the bloody noise and filth in the Mills, can it? I've always had a hankering to give the army a go, so now's me chance.'

Jess immediately thought about Ned. He wouldn't go, would he? Not a married man with a family? And with her . . . He couldn't leave – how could she bear it?

Bert left a few days later, the family hero, for training at Tidworth, on the edge of Salisbury Plain.

Ernie was next. By the middle of August posters were appearing all over town, Kitchener's handlebar moustache, 'Your Country Needs You'. When Ernie came round that Saturday night, Polly knew immediately.

'Oh Ernie – yer haven't!'

Ernie smiled shyly, stroking his beard. Ronny was throwing himself at his legs and Ernie laughed, picking the little boy up and making faces at him so he chuckled.

'Ooh – yer getting too heavy for me!' He swung him to the floor. 'Look, Poll – d'yer fancy coming out, for a walk like?' Jess saw a blush seep into his chubby cheeks.

Olive's eyes followed them as they left. When they came back, Polly was pink-faced and smiling, and both of them looked as if they might burst if they didn't get the words out.

'You two look mightily pleased with yerselves,' Olive said. 'Let's 'ear it then, whatever it is.'

'The thing is, Mrs B,' Ernie said, all blushes. 'What with me going away soon like, I've asked – I mean, Poll and I would like to get wed.'

'Oh, Poll!' Jess cried, delighted for her.

'Oooh!' came from Sis.

Olive was silent.

'Is that awright, Mom?' Polly looked uncertain. 'I mean, since I've no dad to ask for permission like . . .'

'When was yer thinking of? Yer getting married in church, proper like?'

'Whatever you say, Mrs B,' Ernie said fervently. 'I want to do right by Polly, and if that's what she wants.'

'Ar, it is what she wants,' Olive said. 'Well – yer'd best get weaving then, ain't yer? We'll sort yer a frock out, Poll.'

Jess went to them, 'I'm very happy for yer. That's lovely news that is.' She kissed them both, making Ernie go red again.

She was indeed very pleased. Polly deserved to be happy and she liked Ernie. Would have trusted him with her life. But that night there was an ache in her heart for the thought of a wedding of her own. A wedding that she doubted could ever happen with the man she loved.

They still met every week, hungry for each other's company. Their lovemaking had brought them even closer, and they spent their one evening a week locked together, walking, talking. The next Tuesday, they went to Handsworth Park.

'It's daft me bringing you 'ere again,' Ned said. 'Too near home for comfort.'

'But it's so pretty – everyone else's in getting on with their tea this time o' day.'

'That first time I came 'ere with yer – you know – after you nearly threw yerself under that bus . . .' He shook his head in teasing despair at her antics. 'I've never felt more wound up in me life.'

Jess smiled. 'Nor me.' After a moment she said abruptly, 'Ned – you're not going to join up, are yer?'

He was silent, then sighed. 'Not for now, anyroad.' Seeing her dismayed face he touched her cheek, smiling. 'Eh, cheer up! They don't want an old married man of twenty-one – we'll let the young'uns with no family go first and see what 'appens! They say it'll all be over in a few weeks anyroad.'

'I can't stand the thought of you going away. I mean, I'm no one – nothing to yer, am I? Not as far as anyone else knows. If anything was to 'appen to yer, it's the widow they'd tell, not me . . .'

She sounded so wretched, Ned turned and held her in his arms. She breathed in the smell of him, salty, sweaty in the heat.

'That's enough of that. I'm not going anywhere, Jess. I'm 'ere.'

They made love again that evening, in a corner of the churchyard beyond the park, hidden behind long grass and a tree. It wasn't planned, but they sat together in the dusk, under the wide branches of the tree, and were overcome with desire for one another. Jess felt her whole body yearning to be touched and loved. She pulled him close into her, knowing as she did she should be ashamed at being so eager, so helpless with need of him. But she was not ashamed. She was moved that he made love to her so urgently. She didn't care about tomorrow or next week, only now. And now, if this was how they spent it, was enough.

When they had become calmer he lay stroking her, kissing her cheeks, her lips, his hand under her blouse.

'Oh Jess, we need to be so careful.'

'I know. But sometimes I just don't care. It feels as if there is nothing else. Because there ain't—' she turned and looked him in the eyes. 'Not for me.'

She saw Ned close his eyes for a moment. When he opened them again, he said, 'I'm a coward, I should leave her. Go against everyone and go with you, where I really want to be.'

Jess held her breath, waiting, but he did not speak again, not about that. There was a long silence.

Polly and Ernie managed to organize a whirlwind wedding the next weekend, before Ernie had to report to his regiment, the 10th Warwickshires. They were married at St Agnes Church in Sparkbrook, where Ernie's family were regular members and where Olive had attended as a young woman. Polly looked very sweet in a lilac dress trimmed with lace. Ernie's cheeks popped up over the rim of a tight collar. He sweated both with the heat and with nerves and seemed to find the whole occasion an ordeal, but kept smiling valiantly, clearly happy and in love, as Polly was too.

It was also an ordeal for Jess. Ned and Mary were invited, and sat behind her, Mary holding Ruth on her lap. Jess could hear the baby's little sounds as Mary fed her discreetly to keep her quiet. She felt Ned's presence behind her as if a current was running between them. Her chest was tight with repressed emotions.

They were the only guests who came back to the house. Jess tried to stay away from him, keeping busy making tea and cutting cake. Then she sat with Polly and Ernie, who as usual had Ronny on his lap, and they made jokes about the two of them soon having their own children, which made Polly blush and look happier than ever. The couple left in the evening for three days' holiday, staying in a pub in the country.

Polly came back looking very healthy and said bashfully, that they had had a lovely time.

Work changed abruptly. Now they were making battalion badges with a crest at the top: underneath, the lettering, 'Volunteered for Birmingham Battalion'. Evie was full of pride because her new boyfriend had just volunteered. Polly was also proud, but bereft now Ernie was gone, first to Budbrooke Barracks, then on to Tidworth, like Bert.

Summer waned into autumn, but the impetus for war did not fade with it. The papers showed pictures of Belgian refugees arriving in Britain. Ned told Jess that Bonney the fire station horse had been taken to be shipped to France. They started to hear about battles: Mons, Le Cateau, the Marne. Across the Town Hall, a huge banner read: 'RECRUITING OFFICE: WANTED, 500,000 MEN. GOD SAVE THE KING.'

The pressure on young men to join the fighting was becoming irresistible. Jess knew in her heart that it had to happen eventually.

One evening when she met Ned, he pulled out a white card from his pocket and showed it to her reluctantly. It was his enlistment appointment from the Deputy Mayor.

'It won't be for long. They're saying it'll only last a few months, if that. But I can't stand by and let everyone else go and not be part of it, can I? I feel like a shirker, a coward, if I don't do my bit.'

Ned watched her face. Saw her summon strength inside herself.

'I don't want yer to go, course I don't,' she said. 'But I s'pose I'd feel the same.' She smiled tenderly. 'I'm proud of yer.'

As they parted that evening, Ned walked home with a sense of relief, freedom even. All these months he had been torn between Jess and Mary, so that he was worn down with it. He felt unsettled and deceitful, when he had been accustomed all his life to people thinking well of him. Going away from it all was a way out. Just men round him. It would give him time to think, to see if he could forget Jess, and pull himself round to doing what was right. Stick with Mary. Or find the courage to leave her and face the consequences. At the moment that felt the hardest, most heart-breaking decision he had ever faced in his life.

Fifteen

October 1914

Jess slammed the door of the privy shut and bent over the wooden seat, retching. Nothing came up except a thin trickle of yellow bile. Holding her hair back she coughed and gasped until it was over. The stench of the dry privy was awful and she stepped out into the yard, taking in gulps of bitter smelling air. For a moment she leaned against the wall, hearing the chunk-chunk of a goods train coming out from the yard behind. A dark plume of smoke thinned out in the air. The sun was trying to struggle through cloud.

Two months, she'd missed. And sick – for several days now – always aware of her stomach, as if someone had drawn round it in black. At first she'd thought she was ill. But she knew the signs – Sarah's education again. Knew, in a part of her mind that could barely admit it, that she was carrying a child. The sickness. Everything smelt stronger but nothing tasted nice. Her breasts felt heavy and bruised.

She heard someone else come out the back door. Polly, in her slip, younger looking in her nightclothes, legs mottled as brawn, shivering now there was a nip in the air. When she came out of the privy she gave a little shriek.

'Flipping 'eck, Jess, I daint see yer there!'

'Poll – come 'ere.'

'What?' Polly moaned. 'S'cold out 'ere.'

'Poll – I think I'm 'aving a babby.'

'Oh yes – and I'm flying to the moon!'

Jess hadn't said the words even to herself before. Had hardly meant to speak now. Hearing it said frightened her.

Polly peered at her. 'What yer talking about? You're 'aving me on, ain't yer? By Christ, Jess – yer'd better be!'

Jess was shaking her head, eyes filling with tears. Saying it made it sound real.

'But yer can't be! I mean, whose . . .?'

'Ned's.' She only whispered the name, but Polly leaped towards her, clamping a hand over Jess's mouth. She looked anxiously round at the windows of the house.

'What yer telling me this bloody clap-trap for? Eh?' She put her hands on Jess's shoulders, thin fingers digging in. 'Don't ever come out with any of this in front of our mom or she'll knock yer block off, that she will!'

'Poll – I ain't come on for two months.'

For a moment Polly was speechless. She glared into Jess's tearful eyes, then pushed her with all her force round the side of the privy and began shaking her, slapping her face, sobbing, finally clutching her hands over her own face.

'Yer stupid, dirty little bitch!'

'Poll!' Jess hadn't intended to tell her. It had just swollen up in her mouth and popped out before she knew.

''Ow could yer be so disgusting? So bloody *stupid*?'

Polly was beside herself. 'Mom'll . . . she'll . . .' She grasped Jess's wrist. 'She mustn't know. Yer not to say a word to 'er. It'll finish 'er this will.' She turned, her gaunt face looking round the yard as if there might be a solution there somewhere, then turned again on Jess. 'It's not really Ned's, is it? 'E's a married man – 'e's got Mary, the babby...' Her nails were digging so hard into Jess's wrist that she pulled away, wincing.

'Sorry, Poll.' She did feel ashamed, then, hearing it spelled out. 'But Ned and me love each other. I know 'e's married to Mary, but really 'e's mine.'

'For Christ's sake, Jess, yer a bloody dupe, ain't yer?' Polly's voice suddenly quietened, as if with despair. 'Now don't you go saying a word to anyone else. Not a word – got it? I need time to think about this bloody lot!'

Seething with anger and upset, Polly strode ahead of Sis down Bradford Street on their way to the pen factory. How they'd got through breakfast she'd never know, with Jess filling up every few minutes and wiping her eyes on her sleeve.

'What's up with you?' Olive asked eventually. She said it so meaningfully, to Polly's ears, that she thought her own heart was going to stop.

'I think I'm going down with a cold,' Jess said in an almost normal voice. 'I'm awright though – honest. Just me eyes keep watering.'

Polly was so brim-full of emotion she wanted to howl. She was very short with Sis on the way to work.

'Wait for me,' Sis complained.

'Keep yer trap shut, will yer. I'm trying to think.'

'But what's the flaming rush?'

'Oh *shurrup*, will yer!'

Sis looked hurt and decided to keep quiet for the rest of the way.

Polly felt her eyes fill with tears and brushed them away. She'd already been anxious and pent up about Ernie being away. They should be finding a house of their own to rent, moving in together, not parted, not knowing when they'd see each other again. She missed him terribly. His quiet, stable nature steadied Polly. She trusted him absolutely, felt safe with him. Now he was gone she felt alone, and frightened.

And it was only now she was facing up to how worried she'd been about her mom. Those funny turns she'd had. They'd always been fighters, the two of them. Mother and daughter standing together against cold and hunger, getting by with no man in the house. Life so difficult – her begging round the factories for food after school. Just as she'd thought everything was getting better, her Mom had turned strange on her – thank God she seemed better now, at least for the moment.

But Jess – the pressure of emotion welled up in her again at the thought of her cousin. She had great affection for her, but this morning she had felt like killing her. Jess just breezes in, takes everything she wants, makes a disgrace of herself with no regard, no idea ... She felt faint herself suddenly, was afraid she'd fold up, right there in the street, and she leaned against the wall of Clark's, everything fading round her for a second as black panic spread through her. Things were going wrong, getting out of control, when what she needed was to keep order, keep life in check ... Jess was like a whirlwind, stirring everything to chaos. What in hell's name were they going to do?

'Poll?' Sis's voice was frightened. 'Yer face's gone a funny colour.'

'I'll be awright. Just 'ang on a tick.'

She straightened up groggily and took Sis's arm. Sis smiled at her uncertainly.

Later, at work, Polly kept an eye on a woman called Sally. She was a bit simple, Sally was, had been taken advantage of by some factory lad a year or so back. But her mom'd got hold of her, made sure the babby never came to anything. Polly waited until the break when Sally went to relieve herself. There was only one toilet downstairs, out the back, in a filthy state. Polly caught her coming out. Her misshapen face looked first terrified, then perplexed, as if trying to remember something deeply buried.

'If yer breathe a word about this yer gunna get a beating—' Polly had her face pressed up close.

'I'll not, I'll not!' Sally squeaked. From her mouth, the stench of rotten teeth. In a hoarse whisper she told Polly what she wanted to know.

'I ain't doing that! How can yer even think of it?'

'Yer've not got a choice, yer silly little bitch! Yer don't think 'e's going to stand by yer, do yer? With a wife and babby to fend for already! You don't seem to see what a mess yer in! Face it, Jess – yer carrying his bastard child. You're a fallen woman! You don't think our mom'll let yer carry on stopping with us in that state, do yer? She'll 'ave yer out on the street even quicker than 'e put it in there!'

Jess felt the words rain down on her like bullets. 'I've got to tell 'im,' she said stubbornly. Ned would make everything all right. He loved her more than anyone in the world. If she was carrying his child it made her equal to Mary, didn't it? But in that moment all her certainty deserted her and she was filled with a chill sense of despair. He was married to Mary, so where did that leave her? And when would she see him again? For the moment she was alone. Except for Polly.

'Yer can tell 'im all yer like . . .' Polly put her face up close, teeth clenched. ''E'll be as keen to see the back of you, and *that*—' she pointed at Jess's belly, 'as bum boil, that 'e will. Put 'im out of yer mind – where 'e should never've been in the first place. Face it – it's you and that child inside yer. And yer'll not be able to hide it from our mom for long . . .'

The two of them stood staring at each other in silence. Jess's mind raced round and round. What was she going to do?

'Sat'dy night we'll go,' Polly said. Jess thought for a second her cousin was going to spit in her face she looked so angry. 'Then it'll be over and enough said. What in God's name were yer thinking of?'

''E wanted me to – said it'd be awright. And I wanted it as well. I love 'im so much. And I never knew, Poll – honest. I thought it took an age to catch for a babby!'

'Well—' Polly turned away, face twisted with disgust. 'Now yer know better, don't yer?'

'Ow can 'er carry on like that right on top of church!'

The address she'd got out of Sally was in Highgate, close to St Alban's church.

'I'll 'ave to carry the shopping after,' Polly said. 'You'll be in no state.'

It was Saturday, late night shopping in the Bull Ring and lots of bargains. The two of them went most weeks, staggering back with knock down meat, bruised fruit, all they could carry.

'Won't I?' Jess said nervously. She was completely ignorant of what was going to happen. She was just doing what Polly said. Letting her take charge.

'I'll never carry it all,' Polly was complaining, voice shrill with nerves. Both of them had a handy carrier in each hand, loaded down.

Tucked in Jess's pocket was the money she'd got from pawning Louisa's quilt.

'Oh no – not that!' she'd protested. 'It's the only thing of Mom's I've got!'

'Yer can get it back later, before our mom starts on about it. Yer might get five or six shilling for it, it's that nice.'

Jess walked along feeling desperate. She was very frightened, but at the same time, knew she was being given a way out. Things could go back to normal. Life had got knocked out of balance and had to be put back. Anything not to cause trouble and disgrace.

But shamed as she was, Jess still wanted to resist. Inside her was their child, the result of their love. Whatever the disgrace of it, she had something of him growing in her.

'Down 'ere,' Polly elbowed her down Conybere Street. It was cold, foggy, the edges of everything uncertain in the smoky gloom. The streetlamps provided pools of smudged light. They walked down past the almshouses, the church, a gloomy, hunch-shouldered edifice looming over the pavement.

They turned into Stanley Street and Polly slowed, trying to get her bearings. There were dark entries, leading off into the back courts, and all around the sound of human life, children playing, babies crying, doors open along the street to let in some air. They could see into some of the houses, hear the sounds of families carrying on their lives inside: knives and forks, raised voices, children in and out. Normal, Jess thought enviously. A sick feeling grew inside her.

Further on, Polly stopped. 'I think this is it.' Her voice was shaky.

It was a bigger house on the corner of Catherine Street, and even in the murky light its state of decay was obvious. The bottom windows were boarded up, and, blind-eyed to the street, the house looked secretive and forbidding.

'It can't be 'ere, can it?'

'This is it awright.' Polly's voice became hard and practical.

'How d'yer know?'

'I just do. Come on.'

Now she'd seen the place reality really hit Jess. 'Oh Lor', Poll – what's she going to do to me?'

'Yer'll see soon enough. Just think what'll happen if yer don't do it.' Polly had only the sketchiest idea herself. She had to keep her feelings at bay. This had to happen, didn't it? What choice was there: putting things to rights, or bringing a bastard child into the world. 'Come on – round the side.'

The door was not locked, and after knocking and getting no reply, Polly pushed it open, clutching hold of Jess's wrist as if she thought she might run away. The hinges whined. Darkness, and a fetid smell greeted them. The building's decay mixed with something else, cloying and rancid. Jess held the door to the street open. In front of them, very dimly, they could see a long hall and stairs.

'She said it was upstairs . . .'

'Who said?' Jess was only just managing to control her voice, her heart going like a hammer. The smell made nausea rise in her to the back of her throat. She had to swallow hard so as not to retch.

'Never mind.'

Polly edged forwards to the stairs. Broken tiles clicked underfoot.

'Hello!' she shouted. 'Is anyone there?' After the second time she called they heard creaking upstairs and a slow, ponderous movement across the floor. Eventually a door opened and dim, reddish light appeared.

'Who's that?'

'It's—' Polly was thrown for a moment. 'Is that Mrs Bugg?'

Silence, then, in a wheedling tone, 'Is that a wench needing my 'elp? Best get up 'ere. I won't come down to yer.'

The smell had grown stronger, a gust of disgustingly malodorous air wafting down to them.

'I can't . . .' Jess started to say, but Polly wouldn't let go of her, fingers digging into her wrist. Jess's legs were shaking so much she could barely climb the stairs.

They could hear Mrs Bugg's laborious breathing before they reached the top. At the sight of the woman in her dim room, Jess felt her legs begin to give way altogether, and she grabbed at the door frame. The large room was crowded with heavy, dark furniture. At one end, was a ramshackle kind of kitchen, where cooking was done over the fire. Near it was a table on which stood a candle in a red glass jar, like a church sanctuary lamp. On another small table to one side, two more candles burned on saucers. In the thick, blood-coloured light, crouched at the table, was the fattest human being Jess had ever seen. She had turned to look at them, and

147

her eyes were like two stab wounds between her forehead and the welling dough of her cheeks. She spilled over the sides of the chair as if poured there like thick custard.

'Which one of yer is it then, dears?'

She stood up, pulling on the table, grunting and wheezing. It startled them both. The woman had appeared stuck to the chair.

'It's 'er, my cousin.' Polly pulled Jess into the room.

'Ow far gone are yer, bab?' Ma Bugg shuffled, panting towards them, stringy hair dangling each side of her face. The floorboards groaned beneath her. Jess had gone rigid. Couldn't bring any words out.

'Not all that. Eight weeks at the most – ain't it, Jess?'

As the woman moved towards her, Jess recovered her ability to move and, yanking her hand from Polly's grip, ran back down the dark stairs. Outside, she heaved, bringing up teatime stew into the gutter. The breeze felt cold on her sweating face. She stood gulping and shuddering.

'I can't go back up there. The stink...' Polly had followed close behind.

'Oh yes yer can. You're going to or you'll be out on yer ear.' She sounded cruel, brutal. The place, the woman appalled her just as much and she was trembling all over. But she had to be strong. Had to get Jess through this.

'Come on, or she'll think we've done a bunk.'

The woman cleared the table, gave it a rough wipe and made Jess lie down on it. She shuffled to and fro, coughing. Her lungs sounded in a poor state. A kettle murmured on the range and a pot of something was bubbling which was the chief source of the vile smell.

'Just let's see 'ow far yer on. Yer don't look no size

148

but that's no proof. Don't want yer dropping a big'un on me . . . Get yer frock up, there's a good wench.'

Jess moaned at the sharp discomfort as Mrs Bugg prodded her stomach with her slabby fingers.

'I can start yer off. Should 'appen tonight or tomorrer when I've 'ad a go. Five shilling I can do yer for as it's not far on. Shall I crack on?' She held her hand out.

Jess saw Polly give her the money, making a low sound of agreement. She could just see Poll's face, white and pointed in the gloom. Mrs Bugg counted the money. She looked pleased.

'Get yer bloomers off then. And you—' She nodded at Polly, chins quivering. 'Lay the *Despatch* out for under 'er.'

Jess stood up, feeling as if all her bones had been taken out. Her teeth were chattering and the room began to spin, lights appearing at the edges of her vision. She could hear Polly rustling the newspaper. Old Ma Bugg lifted the steaming kettle with a grunt and poured water into a blackened pan.

'Just boiling up a few mutton bones in 'ere—' she pointed at the seething pot on the range.

Just as Jess blacked out she registered the sound of something metal, rattling. Polly broke her fall as she slithered to the floor.

She came round feeling terrible, to find she was lying on the table once more. It was not very big and her head was close to the edge, the knot of her hair pressing on it uncomfortably. Her legs were bent up, heels caught at the other end and she could feel someone's hands holding her ankles. Her knees had swung wide apart and she was naked between her legs and it felt cold.

With no warning, the woman's fingers jabbed

between her legs, pushing up between her lips, cork-screwing round. She whimpered.

'Just a bit o' lard, 'elp it in like.'

After more of the woman's elephantine movements, there was another little clinking sound. Jess rolled her head to one side, saw Polly put her hand over her mouth to stop herself crying out. She raised her head off the table and saw Mrs Bugg had pulled a long meat skewer from one of the saucepans.

'Soon be done, bab . . .'

'No . . . no!'

In a movement that tore at her guts she was off the table, holding out a hand to fend off Mrs Bugg, and reaching for her bloomers.

'Jess!' Polly wailed. Her protest lacked all conviction.

'Don't touch me, yer filthy stinking old witch! I'm not letting yer within a hundred mile of me with that! Come on, Poll. For Christ's sake let's get out of 'ere!'

'Please yerselves,' Mrs Bugg said, throwing the skewer back into the pan. She'd got her money, after all. 'You know where I am if yer 'ave second thoughts – only don't leave it too long.'

Outside, it was Polly who burst into tears, so over-wrought and hysterical that Jess had to hold her on the dark street corner, trying to calm the emotion erupting from Polly's shaking, gulping body.

'Oh, I'm sorry, Jess,' she said, over and over. 'I'm sorry, I'm sorry.'

Sixteen

Rain had been falling hard as Jess woke. There was very little light and it was a bitter day outside. She came inside, coat over her nightdress, still feeling wobbly after bringing up her guts over the lav.

It was only half-past six but Olive was down, stoking the range, empty coal bucket on the floor beside her. She turned as Jess came in and the look she gave her was unmistakably hostile.

'So – what've yer got to say for yerself?'

Jess shut the back door, shaking drops from her hair. Her hands started to tremble and she broke out in a sweat. She couldn't tell Auntie yet! Why was she being so angry? Surely she couldn't have guessed? She looked down, wiping her feet on the old mat.

'What d'yer mean?'

'I mean yer've put no jam-rags in the pail for two month and you're sick to yer stomach of a morning – don't think I ain't heard yer. And you're not shifting from that spot 'til I get the truth!'

Jess felt herself start to shake even harder. The one thing she'd dreaded the most was her auntie finding out! Without looking up, hugging the edges of her old coat round her, she whispered, 'I've just been feeling a bit poorly, Auntie.'

Olive stood with her legs apart, her hands, black with coal dust, clamped on her hips like a wrestler waiting to fight. She was already dressed, sacking apron on top.

'I'm not a fool, Jess, nor blind and deaf. It's no good trying to palm me off with some tall tale. I want the truth, and I want it now!'

She was going to have to tell her. Jess's knees went weak. Eyes fixed on the mucky scrap of mat at her feet, she murmured,

'I might be having a babby, Auntie.'

'Yer don't say.'

More silence. Only when Jess looked up did it dawn on her that her aunt was in as bad a state as she was, white and shaking, having to hold on to the edge of the range to support herself.

'Oh Auntie—' Jess stepped forward.

'It daint get there by itself, did it? Some Factory Jack up an entry, was it, full of blarney?'

Miserably, Jess shook her head. Now her aunt knew, the full enormity of what had happened fell on her like a lead weight. She felt utterly humiliated, but worse, seeing her aunt in such a state she was frightened of what she had caused.

Olive moved closer. Jess looked up to see a terrible expression on her face. For a moment she wondered if her auntie was really mad, she looked so peculiar. The look of her made Jess tremble all the more.

'Spit it out then.'

'It wasn't just – anyone. I love 'im and 'e loves me. I want us to stay together – live somewhere, like.'

'Live somewhere! Stop talking bloody rubbish, wench! Yer don't just go and "live somewhere" with a babby on the way! Yer make 'im marry yer and do it proper. So who is 'e – and where is 'e? What's wrong with 'im that yer've never brought 'im 'ome, eh? 'Cause I'd 'ave a thing or two to say to 'im, that I would.'

'There's nothing wrong with him. It's . . .' She could only whisper his name. 'It's Ned, Auntie. The babby's Ned's.'

The blow her aunt dealt out to her knocked Jess to the floor. She reeled backwards, face stinging with pain, and jarred her lower back as she hit the floor. She sat up, moaning, rubbing it with her hand. Dimly, she saw that Sis had come down and was watching aghast from the doorway.

'Don't lie to me, yer scheming little bitch! Now you tell me the truth before I 'ave to beat it out of yer!'

'I am telling yer the truth, Auntie. I'd swear to yer on the Bible. Ned's the father of this babby and it's me 'e loves, not Mary. He wants to be with me!'

Olive's distress had transformed itself into pure fury, and it frightened Jess so much that she cringed, encircling her knees with her arms and leaning her head on them as she thought Olive was going to hit her again.

'Just like yer mother – no thought for anyone.' Olive's voice hectored at her. 'Ned wouldn't . . .'

'Oh yes 'e would, Mom.' Polly appeared in the back room. 'You may not want to face it, but that's the truth. 'E's the father of Jess's—'

'Keep out of it!' Olive turned on her. 'Ned's a good lad – 'e's got a wife and a babby and I won't 'ear it of 'im. And I won't 'ave 'er in the house – carrying on like . . . like . . .' She couldn't seem to think of an evil enough word. 'I'm not giving 'er a roof over 'er 'ead – she can get out and fend for 'erself and good riddance!'

There was a shocked silence. Then, in a low voice, Jess said,

'So 'ow did Ronny come about then?'

She thought her aunt was going to have a fit. She was quivering all over, her face twitching with uncontrollable emotions. She grabbed a blouse of Jess's that had been drying by the range and hurled it at her. 'Get out! Now! Go on!' Her voice went high and shrill. 'Yer can take everything that's yours and go. I don't want yer coming back tonight!'

'Mom!' Polly cried. Sis started to cry.

'But Auntie!' Jess wailed. 'Where'm I gunna go? There's nowhere for me. I've no one else to turn to!'

'Yer can turn to the real father of that bastard child yer carrying – see 'ow 'e likes to take care of yer. I'm washing my hands of it. Go on – clear out.'

Stunned, Jess dragged herself up off the floor and Polly and Sis stood back to let her pass. She heard Polly trying to calm her mother, to plead with her.

'I'm not 'aving it in the house,' Olive was shouting. 'Not with the blood she's carrying in 'er veins!'

'What're yer talking about, Mom!' Polly was desperate. 'I know Jess's done wrong, but where's 'er going to go?'

Jess was shaking so much from weakness and emotion when she got upstairs, that she could only just manage to pull her few clothes out of the worm-riddled chest and bundle them together. She reached for the quilt, Louisa's quilt, to wrap them in, and remembered they had pawned it to pay for the visit to Mrs Bugg's stinking slum. She sank down on the bed and wept, sharp, dry sobs, pressing her knuckles against her eyes.

Polly and Sis ran up and sat each side of her with their arms round her, both crying too.

'Oh Poll – what'm I going to do? Where'm I going

to find a roof tonight? I'll be on the street! And what'll I do when the babby's born?'

'She'll come round. What did yer go and tell 'er for, eh?'

'I didn't. She guessed. And she'd've 'ad to know sooner or later. I know I've done wrong, Poll – I shouldn't've gone with Ned, even if 'e wasn't married and that. I know it ain't right. But I love 'im so much and 'e loves me. It's all wrong, I know. But I didn't think Auntie'd turf me out like this. I thought she was going to kill me!'

Sis was still sobbing against Jess's shoulder, and Jess slipped her arm round her.

'We'll 'elp yer, won't we, Poll,' Sis said. 'Til she calms down and comes to 'er senses. You can 'ave the two bob she lets me keep every week, and Polly'll give yer some too, won't yer?'

'Course we'll help . . . every way we can.'

Jess was so touched by their loyalty that she cried even more.

'Look—' Polly dragged a hand across her eyes. 'You want to get ready and go to work, or you'll lose yer job an' all. After work, find yerself a room to rent. Yer not showing yet so you'll be awright. And it'll give yer a bit of time to get sorted out. She says she don't want me seeing yer – but don't worry. I won't desert yer.' She squeezed Jess's arm and stood up. 'You're like a sister to me and I'll stand by yer. Meet me after work tomorrow – outside the Market Hall – and you can tell me where yer staying.' Polly stood up, went to the door. She turned, trying tearfully to smile. 'Go on then – get on.'

When Jess came slowly, heavily, downstairs, Sis was

155

waiting, looking round cautiously to see her mom was out of the way.

'This come for yer.' Sis looked, then handed Jess a letter when she was sure the coast was clear.

Jess looked at the envelope blankly. She had never had a letter before in her life. The handwriting was looped and a bit untidy. She hid it in her bundle.

'Get yer breakfast and go,' Olive said. Her face wore an odd, hard expression which brooked no pleading.

Jess left the house with Polly and Sis. There were no goodbyes from Olive. She turned her face away as Jess tried to speak to her.

'Ain't yer going to open that letter?' Sis was full of curiosity.

'Take this.' Jess handed her the small bundle of clothes and slit open the envelope. She read, slowly.

Nov 4th, 1914

Jess—

I've got to make this a short letter or my feelings will take over and I shall change my mind. I wouldn't have written to your aunt's house normally but I've got to risk it.

Jess – I've got to make up my mind to say goodbye to you. I'm a father as well as a married man, with responsibilities. Being here, away from everything, I've had a chance to think and see how wrong I've been acting the way I have. I can't help what I've felt for you. I couldn't say this to your face. If I saw you I wouldn't have the strength. But you can't carry on with two people at once. It's not right or fair and it's turned me into a liar – and you, and I hate myself for it. I don't think that's what we want and I don't see how else we can carry on.

I know I feel more for you than Mary. I'll say that, to be true. That's the worst of it. But she's my wife, mother to my daughter, and I want to find courage to be a better man than I have been.

Goodbye, Jess my love. Don't take this too bad, please. The war will take me away and you can forget me if you will. Don't write and try and make me change my mind. This has to be the way things are.

Yours – maybe in another life when things are different.

Ned.

Seventeen

'You awright, Jess?'

Evie peered at her in the gloomy passage at Blake's, when the two of them were clocking off. She stood back a moment as a large woman pushed past her.

'Blimey – mown over in the rush! Only you're looking down in the mouth today, and I thought … Well what's so funny?'

Jess leaned against the wall, laughing weakly. Down in the mouth! That was one way of putting it! The most endless, miserable day she could remember: pregnant, sick, unmarried, thrown out of home and nowhere to sleep. And worst, by far the worst, Ned's letter. She felt as if her heart was taking up the whole of her body: she was one grieving, aching agony.

Yes, I'm down in the mouth awright! she thought. The only place left for me's the canal! Her laughter became hysterical, tears rolling down her face.

'What's up with 'er?'

She felt harsh slaps, first on one cheek, then the other, and abruptly her laughter stopped. Three women, Evie and two others, gathered round her, staring.

'Eh, Jess—' Evie's arm slid round her shoulders. 'This ain't like you.'

'I'll be awright.' She kept her head down, wasn't going to talk in front of the other two.

When she and Evie were alone outside, she said, 'Oh

Evie – I 'ad such an argument with Auntie, and she's turned me out. I've nowhere to go and I don't know what to do!'

'Oh my word – can't yer go and make it up with 'er? It can't be over much, can it?'

'She won't 'ave me back. She says she never wants to see me again. I . . . I . . .' She was on the brink of telling Evie the truth, but she couldn't. She was far too ashamed. It sounded so bad – her and a married man doing what no girl was supposed to do until she was wed! What had seemed so right when she was with Ned would look disgusting and wrong to everyone else. Evie would never speak to her again.

'Look – come on over to ours. Our mom'll put yer up 'til yer get yerself sorted out.'

Jess seized on this with hope for a moment. She'd visited Evie's family a couple of times over the summer and found them warm and friendly. It'd be so nice to accept, to be able to go and rest somewhere where there would be a welcoming face or two. But she quickly dismissed the thought. Evie's mom, Mrs Cotter, was no fool, and their place was so crowded. With her sick as a dog every morning, Evie's mom'd soon guess what was amiss and Jess couldn't bear Mrs Cotter to know her shame.

'That's nice of yer, Evie – but I'm going to look for lodgings. I've got to get somewhere so I might as well start now.' Jess wiped her eyes on her stiff serge coat sleeve. 'I'll let yer know 'ow I get on tomorrow.'

Evie looked doubtful. 'I'd come with yer, only I said to Mom I'd shop for 'er – look, if yer don't 'ave any luck, yer know where we are.' She squeezed Jess's hand. 'Yer shouldn't 'ave a problem round 'ere. Lots of folk in need of a few bob, and you looking so respectable!'

Carrying her bundle, Jess walked out of the Jewellery Quarter feeling sick and exhausted. On the way she passed Albion Street, and hovered for a few moments outside the fire station. Seeing the place set her off crying uncontrollably. How could he have written to her as he did? She felt destroyed by his words.

Just two weeks ago she'd gone to watch him march with the other lads, all soldiers now. Ned was in the Second City Battalion, the 15th Service Battalion of the Royal Warwickshire Regiment. The three City Battalions were made up primarily of the more educated young men of the city: office workers, accountants, librarians, and Ned had said he felt like one of the nobs! The lads were given a grand send-off with church services, parades, and Jess waited among the crowd along the road to watch them march from the General Hospital to Edgbaston Park, their Commanding Officer on a fine dappled grey horse. Everyone cheered and shouted, their breath white on the air. Jess had stood on tip-toe, straining to catch a glimpse of him as the body of men streamed past, still dressed in civilian clothes and singing a new song, 'It's a Long Way to Tipperary'. He passed quite close to her and she called out to him, saw him look round, just catching sight of her as she blew him a kiss.

She sobbed bitterly at the memory, there in the dark, head pressed against the rough side of the building. She felt as if her life was over. There was no hope in anything. Nothing but trouble, fear and shame.

Come back to me, she found herself begging. Please,

Ned. She wanted rescue and shelter from being abandoned and alone. But of course he wasn't there: he had no idea of the state she was in and now he didn't want to know either. She was alone, and alone was how she would have to cope. Scarcely knowing where she was going, tears half blinding her, she walked on.

She had decided to look for lodgings on this side of town, because it was nearer work – and nearer, somehow, to him. His place. His area of town. Polly had slipped her ten shillings to help her out. Jess tried to argue: she knew the money was from Polly's savings for her life with Ernie.

'Take it – don't be so daft. It's now we need to worry about. The future'll come when it comes.' She told Jess to let her know as soon as she'd found somewhere. Polly'd be over to see her, whatever Olive thought.

She walked out along the Dudley Road. On one side there were houses, and she kept peering at their dingy windows in the poor light to see if any of them had 'Room To Let' signs up. Across the road were high walls, and when she came opposite the gates she saw it was the Workhouse, a huge building which seemed to loom towards her in the dark. Jess felt the hairs on her skin stand up and a shudder went through her. If she wasn't careful she might end up in there! Fallen girls went in there and sometimes never came out! What made her different from any of them in anyone else's eyes? And even if she wasn't thrown into the Workhouse, what in heaven was she going to do after the babby was born? She certainly couldn't hide it then. All the problems she faced swirled in her head like a leaf storm until she was rigid with panic.

She gripped her bundle tighter. Just think about today, she told herself. *Sufficient unto the day is the evil thereof.* Sarah used to say that. *Sufficient unto the day . . .*

She turned back. I ain't looking for lodgings facing over the Workhouse, she thought. Along a side street men were coming out into the slate-grey evening from the factories, a rolling mills, a varnish and colour works. The road crossed over the canal. Jess stopped and looked down at the sludgy line of it. It appeared solid, more like dull stone than water.

How many girls like me have ended up in there? She started to imagine it: turning off the road down that path there, under the bridge, all dark and echoing. Feeling the water first over her boots, fitting close, like freezing stockings sliding up her legs, then her waist, neck . . . Lying down in it, taking it into her and everything would be black, and there would never be anything else but black, and nothing more of her. She found she had been holding her breath and took in a gasp of air as if she really were drowning and hurried over the bridge. No – not that. Not while she had strength and Ned was somewhere in the world. She had to try and survive.

Further on were houses, close-packed little terraces. She knocked at the first one with a sign in the window, where a man appeared, snarled, 'It's already taken,' and slammed the door shut again. In the window of an end terrace squeezed in beside a chapel, she could just make out a card in neat, but shaky writing. 'Room to Let. Single Person. Female Pref.'

She waited such an age after knocking that she was about to move on, but then the door opened a crack. Peering at her was a thin face, wrinkled as an old paper bag, with long white hair straggling down either side.

Jess could tell there was a candle burning in the hall behind. A frowsty smell seeped out.

'Yes?'

'I saw the sign,' Jess said fearfully to this witch-like creature. 'I'm looking for a room to rent.'

The door opened further, and Jess saw that the old lady was supporting herself on a crutch. Her left leg hung, severed off at the ankle, a useless stump with a sock on the end of it. She looked Jess up and down.

'Well, it's not much, I'm afraid.' Her voice was soft, surprisingly well spoken and polite, with a trace of Black Country. 'I can't get about very easily, you see, to keep the place as it should be. But if you'd like to go up and see . . .'

She lurched backwards to let Jess in. 'Have you work round here?'

'Blake's,' Jess was tearful with relief at being treated at least kindly. 'In the Jewellery Quarter.'

'Ah yes. Not far. Well look, dear – take this candle. I shan't come up – takes me too long. My bedroom is at the front – left at the top. If you turn right you'll see it. It hasn't been used for a few months since my last lodger left.'

The lady stood watching as Jess climbed the stairs. A thin runner of green carpet covered the middle of the staircase which creaked loudly at each step. The paper in the stairwell was hanging off the walls and the place smelled of damp and mildew. In the spare room, Jess saw a bare floor, uncurtained windows, an iron bedstead and a wooden chair. The walls were painted white and though it was icy cold and cheerless, it was not unpleasant.

This'd do, Jess thought. And the lady seems kind enough.

She went back down into the front room, which was also sparsely furnished with a table, two wooden chairs, and a small, glass-fronted cupboard. Apart from that was only a little blue and green rug by the unlit grate, and some faded pink curtains. But the old lady, despite her ragged grey frock which hung limp and shapeless on her, and her obvious poverty, had an air of gentility about her which made Jess feel both shy and respectful.

'How much is the rent?'

'Five shillings a week.' She said this with some awkwardness, as if it pained her to talk about money. 'With an evening meal. But not tonight, I'm afraid.'

'I'll take it then.' Jess handed her a week's rent in advance.

'Thank you.' The gnarled hand closed over the money with a slow dignity. 'Now we had better know each other's names.'

Jess hesitated. 'Jess. Jessica Green,' she said. 'My husband and me we're – well, hanging on 'til we can afford a proper place like. 'E's joined up, you see, doing 'is bit – 'e's away at the training camp.'

'I see.' The woman's pale eyes stared back at her. Jess sensed she didn't believe her. There was a kind, homely look to her wizened face, Jess saw. It was her hair made her look like a madwoman.

'Pleased to make your acquaintance,' she said grandly. 'My name is Miss Iris Whitman.'

Once she had taken her things up and unpacked them, Jess was almost fainting with hunger. She found Iris Whitman sitting in her back room, which was as bare and chill as the front.

'I'm going out to get some chips,' Jess told her. Even

if she hadn't been hungry she'd have had to get out. The thought of sitting in that freezing room all evening, when she was a bag of nerves, was terrible. 'D'you want me to bring yer anything back?'

Iris's face brightened. 'Yes, a penn'orth of chips would be very nice, dear.'

Iris told her the nearest place to buy chips, and when she came back, her newspaper parcels smelling of hot vinegar, Iris said, 'Perhaps you'd like to stay down and eat them with me, dear?'

The back room was barely warmer than it had been outside. Not a spark of light or warmth came from the range. Jess was longing for a cup of tea, but it was obvious there wouldn't be any on offer. Miss Whitman sat on her hard chair huddled in a shawl which draped her sufficiently to hide her bad leg. Jess wondered whether she was unable to get down and see to the range.

'Would you like me to build a fire?' she asked timidly.

'I would,' the woman said, in her measured way, 'if I had anything to build it with.'

'Oh.' Jess had not met anyone so poor before that they didn't even have a few handfuls of slack to burn. 'Well maybe tomorrow . . .?'

'Yes.' The lady smiled suddenly. 'Things will look up tomorrow, dear. You'll see. They have a way of doing that.'

Jess suddenly had the oddest feeling that Miss Whitman knew all about her, could see into what she was feeling. But there was no nosiness, no sense of judgement. She asked no questions, but ate her chips, delicately from the newspaper as the smell of them filled the room and warmed both of them.

'If you look in the bottom drawer there, you'll find a little bedding.' Miss Whitman pointed at a battered chest of drawers. 'I'm afraid it's not aired.'

How could it be, Jess thought, in this dank room?

'Not to worry.' She was relieved just at the thought of lying down, never mind aired sheets. But she was grateful to Miss Whitman for the company, for distracting her from her own misery.

She found two sheets and a blanket in the drawer. Turning, she dared to ask,

'Miss Whitman, don't you have no one to 'elp yer – get coal and food and that?'

'Oh yes – there's Miss Davitt from next door—' Iris nodded in the direction of the chapel. 'They're very good people. But I believe she's ill this week. I haven't seen her. And I haven't been any too well myself. Things aren't usually quite so cheerless as you see today.'

Jess was relieved to hear it. 'I was thinking – I could fetch in coal and some groceries on my way back from work tomorrow if yer like.'

Iris Whitman was pulling herself awkwardly to a standing position. She looked across at Jess, as if assessing her.

'Well, that's a kind offer. I believe you're a good girl, aren't you? A little help tomorrow would be very nice, I must say.'

Jess looked into Iris's pale eyes for a second, then lowered her gaze. She could feel herself blushing.

'I'd be glad to help yer if you need it. Goodnight then.'

Upstairs, she made up her bed by candlelight. There were no curtains, and the windows were solid rectangles of black. She laid her coat and other few garments over the blanket for a minuscule bit of extra warmth. She wondered what Iris Whitman had to keep her warm. Precious little no doubt.

Once in bed, she took out Ned's letter again. The pain and confusion of her feelings overwhelmed her. Grief, hurt, but also a sense of injustice and frustrated anger.

He loves me, he told me so, and I'm never to see him again! It was madness, all of it! She wanted to run to him, pour out everything to him, about the child, their child she was carrying, that she'd been thrown out of home and all her troubles. Have him say he belonged with her, not Mary and Ruth. It was *her* he loved . . . But then an awful chilling thought ran through her mind. He doesn't love me at all – he was only saying that to let me down gently, to get out of seeing me again. He was just using me the way Olive says men do. I've no sense, none at all – I've been living in a dream! Of course he wasn't going to leave her and come to me. He was always going to stay with Mary, that was the harsh truth of it. And even if she wanted to see him she couldn't: how could she go to him, force him to come to her when he had a wife and he had rejected her? And when he wasn't even here? Choked with emotion she lay down still holding the letter. She couldn't think clearly about anything, the future, the reality of it. Sleep came down on her suddenly, like a blind.

167

Eighteen

Polly was already waiting for her the next afternoon, after work. She saw Jess coming and ran to her.

'Oh Jess – I've been that worried. I 'ardly slept a wink thinking about yer last night – I should've come with yer, that I should!'

The tears Jess had been suppressing all day welled in her eyes. Everything felt vicious this evening, the hunger in her belly, a cold wind grating on her face like sandpaper. 'I'm awright. Look – 'ere's the address where I'm lodging.'

Polly squinted at the scrap of paper. 'Crabtree Road? Where's that?'

'Near the Workhouse – off of Dudley Road.' She told Polly about Miss Whitman. 'Poor soul. She's quite nice really, I think. Got hardly two farthings to rub together, and she ain't nosey or particular like.'

'So yer set for a bit? Oh thank God for that. Now yer mustn't worry, Jess.' Polly felt the hollowness of her words. If she was Jess she'd be more than worried. Scared half to death more like. 'We'll see yer awright, and we'll try and talk our mom round. I don't know what's got into 'er. She wouldn't treat a dog the way she's turned on you. I can't seem to get through to 'er. I kept on at 'er to change 'er mind, and Sis has, but she won't even listen. Kept shouting at me, telling me she didn't want you anywhere near 'er, and if I didn't keep

168

quiet, I could go an' all!' Jess could see Polly was in almost as bad a state as she was. 'She ain't going to stop me coming to see yer though. I'll come round Friday, awright? Bring yer a few things.'

'Thanks, Poll. Evie said she'd come an' all. But yer don't need to worry yet – I've still got my earnings. Auntie needs yer money, to look after Ronny and that.'

'Oh she's getting 'er usual. I just can't stand to think of yer all alone the way you are—' Polly started to cry. 'It's just not like our mom, Jess. I don't know what's going on. I don't know who I'm most worried about – you, her or Ernie!'

Through those dark days of November and December, Jess went to work at Blake's every day, secure at least in the knowledge that her pregnancy was not yet showing. The sickness left her and she had more energy, but not having the wretchedness of feeling ill to distract her, the full misery of Ned's absence overcame her. She lay in bed at night crying for him, for what they had had before. It had not been much, after all, but to her it seemed like the world now that her existence had become a lonely, dragging round of drudgery and unhappiness, with no hope to lighten it, no love from him to see her through.

Every evening she spent in Iris Whitman's spartan little house. But she did make sure a fire was lit and that they had food. Miss Davitt, the kind lady from the chapel, came to help Iris with her shopping, and Jess would fetch any extras which were needed, so the house was never quite as wretched again as the night when she first arrived. Sometimes Evie came to see her for a while, and Polly and Sis, who Jess introduced as friends of hers, and Iris Whitman let them sit downstairs if they wanted to, to keep warm. They'd tell her any news about Bert and Ernie, who were both still safe training in England. Of course, with Iris about there were things they couldn't say, so sometimes after a cup of tea they'd go up to Jess's room for a private talk. Sis was very sweet, always bringing a little something – a chunk of cake, a couple of apples – and saying, 'It ain't the same at home without yer, Jess.' But so far, nothing they'd said had been able to shift Olive. Jess was still an outcast.

After a few weeks, she got to know more about Iris Whitman. Iris did not have visitors, except for Miss Davitt and Beattie, another elderly woman across the road who looked out for her, when she was well enough to venture out herself. Iris was not able to move far outside the house on her crutches without completely exhausting herself.

Iris was lonely and liked Jess to sit with her, and Jess felt sorry for her and was glad of the distraction of company. Now the evenings were bitterly cold, they sat close to the range cradling cups of tea in their hands, Iris in her shawl, hair straggling round her face so that Jess itched to get the scissors and give it a good cut. She found Iris a strange, disconcerting woman. For days on end their talk consisted of trivial detail about the weather, food, little incidents about Miss Davitt or Beattie, Jess's work, the state of the house ... Iris hopped from subject to subject like a sparrow. Jess never asked her leading questions, hoping Iris would not ask any of her. But one evening, after a long silence, Iris said,

'I was a schoolteacher, you know.'

Jess looked across at her, startled out of her own miserable thoughts. For a second she nearly laughed. Miss Whitman looked so unlike the neat, strict teachers she had had at school! But the well-spoken voice, the gentility of her, once you looked past the eccentric way she was dressed – yes, you could imagine it, almost.

Cautiously, she asked, 'Were you?'

'A trained teacher of young infants, I was. Always liked children. Taught in several schools across Birmingham – one in Sutton Coldfield. Until this.' She straightened her damaged leg, the stump poking out from her shawl, dressed in a sludgy green, handknitted sock. 'They wouldn't have me back afterwards. Said I wasn't fit to be associated with small children.'

Jess tried to control her expression of astonishment.

'Hand to mouth I was, after it. That's why you find me in these straits. Hand to mouth all these years is how I've lived. Faith, hope and bread. That's life, dear. And thoughts. Must have your own thoughts.'

Iris looked very directly at her. 'I'll tell you what happened. You must've wondered, Jessica, although you're too polite to ask.'

Jess nodded, blushing.

'I was engaged to be married, aged thirty. Over the hill, some would say.' She stroked one venous hand back and forth along the thigh of her gammy leg. 'Quite besotted I was. I thought I'd found the only thing in life, pinned all my hopes on him. Anyway, to keep it short: a month before the wedding was due to happen he took off. February it was. Left his lodgings with everything – no letter, nothing. I was told he'd gone to Stafford. Whether that was true now, I don't know, but I was in a desperate state, you see. How I felt about him, I mean. Fit to do myself in – though I don't hold with that, it's irreligious. So, what to do but go to Stafford. Well, it was snowy – inches of it settled for days, banked up in places – and Stafford's a long way to go. By the time I got there this one foot was frozen. They had to have it off at the ankle. Frostbite, you see. I was in hospital in Stafford for weeks. I'd left my school – never said where I was going. They wouldn't have me back – said I wasn't a responsible person. Walking to Stafford like that.'

'But—' Jess sat up straight, appalled. 'Why didn't you go on the train?'

'I was in love, dear. Madly in love.' Iris's pale eyes looked back at her. 'I wanted to show him, you see, what I'd do for him. Find him, wherever. Of course he never knew. I don't even know if he was really in Stafford. Silly young thing, wasn't I? I never saw him again. Thirty years ago now, all that.'

Jess stared back, thinking her way into Iris's life. A life wrecked by love. She was so shocked by what she had heard that she felt as if she'd been punched in the chest.

'So – you never found him?'

Iris shook her head.

'And you never worked again?'

'Oh I did. Of course. Had to, dear. But not as a teacher. Odd jobs here and there. Factories. A bit of private tutoring once or twice. Enough to keep body and soul together. What a fool, you're thinking, aren't you? Everyone does, I know. Mad old Iris. Lost everything for a man. I did – and I regret it. My old life was all gone, of course. But I did *have* love for a time, or thought I did, and that came to the same thing. Had some of the strong stuff for a bit – more than the everyday bread and water of keeping alive and breathing. That's more than some.'

Jess's heart was beating hard, she could hear the pulse of it in her ears. She looked down into her lap. Am I the same: ruined for love? Soon, she thought, the babby's going to start showing and she'll know. Whatever Iris felt for this man of hers, she didn't have a babby . . . But she thought of Iris's leg. A severed leg and a babby came to nigh on the same thing for a woman without a husband.

'I've heard you having a weep up there at nights, dear. I don't know what your trouble is. As soon as I saw you though, I knew there was something. I know a frightened face when I see it.'

Jess couldn't answer.

'Whatever it is, you're a comfort to me, Jessica. I'm not for convention and stoning people for their misfortunes like the woman taken in adultery. No, no. "Let he who is without sin cast the first stone." I could be bitter, but I'm not. God's love and man's – that's all that matters. Loving kindness and seeing into people as they are, that's me. You'll have a roof over your head, my dear, whatever your trouble, have no fear about that.'

'Thank you.' Jess could barely speak, so close was she to pouring out all her woes. Without looking up at Iris, she whispered, 'I'm going up now.'

She managed to control her tears until she reached her room and buried her face in the bed, trying not to make a sound. The blanket was scratchy against her face and smelt mouldy, but it absorbed her sobbing.

Oh Ned, Ned, *please* . . . Over and over again the

begging words spilled from her, whispered into the mattress. Iris's story affected her deeply. It was too late for Iris, but the idea of ending up like her filled Jess with horror: unwanted, disgraced, alone with a child. All because of her love for a man. Are men different? she wondered. Don't they feel? How could he just leave Miss Whitman like that if he'd said he loved her? Perhaps he was married as well? Had a wife and family that Iris never knew about. And hadn't she fallen into the same trap? She curled herself up tight on the bed, lying on her side, banging one hand hard on the mattress as she wept, again and again so that the springs squeaked. How can I go on? she sobbed. How can I live like this, without him, without anyone?

Nineteen

'Mom – you'll let our Jess come 'ome for Christmas, won't yer?'

Polly spoke to her mother's back. Olive was sitting at the table. Sis looked round, watching them both.

There was no reply.

'I don't mean for good, but won't yer let 'er come for the day with us? We can't just leave 'er there all on 'er own! Ernie'll be back Christmas Eve, and Bert . . . family all together like . . . Please, say summat! Why're yer being so cruel to 'er?'

Olive stood up and tipped slack into the range, face turned away from them. The fire flared and crackled. She put the pail down and wiped her sooty hands on her apron.

'Mom!' Sis couldn't bear the silence any longer.

Olive ignored the pair of them. Face blank of expression, as if she was shutting out them and all their words, she took the bucket out to the back yard, went into the privy and banged the door shut.

Polly slammed her cup down on the table. 'I can't stand much more of this. One way or another summat's got to give!'

Jess pulled up her vest and looked down at herself. No doubt about it: it was beginning to show. Not enough for anyone else to notice, but that wouldn't take long now . . . Her nipples had darkened, and there was a little bulge to her stomach that hadn't been there before. She reckoned she'd caught for the babby in August, that time in the park, she remembered bitterly. So she was nearly four months gone. She was starting to feel tiny movements inside her, wrigglings, flutterings, different from anything she'd felt before. She pulled her clothes on, pressing her hand to her stomach. No – no one'd notice for a little while yet. But it was frightening, having something control you from inside, knowing it was getting bigger, spreading.

'I wish I could run away too, just move on and start again.' She buttoned her cardigan with cold fingers. 'But it's done now – there's nowt I can do about it.'

The week before Christmas, she walked home from work, alone as usual. It was dark, with a thick, swirling fog, the lamplight smudged and dim, and the dark walls seemed to close in on her. She was forced to walk more slowly, feeling her way along, able to see hardly a yard in front of her face.

When she reached the fire station in Albion Street, she paused, putting a hand out to touch the cold bricks. Everything else was invisible in the fog. It was not far from here that Ned had told her he loved her. For a moment she leaned back against the building, breathing in the rank, sodden air, and closed her eyes. If only it was June still! How strong and happy she'd felt then, believing in the strength of his feelings for her!

'Yer doing business?'

Jess opened her eyes. A burly man, not much more than her own height, stood just in front of her. His collar was up and his cap pulled low over his eyes. In the gloom she could make out that he had a thick beard.

'What?' She stood up straight, alarmed.

He spoke in a murmur, through the side of his mouth.

'You doing business, are yer?'

'I don't know what yer mean.' She sidled further along the wall.

'A shilling. All I can spare.'

Jess stared at him for a moment, until it dawned on her. That woman in New Street, drenched in perfume!

'No – oh my God, no! I'm just going 'ome, that's all. I'm not what yer think!'

She stumbled away from him, terrified he'd follow. After a few moments she stopped, peering back at the invisible street. She couldn't hear anyone following and she slowed to a walk again, feeling shaky. That'd teach her to stand and dream in the street! It was a horrible feeling, being mistaken for a sordid, fallen woman. The man's words wormed through her mind. A shilling, he'd offered. Just like that. Money for a job. If she did it say six times – even ten times a week . . .

'I must be going mad,' she muttered frantically as she strode along the Dudley Road. 'Right off my 'ead, even thinking such a desperate thing! Never – however bad things get – not in a million years!'

By the time Christmas Eve came there was snow on the ground. For a few hours it made the city look clean and newborn, until the wheeltracks and footprints shovelled it into tarnished heaps and the factories belched their filthy breath all over it.

The lads were due home that afternoon, those with leave. Bert came home from Tidworth, new blue uniform and all, full of himself.

'Awright, Mom—' Bashful, he gave her a peck on the cheek and for a moment Olive's face relaxed with pleasure. Ronny was wild with excitement, pulling at Bert's coat until his big brother took notice, picked him up and dangled him playfully upside down.

'Yer looking well, son,' Olive said.

'In better nick than when I left, no doubt about that.' Bert threw himself down on to a chair and Ronny jumped on top of him, laughing. 'Knocking us into shape good and proper, and some of 'em could do with it, I can tell yer!' He grinned, looking round the room. 'It's good to be 'ome for a bit though, Mom, 'stead of sleeping in a leaky bloody hut ... 'Ere—' He dug into his bag. 'I've brought summat for yer.'

From a paper bag he unpacked a row of brass ornaments and stood them along the table. Olive came nearer, peering at them. Each one was a man's head, moulded in brass, about four inches high. Bert pointed at each of them.

'That one's Kitchener—' Olive smiled 'Oh yes!' recognizing the moustache. 'Then yer've got, let's see – Joffre, Jellicoe for the navy, and Beatty, and that's Sir John French ... They're to go on the mantel – look.'

He helped her line them up, seeing she was pleased.

''Ow is everyone – awright?' he asked as she made tea.

'Ar, they're awright.'

'Poll?'

'Going along. She'll be in soon.'

'And Sis? And what about Jess?'

Olive tinkled a spoon round inside the teapot. 'I've told yer – they're all awright.' She turned, her harsh expression softening again at the sight of him. So like

Charlie he was getting! 'You look as if yer could do with a good sleep, you do.'

'I could an' all. Plenty of time later. After a couple of pints . . .'

There was a knock on the door soon after Polly and Sis got in. Polly dashed to open it.

'Ernie – oh love, it's you at last!'

Ernie was pink-cheeked, bursting with health, though he did look a little thinner in the face, and younger without the beard. He and Polly flung their arms round each other and stayed for some time out in the dark street, hugging and kissing, before going inside.

Polly rested her head on Ernie's shoulder. 'Oh love – I wish you was 'ere all the time, I've missed yer that much. I don't want yer to go away again.' She squeezed him tight.

'Eh – come on, I've only just got 'ere! No need to talk about me going yet.'

Later, the two of them walked out together, to get away from everyone else, holding tight to each other so as not to slip in the street. It had started snowing again, small, dry flakes, falling skittishly.

'I feel I want to hold on to every second,' Polly said. 'The time's going to go in a flash and yer mom's going to want yer over there too . . .'

'Roll on the time when we've got our own place.' Ernie stopped and pulled her close to him, licked a snowflake from her cheek. ''Aving tea and a chat's awright, but it ain't the thing I've been looking forward to all this time, I can tell yer!'

'Ernie!' Polly giggled. 'Cheeky thing – eh, stop it,

not 'ere! There'll be time for that later!' She removed his hand from her bottom. 'Mom says yer can stop over, and turf Sis out of 'er bed tonight.'

'I don't know as I can wait 'til then . . .' He ran his hands over her, feeling for her breasts. 'Oh Poll, I've missed yer.'

'I've missed you too – like anything. But listen, let's walk on a bit. Before we go 'ome I want to talk to yer about summat. It's Jess . . .'

Walking down the Moseley Road, she told Ernie all that had happened. He was far from impressed.

'Stupid bloody fools, the pair of 'em – 'e's got a wife and a nipper! What the 'ell does 'e think 'e's playing at – and 'er! That's disgusting that is.'

'But she's having 'is babby and our mom won't let 'er anywhere near – she's all on 'er own and she's pining and worried sick! She's got no one else, Ernie, and she loves the bones of 'im, 'owever much she shouldn't! I think Ned ought to know. Why should Jess put up with all of it and 'im do nothing? And if 'e knew, maybe . . .'

'Maybe what?' His voice was harsh. 'If you go telling 'im it'll only cause trouble and you'll be caught up in it. It ain't up to you to go interfering. If a woman goes behaving like that she has to count the cost. It's 'er own bloody fault. I must say, I'd never've thought it of 'er, but she's made 'er bed and she'll 'ave to lie on it. Unless – I mean, there's ways yer can get rid of a babby, can't yer, some'ow? Why don't she do that and 'ave done with it?'

''Ere—' Polly's tone became sharp. 'Don't talk to me in that voice – it's horrible! We thought of that. Went to this woman. But oh Ernie, if you'd seen – it frightened the life out of both of us. Yer wouldn't do it to an animal. But someone's got to sort it out. She won't tell 'im 'cause she's shamed and frightened . . .'

'No, Poll – it ain't on. You keep out of it. It ain't your business or mine, and I daint come 'ome to argue with yer. Come 'ere, wife, and give us a kiss!'

For a moment Polly didn't look up at him. She bit her lip. He's wrong, she thought. I've got to interfere. She didn't want to go against her husband, but he couldn't see things the way she could. She didn't want to spoil their time together though. Looking up she smiled.

'Come 'ere then, yer big 'andsome soldier boy!'

Jess spent Christmas with Iris Whitman. She turned down Iris's invitation to go to church with her because she didn't feel like going out, and having people asking questions about her to her face. If they wanted to gossip behind her back, then that was their business.

'You go,' she told Iris. 'And I'll cook us a bit of dinner.'

She hadn't had the heart to do anything about decorating the back room, and the house seemed so dismal in the harsh white light from the snow outside. She didn't want to be reminded that it was Christmas at all, except that somehow it had to be lived through. They did have a small joint of beef as a Christmas treat though, and Jess prepared it for roasting with potatoes and parsnips, sprouts and carrots alongside. But she did so with such a heavy heart. How small were the amounts she had to cook, and how lonely the little cut of meat looked! She thought of everyone in Oughton Place, the family all together. The fact that her aunt hadn't caved in and let her back just for a visit hurt her so much. And there'd been nothing in the way of a Christmas greeting sent from Budderston either. She cried, peeling the three potatoes, scrubbing the few carrots. Of course she was in the wrong: a disgrace to the family. But she'd thought that Olive, after she calmed down, might find it in her to forgive. She would have had her first Christmas with a proper family in such a long time. She knew Bert and Ernie were home on leave, and ... and ... She dragged her mind away from the thought of Ned. He'd be on leave too – going home to Mary, loving her, being a family ... And of course that was the right thing because she was his wife, and whatever Jess felt for him she had no right ... She, and all her deepest feelings and yearnings, were wrong in the eyes of everyone. Worst of all, in his eyes too ... It was a grim, despairing morning, and when Iris came back it took her an enormous effort to conceal her misery.

On the morning of Boxing Day, Ernie went to his mom's for a bit and Polly said she was going out. She looked defiantly at Olive.

'Please yerself,' Olive didn't look up. She had a darning mushroom pushed into one of Bert's socks. She was having to sew again now Jess was gone.

'Shall I come?' Sis asked.

'No!' Polly spoke too sharply. 'Er, no, Sis – not this time. Maybe later, awright?' She gave her sister a wink as she put her coat on and Sis was appeased. They had told Bert Jess was away visiting her father.

She set out across the quiet city, asparkle today in its

new coat of white, screwing up her eyes against its brightness. St Martin's Church seemed made of sugar. Polly felt well in herself. She had had food and rest over Christmas, and her husband home. But the deep breaths she breathed in were as much from nerves as contentment.

'I 'ope I'm doing the right thing,' she said. 'God alone knows – but someone's got to do summat, the way things are!'

Late that night, Jess lay in bed, trying to get warm before she could sleep. She tucked her feet into the bottom of her nightdress, curling up tight, arms folded, hugging herself. It would be a relief to go back to work, get back to the normal routine.

She tucked her nose under the covers, smelling the damp sheet. Nothing in this room ever felt warm. She imagined looking down from outside herself, the sight of her body lying covered by the cold sheet and her black coat, legs bent up trying to get warm. Her body: where she began and ended, the limits of her, so small, so minutely insignificant compared with everything outside. The muffled city, the huge sky flecked with stars . . . what did any of it matter? She lived, she'd die: just like a lump of meat in a big pot of stew. She'd be gone, and none of her problems would matter. Comforted by this, her mind drifted and she was beginning to doze.

The cracking sound seemed loud as a bullet from a gun. She sat up, wide awake again, heart beating like mad. Silence, then it came again. Someone was throwing things at her window. There was a third rap on the pane as she crept across the floor.

She could make out nothing through the pane, and, pulling at the sash, was surprised when the window opened easily.

'Jess?'

She could barely find the breath to answer. His voice, low and cautious.

'Ned!'

'Can yer come down?'

'Wait – I'll come to the back . . .'

She fumbled into her cardigan, fingers almost useless, breath coming in snatches, whispering frantically to herself. 'Oh my God, oh please . . .' It was like a dream, speeding down the stairs in her bare feet, noticing nothing, neither the cold nor the dark. She unbolted the back door and saw the shape of him, faintly silhouetted in the doorway against the snow-covered yard. They both stood quite still. Jess could think straight about nothing, why he was here, what she might say, could only see him standing there where she'd never expected to find him.

'Can I come in? Is it safe?'

'The lady's asleep – ages ago I s'pect.' Jess stepped back and he stamped the snow from his boots as gently as he could before coming in. She took a candle from the cupboard, lit it and stood it in a holder on the table. Across its light they looked at one another in silence.

At last he said, 'Is it true?' His face was fearful, tender.

'Who told you?'

'Polly. She came this morning.'

'*Polly?* Why did she . . .? I daint ask her to come and see yer, honest. I weren't going to force yer . . . to interfere with your life when yer'd said yer didn't want me . . .'

'Jess – for God's sake, tell me.'

Slowly, she nodded.

'A babby . . . you . . .' He went to the back window, staring, for long moments, though there was nothing to see in its opaqueness. Softly, behind him, she started to cry. Eventually he turned round and stood watching her.

'God, Jess – I feel like doing that too.' Gradually, he came over to her. 'I'm frightened to touch you because if I do I shan't be able to let go of yer. What can I do? I can't go on like this any more. I hate myself for it.'

Not understanding, she looked up at him. 'Why did you come then?'

'Because I couldn't stay away. When Poll came and told me . . .' His voice trailed off. 'For heaven's sake – come 'ere.' He pulled her to him so fiercely she gasped, and feeling his arms round her, sank into them, crying wildly. He held her close, rocking and soothing her, one hand in her thick hair, pressing her head close to his chest.

'It's no good.' He was near to tears himself, the tension inside him near breaking point. 'I can't go on with Mary – trying to be a good husband to 'er when all the time my mind's with you, all the time I can think about you and nothing else. Being away and that – away from you – I thought I'd come to terms with it. But I can't. I love yer so much, want yer so much, I'm frightened to death by it, and that's the truth.'

She looked up into his eyes, quieter now, almost forgetting to breathe when she heard what he said, the strength of feeling in it.

'What . . . what d'yer mean?'

'Mary's got 'er mom. It'll be bad for 'er, but she'll

manage. That's if yer still want *me*, after what I've writ to yer . . .'

'*Want* you!' She pulled away from him, standing back, afraid. 'You mean you're going to . . . to . . .?'

He gave a great shuddering sigh, afraid of the words he was about to say. 'To leave Mary and come to you. I'll have to tell 'er. Soon. Before I go. I don't know what's right any more except being with you. I know I love you, Jess. I can't stay away from yer. I married Mary when I didn't know how it was possible to feel, though I can't blame 'er for that. But I've got to be with you. I knew if I saw yer again it'd be like this.'

Jess moved close to him.

'D'yer mean it? You'd really . . .'

'Yes, love, I do. It's all I can do, loving you.'

'And me,' she whispered. 'It's all I can do.'

She put her arms round him and they held each other close, awed by what this meant, by the feeling between them which wouldn't die, however hard they'd each tried to stamp it out.

Twenty

A week later, at work, Jess began to be troubled by low, grumbling pains. On the walk home they became agonizing, and before reaching the house she had to stop, bent over with the cramps in her body and a sudden wetness. Looking down, she saw blood on the ground. Doubled up with the pain, she tried to make sense of what was happening to her. The red stain spread, melting into the snow. She made it home in fits and starts, legs soaked with blood.

Inside the house she fell to her knees at the foot of the stairs, arms pressed into her as the pain tore across her. She heard herself moaning, as if it was someone else.

'Jess?' Iris clumped along the hall. 'Whatever's the matter, dear? Oh, my word . . .' One hand went to her mouth.

Jess was sobbing with pain. 'The babby . . . it's . . . I'm losing—' She broke into an anguished moan. Whatever use was Iris going to be? 'Oh help me!'

But Iris Whitman, in her odd way, couldn't have been a better person to be present at this time, Jess acknowledged after it was over. Unshockable, somehow detached from social conventions, she was calm and practical.

'Miss Davitt will know – I'll just be a moment, dear.' She pulled herself to the door. It closed behind her with a waft of snowy air. There was a moment's lull in the pain. Jess pressed her cheek to the cool lino. She couldn't think about anything, only try to get through those moments, fighting the pain.

Miss Davitt helped Jess up to bed. She was more flustered than Iris, but kindly.

'Poor little thing,' she kept saying. She pressed a pad of soft, folded cotton between Jess's legs. 'I've sent for the doctor – soon be here, dear. Oh you poor young thing . . .'

Jess lay on her side, knees drawn up, biting on a folded corner of the sheet as the pains came and went. Sometimes it was so bad, she cried out. Iris sent Miss Davitt up with warm water for her to sip, but it made her sick. The two women hovered round. Jess heard them talking in low voices outside the door. She felt helpless and completely humiliated.

'Ned,' she whispered. 'Oh Ned – our little babby . . .' Her tears ran on to the pillow. For all the trouble and anguish the pregnancy had caused her, its failure was terrible. She could not give him a child, as Mary could. Mary was a proper woman. He'll go back to her now, she thought. She has a child and I'll have none. He won't stay with me now . . .

She managed to stop crying when the doctor came in, a thin, tired-looking young man with a sharp manner. Iris appeared behind him, which later, Jess saw, was a true act of friendship on her behalf, though at the time she gave it no thought.

'So – miscarrying, then?' The doctor didn't look at her, but put his bag down on the end of the bed and opened it. 'Let's see if we can deal with it all here, shall we, not have to send you into hospital?'

Jess nodded, frightened.

'Much bleeding?'

She nodded again. Miss Davitt had twice had to find replacement strips of stuff to stem the thick flow of it.

The doctor examined her. His fingers prodding her stomach made her moan, she felt so tender.

'So . . .' he eyed her ringless finger. 'Miss er . . .'

It was Iris who spoke up. 'Mrs. Mrs Green. Her husband's in the army.'

Jess felt a kind of love for Iris at that moment.

'Well, Mrs Green. By the looks of what your losing, the miscarriage is a thorough one. You'll need rest – several days, after the bleeding stops. Any problems – your temperature going up, or if the bleeding gets heavier, call me again. Otherwise you should be back to normal.'

Miss Davitt saw him out and, Jess realized, must have paid him as well.

Iris stood by the bed looking down at Jess's white face. Her pale eyes were watery.

'Sad,' she said. 'Very sad. Whatever anyone else might say.'

Jess's eyes filled with tears again. 'Thank you, Iris,' she whispered.

She lay in bed for a week, looked after by Miss Davitt, who prayed at her bedside, and Iris. Miss Davitt was a quiet presence in her flat, silent shoes. She was kind, effective and utterly reserved. Jess never got to know her any better, nor did she know what Miss Davitt believed to be the truth about her situation. One morning she placed on the chair by Jess's bed a little glass containing a few snowdrops.

'Surprising what grows, even in the depths of winter,'

she said, when Jess thanked her. She was touched, tears welling again, as they seemed to so easily in her low state. For hour after hour she looked at the flowers' delicate white, their shading of green underlying the petals. Her mind was hazy and unfocused. The bleeding slowed, but she was weak. She felt scoured and empty.

Iris was much noisier, unable to climb the stairs without the rhythmic thump of her crutch, sometimes an exclamation of 'Ooops – oh dear me!' as she almost lost her balance, or a little argument with Miss Davitt about her going up there when there was someone else to help.

But Jess liked it when Iris came up and sat with her, found her smell of old wool comforting. She didn't say much, often, but she gave off a sympathy of the sort that didn't tut and cluck about how sorry she was, which made Jess just want to cry again. It was something more fundamental. A feeling that she understood about Ned, about love and loss. She went straight to the heart of things.

'Anyone else would have put me out on the street,' Jess said to her one day. Iris sat on the chair by her, holding the glass of snowdrops. Her crutch was propped against the wall, and a wedge of winter sunshine was brightening the room. Outside, the snow was beginning to thaw.

Iris was silent, just held her head to one side in a considering way.

'People are cruel,' Jess said.

'God sent you to me.'

Jess thought about this. Iris said odd things. But it felt true.

'Cruelty is part of life, remember,' Iris said. 'What about his wife? She must feel life is cruel.'

Iris had met Ned, the day before his leave ended. He had gone to Mary, to tell her. When he came back he was in a bad state, agitated, full of shame. They explained to Iris, but even then, hadn't told her about the child. Perhaps she had guessed in any case.

'The way it feels, it should just be between me and him,' Jess said. 'But nothing's like that, is it? Not really private. Things always bring in other people.'

She thought a lot about her father during those long, dreamlike days. His love for Louisa which, as she understood it, had been so strong, so exclusive that it could scarcely encompass the love of a child as well. For the first time she really wondered what her mother had felt for him. That embrace, that private moment she had come upon that time. It was his face she saw, which wore that expression of completion, of bliss. Louisa's face had been turned away from her.

Gradually she felt stronger. She could sit up and eat, then go downstairs. Going outside seemed a possibility.

I'll have to write and tell him about the babby. The thought weighed on her, filling her with dread.

When Polly came, she was full of remorse.

'Oh Jess – if we'd only known! You going through all that with no one round yer!'

'I'm awright.' Jess patted her hand, trying to smile. 'Iris and Miss Davitt have been good to me. And I feel better now.'

At first Polly was wary with Iris.

'No need to worry,' Jess told her. 'She knows everything and she's been ever so kind.' She saw Polly watching Iris when she came into the room, could tell she was thinking how odd she was, wondering how Jess could confide in such a person. Seeing her through Polly's eyes, Jess noticed again what a mess Iris looked, how peculiar and badly fitting her clothes were, her patched old skirt like a sack on her, the enormous, stained blouse and garish blue shawl. Jess had simply got used to her, her looks and strangeness, and grown fond of her.

When they were alone Polly said, 'Mary's been round. If she sees yer she'll kill yer, the state she's in.'

'You didn't tell 'er...' Jess half got to her feet in alarm. The thought of Mary turning up on her doorstep on top of everything else was too much.

'No. Even Mom kept quiet. But yer can't blame 'er, Jess. She's got a child to bring up and you ... Well, you ain't, now, 'ave yer? I mean 'e should really do the right thing and go back to 'er.'

She looked across at her cousin. Jess's hair was loose, lying thick on her shoulders. She had folded her arms, hugging herself, and was crying quietly.

'Oh Jess!' Polly went to her, kneeling to hold her close. 'You don't 'alf get into some messes, you do! Why don't you think for 'alf a second before yer do things?'

'I dunno,' Jess sniffed. 'I never meant – I mean I just...'

'I know.' Polly smiled into her face. 'Yer just can't help yerself. I don't know – I'll go grey early having you around! At least though...' She hesitated. 'You 'ain't got the babby to worry about no more.' Seeing that this made Jess cry even harder, she said, 'I'm sorry, but you know what I mean, and eh – maybe our mom'll let yer come home now?'

*

Ned sat at a scratched table, a thin pad of blank paper in front of him. For their leisure time they had been given the use of the Parish Rooms in Boldmere, a suburb near Sutton Coldfield, and around him was a buzz of conversation from the other lads, someone plinking out a tune on the old piano. He sat with one elbow on the table, cheek resting on his upturned hand, staring across the room, seeing nothing.

'Yer coming out for a pint?'

There was no response.

'Eh, Ned? A pint – yer coming?'

'Oh—' Ned roused himself. 'No, ta Jem. Not tonight.'

'What's up, pal? Not bad news? Your missis ain't playing you up, is she?'

'No. No – you go. I'll stop 'ere tonight.'

'Awright – please yerself.'

Ned watched his two pals go, joking together, to the door. He picked up his pen.

Dearest Jess,
    I'm so sorry to hear . . .

He tore the sheet of paper from the pad, screwed it up, sat twisting the pen round between his fingers. Had it been true? Doubts nagged at him. Had she told him she was expecting to make him leave Mary? But no – no. That night, the night he'd gone to her and they'd lain together she'd taken his hand, placed it on her belly, and he'd felt it, the unmistakable little rise in it, spongy but definite. And that wouldn't be like her, to lie to him. A wave of tenderness passed through him.

Dear Jess,

I got your letter today. Your news about the baby has knocked me for six and I'm sorry you've been so poorly. I hope you feel better now. Don't feel badly about it, love. It's not your fault, you've been under a lot of strain. We'll have other children, you and me, won't we?

I know why you're frightened of what I might do now you're not in the family way, but don't be. I love you with all my heart and I'm coming back to you. I said so, didn't I? It wasn't just the baby that made me decide. It would've happened in the end because I can't do without you.

No time to write more. My mom and dad deserve a letter. But I wanted to tell you not to worry, because you're everything to me, whatever else.

Your very loving,
Ned

Dear Mom and Dad . . .

Again, he sat for a long time, turning the pen round and round. Imagining his parents at their table, eggs in front of them, the morning post propped by the teapot. Reading his letter. His father's incomprehension, his mother crying. Slowly he began, honestly, trying to explain what to them would be inexplicable.

'Jess – there's someone to see you.'

Jess had been lying down upstairs. It was Sunday afternoon and she was gathering her strength to go back to work next day, worrying in case she'd lost her job from being off sick. She hadn't even heard the knock on the door.

From the top of the stairs she saw Olive looking up at her from the hall. Jess stopped and laid a hand on her chest.

'Oh – Auntie!'

'Go in the front room, dear,' Iris said, clump-clumping her way through to the back.

Jess led her aunt into the chilly front room, and they stood looking at one another in the grey light from the window. Olive was wearing her best Sunday frock. She still had her hat on.

'So. Yer better then?' Her voice was gruff.

'Yes, ta.'

Olive walked to the fireplace, stood on the little mat, eyeing the ash in the grate. Jess looked at the thin twist of hair low on her neck. For a moment the only sound was Olive's harsh breathing.

'I didn't want yer bringing a babby into my 'ouse.'

'I know, Auntie.'

'No – yer don't. Yer don't know, and yer don't need to.' She turned, her expression terrible. 'I could spit on yer, Jess, that I could, for what yer've done. Ned . . . were a good lad before you come along.' Her mouth twisted bitterly to one side. 'I s'pose 'e'll go back and patch things up with 'er now, if 'e's got any sense, though that seems to 've flown out of the window from what 'e used to be like. You're a – a – disgrace, the pair of yer. I can't even say what you are . . .' She made a despairing gesture with her hands, holding them up, then letting them drop.

Jess stood with her arms tightly folded. She didn't say anything.

'I came to say, as there's no babby, yer can come home if yer want. I won't have 'im there. You're bad enough but you're family. I don't want to clap eyes on 'im though. I thought the world of him and 'e's – well, 'e's beyond redemption in my eyes now. I won't 'ave it. Is that understood?'

'Yes,' Jess found she could only manage a humble whisper. She cleared her throat. 'Yes, Auntie.'

PART III

Twenty-One

November 1915

'Jess? Wakey wakey – time for a break!'

The other girls were already moving out of the shed but Jess was oblivious to them all, peering into the neck of a grenade, checking it was full of powder. She jumped violently as Sis tapped on her shoulder.

'Oh my word, yer gave me a fright!'

She went with Polly and Sis outside to the canteen shed where they were given a cup of milk and a bun. Polly pulled off the mob cap they were all obliged to wear and shook out her hair before replacing it again. All of them wore khaki, uninflammable overalls over their clothes.

'Flaming milk again,' Polly complained. 'I'd rather 'ave a good strong cup of tea.'

'S'posed to keep us from getting bad from the powder, ain't it?' Jess said. They'd been told that the better their diet, the less they would be affected by the TNT in the grenades.

''Ere – sun's out for a bit,' Polly said. 'Let's drink it out in the yard, eh – get some air?'

All year, with more and more munitions equipment needed to feed the war, factories had been going over to armaments production, and new ones springing up. A friend of Polly's had told them about this one in Small Heath when it was recruiting workers, and offering good wages.

'Why don't we all go?' she said. 'We could work together. 'Ave a bit of a laugh. I could do with a change, and on money like that . . .'

Jess had been very pleased to move away from the Jewellery Quarter. She had seen Mary, more than once, in the street where she worked, and run guiltily away to avoid her. She didn't want to be anywhere where she might meet her again.

The new factory consisted of a collection of wooden buildings built on a piece of waste ground, and they'd spent the summer in the TNT sheds, six or seven girls to each shed. They were moved about: some days they worked together, some not.

They stood out in the weak winter sun amid the clattering from the packing shed behind them. Across the yard, boxes of the grenades were stacked on wooden staging. Some of the other girls came to join them, their faces a sallow, yellowish colour from the powder.

Jess stared into her milk, not joining in the chatter round her. The other girls' eyes followed the foreman, Mr Stevenson, as he walked across the yard. He was tall, slim and dark, in his mid-thirties. He called, 'Morning!' to them abstractedly as he passed.

''E don't look too 'appy,' one of the girls remarked.

'Never does, does 'e?' Polly had downed her milk and was dangling the cup from one finger by its handle. 'Ole misery guts.'

Jess became aware of Sis's freckled face peering round into her own with a grin which was so irresistible, Jess found herself smiling too.

'Cheer up!'

'I'm awright.' Jess roused herself, giving Sis a look of caution. At work she never spoke of Ned or her circumstances. Didn't want to have to explain, or have people judging her. But her thoughts were with him more than ever. Today his battalion was leaving for France. All year the news of the fighting had been so grim, from Ypres and Loos, from the Dardanelles. She dreaded the thought of Ned being sent into it. She still felt he was so close to her after his leave last week. Now she had no idea when she would see him again.

Polly gave her arm a squeeze as they went back in to work. Ernie had been gone since July, and Polly sometimes got very down about it.

'I dunno – 'ere I am, still at home with Mom like a child. I might just as well not be married at all.'

But there had been a big change for her: she was expecting a baby the following spring. There wasn't much to show yet, but the pregnancy had already filled out her face a little, softening the angles of her pointed cheekbones. Ernie had been over the moon at the news, and Polly too, although true to form she worried and fretted. 'When will Ernie ever get to see the babby? This is a rotten time to be expecting. Why does there 'ave to be a flaming war – they said it'd all be over by now!'

They returned to their steady, monotonous work. The women filled the grenades, ramming the powder down inside with an aluminium mallet fixed to a wooden handle. Jess's job was first to check the boxes of twelve to see that each was properly full of powder. Then she inserted an aluminium screw into each, securing it with red sealing wax, and checked the safety catch was in position before they were taken away. She could do the job almost automatically, leaving ample space in her mind for her own thoughts. And those thoughts today were poignant ones.

*

'Jess—'

The day Jess left, Iris had stood forlornly in the gloomy hall watching her come downstairs with her small bundle of belongings. The sight of Iris brought tears to Jess's eyes but she tried to smile.

'I'll come back and see yer, Iris. I hope you get a new lodger soon.'

'Jess—' Iris continued as if no one had spoken. 'What are you going to do?'

'Well – I'm going back to Auntie's.'

'But you and your – and Ned? You say she won't have him there?'

'I – I don't know, yet . . . There's been so much to think about.' After the enormous mental adjustments she had been through, first to the knowledge that she was carrying a child, then to its loss, Ned leaving Mary – then Olive coming to her . . . She didn't feel up to deciding anything. She was nervous about going back, though she wanted to. That Ned loved her, had come to her, had seemed enough. She hadn't, yet, faced all the consequences or made plans.

'You don't think ahead a great deal, do you, dear?'

Jess couldn't help thinking this was quite a criticism from someone who had run off to Stafford in the snow after a man who might or might not have been there, but she looked chastened. 'No – I s'pose I don't.'

'Well,' Iris made a twitching motion with her shoulders, pulling her shawl closer round her. 'I'd like to say this. You'll have difficult times ahead of you, dear, any way you look at it. Now, I shall look to rent out your room up there. I have to keep going, you see. But there's the front room. Never gets used very much. I'd like to offer it to you whenever you need it.'

'Oh Miss Whitman! You're so, so kind!'

'Don't go all weepy on me, dear, please. That's the last thing . . .'

'We'd pay you – to use the room, and . . .'

'Pay me or not. No, pay me – then you won't feel obliged. Keep it as business.'

'But what about your lodger – what would people . . .?'

Iris waved a hand dismissively at this. 'Oh – people. You soon find out who's worth anything.' There was a pause. With dignity, she added, 'You will come and see me?'

'Of course. As often as I can!' Jess almost went to kiss her, but stopped. Iris was somehow untouchable. But her lined face lit into a smile and for a moment she was transformed, like an angel.

Jess kept her promise and visited Iris almost every weekend. Once she was earning better she took her little presents: fruit, or flowers, or a nice cut of meat, now things were becoming scarce in the shops. By February Iris had found a new lodger, a typist working in one of the firms nearby, a stodgy, very private woman.

'Not much to say for herself,' Iris whispered to Jess, raising her eyes to the ceiling where the woman remained silently in her room. 'No trouble though.'

Jess was glad to be back with the family, but life over these past months had been full of tension. Living with Olive had become a difficult, delicate business. The woman was so wound up that the slightest thing made her lose her temper and Jess still felt she was an irritant to her by her very presence. Bert had sailed for the Dardanelles with the 9th Warwickshires. Ernie was gone, Polly pregnant, all things to make Olive tense and worried. Her sense of betrayal by Jess and Ned seemed to underlie everything that was said and no one dared mention his name.

Now and then, Mary appeared. She came twice, when Jess was out: both times when Ned was still in Sutton Coldfield and was back on weekend leave. Jess was with him at Iris's, her snatched, brief taste of life with Ned, and the family did not tell Mary where they were. Then one spring day Jess opened the door and there she was, with Ruth sitting up in the pram. Her face was very thin, those arched eyebrows giving her the look of a frightened animal. Jess thought her heart was going to stop. Seeing Mary, her bereft sadness, her hurt and anger, she knew that what she and Ned had caused was terrible.

'Oh God.'

She expected Mary to leap on her, swear at her, scratch her face. But whatever fury had possessed her for weeks on end, it seemed now to have burned itself out. Now the moment had come, she didn't seem to know what to do with it.

For a time she didn't speak. She and Jess stared into each other's eyes, until Jess had to look away.

'Yer bitch! I don't know how you can even . . .' Mary started to say, but burst into tears before she could finish. Slowly, weeping, she pushed the pram back along the road. Jess saw her shaking her head from side to side as if it was the only thing she could do. Horrified, she watched Mary walk away.

That weekend was the last time she saw Ned for a while, and it was an emotional one. He went, once more, to his family, to talk to them, to try and explain himself, and it left him distraught and tense. It was some time before he would talk when he got to Iris's.

Eventually they made a makeshift bed on the floor with a few covers, and lay holding each other in the strained light through the net curtains.

'I've done the worst I could do – to everyone.' He lay on his back, one arm round her, one bent to rest his head on. Jess fitted beside him, head on his chest. 'I've been a good son to them – the favourite really. Our Fred'd say that if yer asked 'im. 'E was always more trouble. But me – I've done what I'm told, gone on awright with my job. Married the way they wanted me to. I mean Mary was just ... she was chosen for me before we'd thought really – either of us. And now, when I do the one thing I do for myself, out of ... of *desire* for it, they don't want to know – can't see it. I don't know, Jess.' He looked back at her. 'What're yer s'posed to do – stick with things even if yer know they're not right?'

'We've done wrong,' she said gently. 'We have.' Mary's face haunted her, though she hadn't told Ned she'd seen her. She couldn't bear to talk about that and see his eyes fill with longing to see Ruth. She couldn't face hearing how much he was missing his daughter.

Ned's expression froze. 'Are yer sorry – d'yer want out of it?'

Jess put her arms round his neck, pulling him close. 'No ... no,' she murmured. 'I don't want anything 'cept you.'

'Come 'ere.' He rolled over and looked into her eyes, then laid his cheek against hers, taking in a deep breath, smelling her skin, nuzzling against her. 'I don't know how long it'll be before we can ever be normal – live without worrying.'

She knew he was thinking of his marriage, how long it would take to end it.

'Don't think about it,' she said. 'Just be here, now, that's all.'

He moved his head down, seeking out her breast. They made love carefully. He waited until the pleasure mounting in him became impossible to contain, then, with an enormous effort of will, pulled himself from her, burying his face in her, gasping. She held him, kissing him tenderly. There must be no more babies – not now.

That week his battalion were transferred to Wensleydale. He wrote to say they had at last been issued with khaki uniforms, although there were still very few rifles. And to say he loved her, that he did not regret it. The letter made her ache for him. Throughout the summer he was moved around: Wensleydale, Hornsea, then in August, to Codford Camp on Salisbury Plain. While he was away, things were less tense at home, but Jess fretted, not knowing when she would see him again.

He had some time away on embarkation leave. Once more a difficult visit to his mom and dad who were begging him to heal the breach with Mary, to go back to her.

'They talk as if you don't exist – like I've left Mary for nothing, for a ghost. I can't seem to get through to 'em.'

At the station, when he left, Jess couldn't help her tears. The war was real now. Casualties had been coming in from Loos – one of the Bullivants from next door, a lad of seventeen, had been killed. She and Ned stood looking into each other's eyes, then hugged, closely, in silence, for as long as they had.

'I'm with you,' she said, as he left. 'Everywhere you go.'

He smiled wistfully, waving.

That was the picture of him she carried in her head. The uniform – not a black-clad fireman any more, but a soldier, smart, dignified, yet somehow passive: waiting for what was to come. There was nothing she could do about any of it except wait too, and hope, just the same as Polly waited for Ernie, the two of them making bombs day after day.

She tightened the screw hard into the neck of the grenade in her hand and sealed it up. There you go, she thought. One more for the Hun.

Twenty-Two

A new brick building was put up at great speed, some distance from the wooden work sheds, and shortly before Christmas 1915, a Lieutenant Michaels from the Woolwich Arsenal visited the works and announced that there was to be a new process for dealing with detonators.

Soon after, one morning while Jess was working, she sensed she was being watched, and looked round to find the foreman, Mr Stevenson, observing her.

'I've a new job for you,' he was softly spoken, polite, not like the cocky sods you found in some factories. 'Would you come with me, please?'

Polly, who was in the same shed that day, winked and pulled her mouth down mockingly as Jess was led out, as if to say, 'Well aren't we the lucky one!'

Jess and two other girls followed Mr Stevenson as he led them with long strides into the new building.

'You can hang your outdoor clothes here when you come in,' he told them. He stood with his hands pushed down into the pockets of his overall while the three of them moved into line, facing him. Jess was rather in awe of him. He was so tall she had to look up to see into his face which was a handsome one, she realized, with dark eyes and strong black eyebrows. But she thought how tired he looked. Even the way he talked seemed to imply an infinite weariness. 'And you'll need to wear these over your ordinary shoes.' He freed his hands from the pockets and turned to reach for pairs of rubber overshoes which he handed to them, and the three of them bent to put them on. Jess's felt rather big and floppy.

'This is dangerous work you'll be doing. I've picked out you three because so far you've been sensible, and good workers. I'm going to take you through each stage and you must listen very, very carefully, for your own safety. Now – come through here.'

The shed was divided up by two brick walls. A doorway led through to the next section, with a high brick barrier that they had to step over. Jess followed, walking awkwardly in the oversized rubber shoes.

'If you look, you'll see only three walls are brick,' Mr Stevenson pointed to one side. 'That one's plywood. In the event of an explosion . . .' He finished the explanation with a gesture which implied that one wall, at least, would rip off like paper. The three girls looked at one another.

'You two will work in here,' he told the others. 'This is where they're varnished, then heated in the oven. So – you wait here, please, and you . . .?'

'Jess,' she said shyly.

'Jess – come through here.'

Behind another wall, in the third section was nothing but a large metal drum, attached to a spindle which passed through the wall, allowing it to revolve at the turn of a handle. Above it a clock hung on the wall and nearby on the floor stood piles of boxes. *White and Poppe, Coventry*, Jess read on the side of them.

She listened carefully as Mr Stevenson explained that she was to put forty detonators – 'no more than that, all right? There're forty in a box but I still want you to count' – into the drum, which was full of sawdust. 'That'll polish them up in there. You'll be surprised at the difference when they come out.'

He showed her how to rotate the drum. Jess watched his long fingers close round the handle, became mesmerized by the circling motion. She imagined writing to Ned about this. So many of her thoughts were a commentary to him in her head. I've a new job finishing the detonators for your grenades, so I'm doing it the best I can. I have to wear shoes that make me feel like a duck . . .

'Are you listening?'

She jumped. 'Er . . . yes.'

Mr Stevenson looked at her in silence for a few seconds as if reappraising her and Jess found herself blushing. 'I said turn it for three to four minutes – look, you've got the clock up there. D'you think you can manage that?' He wasn't being sarcastic, she realized. He spoke with a kind of detachment, as if his mind was partly elsewhere. She found herself wondering what he would look like if he smiled.

'Yes, Mr Stevenson.'

'Then you count them out again – carefully. You don't want any left in there. They go through next door then for varnishing. You might as well come and hear what I tell them – you can't start 'til we're all ready.'

Jess didn't take in much of what he told the other girls. She felt how cold it was in the shed and stood hugging herself, hoping the work would warm her up. The varnish smelt strongly of methylated spirits.

'. . . heated for ten hours,' Mr Stevenson was saying. 'When they've cooled they'll be picked up from here to have the fuse caps fitted. Now – have you got all that?'

The detonators went into the drum looking dark and

tarnished, and emerged as if reborn, a shiny copper colour. Next door the girls varnished them and stood them to dry on racks. Jess rather liked the new work, the fact that she was alone, the rhythmic rumbling of the drum.

When they got home that evening, a letter had arrived from Bert. The Dardanelles had been evacuated earlier in the month and he'd been reposted to Mesopotamia, had had a bad dose of fever but was feeling better. Olive seemed as if a weight had been lifted from her, and was in a good mood. When Jess told her about the new work, she made a face.

''E put a dreamy so-and-so like you on doing that? Heaven help 'em – I just 'ope yer don't send the whole place sky high!'

Jess laughed, happy at her aunt's warmth towards her.

She settled into the work, in the 'Danger Shed' or what quickly became known as the 'Rumbling Shed', and managed it without mishap. She was happy in the job. But even working alone, she soon picked up the fact that there was discontent growing among some of the other women, through murmurings during the breaks or through Polly and Sis repeating the gossip.

One morning when they got to the factory they found a group huddled round the entrance, arms folded, their faces defiant.

'We've come out on strike,' one of them said importantly. Vi was one of the older women at the works, the sort you didn't tangle with and a natural leader. 'We reckon we'd all be better off on piece work, so that's what we're asking 'im for, when 'e comes in.'

Jess and Polly hesitated, but by the look of it, with

everyone else out, they didn't have much choice but to join in. The morning was damp and very cold. They stood in groups, their breath billowing like smoke.

'Are they right?' Jess asked Polly. She didn't know what to think about it, but most of the women had years more experience of factory work than she did. 'D'yer think we'd be better off? We don't seem bad off now, compared with before.'

Polly hunched her shoulders to raise her collar higher round her ears. 'I dunno – it's worth a try anyhow. They could've chosen a better day for it though.' Her nose was pink with the cold, eyes watering in the chill wind and her skin yellow. Although among some of the 'canaries' the yellowness was a sign of pride, a sign of what they were doing for the war effort, Polly loathed it. 'Makes me look really poorly and ugly,' she complained sometimes, looking in the mirror. 'Blasted TNT. I'm all sore and itchy round me collar from it an' all. Maybe I should look for another job.' But it suited them all for now, going off to work at the same place.

Sis looked round at the crowd filling the yard. 'Oh well – this makes a change from being in there, don't it?' she said cheerfully. 'Ooh, I wonder what old Misery Guts is going to say when 'e gets in!'

A few moments later Mr Stevenson came round the corner, the collar of his black coat up to keep the wind out, hat pulled well down to stop it blowing off. Though a quiet man, he had a strong presence and the women fell silent as he approached, all watching him. Jess felt her stomach tighten. It was only then it occurred to her that Mr Stevenson was a nice man and she liked him, didn't want to make him angry.

'O-oh,' someone said. ''Ere we go!'

Seeing them all standing there by the sheds he faltered

for a moment. Jess saw the surprise, then concern register on his face, eyes scanning the sheds as he hurried towards them.

'What's wrong?' He looked over at the Rumbling Shed. 'Has something happened? Is everyone all right?'

He didn't sound furious at all. Jess had expected him to lose his temper at the loss of time and order them all back to work. But then she saw by the way his gaze swept over the sheds that he was worried there might have been an accident.

'It's nothing like that.' Vi moved forward, arms folded. She was a broad, muscular-looking woman with black hair on her top lip almost like a 'tache. 'We've come out to ask yer to put us on piece work, like they've got over at Dalston's. We ain't happy with it being a fixed wage, like, and we're all fast workers. We think we'd do better on piece work.'

'Oh, I see.' Mr Stevenson took his hat off and looked down, obviously considering this, his dark eyes scanning the muddy surface of the yard. His black hair blew boyishly down over his forehead. After they had stood waiting for a couple more moments he looked up at them.

'The thing is, ladies—' He spoke in a reasonable tone, and rather quietly so that some of the women moved closer to hear, leaning towards him. 'I know every one of you is working very hard here – not much in the way of holiday time and so on . . .'

'None at all, yer mean,' someone mumbled behind Jess.

'Sssh,' Jess turned to them, without thinking.

'Oi – who d'yer think you're telling to shoosh? Think yer above the rest of us now yer over there, do yer?'

213

Jess blushed, and stared straight ahead of her.

'I do want to do what's best,' Mr Stevenson was saying. 'But the problem is, we're going to find that the amount of work coming to us varies from time to time. Sometimes you might be right about earning more on piece work – fractionally more anyway. Other times when things're slower, it'll be less. So if you stay on the regular wage . . .' He looked round at them with genuine, disarming concern. He knew, and they knew, that they were now earning better than most of them had ever earned in their lives before. 'You'll be guaranteed that coming in every week instead of it going up and down – especially down.'

There was silence for a moment as the women digested all this.

'So 'ow come Dalston's do it the other way?' Vi didn't want to give in too easily.

Mr Stevenson shrugged. 'Up to them, isn't it? I'm just telling you what I think's the best for you. So – that's my point of view.' They could tell that, for all the gentleness of his tone, he was not going to be argued with. 'Are you in agreement?'

Again Jess's mouth leaped ahead of her. 'Yes!' she cried.

Mr Stevenson almost smiled. The corners of his wide mouth twitched as Jess's face went even pinker.

Vi, after conferring with her neighbour, gave a nod. 'If that's the way it is, we'll stick with the wage.'

'Thank you,' Mr Stevenson said. He put his hat back on firmly and turned towards the shed that served as an office. 'Good morning, ladies.'

This was his way of telling them to get to work.

*

214

A card had come from Ned to Iris's saying he'd arrived in France and would write properly soon, and Jess tried to fill her time so that it would pass more quickly, keeping herself as busy as possible.

On Christmas Day she went to see Iris Whitman, who was under the weather with a cold. Jess stoked up the fire for her, making her tea and pampering her as much as possible. She'd considered buying her a little bottle of brandy to help warm her up, but thought the better of it because of Iris's religion. Iris had no desire to possess knick-knacks of any kind, so instead, Jess found her a nice second-hand blanket for her bed, and bought a few groceries to go with it.

'Ooh,' Iris was childlike with delight, her face rearranging itself into one of her rare and beautiful smiles. She spread the blanket over her lap, stroking the soft wool. 'My goodness, they must be paying you well nowadays.'

'They are,' Jess beamed, warmed by Iris's pleasure. 'When I got my first wage packet I went and got my mom's quilt back.' She'd told Iris long ago that she'd pawned the quilt, though not the full reason why.

'Well—' Iris said, holding up her teacup as if it was a champagne glass. 'Here's to happier times. Pity we haven't got something a wee bit stronger to toast ourselves.'

Jess grinned. 'I thought you'd most likely signed the Pledge.'

'Oh no—' Iris was spooning extra sugar into her tea from the bag Jess had brought. 'Why should I want to do that? Do you think of me as an immoderate person – someone who wouldn't know when they'd had enough?'

She seemed rather indignant.

'Er – no, I don't.' Jess raised her cup too, to change the subject. 'Different from last year, eh?'

'Yes,' Iris gulped the tea. 'Yes indeed, dear. Best to be friends with your family, if you can manage it. Though that Ned of yours . . .' Iris had taken to this particular phrase for talking about him. 'He's used to approval, isn't he? Not easy, if you have to become a fighter all of a sudden. Rather different for you, of course. Seems to be more of a habit for you.'

Jess laughed at Iris's sharpness. 'It's one I wouldn't mind breaking though, Miss Whitman.'

One evening they were all sitting round at home. Ronny was asleep upstairs, Olive at the table thumbing through the paper, and Jess was sewing a soft little nightshirt for Polly's baby, squinting in the poor light. Polly had her feet up on a little stool, yawning frequently. She didn't have the energy to do anything much once she got home from work. Her belly was like a neat little football now and she sat stroking one hand over it. Jess looked at her, wistfully.

'Is 'e kicking?'

Polly nodded. 'Got 'is feet under my ribcage and 'e don't half thump about.'

'Let's 'ave a feel . . .' This was one of Sis's favourite pastimes at the moment. Polly took her sister's hand and laid it in the right spot. Sis waited, leaning forwards solemnly, long hair falling over one shoulder. She looked sweet, and was always the most carefree of them, although her young man, Perce, had now joined up as well.

'I can't feel . . . ooh yes, there! Oh, and again! Blimey, Poll,' she laughed. 'Getting a belly like a cow on yer – I

216

'ope it goes down after!' Sis had the kind of laugh that made everyone want to join in and even Olive looked round and smiled rather dryly.

'You just shurrup—' Polly whacked at her and Sis dodged. 'Wait 'til it's your turn.'

Jess watched, forcing herself to smile, but her feelings were very mixed. How did it feel when the baby grew that big? When you could really tell there was a robust life in there? She knew things were infinitely easier for her than they would have been with a child of her own, that her loss was really for the best, but that little person who had inhabited her was like a shadow that still followed her. An unseen ghost. Who would it have been?

Polly gave another huge yawn.

'Go to bed, why don't yer?' Sis said.

'When I'm ready.'

Polly sat back with a disgruntled expression. She was used to being the bossy elder sister: she wasn't having Sis telling her what to do. And she felt tired and vulnerable. Her ankles were swelling up in the evenings and her back ached. She wanted Ernie. Sometimes, just for a second, she envied Jess. Losing a babby was a terrible thing, but at least she didn't have to have it and bring it up on her own with a war on, not knowing if its father was ever coming home. She tried to push away such wicked thoughts, but she hadn't reckoned with the way carrying a child made you feel so tired and uncomfortable and at the mercy of everything. So old, suddenly.

'I s'pose I'd better get up there before I end up spending the night down 'ere.'

She was just hoisting herself out of the chair when Olive made a strange, involuntary sound. A gasp or moan, it was hard to tell. Her back was to them, head bent over the paper. Everyone looked at her.

'What that, Mom?' Sis looked over her shoulder at the paper.

Olive had one hand over her mouth, as if to stop any further sound escaping.

'Deaths . . .' Sis read. 'What's up – is it someone we know?'

Polly and Jess both moved in closer.

As if reluctant, Olive slowly moved her finger to a name on the page.

'Arthur Tamplin, seventy-two, of South Road, Erdington,' Polly read, slowly. 'January the ninth. Leaves wife, Elsie and four children. Well who's that then?'

All eyes were on Olive. Without meeting their gaze she said, 'Your grandfather.'

Polly straightened up, wincing at the pain in her back.

'But we ain't got a grandfather – I mean, we never have had one. They're dead, you've always said – ain't they?'

'Well they are now,' Sis said.

Polly frowned furiously at her.

'Four children,' Olive murmured. 'I don't s'pose 'e ever knew about Louisa passing on . . .'

'But why . . . whose . . .?' Polly couldn't get a whole sentence out.

'My father, that was. Gone now then. Well, well.'

The loathing in her voice was barely concealed. Jess's eyes never left her aunt's face. Their grandfather.

'But I thought 'e'd been dead years. Didn't you think 'e was dead, Jess?'

'I s'pose – yes,' Jess said. There'd never been any

218

mention. But then she'd barely managed to get Olive to talk about the family at all. It was just as if they'd never existed. 'Yes, I did.'

'So 'e was living just nearby and we never even met him! Why the hell not – didn't yer get on or summat?'

Olive stood up, closing the paper, pressing her hands down on it.

'After our mother died – Louisa's and mine – our father remarried. 'E didn't want us and 'e threw us out. It were his sister, Bella, brought us up, in Sparkbrook. So no – I never went and saw 'im after that. Why should I? I weren't wanted.'

Jess watched her aunt, full of pity.

'Well, how old were yer when she died?' Polly's tone was still harsh, as if she felt cheated.

Olive's expression became guarded. She seemed to calculate in her head. 'About twelve or thirteen, I think. Yes, thirteen. Louisa would've been ten or eleven.'

'So were there any more of you? Any other cousins or missing relatives we ain't been told about?'

'Poll—' Sis said softly. She had tears in her eyes. 'Don't be like that.'

'No. No others.' Olive moved from behind the table and thrust the newspaper into the fire. Jess saw that her hands were shaking. Sis went and stood beside her as the paper caused a brief blaze, but didn't touch her.

'It wouldn't've gained yer nothing if yer'd met 'im.' She turned, including Jess as she spoke. 'None of yer. Some things are best left dead and buried. Now I don't want to talk about this no more.'

'But—' Polly began, but was silenced by the look on her mother's face.

Twenty-Three

Polly worked all the day her baby arrived. That morning she was flushed in the face, the picture of health in fact, even with her jaundiced skin. She was also very restless and talkative.

'You got the chats today, ain't yer?' one of the older women said, grinning at her. 'That's a sign the babby's on the way, that is.'

'I 'ope so,' Polly grimaced at her swollen belly. 'Be glad to get shot of it now, that I will.'

The timing was perfect. Soon after she got home the pains started.

'Oh Lord,' Olive said, ''Ere we go.'

Jess saw that despite her gruff attempts to seem matter of fact about it, Olive was nervous, and flustered. Jess felt her own stomach turn with dread at the sight of Polly as she sat by the window, face screwing up with pain. She remembered that pain, the agony which had spelt loss for her. It was going to get a lot worse. They had to keep Ronny away from Polly as he kept worriting at her.

'Come 'ere,' Jess said, feeling sorry for him. He couldn't understand what was happening. To Olive she said, 'Shall I take 'im to fetch Mrs Cooper?'

'D'yer think yer need 'er yet?' Olive was laying the table, the forks all upside down.

'No, I'll be awright for a bit. You 'ave yer tea. I don't

'fancy none just yet.' Polly sat back with a sigh and Jess went and rearranged the cutlery, getting Ronny to help her. His freckly face, topped by the carroty hair, was only half visible above the table.

'I'll go and 'ave a lie down for a while.' Bent forwards, Polly carefully went to the stairs.

'You shout if yer need anything, won't yer?' Sis said. She touched her sister's shoulder nervously. 'Never mind, Poll – soon be over now, won't it?'

None of them had much appetite, except Ronny who tucked into pie and potatoes, oblivious of what was going on. Olive tried to behave as normal, but after a few mouthfuls, laid her fork down. They were all quiet, listening for sounds from upstairs.

'Ooh Mom – it's exciting!' Sis said, all aquiver. 'I can't eat – shall I go and see if she's awright?'

'Leave 'er. We'd soon hear if she wasn't.'

As they finished there was a wail from Polly and Sis and Jess rushed upstairs, Olive panting behind them.

'I must've gone and wet myself!' she cried, mortified. 'I dunno how – I never meant to – oh!' She was seized by a severe pain.

'That'll be yer waters,' Olive said, nodding her head at Sis to run down the road for Mrs Cooper. 'Yer awright – that's natural. Should get yer on the way that should. Jess and me'll give yer a clean bed. We'll get Ronny down for the night after.'

From then on things happened quickly. Mrs Cooper was a cheerful little lady with fading blonde hair who talked non-stop, so much so that at the height of her pain, when Mrs Cooper was gassing unstoppably on, Polly croaked,

'Can't yer just bleeding well shurrup for a bit?'

The lady seemed not the least offended.

'Everyone likes to curse a bit when it comes on bad,' she said. 'They don't remember a thing about it after.'

'Well I bloody sodding well will!' Polly yelled.

Jess watched her cousin writhing around. It was all so ungainly and undignified and she trembled at the odd sounds of pain she made. She wondered if Polly minded them all in and out but she didn't seem to care. They took it in turns to keep an eye on Ronny downstairs. He was wide-eyed and full of questions. Sis had a hard job getting him to go to sleep as the night wore on.

But soon after three in the morning, the baby arrived, long, mauve and shrieking.

'Another lady of the house!' Mrs Cooper told them. 'Yer got a healthy little wench there, Poll – 'ark at 'er!'

Jess cried. They all cried, standing in a snivelling ring round the bed until Polly, who was now quite composed, looked up and said, 'What the 'ell's got into you lot?' and they all started laughing and crying at the same time.

Mrs Cooper washed the baby in a basin and wrapped her carefully.

'There yer go—' She handed her over to Polly who took her confidently as if she was born to it. Her face was transformed – exhausted, dark under the eyes, but smoothed out and happy.

Once Mrs Cooper had gone they sat round in the candlelight, listening to the baby's tiny, fluttering breaths. Their sense of wonder filled the room like incense. Jess saw that Olive's tough face softened at the sight of her first grandchild.

'I wish Ernie was 'ere to see,' Polly sighed tearfully.

'Yer've good news to write and tell 'im anyway,'

222

Sis said. 'And p'raps 'e'll be home soon. Yer never know.'

Polly smiled down at the little one nestling close to her. 'I think I'll call 'er Alice . . .'

'No!' The harshness of Olive's tone cut into the serene mood, making Jess jump.

'Mom?' Sis looked round, startled.

Olive lowered her voice. 'No, Poll – not Alice.'

'Why not for goodness sakes?'

'Just not Alice. It's . . .' For a moment she couldn't speak, as if the words had to be found from somewhere deeply buried. 'Your grandmother was called Alice, if yer really must know. It's unlucky . . . I won't 'ave yer calling 'er that.'

She sounded really upset at the idea. Jess's eyes met Polly's. Another of those areas of knowledge about their family that had been kept from them, about which Olive refused to speak, and almost violently resisted their asking.

'Well awright – not Alice then,' Polly said carefully. 'It's just I know Ernie likes it. What about Grace?'

'That's pretty,' Jess said.

'Lovely,' Sis added.

They looked at Olive. She nodded, reclaiming her dignity.

'That's a good enough name. I've nothing against Grace.'

'Grace Violet – after Ernie's mom. That'll please 'er.' She leaned down and kissed the child's head. 'So soft,' she murmured.

'D'you know what?' Sis said. 'I'm starving.'

Polly looked up. 'So'm I! My belly's gurgling like mad!'

They ate bread and jam in the bedroom at four in the morning, laughing like children on a forbidden picnic.

Jess had the job of relaying the good news at work. The other women were overjoyed for Polly.

'Tell 'er to stay home as long as she can,' one of them said. 'Old Stevenson's quite good about that sort of thing.'

That week, they had another inspection visit from the Woolwich Arsenal. A party of officers would arrive every few weeks to check the work, explode a few detonators and, as some of the women put it, 'hang about poking their noses in everywhere.'

Jess was hard at work rotating the handle on the drum when they came. She got quite a sweat up doing it now spring had arrived, and she wasn't looking forward to the summer heat. The elastic holding her cap rubbed, making her forehead itch. She finished turning and stopped the machine, breathing hard, and wiped her face on her handkerchief.

She heard voices in the varnishing section of the shed. She didn't think much of this and carried on emptying the drum of the last of the detonators, when there came a bang from next door. She ran through to see what had happened.

'Oh my God!' she heard one of the other girls cry.

One of the inspectors, a woman, was standing, stunned, blood pouring from the end of her finger down into her sleeve.

Jess pulled out her handkerchief and gave it to the woman who wrapped it round her finger.

'I'll go for Mr Stevenson!'

She ran out of the Rumbling Shed, her feet slapping

across the yard, trying not to trip over the rubber overshoes, and wondering whether Mr Stevenson would be in the office or in one of the sheds with other inspectors.

She knocked softly on the office door and immediately pushed it open. Mr Stevenson was sitting side-on to her, bent over on the chair, and for a moment she thought he was searching for something in the bottom drawer of the desk. But as he straightened up on hearing her, she saw that she had disturbed him sitting with his head in his hands.

'What is it?' He looked dazed, she thought, as if trying to remember who she was.

'There's been an accident. One of the inspectors.'

He ran ahead of her, his long stride far outstripping her, the First Aid box clenched under one arm.

The woman was still standing, ashen-faced, trying to staunch the flow of her blood.

'A chair – please,' she said. It was only as Mr Stevenson examined her that Jess saw the tip of her finger had been blown right off.

The girls told Jess afterwards that the woman had been examining one of a new range of tiny detonators which they had been processing of late, which was placed in a fuse cap to explode a larger detonator.

'She picked up this one, and she must've seen summat on it – looked like a hair. Anyroad, she went and took off this brooch she 'ad on and started prodding at it to get it off – I mean I should've stopped 'er, but I couldn't believe my eyes! The thing just went up in her hand!'

Afterwards, when they'd gone, Mr Stevenson came and spoke to Jess. 'I should've been there myself really. I'd've been able to stop her.' He shrugged. 'But there it is. I can't think why she started messing about like that. You did well fetching me so promptly.'

'That's awright.' Jess smiled shyly.

Something resembling a smile fleetingly passed across his face as he walked away.

'Oh—' he turned. 'Those overshoes'll need a clean up.'

That evening, when Jess thought back on the day she remembered the expression on Mr Stevenson's face as he looked up at her in his office. She sensed, without knowing the cause, that what she had witnessed was a moment of private desperation.

10th Royal Warwicks
2.6.1916

Dearest Poll,

I'm happy to hear you're recovering well and our little Grace is coming along. We've drunk to her health a few times, I can tell you! I'm sad at the thought of how long 'til I see her but what you've said gives me a picture. My eyes, has she? Quite a thought that. Give her kisses from her loving dad for me.

Weather's warm here – a nice change from sleeping in the wet and snow. The mud's drying out at long last. We're still as lousy as a load of old rooks – one favourite pastime is burning the so-and-so's off our clothes with a candle! Good bunch of lads here though.

We moved on again in the last few days and much talk of build-up to what's ahead. Not sure what we're in for but it feels like high time to give them a good pounding – we're ready after waiting all this time.

I'm being used as a delivery boy at present, better than all the waiting. You know me, I like to be on the go. Up and down the trenches with supplies day and night. We bought a pig off one of the farms nearby a couple of days ago. What a feed that was, I can tell you. One nearby's got a cherry orchard. Next it'll be . . .

The door flew open and Polly jumped. Grace stirred at her breast.

'I won, I won – I got the Lucky Potato!' Ronny shrilled into the room with the natural ecstasy of a three-year-old who's just acquired a stick of sugar-pink rock, no charge.

Polly swallowed her irritation at being interrupted and smiled. 'You get the Lucky Potato number? Lucky old thing, ain't yer?'

Ronny already had the wrapping off and was going at the end, cheeks hollowed with sucking.

'Keep yer quiet for a bit any'ow.' She looked across and saw Olive's face, felt a moment's terror clutching at her innards. Ernie! No, it couldn't be – she had his letter in her hand . . .

'Kitchener's dead. Drowned. Ship went down off the Orkneys.'

'Oh—' Polly sighed with relief, then saw it was indeed awful news. General Kitchener, hope of the nation. 'Oh Lor',' she said.

Olive went to the mantel, picked up the brass moulding of Kitchener's head and leaned it face to the wall.

Ned had passed some of the winter of 1915 on a quiet part of the Western Front, firstly around Suzanne, camped in the grounds of the Chateau, but also later spent a month in the appalling trench conditions of the front line at Maricourt. Now summer was here and the war had moved on once more. Jess still collected his letters from Iris, who said, 'Here you are dear,' with some pleasure whenever there was one. Jess was touched by her loyalty to her and Ned, when she could have been bitter on her own behalf.

> *15th Royal Warwickshire Battalion*
> *10th June 1916*

My dearest Jess,

A few days' rest and clean-up once more, so time to write. I hope you're all right, all of you, and Polly's little one?

Things got very lively here Sunday. Such a pounding the trenches in parts are all knocked for six and quite a few losses of our lads. At the same time it made you feel full of it, somehow. Never felt anything like it before. Shook me after, when I thought about it and roll call was—

There was a sharp jerk of the pencil, scraping a line across the page.

That's some silly sod in the barn behind me. Shooting rats, I'd take a guess, made me jump. Anyway – we've had a memorial service. Poor lads. But don't worry about me. Everything's all right and it's very pretty round here now spring's come. Birds in the hedges. Larks over the fields, rooks. A couple of the lads are good on naming birds so I'm picking up some knowledge. I wish I could show it all to you – without the company we've got watching out for us in the trenches over the other side, of course.

Did I tell you they've made me a Corporal? Going up in the world, me. I wouldn't mind being a Sergeant and giving some of the orders for a change.

There's talk of us moving on soon. We're being trained up for something big though none of us know exactly what yet. There's a feeling about. I suppose we'll find out soon enough.

I've been wondering, when I get home leave, whenever that will be, if you and I should go and see my family together and try to put things right a bit. Let them see you as you are. It'd be an ordeal for you but let's plan to do it. Or am I mad even to think of it? If the war wasn't on we'd have had to sort it out somehow and we can't just go on as we are forever.

Will close now. I think of so many things to tell you but when I come to write them I can't remember. Send my regards to Miss Whitman – and Polly and all. To you my love, as ever, missing you,
Ned

Jess folded up the letter, gazing at the pale grey lines on the cheap paper. His hands had touched it, sealed the envelope. She pressed the paper to her face and breathed in, searching for some trace of him. She felt as if she was always living in the future when he'd be home, all her energy directed towards that. Now she was earning better she was saving a little money every week so that month by month it grew: her nest-egg for their future life together.

She sighed walking home from Iris's house in the

warm evening, the letter in her pocket. It was hard to admit to herself but she also felt a bit disappointed. The parts of his letters which she longed for, apart from his news, were his expressions of affection for her, his feelings pouring out. They warmed, fed her. But they were never enough. He felt so distant and she needed to see him, to be reassured constantly of his love. It seemed to her he was being drawn farther and farther away into the companionship of men, the clutches of the war, and she even had to strain to see his face in her mind.

Just let this war be over soon, she thought. Let them all just come home. Let us be able to live properly, not wasting our days waiting for life to begin.

Twenty-Four

That morning, the first weekend in July, Jess and Polly said they'd take Grace and Ronny out while Olive went to church. Perce, Sis's sweetheart, was home on leave and she was spending every moment she could with him.

The two of them set off for Calthorpe Park, both in summer frocks, Ronny skipping back and forth along the pavement. Mrs Bullivant had let Polly use her old pram, which had served for most of her children and she hadn't parted with it. It was a deep, clattering contraption which had come to them with patches of mould on the hood and dirt and cobwebs inside, but Polly had cleaned it up as best she could.

Jess smiled as the wheels went clunking round. 'She don't seem to take any notice of the noise.' Grace's tiny, mauve-tinged eyelids had fluttered closed almost the moment they started moving.

'Nah,' Polly peered over adoringly at her. 'It rocks 'er to sleep. Any'ow, she was playing about that much in the night, she ought to be tired out!'

They decided to cut through the back, past the sweet factory on Vincent Parade. Further along, outside the houses, a man had wheeled out his hurdy-gurdy and they stood with the crowd, letting Ronny go to the front to watch the monkey on top of it, with his little fez falling down over one eye, prancing along the top on his bony legs to the tinkling tune. Ronny giggled and jumped, copying the monkey's old man gestures.

'Bless 'im,' Polly said. There was a wistful note in her voice as she watched him.

'Poll – don't snap my head off – but who *is* Ronny's dad?' Jess spoke nervously in a low voice, wondering if she'd get an answer this time.

Polly carried on staring ahead, eyes on her little brother. 'Hand on my heart, Jess, I don't know for sure.'

'But – I mean, the colour of his hair . . .'

'I've told yer, I dunno. I can't think of anyone we've ever known who it could be. It was a mistake, that's all. I don't dare ask.'

'There's a lot of things none of us dare ask.'

'She's ashamed of it. She ain't that sort of woman . . .' Polly trailed off, turning red, as she realized what she was saying, and to whom. She called Ronny to her and they walked on down the road in the sun.

'Sorry, Jess – I daint mean . . .'

'I know what yer meant.' Jess was stung, her cheeks flushed pink. 'I know what yer all must think of me. But it's as if there ain't nothing yer can ask Auntie about. She's a closed book: the family, our grandmother. Why shouldn't we know about 'er? I mean, I barely had my mom for any time – I want to know about everyone else.'

'Well *you* try asking 'er then!'

'I can't, can I? She's funny with me all the time – nice as pie one minute, huffy the next. I only have to do one thing wrong . . . Yer never know where you are with her at the best of times, but after what I've done – sometimes I think she can't stand the sight of me, and other times she's awright . . . But Polly, ain't she *ever* talked to you about our grandma?'

Polly's brow crinkled. 'The only thing I can remember is, she was marvellous at baking – bread and that. Mom used to say that sometimes.'

Jess took Ronny's hand as they crossed the road into the park. 'Well there must be more to know than that.'

Polly breathed in the flower-scented air of the park. 'We ought to come in the afternoon. There'll be a band.'

'I'm going over to Iris.'

'Yes – course. Oh Jess . . .' Polly linked an arm through her cousin's, both of them pushing the pram together. 'Never mind our mom. She don't seem too bad at the minute. Let's just make the best of today, eh? It's lovely in 'ere.'

They chose a place to sit, legs stretched out comfortably, and Ronny found another little boy to play with, tumbling on the grass together and chasing one another. Jess and Polly turned their faces up to the sunlight, talking intermittently. Nowadays their favourite talk always began, 'when the war's over . . .'

'I want to go and live in the country.'

Jess snorted. '*You?* That's a laugh!'

'Get a little house, bring our family up where the air's better. Cleaner, like where you grew up. Don't you want to go back?'

'Yes, I s'pose so. All I can think of at the moment is getting Ned back safe.'

Polly watched her cousin's thoughtful face, her brown eyes fixed on the trees at the far side of the park. Jess's sweet looks, her tendency to stare dreamily ahead, gave her an air of vulnerable impracticality which sometimes made Polly want to shake her. But she knew that Jess was much tougher and more determined than she looked.

'I reckon you'd do anything for 'im though, wouldn't yer?'

Jess nodded. 'I feel ever so bad about Mary, though. I think about 'er a lot, how she's getting on. She must hate me so much.' She was silent for a moment, looking at the pram. 'Mrs Bullivant carried nearly all her babbies in there, didn't she?' Their neighbour had had nine children. 'Now there's five at the Front, Stanley already dead. What was 'e – seventeen? It's frightening, Poll.' She turned, looking her cousin in the eyes. 'Life's like paper on the fire – gone, fast as that. I could've married Philip if I'd wanted just an arrangement, no feelings to speak of. If we've done wrong, me and Ned – well there's no if about it, we have – it's because we love one another and we want to spend our lives together. Is that wrong? *Is* it?'

A few nights later Polly lay in bed with Grace tucked beside her. Grace had finished feeding and was sleeping in the crook of her mother's arm, Polly curled beside her so that her face was close to the child's, hearing the sweet sound of her breathing.

Polly was in the half-wakeful, alert sleep of early motherhood. She stirred, moving carefully to ensure Grace's safety beside her, and woke, opening her eyes suddenly in the dark. A moment later a sensation passed through her as if an icy wave had sluiced over her body. She pulled herself up and sat hugging her knees, teeth chattering, her hands and feet as cold as if she had walked the streets in midwinter. But worse than the cold was the terror that took possession of her, a fear that made no sense but which turned her body rigid, filling her with a terrible certainty.

She got out of bed, covered Grace and stumbled next door to where Jess and Sis slept. Jess woke to find icy fingers clutching at her hand.

'Poll?' She sat up immediately. 'What's up? You're freezing! Is everything – Grace . . .?'

'She's asleep – I just . . .' Polly sank down on the bed, still shaking. 'Summat terrible's happened.'

'What – what's the matter?' Hearing the fear in Polly's voice Jess could feel herself beginning to panic.

'I was just lying there, and I just went cold, and it was then I knew. I'm so scared, Jess!' She began sobbing. Jess moved beside her, wrapping her in her arms. 'It's Ernie – I'm sure that's what it is, summat's happened to 'im.'

'Oh Poll – how can that be? You've likely caught a chill and yer imagining things – you know 'ow yer get delirious when yer poorly. All them bad dreams you had last winter when you was bad—'

'I'm not sick,' Polly interrupted. 'Jess, there's nothing wrong with me. I was perfectly awright when I went to bed. It's a message from Ernie – he's calling out to me, I can feel it!'

A letter arrived that Saturday. Olive brought it to her. One of Polly's hands went to her throat. She didn't say a word, and her hand shook as she reached out to take the envelope.

> *10th Royal Warwickshire Regt.*
> *B.E.F.*
> *July 6th, 1916*

Dear Mrs Carter,

It is with deep regret that I have to inform you that your husband Pte Ernest J. Carter 10/612 died of wounds last night.

His Company showed great bravery and he was a gallant man who will be missed by his comrades.

Please accept my very sincere sympathy for your loss.

The letter was signed by the Captain of his Company.

Polly's legs went from under her and she sank groggily to the floor. Gently, Olive helped her up on to a chair.

Ronny stood staring, not needing to be told he must keep quiet when Polly, who was usually full of jokes, was sitting absolutely still, her face stony with shock.

Grace was crying upstairs and Jess fetched her down. 'She wants yer,' she said, holding her out to Polly who took her, automatically latching her on to feed, hardly seeming to notice she was there.

'Oh Polly, bab . . .' Olive whispered, watching her. Her own legs were trembling, but she forced herself to be practical: get the kettle on, hand Ronny a finger of crust to keep him quiet.

'I knew . . .'

'What's that?' Olive was putting cups out.

'I knew summat had happened. I had a message, the other night, from Ernie. 'E were trying to tell me . . .'

'Don't start talking like that,' Olive said sharply. She didn't mean to. Her daughter's suffering was unbearable to her. It made her hands shake so she could barely put out the cups. She wanted to take that agony on herself and knew there was nothing she could do. Polly had had just a few days of proper marriage with Ernie, and now it was over.

For a second, as she went to the hissing kettle to warm the teapot, another loathsome thread of recall from the past forced its way up through a crack in her mind as if one cause for distress brought back the memory of another. Images chasing one another, the staircase, sound of footsteps on the bare stairs, that dark room, the woman with her back to her at the window ... but there were curtains drawn, closed, she was staring at nothing. And there was a smell ... that smell ...

She found she was shaking her head hard from side to side – forget, forget ... don't let it come back, keep it down, down ... It was Polly she must think of now.

'What're yer doing, Mom?' Ronny said.

'Yer mom's upset, darlin',' Jess told him. 'Don't you worry.'

'I'm so sorry for yer, love.' Olive left what she was doing and went and stood by her, pressing Polly's head to her and stroking her hair with her rough hands. 'So sorry. I don't know what to do for yer.' Polly began to cry, high sobs like a little girl. Ronny came to her, his eyes full of sorrow, and stroked her too.

'I'd just sent him them nice things,' Polly sobbed. 'And now 'e won't get 'em. Oh Mom, I want 'im back – I hadn't even seen 'im, not for ages. And now I shan't ever see 'im again. Never!'

Polly had been thinking about weaning Grace early and going back to work, but now she didn't want to be parted from her. Jess had to tell Peter Stevenson what had happened.

She stood in his office, feeling as if she was going to teacher for a telling off, her cap held in front of her, aware that her hair was sticking out in wayward wisps. Mr Stevenson's face looked bruised with exhaustion. He listened quietly as Jess explained what had happened.

'There's no need for her to worry, tell her.' He spoke kindly, but it seemed somehow an effort for him to bring forth the words. 'We've almost more work than we can manage all the time. I'll happily take her back when she's ready.'

'I'll tell her,' Jess said. 'That's nice of yer.'

He shook his head with such a sad expression in his brown eyes that Jess was touched by his sympathy. 'Not at all. Poor thing – with the child to look after as well.'

'Yes, she's upset 'er husband never saw Grace – that's the babby. It's been a terrible shock for all of us. You don't think it's going to happen to yer 'til it does.'

'That's true, you don't. Terrible for her.'

There was an awkward silence during which Mr Stevenson seemed to sink into his own thoughts, and Jess wondered whether she should be gone.

'Well, thank you,' she said, turning away.

'Oh, Jess?'

She turned back.

'Is everything all right out there?' He nodded towards the Rumbling Shed.

'Yes, thank you. I think so.'

'Good. That's good,' he said distractedly. Jess went back to work, grateful for his genuine sympathy.

She was full of sorrow for Polly, and of unease. The Big Push everyone had been talking about on the Somme had begun on the first of the month, and that was where Ernie had been with the 10th Warwicks. Jess felt sure that was where Ned must be, and as the Casualty lists poured in, taking up more and more column inches in the newspapers, she became increasingly frightened and uneasy. Death had already come to the heart of the family: sudden, arbitrary, final. The image of Polly sitting at home, so numb and bereft, haunted her all the time. They were helpless, unable to argue with anything that was happening. Nothing could be done to change the fact that they would never see Ernie's chubby, cheerful face again and Grace would grow up without her father. Jess's eyes kept filling with tears thinking about it. It touched on her own deepest feelings, her memories of Louisa's death, and her desperate longing to have Ned home, safe, loving her and alive.

Twenty-Five

Weeks passed. Casualty lists kept on and on coming from the Somme. Each day they looked at the newspapers in silence, the long columns of names, seeking out, in dread, any that might be familiar. Polly had kept the little cutting of Ernie's name, had stuck it into the frame of their wedding photograph. In August the name Bullivant appeared twice: this time Frederick, who had been the youngest to go, a bright-eyed, muscular sixteen-year-old, and their oldest son John, who was wounded. Olive steeled herself to call next door and see Mrs Bullivant.

'I'll come with yer,' Polly said.

'Oh no – yer awright. You stay 'ere with Gracie. I want to go now while '*e*'s not there.' She was none too keen on Mr Bullivant, a sullen man who was working in munitions.

'I'll bring the little'un with me – I want to come.'

Polly had scarcely been out since the news of Ernie's death. Olive eyed her pinched face. She didn't want to inflict any more misery on her, but thinking it might do her good to give sympathy to someone else, relented.

'Awright. But none of that clap-trap you've been on about.'

Polly carried Grace next door, where they found the lady with her younger children. The house smelt of cabbage water. Mrs Bullivant was a quiet, stoical lady, broad in the beam, with a ruddy complexion and a mound of thick, dusty-looking hair fastened into a bun. She was trying to be brave, admiring little Grace and sitting them down while she made tea. But she was clearly not far from tears, and their sympathy started her off weeping.

'I should never've let 'em go,' she sobbed. 'Not the two young'uns. Fred never said 'e was joining up, not before 'e'd gone and done it.'

'You couldn't've stopped 'im,' Olive said, reaching over to pat her hand. 'Not once 'e was signed up. And 'e thought 'e was doing the right thing ... There's no telling 'em, not at that age.'

Mrs Bullivant mopped her tears with a large crimson handkerchief.

'Has 'e tried to get in touch with you at all?'

'*Don't*, Poll,' Olive seemed to swell with anger. 'I told yer not to ...' Her eyes flashed fury at Polly, who ignored her. Since Ernie's death she had started coming out with some notions which filled her mother with horror and distaste.

'What d'yer mean?' Mrs Bullivant sat turning the handkerchief round, kneading at it.

'The day my Ernie died 'e tried to tell me – get in touch with me. I know 'e did.' Polly spoke with great intensity. 'All them boys dying out there – their souls don't just disappear, you know. Not when they can't rest. They're all out there, round us, trying to find a way back to us ...'

The woman stared hard, as if stunned. For a moment Olive thought she was going to lash out and hit Polly. But she said, 'D'yer really think ...?' Mrs Bullivant wanted to believe it. She wanted desperately for her sons not to be gone from her forever.

241

'I do,' Polly sat with Grace in the crook of her arm, a fact which somehow increased the impact of her earnestness.

'Stop it,' Olive hissed at her. 'I've had more than enough of yer nonsense and yer carrying on. You'll only get 'er all upset!'

'She ain't upset, are yer, Mrs Bullivant? Least, not about that. Whatever you think, Mom, it's a comfort to know we might not've heard from the ones we love for the last time. You wait and see, Mrs Bullivant, if your Stan and little Fred don't send you a sign from where they've passed on to.'

Olive held on to herself until they got home. She closed the door and stood leaning against it as if in need of support or containment for her feelings.

'Don't you walk away from me, my girl!'

Polly turned by the door of the back room, still holding Grace. Her face held a kind of blank defiance.

'You've got to stop this – stop it now! I can't stand any more of it. You're making yerself bad with it.'

Polly sensed the suppressed fear and panic in the way her mother was talking. What was the matter with her? Why couldn't she see how simple, how beautiful it was that Ernie was taken from her but was still here, still loving her, watching over her?

'I'm not making myself bad, Mom.' She tried to sound reasonable and calm. She moved back along the half-lit hall. To Olive she looked like a ghost herself, her face long and white in the gloom. Olive shuddered. 'I don't know why yer getting in such a state. I just know Ernie's still 'ere, somewhere, trying to get through to me.'

242

'I wish *I* could bloody well get through to yer!' Olive summoned her last shreds of patience and tried to speak gently. 'I'm worried for yer, Poll. Girls sometimes turn funny after birthing a child. And now Ernie going too. Yer need to try and get hold of yerself, Poll, or people'll start talking if they see yer acting peculiar . . .'

Polly gave a bitter laugh. 'That's a good'un coming from you!' She backed away down the hall. 'I'm not the one who's peculiar, don't you worry . . .'

'Yer not the first woman to be left on 'er own, yer know!' Olive couldn't hold back her feelings any more, felt that if she raged and screamed loudly enough she could batter some sense into her daughter's head, make her put a stop to all this nonsense. 'I lost my husband and I weren't going on the way you are! You 'ave to keep going – put it behind yer, or yer going to end up in the nut house, that you are!'

Appalled to find she was bawling along the hall at the top of her voice, she pressed a hand over her mouth to stop anything else escaping from it. Would they have heard next door? Her breath rasped unevenly in and out.

There was no response from Polly. As Olive stood there trying to collect herself, the door opened behind her and Jess and Sis came in.

'What's going on, Mom?' Sis asked cautiously.

Olive tried to pull herself together. She jerked her head in the direction of the front room.

'I was having words with Poll. More of 'er carry-on about spirits and ghosts and such. Came out with it to Mrs Bullivant. It's got to stop.'

*

The atmosphere was uneasy as they sat down for tea that night. Polly had Grace on her lap.

'Why don't yer put 'er down while yer eating,' Olive suggested brusquely.

'She's awright. She'll only blart. It's quieter keeping 'er here.'

Olive pursed her lips, carrying a pan to the table. In it were pieces of pig's liver, onions gleaming in thick gravy, a great treat nowadays when things were short.

'Ooh – liver!' Sis cried. 'Did yer have to queue long for it, Mom?'

'Long enough.'

Jess took a potato to go with her liver and gravy, not looking at her aunt. She didn't dare say anything about the latest row with Polly. Over the past weeks Olive's temper had been even more uncertain than usual. Jess felt she had to be secretive about so many things so as not to provoke trouble: her visits to Iris, letters from Ned. One day, the week after Ernie was killed, Olive said to her, 'So 'e's awright, is 'e?'

Jess was startled. She had had a letter from Ned, but had not breathed a word about it.

'Er – who?'

'Who d'yer think?'

Somehow neither of them could speak Ned's name in front of the other.

Olive was looking at her, waiting for an answer.

''E's awright, Auntie, yes. Says he's . . .'

Olive held up a hand.

'Yer can keep the detail to yerself. I don't want news of adulterers in my 'ouse.'

They all ate in silence for a time, until Jess said,

'We heard some sad news today, didn't we, Sis?'

'Oh ar – I'd forgotten . . .'

'What?' Polly was always interested to hear gossip from the factory.

'Mr Stevenson's wife died,' Sis said.

Polly looked surprised. 'I never knew 'e had one.'

'Nor did we,' Jess said. 'Never thought about it, I s'pose. Apparently 'er's been bad for months. 'E's got a little lad an' all, only two years of age, poor little lamb.'

'Oh *dear*,' Polly said, with genuine sympathy. 'What a shame for 'im.'

'No wonder 'e's always looked so miserable,' Sis said. 'Poor thing. 'E's probably quite a nice man really, under it all.'

Olive shook her head. 'Bad thing, that, a man left on 'is own with a child. With all them dying over there you forget people're still dying here like normal.'

Jess had felt shocked by the news, suddenly seeing her employer as a real person with a whole life outside the works.

'He must've been going through hell, and never said a word,' she said. She had found herself thinking about him all day, seeing him in a quite new light and moved by the sadness that she'd felt from him.

Two nights later, when Jess came home Polly beckoned her to go upstairs, peering round to see whether Olive was listening.

'Go and see Mom for a minute,' she whispered to Sis. 'I've summat to say to Jess.'

Jess hung up her hat and went up to the room she shared with Sis. Polly slept in Bert's room now, with Grace, and through the wall at night, they often heard Polly sobbing. Sometimes she went to her and tried to comfort her, other times just left her alone. Polly's loss aroused strong, conflicting feelings in her: sorrow, help-lessness that there was nothing any of them could do or say to ease her suffering, but along with these emotions also a tangled mix of relief and fear. Relief because she felt, superstitiously, that if death had come to them once, then Ned was the safer for it. Death should spread itself out fairly, should strike somewhere else. But fear also at the danger Ned was in, and at the violence of Polly's grief and loss. Polly had crossed the black river into the land of mourning and it made her seem older and separate.

'You awright, Poll?'

'I'm awright. More than Mom thinks. Look, I wanted to ask if you'd mind Grace for me tonight. I want to go out.'

'Course. Why're you asking me though?'

'I don't want Mom knowing about it – not 'til I get back. I'm going to a meeting – she won't like it.'

Jess sat down on the bed, her face serious. 'What is it?'

Polly hesitated. 'Look, I'll tell yer if yer don't start on me. They call themselves Spiritualists. There's some-one there, a Mrs Black, can get messages from – you know, the other side. Mrs Bullivant told me – she's going as well.'

Jess looked closely at her. She knew Olive was worried Poll was going off her head, but Polly seemed calm enough.

'Poll – after Mom died, for a long time after, I used to talk to 'er. I mean, there wasn't anyone else I could talk to, 'cept sometimes Mrs Hunter at the farm. I used to tell 'er how I was feeling and that. And it felt as if she was still there, some of the time, close to me. I mean, I never heard her voice or nothing like that, but I thought she

246

could hear me. So I know 'ow yer feel. It's natural to feel like that. But d'yer really need to keep on about it so much – going to meetings? They're most likely all barmy and if Auntie finds out you'll be for it.'

'I'm not going to hide it from 'er – I'll tell 'er when I get back in. I just want the chance to go, find out. If I say beforehand she'll kick up one 'ell of a fuss. I'm just going to slip out – tell 'er later. So will yer, Jess – please? If I give Grace a feed I'll be back before she's ready for the next one. It's just if she cries . . .'

Jess could feel herself giving in. Polly didn't seem any madder than the next person, she just wanted comfort. Who was she to stop her going out?

'Awright then. But for 'eaven's sake watch what yer getting into.'

After tea, Polly slipped out into the light, warm evening, without announcing she was leaving.

'Where's Poll?' Olive said after a while. 'She still in the lav?'

'I think she went out – said she was going to see someone,' Jess said, her heart thumping hard. She saw Sis frown. Polly hadn't been out to see her friends for weeks.

'She didn't say.' Olive wasn't sure whether to be encouraged or worried. 'What about Grace?' Jess saw her aunt's expression change and Olive was on her feet and across the room. 'Grace – where is she? Has she taken the babby?'

'No—' Jess was bewildered. 'She's upstairs, asleep.'

They heard Olive's frantic tread on the stairs.

'Well where's she gone?' Sis demanded. 'What's all the flaming fuss about?'

'To a meeting,' Jess hissed. 'Some Spiritualist thing or summat. For God's sake don't say nothing.'

Sis rolled her eyes to the ceiling. 'Oh blimey – there'll be all hell let loose.'

Olive came back, her face relaxed again, having found Grace splayed peacefully on the bed upstairs.

'So why'd she go out and not say then?'

Polly came in at half past nine, her cheeks pinker than they'd been in weeks, and a slight smile on her lips.

'Is Gracie awright?'

Jess smiled, holding Grace, who was staring mesmerized up at the sputtering gas mantle. 'You can see.'

'Well – where've yer been?' Olive asked fairly cheerfully, but Jess and Sis eyed each other, both holding their breath.

Polly leaned over and lifted Grace off Jess's lap. ''Ello, my pet! How've yer bin – awright?' She rubbed noses with the baby and kissed her. 'Ooh, I've missed yer, I 'ave!' She turned to her mother. 'I'll tell yer, but yer not to bite my 'ead off.'

'Oh yes?' Olive said suspiciously.

Polly looked at Jess as she spoke, as if feeling that was safer. 'There was this meeting – just in this woman's house, down in Balsall 'Eath. She's got a special gift like, she can get messages from people who've passed away . . .'

This was an immediate red rag to a bull. Olive was tutting loudly straight away.

'It's awright, Mom – really. Mrs Bullivant came with me, and they were all very nice. And I got a message from Ernie . . .'

But her mother got up and walked out of the room. They heard her going upstairs.

248

Polly looked at Jess with desperate appeal in her eyes. ''E said 'e's in the pink where 'e is and I'm not to worry and that 'e loves me and is looking out for me ...' As she spoke her voice cracked and tears ran down her cheeks. 'I know it ain't much and Mom don't want to hear about it, but it's everything to me, to know e's getting on awright and 'e's still with me! I hadn't seen him for such a long time and it felt as if 'e'd gone forever without us being able to say goodbye ...'

Jess felt a lump rise in her throat, seeing the pain Polly was in, the joy that this simple message had brought to her, whether it was real or not. She got up, saying 'Oh Poll—' She and Sis went to her and took her in their arms.

Twenty-Six

Monday morning. Jess stepped into the Rumbling Shed and exchanged her cardigan for the overall and cap. It was going to be a hot day. Work started at eight and even on the journey she had felt almost too warm. As she slipped the rubber overshoes on, the other two girls came in saying 'Morning, Jess!'

She greeted them absent-mindedly and stepped through into her section of the shed at the end. The other two exchanged looks which said, 'What's up with 'er?'

'Yer never know with people from day to day nowadays, do yer?' one of them said. 'Anything could've happened.'

'It could. Or maybe she's just mardy 'cause she is.'

'Nah – she ain't like that.'

In the few moments before work was due to start, Jess leaned her back against the brick wall of the shed and pulled Ned's latest letter from her pocket. She had collected it from Iris's the evening before. Each time she read it hoping she'd missed something. A postcard fluttered to the floor and she bent to pick it up. It was a view of a French town, its church spire standing tall and noble. Small grey print on the back said, '*Albert – la basilique*'. He had enclosed a second card of the same view, but this time most of the buildings were wrecked, heaps of crumbling brickwork: the spire of the basilica

250

was smashed away at the sides, its statue at the top lurching sideways at a right angle to the spire.

She read Ned's letter again, urgently trying to find in it the warmth of the man she loved from this foreign country which felt so far away. Her eyes moved quickly over his sloping hand and settled on the end of the letter, needing his parting words which always meant so much to her. But they were so brief, matter of fact almost. And things he said in the letter: '*bombed it to hell*,' ... '*we were dead beat* ...' It didn't sound like him. It was almost as if it was written by another man.

She folded the letter away and went to work, counting the detonators with half her mind, distracted. She turned the drum fiercely, feeling her cheeks turn pink with exertion, pounding all her misery and frustration into it.

For a while she fought against giving in to her emotions, mechanically doing her job. But after a time, going to re-load it she turned too sharply and caught her elbow hard on the edge of the drum.

'Oh sod and damn it!' She doubled up nursing her elbow and gave in to her feelings, tears running down her cheeks. 'Oh Ned, I want you – I want you here now, just to see you!'

She was barely aware of the door opening.

'Jess – are you all right? What've you done?'

She straightened up immediately, rubbing her elbow, then quickly wiping tears from her face. 'Nothing. I just caught my elbow. I'm awright.'

Peter Stevenson looked closely at her. He had dark, sleepless rings under his eyes. The kindness in his expression, when she knew the loss he must be suffering, made Jess fill up with tears all over again.

'It's not just that, is it? Has something happened?'

'No—' Jess pulled out her hanky and mopped her eyes. She felt very stupid and her hands had gone all clammy. 'No – not really. I mean . . .'

Peter Stevenson hesitated, struggling to overcome his natural shyness. 'Perhaps I shouldn't be asking, but do you have a young man at the Front?'

'Yes . . .' She was in an agony of indecision and embarrassment. Mr Stevenson catching her in this state – but she could hardly tell him anything about Ned! Yes, I've got a young man at the Front who I love like crazy and he's married to someone else and he's left her and his child for me and everyone thinks we're wicked . . .

'Nothing's happened, I don't think. It's just I had a letter and . . . and . . .' Her cheeks were on fire. She had no idea how lovely she looked, face glowing, her eyes wet with tears. 'I just want the war to end,' she added lamely. 'It's silly of me. And compared with what you must be going through with your wife and every-thing . . .' Then she wanted to bite her tongue out. She shouldn't have said that! They'd all put together a card for him, from the works, but she'd never imagined saying anything to him. It'd never've happened before the war, she thought. So much was nearer the surface now.

'Oh . . .' Peter Stevenson looked at the floor. Oh God, Jess thought, don't let him start breaking down or carrying on as well because I shan't have the first idea what to do.

'Her name was Sylvia.' He looked up at her again. 'Everything feels pretty grim, at the moment.' Jess felt her heart contract at the tender sadness in his voice. Ned was alive – what did she have to complain about? 'But you know, although I miss her a great deal, what

252

was worse almost was when she was very sick and we didn't know how long she had left. How much she was going to suffer. Not knowing is terrible – the waiting.' He tried to give a rueful smile but it reached no further than his lips. 'So I do understand. There're so many people waiting at the moment . . .'

'I'm sorry.' She didn't know what else to say.

'Thank you.' For the first time she saw him really smile, a wide, rather melancholy uplift of his features, but wholehearted. It reminded her of the way Iris's smiles transformed her face. What a lovely face, she thought. He's a nice man. His kindness warmed her and she felt better for having let out her emotion.

Peter Stevenson's tone changed, became businesslike again. 'I really came to say – to warn you – that there's another group here from the Woolwich Arsenal.'

He rolled his eyes half comically to the ceiling.

'What, again?'

'I'm afraid so. They're over in the filling sheds at the moment so I thought I'd pop in and let you three know.'

'Oh well – I'd better get to work then.' Jess paused. 'I'll do my best, don't you worry.'

Peter Stevenson turned away, smiling faintly again. 'I know.'

That night, Jess lay in bed listening to the rain. The day had been intensely hot and close. Her temples throbbed and her body felt clammy and heavy. It was an effort to move.

The atmosphere at home was fraught. Polly had sloped out again, and though Olive didn't say anything, the strength of her feelings seeped out in the way she slammed pans down on the range, chewed at the edges of her fingers when they were sitting together after tea. The sense that she was charged, ready to explode with some fearsome emotion, increased daily, making all of them nervous of her, not just Jess.

Jess and Sis had carried pails of water in from the tap and poured them into the tin bath so they could all have a wash to cool down. Ronny always loved it when it was bath night, and chuckled as they stood him naked in the tub like a little white freckly fish, to pour water over him. Their splashing and activity relaxed the atmosphere a little, and afterwards, Sis bundled Ronny up in an old shirt of Bert's and rubbed him dry. Jess sat by her aunt twisting the long, wet skein of her hair between her hands. She liked the summer: they had bare legs so she didn't have to keep darning stockings every night.

'Yer know, Auntie—' Jess reached out and dared to touch Olive's hand for a second. 'Poll's awright. I know she's picked up a few odd notions for the moment, but . . .'

Olive jerked her hand away and Jess retreated, chastened.

'She said she'll come back to work if Grace can stop with you and Ronny.'

'She knows she can,' Olive snapped. 'I've said enough times, ain't I?' She was keen for Polly to get back to work, thinking it would help restore her to normality.

Polly got in just as the first growls of thunder echoed round the sky.

'It's flaming dark out there already!' She sounded cheerful enough.

Don't say nothing, Jess pleaded with her eyes. Don't tell us about messages you've had from the 'other side' for goodness sake. Just keep them to yourself for now 'cause we need that like a hole in the head.

The storm distracted everyone. The strange quietness, as if the whole city was waiting for each lightning flash, for the loud wrenching of the thunder, as a release from the fetid stillness which had settled over everything. They sat in the gloom, not even lighting the gas. Their horizon was limited by the row of houses opposite, only a thin border of sky visible to them, but they watched, sometimes glimpsing the lightning across the thick swirl of clouds. At last the rain came in force, a hissing, sighing sound sweeping over the rooftops, swelled by the wind. Grace slept on despite the noise, but Ronny was too excited and frightened to go to bed and sat cuddled up on Sis's lap, cowering when the thunder came.

They went up for the night when the worst of it had passed, but Jess could not settle. She lay for a long time with her eyes shut but no closer to sleep, feeling stirred up by the force of the storm outside. Storms visited themselves on you, powerful and out of your control, and it brought to her mind sharply the other events going on beyond them all, yet touching them, over which they had just as little influence. People said the guns sounded like the thunder. The feeling of her own insignificance which sometimes came over her at night filled her now. Sometimes that was comforting, but tonight her nerves were on edge with worry and longing and she felt small and frightened.

All she could hear was the steady fall of rain. But a few moments later there came a cry from the other end of the house, so agonized that it made her skin come up in goose pimples. She jolted upright, her heart banging, and found she was drenched in cold sweat.

Sis stirred, her bedsprings creaking as she half sat up. Jess could see her, dimly, across the room, hair hanging dark each side of her face.

'What was that?'

'I dunno. God, it was horrible. Sshh.'

They both sat absolutely still. The cry was not repeated, but gradually they heard the sound, at first low and intermittent, then louder, of anguished, un-stoppable weeping.

Sis gasped. In a small, frightened voice she said, 'I think it must be our mom.'

Twenty-Seven

The two of them tip-toed along the landing, sliding their hands along the walls in the dark. As they passed Polly's door it opened and Jess and Sis jumped, clutching at each other.

'Poll!' Sis whispered furiously. 'Yer nearly made my heart stop coming out like that!'

Polly was holding Grace, who was awake. 'That ain't just Ronny, is it?' She sounded frightened. The crying was childlike and utterly desolate.

'I think 'e's blarting as well now,' Sis said. 'She must've woke 'im and set 'im off.'

'What're we going to do?' Polly held Grace close, the baby's head tucked under her chin.

'God only knows. Let's get Ronny out of there anyhow.'

Sis pushed open the door of Olive's room and felt around in the darkness for her distraught little brother, lifting him into her arms. He sobbed into her neck and she stroked him, murmuring comforting things to him. Olive was still weeping, more quietly now, sounding tired and defeated.

Jess, the only one with her hands free, knelt down by the bed.

'You ain't going to wake 'er, are yer?' Polly said, alarmed. She moved Grace who was rooting around for milk and began to feed her.

'She sounds so sad. What's the matter with her?'

'I don't know. Honest I don't.'

'Sis – fetch us a candle, will yer?'

Sis persuaded Ronny to get down and in a couple of moments they were back with a lighted candle.

'Auntie.' Jess's hands were shaking as she very gently prodded Olive's shoulder. 'Auntie, wake up.'

Olive's eyes opened but at first it was as if she couldn't see them or make sense of their presence in the room and she was still crying. After a moment she sat up, knuckling her eyes like a child. Her arms were bare and she had on an old vest which was tight across her slack breasts. Sitting close to her, Jess could feel the moist heat coming off her body.

Gradually she quietened and sat with her head in her hands. Minutes passed. At last, more composed, Olive spoke quietly through her fingers.

'What've I been doing?'

'You were crying out, Mom,' Polly said gently.

They all waited. Jess expected Olive to say she was all right now, it was nothing, just a dream and what were they all mithering round her for in the middle of the night. But instead she continued to sit there, rocking gently back and forth, her breathing still ragged from crying. Jess thought how vulnerable and broken she looked in her yellowed old vest, her hair hanging down, no longer on her dignity, the fight gone from her. She wanted to embrace her, but didn't dare.

After a time Olive wiped her eyes. 'I can't keep on like this.'

'Auntie—' Jess dared ask. 'What're yer so sad about?'

Olive's hand went to her mouth as her emotion began to well up. Tears spilled from her eyes again.

'I can't stop crying,' she shook her head helplessly.

'Don't know what's got into me. I've tried never to think of it, never burden anyone with it, but lately I can't . . . it keeps . . . I keep remembering.'

'What, Mom?' Polly moved closer. She sounded near to tears herself. 'Why don't yer tell us – get it off yer chest, 'stead of bottling it all up. Is it summat about our granddad?'

Olive shook her head. 'No – not 'im. Not exactly.'

'If yer tell us,' Jess at last found the courage to touch her aunt's arm. 'Maybe it'll make yer feel better.'

'I worry I'm going off me head, that I do.'

'We've worried about yer an' all, Mom,' Polly said.

'And then you started on about all this . . . after Ernie died and I've been frightened to death you was – poorly . . .'

'I ain't, Mom. I just miss him so bad, that's all.'

Olive looked at the stricken faces of the girls gathered round her. They're not children any more, she thought. None of them.

'If I'm coming out with it it's now or never. By morning I'll've changed me mind.' More in command of herself, she beckoned to Sis who was still holding Ronny's hand. 'Bring 'im here.' She gave the little boy a kiss. Jess was touched. She'd seldom seen her aunt show the boy much warmth.

'Get 'im into bed, I don't want 'im listening. He'll soon be off to sleep and we can go in the other room.'

Sis settled Ronny back in bed and kissed him too, and they went into Jess and Sis's room, and Olive got into Sis's bed.

'It was your grandmother,' Olive began when they were all gathered round her. 'My mother. Ours, Louisa's and mine.'

Jess's attention was fixed so absolutely on her aunt's

face and her voice, that she was conscious of nothing else. If another storm had taken the roof off she might not have noticed.

'Alice, she was called. Alice Tamplin. Louisa favoured 'er but—' Jess felt her aunt touch her hand for a second. 'You're the image of 'er, Jess. When I saw you again, that night you turned up 'ere, I thought you was a ghost. It was you coming seemed to set it all off. I'm not blaming yer – 'ow could you know? All the things I kept down, didn't want to think about ever in my life again. I'd be standing there one day, getting on with things, and summat'd come flooding into my head, just for a second . . . And then it'd be gone. But it'd be so strong – like the past coming back, as if it's still 'ere. You know – if you've got memories, people who're dead're still alive like, in a way, ain't they? Almost like it's still happening to yer.'

Jess saw Polly was about to speak, but she silenced herself. None of them wanted to stop Olive talking.

'Our mom, Alice, had us – there was about two years between me and Louisa. I'd've been four – so that'd make Louisa two – when she had another babby. I don't remember much before the babby came. Just odd things. But then there was three of us. Another girl, Clara. Our mom liked fancy names. She was bad after Clara. Louisa was taken away to stay with Auntie May. She was always the pretty one, see, the easy one, and the aunts liked her. I was plain and quiet. They never liked me as much.' She pressed the large mole on her cheek with her finger. 'They used to say it was a shame, me 'aving this. Said it spoilt me looks. But Louisa'd dance for them, like, and sing, even at that age. Queer how different sisters turn out when yer think of it. I was the older one who had to be responsible, even then.'

260

Olive spoke looking down into her lap, hands still moving restlessly on the sheet, alternately twisting and smoothing it.

'I don't know exactly what was wrong with 'er in the beginning. She was really sick like – poorly in herself. Lay in bed all day, feverish. Whiteleg or summat, I s'pose. Our dad came in and out, carried on going to work – 'e had a good job then, in a Japanning works. She got better so's she could get up but she was still bad. Course I didn't know. Not at that age. And then . . .'

Her breath caught. Until that point she'd been telling the story calmly.

'All I remember is, she was carrying the babby about with her. Not just in the 'ouse. She'd been down the 'orse road carrying her in 'er arms. And she'd gone up and said to people – it just shows 'ow bad she was – showed 'er to people she met before she came home. What she'd done. She was upstairs – I was up there . . . just standing . . .' She stopped, unable to speak. All that came from her was a moan of distress. Her need to speak battled with a terrible fear, swelling and filling her until she was gulping for air, couldn't breathe. She threw back the covers and tried to climb out of bed. Jess moved quickly out of the way—

'Auntie, where're yer going?'

'Oh God!' Polly cried. She tried to restrain her but Olive flung her off.

'I can't!' Olive gasped. 'Oh that smell – I can't stand it!' She wanted to go to the window, to fling it open and get some air she was so hot, so desperate to breathe, to escape this mounting pressure inside herself. But as soon as she stood up she was dizzy, the room swaying and lurching round her. Sis and Jess caught her as she began to fall. She was both heavier and softer than Jess would have imagined, and hard to keep a hold on. It took all their strength to ease her back on the bed.

'Get 'er head down!' Jess instructed.

While Olive recovered, Sis went down and put the kettle on.

'Auntie?' Jess sat beside her, supporting her, stroking her shoulder. She felt more able than her cousins who found it harder to face all this emotion locked away in their own mother. 'When you feel a bit better shall we go down and have a cuppa tea? Then you can tell us . . .'

They sat round the table downstairs with the candle in the middle. Jess looked round at them all: Olive, her face washed with tears, and Polly and Sis, both looking like little girls with their hair loose on their shoulders. The storm had long passed over but there was still the soft sound of the rain outside.

'Will yer tell us, Mom?' Polly said. 'Did she do summat to the babby?'

Olive was able to speak more calmly now. 'We was upstairs. I don't know why. It was later on and I followed her up there. I was stood behind her and she had Clara in her arms. We had curtains on the upstairs windows, made out of this thick mustard-coloured material they were, and she was stood by them. Not looking out the window. They was drawn closed. She was holding this bottle of smelling salts to Clara's nose, and the smell of it was all in the room . . . She must've thought it'd bring 'er back . . .

'They came to get her. I don't know 'ow long it took, 'ow it happened exactly. I heard 'em coming up the stairs. Two coppers. There was one of 'em, very tall, said to me, "Are you all right?" And then one of them took her arm and she walked down the stairs with them . . .'

She was crying again, but quietly, the tears simply flowing as she spoke. Polly and Sis were crying too. Jess reached over and took her aunt's hand as tears poured down her own face.

'See, it weren't like – yer know, one or two you hear of get desperate, nowt to feed another babby on, roll over on it and say it were an accident. And there's some'll guess what might've happened but no one can say for certain. But our mom – Alice – she walked round the streets telling them what she'd done, pressed a pillow over 'er babby's face 'til she went blue, and she weren't newborn, she were a good four month by that time.

'They wouldn't leave us alone. Everyone knew. They were that cruel. Stones through the windows, shouting and making a display of us when we went out. Not everyone, but enough of 'em. And at school, because I'd just started going by then. My mom was a murderess so far as they was all concerned. She'd killed her child. Never mind that 'er mind was disturbed. Oh you don't know what people can be like. Course, Louisa wasn't there, she was still with Auntie May and Uncle Bill and they hung on to 'er after it happened. Louisa never remembered any of it too well. By the time she started at school we'd moved on. But in the beginning . . . They copped 'old of me once, bunch of kids held me down – there was this pothole in the road on the way back from the school, a real big'un, and when it rained, course it filled up with filthy water. They shoved my face in it and held me down. I thought I was going to drown. Yer can drown in a teacup, our dad used to say. 'E moved us on a few times – just nearby to begin with, but there was always someone found out where we'd gone. There was two of 'em, Doris Adcock and a Mrs Dobson. Doris 'ad these peculiar eyes...' A shudder passed through her. 'They daint 'ave one black bit in the middle like normal – there was two, sort of double. Looked more like a cat's eyes and she frightened the life out of me. I don't know why they did it, why they wanted to be so cruel, tormenting a man and his children. But Doris always found us, after a time. To this day I don't know 'ow. She'd come and leave a note through the door, "I know where you are..." At first we'd not move too far. Round Saltley or Bordesley. I saw her once, in the street after we'd moved on, and I wet myself I were that terrified of 'er—'

'Mom—' Polly interrupted suddenly. 'Is that the woman you saw, that day when you went shopping?'

Olive hesitated. 'If it was her she'd be well into 'er eighties by now. I don't know, Poll. It might've been her and it might not. Anyroad, in the end we went and lived the other side of town. Our dad only went back over that side when we was growed up. Once 'e thought everyone'd 've forgotten. Louisa ran off and got married the second she was asked.' The bitterness in her voice was unmistakable. 'Left me to it as usual.'

'Where did they take our grandmother ... Alice?' Jess asked softly.

'They put 'er in the asylum. In Birmingham first, and after we was told she'd been taken out to somewhere in Staffordshire. I don't know why that was. I never knew any of the ins and outs. We just wanted 'er to come back to us. She was our mom. But we never saw 'er again, Louisa and me, although I think our dad went out there a couple of times. We never saw the babby,

264

little Clara, again neither. Never 'ad her to bury so what they did with 'er I don't know. And I never knew how our mom carried on or what state she were in after. Seven years she were there. She died in there, never came out. Pneumonia, our father said. 'E'd moved 'is new missis in with us by then, not that they was married or anything. Not 'til after Mom died.' She seemed to notice then that she had been crying again, and wiped her eyes.

'Oh Mom,' Polly's face was blotchy from her own tears. 'What a terrible thing. Why didn't yer tell us all before? We'd've understood – what yer went through and that.'

Olive gave a deep sigh. 'I tried to put it all out of my mind once I was older – then married to Charlie. Past was past. And what good would it've done yer to know a thing like that? 'Specially when you was having bab-bies yourselves. When you turned up—' she looked at Jess. 'And then when you said you was expecting, out of wedlock – never mind who the father was – I just . . . It did summat to me nerves. I just couldn't 'ave yer in the house. It was as simple as that. I know you thought it was just 'cause you was in trouble, but it weren't that, though I was angry about yer leading Ned astray. But God knows, I've made mistakes in my time. You'll've worked out that Ronny's father was one of 'em. But you're the mirror image of 'er . . . I thought history'd start repeating itself and I couldn't even bear to look at yer, not knowing you was carrying a child. You'd come back to haunt me, that's what it felt like. And I've been that frightened for you as well, Poll. I never 'ad no trouble after I had all of you, not being bad like, and I was scared of 'ow things would go then. But I had Charlie then and I was safe with 'im – solid as a rock, he was, whatever 'appened. When you started on all this talk about spirits and ghosts I thought yer mind was going . . . Don't get that upset, love—'

Sis was sobbing. 'But Mom, why did she do that to 'er little babby?'

'She weren't 'erself. Sometimes it does summat to a woman's mind 'aving a child. And our Dad was no help to 'er. Took no notice. I s'pose 'e daint know what was happening, what to do. No one else could understand it – t'ain't a natural thing to do and that's why they were so cruel. But she weren't a wicked woman—' Her voice caught as she spoke. 'She were our Mom and we loved 'er. And she was your grandmother.' She looked across at Polly whose eyes were fixed on Grace. The baby had finished feeding and was sleeping snuggled close to her, a tiny fist curled by her face.

'I know what yer thinking,' Olive said. 'Clara would've been about that age. But yer grandmother needs yer sorrow, not you condemning 'er.'

'That was what I was thinking, Mom,' Polly said. 'With Ernie gone, Grace is all I've got. I'd kill anyone to protect her, that I would. Someone should've helped our grandmother and taken that babby off 'er for a bit.'

'They didn't know she were that bad. Not 'til it were too late.' Olive looked round at them. 'So now yer know.'

'You should've told us, Mom.'

'I didn't think it'd do yer no good.'

'No, but it might've done you some.'

'It might.' Olive sat up and let out a long, tremulous sigh from the depths of her. 'Ar, I think it might.'

Twenty-Eight

'I tell you what, Auntie,' Jess said a few days later. 'If you'll look after Gracie, I'll go with 'er and see what this Spiritualist business is all about.'

'Can I go too?' Sis asked.

'No,' Polly retorted. 'You'll only get the titters, I know you.'

Mrs Bullivant was not going tonight as she was visiting her son John, who had lost his legs on the Somme and was now in hospital in the city. Jess and Polly set off along the road in the smoky dusk. As they passed a bus stop on the Moseley Road a bus drew up alongside, letting a passenger off.

'Yer getting on or what?' the conductorette shouted.

'What does it look like?' Polly snapped at her. The bus chugged off in a cloud of fumes. 'Think they're the Lord God Almighty, some of 'em, once they've got a ticket machine over their shoulder.'

Jess laughed. 'You sound more like yerself.'

Polly smiled faintly. 'I'm up and down. Natural though, ain't it?'

'Auntie's better in 'erself too.' Over the fortnight since Olive had told them about Alice she had been emotional. Sometimes she'd start crying unexpectedly, and was bewildered and embarrassed by it, but she was more relaxed than Jess ever remembered her and somehow softer. It had been a release.

''Ow's Ned?'

'Awright, so far's I know,' Jess said carefully. She kept her feelings to herself, the worry that was constantly with her. All that year there had been little news but that of slaughter: the French at Verdun, now the Somme, day after day.

'Come on—' she changed the subject. 'How much further to this barmy Mrs Black of yours?'

'It's no good thinking like that,' Polly was on her high horse straight away. 'Nothing'll ever happen for yer if yer think that way about it.'

Jess nudged her. 'I was only kidding.'

'Remember what they said after Mons? There was that queer light in the sky, like an angel watching over them?'

Not the Angel of Mons again, Jess thought. 'Yes, you 'ave mentioned it before – just a few dozen times.'

'Anyway – 'er lives on Runcorn Road. Nearly there.'

Runcorn was a road of respectable terraces, intersected every half dozen houses with little avenues leading to houses behind, all bearing the names of trees.

'I wouldn't mind living here,' Jess found herself talking in a slightly hushed voice, even though there was plenty of neighbourhood noise from children playing out in the avenues and on the pavement. They walked a good way down the road. As they passed under the railway bridge a train thundered over their heads. The loud sound brought Jess's arms up in goose pimples.

'Lilac, May, Myrtle . . .' Polly read off the names. ''Ere we go.' She knocked on the door of a house between Myrtle and Vine Avenues and it was opened immediately by an elderly man with a drinker's complexion, who must have been standing just behind it.

There was no hall and they stepped straight into the

front room, which was gloomy and sparsely furnished, with brown lino on the floor, and obviously used more as a passage than a room.

'Evening, Mr Black,' Polly said respectfully.

'Oh – Polly, it's you! 'Ow are you then? And who's this you've brought with you?'

'This is my cousin Jess.'

Jess shook Mr Black's sinewy hand. He had a quaint, gentlemanly way, but it didn't seem to come quite naturally, as if he'd trained himself in this rather starchy new way of behaviour.

'Have you had a loss, my dear?'

'Er . . . well, no,' Jess said. 'Least, not for some time.'

'She's just come along to keep me company,' Polly said. She handed over the money and Mr Black stowed it in a jar which had once contained barley sugar.

'Go inside,' Mr Black pointed to the back room and returned to his post behind the door. 'There's a few waiting.'

Three rows of upright chairs had been fitted in at the nearest end of the room, and several of them were already occupied. Facing them was another more stately seat with arms, built solidly in oak. At the far end an upright piano stood against the window, but Jess's eyes were immediately drawn to a strange, pavilion-like construction in the other corner. A wooden frame was draped in white sheeting, creating a shrouded oblong area which Jess realized must have covered the door to the stairs. On the long wall beside them was a painting depicting the afterlife. As well as lots of swirling cloud and what looked like a vivid blue lake in the middle, there were crowds of people in white, flowing clothes, and small, plump angels hovering above their heads.

Jess squeezed into the middle row between Polly and

a middle-aged woman in black, who had apparently dozed off to sleep. Everyone else was very quiet and a rather resigned, gloomy atmosphere hung over the place which was stuffy and smelt overpoweringly of mothballs, although this didn't overcome the stale odour coming from the lady on the other side of Jess. The woman behind them kept coughing. Jess felt self-conscious and not very trusting of what was going to happen. She nudged Polly, pointing at the sheets.

'What're they for?' she whispered.

'Mrs Black always comes out from there. I s'pect she's upstairs getting ready.'

Jess jumped violently as the lady on the other side of her roused herself and laid a hand on her knee. She greeted Polly, then said to Jess,

'My name's Irene Crawford. 'Ave yer suffered a loss?'

'No.' She felt almost guilty at this admission. 'I've just come with Polly.'

'My 'usband and my son have passed on to the other side. Only me and my daughter left now. My son William was killed at Suvla Bay.'

'Was your husband killed in the fighting too?' Jess asked.

'No, bab, 'e fell off of a roof on the 'agley Road. The two of 'em keep in touch though. Always were good to me, both of 'em.'

As they waited a few more people arrived, all – with one exception – women, who seemed to know each other at least by sight, and there was a low murmur of conversation.

At half past seven on the dot, Mr Black disappeared into the white, tent-like structure and they heard him calling up the stairs,

'Yer ready now then, Dora?'

There came a muffled reply, then they heard what sounded like at least two pairs of feet on the stairs. Jess, in a slightly hysterical state, found herself picturing Mrs Black having four legs like a pantomime horse and had to force down the powerful urge to laugh which swelled up inside her.

Mr Black held the sheet aside, closing it behind his wife as she appeared. She was a small, neat woman, quite a bit younger than her husband by the look of her, dark-haired, with bold, shapely eyebrows. She was also dressed in black, and her hat was trimmed with black net. There was a stiff elegance about her movements.

'Good evening, everyone,' she said, looking round at them with composure.

'Good evening,' they all muttered.

'We shall start with our hymn.' She moved to the piano and began to play it rather well, but there were not many voices to make a swell of sound and their efforts at singing turned out as more of a mumbling,

'Jesus lives! no longer now
Can thy terrors, death, appal us;
Jesus lives! by this we know
Thou, O grave, canst not enthrall us.
Alleluia!'

By the end of the first verse, Mrs Crawford and Polly were both crying and some of the others soon joined in. It was so sad it set Jess off crying too, thinking of Ernie's sweet, friendly face and how happy he and Polly had looked together and now they'd never see him again. And it called to mind the day her mother died and she found she was crying for her too, and for her grandmother and baby Clara, until she was at least as upset as everyone in the room, and needed something to blow her nose on. She had to borrow Polly's handkerchief.

They all sat down. The room was rather shadowy now, although there was still some silvery grey evening light coming from the window. Mr Black lit the three candles in a brass candelabra and placed it on the piano. For a moment they all sat quietly, except that Jess heard someone give a sniff and she frowned. It sounded as if it had come from in front of her, but that would mean someone who they couldn't see was waiting behind the screen of sheets. The thought was rather spooky. She wondered at Polly coming here on her own: she must truly have been desperate.

Mrs Black sat down on the rather grand oak chair and took several deep breaths. Her little round tummy seemed constrained by her frock, and her full bustline looked fit to erupt out of it too. She closed her eyes.

'I can feel the spirits are close to us tonight.' She kept her voice low, intoning in a rather posh voice so it didn't seem like natural speech. Despite her unease, Jess found she was reluctantly full of curiosity. If it was real it would be very nice to hear from Ernie again.

'Who has grief pressing on them at this moment? Who shall I summon from the spirit world, the land of blessed light? Those on the other side are only gone before: they are watching over us, and they are still needful of our love and our communion with them.'

'I . . .' Polly sniffed. 'I'd like to 'ear from Ernie . . .'

'Ernie . . .' Mrs Black said meditatively. Then opened her eyes and said in a normal voice, 'You mean yer 'usband?'

Polly nodded. 'Ernest Carter. Same as last week.'

'Ernest Carter . . .?' The eyes closed again. 'Your wife would like to hear from you. Ernest, come to us: cross back from the other side to where your wife waits faithfully for you . . .' Her tone turned incantational, like someone pretending to be a ghost.

'I'm here,' a voice said.

Jess nearly jumped out of her skin. She gripped Polly's wrist.

'Oh Ernie!' Polly whispered.

'I've come to see yer again . . . er, wife. I'm awright. It's very nice over 'ere. Very comfortable and er, pleasant. Wish you could come and join me . . . well, when yer ready and that, I mean. I hope everything's going along at home. Don't worry about me. The wounds don't hurt any more. Well – love for now then . . .'

The voice seemed muffled during the last sentence, in a way which sounded to Jess as if the person speaking was backing away up the stairs.

''E sounds different,' she whispered to Polly.

'Dying does that,' Polly said tearfully. 'Mrs Black told us that. They've gone to another place. They have astral bodies.'

Irene Crawford, next to Jess, was asking about her husband and son.

'I'd 'specially like to 'ear from my son if you can manage it again. I know the Dardanelles is a long way.'

Mrs Crawford's son William did want to speak to his mother and he seemed to be having a quite similar experience of the other side to Ernie. Jess found, after several encounters with the spirit world, that life over there didn't seem to be any more varied or interesting than existence in this one and she began to lose interest. Until a thought struck her.

When there was a gap in the proceedings she said,

'I'd like to call someone.'

Polly's head whipped round. 'Jess – what're yer doing?'

'I'd like to talk to my grandmother. She was called Alice Tamplin.'

She heard Polly gasp.

'How long has she been gone from this world?' Mrs Black asked in her strange, sing-song voice.

'Er . . .' Jess looked uncertainly at Polly. 'Oh, at least twenty years.'

'I see.' Mrs Black was sitting with her eyes closed, obviously concentrating. There was a long silence. Jess was torn between amusement and nervousness. This would be a tough one for the man behind the screen! But still she found she was tingling with a strange sensation. Everyone was silent. An atmosphere of intensity had come over the room.

She'll have to give up on this, Jess thought. She's not asked me anything about her. How's he going to know what to say?

She was looking expectantly at the little sheeted box, when Mrs Black abruptly put her head back, her body went rigid and she gave a long, horrifying howl. Jess felt her limbs turn to water. The howl was followed by a high keening of grief and distress and Mrs Black's body jerked about as if in pain. Then they heard the sound of a woman sobbing as if her heart would break. There was nothing going on from behind the screen: it was all coming from Mrs Black. Jess couldn't see her moving: her lips and throat were still, the noises shrill and disembodied. She and Polly sat rigid, gripping hard on to each other's hands.

The desolate weeping went on for a short time, then

stopped abruptly. Mrs Black relaxed into the posture she had been in before.

'She is not quiet.' She spoke softly. 'She is not at peace. She cannot speak to you.'

'Oh my God,' Jess whispered. She was shaking all over.

Both of them were sober and shocked on the way home. Polly tried to talk. 'You see? Marvellous, ain't she? It does me so much good to know I can hear from Ernie.'

Jess didn't reply. Away from the confines of the Blacks' dark house she was struggling to make sense of what had happened. She had felt frozen in there, although the night was not chill. All the grief and sorrow and desperate hope congregated together seemed to cast a cold pall over the atmosphere. But she didn't really believe in all that sort of thing, hadn't until tonight. She'd been certain they hadn't really heard from Ernie. It was clear as anything that there was a man behind the sheet doing all the voices. Why could none of them see it? Was it because they needed so badly to believe what Mrs Black told them, because they were so bereft and lonely? And if that was the case, did it really matter that she was a fake if she brought comfort?

But Alice . . . Had Mrs Black taken over the act of being Alice because she'd only got a 'ghost' who could do men's voices? But how had she known what sort of person Alice would be? Was it luck? But the sound of that weeping, when Mrs Black had been sitting so still, not apparently moving a muscle . . . The sound of it was locked, echoing round in Jess's head. What if it was real, if their talking about her had somehow brought her spirit closer to them? Poor, unquiet Alice. Was she still out there somewhere, mourning, needing them in some way? With all these thoughts turning in her mind Jess was silent almost until they got home. At the end of Oughton Place she turned to her cousin.

'Well Poll,' she was trying not to show how uneasy she felt. 'I'm glad I came with yer, but I shan't come again.'

'What'll yer tell our mom?' Polly stopped her for a moment. 'You won't make things difficult for me, will yer?'

Jess shook her head. 'Course not. But Polly – what about Alice?'

'We'll 'ave to do summat to help her rest in peace.'

'But what?'

Polly frowned. 'I dunno. We'll 'ave to put some thought into it. P'raps we could find where she's buried, when we get the chance. But Jess – don't let on to Mom. She's been in enough of a state lately. Knowing this won't help 'er.'

When they got home, Olive said, 'Well – what was it like?

'Oh,' Jess managed a grin at her. 'It weren't too bad. Nice enough people, no madder than most. I don't suppose it can do any harm.'

PART IV

Twenty-Nine

June 1917

'Right, girls – come on over 'ere and gather round – I've got summat to say to all of yer!'

Vi, who was still the unofficial gaffer at the factory, was out in the yard, waving her brawny arms to get their attention.

It was a bright day, with a feeling of warmth and promise peculiar to early summer. It had rained in the night and there were puddles dotted about, but now they could hear birds on the waste ground beyond. Pigeons were muttering on the roof of the Rumbling Shed.

Sis winked at Jess as they met outside the office on their way to the canteen.

'What does she want then?'

Jess shrugged. 'Soon find out.'

There was already a crowd of women round Vi, and a sallow, jaundiced-looking lot they were, a number obviously full of cold even though the winter was long over, some with red, itchy skin from contact with the powder. They were all squinting, coming out of the sheds. Quite a few were coughing, including Sis who complained continually of having a sore throat. In the bright light Jess saw she was thin and tired-looking. Perce had been posted now and she had joined the ranks of the permanently worried.

Someone handed Vi a chair and she stepped up on to

it, wobbling and flailing her arms before standing upright as it creaked under her.

'To my mind,' she bawled across the yard, 'we're all in need of a bit of a day out.'

Jess and Sis looked at each other and raised their eyebrows. 'We've had a long, hard winter,' – murmurs of agreement – 'and yer all looking like yer've bin locked up in the cellar for six month—'

'Feels like it an' all!' someone shouted.

'So 'ow about a picnic out somewhere Sunday? Bring some grub—'

'That's if yer can get 'old of any!' There was laughter.

'—and we'll go over the park . . .'

A discussion broke out about where it should be. Some wanted more of a day out, right out of town, and eventually it was decided that they'd go across to Sutton Park.

'Ooh—' Jess said. A quiver of pleasure went through her. 'How lovely. It's s'posed to be real nice up there.'

'Poll could come, couldn't she?' Sis said. Polly was back at work, but had decided to find another job nearer home so she could pop back at dinnertime and look in on Grace. She found it difficult enough to be separated from her for even an hour or two.

'I should think so,' Jess said. 'And Ronny'd love it.'

She went up to Vi. 'Can I bring me cousin – 'e's five?'

'Bring who yer like, bab, so long's yer can get 'em on the bus.'

As they dispersed to go and fetch their daily cup of milk, Peter Stevenson was standing watching, leaning against the wall by his office door. Jess saw Vi go up to him. A few moments later she came in to the little canteen.

''Ere – guess what. 'E wants to come along an' all.'

'What – Mr Stevenson, on a picnic with us lot!'

'Blimey – 'e must be lonely.'

'Did yer say 'e could?'

'Well I could 'ardly tell 'im 'e couldn't, could I?' Vi grunted, lowering herself on to a chair, the enamel cup in one hand. 'Oh me legs! Flamin' 'ell, I'm old enough to be 'is mother! Now there's a thought.'

It had been a dismal winter indeed. The cold and shortages of food, the queueing, the triumph of finding a potato in the shops when there was such a scarcity of them, the long, grinding hours at work day after day made nearly every aspect of life a struggle. Added to that was the yearning for loved ones, some had now been absent so long, and the constant gnawing anxiety for their safety.

My life, Jess thought sometimes, is made up of work and Ned. She dreamed about him as she worked, hour after hour, her arms and back aching. Of their future, when the war was over. Some days she burned with optimism, others she was full of fear and insecurity. He might be killed. He might change his mind. Perhaps already he'd decided he didn't love her any more but couldn't bring himself to tell her? On days like that she felt low and hopeless and tried to put him out of her mind. It was too unbearable to think about. If he was taken from her, her life would be empty. It would have no meaning.

She was comforted though, with regard to his safety, by his letters throughout the winter. He was at a quiet part of the Front, he told her. It was bitterly cold for a large part of the time, frosts which broke French records, but there was little in the way of shooting and shelling.

She tried not to ask more than to know he was all right. In the April his Company were involved in the fighting at Arras, helping to capture Vimy Ridge. Soon after he wrote and told her he was safe. Just occasionally he managed to say more to her than the facts and these parts were the greatest treasure to her.

Sunday started off cool and misty but they had hopes of finer weather. Jess, Polly and Sis piled on to the bus with Ronny. Polly had Grace in her arms.

'You can come too, yer know,' Jess had said to Olive. 'It don't matter who goes so long as they make their way and bring their food.'

Olive smiled. She was sitting back comfortably in anticipation of a day on her own. 'Nice to be asked, but I'm going to 'ave a day's peace without them two.' She nodded at the two little ones. 'No one keeping on at me or causing trouble.' She fixed Ronny with a dire look.

There was a festive atmosphere on the bus as quite a few of the other workers had caught the same one. Ronny sat on Jess's knee and Polly was next to her with Grace. Ronny had lost all his baby fat and was now a thin little thing with white, stick legs and knobbly knees, hair a vivid carrot colour and freckles all over his face. And he was trouble in motion, despite the innocent expression.

'You're not going to run off and be a nuisance, are yer?' Jess spoke close to his ear over the noisy rumble of the bus.

Ronny shook his head absent-mindedly, knowing this was the right answer.

'I wish this one'd get up and run about,' Polly nodded at Grace. She was over a year now, and despite the limited amount of food about, was a rounded pudding of a child with thick brown hair and big blue eyes, who was barely showing any inclination to walk. 'Tires me out lifting 'er, that it does.'

They'd got no sense out of Sis who sat reading and re-reading a letter she'd had from Perce and grinning to herself.

'From the look of yer I take it 'e's awright,' Polly said.

''E's being trained up to work in them tank things,' Sis said proudly. 'In the Tank Corps.'

'Blimey,' Polly made a face. 'Well p'raps 'e's safer inside one of them.'

As the city fell away and they moved towards the old town of Sutton Coldfield, things started to look more cheerful. The sun found a chink in the clouds and shone in a determined sort of way. When they got off the bus and walked into Sutton Park, the smell of the grass rising to meet them, Jess suddenly felt her spirits lift further than they had in a long time. She wanted to drop everything and run across the open expanse of green, over to the fresh spring trees at the other side, but knew she couldn't leave Polly to carry the bags as well as manage Grace.

They strolled across among a crowd of other women from the works with their families around them, calling out noisily, the children chattering with excitement. Ronny, for the moment, seemed awed by the space round them.

Vi was there with two of her daughters, and a carrier in each hand, swaying from side to side as she walked across the grass. As usual she took charge.

'Best stay in the sun,' she squinted up at the clouds. 'There ain't much point in sitting in the shade when the sun's hardly shining.'

Jess, Polly and Sis settled with a group of others. There were more arrivals from another bus and gradually the group grew, snaking across the grass, everyone close together but gathered into smaller clusters here and there. Some laid out mats and coats on the damp grass. Behind them, a short distance away was a row of trees edging a stream which ran through the park, and in front stretched the wide swathe of grass.

It was only mid-morning and too early for dinner, although that didn't stop a few having a nibble of the food they'd bought. At first Ronny sat quietly between Jess and Sis as the women chatted, enjoying the freedom to loll on the grass and talk for as long as they wanted without having to go back to the sheds and fill grenades. Then a set of identical twin girls, both about seven, with ash-blonde hair and freckles, went up to Ronny and pulled him to his feet, each hoicking him by the hand.

'We'm gunna play tag,' they commanded. 'So come on with us.'

Jess smiled over at the twins' mom. 'No saying no to them, eh? Bet they give you the run around?'

'Not 'alf.' The woman smiled wearily.

'Eh—' Vi said. 'Look – 'e's come an' all!'

Peter Stevenson was walking towards them, a little self-consciously, Jess thought, one long arm raised in greeting. He was dressed casually in grey flannel trousers and a dark green sweater, with a jacket over one arm. Beside him, holding his spare hand and walking with stolid, rather uncertain steps, was a young boy.

'Oh look,' Sis said. 'His little lad. Poor little bugger.'

284

'Oi,' Vi said. 'Watch yer mouth.'

'Morning!' Peter Stevenson put his bag down. They all replied, cheerfully though with a shyness that his own reserve brought out in them. He wasn't like some of the men they were used to, full of lip, and they weren't sure how to talk to him.

The whole group must have numbered about sixty or seventy people, and now they were closer, the little boy was overcome and turned away, pressing his face into his father's thighs.

'Now, Davey – there's no need for that, is there?'

Peter Stevenson gradually prised the boy away from him and squatted down to look into his face. The child tried to move close again and hide his eyes.

'These are the ladies from the factory and their families,' he said gently. 'They all want to see you, and we're going to have a picnic together, remember? Maybe have a game or two.' He turned, smiling. 'He's always been shy, but recently . . .' He stopped. They all knew what he meant.

Jess watched the careful way he looked into his son's face, reassuring him. But David's eye was caught by a movement beside him. Grace had crawled across the grass and was looking up at him with her mouth open, drooling. The boy squeaked with alarm and clung to his father again.

'She wants to play with yer!' Polly said. Grace moved closer, kneeled up at the side of him, wrapped her arms round the boy's legs and started sucking experimentally on one of his kneecaps. He started to giggle.

All the women laughed too, and for the first time Jess could remember, so did Peter Stevenson.

*

By the time they ate dinner the sun came out, coats and cardigans came off and everyone relaxed visibly in the warmth. Jess lay back, straw hat on the grass beside her, feeling the sun on her eyelids, warming her stiff limbs. She stretched like a cat. It was so nice to lie still! She knew in a while she'd have to give Polly a rest and take her turn traipsing round after Grace who wouldn't sit in one place for a second. But for now she felt drowsy, half detached from the shrieks and laughter around her, the distant chug of a bus on the road. She could hear women talking lazily round her, and mixed with their chat, the occasional low sound of Mr Stevenson's voice which she found reassuring. She remembered the tender way he had looked at his son and for a moment a great longing filled her. When had her own father ever looked at her like that? The sunlight and country smells of grass and earth took her mind back. The orchard at Budderston, the hayfield, Louisa ... And Alice. She recalled Olive's sudden, so far as she could see, unprovoked anger that day. Had it been out of bitterness at all Olive had endured, when Louisa had escaped so much of it? The three women haunted her. Even though Olive was part of the present, the past felt mysteriously, nudgingly present. But shortly the actual present crashed in on her.

'Oh, take 'er off of me for a bit, will yer, Jess – she's running me ragged!'

Jess sat up drowsily. Polly was clutching a beaming, grubby-faced Grace whose arms and legs were pedalling frantically in her eagerness to be off.

'Come on then, Gracie.'

It was a little later, while Jess was trailing round after Grace as she half crawled, half staggered holding Jess's hand, ferreting into people's bags and picking up odd bits of soil and leaves to eat, that some of the older children tired of games and discovered the stream.

There were four boys all about Ronny's age, including David Stevenson. Ronny, who had quite recovered from his quiet moments of awe and wonder, was the undoubted ringleader. Jess saw them hurtle down into the shade which shrouded the low banks of the stream. After a second or two's uncertainty they pulled their shoes and socks off and their shrieks of agony and delight could be heard at the coldness of the water.

'Let's go and keep an eye on 'em,' Jess said, picking Grace up. 'Ooh, you're a lump. And don't go thinking you're going in with them 'cause yer not.'

When she reached the stream the boys were all bending over something they could see in the water, prodding at it with their fingers. She stood watching, Grace struggling in her arms. In a moment Sis came to join her.

'They awright? Not getting into any mischief, are they?'

'Not so far, but there's no telling.'

A couple of other women were looking across towards the stream, but seeing Jess and Sis there, sunk down again thankfully. Peter Stevenson had got up and was also walking towards them.

'Is David in there?' he called, sounding anxious.

Jess nodded. 'They're all awright.'

He had taken his hat off and his black hair was blowing waywardly about. He seemed aware of it and tried to smooth it with one hand but it sprung up again. When he reached them, Jess felt small again beside his tall, rangy figure.

'Don't get your clothes wet, will you?' he called to the boys.

287

They ignored him, their eyes fixed on the water in search of tiddlers.

There was silence for a moment. Jess felt self-conscious beside Peter Stevenson. He was staring across the stream, out through the trees the other side, to the grass beyond. His face was sad and her heart went out to him.

'Who's looking after Davey?' she asked. 'I mean when you're at the works.'

'Oh – I've got a housekeeper. Very kind lady. And sometimes my mother comes – she's been very good too. Things could be worse,' he finished valiantly.

Could they? Jess wanted to ask. Instead she said, ''E's a lovely little lad. Got your eyes.'

She saw him smile. 'He's a good boy. We help each other along.'

Ronny spotted them watching and grinned.

'Oi, Jess, Sis – come on in 'ere with me, it's bostin'!'

'No ta, Ronny,' Jess said. 'I've got to hold on to Grace.'

'I'll take her if you like,' Peter Stevenson offered.

'Oh – no, yer awright. I'm not keen on cold water.'

'Oh—' Ronny pleaded. 'Go on!'

'I'll go in with them.' Sis had been rather hoping for a paddle. She slipped her shoes off and slithered down into the water. 'Oh my God – it's flipping freezing!' She laughed, holding up her skirt, trying to tuck it between her knees, and waded unsteadily over to the boys.

'You're close, you and your sisters, aren't you?' Peter Stevenson observed. He stood in a relaxed manner, hands loosely clasped behind his back.

'Oh we ain't sisters,' Jess laughed, rearranging Grace in her aching arms. 'Well, Sis and Poll are – I'm their cousin. Their name's Beeston – well, Poll's was before she was married. Mine's Hart.'

'Oh – sorry. Too many names to take in. But I thought you all lived together . . .' he trailed off, afraid of seeming too nosey.

'We do. I came to Brum to live with my auntie just before the war. She sort of took me in when I . . .' She had been about to say 'ran away' but it sounded bad, she thought. Flighty. 'I er, didn't get on too well with my stepmom so I thought I'd just get out of 'er way. Auntie's been good to me.'

'That's a hard thing to do. Your mother . . . ?'

'She died years ago. Only Sarah – that's my step-mother – well, the older I got the worse we got on.' She spoke matter of factly, not thinking she gave away any of the pain of the situation, but Peter Stevenson could sense it in the way she looked away at the ground, touching her cheek against Grace's.

'I lost my father when I was ten,' he told her, his eyes on Sis who was holding hands with Ronny and Davey, larking about with them. 'Changes everything, doesn't it? If he'd lived I'd've stayed on at school, but as things were, it was out to work as soon as possible. Still – could be worse,' he said again. He smiled, and Jess smiled back shyly.

'I'll have to move back and put this one down,' she said, looking at Grace. 'My arm's'll drop off else.'

As she spoke, there was a great yell from Sis. The two lads had been pulling playfully on her arms and Sis had slipped on one of the rounded, slimy stones at the bottom and was now sitting down, laughing and shriek-ing at the same time.

'Oh my – oh flippin' 'ell, it's icy cold! Oh, you little perishers . . .' She struggled to stand up, water pouring from her clothes.

Jess started laughing, but Peter Stevenson said, 'Oh

goodness – let me help you.' And stepped into the stream, wading along without even rolling up his trousers.

Sis was still trying to get to her feet, splashing about almost hysterical with laughter.

'You've still got yer shoes on!' she cackled, pointing at Peter Stevenson, seeming to find this the funniest thing of all. 'Oh my word, look at that – they'll be ruined!'

Peter Stevenson took a couple of strides then looked ruefully down at his feet. 'Oh dear!' he said. 'What an idiot!'

Jess and Grace walked back up the grass with Sis and Peter Stevenson dripping alongside them, all of them unable to stop laughing. Ronny and David, having expected a serious ticking-off, were laughing as much from relief as anything.

Polly looked at them with amused incomprehension as they approached, holding out her arms to take Grace. 'What in the . . .?'

Having all been released into laughter, none of them could seem to stop.

Jess and Peter Stevenson's eyes met as they laughed, each enjoying the other's mirth. As he looked at her pink cheeks and wild, wispy hair, the thought came to him, what a lovely girl she is, that Jess. Somehow sad, but lovely.

Thirty

France, October 1917

The hospital train approached the railhead at a shrieking pace, smoke puffing out into the chill blue sky. As it drew nearer it slowed, with an intermittent screech of brakes, eventually to ease its way alongside the platform with a glide which barely suggested it was moving, and halt with a final swooshing climax of steam.

The orderlies awaiting its arrival were working against the clock, each carrying a clipboard, making their way back and forth along the tightly packed rows of stretchers, several deep, which occupied the length of the platform. The wounded men on the stretchers were covered with grey blankets, only their faces visible, some appearing swaddled like babies and just as helpless. They had been assembled from the Casualty Clearing stations and many were deep in post-operative shock, glassy-eyed, silent. But amid the terse calls of the orderlies and the hiss of the engine, low groans and an occasional cry of pain cut through the cold air.

By and large the orderlies treated the wounded men with gentleness and respect. Just one or two were brusque, unable or unwilling to see into the extent of their shock and incapacity. The embarkation details had to be completed before their patients could be entrained and they were under pressure, so that for the less sensitive of them the prostrate men became a mass of spiritless items with which they had to deal.

'Name?'

A ginger-haired orderly stood over one young man with full lips and cropped wavy hair who was one of those evidently suffering from shock, his face deathly pale. The lad stared up at him with a frozen gaze, straining to make sense of the question.

'Can you tell me your name, chum?'

His licked his lips. 'Jem . . .?'

'Jem? Jem what?'

'No . . . not . . . My name's . . .' He frowned desperately. 'Green. Ned . . . Edward Green. 15th Warwicks. D Company . . .'

'That's a good lad. Now – what's your address?'

After a moment he managed to say, 'Oak Tree Lane, Selly Oak, Birmingham.' His childhood address was the only one that came to him.

'Right. District Three. That's it then. Soon be on your way to Brum, chum.'

The train rumbled along at a more careful pace with its full load en route to Boulogne. The men lay trussed up three layers deep along the sides of the compartment. Ned was on a middle berth. He was aware of what was going on around him only in a dreamlike, distanced way. Nurses moved about the carriage, holding on where they could as they went about their duties to keep from lurching over. One of them, seen sideways on, had a pale, sharp face and when she turned, Ned was convinced in his delirious state that it was his wife. She must have come on the journey to look after him, he thought. Despite everything. He was filled with enormous shame and humility. Who was looking after Ruth, he wondered, and supposed Mary had left her with her mom so that she could be here to look after him.

There was a ghastly smell in the compartment, the suppurating odour of gas gangrene. He heard groans, the sound of retching, a shout here and there. He didn't know how far apart the cries came but they seemed to clang into his brain, unbearably loud, making him moan quietly. The stench seemed to intensify with every mile, even though the nurses, sickened, slid windows open. It mingled itself with the fractured images in Ned's head.

'Gas!' He tugged at the bed covering, trying vainly to find his respirator.

'What is it? Are you in pain?'

Mary's face loomed close, level with his, wearing a nurse's veil. She was so young, so sweet. 'Is it your leg?'

'I'm sorry,' he sobbed. 'I'm sorry, Mary, sorry ... sorry ...'

'Sssh.' Accustomed to incomprehensible outbursts of woe, the young woman squeezed his hand, the other going to her nose and mouth at the smell of decomposition. The gas gangrene case was below him. 'Try and sleep. We'll soon be there.'

During that autumn, John, the oldest son of the Bullivants, had come home to Oughton Place after months in hospital. Olive saw him arrive. She was coming up the road with a bag of shopping when the ambulance pulled up and saw them bringing a wheelchair out of the back. The rest she watched from inside, standing a little back from the window, the handles of the bag still cutting into her hand.

Mrs Bullivant stood in the road holding a bundle of clothes in one arm while the other made nervous gestures as if in an attempt to help, but there was nothing she could do. They lifted him out and placed him in the chair. No legs, or at least, two bits of legs which ended mid-thigh and stuck out a little bit over the seat. His trousers were folded up at the bottom and pinned. As they put him down he cried out, and Olive saw the bones of his skull move under his skin. Her hand went to her mouth. Almost more shocking than the legs was the sight of John Bullivant's face which had once been solid, almost bullish, with a thick, black moustache, and was now clean-shaven, cadaverous and twisted with pain.

There was a low step up into the house, and they had to manoeuvre the chair up over it while John clung, obviously petrified, to the arms. They disappeared inside.

Olive went through unsteadily to the back, put her bag down and reached for the kettle, overcome by the pity of it. She found her lips were moving, praying for her own, for Bert, for Sis's Perce, for Ned ... Her bitterness towards him seemed petty, horrible, when his wrongdoing was set against the disfigurement she had just seen. Her heart ached for Mrs Bullivant. Two sons dead, one maimed, how much more was there for her to bear?

It was quiet for the first few days after John arrived home. Mrs Bullivant told Olive he was starting to get used to things at home. Her face was strained and she looked exhausted.

'Mr B's not finding it easy seeing 'im like this, yer know,' she confided. 'John used to be such a big strapping lad.'

'Look, Marion,' Olive said, drawn to her neighbour by her staunchness. 'I'm always 'ere. Anything yer need 'elp with. You know that. I mean if yer wanted to get him out for a bit of air and that – when yer ready. You'd need help shifting the chair out, wouldn't yer?'

'That's good of yer,' Mrs Bullivant said resignedly. 'It's nice to have a good neighbour and I'll let you know when 'e's ready. But 'e's dead set against anyone seeing 'im.'

Not long after, when they were all home having tea, they heard shouting from next door. Polly paused, a spoon halfway to Grace's mouth.

''Ark at that – is that . . .?'

'Well, 'e sounds back to normal any'ow,' Sis remarked. John Bullivant always had been a mouthy so-and-so before the war.

'No,' Jess said. 'Listen.'

It was a man's voice all right, but the way it was raised, the rage and anguish registered in it was that of a small child or a lost soul. None of the words was comprehensible, but the emotion was. Jess had not seen John since he was home, but the sound of his distress, the softer sounds of his mother trying to comfort and quiet him brought tears of pity to her eyes.

'Poor, poor man.'

''E's twenty-four,' was all Olive said.

As the days passed, there were more outbursts next door. Olive thought about how Bert had been when he had left: strong, upstanding, full of physical confidence. So far as she knew he was still full of life, although having suffered bouts of fever. He wrote her short letters full of wry details about Mesopotamia which he summed up as 'flies, beggars and s—t'. The thought of him coming home in the same state as John Bullivant was almost beyond imagining. But then she thought of Mrs Bullivant's other sons. At least John had come home.

She took courage one morning when she knew the younger children would be at school, and went next door and knocked. The step was newly scrubbed and Mrs Bullivant came out calmly to her, but didn't invite her in.

'I wondered if John'd like visiting,' Olive ventured to say. 'You know – stuck in there all the time. Would 'e like a bit of young company? The girls'd sit and chat with him for a bit if 'e'd like?'

Mrs Bullivant began to wring her hands in an agitated way.

'It's nice of yer, Mrs Beeston, but I don't think . . . I mean, I don't think 'e's up to it. 'E's still in a bit of a state, and . . .' Her emotion flooded to the surface, and she was fighting back tears as she spoke. 'I really don't know what I'm going to do with him!'

Trying awkwardly to offer comfort, Olive said,

'Yer going through a bad time, I can see. It's terrible for yer. But 'e'll get adjusted to it by and by, won't 'e? Things'll get better.'

'They will, will they?' Marion Bullivant's eyes blazed with sudden, bitter fury. 'How? You tell me that!'

Thirty-One

Jess was growing more and more worried and despairing. She hadn't heard from Ned for three weeks.

She went over to Iris's every other day now, each time full of hope, only to be greeted by Iris sorrowfully shaking her head. The third Sunday in October, a lowering grey afternoon, she hurried over there, sodden leaves underfoot and a bitter wind in her face, in such suspense that she could barely contain herself as she ran alongside the Workhouse wall, past the factories and into Crabtree Road. There had to be a letter from him this time! Perhaps he'd been too busy. The news was full of the fighting at Ypres. If that was where he was he most probably hadn't had the chance ... But then if that was where he was ... Never had there been a gap in their communication this long before. He had to have written by now – had to!

Iris was expecting her, and the door opened almost straight away to let her in. Jess didn't need to speak.

'I'm so sorry, my dear. Still nothing.' Iris looked upset.

'Oh Iris, I can't bear it!'

They went through to the back room where a meagre fire was burning. The coal shortages had become acute and now the cold weather was drawing in it was increasingly hard to get hold of any. Iris, being Iris, dealt with the shortages imposed by the war with equanimity. Her life had long been one of privation. She stood watching Jess with her arms folded.

'I know there's summat wrong!' Jess paced the floor, wringing her hands. She found it impossible to keep still these days, her body full of restless agitation. 'Anything could've happened.'

'Not the worst, necessarily, remember,' Iris reminded her.

'But it could be, Iris. Oh it's so horrible – never knowing, not being able to *do* anything!' Her anxiety and frustration, which she tried to keep in check at home, poured out now.

'In any case, if anything's happened to 'im, I'm going to be the last one to know. They'd send word to his mom and dad, or Mary, but they're never going to tell me. So far as they're concerned I don't even exist.'

She sank into a chair, looking woefully up at Iris, arms wrapped tightly round herself as if to contain her emotion. 'I'm sorry, Iris – my troubles always seem to land on you one way or another.'

'His family really should be the ones to be told in the first place if anything's happened,' Iris pointed out. 'It's only natural.'

'I know. But how am I ever going to find out if I don't hear it from Ned?'

'Well . . .' Iris hesitated. 'I suppose if the worst comes to the worst . . . and God forbid,' she added. 'You'll have to go and ask them.'

'But I can't – they'll never speak to me! They think I'm the *devil* – or worse!'

*

The next day, Jess bought an evening paper as she had all the week before, and scanned frantically through the columns of names.

Sis peered over her shoulder as they walked home, just as anxious not to see Percy's name among the casualties.

'Nothing there,' she said.

Jess closed the *Mail* and tucked it under her arm. 'But I could've missed it. It could've been in earlier.'

The days were torture. Fear and dread seemed to swell inside her like a physical sensation and she found it difficult to get any food down her. Her emotions ran out of control: at home, snapping at everyone, bursting into tears and running upstairs to hide her emotion, and at work she was a bag of nerves, jumping at any sound. While before she was glad of her solitary job so that she could think her own thoughts, now she wished she could be in the filling sheds again among the chatter of the other women to help keep her mind off it. Apart from the breaks, the only people she saw from one end of the day to the other were the two girls next door when she took batches of detonators through for varnishing, and Peter Stevenson when he popped in to check on things, which he seemed to do more often nowadays. She was glad of the interruption. She found his strong, kind presence soothing, and was always aware that while she felt sorrow and dread, he was also grieving and had plenty of problems of his own.

By the time another few days had passed with no news, Jess's nerves were ragged to a point where she was beyond fear of any reaction from other people. Whatever it took, she had to find out if something had happened to Ned.

'I can't live like this,' she said to Polly. They were sitting on Jess's bed, Grace lying kicking behind them. 'It's like Mr Stevenson said to me – not being sure's almost worse than knowing . . .'

Polly looked round at her. Jess's usually rosy cheeks were white and drawn with tension, her eyes dull from exhaustion and lack of sleep. Pitying her, Polly put her arms round her shoulders.

'How much longer's it all going to go on for?' she sighed. 'There's hardly anyone yer meet not grieving, or in a state. I mean, look at 'im—' She jerked her head towards the wall which they shared with the Bullivants. 'I hear 'im nights, sometimes. Crying. Sobbing like a child. Must be the pain. They say it's worse at night.'

Jess shook her head. 'Poor bloke. Auntie says 'e's not been out since 'e come home.'

'I'd go and call . . .' Polly said hesitantly. 'Only his mom said he don't want anyone round.'

'Maybe you should. Leave it a bit though. See if 'e settles in.' Jess wiped her face, sniffing exhaustedly.

'What is there you can do?' Polly asked.

Jess bit her lip, staring at the floor, then roused herself and stood up with sudden purpose. 'I'm going to his mom and dad's. They may hate my guts, but the least they can do is tell me what's happened.'

'What – now? But we haven't had tea!'

'It'll keep. If I don't go straight away I'll lose my nerve.'

Riding the tram out along the Bristol Road, Jess felt calm, resolved. Courage in the face of the hangman, she thought. After all, Ned's mom and dad were only people. What could they do except shout and curse at her? She thought she could manage loathing: her childhood had given her practice at that. And she knew it was no worse than the fear and worry she was living with now.

But climbing down from the tram in the tranquil suburb of Selly Oak, with its genteel High Street, she immediately felt out of place and very frightened. She hadn't even changed out of her work clothes! What a mess she must look. She wanted to get back on another tram straight away and go home. But she just couldn't go back to waiting, dreading, still with no idea where Ned was.

Ned had told her his family lived in Oak Tree Lane, but she didn't know the number. A lady was coming towards her as she turned into the road and passed the Oak Inn. Jess quickly tucked some loose ends of hair under her hat.

'Excuse me – do you live along 'ere?'

'Yes,' she replied pleasantly, and Jess was momentarily reassured. When she asked for the Green family the woman laughed and said,

'It's yer lucky day – I live a few doors up from 'em.' She pointed. 'On the left there – the blue door.'

Once she'd knocked, Jess felt as if her chest had caved in, she was finding it so difficult to breathe. As Mrs Green came round the door she took in a great gulp of air.

She found herself observed, scrutinized in fact, by Ned's mother. She was a little taller than Jess, a gently rounded woman dressed in a soft, brown wool frock with a cream collar and brown leather shoes. Her hair was thick and fastened back into a soft, dignified pleat.

Jess could see immediately where Ned had inherited his clear blue eyes from. Her face had a natural gentleness, and in the seconds that they looked at each other, Jess felt a pang of great sorrow. If she had married Ned, if this woman was her mother-in-law, she sensed instinctively that she would have felt great fondness for her.

'And who are you?' Mrs Green's tone was polite, but already held suspicion, as if she guessed or was beginning to.

Jess saw herself through Mrs Green's eyes: young, unkempt, a stranger on her step, but not one who was nothing to her. She was much more than nothing: she was an object of loathing. She opened her mouth to say her name, finding it as hard as coughing up a chicken bone.

'I'm Jessica Hart – please . . .' Seeing the hostility provoked by the mention of her name she reached out to put her hand on the door so Mrs Green couldn't shut it on her. 'I know what you must feel about me, but just tell me where 'e is and how 'e is! I ain't heard a thing from him for weeks and I've been nearly out of my mind worrying. Just tell me 'e's alive, Mrs Green, I beg yer . . .'

The woman folded her arms tightly across her chest and stood back.

'Step inside. I don't want the whole neighbourhood watching.'

Jess walked into the narrow hall. It was covered with brown linoleum and there was a nice, homely smell of cooking, apples and onions mixed.

'He's alive,' Mrs Green said, hoarsely.

'Oh thank God!' Jess put her hands over her face and sobbed, unable to stop herself. For a few moments there was no sound but that of her weeping. Mrs Green watched her.

'Do you have any idea,' she started speaking quietly, but her voice rose until it was shrill with emotion. 'Of the trouble and pain you've caused? To all of us? His family, his wife and child?'

Jess took her hands from her face and looked into Mrs Green's eyes, unable to reply. Whatever answer she gave would be offensive, and the truth, the most honest answer of all was no. No she didn't know. Hadn't wanted to know because she'd believed she loved Ned with all her heart and that had been all that mattered. Guilt, consideration of the consequences to others had been there, had lain constantly between them, but nothing, not even those things had been enough to quell the power of attraction, the passion she felt for him which dictated that they had to be together whatever else.

Mrs Green took a step towards her and Jess cowered.

'My son was married – happily – to a girl he's known most of his life. They made their vows in church. He had a child, a good job. He'd never thought of anything else. Why should he? What more could a mother ask for her son? And then *you* came along. Have yer thought for one second what it's been like for his wife, for Mary, to be deserted with a child to bring up? Have yer?'

Jess hung her head, unable to meet the woman's eyes. 'Yes,' she whispered. 'I have, course I have, but . . .'

'But what?'

There were more footsteps from the back of the house and a man appeared who Jess saw was Ned's father.

'What's all this?'

Mrs Green gestured towards Jess. 'This is – the girl. The one – Jessica. Look, you deal with it. I can't . . .' Hands over her face she went into the front room and Jess heard her weeping.

Faced with Mr Green, Jess could feel the fury emanating from him. He was quite a tall man, though perhaps an inch or two short of his son in height, his hair still mostly brown, though greying round the temples. Jess saw Ned's chiselled features, the generous mouth.

'So you're the one.'

'I know what you think of me. I just want to know he's all right. I hadn't heard . . .'

Mr Green was by nature a mild, gentle man, qualities Ned had inherited from him. But he was outraged at what had happened to his son's marriage. Mary had been a sweet girl as a child and the two had been friends for such a time. The arrangement had felt safe and right. Everything had been well sorted out until Ned went off the rails like a weak fool. How could he admit what had happened, his son running off with some factory bint, deserting his new family and asking for a divorce? As well as this reservoir of anger and disappointment, his emotions were twisted further by the sight of this pretty, distraught girl in front of him. For a second, before he repressed the feeling, he understood his son's desire, his wish for this lovely girl who was crying so passionately for him and he found himself speaking more harshly to her than he ever had to anyone in his life before.

'How can you dare even set foot in my house?' He paced the floor in front of her, trying to steady himself. He fished around in his pocket for his pipe and took

refuge in lighting it. 'After what you've done. You're a
. . . a bloody disgrace!'

Jess almost had the impulse to go down on her knees.
'All I wanted was to know if 'e's alive. I didn't
know . . .'

'Well of *course* you didn't know, yer stupid girl.
You're not family. You're nothing to us!'

'*Please.*' She wrung her hands.

Mr Green held a match in the bowl of his pipe,
puffing at it to get it lit up. The sweet smell of tobacco
curled round the hall.

'He's wounded.' Ned's father spoke as if against his
own will, without looking at her. 'Smashed up thigh – a
shell caught him.'

Jess's hands clawed at the air. More, tell me more.

'I'll tell yer, and then you're to go for good. D'you
understand? And I mean for good.'

She nodded. Anything. Just tell me.

'He's home – in hospital, at least. Things haven't
gone any too smoothly – infection set in. It was touch
and go at one point. He's coming out of it now but for
a time he didn't know us. His mother's been worried to
death. They think it'll be a good few months in hospital
– then home, and who knows. It may all be over by
then.'

Jess was listening with absolute attention, quite still
now.

'He's going to be all right?'

'Depends on how the leg heals. There may be a limp.
But he's going to live, yes.'

'Thank God,' she gasped. 'I thought . . . oh . . .' She
was weeping again, quietly. 'Thank you,' she said softly,
then looked up. 'Where is he?'

He jabbed the pipe at her. 'He doesn't need disturbing – what 'e needs is rest and settling back down with his family where he belongs!' Mr Green looked down into the bowl of his pipe, evading her eyes. 'I'm not going to tell you where he is. His wife's going – that's all he needs. You're to keep away. Ned's married. He and Mary can ... well, this is a chance for them. Patch things up and put the mistakes behind them. He's finished with you. Is that clear?'

He looked across at her with a terrible sternness that made Jess shrink inside.

'I've told you what you want to know. Now, if you've any real consideration for him, for all of us, you'll keep away. You've done enough harm to us all already.' His voice became ever sharper. 'Keep away – you're not wanted. By anyone!'

Thirty-Two

That same night, Peter Stevenson sat staring into the grate in his back sitting room. He had drawn the chair in close to catch the last of the heat from a smouldering log and was hunched forwards, elbows resting on his knees in a sad, sagging posture similar to that in which Jess had once come upon him in his office. Mrs Hughes had long since put David to bed and the house was quiet except for the fire still hissing quietly and the clock on the mantelpiece with its slow, mellow ticking. Either side of it were arranged framed photographs: a small, oval, silver frame held a picture of David as a baby, and the other, a rectangular frame wrought in silver-plated filigree, was a portrait of Sylvia. She had had a soft, reassuring beauty, long fair hair brushed back and fastened elegantly for the photograph. Every so often his gaze moved up to take in that picture. Even now, so many months after her death, he had to stop himself expecting to see her seated opposite him on the chair by the fire, legs comfortably crossed, with sewing or knitting for David in her lap. When he looked at the photograph the day it was taken always came to mind, how she couldn't stop laughing: for some reason the sight of the photographer disappearing under the black hood of the camera tickled her, seeming absurd in some way, and they had to make several attempts. Even in the finished portrait her face had a look of repressed mirth.

Peter Stevenson put his hands over his face and rubbed his eyes. At last he sat back in the chair, crossing one long leg over the other. The eyes of the picture seemed to watch him relentlessly, as if she were seeing into his thoughts, and with a sudden movement he stood up and picked up the frame.

'You know I loved you, Sylvia, don't you? Always . . . I wish I still had you here, God knows I do. There's nothing I wish for more.' For a moment he held the picture over his heart, smoothing the back of it with his hand, then replaced it, turning it away from him towards the wall. He went to the glass door which looked out over the bleak little garden, but in the dark, could see only his own, long reflection, and he pressed his forehead against the window, shocked for a second by the coldness of it.

He had expected grief to go on, undiluted, forever. The extent of his anguish when Sylvia first fell ill, then lay dying and was finally taken from him, leaving him with a motherless child, was so acute that he could not then imagine life without the agony of it inside him. The early mornings were the worst, waking alone, and these silent evenings. Sylvia had liked music, would sing to herself, and the house had felt full of life. The pain of losing her had been his one certainty. It was still present, waves of loss and bereftness building and receding within him. But already he found that other feelings could exist mingled with grief: he could begin to move on without her, and this made him feel guilty and ashamed of his disloyalty. Chiefly these emotions were directed towards Jess Hart. At first he simply noticed her, the way some people in a group stand out while others fade. Her presence drew his eye, her prettiness, her shape. And he liked her, enjoyed the way their brief conversations seemed to fit with each other's, her smile which had become, along with seeing David, the main thing which could brighten the day. She could make him laugh. More lately, she had aroused his tenderness, finally his desire.

He found himself looking for opportunities to talk with her. He wondered now at his decision to put her in the 'Rumbling Shed' as the women called it. At the time it had been nothing whatever to do with being able to see her alone. But had some deeper instinct, riding ahead of his knowledge of his own feelings, prodded him to do it? Whatever the case he was thankful daily that he had placed her there, and found himself looking for excuses to visit the shed.

'Is there bad news?' he had asked her again, cautiously, earlier in the week.

It was clear to everyone that Jess was in a state. Of course, so were a lot of people, but it was her that he particularly noticed. Her expression was tense and she looked pale and drained. He knew there was something – someone – for whom she worried and suffered constantly, yet she would say nothing about him except that he was on the Western Front. He wanted to know who it was that took up her thoughts and feelings, but why should she tell him anything about her private life? He was only her boss, and he must seem like an old man to her!

But when he asked, she turned to him with such a look of desperation in her eyes that he wanted to take her in his arms.

'No – no news at all. That's the thing – I just don't know.' Her eyes, already pink from crying, filled with tears.

'Oh dear,' he said. 'I'm ever so sorry.' He wanted to

add some platitude about no news being good news but it felt the wrong thing to say. 'I hope you have some good news soon.' The words sounded hollow. He turned to leave.

'Mr Stevenson?' She was hurriedly wiping her eyes. 'Is there anything the matter with my work?'

'No!' He sounded too emphatic and corrected himself. 'No – not a bit. Why?'

'I just wondered if you was feeling you had to check up on me.'

He cleared his throat, finding himself reddening a little.

'Not at all, Jess. You've been doing that job more than satisfactorily for a long time now. I – er, just like to keep tabs on things . . .' He knew he was not bound to explain but found himself doing so anyway.

'Oh,' Jess gave him a wan smile which simply jerked at her mouth and didn't alter the rest of her face. 'That's awright then.'

She turned back to the drum, already oblivious to him. He watched her, the sturdy determination of her movements. Finding he had been standing there too long, he hastily moved away.

Staring into the fire he went over what had happened. Had he made a fool of himself? She wouldn't have noticed, he told himself. She was so worried she barely even saw him. But all evening he was full of longing thoughts of her.

Jess walked through the gates of the infirmary, the blackened brick building on the Dudley Road next to the Workhouse and near Iris's house.

She still had a sense of disbelief that she had found

310

out so quickly where Ned was. When she left his parents' house her emotions were in such turmoil that no single one seemed able to master the others. She had expected the anger and bitterness they felt, but she was taken aback by how much this bruised her, made her feel worthless and rejected.

What did you expect? she ranted at herself on the way home. Considering what you've done they could've been a lot worse! But still she felt winded by it, and tearful. However wrong she and Ned had been in what they'd done, however much they had hurt and betrayed Mary, she had wanted them at least to understand the strength of her feelings for Ned and his for her. That her love was enduring and genuine. But while this seemed so important to her, in their eyes it counted for nothing.

But with the pain of this, there was also her enormous relief after the tension of the last few weeks, and she was full of joy.

She burst in through the door at home, her face alight with the news.

'Ned's alive – 'e's awright! 'E's home!'

Everyone stopped what they were doing immediately.

'Oh Jess!' Sis said. 'Thank God for that!'

Polly smiled bravely at her and Jess saw Olive's face relax. Though she seldom ever mentioned Ned, the war's months of slaughter had softened her attitude. Life was too short to bear grudges. Just getting those lads back alive, that was all that mattered.

'So 'e's out of it?' she asked.

'Yes!' Jess was dancing round the room. 'He's been wounded – one of his legs, they said. He's in hospital.'

'Who said?' Olive frowned.

'Mr and Mrs Green.'

'*You went to their 'ouse?*'

Jess's face fell. 'I had to find out, Auntie.'

Olive sank down at the table. 'Well, what did they make of you turning up?'

'They were none too pleased.'

'I'm not surprised! Oh Jess, how could yer've done it?'

'I couldn't stand it. No one'd ever've told me, would they?'

'So where is he then?' Polly said, eyeing Grace, who was walking now, round the room.

Jess shrugged. 'I don't know. Yet.'

At first she almost despaired, realizing the number of hospitals in Birmingham, and especially the additional mansions and private houses which had been converted for nursing the war wounded. She'd have to go round every one and ask. She might never find him!

But luck, in this instance, was on her side. The next evening she went to tell Iris the news. When she described her visit to the Greens, Iris seemed to withdraw from her a little, as if the reality of Ned's situation, of his parents as live flesh and blood people, had impinged on her properly for the first time.

'You must be careful,' she cautioned. Her injured leg was troubling her and she leaned down, massaging it as she spoke. 'You've upset people badly, the two of you, and you must think seriously of what you're going to do next.'

Jess was in no mood for a sermon from Iris.

'But you've always stood by us, up 'til now.'

'I know, dear. I am standing by you, but the facts don't alter. Happiness should never be at other people's expense.'

Jess moved restlessly about the room.

'It's a bit late for that, Iris. Look, I've got to see 'im. I can't think of anything else until I've seen how he is, what he feels. Can't you understand that?'

'Yes. And I know what you've suffered on his behalf . . .' Iris sighed. 'But it's all looking rather a mess.'

'I don't even know where to start – he could be anywhere.'

'Well,' Iris said simply. 'Why not try the nearest? It's a big hospital. There's a good chance he could be there.'

Before going home Jess went into the hospital to enquire and was told that a Corporal Edward Green of Oak Tree Lane, Selly Oak, was indeed in the hospital. Visiting, she was told, was for close relatives only.

'That's awright,' Jess smiled. 'I'm 'is sister.'

So now she stood looking at the brightly lit windows of the infirmary, wondering which of the high rooms contained him. A thrill passed through her. He was here, so close after all this time! She could see him, touch him! She knew there would be very little time, and was terrified of meeting a member of his family, but her determination was absolute. If she had to come every day, waiting for a chance to slip in and see him alone, she would do it. Nothing was going to stop her.

She pulled the belt tighter round her coat. She had on her close-fitting hat with the cream band, and under the coat a purple velvet skirt which she had made, with a white blouse and a little blue waistcoat. She knew she was looking her best, her hair brushed and tied back.

As soon as she was inside the hospital, her excitement faded and was replaced by terror. Her heart was pounding, hands horribly clammy. In these long, echoing corridors there was very little place to hide and she expected any moment to find Mr and Mrs Green walking towards her. But she had to see him . . .

Ned's ward was upstairs. Every bend of the staircase, with people moving up and down, was a source of fear for her. She felt like a criminal about to be arrested at any second. By the time she'd reached the door of the ward she thought her heart was going to give out on her.

The door was open and she stepped in. A nurse near the door seemed to be in position to direct visitors.

'I've come to see Mr Green.' Jess found that she could sound calm. 'Ned Green. I'm his sister.'

The nurse looked confused for a moment. 'Oh – er, I see.'

'Is there anyone here – my mother and father may have beaten me to it?'

'No one's come in yet.' She leaned back and looked along the ward. 'He's alone. He is very tired today though. Still very up and down. Not too long a visit, please.'

'Yes of course,' Jess said. 'I'll just pop over and say 'ello.'

Her heels sounded to her like hammers as she walked along the long Nightingale ward, wishing she was invisible. Some of the lads were sitting up talking quite cheerfully to their visitors. One or two lay quiet, some with one or both arms bandaged. One, who smiled at her, had lost most of his right arm, and was nursing a short, bandaged stump. She found this less shocking than she would have expected, and realized that knowing Iris had accustomed her to such sights. She smiled back as she passed. On some beds there was a frame under the bedclothes holding their weight off the injured legs beneath like a tent, and there was one on Ned's bed when she reached it two-thirds of the way down on the right.

He was propped in a reclining position on his pillows, his eyes closed, head tilted a little to one side. Jess stopped. Seeing him was a shock: she didn't know whether he looked different or the same. She was not used to observing him in a lifeless position like this, unaware that she was there. For a moment she did not want to speak, afraid of what he might say when he saw her. But she longed to move closer, to touch him. And there was no time to delay. She glanced behind her, terrified his family might be bearing down on her, then moved quietly to sit beside him.

'Ned.'

He opened his eyes at once, and she saw his face register who she was. 'Jess . . .' Immediately he tried to push himself up, wincing at the pain he caused himself. To her horror, she saw his eyes fill with tears and his face, at first startled, crease with anguish. Supporting himself on one elbow he covered his face with his other hand, trying to hide his distress from her.

'Oh Ned!' She leaned close, putting her hand on his shoulder, tears running down her own face. She would never have believed she'd see him like this. 'What is it? Oh Ned! Look, my love, I can't stop 'ere long – if your mom and dad were to come . . .'

Hearing what she said he managed to control himself, wiped his face and looked up at her almost as if he was afraid of her.

'Does it hurt?'

'My leg?' He lay back, grimacing for a second. 'Sometimes, now. Didn't at all when it happened. Just

315

like a little knock. And all the way back from France. Not a thing. But now – at night mainly. Oh God, Jess . . .'

'I was so frightened . . .' It was she, now, who couldn't stop crying. 'So frightened for you!' She leaned down and kissed him, stroking his hair, his face. 'I love you so much and now you're safe, back with me.'

He looked back into her eyes with a bewildered, hungry look, as if hanging on every word, needing to hear what she said.

'I saw your mom and dad—'

He started to speak, but she held up her hand.

'It's awright. But they mustn't find me here. Are they coming today?'

'I don't know . . .'

'They said you and Mary are going to start again . . . Is it true, Ned?'

She saw panic in his eyes. 'No, Jess. No! They've not said a thing . . .' He grasped her hand, and to her confusion said with strange intensity, 'You're good – a good, good thing. You are.'

'Tell me you love me, Ned. Please. It's been so long . . .' She felt and sounded plaintive.

He began talking fast, a desperate note in his voice. 'I do. I love you. Oh Jess, I just want to get out of here – away from them all. To come out with yer. You're my love, you are. Let's go somewhere where none of them can find us.' He gripped her hand so tightly that she gasped.

'Are you still feverish?' she felt his forehead. It was overhot, but not extremely so. But she knew he wasn't himself, and could see how ill he'd been, this odd excitement in him. He lay limply now, as if he'd exhausted himself. Jess kept her hand on his forehead.

'Never mind, my love. You'll soon be better. It'll be awright, I promise you.'

'You mustn't come in here again, Jess.' She was terribly hurt by the sudden aggression in his voice. He was becoming agitated again.

'But why . . .?'

'I've told yer – yer mustn't – it'll cause trouble. I've hurt them all enough and I can't face it, not stuck lying 'ere like this. Please – stay away. Wait 'til I'm better and then I'll come to you.'

'But what can they do to me?' She felt burningly defiant.

'Nothing – not to you. I just – I'm a coward, Jess. I don't want it going on in here. Fighting, arguments.'

She understood. He was too weak, too low to have conflict going on around him.

'It's ain't just them, it's Mary . . .'

Jess had a sensation like a cold hand closing round her heart.

'Has she been to see yer?'

'Not yet, but she will. They'll make sure she does. Look, just keep out of it for now – please. Don't make it any worse, Jess.'

She swallowed. There was desperation in his plea. 'Whatever you want, Ned. Whatever'll get you better sooner. As long as I know you love me I can put up with anything.'

Ned looked stricken. 'I *know* yer can . . . oh God.' He was sobbing again, clutching at her.

She held him close, kissing him, pressing her cheeks against his, trying to will all her strength into him. 'I can't stay now, Ned – just remember, I love you. You get better – that's your job. I'll be waiting, however long it takes yer. I promise.'

She felt him nod as she kissed him goodbye.

Jess left the hospital with the image of his face in her mind as she left him, pale, but calmer. When she turned back to look, he had already closed his eyes. She was disturbed by the state of him, one moment calm, the next distraught. What in God's name had they done to him over there? But she was so full of resolve now, that she felt unbreakable. If she couldn't see him for a time now, until he was healed, if that was what he needed, she could bear it. Knowing he was safe, away from the trenches, and that he still loved her, those were the main things. For their own good she would keep away until they could be together. She would wait. She had borne so much for him already that this seemed only a small thing.

Later that week, Olive pointed to a few lines in the paper which said that Lance-Corporal Edward C. Green, had been awarded a Military Medal for courage under fire.

'Oh Auntie!' Jess cried. She burned with pride for him. 'See how brave 'e's been – oh ain't that summat special!'

And she could see that, though she tried to hide it, there was also pride in Olive's eyes.

Thirty-Three

December 1917

'When're things ever going to get better?' Sis groaned, eyeing the evening meal Olive was dishing up, which consisted of a thin broth with a few bits of vegetables in stock made from boiled up chicken bones and a bit of bread and cheese. 'We'll be starving hungry again an hour after tea!'

'I was in the line for some stewing beef today,' Olive ladled out the broth, glowering round the table in a way that dared anyone else to complain. 'Stood there over an hour I was, and then they shut up shop and said it'd all gone – and that was with *her* mithering at me the whole flaming time.' She nodded at Grace. 'Half the morning gone, nothing done back 'ere, and it'll all be the same tomorrow. 'Ere – save some of it to go with yer broth!' She rapped Ronny's hand gently with the ladle as he went to cram his share of bread into his mouth.

'Ow, Mom!'

'Eat slower – it'll last yer longer.'

It was a couple of days before Christmas and everyone round the table looked sunk in gloom, exhaustion, or both. The fighting on the Western Front had ground to a halt for the winter months. Everything felt as if it was everlastingly stuck: the grim news, the grief and worry, the sheer drudgery of war seemed set to go on and on.

This evening was pitch black and wet. Jess and Sis had been soaked through by lashing, ice-cold rain as they came home from work, and even after they changed into dry clothes, sat shivering for ages before they felt warm again because there was barely enough fuel to keep a fire going. Now Grace was toddling, Mrs Bullivant had her pram back and it had found a new role as a coal cart for both families so they could at least get some warmth in the house.

But day-to-day living had become even more tiring and gruelling than usual. And everyone had the worry of a loved one on their mind: Sis was fretting about Perce, Olive and the girls worried for Bert, Polly was still grieving and Jess waiting for Ned to be released from hospital, on tenterhooks, longing to know how he was and what was happening. Through an old acquaintance of both Olive and the Greens, Olive had heard that he had been moved out of Dudley Road to a convalescent home in Bromsgrove, which would have been difficult for Jess to get to even had she been allowed. But she was tormented by the thought of Mary being able to see him. It was terrible to be banished, pushed into the background, a dirty secret in a corner of Ned's life. Almost daily she was tempted to go against what he had asked of her, and try to travel over and see him. She didn't even know the address to write to and she had not heard from him. She understood that while he was convalescent and needing help, he was at the mercy of his family, but his weakness frustrated her when she felt so strong. She was caught between jealousy and worry and shame that she was being so selfish when he had fought and suffered. He needed his leg to mend, she told herself, to get his strength back. Then they would face everyone and fight them together. The two of them could overcome anything. And every day she was thankful that he was at least home, alive and safe.

The rain was still pelting down. Jess looked at the clock. Normally Polly would be on her way out by now. It was her night for going to Mrs Black's.

'Not going out tonight, Poll?' Jess asked, wiping the bread round her dish.

'No—' Polly had Grace on her lap and was dipping little bits of bread in her broth, feeding them to Grace on a teaspoon while trying to feed herself and keep her daughter's inquisitive hands from tipping the bowl over. 'One soaking's enough. Hark at it out there! I'll leave it for this week.'

She still clung to her messages from Ernie as one of the few things that kept her going. Jess once asked her whether it might be a good idea to stop, try and put his death behind her for good.

'I can't, Jess,' she said. 'Not yet. It's too much for me on my own. I need him to help me – I know that sounds like nonsense to you, but it's true. It'd be different if we could bring his body home – have a proper burial and a funeral and that. But being out there – I know 'e's gone really, in my heart. But it ain't finished. There's too many of 'em all just to go like that, for good.'

Jess half understood Polly's need, although she'd never gone back to the Blacks' spiritualist sessions with her. The experience of going once had been unsettling enough. Most of it was a trick, she was sure: so obvious to anyone who didn't desperately want to believe it wasn't.

'It gives them comfort,' she told Olive. 'You can feel it. Everyone's so sad, and it makes 'em feel better.

I think it's harmless enough.' But what about what happened when she'd asked to hear from Alice? What if that had been real? It had certainly seemed convincing at the time. She hadn't mentioned the incident to Olive.

Sometimes, usually in the dark of the night, she found herself wondering about Alice, fancying a plea, a cry coming from her, something unfinished that it was her responsibility to act upon.

That's just daft, she'd say to herself when daylight came. Getting the heeby-jeebies in the night! But she knew instinctively that she wanted to know more, as if her grandmother's fate was a key to something in herself. She found nowadays that she could ask Olive more about the family. A dam had been breached and she would try to remember details about Alice, about Louisa. Jess was hungry for the information, was beginning to understand more fully her aunt's contradictory feelings towards her sister: the great protective love for a younger sister, mixed with enormous bitterness and resentment that Louisa had been absent through so much of the grief and trouble they'd endured, that in marrying first, she had escaped it again. Jess was watching her aunt, thinking about these things, when Polly looked up, her chin close to the top of Grace's tufty head.

'I thought I might pop in next door again – a bit later on like. When the younger ones've gone up.'

Olive paused, spoon halfway to her lips. She looked concerned. 'Why don't yer leave it for a bit, Poll? Yer said 'e daint take too kindly to yer going last time.' She was worried about Polly's preoccupation with John Bullivant.

'I hear 'im – the way 'e keeps moaning and carrying

322

on. It's terrible, Mom. Heartbreaking. No one should 'ave to suffer the way 'e is. 'E was a big strapping bloke before. And she's at 'er wits' end. I know 'e'll most probably tell me to get out. But how's 'e ever going to have any sort of life again if all 'e does is sit there?'

Polly leaned in close to the Bullivants' front door, trying to shelter from the rain. Mrs Bullivant opened it cautiously, unused to visitors at this time of night, and hurried her quickly into the hall out of the wet. She held a lamp in one hand and they stood in its arc of light.

'Anything the matter?' She sounded tense, had guessed why Polly had come. Polly's hands had gone clammy. He's only a man, she told herself. An injured man, that's all. What was there to be so nervous about? But she was frightened: at the same time she felt compelled to be here.

'I just thought I'd pop in and say hello to John again. Wondered if 'e'd like a bit of company? I know it's late, only I'm at work again now.'

'Well, I don't know...' Marion Bullivant kept her voice low. ''E's not been too good today.' She worried at her lower lip with her teeth. Polly's heart went out to her.

'I'm ever so sorry.'

'Oh, you've got yer own troubles, Polly. I know that. Look, come in, but I don't know what sort of welcome you'll get.'

Through the back, Mr Bullivant, a dark, stocky man, was asleep in a chair beside the same sort of puny fire that burned in their grate next door. The room was cold, although it had a cosy atmosphere, plates and cups tidy on shelves and the range and little ornaments on the mantelpiece. Close to Mr Bullivant sat Lottie, who was twelve, fiddling with a tangled skein of wool. She looked up at Polly and smiled, but also glanced anxiously across at her brother.

'Awright, Lottie?' Polly greeted her. ''Ello, John.'

There was no reply from John Bullivant, seated in his wheelchair which was pushed up close to the table. The way he was sitting you couldn't see his injury. He just looked like a man reading the paper, elbows on the table, hands making a frame round his face. For a second Polly imagined him getting up, walking across the room, like before.

She pulled up a chair to sit down by him. As she did so she saw him wince as if she had hurt him, or he was afraid she would.

'For Christ's sake watch it!' He bellowed so loudly that Polly jumped. Mr Bullivant stirred, opening his eyes. John's face was contorted with rage and pain.

'I'm sorry,' Polly stood gripping the back of the chair. 'What did I do? Did I hurt yer?'

She knew she hadn't touched him. It was as if pain surrounded him like a magnetic field.

'What do you want?' he said, more quietly, but with such contempt that Polly cringed.

'John—' his father warned.

'I just came to see yer. Thought you might like a bit of company.'

'Come to have another look at the cripple, 'ave yer?' he propelled himself back from the table. 'There yer go then – 'ave a good look.'

'I didn't come to . . .'

'LOOK, I said!' Again, a loud bawl, which sent his

324

mom and dad into protests that he should stop it and calm down, Polly was trying to be kind.

Polly clung to the back of the chair and did as she was ordered. John sat with his shoulders thrown back in an awkward, helpless posture. Polly thought, you don't see how much the legs do, even sitting down, until they're gone. She looked down, past his strong, barrel chest to the thick stumps, sawn off mid-way between knee and groin. There was nothing repulsive in the sight, barely even shocking. He was covered, dressed. It was unnatural to see, but the full horror of it came when she slowly moved her gaze upwards, over his thin, taut face. He had grown back his moustache, but when their eyes met, she felt herself go cold at the expression in his.

'Now get out.'

'Oh don't, John!' His mother stood over him, her hands squirming round each other. 'Polly's just come out of friendliness – to see if yer'd like a chat.'

'A chat! What in hell's name does she think I've got to chat about? Go on – out. Bugger off out of 'ere!'

'Awright—' Polly shifted towards the door. Her knees had gone weak. 'I'm going . . .'

'I'm sorry,' Mrs Bullivant said in the hall. 'I did warn yer. I just don't know what to do with 'im for the best, that I don't . . .'

'It's awright.' Polly was shaken by the intensity of John Bullivant's self-loathing. 'I s'pose I shouldn't've come.'

'No – I'm sure it's what 'e needs. It's just – well, it's taking a bit longer than we thought . . .' She trailed off, her voice desolate.

'Any news of the others?' Polly asked.

The woman nodded. 'They're awright, for the moment. Look—'

Polly stopped with her hand on the door handle.

''E won't see anyone – pals of his, nothing. Course, most of 'em ain't home anyhow. But the couple that are've given up . . . I hardly dare ask this, but . . .'

'I'll come again,' Polly promised. 'In a while.' She squeezed Marion Bullivant's hand. ''Ave the best Christmas yer can manage, love.'

Thirty-Four

Ned was let out of the convalescent home at the end of February 1918. His leg was healing reasonably well, and the doctor said he should soon be able to progress from walking with a crutch to a stick. Eventually, perhaps barring a very slight limp, he should be back to normal. He didn't say 'fit for duty' but Ned knew that was what he meant.

'You'll be able to come and stop with us, son,' his mother said. She was looking forward to having him there, he could tell. His brother Fred was in France, and she had at least one of her sons where he belonged – at home. She was longing to look after him, fuss round him.

He felt like a stranger in his parents' house, although every inch of it was disconcertingly familiar. He spent the first few days resting, waiting to feel normal, to find himself again. More mobile now, he soon became restless. He couldn't concentrate on anything, and found himself wandering without purpose from room to room, looking at things. There was the table at the back where he had eaten breakfast and tea every day of his childhood. His bedroom – also at the back – overlooked a short strip of garden where his mother grew marigolds and pansies in neat beds, though now she had taken some of them up for vegetables. He saw the same old wooden bedstead, the faded hazelnut brown eiderdown, the little table where he had done his homework with scratches and ink marks and in the top right-hand corner, a hardened patch of glue. His father's chair with the round patch worn thin and oily where his head rested. Things from which he now felt cut off: a past when he had been innocent of both love and war.

'How d'yer feel today?' his mother asked every morning, carrying him up a cup of tea on a little tray. Even the cups and saucers were unnervingly familiar.

'Not too bad,' he'd say. 'Better.'

In truth he felt nothing, or rather could not find the place in himself where feeling should be. But he couldn't say this. It was too strange and difficult to make sense of this state he was in.

In the hospital there had been the other men, the ones who knew the Front, had seen the same sights, the commonplace horror, the things impossible to describe – or perhaps possible if anyone ever asked, which they did not. They avoided the subject as if it was personal and embarrassing. It was too far from them. Back here he was supposed to put it behind him, to forget: he protecting them and they him. Here at home, he reverted to the state of a child, sitting for hours at a time in the back room, watching thin winter sunlight etch the bright, distorted shape of the window on the carpet. His mother brought him food on invalid trays. She would come and sit opposite him with her own dinner balanced on her knee, and he learned, watching her hold her knife and fork, that her knuckles had begun to swell and she told him they ached. She looked much older than when he'd left, her hair steely grey, the white catching the sun from the window. She talked about the neighbours, snippets of amusing or reassuring – never bad – news. In the evening his father came home. Sometimes they went down to the pub together where Ned went through the motions of talking to people, being modest when they called him a hero because of his medal, being cheerful and grateful to be alive. He *was* grateful – of course he was. He was also thankful for their affection but he could barely breathe at home. He knew he had to get away.

The pressure they put on him was gentle at first. It started in the hospital, after the delirious days of fever had passed and he was cooler, weak, but able to talk.

'We thought, in a day or two, Mary could come in and see you,' his mother said.

Ned looked into her face. At that moment he didn't care who came. 'What good will that do?'

'Well – she wants to see you. I don't think they'll let Ruth in here, but all in good time. It'll give you two a chance to have a talk together, won't it?'

'But Mom—'

'She wants to see yer.' In a sterner voice she added, 'She's your wife, Ned. Of course she's going to visit yer.'

He had started to cry.

'There, there.' His mother kept patting his arm. 'Oh dear, never mind, love, never mind. Least said soonest mended.' She interpreted his tears as those of remorse. They had decided to act as if Ned's behaviour before he went away had been a few weeks of madness, an aberration so offensive to their respectable social standards that they could ignore it and treat him as if it had never happened. They wanted their son back from years before: a good lad, biddable, settled.

Jess's visit now seemed like a kind of dream. Her lips on his cheek, her face ... One small crack which had opened in him, letting emotion crowd through. But now that too was distant from him. He couldn't seem to rouse any emotion towards any of them.

Mary came dressed sweetly in a sea-blue skirt gathered at the waist, a white blouse with an Eton collar tucked over her navy coat. She was still painfully thin and obviously very tired. Ned saw how much she was coming to look like her mother.

'Hello, Ned.' She tried, uncertainly, to smile as she sat beside him. He realized as he answered, that she was fighting tears, but she won against them, looking down for a moment, controlling herself.

'How are yer – the leg and that?'

'Oh – coming along, you know. I weren't myself for a while I think.' He tried to move the leg and clenched his teeth at the pain which shot through his thigh. 'But they say it'll be awright.'

There was a long silence, before he remembered to say,

'And how're you?'

'We're getting on awright,' she spoke carefully. Everyone seemed in a conspiracy to spare him any feeling, to pretend everything in life was smooth and quietly contented.

'You wouldn't know Ruth now,' she said. 'She's ever so pretty. Got your eyes. I'd've liked to bring 'er in but they don't want children in 'ere. She'll be four before long.'

Ned nodded. 'Yes. I know.' He licked his dry lips.

'Would yer like to see 'er?' There was a tremor in her voice.

'Yes, awright,' he agreed, dismissively. 'Mary?' He looked into her face.

Mary kept her expression calm. 'What is it?'

'I'm sorry.' He knew he should be sorry, that he *was* sorry. He had the memory of sorrow and knew it was for her. 'What I did ... you and Ruth. It was terrible ...'

Tears welled in her eyes again. 'Yes it was.' She pulled out a handkerchief. 'It bloody was, Ned.' She sat waiting for him to say more.

'I don't know—' he hesitated. 'I don't know what else to say to yer.'

She shook her head, wiping her eyes. 'One minute you was there – Ruth's dad, my 'usband. And the next you'd just gone – with *her* ...'

She was really crying now, unable to control it. 'I wanted you to die,' she said bitterly, through her tears. 'For what you'd done to us. I thought if I couldn't have you then neither would she. How *could* you've done it?' She clasped her handkerchief over her mouth for a second. 'Oh – I said I wouldn't ...'

'It's awright – I deserve it,' he said dully. He watched her, trying to enter into the situation. It must be because I love Jess, he thought. I can't pity Mary as much as I should.

In a short time she stood up. 'I'll come again. Let you know 'ow Ruth's getting on. I'll bring a picture of 'er.'

As she left he turned his head away, exhausted, and closed his eyes. As soon as he did so the ward vanished and he was back there, as ever among the dead, standing completely alone, it seemed, heat hammering down on him. The only sound he was aware of was the roar of thousands of flies moving over the scorched waste of No Man's Land.

Mary walked out to catch a tram on the Dudley Road, back to her mother's house where she had lived with Ruth for the past three years. As Ned's wife she had received her share of his army pay, but it had made no sense to rent two houses next door to each other and she could barely afford it anyway.

When Ned left she had felt disbelief for a long time, then anger and jealousy. If she thought back now to that time, to what she had suffered, she could still get herself worked up into an almost hysterical state of bitter fury. But after three years of bringing up Ruth on her own, yet being also back in the position of child in her mother's house, her emotions now included a shrewdness towards the practicalities of life.

I don't want to spend the rest of my days like this, she thought. I've got the worst of all worlds. I want a house of my own and a husband. She knew that Ned's mom and dad had always been on her side when he left, and when he came home, injured, it was they who told her of it and suggested she should be beside him in his weak state to tell him how his little daughter missed him.

'Take it slowly,' Mrs Green said. ''E's been ever so poorly since 'e's been in hospital. But if you're prepared to make a fresh start with him, now's yer chance. Be gentle with 'im and I reckon you'll soon win him back.'

I was gentle enough, she thought. Gentle as I could be, when I think of some of the things I might've said to him! And I'll be back, so he'll have to get used to me. Seeing him lying there helpless, she knew she could still feel for him, despite the hurt he had inflicted on her. He's still mine – my husband, the only one I'm likely to get now. I want him back and I'm going to see I get him!

Every week throughout the winter, Mary travelled out to visit him in the convalescent home. She brought in photographs of Ruth, with her hair waving round her mischievous little face. He smiled when he saw them, a little uncertainly, but when she said,

'She's a lovely little thing,' Ned agreed, yes she was. She talked lightly to him, getting him used to her being there, herself getting used to him again, told him about what Ruth had been doing, things she'd got up to as a baby, and as an older child, toddling around. She told him news of her mom, the family, as if he was still part of it, and he seemed to listen with interest, pleasure sometimes. She was, she thought, being as saintly and patient as it was possible to be, in the circumstances. She knew Jess had been to see his family, had been told to keep away. So she, Mary, was the one with a chance. He would come to his senses and come back to her.

As the weeks passed though, she began to get impatient. It would take time, she knew, but as 1917 turned into 1918 and she was still visiting Ned in the convalescent home, nothing seemed to change. He smiled when he saw her, listened to her, talked a little about his injury, the ward routine, all little everyday things. But never did he show the emotions she'd hoped for, the remorse, the begging her for forgiveness and asking for her to have him back. And she was afraid to ask, for fear of his reply. She was in fear of him, a little, for all that he was wrong, because he had the power to hurt her so badly. At least though, she thought, he's not turning me away. He's used to me being around.

Soon after he came out of the home and was at his parents' she went to see him. She found him sitting bent over the table in the back sitting room, writing. He looked different. He had been to the barber's and his hair, which had grown in hospital, was now cropped short again. Startled, she realized it was the first time she had seen him fully dressed since his return and suddenly felt intimidated. Before, sitting there in pyjamas, he had been defenceless like a child. She'd stood over him and been able to pity him. Now he was fully a man again: tall, stronger, a soldier, the man who, in spite of his dutiful nature, had felt such overwhelming desire for another woman that he had left her, his wife.

He turned as she came in and she saw him swiftly close the pad of paper he was writing on and arrange a smile for her on his face.

'So – yer out,' she said, stupidly. She felt gawky and awkward, like a young girl asking to be wooed.

'Yes.'

'That's – well – it's good, ain't it?'

His hand was spread on the writing pad as if he was afraid of her looking into it.

'I've brought someone to see yer,' Mary said softly. She stepped out into the hall where Mrs Green was holding Ruth's hand. She was squatting down with her finger pressed to her lips and Ruth was copying her game of being quiet, keeping her presence there a surprise.

Ned's mom led the little girl into the room.

'Now, love – this big man here is *my* little boy – yes, he is! And you won't remember him because he's been

334

away fighting in the war. But this is your Daddy, Ruth.'
Eyes on Ned's face, she led the child over. 'Come and
say hello to Daddy.'

Ruth came over to him, led by Mary, one finger in
her mouth, walking with a child's shy, dragging steps
until she was right up close. She was a leggy child with
wide grey eyes and thick, wavy hair cut level with her
chin. Ned thought of the night she was born, remembered that he had had strong, protective feelings towards
her and Mary and he tried to summon them up in himself now.

He told himself he should smile at her, and commanded the muscles of his face to bend for him. The
smile was achieved and now he knew everyone was
waiting for him to speak. Ruth was standing, wide-eyed,
at his knee.

'Hello, Ruth.' She rocked slightly from side to side,
body half-rotating, feet planted firmly, plucking at the
back of her skirt with the other hand.

She removed the finger and said, ''Ullo.'

Suddenly he could no longer stand the child's stare,
the naked enquiry in her eyes. Unlike the others she
was not careful with him, not in a conspiracy to keep
him calm. She gazed right into him, looking for a father,
wanting to know from him the meaning of 'father'.

Ned put his hands over his face. 'Please. I can't. Take
her away.'

He heard her being taken out of the room, pacifying
promises of cake and 'never minds' and 'Daddy hasn't
been very well – you'll see him another time when he's
better . . .' His hands were trembling. When he moved
them away from his face his fingertips were moist from
the cold perspiration on his forehead.

He pulled his chair close to the table again and with
desperate haste opened the writing pad. With fast, hard
strokes of the pencil he finished the note.

Dear Jess—
    I'm out of hospital and at home. I've got to see
you – please. Can you meet me Sunday p.m. – at
Iris's? No – I'll wait in town, by Nelson's statue,
from 2 p.m. Please come – please.
    Ned

Before they could come out of the kitchen he limped
quickly to the hall, pushing the note into an envelope.
The door slammed behind him.

'I'm ever so sorry, Mary,' Mrs Green was distressed at
the scene she'd just witnessed. She stroked Ruth's hair
as the child sipped a cup of milk. ''E's just not 'imself.
I thought 'e'd be over it by now.'

Mary dried her tears. 'I dunno what 'appened to 'im
over there,' she said. ''E's like a different person. But
I've waited this long, Mrs Green. I want him back and I
know he can be a good father to Ruth – like the Ned
I used to know. I'll stand by 'im. After all *she* soon
vanished out of sight as soon as there was any trouble,
daint she? 'E's got no one else now – 'e's got to come
back to me.'

Thirty-Five

That Friday, Peter Stevenson woke to hear a bird singing outside his window. There were only a few days of February left and that morning felt light and springlike. Sunshine came strained through the thick weave of the curtains. It was early and the house was quiet, David not yet awake. He closed his eyes again, still half inside a dream, a pleasing one, though he couldn't remember it now, its images flickering elusively in his head. He turned on his side and out of old habit stretched out his arm to the left to embrace Sylvia, hard with desire for her. The cold of the empty bed shocked his hand. Sleep tricked him so often. Waking alone, no warm female body beside him, still gave him moments as raw and terrible as in the early days after her death. He brought his outstretched hand up and laid it over his eyes, letting out a low groan.

By the time he had eaten breakfast and Mrs Hughes was there, bustling round David, insisting he ate all his boiled egg because her chicken had laid it especially for him, Peter felt better. Light was pouring in dust-laden bars through the window and his early morning phantoms receded. But there was still the thought of Sunday, long and empty before him. Often he and David went to see his mother, but today, somehow he couldn't stand the thought. He longed for other company, something difficult to achieve for a rather reserved man so busy working long hours, and with a young son to care for. But today the need of it was on him like an itch.

'Tell you what, Davey—' He was excited suddenly. 'How would you like to see Ronny again? D'you remember – the little lad you played with on the picnic, in the stream?'

David smiled slowly, and nodded.

'I'll see if he'd like to come out with us on Sunday – how about that? Just for a play in the park. That'd be a change, wouldn't it?'

Cycling to work, the idea grew in him. He could ask all of them if necessary – Sis, Polly, Grace. So long as Jess could come. He'd be grateful for the others being there. He knew she was spoken for, and nowadays he felt nervous in her company, afraid his own feelings towards her were obvious, that he would make a fool of himself. He hoped the difference in their age would stop anyone suspecting how he felt. She could bring a whole crowd if she liked – so long as she was there and he could see her and be near to her. He found himself whistling as he came closer to the works. She'd be on her way too – he was moved by the thought of Jess and himself travelling towards the same spot.

'Silly fool,' he said to himself, wheeling his cycle round to its spot by the wall. But the very thought of her made him happier.

As he turned to go and start work he saw Jess and Sis turning in through the gate and his heart began to thud rapidly. Her expression caught his eye, because she was laughing, looking pink and radiant. She always stood out among the other women, not just in his enamoured eyes, but because it was a long time since she had worked in the filling sheds and her skin had returned to its natural, healthier colour. And today she was all smiles. She leaned towards Sis and another of the girls and said something and they all laughed.

He didn't speak to her until later, enjoying the anticipation of seeing her, but all morning the thought of asking her made his stomach flutter with nerves, however much he told himself he was being ridiculous. Eventually he told himself, casually, it was time to have a look in the Rumbling Shed, see everything was working as it should be . . .

He found Jess filling the drum with fresh sawdust and humming to herself. She didn't notice him for a moment and he stood watching her profile, the upturned mouth, pink cheeks. She looked animated, happy, even working here on her own. Her expression was no longer drawn and tense as it had been over the past months. She seemed to glow.

Something's happened, he saw, and had a sudden cold sense of foreboding. Whatever he felt for her, however much tenderness, however much he would do anything for her, he saw in that moment that it was hopeless. Her mind, her whole being was centred elsewhere. He was invisible to her.

Somehow this enabled him to speak to her more calmly.

'Er – Jess?' She turned, smiling.

'I just wondered if you and the girls – your cousins – would fancy a walk out on Sunday. My David's a bit short of pals and he and little Ronny got on so well – I wondered if you'd all . . .?'

'Sunday?' Her forehead wrinkled for a second, then a smile of vivid joy spread across her face. 'Oh no – not Sunday. Sunday's busy. Sorry . . .' She spoke abstractedly and he sensed enormous excitement pent up in her. 'Maybe another week?'

'Yes, course,' he said with overdone cheerfulness. 'It doesn't have to be this week – any time'd do.'

Jess could barely contain herself on Sunday. She didn't give the others a chance to ask where she was going, though she knew Polly would guess. Once dinner was over she tore along the road into town, setting off far too early, but unable to sit still any longer. Ever since Ned's note had arrived – at Olive's house this time – she'd moved round in a cloud of happiness and anticipation. He was out – free! He was asking – begging, almost, to see her. He'd written 'please' twice at the end of the letter. She was moved by the urgency of this. Her body quivered with excitement and longing for him.

The Bull Ring, usually teeming and loud with the raucous shouts from the market stalls, was a peaceful place to meet on a Sunday, when instead, it became a place for people to go to church at St Martin's, its spire a landmark at the lower end of the street. The statue of Nelson was a little further up and usually attracted hawkers and street musicians trying to earn a few pennies, and was a meeting place for lovers and friends. Today though it was deserted, except for an old man, asleep with his mouth open, leaning against the railings.

Jess waited. Pigeons toddled round her, some making half-hearted attempts to take off and fly. Mostly they just stalked aimlessly back and forth across the filthy cobbles pecking at odd leftovers of food on the ground. Jess looked up at the church clock. A quarter to two. Despite the plea in the letter she was so afraid he wouldn't come.

*

Limping, with his stick, up Spiceal Street, Ned saw her before she caught sight of him. She was dressed much as she had been that time she came to the hospital: black coat, a glimpse of her rich purple skirt showing where it fell open at the bottom, white blouse at the neck. Her neat little felt hat. He stopped. She was looking down at her feet. He willed her not to look up for a moment, to give him time to locate his feelings, to gather himself. Again there came the sense of utter familiarity, her wide, pretty face, the shape of her, her way of standing. How lovely she was! She was the one, if anyone, who could restore him, bring him properly back to life.

Help me, was his silent plea to her. Please help me.

And then she saw him, moving slowly towards her, supporting himself with a stick, dressed in the blue uniform issued to soldiers recovering from wounds, with a coat over the top. His eyes were fixed on her and she walked forward a couple of paces, her breath catching, unsure for a moment. Then she saw the corners of his mouth turn up.

'Ned! Oh Ned!'

She ran down to him, her arms held wide to embrace him. He dropped the stick, his arms came round her and she was laughing, crying, nuzzling against him, so starved was she of the feel and smell of him.

'Oh Ned, at last – at last!' She turned up her face towards him and closed her eyes as his lips met hers, the moment she had waited for all these months, years. They stood locked together.

But she was eager to talk, beaming up into his face. 'You're here – oh God, you're really here!'

She saw him smiling back at her, as she drank in the

sight of him, his face, thinner now, the thick, wavy hair, the eyes that she so loved looking down into hers, flecked pebble-grey in the sunlight.

'It's so good to be out of that hospital, and out of 'ome too for that matter.' He bent to pick up his stick, then took her arm. She was relieved to hear that he sounded more normal, more like the old Ned.

'How's yer leg now?'

'Pretty good.' They made their way slowly up the road, no particular destination in mind. The light was hard and bright, casting sharp shadows. 'I reckon it'll be just about back to strength before long.'

She looked up at him sharply. 'You mean . . .? They ain't going to send you back, are they?'

'Dunno. S'pect so.'

She tried not to feel deflated, chilled inside by the offhand way he said it. So much time has passed, she told herself. I don't know what it's been like for him out there. It takes time to get used to someone again. She squeezed his arm, smiling up at him.

'Saw about your medal – in the paper. Ooh, we was ever so proud of yer! "Courage under fire." So – does it feel nice to be a hero?'

'No!' He spoke more harshly than he intended. As he did so, an image of his friend Jem, the dead Jem, sitting beside him in that trench with a bullet hole in his head, flashed through his mind. He closed his eyes for a second. 'No,' he said more quietly. 'It weren't like that, Jess.'

This conversation seemed to be turning into a quicksand. She struggled to say the right thing. 'I'm sure you were brave though.'

'No,' he insisted. 'There ain't no heroes and there

ain't no cowards. Yer a coward one day, a hero the next and yer never know yerself which it's to be. I just didn't notice I'd been hit.'

She was silent for a moment. 'I've missed you so much,' she appealed to him.

Ned stopped. They were at the bottom of New Street.

'I'm sorry, Jess. I didn't mean to be short with yer.'

Ignoring passers-by, he pulled her to him and kissed her hard on the mouth, and Jess responded, full of relief and desire for him. Her young body came alive at the feel of him close to her. She ran her hands up and down his back. Then he released her.

They strolled round town arm in arm, talking of this and that, unsure where to begin.

'It's a long time since I've been in 'ere,' he said. 'Bit of a mess, ain't it? Any bombs come down here?'

'No. They bombed a few times but they missed – kept dropping 'em out in the fields.'

By the cathedral they sat on a bench with their coats pulled tight round them and Ned's arm round her. Small clouds moved across the sun. Jess did most of the talking, told him about how things had been at home since Ernie was killed, and about Alice, about how upset Olive had been.

'She's forgiven you, yer know.' She turned to face him. 'Give 'er a bit of time and she'll be back to letting yer come round again.'

'That's good of 'er,' Ned said, but his voice sounded flat. There was silence for a moment.

'Has Mary been coming to see yer?'

Ned sighed. 'Yes.'

'She still want you back?'

'Seems that way.' There was a pause. 'I didn't think she'd – well, after all this time ... forgive me like she has.'

Jess froze. She forced the words out. 'Are you going back to her?'

Ned pulled her close to him with a fierce, hard movement. '*No!* No, of course I'm not. Christ, look I ain't got no words – just come 'ere ...'

Again he kissed her so hard she was gasping, his arms almost crushing her. She tried to pull away.

'Ned, you're hurting ...'

'Sorry.' He relaxed his grip. His intensity, his need of her, filled her with desire.

'I began to think I'd never feel like this again,' she pressed herself close to him. 'I needed you to come home and wake me up!'

His lips moved close to her ear. 'God, Jess, it's more than waking up I need.'

She went weak at the urgency in his voice. 'Iris'll let us go to hers—' Their eyes met. 'We can't just turn up today. I'll have to ask 'er ... Next week.'

He closed his eyes. He wanted her now, here on this bench, as if it would sort everything out.

'Seven days is too long.'

'I know.' Jess laughed. 'But it'll come round.'

Thirty-Six

When Peter Stevenson asked Jess again that week whether she and her family would like to meet him, she tried to drag her thoughts away from Ned and take a little more notice. This time he came in late in the day, just as she was in the outer room of the Rumbling Shed, unbuttoning her overall. The other two women always left in a great rush and he had waited until they'd gone.

Jess hung her overall on the peg. Peter Stevenson felt ludicrously bashful just asking if she and her family wanted to take their children to the park, but this was not evident to Jess. To her he seemed calm and dignified.

At the thought of Sunday Jess felt a blush spread right through her and wondered if Mr Stevenson had noticed.

'Oh dear, I'm sorry – this Sunday's not much good either.' She pulled off her mob cap, releasing her hair down her back. Peter Stevenson watched, longing to step forward and take her head, with the long, soft hair, between his hands and turn her face up to him to be kissed. Emotion twisted in him, an actual physical pang. She was so lovely, and she didn't even see him: had no idea how he felt.

'You having a busy time then at the moment?' he asked carefully.

Jess put her head on one side. 'To tell you the truth, Mr Stevenson, I've got my ... my friend home from the

Front. He was wounded before Christmas and 'e's just out of hospital. Sunday afternoon's the only time we've got.'

'Oh I see,' he said brightly. 'Well of course you're busy then. That's nice for you – you should've said, then I wouldn't't've kept pestering you.'

Jess frowned, puzzled. 'But you ain't. And it'd be nice to take the lads out. Ronny and David got on like a house on fire, daint they? Tell you what.' She shouldered her coat on, pulling her hair out over it at the back. 'As soon as there's a free Sunday I'll tell yer. When it gets warmer, we could have another picnic or summat like that? I enjoyed the last one ever such a lot.'

'Yes, me too.' He hesitated, bathed in her smile. 'To tell you the truth, Jess, Sunday hangs very heavily for us now. David misses his mother. It's good to have some company.'

Jess saw suddenly how thoughtless she'd been, how lacking in imagination. Mr Stevenson looked so sad and dejected sometimes, and he was such a nice, kind man. She wanted to cheer him up. But nothing could stop her seeing Ned this Sunday, and any other Sunday she could.

'I'll talk to Sis and Polly,' she said. 'And we'll plan an outing as soon as we can, shall we?'

Peter Stevenson smiled. 'It'd be a treat.'

Iris gave her a surprisingly disapproving look when she went one evening and asked if she and Ned could come and be together in her front room on Sunday as they had used to do when he had leave.

'Well you did say we could,' Jess protested. 'Like before.'

'Yes – yes I did.' Iris clumped along the hall and flung the door of the room open. 'You do what you like – light a fire if you can find anything to light it with. Nothing to do with me.' She stood back leaning on her crutch and sniffed. 'I think my morals have slipped.'

'Iris—' Jess tried to appease her. Miss Davitt's been on at her about us coming here, she thought. 'We're not here to plan a bank robbery. We just want somewhere we can be on our own for a bit.'

'Well, as long as you both know how to behave . . . I shall probably go out to see Beatt. As for her—' She rolled her eyes up in the direction of Hilda the stodgy clerk's room. 'You won't have any trouble. You'd barely know the woman's alive.'

Jess tutted at Iris's contrariness and looked round the room. It was bleaker even than she remembered, but she and Ned had made do there before, barely noticing their surroundings in their hunger for each other. But now she felt more effort was needed. The floor was bare boards except for a little woven rug by the grate and the only furniture was two upright chairs and a worm-ridden chest of drawers in the corner. The window was shrouded by an old net and there was also a pair of limp curtains which had once been pink but were now almost grey.

I'll have to do better than this, she thought. This has got to be as cosy and nice as I can possibly make it.

That Sunday morning, Ned agreed to go to church with his mom and dad. His father was a sidesman and Ned had grown up well known by the regular congregation. Still dressed in his convalescent's uniform, he hobbled into the familiar building, taking in the smell of the place, a mixture of polish and old books and stone which had stood, unaired, for many years. His father, after he had shown people to their seats, sat at the end of the pew dressed in his Sunday suit and well-polished shoes, the green and gold collection pouches on the seat beside him. Ned sat between him and his mother. He felt like a child sitting between his mom and dad, but this time the feeling was welcome, as if all responsibility was taken from him, no decisions or commitments expected.

As they sang the first hymn: 'Oh for a faith that will not shrink, though press'd by many a foe', he felt his mother glancing anxiously at him. Her worry and concern had increased since he had come home. She had thought he would immediately be restored after so long in hospital, but he was withdrawn, silent. Perhaps it was only to be expected. It was his reaction to seeing his daughter which had really distressed her. She had thought at first that he was going to break down, but he had simply gone quiet again. Mary had brought the little girl a number of times since and the first time Ruth screamed and said she didn't want to see 'Daddy' – she didn't like him. But on these occasions he had been calmer, if not animated. He had talked to her, shown her a little wooden puzzle, tried to befriend her. Mrs Green and Mary had given each other nervous looks of relief.

'It'll take time, son,' Mrs Green said to him afterwards. 'It's hard for her as well, the little lass. Growing up without yer. Not that that's your fault,' she added quickly. 'That's the war, done that.'

Ned could see their pain, their anxiety: his mother's worn face and her constant fussing, his father's attempts to have conversations with him, heart-rending in their awkwardness. He asked about France, but in such a sidelong way that Ned deduced from it that he didn't want to know.

'I s'pose you got through the winter all right there? They looked after you?' Such questioning demanded the reassuring answer 'yes'.

'They gave us leather jerkins,' Ned told him. 'And goatskin jackets.' He could not tell him how impossible it was ever to get warm day after day on an inactive part of the front where the ground was either stone-hard with frost and snow or thigh deep in water, and any careless raising of your head too high could result in your being shot.

But he recognized his parents' agitation, their need to see things put to rights, for him to be well and back with his wife and daughter. He heard barely a word of the service, thinking of these things.

Afterwards, he was greeted like the conquering hero by the parish. A soldier, wounded, with a medal: he was their pride and joy. He smiled and shook hands. By their questions he saw that none of these people had any idea that he was the object of shame and trouble who had deserted his wife and child. Of course, his mom and dad had kept it to themselves. Partly the shame, partly because they believed it would not last, that he would come back to Mary and things would be smoothed over. To everyone else, things were as they had been before.

The church warden, a jolly, elderly man with a red face, pumped his hand up and down.

'Very good to see you, Ned. I hope when all this is over you and your wife'll move over closer to home again. We've missed seeing you – and the child.'

Ned nodded and smiled, murmuring, 'We'll have to see.'

Deeply ashamed, and desperate to escape, he edged to the door.

As they finished dinner later on, his mother said, 'I thought we'd go and see Auntie Joan this afternoon.'

'Oh – I can't,' Ned said. 'I'm off out.'

'Are you. Where?'

'Just – out.'

He knew they wouldn't ask. He saw the way they exchanged worried glances, and a great weariness came over him. He stood up and forced a smile. 'See you later.'

Jess spent the morning at Iris's getting ready for his arrival, dressed in her old work clothes, a black skirt worn so threadbare that it was grey, and a scarf tied in her hair to keep the dust out of it. Her best clothes lay folded on a chair ready to change into later.

First of all she swept the front room out and dusted it. During the week, on her way home from work, she had bought a couple of bundles of kindling from a half-starved looking boy. They were obviously chopped up bits of orange boxes, but beggars couldn't be choosers. She'd managed to scrounge a few small pebbles of coal and wrapped them in a newspaper which she used when she arrived, to twist into fire lighters. She swept out the grate and laid a meagre little fire.

With her she had also brought Louisa's quilt and another blanket and she laid them on the floor, the colourful quilt on top. She took two candles and brass candlesticks from her bag and stood them on the mantelpiece. She'd also brought a twist of paper with some tea in it, and a bag of buns – one extra for Iris.

As she worked on the room she hummed to herself, imagining, as she used to do before, that this was her own house and she and Ned were soon going to live together and make it their home. Soon, she thought, please God. If only the war would end, we can all get sorted out and start our lives over again, together, where we're meant to be.

She stood by the window for a while to get her breath back, hugging her arms across her chest, looking out at the pale blue sky. She pretended to herself that she was already married and was waiting for Ned to come home from work, his dinner in the oven. That's all I want, she thought. Husband, babbies, just normal. Bring 'em up right. Family life, not like my childhood. Excitement bubbled in her, her pulse racing. Soon he'd be coming along that road, she'd see him, the tall, wondrous shape of him, be able to touch him, lie beside him . . .

'Come on,' she said to herself. 'Daydreaming all morning ain't going to get the babby bathed.' She went to fill a bucket of water and wipe down the windows, singing 'Keep the Home Fires Burning' at the top of her voice.

Jess waited. An age seemed to pass. He's got a long way to come, and there's not a lot of trams on a Sunday, she said to herself, trying to contain her impatience. She'd waited so long to be reunited with him that these last minutes, once Iris had taken herself off across the road, were suddenly unbearable. She kept going to the window to look down the street, which remained sunlit but stubbornly empty.

She was becoming desperate when at last she saw him and ran to open the door. There he was on the doorstep, tall, handsome, here at last. Her first impulse was to throw her arms round him but she cautioned herself to be careful, and she stood aside to let him in. Once the door was closed they stood in each other's arms.

'So—' he said eventually, looking about him. 'Back 'ere again.' Their eyes met for a second, each remembering other afternoons here, and the night he had come to her in the snow and they had lain upstairs, clinging to one another. 'Not changed much, has it?'

'Not at all, I shouldn't think,' she laughed.

For a few seconds they were at a loss.

'Come on in – to our room.' Jess opened the door. The colours of the quilt seemed to leap out at them in the bare room. 'I can light a fire, but it won't last long, so I thought we'd save it.'

Ned nodded, looking round the room.

'What's up?'

'Oh – nothing much. It's only that it's still a bit hard for me to sit – on the floor like. I can lie down, or sit on a chair. I don't think I could manage sitting down there though, that's all.'

'There're chairs—' she pulled one out from behind the door, wanting everything to be right for him. 'Look – shall we see if we can breathe enough life into the range for a cuppa tea?'

Ned nodded. 'That'd be nice.'

He followed her out to the kitchen, his presence seeming to burn through her back. He felt so distant from her. They needed time to get back to where they

352

were again. She longed just to hold him, to lie with him and get back to the closeness they'd had.

They talked a little as she made the tea, the sort of polite, careful conversation she might have had with anyone.

'Where's Iris?' he asked.

'Over at Beatt's.' She decided not to mention that Iris had turned a bit sniffy about the two of them being there. Before she would have told him and they'd have laughed about it, but the situation felt delicate enough already.

'How're things at home?' she asked.

'Oh – awright.' He was staring out through the back window. 'Mom's carrying on as if I'm made of bone china. With Fred out there an' all she's always worrying. I'll be glad to get out though. Gets a bit much after a while.'

Jess tipped some of her precious tea into the pot. She looked at Ned's pale profile by the window, the face she loved so much. She longed to know what he was thinking. There were so many questions buzzing in her head that she was afraid to ask. Where did he want to get out to? Had Mary been, and how often? Were they all trying to force him back to her, and if so, what chance did she stand in the face of all of them? And how did he feel – did he love her as she so desperately, devotedly loved him, so that he was all of her life? Tell me, tell me! her thoughts screamed, so that for a moment she felt choked by panic. She fought to speak calmly.

'Must be nice for 'er though – being able to look after you.'

There was a long silence as she brewed the tea, that

353

neither of them seemed able to break, and the tension grew until the very air between them seemed brittle with it. Jess fiddled with spoons, cups and saucers and poured the pale tea. He still stood at the window, hands in his pockets.

'Ned?' She held a cup and saucer out to him, but the tone of her voice asked him so much more.

As he took the cup and saucer from her his hands were trembling so much that he couldn't hide it. He had to put them down. He stood by the table, pressing his palms against his thighs to try and control the tremor.

'Ned – love?' She stooped to look into his face. 'What is it?'

He shook his head, unable to find words for the confusion inside him.

'I so want to make things better,' she said. 'I want to be close to you.' She took one of his arms and firmly helped him stand upright. He couldn't look into her eyes. He was breathing hard, in panic, distress.

'Love, oh my love – don't! There's nothing to worry about.' Overwhelmed with feeling she pulled him to her, felt his trembling. Into his chest she said, 'Let me love you . . .'

She looked up at him, needing reassurance herself, needing him to desire her. 'I'm bad, I know. But I want yer so much – all this time I've waited and I love you more than anyone, anything . . .'

He seemed to relax, and smiled properly for the first time, gently kissing the tip of her nose. 'I like your badness. Oh Jess, you're what I need.'

'Come with me.'

She led him into their front room and closed the door. As he stood watching she knelt by the grate to light the knotted twists of newspaper. The flames bit into them and soon they could smell smoke. She turned, and saw how intently he was watching her, his eyes moving over her.

'That'll help – for a little, anyhow.' She drew the curtains, then sat on the quilt, her legs stretched out, hair falling over one shoulder. 'Can you get down 'ere with me?'

He managed it, slowly. Once he was comfortable he reached out for her. 'You're so lovely.' His voice held a desperate mixture of longing and regret.

They bunched up the edges of the quilt and blanket to rest their heads on. Ned eased himself down beside her, settling on his back, where he was most comfortable. It was only after a moment that he realized his body was so tense that he was holding his arms and legs almost rigid, and he tried to relax and let them sink closer to the floor.

'You awright?' she moved her hand across his chest.

'Yes – just stiff.'

Jess leaned up on her elbows beside him and looked down into his face. She reached round and pulled the ribbon from her hair and it fell in long, thick waves over her shoulders. Teasing, she took an end of it and tickled his nose.

He shook her off, still taking deep breaths, trying to calm himself out of a sense of panic that he didn't even understand. He looked into her face, seeing the love in her dark eyes, a tiny freckle on her left cheekbone, her soft, radiant skin. She leaned down and kissed his lips and her hair hung over him, further darkening the room.

'I love you,' she said, her face close to his.

'I love you too.' He searched inside himself for the meaning of the words.

'You lie still,' Jess said. 'And I'll make it better.' She

knelt up and simply took charge of him. Stroking, circling her hands, she moved over his body – his shoulders, his neck, arms, smoothing and kneading with her palms over his clothes, stopping often to turn and kiss his face. She felt him watching her, submitting to her, waiting. When she reached his injured leg she softened her caress to a light, fluttering stroke. She confined her touch to parts of his body which showed she was not impatient to arouse him. She simply loved him with her hands, her face intent. At first he felt foolish, passive. Then, under the warmth of her hands, sensations flooded through him.

She heard his breathing change and smiled into his eyes.

'Oh God, Jess,' he whispered.

Seeing the longing in his face, Jess unbuttoned her blouse and took it off, then her vest, with neat, graceful movements. Her skin was naturally slightly sallow across her shoulders and down her outer arms, but her breasts were very white, the nipples pink.

Clumsily, he pulled off his clothes, then reached out to touch her, heard her gasp as his flesh met hers. She clung to him, laughing, lips, tongue, hair moving over his flesh. Seeing her desire for him increased his own and he urgently pushed her down on to her back. She looked up into his eyes, giving her wide, delicious smile.

'I don't think there's much wrong with you, is there?'

He pulled away after, leaving her abruptly cold after the heat of their lovemaking, drew his knees up and sat with his elbows on them, hands supporting his head.

'I shouldn't've done that. Not the full way. You should've stopped me.'

'I didn't want to.' Jess hugged her arms across her breasts, shivering, inching herself closer to him again.

'You could 'ave another babby.'

'I don't care.'

'Well yer *should* care. Christ!'

She had thought that he was with her, that they were back where they used to be, and then it was lost. She had let him make love to her, holding in the back of her mind a tiny hope that she might carry his child again, perhaps be able to lay to rest the phantom of the one she had lost.

His mind was in turmoil. With her, he had experienced the first real depth of feeling, wholeness, that had come to him since he came home. For those moments he had at least had the physical evidence that he was well. He was a man again. He had been able to perform with a woman. But then the desire was replaced by remorse. This was wrong. Since he had met Jess his life had buckled out of shape. It was all wrong. He thought of his mom and dad and Mary and Ruth: he'd let down and betrayed every one of them. He thought of all the good, weary-faced people who had greeted him that morning at the church, who all thought so well of him. Ned Green, the splendid lad they all knew. And this Ned here now – who was he?

He looked round the rotten little room, feeling as he did so, Jess's caress on his back. He leaned away from her. What was this life with her? Lying and squalor and turning everyone against him. No – it was impossible. It couldn't go on. The thought came to him, *I want to be safe.*

He got up, with some difficulty, and started to dress. Jess watched him uneasily, her teeth chattering with cold. The feeble little fire had gone out. When they were both dressed she could no longer bear the silence, the way he had closed himself against her so completely. She went to him and held out her arms, her face appealing to him.

Slowly, with infinite regret, he held her close for a moment.

'I've got something to eat,' she said, trying to be cheerful, to tell herself it was early days. He had been so passionate for her while they were making love. Things would get better.

They had more tea with the buns in the kitchen, huddling close to the range.

'We need time to get used to each other again, don't we?' she said. 'Will you come here – next week?'

Ned swallowed. He could think of nothing else to say, not in the right words, so he said, 'Yes.'

Thirty-Seven

'I don't want yer pity. Get out of 'ere and don't come bloody mithering round me, woman!'

John Bullivant had shouted these words, and variations on them, at Polly through the winter as she continued to try and visit him. At first she had gone tentatively, once a week, her heart pounding, frightened of him, but somehow unable to keep away.

'Leave 'im be if 'e don't want to see yer,' Olive said. ''E'll have to get over it in 'is own way.'

'I can't leave it, Mom,' Polly said. 'If you'd heard 'im like I do, and seen the state 'e's in . . .' She couldn't easily explain how John had touched her heart, how she felt she couldn't just abandon him to suffer like an animal in a cage, never going out and seeing the sun. And his family couldn't get anywhere with him and didn't know what to do for the best.

'When yer come down to it,' Polly said to Jess, 'that's all the war'll amount to when it's over and done with. Widows like me left to grieve or a wheelchair in the corner of a room. There's nowt we can do except help each other.'

'I think yer brave,' Jess said. 'I don't think I'd have the courage to go in there and have 'im shouting at me. I wouldn't know what to say to him.'

'I think I'll go more often,' Polly smiled ruefully. 'Get 'im used to the idea that I won't give up!'

She'd call in and sit beside John. The rest of the family got on with their lives around them, timidly, obviously afraid of John, his suffering and his moods. He was so down in himself that he barely ever answered her, sitting with his dark head sunk on to his chest. Mrs Bullivant whispered to Polly that she couldn't get him to do anything. He wouldn't even sit and read a newspaper. After a time, instead of shouting at Polly he seemed to realize that it would do no good so instead he sat quiet, seeming indifferent, just tolerating her presence.

Polly talked to him about all sorts: the news, work, what happened when she went to see Mrs Black, Ernie and how they'd got the news about him, where he was when he died. She asked him how he was keeping, never really expecting to get an answer.

The week before Jess met Ned though, John had seemed particularly low. Polly sat beside him, chatting away. John didn't answer her, although she did feel he was listening. After a while, running out of news and gossip, Polly said,

'D'you know, your moustache has grown nice and thick again now – and yer face ain't so thin as it was. You look more like yer old self.'

To her bewilderment, John's shoulders began to shake and she thought he was beginning to weep, but instead she realized he had been overcome by a desperate mirth. He put his hands over his face, the dry laughter escaping from him.

'What've I said?'

Eventually he looked at her.

'My old self? Oh that's good, that is! Look at me! A man with no legs, who can't walk, can't work, can't even dress or get out to do me business without someone seeing to me. I'll never be any use to anyone ever again, so for God's sake, woman, leave me alone – why d'yer keep coming, carrying on and on at me?'

Something had broken through the rage, the bitterness. The face that Polly saw before her showed all his agony, his vulnerability.

'John—' Polly spoke softly, laying a hand gently on his arm. She could tell Marion Bullivant was listening, but she didn't care. 'I lost my 'usband on the Somme. You know that. My life'll never be the same again now. Grace'll never know her father and I'm so sad and lonely that sometimes I don't know what to do with myself. Many's the time I've thought of finishing it altogether, to tell yer the truth. But I've got Grace to bring up – and I've got a life to live the best I can. And you've got one too, John. It'll never be the same again for you neither, but it's still a life. You know – if yer'd just go out of the house for once you'll see there's lots of boys on the streets with one leg or both missing. You're not the only one. But I still reckon if it was me I'd sooner be 'ere with no legs and all my family round me, than buried in French mud.' Her voice was fierce as she finished.

He didn't say anything, just continued to stare into her face. A nerve in his cheek twitched. He was in a tumult of confused emotions.

'Maybe . . .' Polly said. 'If you was to get out and see some of the other lads – you know, a trouble shared . . .'

He tutted, suddenly furious, and looked down at his lap. 'I'm finished . . . I'm not a man . . .'

Polly hesitated. Very quietly she said, 'You are to me, John.'

*

On the Sunday he agreed, at last, that she should wheel him out for a walk.

'Shall we all come?' his mother said nervously. 'Make a bit of an outing of it?'

'No!' John protested sharply. 'I'm not being taken out with yer all like a freak in a fairground. Just Polly on 'er own. That's all I want.'

'It'll start getting him used to the idea,' Polly spoke to Mrs Bullivant quietly in the hall, hoping she wasn't offended. But she was only relieved.

'It's marvellous him agreeing to go out of the house!' she said gratefully. 'Where'll yer take 'im?'

'Cannon Hill Park.'

'Oh no – that's too much for yer, Polly – it's a hell of a walk, and pushing that chair! You've no flesh on yer bones as it is!'

'I'll manage,' Polly said determinedly. 'I'm feeling strong today. And I want to take 'im somewhere really nice. Get some fresh air into 'im and summat pretty to look at. There might be a few daffs out by now.'

The two of them manoeuvred the wheelchair down the step, with John clinging tensely to the arms, cursing at them as they landed it rather joltingly on the pavement. They'd wrapped him up in blankets over his coat because although the sun was shining weakly, it was still a bitter day.

'Have a nice walk,' Mrs Bullivant said, then looked as if she wanted to cut her own tongue out. 'I mean . . .'

'See yer later.' Polly smiled ruefully, waving at her.

They didn't talk much on the way, as Polly needed to concentrate on learning to steer the chair and she could sense that John was having to get used to all sorts of sensations. All these months he had not been outside for more than a few moments. He screwed up his eyes, which watered in the bright winter light. The air felt strange on his pallid skin, everything felt so wide and spacious, even in the streets. And above all, he was not the man who had left Birmingham, full bodied and vigorous. He had to face meeting people outside, being seen for what he was: a man who had been mutilated, changed forever on the battlefield.

'There at last,' she said, and saw him nod.

She pushed the chair into the wide, green space, and along the path which led to the pond, pausing to look across the water. As they did so, both of them caught sight of a young man and woman, arm in arm together. But instead of moving with the easy strides of a young couple in love, the man was taking tiny, shuffling steps, and clinging to the girl's arm as if terrified that a great crevice was about to open in the ground in front of him. His free arm waved in front of him, feeling the air like an antenna. It was immediately apparent that he was newly blind. As the two drew painfully nearer, Polly saw that while the girl was holding his arm, talking to him calmly, reassuring and guiding him, tears which he could not see ran ceaselessly down her face. Polly and John watched silently as they passed.

She wheeled him to the far side of the pond, so that the water was to their right, the park on their left, and it presented a beautiful sight.

'No daffs yet,' Polly said. 'But just look at that.'

Planted in huge numbers, in great patches across the grass were crocuses, all flowering at their perfect best in purple and mauve, rich golden yellow and the purest white. The thin sunlight caught them, illuminating the perfection of their shape and colour as if they were jewels scattered across the green.

John had been looking round, taking everything in,

but suddenly Polly saw him lower his head and clasp his hands to his face.

'John?' In concern, she leaned down, her face close to his. She stood up and gently laid her hands on his shoulders. After some time he reached round and clasped one of his hands over hers.

Thirty-Eight

Sunday came at last. As before, Jess made preparations for Ned. She took time over it, arranging a few sprigs of forsythia in a jam jar, brushing out the room, singing and humming. She took a warm, caressing pleasure in the homely activity. Soon she'd be doing this properly, in a place of their own.

I'll talk to him about it today, Jess thought. Tell him about the money I've been saving for us. But then she changed her mind. The war wasn't over. Ned had said they'd most likely send him back once he'd recovered fully. Though she longed with all her heart for the love and security of marriage to Ned, of a home, it would be tempting fate to start planning now. There were still so many hurdles in their way.

She was lost in thought, kneeling by the grate, sweeping out the ashes from last week, when she heard Iris come and stand in the doorway and turned, smiling. Iris had washed her hair that morning and got Miss Davitt to cut it, and it hung just below her ears, severely chopped, but clean and almost pure white. Once again she had promised to pop out for a bit, although Jess told her there was really no need.

'This can't go on forever, you know.'

'I know that,' Jess stood up and came over to her. 'Of course I do. I was only thinking that myself. But the war . . .'

Iris just sniffed.

'The man you loved, Iris – d'yer think *he* was married?'

'I don't know, dear. Quite possible. I expect he was lying to me all the time. I was such a foolish, innocent little thing. I just wonder ...'

'What?'

'How serious your young man Ned is after all, carrying on in this hole in the wall sort of way.'

'Oh 'e is!' Jess didn't feel she could say, you should see his face, the way he looks at me and loves me! 'It's only that he's living with his mom and dad and they don't approve of me. But when we're together, there's nothing to worry about there!'

She was expecting him at two o'clock. We'll go out, she thought. They'd walk arm in arm round the park, close, loving, stopping to kiss. Then come back to the house. As the time approached she went through to the back and put a kettle on the fire. Between them, Iris's helpers seemed to be making sure she had enough fuel, and Jess had paid her a few pennies for the use of some of it. She had put the lid back on the kettle and was brushing soot off her skirt when she heard him rapping on the front door.

She danced along the hall singing out, 'I'm here – I'm coming, my love!'

She flung the door open with a flourish, a smile of joy and welcome on her face. In a second the smile froze. Jess felt as if she had been punched. Her breath seemed to get stuck in her chest. It took her a couple of seconds for her mind to process what was in front of her eyes.

'What're *you* doing 'ere?'

Mary stood before her, thin as a park railing and

dressed in grey. The arched eyebrows which before had made her look friendly and enquiring now gave her an expression of superiority and triumph.

'I'm 'ere to give you a message.' Jess could feel her enjoyment, the way she was savouring what she had to say, almost delaying the moment. 'A message from *my husband*.' Mary gave a knowing, calculated smile.

'Ned and I have been spending a lot of time together over the past months. With our daughter. I don't s'pose he told you all this? Anyway, he sent me to tell yer that he's decided to come back to me. He's come to his senses and he's coming back home for good . . .'

'No!' Jess's hand went to her throat. 'It's not true!'

'He never really left me in the first place,' Mary said spitefully. 'After all, he's been away fighting like everyone else so yer've never really 'ad 'im at all, have yer? Don't go getting any ideas that you can go changing his mind – 'e says 'e wants to live a decent life now with his wife and family – 'stead of with a whore like you . . .' She spat out the word.

'I don't believe yer – he wouldn't . . .' Jess could barely get a sentence together.

'Oh wouldn't 'e? And you think you'd know, do yer?' She came up very close so that Jess could feel the woman's breath on her face as she spoke. 'You know nothing. And yer'd better take my advice and keep well away from us. Keep out of our lives – yer not wanted!'

She began to turn away, then looked back. 'I'd tell yer 'e said 'e was sorry – but come to think of it, 'e never said that.'

Mary stalked off down the road without looking back, her head held high.

Jess shut the door and leaned back against it. Her limbs seemed to have turned to water, her shocked mind telling her she had found herself in a crazed dream. Here, where he'd come last week, loved her, held her ... suddenly everything was shattered.

She hugged herself, trying to force from her mind the memory of Ned's back turned away from her after their lovemaking. It couldn't be true! Mary had wormed out of him where she was meeting him, had come to spin her a pack of lies ... Ned would never do this to her, he loved her! She shook her head, moaning gently to herself.

'He loves me – just me ...' She couldn't stand the pain of what she had heard, nor would she ever believe it unless she saw Ned herself. She had to hear the truth from his own lips.

Afterwards she couldn't remember the journey to Selly Oak. It was as if she had done it in her sleep and wakened to find herself outside the Greens' house, wondering how she got there.

She hammered on the door, past caring about anything: that it was Sunday afternoon and that his mom and dad loathed and despised her, that Mary might well be there as well by now ... In her desperation none of this mattered and only one thing in the world did: she had to see Ned and talk to him.

It had begun to spit with rain as she walked up Oak Tree Lane and the wind was getting up. As she waited for someone to open the door she thought, we'd've got wet. We couldn't've gone for a walk in the park after all.

Ned's mother opened the door. She gasped when she saw who it was.

'You've got some nerve coming here! Don't you

think you're coming in because you're not. Clear off and don't you ever come near this house – breaking up families. You're nothing better than a common little tart!'

She went to shut the door, but Jess ran against it with her full weight, making sure she got her foot wedged in the doorway.

'I've got to see him!' She found she was right out of control, shouting at the top of her voice. 'I'm not going away 'til I've seen 'im and 'e tells me the truth with his own lips – 'stead of sending a cowing messenger round – if 'e did send her! Ned – Ned!'

'Mom—' She heard his voice, very tense sounding in the hall behind.

'Disgusting little trollop, coming round here!' Mrs Green's face was contorted with anger and disgust. The sight of it made Jess feel dirty and sordid. Something in her shrivelled and died, knowing so clearly and brutally what they all thought of her.

'I don't care what you think – I love 'im!' she sobbed, distraught. 'I want to see 'im!'

Ned pushed past his mother, gesturing for her to go inside. Jess heard him say, 'Let me deal with this.' Being referred to as 'this' wounded her more than anything else had done so far. She found herself weeping uncontrollably in the street as Ned seized her arm, leading her away from the house as the rain began to come down in earnest.

'Tell me it's not true. Tell me yer love me! Yer love me, Ned!'

But he didn't speak. He pulled her along by the arm, the rain pelting into their faces, turning down towards the Infirmary, walking very quickly until they passed the gates and reached a green space under the bare trees at the end of the road where there was more shelter. Then he stopped and faced her. Jess, her face wet with rain and tears, looked up into his eyes.

'Oh God—' she put her hand over her mouth, feeling for a moment as if she was going to retch. She swallowed hard before she could speak. 'It's true – what Mary said? You're going back to 'er?'

For a moment Ned seemed frozen, as if in those seconds he had to make the decision all over again. They heard the rain falling through the trees. He looked away from her, down at the rotting leaves under their feet, and nodded.

'And you – you—' Jess was panting, so beyond herself she could barely get the words out. 'You sent *her* to tell me – of all people. You come to me, you tell me we're going to have a life together, you come and love me as if I'm the only woman in the world, *use* me – and then you—' She ran out of words.

'Jess—' He went to touch her shoulder.

'Don't!' she screamed. 'Are you going back to Mary? I want to hear it out of your own mouth.'

'Yes.' He sighed resignedly. 'Yes. I'm going back to Mary. She's my wife.'

'But why? You don't love her – you love me!'

He spoke dully, but she could tell from his tone that the decision had been made. He was unshakeable. 'I do love her – in a sort of way. She's always been there. There's a lot in that, Jess. And there's Ruth . . .'

A man appeared, cutting through the trees, shaking the wet off his cap, but she was too overwrought to wait until he'd passed.

Scalding tears stung her eyes again. 'You're a coward, Ned! You're the worst sort of coward there is. You didn't even have the courage to come and speak to me, after all this – all that's happened. I've devoted myself to you. I carried your babby – or have you already forgotten that? And I would've kept quiet and suffered bringing it up alone to spare you, so's not to force yer into anything because I loved yer that much! I was turned out of home for you – on the streets, with no one. I turned Auntie against me, I've waited for you and lived for you. You're my life, Ned! I would've done anything for yer – and you send Mary to me. You treat me like ... like *nothing*, and you didn't even have the guts to come and tell me yourself ...' She could say no more, she was crying so uncontrollably.

'I didn't come because I couldn't – can't you see that? I couldn't do it. Not after last week – seeing you. I just wouldn't have been able ...'

'Because you're a bloody, sodding coward!' she screamed at him. 'I hate you – hate you for being so weak that you can't stand up to them all!'

'Yes—' he held out his hands helplessly. 'Yes – I am, I know. But Jess, I've got a wife, a daughter – there're my mom and dad to think of. Everyone – everyone we know – it's like my whole life falling apart if I leave it and go with yer. You're so good, so beautiful ... That's the thing. Choosing between good and bad's not the hard thing – but how d'yer choose between two good things? Things which both feel right? When either way the choice hurts someone – lots of people.'

Jess stood quiet, feeling despair come over her like great weariness. Because for all her hurt, her anger, her love for him, she understood what he was saying, and that cut her more than not understanding.

'It's like the war.' He looked at her again. 'You kill them or they kill you. Which is better?'

'Oh, you have to kill them.'

'That's where we're different. You're a born survivor. I don't know how I've lasted this long in life.' He looked into her eyes and she saw his, at last, fill with tears.

'God, Jess – this is the most horrible thing. I hate hurting people, you more than anyone.' He reached out for her but she kept back, standing stiffly. She could not bear for him to touch her. She felt as if she would go crazy, thump and kick and scratch him if he came nearer, to release her pain on to him.

'I should've known I could never have you,' she said. Her voice sounded strangled. 'Not really. Not a proper life, happy ever after. It's always been a dream. Just a dream.' She paused looking up at him. 'You won't change yer mind – not even now? We could just go . . .'

He was solemn. 'No. I've got to stay. No more lying and letting people down. I want to live decently.'

These words winded her as if he had punched her. Decently. He wanted to live decently. For a moment she closed her eyes. When she opened them he had stepped closer to her. 'Jess – I'm sorry . . .'

'I know.' She looked down, tears running down her cheeks. She pressed her hands over her face to shut out the sight of him. 'Ned – go away. I can't stand seeing yer.'

'I can't just leave yer here . . .'

'Why not? You're leaving me anyhow. Just get away from me – leave me!' At last she was screaming.

Ned paused helplessly for a second, then walked away under the trees without turning to look back. Jess watched through her fingers, saw the strong shape of him darken further for a moment in the shadows. Then, with his head down, moving slowly and sorrowfully, he stepped out into the rain, taking himself out of her life. She wondered if she would ever see him again.

She gave way then, her legs folding so that she crumpled forward on to the sodden leaves and twigs, sobbing in anguish. She curled into a ball, incoherent cries of grief tearing from her. Her forehead was pressed against the wet earth as she wept, arms clenched tight round her body as if to hold within herself a heart that was shattering apart.

Thirty-Nine

The fighting began again in earnest in March with a
German offensive, once more on the Somme, and
through the summer of 1918 the numbers of casualties
on the Western Front soared again to the highest they'd
ever been.

It was Sis's turn to spend her life in a state of acute
worry about Percy. Tanks were being used more and
more often in the fighting to try and break through the
Hindenburg Line. In parts the Germans had dug
trenches so deep and well defended that the line seemed
impregnable. And in the early spring it was the Germans
who were pushing west, forcing a bulge in the allied
front. By April though, they had still not broken
through. The war had taken on a terrible, unresolved
permanence and everyone was worn down with it,
sickened, exhausted.

Jess did, after all, see Ned again, and quite soon. One
Sunday in May, he and Mary arrived at the house, Ned
carrying Ruth in his arms. It was Olive who opened the
door.

'Oh. It's you.' She stood firmly on the step. 'What
d'yer want?'

The cousins heard her voice from the back room and
looked at each other. Ronny ran through to see.

'We wanted to come and see yer, Auntie,' Ned said,
hesitantly.

Mary was obviously eager to take over the talking. 'Only – Ned knows what yer've thought of 'im over the last years, and 'e wanted to try and patch things up, for the best like.'

Jess seemed turned to stone. For the last two months she had felt like a dead person, full of leaden despair, and her cousins were helpless in the face of her misery. For a moment, hearing his voice, hope sparked in her. He had come back for her. It was all a mistake and he loved her after all, couldn't live without her as she couldn't without him! But then she heard Mary speak too.

'Dear God, no!' She got up to escape upstairs, but it was too late. Olive had stood back, grimly, and they were already coming along the hall.

'They've got a bloody nerve coming 'ere!' Polly said, enraged. Although they had always known Jess was wrong to go with a married man, her obvious love and devotion to Ned, the suffering they had witnessed in her since, had drawn all of them, even Olive, on to her side.

As Ned and Mary's footsteps came closer, Jess stood behind the door, arms tightly folded, trying to keep her emotions closed down. As soon as Ned came into the room he shot her a look of apology, but Jess wasn't looking at him to intercept it.

Olive didn't ask them to sit down, though she greeted Ruth kindly enough and let her perch on a chair by the table.

'So – what've yer got to say?'

The smug look on Mary's face dropped a bit. She could feel Polly and Sis's eyes boring into her with loathing.

'Me and Ned want to say a few things to yer,' Mary said. There was satisfaction in her voice.

'Oh yer do, do yer? Why should we care, yer smug little bitch?'

'Poll—' Olive shushed her and looked at Ned. 'Yer've made a right mess of things, my lad.'

'I know . . .' he looked round her and spoke to Jess. 'I didn't come to upset yer – I wouldn't've come . . .'

'What're yer talking to '*er* for?' Mary snapped. 'Don't go crawling to 'er!'

Jess couldn't look up or answer. Her cheeks were burning. Just go, she prayed. Please. Leave me in peace.

'I wanted to say to you, Auntie, that I'm sorry for all I've done to upset you, and your family—'

'It's not as if things were easy for me,' Mary interrupted, unable to keep quiet. 'Having *my husband* stolen by some common little—'

Ned laid a hand firmly on her arm. 'Mary, you said we was coming to make our peace, so just keep out of it, will yer? Auntie—' he looked appealingly at her. 'Can yer forgive me?'

'You've got a bleeding cheek!' Sis exploded. 'Coming 'ere, trying to make everything awright for yerself! That's all you ever think of, ain't it? Never mind all the misery you've caused . . . you just want to go off thinking you're bloody marvellous Ned Green again . . . Well you ain't, I can tell yer – your name's muck around 'ere.'

Olive waved an arm to shut Sis up. Jess seemed to shrink further into herself. There was a silence as Olive stared at him so intently that Ned had to look down.

'I might be able to forgive yer,' she said slowly. 'In time. But not yet. There's too much heartbreak round here for me to wave you off with my blessing. It takes two, Ned, and you was every bit as much to blame for all that's 'appened. So you can put up with a heavy conscience for a bit. I ain't handing out my blessing just on your say so. It's Jess yer should be talking to.'

'Well 'e ain't doing that,' Mary said. She looked round at them all, then announced, 'Ned's been redrafted.'

This stopped Olive in her tracks. Less harshly, she said, 'You going back to France?'

'No.' Ned spoke quietly, almost shamefully. 'In the Reserves. My leg's not fit. They're sending me to Dover.'

'Well you ain't going to get killed there, are yer?' Sis said.

Mary looked as if she was about to say something that would have started a slanging match, but she thought the better of it.

'Come on,' Ned said quietly. 'I think we'd better go.'

As they were shown out, Polly said, 'I think we did well not to 'ave a proper old ding-dong with 'er. How I didn't put my fist through 'er cowing smug gob I'll never know!'

Jess sank into a chair, trembling like someone who's been in an accident.

Those last months of the war were a time of mourning for Jess. She felt hollow, lost. Sometimes she confided her feelings to Polly and Sis. One evening they were standing out in the little yard behind the house, catching the last of the sunshine. The sky was a pale yellow with a few sludgy wisps of cloud across it.

'I've spent four years thinking of no one but 'im. I feel as if life's empty and it'll be empty forever.'

'I know yer do,' Polly laid a hand on her shoulder. 'And I know 'ow yer feel. Even though I've got John to

377

think about now, I still feel it's Ernie I'm married to. I can't help it. And every time I think about it I feel really bad inside. It's like 'e's not dead and buried – I don't feel I can ever believe 'e's really gone. I mean, if John and I was to ... well, you know – I'd feel like a bigamist.'

'Least Bert seems to be awright for the moment,' Jess turned to Sis. 'And you heard from Perce yesterday.'

Sis nodded despondently. 'But God knows how much longer they'll be out there ...'

Jess squeezed Sis's hand. It was no good telling her everything would be all right. You never knew. They just had to hope.

As the months passed, the war began to turn. The Germans began many successful attacks, their artillery bombardment devastating the allied lines, but as soon as their infantry tried to move forward they lost the initiative. By September the whole Front was ablaze, and at last, the allies ruptured the Hindenburg Line. The newspapers began to trumpet successes. A breathless, almost unbelieving hope began to break through the gloom.

During that summer, Jess and Sis also honoured their promise to invite Peter Stevenson and David out with them. They spent several hot Sundays picnicking in Cannon Hill and Highgate Parks, the two boys scrapping on the grass like pups or playing ball, with Grace trying to join in and annoying them.

One hot afternoon in August they all went to Cannon Hill, taking a picnic of sandwiches and cake and some cold mutton contributed by Peter Stevenson. John Bullivant agreed to come. He was wary towards Peter

Stevenson at first: a man who hadn't been in the fighting, who was an outsider, a shirker even, so far as John was concerned. He was also mortified at his disability in the presence of a strong, able-bodied man, and it took some time to break the ice. John scowled when Peter offered to push the wheelchair and Polly indicated gently that it might be better if she did it.

They all set off, Jess and Sis with a bag each, Olive and Peter looking out for the boys and Grace riding in pride of place on John's lap in the wheelchair. She loved it sitting up there, with John tickling her and trying to remember little rhymes to sing to her. Grace thought 'Uncle' John was wonderful.

For a long time, Jess scarcely noticed that whenever they went out together, Peter Stevenson always seemed to gravitate towards her. Walking down to the park that day, he appeared at her side with David.

'Looks set fine, doesn't it?' he said.

Jess managed a smile. 'Yes, nice and warm,' she said absently.

David reached up for her hand. She transferred the bag to her left hand and took his.

'And how're you, young man? Getting big now, aren't yer? You'll be taller than Ronny, I reckon. You two can have some nice games.'

David grinned. 'Football.'

'You gunna play for the Blues when you grow up?'

'Yep—' Davey kicked an imaginary ball along the road.

'He's dead keen,' Peter said. 'Course, at that age you think you can do anything in the world, don't you?' Jess gave a little chuckle. Peter thought how long it was since he had heard her happy, full hearted laugh. By now he knew what had happened, or some of it, from Sis. That Jess had been let down badly, was rejected and sad. He longed to bring the smile back to her face.

They made themselves comfortable on the long sward of grass which sloped down to the pond. The grass was parched and worn from the crowds of people out enjoying the summer sun. Between them, Polly and Peter lifted John out of his wheelchair and on to the grass. He had to accept their help, but a distant look would come over his face as if to dissociate himself from what was happening. The children romped around and Jess and Sis kept an eye on them while Olive opened the bags and sorted out the food, her hat well pulled down to shade her eyes. Polly got up to chase after Grace.

Jess felt the sun pressing on her back as she sat on the grass and the warmth made her feel drowsy. She became aware that Peter was talking to John behind her, gently asking him questions. What had happened, how had he lost his legs. Did he mind being asked?

'I don't mind – there's not many ask as a matter of fact. They was blown off. A shell came down and the next thing I knew I were in a bed in a hutment hospital – that's what they call 'em – sort of makeshift places out there. Left the rest of my legs somewhere near Plugstreet – that's Belgium.' Jess could hear a kind of pride in his voice: he knew about the war first hand, Peter didn't. 'Lot of lads gone the same way. Nothing like them lads: bloody golden, the whole lot of 'em.'

'Sometimes I think I should've kicked up and gone. I was fit enough, after all.'

'No.' John was angrily emphatic. 'Oh no. Mind you, nothing would've kept me from joining up. Not at the time. But we shouldn't've been there – not a single one of us down to the last man. No – you're best out of it, pal. It's just one long f—.' He bit back an expletive. 'Scuse me, Mrs Beeston . . . It's a nightmare, Peter, that it is.'

'Yer awright,' Olive said. 'Any'ow – there's dinner ready now. Go and get the others, Jess, will yer?'

'I'll come and get Davey.' Peter was on his feet as Jess got up.

'No need,' she said. 'I'll get 'em.'

'I'd like to,' he smiled at her.

They wove through the lazing family groups on the grass. Polly and the children were at the edge of the pond watching the ducks.

'He's a brave man, your friend John,' Peter said. 'He must be going through hell.'

'Yes, 'e is brave,' Jess glanced round at John. 'But 'e has suffered such a lot and 'e feels useless. Polly was wondering if 'e could maybe get a job somewhere – get 'im out and keep 'im busy like. Otherwise 'e gets ever so down at home, thinking he'll never do anything again.'

'I'm sure he could. There's munitions factories crying out . . . Tell you what, Jess. I'll ask around.'

Fleetingly, she smiled. 'That's kind of yer.'

He wanted to say, I'd do anything for you, Jess. Instead he said, 'I'd be glad to. It'd help make him feel part of things again, wouldn't it?'

They helped Polly gather up the children and went back up to eat dinner. Jess was conscious of Peter striding tall at her side once more. She found herself noticing the warmth in his eyes when he smiled at her, and was suddenly cheered and comforted by his presence.

Forty

'It's over!'

Sis came tearing into the Rumbling Shed, bursting with the news, her face pink through the canary yellow. She threw her arms round Jess, jumping up and down in excitement.

'Oh Jess, I can't believe it – it's finished, over at last! And Perce can come 'ome!'

'Are you sure?' But she could already hear the shrieks of excitement from outside.

'Yes – definite – they signed this morning! 'Ere, come on – everyone's out!'

They pulled off their caps and overalls. All the other women had come out from the sheds and were hugging, laughing, shouting all at once in a great commotion. Jess saw Peter Stevenson among them, being grasped hold of and kissed by all and sundry, all of which he seemed to be rather enjoying.

'Go on!' Sis shouted down her ear. 'Go and give 'im a kiss – make 'is day!'

'What d'you mean?' Jess shouted back.

'You blind or summat, Jess? Ain't yer seen the way 'e looks at yer?'

Jess shook her head. 'No!' She'd been so wrapped up in her hurt, her misery over Ned, that nothing much else had got through. At the edge of the crowd with Sis she watched him, standing at least a head taller than the women, in his khaki overall, his eyes crinkling with laughter as a group of them milled round him. She saw he was looking round, searching, and after a moment his eyes rested on her for a second, with a questioning, uncertain look. Jess managed to meet his gaze, equally uncertain. Was Sis mistaken, and was she imagining the special tenderness in his eyes when he looked at her?

She saw he was coming over and she felt panic rising in her. But Sis saved her, launching herself at Peter Stevenson, throwing her arms round him and just managing to reach up and kiss his cheek.

'Ain't it *bostin*!' she cried. She couldn't keep still at all.

Peter laughed, pretending to stagger with her hurling herself at him. 'Yes, Sis – it's bostin all right – couldn't be better. Could it, Jess?'

'No.' To her annoyance Jess felt a heavy blush spread across her cheeks and hoped Peter Stevenson would think it was just excitement about the news. 'It couldn't, could it?'

'Why don't yer come round ours and help us celebrate later on?' Sis said irrepressibly.

'Sis!' Jess reproached her. 'Mr Stevenson's got his own family . . .'

'Well – Davey can come with him, can't 'e? The more the merrier!'

Peter Stevenson came round that evening to join in the celebrations, which spread out all along the streets, with singing and dancing, drinking and cheering. But the poignancy of the occasion, its combination of joy and grief, was too much for Polly and she broke down during the evening. The truth that Ernie would never come home now peace had broken out hit her even harder.

When they had all been out partying in the cold long enough, Olive suggested everyone go in for 'a cuppa tea and a nip of the hard stuff'. They crowded into the back room, Ronny and Davey both up long after their bedtime although Grace had given up the battle with sleep some time before and was tucked in upstairs. Olive poured celebratory tots of brandy, they had glasses of ale and later on, boiled up the kettle.

'It's nice to 'ave yer with us,' she said to Peter Stevenson. 'I 'ope you'll come and see us, even when the factory's gone and that – they won't be needing it no more, will they?'

'I s'pose not, no. I haven't had time to think yet, to tell you the truth!'

'Poor old John,' Sis said. John had got a job making Lee Enfield Rifles – now there wouldn't be much call for them.

'What'll you do then?' Jess asked Peter.

'Look for another job, I s'pose – even start summat up myself in the long run. I've always fancied that.'

It was a happy, if poignant evening, so much ending, so much lost, yet such an enormous relief still tinged with disbelief that it was finished. Eventually, when David was beginning to look glazed with sleepiness, Peter stood up.

'Come on, my lad. High time we were off.'

'Jess'll see you out,' Sis said, wickedly. Jess glowered at her, blushing, but stood up.

Once they had coats on, Peter picked David up and the boy leaned his head thankfully against his father's shoulder and closed his eyes. Peter carried him carefully out through the front door and turned to say goodbye.

Jess stood on the step. A candle was burning in the hall and against the soft light she looked so sweet, so soft and deliciously feminine. He could just see her face, her teeth gleaming as she smiled at him.

'Goodnight then,' she said softly. There was a wistfulness in her voice that he was unsure how to interpret.

'Jess?' Thank God I'm holding Davey, he thought, otherwise I'd be unable to stop myself taking her in my arms.

'Umm?'

'When the factory closes – I mean it's bound to be soon – I wouldn't want to – not see you – and the family, of course.' He paused, then added, 'But especially you.'

Jess was deeply touched by his care for her, but in her own heart there was still such hurt and confusion. She wasn't sure exactly what Peter felt for her, let alone what she could feel in return.

'I–' she swallowed. 'No – course not. You must come and see us. I'm glad you came tonight. It's hard to believe it's all over.'

'Yes–' All evening they had been saying things like this. 'Maybe tomorrow it'll sink in.'

'Well . . .' Jess pulled the door closed a little. 'Goodnight then. Give Davey a kiss from me.'

'Jess, I . . .' He saw her hesitate at the door. 'Goodnight.'

'Goodnight, Peter.'

His face didn't register his disappointment. He heard her shut the door gently behind her.

After all, what else could she say? he demanded of himself as he carried his sleeping son home through the streets still full of jubilant, carousing people. There were moments when he thought he saw her eyes respond to his, to his feeling, but so fleetingly that he wasn't sure.

I'm so flaming old, he thought. Maybe I'm just making a fool of myself. Why should such a lovely girl want a man more than ten years her senior? And when she's grieving for someone else? I ought to keep away. Leave her alone. But I can't.

He let out a groan of longing and frustration that got lost in the clamour around him.

God, I love her, he thought. I do – I just can't help it.

The following weeks were spent adjusting to the idea of peace after the long, dark years of war. The munitions factories closed or reverted back to pre-war production and all the cousins had to look for new jobs. Polly managed to get taken back on at Clark's Pens, Sis found a job at Wicker Carriage and Basket Manufacturers, and Jess found a firm needing experienced enamellers that was the right side of town, not in the Jewellery Quarter. She knew, guiltily, that if she'd gone back over there to work, she could have seen more of Iris. But fond as she was of her, she had avoided going over there too often. Iris was sympathetic about what had happened, but for Jess, Iris's house held too many memories of Ned.

As the weeks passed, the boys came home. First one of Mrs Bullivant's remaining sons, Ed. The other, Lol (short for Laurence), was wounded and in hospital in France, but would be following later.

The family were waiting on tenterhooks for their loved ones to come back. Perce was the first. There was a knock at the door one evening after they'd finished tea.

Polly led him through to the back crying out, 'Look who's here!'

Percy looked bigger and broader in the shoulders, blond hair cropped, a man suddenly, instead of a boy. He stood beaming in the doorway, arms outstretched.

'Perce!' Sis shrieked. 'Oh my God, Perce!' She almost flattened him, hurling herself on him with full bodied ardour and covering his face with kisses which he enthusiastically returned. Everyone else might just as well not have been there. Polly and Jess grinned at each other and even Olive's face softened at the sight.

'Sis—' Perce held her by the shoulders as soon as they both got their breath back, although Sis couldn't keep still.

'What?' She was tearful and giggly all at once.

He had been about to say something else but he stopped. 'Bloomin' 'ell! Yer've gone all yeller!'

Sis laughed, wiping her sleeve across her eyes. 'It's the powder goes in those grenades – it'll go in the end!'

'I should 'ope so, yer look like a flaming budgie! Anyroad, Sis – you're my girl and I want to ask yer, 'ere and now – will yer marry me?'

'Oooh yes! Yes I will, Perce!' Her arms snaked round his neck again and she squealed with excitement, then burst into tears all over again.

''Ere – steady on,' Olive said. 'You've only just got through the door!'

'I know, Mrs Beeston – but it's been a long, long war and we've had time enough to think,' Perce said seriously. 'I spent hours sitting in them tanks, sick to me stomach from the stink in there, thinking, when I get out of 'ere, the first thing I'm gunna do . . . I love yer daughter and we've lost enough time. I don't want to waste another second. That's with your permission, of course.'

'Oh Auntie!' Jess said, more animated than she'd

looked in ages. 'Of course you'll give yer permission –
look at them!'

Olive, on her dignity, paused before nodding, though
a smile was spreading over her face.

'I reckon the pair of yer are sensible enough after all
this time.'

'Oh *Mom*!' Sis cried in delight. 'Oh Perce! When
shall we fix the day for?'

''Ow about sitting the poor lad down and offering
him a cuppa tea?' Olive said. 'After all – 'e's come a
long way to ask yer!'

The next thing, a week later, while Olive was alone with
Grace, was the door opening and a lean figure walking
in, a greatcoat over one arm.

'Mom?'

'Bert?' For a second she didn't recognize him. 'Oh
Bert, at last!' She flung her arms round him, more
emotional than he'd ever seen her before. 'What's 'appened to yer – you're all skin and bone!'

'Oh I'll be awright, Mom, with some decent 'ome
cooking inside of me.' He was in good spirits. 'Eh – I'm
dying for a decent cuppa tea. You got the kettle on?'

As she heated up some food for him and brewed
tea Bert sat at the table looking round, chattering to
her, although his face looked grey and drawn with
exhaustion.

'The 'ouse looks smaller, Mom. It's a queer thing but
yer come home after all this time and everything looks
the same but different some'ow.'

Olive was watching him, frowning. 'What's the matter with yer, Bert? Yer look like a death's head.'

'Oh I'll be awright. It were just one damn thing after

another out there. Poxy bloody place the east is – I never want to set foot there again, what with the heat and the flies – and I was sick like you'd never believe. Fever and dysentery and Christ knows what. Blokes dying all round – not just from the fighting, mind – from all the diseases out there. Terrible. Anyroad . . .' He sat back, breathing in contentedly. 'Home at last. I wouldn't go back in the army if yer gave me a fortune to do it, I can tell yer!'

PART V

Forty-One

Spring 1919

'You go,' Polly said to Jess. 'I'll stay and mind Ronny and Grace. Might cheer you up a bit.'

It was Saturday morning and Olive and Sis were off to town to choose material for a wedding dress for Sis. Polly stared commandingly into Jess's pale face. 'Go on with yer – get yerself out. I'll trust yer to get summat nice for Gracie.' Grace, now three, was to be Sis's little bridesmaid. 'You're the one that's doing the sewing anyhow. And you never know who yer might meet!'

Jess managed a wan smile. 'That's what I'm worried about.'

'Look, Jess—' Olive buttoned up her coat with her gnarled fingers. 'It's high time you put it all be'ind yer, instead of mooning and mooching round 'ere. Ned's gone and now 'e needs to be forgotten. You've got yer own life to lead. Get yer coat on and come and give us a hand.'

'Awright,' Jess said listlessly. She knew her aunt was right. They had all been nothing but kind over the winter. She owed the family everything. But she felt so low and raw inside, as if Ned had taken away her youth and energy, her capacity to love.

For Sis's sake she tried to put on a cheery smile.

'Two weeks!' Her cousin could barely prevent herself from skipping along the pavement. 'Two weeks and I'll have a ring on my finger and be Mrs Bolter!'

'An old married lady,' Jess teased her.

'With her own little house!' Sis hugged herself.

'Ar – and 'er own scrubbing brush and mangle,' Olive added.

Listening to Sis, Jess felt such a pang of longing. How close she had thought herself to a settled life with Ned, and how much joy the thought of that had given her. To be loved, to have a home and feel secure!

'You make the most of it,' she told Sis. 'Scrubbing brush an' all.'

Sis grinned gladly at her. 'Ta, Jess. I will. I know I'm one of the lucky ones.'

The three of them walked along companionably in the bright March sunshine. A few trees they saw along the way were coming into leaf and though the sunlight still had the thin, strained feel of winter, it was good to feel its warmth on their pale faces.

'I still can't get used to it,' Olive said. 'Having time to walk about and shop – not queueing for hours for everything. Just not 'aving the war on.' Things had returned, in so far as they could, to normal. Bert was one of the fortunate ones who had his old job back at the rolling mills. The three girls had all squeezed into one room to let him have a bed, although Sis would soon be gone, and the house had settled into a routine again.

'It's lovely, ain't it!' Sis was truly full of the joys of spring and everything else too. 'Ooh – this time in two weeks! Let's hope and pray none of us go down with the influenza.'

'There's a lot bad with it,' Olive said. 'No good thinking about that.' She made a wry face at Jess. 'Come on – let's go an' put 'er out of 'er misery.'

They spent a leisurely few hours combing through the rag market and along the shops, looking at bolts of cloth, hats and shoes, weighing up what Sis had already and what would need to be bought. When it came down to a choice between two materials, Olive favoured a plain lilac cambric.

'Oh no!' Sis protested. 'I'd look like a flaming nurse-maid or summat in that. Look – what about this? It's really pretty – for a spring wedding.'

She ran her hand over a soft lawn with a pattern of honeysuckle and roses on it. Jess smiled. Despite Sis's desperation to get married, she'd said she wasn't going to do it in December, oh no. It had to be in the spring with flowers and sunshine. Jess could immediately imagine Sis in the floral material, flowers, or perhaps even a little tulle veil in her hair . . .

'Oh Auntie!' she cried. 'That's Sis to a tee.'

Their eyes met for a moment and Jess knew they were both thinking the same thing: Louisa. It was just the pretty, romantic sort of stuff Louisa would have chosen.

Olive fingered the price label. It wasn't too expensive: Sis had made quite a simple choice.

'It'll be easy to work with, that will,' Jess cajoled her aunt. In the end, Olive nodded.

As the morning progressed, Sis chose a pretty straw hat which she could decorate with flowers, and settled for a pair of second-hand shoes, white, with a ribbon bow on the front.

'They're a bit scuffed.' She eyed the toes of them.

'We can stick some whitener on 'em,' Jess encouraged her.

'They're ever so comfy.' Sis was clearly delighted with them. 'Must've been pricey new.'

'I could do with a sit down,' Olive said, after all these deliberations. 'Let's treat ourselves to a cuppa tea and a bun.'

As they sat together chatting and sipping tea, Jess looked at her aunt. If there's one good thing, she thought, that's come out of Ned leaving me like he did, it's me and Auntie getting on again. That tension between her lover and her family which had torn at her for so long was gone now. She felt a great surge of affection for the stout woman in front of her with her worn face and hands. Her sad past. As Sis chattered on about Perce and the house they were going to rent together in Balsall Heath, Jess thought, she's been my only real family, Auntie has. I owe her everything.

'My treat today,' she said, handing over the money for the tea. 'Since you've got to put up with me about for a bit longer yet.'

'Oh—' Olive hauled herself up from the table. 'That's awright, bab. I shan't like an empty 'ouse, that I shan't.'

They ambled down along Spiceal Street and Sis, catching sight of the flower ladies, surrounded by their bouquets and all yelling in raucous competition, moved on to the subject of what sort of posy she was going to carry. Jess was just about to remark that she'd already have flowers in abundance all over the dress, when she noticed Olive was no longer walking beside her. She turned.

'Auntie?'

Olive had stopped and was standing quite still, one hand laid over her heart. Her eyes were stretched wide with an expression which Jess read as pain, and she hurried back to her.

'You feeling poorly, Auntie?' she asked, frightened. She took Olive's arm and her aunt didn't shake her off.

Sis came rushing back too. 'What's up, Mom?'

'Over there . . .' Olive was staring across towards a fruit and veg stall.

In that second Jess understood that her face was full not with pain but with fear. They followed her gaze and Jess saw a thin, stooped old lady in a black coat and hat. She was buying spuds and the stallholder was tipping them into her carrier for her. They could only see her in profile, but Jess made out a sharp face with a pointed nose and slack, yellowish skin.

'Oh God alive . . . It is – it's 'er . . .' Jess felt Olive sag as if she was going to collapse, and grasped her arm more tightly under Olive's, feeling her trembling. Her face had gone sickly white, perspiration breaking out on her forehead.

'Who?' Sis was staring across wildly, not understanding.

'It's that woman,' Jess said. 'Doris . . .?'

'Adcock,' Olive added, her eyes still fixed on her. 'She's there – I ain't imagining 'er, am I? She really is there?'

'That lady in the black hat?' Sis frowned. 'You sure it's 'er?'

'Yes . . . oh . . .' Olive gave a moan, a hand going to her mouth.

'My God, Auntie—' Jess squeezed her aunt's arm fiercely. 'What in God's name did she do to yer?' She was appalled to see Olive, so strong, so brave, reduced to this by the memories of this woman's cruelty. She saw that no one has power like that of an adult over a child.

Olive shook her head. 'Just the sight of her . . . Oh, I feel bad.'

Sis handed her mother a handkerchief and Olive mopped her forehead.

Jess felt as if she was swelling inside with rage and indignation.

'We'll go and give 'er a talking to, that's what we'll do.'

'No!' Olive said faintly. 'I can't . . .'

'She's just an old woman,' Sis said.

'So what if she's old – what excuse is that?' Jess was on fire. 'You might be frightened of her, Auntie, but I'm certainly not. Come on – she's moving off. We'll lose 'er else.'

The old woman had begun to shuffle off with her walking stick along towards St Martin's Church, her lips seeming to move in an endless mumbling patter as she did so. Jess pulled the others along, following until they reached a less crowded little spot near the church gate, and released her aunt's arm.

'Oi – you. Missis!'

The old woman took no notice so Jess tapped her on the arm and she stopped abruptly. In that second Jess saw two watery eyes peering at her from under the hat brim with a steely hostility. Startling, horrible eyes with their double pupil, giving her the cold, glassy look of a cat.

'Doris Adcock?'

'Who're you?' She squinted at Jess.

'You deaf? I said are you Doris Adcock?' Jess experienced almost a sense of ecstasy rising in her. Her fury was so strong, so complete, her body so taut with it, there was a kind of perfection in it. It was the most soaring emotion she had felt in a long time and she was ready to knock the old crone into the day after tomorrow.

She saw the old woman nod reluctantly. The whites of her eyes were a sludgy yellow, lips mean and crinkled as pastry cutters.

'D'you know who this is?'

She heard Olive say, 'Oh Jess – no . . .'

Doris turned and looked at Olive with a vague bewilderment. Olive quailed under her gaze, gripping Sis's arm.

'This is Olive. Olive Tamplin, she was. From your old neighbourhood. Remember?' Jess had her hands on her hips. She wasn't speaking loudly, but she could hear the menace in her own voice. 'Had a sister called Louisa. Their mom was called Alice. Alice Tamplin. Bet you remember her awright, don't yer?'

There was a horrible moment as recognition seeped into the old woman's expression, a look of unguarded malice which narrowed her eyes and contorted her face.

'Yes.' She tapped the stick vehemently on the ground. 'The babykiller.'

Jess heard Olive give a whimper just behind her, and for a moment she had an urge to tighten her hands round Doris's scrawny throat and crush the life out of her.

'And you thought it was your business to follow 'er children and hound them, torment them until they was too frightened to live in that neighbourhood so they moved on, and even then yer'd still follow 'em and spread yer poison about them until life was hell for them. A worse hell than it already was without their mom because you saw to it she was locked up and the key thrown away!'

Jess had her face right close up to Doris's. She could hear the woman's whispery, agitated breathing, but her eyes looked back as cold as stones.

'Have you got children, Doris?'

'Yes.'

'Well you never should 'ave!' Jess spat at her. 'Nature should've dried your womb up before it let you breed any more of you. You're a cruel, vicious bitch and you made life hell for my auntie for no reason. You just had nowt better to do than be cruel and make life as rotten as possible . . .'

'She killed a babby,' Doris croaked. 'Murdered it with 'er bare hands. People 'ad a right to know what was living in their neighbourhood . . .'

'But you carried on when she weren't even there!' Olive spoke, crying, and Sis was holding her arm. 'On and on, never leaving us be. She was gone, our mom, and we never saw 'er again.'

'What's bred in the bone . . .' Doris said. The very sight of her filled Jess with horror. She had viciousness stamped through her like a stick of rock. 'I'd do it again tomorrer, that I would. She was a wicked woman, that Alice was . . . she walked the streets parading 'er crime. She were proud of it. Don't tell me that ain't evil in a woman.'

'She was sick,' Olive moved closer, sobbing. 'She was poorly, our mom was – after the babby . . .'

'Not half as poorly as you are though, Doris,' Jess snarled. 'Sick in the head, you are, ain't yer? This is who you've been afraid of all this time, Auntie: a broken down, mumbling old biddy so eaten up with nastiness towards other people you can read it in her face. Auntie—' Jess held out her arm and pulled her forwards.

Olive was trying to calm herself, wiping her eyes with the handkerchief. 'See – she ain't nothing to be afraid of. She's an evil old bitch who likes to make other people suffer.'

Doris tried to take a step back as Jess, Sis and Olive half encircled her, but there was a wall behind her. Olive stood staring into her face, taking deep, shuddering breaths. It was a moment before she could speak.

'You made life hell for us,' she said at last. 'It was wrong and cruel of yer. I 'ope you rot in hell for eternity for yer wickedness, that I do. But whatever happens, there ain't nothing more you can do to me. You're nothing. You're just a speck of filth and soon time'll sweep yer away and you'll've left nothing good behind yer.'

Doris was making vicious sounding mumblings, 'get away from me, yer bitches ... get away!' Jabbing her stick at them, her head making little jerks which reminded Jess of her stepmother's hen-peck nod.

Olive straightened up. 'Leave 'er. Just leave 'er. I've seen 'er now and I don't want to look at 'er no more. Let's get 'ome.' She took Jess and Sis's arms and they turned away, Sis making sure they'd got all the right bags.

They had walked a little further on towards Digbeth when they became aware of a small commotion behind them. Nothing loud, but a ripple of different sounds at the end of the Bull Ring, and they turned. A couple of people were running and a little knot of passers-by was gathering round. The three of them stared for a few seconds at the little they could see of what was on the ground: what looked like a little pile of crumpled black clothing lying very still. A walking stick lay discarded nearby.

They looked at each other.

'We killed her,' Olive said. Her tone was of disbelief mixed with fear. Sis looked absolutely horrified. They stood stock still, watching as two of the crowd bent over Doris. A few moments later they saw she was being helped groggily to her feet.

Jess pulled on their arms, forcing them to turn away and walk on with her.

'She must've come over dizzy, we never killed her.' She squeezed each of their arms, certain, reassuring. 'But even if we 'ad, she'd've bloody well deserved it.'

All the way home Olive chattered, 'Oh Lor' – oh my, I can't believe it ... And the way you carried on, Jess, I never knew you 'ad it in yer!'

'Well I 'ave – and the way I feel about 'er I could've broken 'er flaming neck, the evil old cow.'

They found Polly giving the children their dinner at the table and John Bullivant was there too. His face had filled out more and he was a calmer, slightly more cheerful man though still suffering times of deep depression.

Polly looked at her mom with concern.

Olive sank down on to a chair as if none of the rest of them was there.

'She awright?' Polly whispered to Jess.

'My legs,' Olive murmured. 'They won't hold me.'

'What's happened?' Polly demanded. 'Did yer 'ave a nice time?'

'We, er ...' Jess looked at Sis who was still holding her bags of purchases, over her arm.

But Olive had put her face in her hands and burst into tears, crying with all the abandon of a young child.

*

Later, when they were alone, Jess said to Polly, 'There's one more thing for 'er now. For all of us. When the wedding's over, we've got to get things finished for 'er. We've got to find Alice.'

Forty-Two

'I now pronounce you man and wife!'

The vicar's thin face lit up as Sis and Perce flung themselves joyfully into each other's arms in the aisle of St Agnes' Church. Jess felt a smile spread across her own face. She wanted to clap but that wouldn't be right.

Sis, for all her passion to marry Percy, had been all nerves that morning. When they reached the church she'd come over wobbly and tearful and Olive had had to calm her down outside before they could go in, while Polly reminded an over-excited Grace that she was going to have to walk quietly up the aisle with her auntie Sis in their pretty dresses.

They'd all been on the edge of their seats as Sis and Perce took their vows. At the moment when the vicar asked did he, Percival James Bolter, take Louise Joan Beeston, Perce's head shot round to look at her in astonishment. He'd forgotten Sis's proper name – was he marrying the wrong woman? Little Grace had stood fidgeting and twisting round to receive encouraging looks from her mom, and they all thought Sis was going to get the weeps or the giggles again. But now she had got through it. She was married! She paraded back along the aisle on Perce's arm beaming at everyone.

As the rest of them turned to follow the couple out, Jess saw Peter Stevenson standing a couple of rows behind them, dressed smartly in black, following Davey out from the pew. He was turned slightly away from her and she had a couple of seconds to observe him, dark eyes fixed on his son, his tall figure stooped to guide Davey. The sight of his large, gentle hands on the boy's shoulders sent a sudden sensation through her, a kind of melting, a longing. What care, what kindness there was in the man, she thought. He didn't look round at her, and following him to the back of the church she thought how little they'd seen of him recently. Last summer he'd been round, or out with them almost every week, had been so often by her side, but she had been so preoccupied with Ned she had barely noticed, had taken his presence for granted, oblivious of the feelings which Sis said he had for her. She realized that until today they hadn't seen him for well over a month. Everyone was busy with new jobs and they no longer worked together. Peter had found another job as a foreman in a machine tool works. Perhaps he's feeling better in himself now, Jess thought. He just needed company then, that was all.

'Wasn't it lovely?' Polly was chattering down her ear. Grace, who had run to her the second the service was over, was in her arms. 'And didn't you look just like a princess, Gracie? You did them dresses lovely, Jess.'

Grace's yellow, flowery frock matched Sis's and the colours had looked warm and lovely in the dim light of the church.

'It was perfect,' Jess said absently. I miss him, she found herself thinking. Miss him being there with us.

After Sis and Perce had been duly showered with rice and congratulations, the families went down to the Ship Inn for a drink or two before going back to the house for some food. Jess hurried home with Olive to make sure everything was ready for them. Polly followed them more slowly, pushing John, Grace riding on his lap and Ronny running alongside.

'Is, er – is Peter coming back?' Jess asked.

'Oh, I s'pect Sis'll bring 'im along,' Olive panted. 'God, it's warm today, ain't it? I 'ope we've got enough, Jess, I want them all to 'ave a good feed.'

The tables were chock-a-block with meats and pies, sandwiches and cakes, and a vase of spring flowers stood by the front window. Olive whisked the cloths off the plates and set out as many cups and glasses as she could lay hands on, Marion Bullivant having provided her with all hers. When Sis and Perce and the rest of them arrived from the pub, full of jollity, everything was looking ready and welcoming.

'Oh Sis!' Jess kissed her, then Perce. 'That was lovely. You look so beautiful, don't she, Perce?'

'Like my very own angel,' Perce said quaintly, and Sis, still clinging to his arm, said, 'Oh Perce, that's lovely, that is. I 'ope yer'll still be saying that when I'm an old lady and me teeth've all dropped out!'

Over their shoulders Jess saw Peter arriving. Her pulse picked up speed at the sight of him. I never thought this'd happen again, she thought, not for anyone. She waited for him to come to her, as he always had in the past, looking for excuses to be at her side. But instead he looked round the front room, his eyes skating over her, as if he was looking for someone else, and he went out, through to the back. Jess found herself feeling bereft.

Oh well, she thought. No point in me thinking about him. Sis was imagining things about Peter. He was just lonely. And anyway, I must seem almost like a child to him.

She moved round the room offering sandwiches,

chatting to Perce's mom, dad and sister, and his brother who had lost an arm on Vimy Ridge and had to stand next to the table to rest his plate on it or he had no spare arm to eat with. Jess liked Perce's family. They were all relaxed and friendly and full of jokes, but all the time she was aware of where Peter was in the house. He chatted to John, to Polly, to Sis and Perce. He played with the children, helped Olive bring in water from outside. Once or twice as they passed one another he nodded and said hello with a tentative smile. But not once did he come to her as he used to do, to talk and spend time with her. If Peter had ever felt anything for her, she thought, he didn't any longer. Now they were working apart that had changed. The chance was gone. By the end of the afternoon, happy as she was for Sis, she found herself feeling empty and disappointed.

They saw Sis and Perce off for their little weekend holiday with much cheering and kissing and good wishes. They were off into town to catch a train out to the country. Sis, her moods changing with great rapidity that day, was a bit tearful again as she embraced Olive.

'I'm not really leaving 'ome, am I, mom? I'll only be down the road!'

'Go on with yer and enjoy yerself,' Olive sniffed, giving her a watery smile. 'Time to worry about all that when yer get back.'

'Bye, Jess,' Sis hugged her tight. 'You next, eh, you and Polly?'

'Polly maybe,' Jess laughed. 'I don't know about me – I think I'm going to end up an old maid!'

'Poll?' John Bullivant called to her from where he was positioned by the table in the back room. Much of the afternoon he had been having a good chinwag with Bert and with Perce's brother, the other old soldiers present. Now things had quietened down a bit, the light was beginning to die outside and he wanted a few moments' privacy.

'Take us out the back for a minute, will yer?'

Polly, thinking he needed to use the privy and didn't like to say, tactfully opened the back door and manoeuvred the chair through it.

'Close the door, wench.'

Obediently she fastened it and went to push the chair closer to the door of the privy.

'No – I don't want that. I wanted to talk to yer, alone like.'

John found his hands were quivering and he gripped the arms of the chair. Polly stood in front of him in the half light, thin, kindly, waiting to hear what he had to say. For a moment he was overwhelmed by the sight of her. How could he even be thinking of offering himself to this woman: injured, useless, half a man as he was? How could he even dare think it?

'What did yer want to say to me, John?'

Best spit it out, he thought. Only way. 'Polly – I'll never be able to walk again. I can't work. I'm next to useless. But I love yer. I want to ask you to be my wife.'

There was a long silence as she looked into his face. For a moment John could barely meet her eyes, but he looked up to see her lips trembling and she turned away from him, putting her hands over her face.

'Yer can't face it, can yer? Being saddled with a cripple for the rest of your life! For all yer fine words that's what I am to yer – a lump of meat in a wheelchair, not a man!'

'No! It ain't that, John – truly!' Slowly she moved round to face him again, hands still held in front of her as if to replace them over her face at any moment. 'It ain't you. I love yer, John – I do. You're a lovely man and I'd give my life to yer with pleasure. But—' She couldn't put into words what was stopping her, was tearing her emotions apart. I'm still married: Ernie's still with me as if it were yesterday and until I can believe he's dead I can't marry you with a clear conscience. I'm haunted by him and he won't let me rest . . .

'But . . .' The grief and bitterness in John's voice as he echoed her made her distraught. She went to him, kneeling to take him in her arms.

'I do love yer – just give me a bit more time, sweetheart. That's all. I want to be yer wife. I just can't agree to it yet.'

John put his arms round her bony shoulders and his eyes met hers. 'Don't hide anything from me, Poll. I couldn't stand that. Is there someone else yer want more?'

'No! Oh John, no! I mean, not anyone like you mean. It's Ernie. I know it seems stupid to you but I can't marry yer 'til I've found a way to lay 'im to rest. Once and for all.'

Everyone looked up as they came back in. Perce's family had all gone and the rest of them were sitting round the back room looking relaxed and happy. As they came in, Peter Stevenson got up.

'Time we were off, Davey,' he said. 'I'm sure we've outstayed our welcome already.'

The little boy groaned. He and Ronny were playing together on the floor. 'Oh Dad – not yet!'

'Course yer staying,' Olive commanded. 'There's plenty more to eat and drink and we've 'ardly seen yer since Christmas. We'd thought you'd gone off us!'

'Don't talk daft,' Peter said, putting his hat down again. 'Course I haven't. I thought you might just want to be family . . .'

'You're almost part of the family,' Olive insisted, eyeing Jess meaningfully. 'How's that kettle coming on?'

'Slow,' Jess said. She was glad of something to keep her busy. All day she had felt an emotional pressure growing between herself and Peter Stevenson. She was sure now that he was not avoiding her by accident. But she hadn't approached him either. She didn't know how to be with him any more, what to say. She didn't know what he felt and was just as unsure of her own feelings. She found herself struck dumb in his company.

As John and Polly came in Bert got up to help. He took in Polly's emotional expression.

'What's up, Poll?'

Polly looked round the room, then down at John as if asking his permission. Jess saw him nod.

'Go on,' he said. 'Yer might as well.'

'John's asked me to marry him—' Polly held up one hand as the others began to exclaim at the news. 'But I've said to 'im I can't yet, things being as they are. You know 'ow things were for me after Ernie . . . after 'e were killed. I know you thought I were going off me 'ead, Mom. But it were the only way I could face things then. But the thing is . . .' She began to get emotional again. 'I still feel as if 'e's about. As if it's a mistake and 'e ain't really . . . dead. I know it sounds daft, but it's not knowing where 'e is or what happened . . .'

She stopped, looking round at them.

Bert spoke gently to her. 'You don't think 'e's not dead? Don't waste yer time thinking that, Poll. 'E'll be dead all right – you know that, don't yer?'

Polly nodded. 'I do really. It's just – if I could see his grave – you know, like you do with a normal death. I mean, even if we knew where 'e was, they ain't going to bring any of them back over 'ere, are they?'

Jess listened, one hand on the warm handle of the kettle. She thought of all her visits to her mom's grave, what strength she had taken from it. Things need finishing properly, she thought. For all of us.

Olive sat massaging her sore knuckles. 'Well there ain't no chance of that, Poll.'

'There might be, you know.'

Everyone looked at Peter Stevenson.

'What d'yer mean?' Polly said.

'People do go. Some even went before the war was over.'

'Well I know *some* do, like with money and that, but I mean it's right over there – across the Channel. It's *France*.'

Peter smiled. 'It's not the ends of the earth. People do go to France.'

'Not people like us.'

'Well I went,' John said. 'For a start.'

'But it'd cost the earth,' Olive said.

'There's a fund started up, I think.' Peter rubbed his forehead as if it would help him remember. 'Some feller at the works was talking about it. Look – I'll ask around, see if there's anything we could do.' He smiled suddenly, his gaze directed across at Jess who had not realized until that moment that she had her eyes fixed on him. It was as if each of them forgot for a second that they were not supposed to feel for each

411

other. Shyly, she smiled back, instantly full of a warm sense of joy.

A few days later he called again, quite late in the evening, without David who was asleep at home. Polly let him in and Jess was startled at his sudden appearance, hat in hand, ducking his head to come through the door. For a second his eyes met hers, then he looked quickly away. Jess moved briskly across the room, finding things to busy herself with. He hasn't come to see me, she told herself. He's come out of kindness for Polly.

'There is a fund, like I said. Just starting up.'

Polly was watching him, her expression full of misgiving.

'If you go with a London travel company it'll set you back thirty-five pound – more even. If you go through the fund it's fourteen.'

'Struth!' Olive exclaimed.

Bert was shaking his head. 'Fourteen quid! The bloke's dead!'

Polly ignored him. 'That's still an 'ell of a lot of money.'

Jess moved over and put her hand on her cousin's shoulder. 'Poll – if you want to go that bad and put your mind at rest, we'll find the money for yer. I've got some savings – put away for a rainy day, like.'

'But I can't go to France on my own!'

Peter Stevenson cleared his throat. 'If you don't mind – I've got a suggestion to make.'

Forty-Three

May 1919

Jess leaned her head against the grimy window, feeling
the rocking rhythm of the train as it chugged through
the Staffordshire countryside. It was two weeks after
Sis's wedding and she and Perce were home and getting
settled into their tiny house on Sherbourne Road,
though she was forever popping back to see them. She
seemed happy and lively as ever, but missed the girls'
company.

'Perce's lovely to me,' she said. 'But 'e don't *talk* all
that much. I don't even know as 'e's listening to me 'alf
the time.' She'd said she was too busy getting straight
to come with them.

Polly and Jess sat side by side, each of them with
their hats in their laps. Olive was opposite, dozing,
mouth slightly open, hands slack. On the seat beside her
was a posy of spring flowers. Outside was cloudy but
dry, sunlight through breaks of cloud. They had started
off very early that morning, taken a train up through
the Black Country, seeing the red glow of furnaces in
the grey morning, a pall of soot seeming to engulf
everything, buildings, grass, trees. They changed at
Stoke-on-Trent and were now on the branch line looking out at the fields green with young wheat, at tarnished churches, stone buildings. It's peaceful round
here, Jess thought, and solid. She liked things to be
solid. Sure. The nature of their visit filled her with a

great sense of poignancy. Travelling by train made her think of the passage of time, of life itself passing by in a way she seldom had time to do normally. She thought of Alice and Louisa. Her mother and grandmother, their lives cut short so young, and both, one way or another, because they were women. She found herself thinking of her own dead child. Ned's child. It came to her that every time a woman fell pregnant she took her own life in her hands, forever. Whether the babby lives or dies, none of us is ever the same again, she thought. And will there ever be any more children for me? Any more love for me?

Peter Stevenson's face came into her mind, the look he had given her that night outside the house, when he left with David asleep on his shoulder. She had been too frozen inside then, too full of grief to respond. Whichever way her mind turned it seemed to fasten on something sad: children, Ned, Peter. She turned to Polly who was looking across at Olive.

'Be there in a minute,' Jess said. 'It's no distance.'

'I hope this ain't going to upset her again.' Polly looked anxious. 'Mom's been through enough.'

'She wanted to come. Like you and France.' They were making arrangements, with Peter's support and help.

'I know it's the right thing to do. She should know where 'er own mom's buried. I think it's terrible our granddad never took 'er to see. I feel ever so churned up though, thinking about it.'

Jess nodded. 'I do an' all. Sort of touching the past. Gives yer a peculiar feeling.'

The train slowed and Polly leaned forward and gently prodded Olive's knee. 'We're there, mom.'

Olive opened her eyes, bewildered for a second as

the train braked abruptly. 'Feels as if we've been travelling for days.' She gathered her coat stoutly round her, picked up her bag and they hurried off. Polly had picked up the flowers.

As they stepped out on to the little station, a goods train made up of trucks full of sand rumbled past, the wind lifting a light silt of it sharp against their faces, making them blink their eyes.

'Ugh!' Polly said. 'It's windy up 'ere – let's get on.'

On the street, they stopped, at a loss.

'How do we know which way to go?' There was a tremor in Olive's voice. 'Oh Poll, we can't ask – not for that.' The terrible shame of it filled all of them. They would have to go and ask for the Mental Hospital. As good as admit that someone, one of their own, had been in an asylum, locked away from the world. For a moment they were completely at a loss.

'Maybe if we was just to walk round for a bit?' Polly suggested.

'No.' Jess pushed her chin out with furious defiance. 'She was our flesh and blood, Alice was. I'll find out. I'll go back in there and ask.'

They had to walk out of the village, the stationmaster told Jess. He was a middle-aged, kindly sort who set them on the right road.

'You can't miss it,' he said. 'Look for the tower.'

The blackened, brick tower was the first they saw of the hospital. Once on the long drive the rest of it came into view, tucked in with hills behind, a low collection of buildings so desolate, so marked in its isolation from everything around it that the sight made the three of them reach for each other's hands. They had not spoken much on the walk out there, each of them too full of feeling. Jess breathed in deeply, trying to calm herself. Was this Alice's place? The walls behind which pretty, young Alice had lived out the rest of her days? She looked anxiously at her aunt and saw Polly was doing the same. How much more Olive must be feeling!

Olive showed no outward sign of emotion.

'This is it then?'

'Yes,' Jess said gently.

'I can't really take it in.'

'You awright mom?' Polly had a catch in her voice.

Olive's eyes moved over the collection of buildings. 'This is where they put 'er then. Where they took 'er. All that time . . .' She shook her head, beyond words.

When she had taken in the sight of the place for a time, Jess said,

'Shall we go and ask to see the graveyard?'

Olive seemed to steel herself for a moment, then nodded. As they walked along, arm in arm, she pulled the two of them closer to her. Jess looked round at her, remembering holding her aunt's hand the day they buried Louisa, when her head only reached up to Olive's elbow.

The main door was black with a small grille set in it which opened quite some time after they had pulled the bell. A man's face appeared, eyes narrowing against the light.

'We're expected,' Jess said. 'Mrs Beeston. We wrote to say we'd be coming.'

After a long process of rattling bolts and turning keys, they stepped inside, as if into another life.

'Follow me,' the man said. 'It'll be Mr Lang you want.'

He led them halfway along a deserted, echoing corridor and into an office where a dark-haired man with thick horn-rimmed spectacles sat owlishly behind a desk. Seated at another desk behind him, a woman was typing at high speed.

It was Polly, in the end, who did the talking. Olive found herself incapable and sunk down on to the chair opposite the desk. Jess found Mr Lang a little strange at first. He didn't look them in the eye, and he spoke slowly, as if unused to it, in a low, gravelly voice, but he was obliging enough. He searched through a pile of papers for Jess's letter.

'Let's see – you say you want to look for the grave of an Alice . . .' he strung out the words, 'Tamplin. Hmmm. Now I don't know anything about her, of course. You're certain she was here when she died? Good, well, I'll get someone . . . no, look, let me take you. That would be easiest.'

He stood up and put his coat on and a hat over his thin black hair. 'I shan't be long,' he told the typist.

To Jess's relief he led them, with loping strides, back the way they had come to the front entrance. She had been afraid they would have to walk through the labyrinth of the hospital, and the place appalled her. The man asked no questions, just kept walking, slightly ahead of them. Once they had walked out and round the side of the building he pointed and said,

'You can see the hospital chapel there.' The geometry of that part of the building differed from the rest, the roof curving up to a point, rather like the prow of a ship, with a cross on top, and the end wall, which jutted out, had crosses built into the pattern of the brickwork. 'We need to go just round behind there.' His tone was low and considerate.

'It's very quiet,' Jess said uneasily. 'Where is everyone – all the inmates, I mean?'

Mr Lang pulled out his watch as he walked and looked at it. 'They'll all be inside on the wards. Except a few who're out working in the grounds, but that's over the other side.'

The graveyard looked neglected, the grass long and full of clumps, and a riot of weeds and wild flowers had colonized all over it. Mr Lang explained that part of the hospital had been vacated for use as a military hospital during the war, the inmates moved elsewhere.

'Everything went downhill as you can imagine. Still recovering. I'm very new here myself, of course. Now – perhaps you'd like to have a look . . .'

He stood aside with his hands clasped behind his back as if to dissociate himself from their emotion as they began to wander up and down the rows of graves together, reading the plain little crosses and headstones, some of them wood, a litany of strangers' names, waiting for the words, 'Alice Tamplin' to be there, to jump out at them. Row by row they looked, reading along the fifty or sixty graves until they came to the last.

'Must be here,' Polly murmured. ''Ow could we've missed it? We can't've done, can we?' Jess felt she was studying each one more intently than the last, as if to force the name on it to be Alice's. When they reached the last stone, it read, 'Susannah Peters'. They looked up at each other.

'Well where is she then?' Olive said shrilly. 'What did they do with her?'

Mr Lang was beginning to sound weary of the whole affair. He led them back to his office.

418

'You say she died – when?'

'It'd have been eighteen eighty-four,' Olive said. She couldn't hide her distress. 'That's when my father told us. I was thirteen ... She must be 'ere somewhere. I've always known of 'er being 'ere ...'

'One moment Mrs – ?'

'Beeston.'

Olive sat, breathing audibly as Mr Lang went through a door at the back of the office and returned with two leatherbound ledgers which he opened on the desk and stood leaning over them like a carrion bird.

'What year was the lady in question sent here?'

Polly and Jess looked at Olive.

'Eighteen seventy-seven. August eighteen seventy-seven – no, 'ang on, that'd be Birmingham. She came out 'ere the following year. Eighteen seventy-eight, early on, about February.'

He replaced the ledgers with others, opening yellowed pages and running his twig-like fingers down inky lists.

'Ah.' He stopped. 'Yes. Here we are.'

Olive's right hand went to her throat.

'Alice Tamplin – from Birmingham? They brought her all the way out here?'

'Was that unusual?' Jess asked.

'Rather – but not unheard of. There are hospitals in Birmingham, of course. But if they were over-full, for instance ... Or a request from the family. Now ...' He turned over a few pages, musingly. Jess felt as if her eyes were trying to bore through the pages. Show us! she wanted to shout. Show us what it says!

Mr Lang turned another page and a sheet of paper fluttered to the floor. The woman who had been typing had stopped to listen, and she picked it up. Mr Lang peered with sudden attention at the page.

'Oh! Ah – now, here we are! Well well . . .'

'What does it say?' Jess couldn't keep quiet.

'No wonder we couldn't find her in the grave-yard.' He looked up at them over his spectacles. 'Alice Tamplin did not die in this hospital.'

They gaped at him.

'What d'yer mean?' Polly could barely do more than whisper.

'On the fifth of May eighteen eighty-seven, an Alice Tamplin quitted the hospital.'

'Quitted?' Olive said faintly.

'Yes, left. Was allowed to leave. Discharged.'

They looked back at him in sheer disbelief.

'But—' Jess said eventually. 'How could she just *leave*?'

'It seems that she was considered of sound enough mind, of no danger to others or to herself. It does happen occasionally. But someone must claim responsi-bility for any inmate who is to be released. In this case,' he looked down at the page again. 'The person named is a Mr Arthur Tamplin.'

Shock came so fast upon shock that they hadn't the time or capability of making sense of it. Olive sat quite silent, quite still.

'But where did she *go* then?' Polly asked. 'She never came 'ome, did she?'

'No,' Olive whispered. 'Never.'

'She may have gone to Leek to seek employment. Or even as far as Stoke. I'm afraid there's no record of that.'

'I think this might shed some light on it.' The woman at the typewriter was peering at the yellowed slip of

420

paper which had floated to the floor. Mr Lang turned to take it from her, but she got up and handed it straight to Jess.

It was a cheap piece of notepaper with a few lines of looped writing on it. It was addressed to a 'Miss Harper'. Jess gave it straight to Olive and she and Polly leaned over her to read it.

1887

I got to Whitall orite He got me a plase to live and Im making a start on the baking He said he'd see me orite wich he will in case i deside to goo back home wich he dont want I wont goo, too much water under the brige Ill get on here its nice and quiet

Thankyou for waht youve dune for me ill niver forget you.

sincerly, Alice Tamplin.

When she'd read it, Olive went very pale and her hands were shaking so much that she couldn't hold the flimsy sheet of paper. 'That's her writing,' she kept saying. 'Oh yes – that's her writing.'

Polly handed it back to Mr Lang and laid her hand on her mother's shoulder. She helped Olive lean forwards, supporting her as she tried to recover herself.

'D'yer think . . .' Jess's mind was racing. 'I mean, might she still be alive?'

The man shrugged. 'I'm afraid I have no idea. This was all before my time. I don't know the age of the woman in question, or her circumstances.'

'No – course you don't,' Jess said. 'Only this is such a shock for us, yer see. All these years . . .' She stopped, shaking her head. 'Where is Whitall?'

421

'Not far at all. Between here and Wetley Rocks. A couple of miles at most.'

She and Polly helped Olive to her feet and they left, thanking Mr Lang. The main door closed thunderously behind them.

Walking back down the long sweep of the drive, their minds were seething with all they had just learned. Olive, so silent before, couldn't stop talking, repeating over and over the anguish of the truth she had just learned, tears streaming down her face.

'All that time 'e knew our Mom was alive and 'e kept her hidden out of the way so 'e could live with that Elsie instead! Louisa and me'd 've done anything to have our mom back. Oh Poll – can yer credit it? She was out of 'ere and 'e never said. I can't believe 'e could be that cruel, that I can't. If 'e was still alive today I'd – oh, I don't know what I'd do!' She stopped, turning to look back at the hospital with its black, secretive windows.

'What if—' Jess said. She and Polly were nearly as overwrought themselves. 'What if she's still living there, in Whitall? I mean – she'd be what, seventy?'

'Nigh on. No – oh Jess, yer don't think ... No, she can't be, can she? I mean, she ain't come to us in all this time. We can't – she daint want us ...'

'Auntie—' Jess took Olive's arm and spoke gently to her. 'She'd been in this place for ten years. *Ten whole years.* Of course she wanted yer, but it must've felt like a lifetime she'd been away. And she knew she weren't allowed to 'ave yer.'

'Granddad would never've let 'er out if 'e thought she'd ever come near Birmingham again,' Polly said. 'She must've thought of you and Auntie Louisa with a new step-mom, all settled like ... How could she just come back? She was dead to them and she had to stay dead even if it broke her heart.'

Olive's face crumpled again. 'Oh God, and it breaks mine just to think of it . . .'

Jess and Polly held her close to them. Jess felt the rough weave of Olive's coat under her fingers, and could feel her trembling.

'Mom,' Polly said. 'D'yer want to leave the flowers here somewhere? Where she was? I know she daint die here, but just in case?'

Olive drew back, tears on her face.

'I don't know.' She looked round. 'No. We can't leave 'em 'ere. I wanted somewhere with the feel of 'er in it, but I can't feel it. She ain't 'ere.'

Forty-Four

It took them nearly an hour to walk to Whitall. On the
way they persuaded Olive to stop for a few minutes in
a gateway by the road to rest and eat some of the bread
and cheese they had brought.

'I couldn't eat,' she said.

'You must, Mom. It's hours since we had anything
and we'll be dropping else. You need to keep yer
strength up for this.' Polly handed round food from the
bag. 'Ooh, I could do with a cuppa to wash it down,'
she said.

The grass was wet and muddy underfoot so they
stood up to eat. A horse and cart passed by on the road
and a lad sitting at the back with his legs dangling down
stared open-mouthed at them. Birds dived twittering in
and out of the hedgerows and Jess breathed in the smells
of grass and wet earth.

'Louisa took to the country,' Olive said, seeing Jess
gazing round at the fields, a soft expression in her eyes.
'It were like she was born to it.'

'P'raps Alice liked it too,' Jess said.

The village of Whitall sprawled along the road which
ran through it like a spine. They passed farms, then
cottages, widely spaced at first, then huddling closer
together, making a proper street. A few people were

about, and some looked curiously at them. The road was muddy and churned up by cart tracks. At the heart of the village smaller lanes branched off the main road and to one side, and behind the cottages, they could see the square tower of the church, topped at each corner with little gold flags. They turned off down the lane to the church, hawthorn and young trees on each side of them. At the end the path widened and divided to run in each direction, forming an oval-shaped path round the graveyard.

Olive immediately began looking at the names on the graves. Watching her aunt's quest, her stopping, looking so intently, sometimes even tracing over the letters with her finger then straightening up, each time hoping, Jess felt suddenly that she couldn't bear it. Even if Alice was buried here, a stone would tell them nothing of her.

'That must be the vicarage.' She pointed at a large, gabled house behind the church. 'Let's ask, Poll, shall we? It's such a small place we must be able to find someone who knew 'er and could tell us summat.'

Olive began to protest.

'Please, Mom,' Polly touched her arm. 'We've come all this way.'

There were yellow climbing roses in the front garden of the vicarage and they could hear the sound of children from the back. The house was so big and grand that for a moment they hesitated. Then Jess lifted the heavy knocker.

The maid told them the vicar was in, and took them into a homely parlour evidently reserved for visitors. Soon they heard a voice in the corridor saying, 'Strangers, you say. Well, well. How exciting—' and round the door appeared the plump, boyish face of a

425

man who appeared ready to befriend anyone in the world.

'Good afternoon – I'm Mr May. Archie May. Vicar of the parish.'

As he stepped forward to shake hands, it was immediately apparent that his left arm was missing, the sleeve of his shirt pinned up at the shoulder. Seeing their gaze immediately fix on this as they shook hands, he said,

'Yes – lost the other one. Ypres.' He pronounced it Wipers. 'Army chaplain – one of the Staffs battalions. Damn lucky it wasn't the other one, since I'm right-handed, eh?'

He indicated that they should sit down. 'Now – can I help you in any way?'

Between them, Jess and Polly began to explain, and the Revd Archie May listened attentively.

'I say—' he interrupted after a moment. 'You've travelled all the way from Birmingham! You must have a cup of tea – just a moment.' He went to the door and summoned the maid and in no time a tray of tea appeared. Jess felt like hugging him for his thoughtfulness. As they drank it, they explained that they were looking for a relative who may have lived in the village.

Archie May stroked his chin. 'Alice Tamplin?' As he spoke, Jess felt her innards contract. It was so strange hearing her name on someone else's tongue. It made her real. Out of the corner of her eye she could see Olive's hands tightly clasped on her lap. But the vicar shook his head. 'No – doesn't ring a bell. Thing is though, I've only been the incumbent here for a matter of months, so my memory doesn't stretch back all that far. Tell you what—' he jumped up boisterously. 'Soon as you've downed that tea – I've got just the chap for you. Just have a word with my wife – let her know I'm off out.'

He left the room for a moment and they heard his voice shout 'Darling?' distantly at the back of the house. They looked at each other in silence, sipping the hot tea from bone china cups as fast as they could manage.

'Now—' Archie May looked the sort of man who would have rubbed his hands together frequently had he been able to do so. 'Let me take you to meet Revd Chillingworth. He was vicar here for – oh, thirty-five years or more, and he still lives in the village, just across the green. If there's anything to remember about any soul in the parish, he's your man. Marvellous fellow.' He led them out of the front door. 'In his mid-seventies and still turns out to make up the Whitall eleven, cricket mad, all his life.'

Polly took Olive's arm and they followed Archie May's springy walk back along the lane to the road and along another short path running off from the opposite side, which led to the village green. Round it stood four cottages and he took them to one which had a riot of buddleia bursting out of its front garden, alive with cabbage white and tortoiseshell butterflies.

The Revd Thomas Chillingworth was, even at his advanced age, a magnificent-looking man. Tall, slightly stooped, with the bushiest white eyebrows Jess had ever seen, vivid blue eyes and a large, hooked nose. His face and hands were so lined and gnarled they made Olive's look quite youthful.

'Come in, come in!' He led them into a sitting room at the back looking out over a lawn edged with flowering shrubs. The three of them quailed at the sound of his loud, autocratic voice, but to Jess's astonishment,

Archie May turned round and winked conspiratorially at them. 'He's a proper old lamb in wolf's clothing,' he murmured. 'Very deaf though.'

They were invited to sit in this room, already so stuffed with books and papers that there seemed barely space to move. The wall was covered with pictures with leprous-looking mounts round them, mostly of cricket teams. Thomas Chillingworth sat grandly before them, a prayer book resting on the arm of his chair, and leaned forward to listen to what Archie May had to say, one hand cupped round his right ear to increase his chance of hearing.

'Alice?' he boomed. 'Oh yes – I remember Alice all right.'

All of them felt their hearts race violently, but intimidated by the old man they left the young vicar to question him.

'Alice Tamplin?' Archie May asked.

'What's that? Tamplin? No – no recollection of a Tamplin. But Alice – now I remember her. Could hardly forget her – practically lived in the church. Only one who came to evensong every night of her life . . .'

'But her name wasn't Tamplin?' Archie looked regretfully at them. No luck, his expression said.

'No – she was . . . Brodie. That was it. Alice Brodie.'

They all heard Olive's breath catch. Even Thomas Chillingworth seemed to sense the impact of his words.

'That was 'er maiden name,' Olive said, gripping Polly's hand. 'She was a Brodie – 'ad a brother, Joe Brodie all 'is life.'

'She's . . .' Jess hesitated. 'She's dead then?'

'Dead – oh yes,' he continued loudly. 'Died a good while back, poor old Alice. Before the war. She was taken with one of those wasting diseases and faded

428

away. Never would have any help from anyone. Baked bread – that was her living, you see – right up to the end. Always like that. Very reserved woman, very quietly spoken. Strong as an ox though, I reckon. She came to me two or three times—' His voice slowed, musing on the memory. 'Odd, it was – I thought so at the time. She'd look into my face as if she'd come to offload something particular, but in the end she'd never say anything much ... In all the years she was here she barely ever said a word about herself. Not to anyone, so far as I know. I knew she'd been in the asylum over there—' He jerked his head. 'That was common knowledge. Heaven alone knows what effect that had. But she just went along, you know, lived a quiet life, no harm to anyone ... that was all really.'

There was silence for a moment. He sat nodding, remembering.

'One thing I do recall, now I think of it. Early on – probably the first Christmas she was in the village though the Lord only knows now when that was ... She was a very devout woman as I say, attended everything. But on that Christmas Eve she came to the midnight service. She was deeply upset by it. It sticks in my mind because she was in such a state when she came to take communion. Weeping, distraught. And upset at attracting notice to herself. It's a season which does heighten the emotions, of course. Especially these days ... but I never saw Alice like that at any other time. She never came to the Midnight Eucharist again. Not in all the years she lived here.'

He became aware of the intense, rapt attention of the three women in front of him. 'So what have you to do with Alice?'

'She was ...' Jess had to shout to make him hear. 'A

relative. A long-lost relative.' She looked at Archie May. 'Will you ask him – did Alice marry? Are there any children?'

'Marry? Alice?' For a few seconds his body shook with silent mirth at the idea. 'Alice wasn't the marrying kind. Oh no – you couldn't imagine Alice marrying. I don't know what was in her past – perhaps you do. But she was an island on her own, Alice Brodie was . . .' Again, he shook his head. 'An isolated being. That was Alice. Cut loose, somehow. Strange creature.' He looked directly at them. 'But a good soul. Of that I'm sure.'

A thought struck him and he pulled himself spryly out of the chair.

'Let me see now – d'you know, I do believe . . .'

He fumbled round amidst the utter chaos of the shelves, limping along them stiffly, running a finger along the dusty leather bindings.

'There are a couple of albums from the parish – I must hand them over to you, Archie. Not really mine to keep after all. Ah – here!'

Yellowed pages crackled open under his hands displaying faded sepia photographs. He looked through, murmuring to himself.

'Yes – that's the one! The only time we could persuade her to come along. This was the annual parish picnic – nineteen hundred, look. Now that—' his arthritic finger quivered lightly over a face at the end of the solemnly posing line, 'is Alice Brodie.'

The tiny, indistinct face of a fifty-year-old woman looked out at them from the picture from under a dark hat with a brim. Jess could hear Olive's jerky breathing close to her as they peered forward to look.

'Oh God.'

'Is it?' Polly asked.

'It's so small – I can't be sure . . .' Olive laid her hand over her heart, trying to calm herself, staring rapt at the picture. 'It could be, but then – oh my Lord, yes it could easily be . . .'

They all pored over the picture, unable to move away from their one glimpse of Alice, Alice who, after all, had made some sort of life. Jess couldn't stop staring at the faded sweetness of the face, its closed, unsmiling gaze, the thick hair escaping from under the hat. She could sense that had Louisa lived long enough, she too would have looked like this, and that in turn, one day, she herself . . . But the woman's face told so little. Another face among a throng of faces giving nothing away. No clue on the outside, Jess thought. No scars to show us.

'I say,' Archie took in the acuteness of their need to see. 'Thomas – how about giving them the picture? The parish won't miss one photograph – they'll only moulder quietly away on the shelves in the vicarage.'

'Would you like it?' Thomas Chillingworth asked. 'I don't see why not, after all, if it means so much.'

He took an ivory-handled paper knife from his desk and carefully cut the page from the album. Olive took it from him as if she hardly dared touch it, looking up at him in awe.

'I'm ever so grateful – I don't know what to say,' she said tremulously. 'You see – Alice Brodie was my mother.'

They found her name in the graveyard, 'Alice Brodie', carved on a simple stone, positioned close to a young lilac tree which was pushing out fragrant white blossom.

They had left Archie May with their stumbling gratitude, and come to kneel on the spongy grass round the grave in the afternoon sun.

On the stone it said simply, 'Alice Brodie 1850–1912. Faithful Child of God.'

Olive sat, transfixed by the sight of it. They were silent for a long time, staring at the little grave, the high emotions of the day still coursing through them. All that remained of Alice, then, they could locate here. This had been her place where she settled at last, and this what finally remained, this little stone already green with lichen.

But we remember you, Alice, Jess said, in her mind. Your family remembers you and you live on with us. Now you can rest in peace.

At last, Jess gently nudged Polly. The two of them got up and walked a short distance away. The graveyard was ringed, beyond the path, with dark yew trees, but among the graves were lighter, young blossom trees. They went and stood near one, a flowering cherry still wearing the remnants of its blossom.

For a moment the two of them put their arms round one another and held on tight, not speaking. When they released each other they stood watching Olive still kneeling by the grave, her bag and the flowers beside her. They could tell she had begun to speak, the low murmur of her voice just reaching them though they couldn't hear her words. After a time, she picked up the posy of flowers and laid it carefully beside the humble headstone. Then she got up and walked towards them, and there was an enormous tiredness about her.

Forty-Five

Picardy, France – June 1919

The car lifted lazy sworls of dust behind it that hot, still midday, the sound of its engine breaking into the silence of the countryside. They had the windows open, so that the burring sound of the tyres over the pavé road came to them more loudly. The sun was almost at zenith, so that the car moved through an arcade of grey shadow thrown down by the trees with knobbly trunks which grew along the roadside.

They had taken the first morning boat to Boulogne, where the lady from the St Barnabas Fund met them to take them south: past Montreuil, through the old city of Abbeville and along the line of the Somme Valley towards Amiens. Now the war was coming very close to them. The names of towns were taking on a terrible familiarity, and as they motored away from the comparative tranquillity of the coast towards the battlefields of North Eastern France, they began to see clusters of graves marked with wooden crosses.

Jess, who was seated next to the rear left window, shifted her position a little, her cotton frock damp with sweat under her. Polly was asleep, leaning heavily against her shoulder, and Jess could feel the moist warmth between their bodies. She felt protective towards Polly, travelling here to face her grief head on. John was also asleep with his head back next to the other window. In front, Peter Stevenson made desultory conversation with Miss Baxter, the St Barnabas lady who was driving the car. She had rich brown hair taken up into a pleat and held tenuously by tortoiseshell combs. They looked so insecure that Jess, sitting behind her, had been waiting all day for them to fall out and her hair collapse, but so far they had held on, letting more and more strands of hair escape from them and blow round her head in the breeze from the window. Jess felt almost a sense of worship for Miss Baxter. She had thought of everything: the route and accommodation and the need to strap John's wheelchair to the roof of the chesty old car. She anticipated their needs, even their feelings. To Jess she seemed one of the most wonderful people she had ever met.

'Not too far now,' she called over her shoulder. Jess loved the sound of her Scottish accent. 'It's a pity we have to make these visits so brief,' Jess heard her say. 'But of course it's a question of the expense, and the sheer numbers of folk wanting so desperately to come. We hope to charge less as things get established.'

Peter nodded. Jess watched him out of the corner of her eye. She had an oblique view of his profile, the slant of his cheek, and she could just see the tip of his nose. She looked out of the window, but kept feeling her gaze drawn back to look at him, at the line of his dark hair at the nape of his neck.

'Were you on the Somme yourself?' Miss Baxter asked.

'No.' Jess heard a stiffness in his tone, his shame at not having done his bit. Peter raised one hand to ease some irritation on his cheek and she saw his long fingers rub the skin back and forth for a moment. 'I was reserved to oversee a munitions factory.'

'Aha. Well – the body is composed of many organs,' Miss Baxter said enigmatically.

Jess sensed, rather than saw, Peter smile faintly. She felt a huge surge of gratitude to him as well. It was because of him they were here. He who had sought out all the possibilities of getting them to France, who had made the arrangements. What had clinched things was that John Bullivant, hearing them discussing the possibility of going to the battlefields, had begged to be allowed to go.

'What on earth d'yer want to do that for, John?' Marion Bullivant had seemed quite alarmed.

'I can't explain it, Mom. I just do. I left me legs over there and I weren't with it when they brought me back. I don't remember 'ardly a thing about it.'

'But John,' Polly said gently. 'Ernie died on the Somme. We won't be going to Belgium.'

'I know that, Poll. But it's still over there, ain't it? The state the place'll be in I should think Ypres and the Somme'd look pretty much alike. I just feel I'd like to come and see it. It took years of my life as well as my legs.'

Polly had glanced across his head at Jess. We can't refuse him, her expression said. But how on earth are we going to manage?

It was Peter who had found out about the recently founded St Barnabas fund. Peter who had then said that he would come at his own expense to help John. Ernie's family had been all for Polly going and they chipped in to help. All of them had savings from the war and in the end they put together enough for the four of them.

Those weeks, as the spring had passed and turned into early summer, were a time of churned up feelings for all of them. Mixed in with the preparations for the journey to France was all the emotion over Alice, the rewriting of her past in their minds. Slowly they grew more used to the idea. It was hardest of all for Olive: to have to accept that her mother had been alive and had not come back to them, and grow to understand and forgive her. Jess saw her quite often just sitting in silence, staring, and knew she was thinking of it. When she did talk about it it was with enormous sadness and regret, not with bitterness. She put the photograph from Whitall parish in an old frame and it stood on the mantelpiece. Having that seemed to reclaim Alice as part of the family.

And there was other turmoil. Bert, after coming home and gleefully returning to civilian life, was now restless and discontented. His face wore a frown almost all the time.

'I'm back 'ere,' he complained. 'Back where I started in a bloody 'ard, filthy job. Four year of my life I fought and for what? What did I get out of it?' Though he had left the army cursing it high and low, he was now talking about joining up as a regular.

'You get used to the life, sort of thing. Moving about. Seeing a bit more of the world. And there're some good lads . . .'

By May he had re-enlisted and said his farewells to them.

'I don't blame 'im in a way,' Perce said when he heard.

Sis looked indignantly at him. 'Well I 'ope you ain't getting any ideas of going off!'

'Not on your life!' He gave her a saucy, affectionate pinch so she squealed. 'I know when I'm well off!'

Jess turned to the car window again, seeing now that

the scenery was changing. They had reached the edge of the town.

'Now you can see,' Miss Baxter said. 'We're getting close.'

Jess nudged Polly who stretched, yawning loudly, and woke John. They sat in absolute silence as Miss Baxter steered the motor car slowly, almost reverently along the ruined main street of Amiens, still following the river.

'They make beautiful wool and velvet here – or did,' Miss Baxter said. 'Before it was shelled to blazes. And Albert's even worse. Almost completely flattened.'

It was hard to imagine that anything would ever be made in Amiens again. So many wrecked and ragged buildings, the rubble of stone, the smashed remains of life as it had been before.

'They didn't get the cathedral though – look, quickly, to your right. We're turning off here in a minute.'

Before them, the lead covered spire of the cathedral soared up out of the rubble against the blue sky with a kind of majestic defiance and in it they caught a glimpse of the city's real face, its splendour before the war.

Jess felt a moment of empathy with the huge building as if it were a big strong lady, squatting there, flanked by its flying buttresses like petticoats. She survived! Wouldn't let them crush her. It gave her strength, this thought, as they drove along the sleepy country road towards the ruined town from where Ned had sent her postcards of the basilica, when she had believed love was a sure, unchanging thing.

*

They stopped outside Albert in a tiny roadside café, ate bread and drank black coffee brought to them by a wordless girl who then stood with her back against the wall, watching them. Jess winced at the bitterness of the coffee but it refreshed her. They were seated at a rickety table in a little stone floored room where flies moved above their heads. Peter was beside her. Miss Baxter opposite.

'How did you come to be doing this work?' Peter asked her.

'Well . . .' She spoke slowly, as if reluctant. 'My fiancé was killed not far from here – at Grandcourt.' It came as a revelation to Jess that Miss Baxter was a great deal younger than her old-fashioned manner and style of dress made her appear. 'My family are not without money – I was able to come almost as soon as the war finished. It meant everything to me to know where Duncan met his end. There was no grave for me either—' She looked at Polly. Neither the Red Cross nor the Graves Registration Committee had been able to locate exactly where Ernie was buried. 'But to see the place – be close to him somehow . . .' She spoke with great sadness, but with a kind of resignation, and looked calmly round at them. 'I had to find a worthwhile way to fill my life. You see, Duncan and I were going to go abroad. He'd planned to train for the ministry and I was to teach – in India. I didn't want to go alone: it was our project, our dream to carry out together. So when I heard about St Barnabas I volunteered straight away, to help other people find some sort of peace of mind.'

Polly's eyes filled with tears. John put his hand on her shoulder. Before they left she had gone to a seance at the Blacks' house for what she said would be the last time. John didn't like her going. She had asked Ernie what he thought of her going to France and he had given her his blessing. Miss Baxter's round face looked with great kindness at her.

'It's a sight you'll never forget – out where they were fighting. Beyond belief. But it does help, in a strange way.'

'I just need to know – to see,' Polly said. 'To lay him to rest in my mind.'

Miss Baxter leaned across and laid her hand over hers. 'I know, dear. I know.'

They left behind the ruins of Albert, straddling the River Ancre, and drove the few miles to La Boiselle through a landscape which looked ghostly even on this sunlit afternoon. The fields lay uncultivated along the Front, for the land had to be combed further for the dead. For miles on end stretched the churned up earth, pocked with shellholes. Shoots of grass, wheat and weeds had sprouted across them in uneven patches and here and there, tiny, fragile poppies blew in the breeze. They passed thin clumps of tree stumps, pathetic sticks poking up, barely a leaf in sight, and along the road still, lay the rubble and the human debris of the front line: sandbags, twisted chunks of rusting metal, wrecked wagons, sprawls of barbed wire and discarded belongings – a bleached scrap of khaki cloth here, an old water bottle or rusting mess tin there.

'My God,' Polly breathed. 'What a mess.' She had taken Jess's hand. They were almost afraid to see, much as they wanted to.

'We thought we had it bad,' Jess said soberly. 'But my God, the poor French!'

'There is a little money to be made out of the debris,'

Miss Baxter told them. 'I gather copper wire fetches a good price. And uniform buttons, guns – you'd be surprised.'

'Can't say I blame 'em though,' Polly said.

The road climbed gradually upwards and on each side of the road were gentle hills. Miss Baxter pulled the car into the side of the road and swivelled round to face them. She looked at Polly.

'We're very close. Up here the road will cross the line of trenches the Germans were holding in July 1916 when the Big Push began. You can see one of the craters where our boys mined underneath it prior to the attack. It's a massive hole – still full of what they left behind, helmets and so on. And just over the way are our trenches – they were very close together here. Just in the village there's a spot they call the Glory Hole where they were only yards apart.'

Polly gripped Jess's hand. Jess could see Peter watching her cousin, a gentle expression on his face. He sensed her looking at him and his eyes moved to meet hers for a second.

'Can we get out 'ere a minute?' John asked.

Miss Baxter hesitated.

'I'll help him,' Peter said. 'You stiff, John?'

'Ar – bloody stiff.' His voice sounded harsh after Miss Baxter's soft tones. 'And I want a look round.'

Polly and Peter levered John out of the car again and eased him down to sit on the ground. Polly got back into the car, leaving the two men to talk.

'I was going to say to you, Mrs Carter—'

'Please – my name's Polly – this is Jess. You don't need to call me Mrs Carter all the time. 'Specially the way things are and you being so kind to us. You feel almost like family.'

Miss Baxter smiled. 'All right. Thank you. And I'm Isobel. I'd be just as happy if you called me that too. I was saying – as there is no grave as such for your husband, and you can't be certain of the exact spot where he died . . .' She brought the words out painfully. 'There will be memorials of course, eventually. None of them will be forgotten. But for now, I'd suggest you choose a place, when you find somewhere appropriate, to make your peace with him. People find that helps.'

This time Jess squeezed Polly's hand to give comfort.

'Awright, I'll do that,' Polly said huskily. She turned to look out at the fields. 'Oh my God – what're they *doing*?'

Already yards away, on the rough terrain beyond the road, were Peter and John, beginning to climb slowly up the side of the nearest low incline. Peter was bent forward, taking short, determined strides, as John clung to his shoulders. He looked a pathetic sight, flung across Peter's back, the remains of his legs dangling helplessly, Peter's elbows sticking out as he held on to him.

Isobel Baxter was out of the car in a second and Jess and Polly followed.

'Stop – for heaven's sake don't go any further! STOP!' The young woman jumped up and down waving her arms frantically above her head. They saw Peter stop and swivel round. For a moment he loosed John with one hand and waved at them.

'Shan't be long!' they heard him shout. 'It's not far!'

'But there're BOMBS!' Isobel shrieked. She seemed almost beside herself. 'Please stop, you could be killed!' But Peter had turned away and continued to clamber up the slope, a rough rubble of stones, exposed roots, tree-stumps and debris, so that he had to watch every step and it took all his attention.

Isobel wrung her hands. 'It's quite, quite wrong to leave the roads and the designated paths. There are unexploded bombs everywhere . . . bodies . . . Oh dear. Perhaps I ought to go after him.'

'I'll go,' Polly said.

'No.' Jess laid a hand on her arm to stop her. 'Don't. Leave them.'

'You're right,' Isobel said, her eyes never leaving the two men. 'If we all start going it increases the risk. But oh heavens . . .' She pressed her clenched fist to her lips.

There was a kind of indistinct path which Peter was following through the rubble. Slowly, ploddingly he climbed. Jess watched, her body so tense she felt she might snap, every fibre of her willing him to reach the top safely, to turn, to come back. She found herself overwhelmed with feeling that she had only dimly known was in her.

Be safe, be safe, Peter, oh Peter, her mind hammered, beyond her willing it. Come back to me . . . She laid a hand over her fast-beating heart. She didn't really know how big the risk was that Peter was taking with his own life and John's, but she found herself chill with fright. It was as if all the same kind of longing, the hopes and prayers she had sent out to Ned during the war distilled together in her mind, the intensity of it startling her. Come back to me, Peter my love – please . . . This time the words, the longing, was for someone else, and she was shocked by the extent of feeling towards him that had been growing, deep in her.

The three of them watched every move of the two men as they reached the highest point. Peter turned this way and that, so that they could look back towards Albert, then over to La Boiselle. Jess saw him pointing across the landscape with its scarred fields and clumps

442

of razed woodland, its pimples of hills. For a few moments he put John down and they rested, apparently without talking. Jess watched them, saw the curious camaraderie that had formed between the two men. Soon, Peter hoisted John back on to his shoulders and they began the descent. For a moment, halfway down he slipped and almost fell and they all gasped, but he managed to right himself.

'Oh Lord!' Isobel murmured. But soon they were down the hill, safe, and Peter was walking across to the car. Both men were smiling.

'I ought to give you a thorough ticking off!' Isobel ran to them, laughing with relief. 'Please don't ever, *ever* do anything like that again, will you promise me?'

'I'm sorry, Miss Baxter,' Peter backed in through the car door, depositing John on the seat. Jess heard the jubilation in his voice. 'Didn't mean to get you so worried. Got a bit of a better picture up there.'

'You can see our lads' trenches,' John said through the open car door.

Jess looked into Peter's face and he smiled at her.

'Don't suppose you were worried?'

Jess felt her cheeks burn. She had known, in those moments, how much she felt for Peter Stevenson, and now she was vulnerable in front of him.

'I was. Course I was,' she said testily.

'I just wanted John to be able to see . . .'

She could see in his face that it was not just John. Carrying him up there had been a test for him: the duty of a man who had not endured the trenches to perform a service for one who had. A different pilgrimage from the one the rest of them were making, but a pilgrimage none the less. There was a relief, a satisfaction about Peter as they got back into the car.

'Now,' Isobel said. 'Time is marching fast onwards. We have to return to Abbeville this evening, so no more delays – please.'

Polly chose a spot just outside the village of La Boiselle to consecrate a little piece of ground, in her own way, for Ernie. La Boiselle had been fought over so heavily that most of it was a ruin. Looking along what must have been the main street was a poignant sight. So little remained of the buildings of the flattened village and what did was mostly rubble.

'These poor people,' Polly said, even more moved by the sight than she had been in the towns. 'All their homes gone. I think I'll do it somewhere 'ere.'

They walked until she found a little spot at the edge of the field nearest the southern end of the village.

'I shan't be able to keep coming back 'ere,' she said. 'So it don't matter to me if it's only me knows where it is. Look – by that little tree. That's where I want it.'

Close to what looked like the remains of a barn, a young sapling had been smashed, leaving its trunk a sharp stump not much more than a yard high.

'Cut off in it's youth – like Ernie. Like all of 'em.'

Peter helped her, digging a little hole in the ground near the tree with a trowel, which Isobel had had the foresight to carry in the car. John sat in his chair and Isobel and Jess stood nearby watching. Polly had a little wooden box with '*Pte Ernest Frederick Carter – Royal Warwickshire Regt*' carved on the top. Inside, she had told Jess, she'd written a letter to Ernie saying how much she loved him, would always love him, and wishing him goodbye. With it she'd put her wedding ring with a picture of Grace and a lock of the little girl's hair. She broke down as she laid the box in the ground, and knelt by it sobbing.

'Oh Ernie,' they heard her murmur. 'Oh Ernie ...'

Jess went forward and knelt beside her, her arms round Polly's shoulders, while Peter retreated to stand next to John. Peter knew as well as any of them the need to relinquish the dead in order to love the living, but he also understood how hard it must be for John to watch Polly's grief over another man.

Polly accepted Jess's embrace for a moment, then turned back to cover over the box with earth.

'Goodbye, my dear Ernie,' she whispered. 'I can't do no more for yer now. I wish you'd lived and come home, I do with all my heart, but I know you're gone. Rest in peace, my love. I'll bring up our Gracie right, and I'll never forget yer.'

She patted the surface of the little grave and got up to gather some stones, which she laid in the pattern of a cross over the top of it. Peter came close and took some photographs.

'Grace might want to see when she's older,' he said. Jess saw Polly give a smile.

'Well done,' Isobel said softly. Jess saw that she too had tears in her eyes. 'Shall we all just take a bit of time to walk with our own thoughts before we go?'

They all spread out, each of them leaving the others with their private griefs. Peter pushed John's chair to a place next to the road where he could sit and look. Jess walked back a short distance, and stood with her arms folded looking out across the sombre French fields. The light was fading: it was almost dusk and very quiet, the only sound the gentle breeze which played with the light skirt of her dress. The end of a warm summer's day. They were days like this in 1916, she thought. And only last year guns were firing across these fields. She felt full to the back of her throat with emotion: grief and anguish for Polly and John, and an immense sorrow for all the dead who still lay round. But mixed with the sadness came also a sense of wonder, a restless longing.

Inevitably she found herself thinking of Ned. He fought near here somewhere, she thought. He had mentioned High Wood, and she wasn't sure where that was, how far away, but he had undoubtedly been through Albert. Here, so many miles away from her, when in feeling they had seemed so close. And now she had come to this place herself, he was lost to her forever. How long, how faithfully she had devoted herself to him! She had lived for him and for his love, for their future together, and what had happened to all her high ideas of passion and devotion? She saw Polly, in the corner of her eye, walking along the edge of the field with her head down. Polly with her clear grief. For a moment Jess even envied her. If Ned had died on the Somme, how sweetly she could have remembered him! His life cut short, a decorated hero of the war, preserved for her like a tinted photograph, enshrined in all his perfection. If he were gone, she could still remember him as loving her. As it was he had had to go on, carry his wounds, his confusion into the imperfect future. He had left her a more bitter remembrance than Ernie, who had given everything to the French earth and who by not returning, had lit his own life with a glow of glory.

But Ned *is* gone, Jess told herself. Just as much as Ernie is. She too, had to bury him here and look to the future.

She turned to go and join the others, and as she did so, heard her foot tap against something wooden. Looking down she saw a short plank, painted as a rough sign board. Curious, she squatted down and turned it round, rubbing off some of the dried mud. In black paint, above an arrow, it read, 'Sausage Valley'.

Peter came and stood over her. 'What's that you've found?'

'An old sign – look.' She stood up.

Peter read it and chuckled. 'Did you know there's a "Mash Valley" somewhere near it as well?'

'No!' she laughed.

There was silence for a moment as they looked out together across the haunted landscape.

'They're still here,' she said. 'All of 'em. I can feel it. As if they're begging us not to forget them.'

Forty-Six

By the time they arrived in Abbeville the sun had long set. Jess and the others all slept on the journey, while Isobel Baxter drove on steadily, car headlamps pushing on into the darkness. When Jess woke, the engine was switched off and they had pulled up in a dark street. She could make out almost nothing outside except that there were buildings on either side of them.

'Here we are.' Isobel opened her door and Jess stepped out feeling muzzy and confused. The air was warmer than she expected. 'This is our stop for the night. We're rather late, but Madame Fournier should be waiting for us.'

Peter Stevenson and Polly attended to John, and Jess and Isobel carried the luggage into the dim little vestibule, where Isobel, with obvious affection, greeted an elderly woman with hunched shoulders and steel-grey hair. Even in her only just awake state Jess marvelled at Isobel. She seemed to manage everything: even spoke fluent French!

Madame Fournier showed them to their rooms up a staircase with an intricate wrought-iron bannister, shadows leaping around them in the candlelight. It was a sizeable old house and their footsteps sounded loudly along the wooden floors. There were engravings in heavy dark frames along the upper corridor, which smelt strongly of beeswax polish.

Polly carried a candle into the room she and Jess were to share. There was one, grand-looking bed, the bedstead high at each end, made of carved wooden panels, and a crucifix was nailed to the wall above the head of it.

'Look at this!' Jess lay down on the bed. 'Be a bit like sleeping in a ... box.' She'd been about to say 'coffin' but in the circumstances, thought the better of it. A hard, well-stuffed bolster lay along the top of the mattress.

'Ain't it *nice*?' Polly said, looking round. There was a marble topped washstand, a wooden chair with curved arms and a tarnished mirror on a chest of drawers near the foot of the bed. She rested the candle on the washstand and sank down beside Jess. 'This feels like the longest day I've ever had in my life. I'm all in.'

Jess rolled over on to her side, closer to her. 'How d'yer feel, Poll?'

Polly was rubbing her hands over her face. She paused a moment as if trying to assess her feelings. 'Better. I'm ever so glad we came 'ere. I mean, Ernie's been dead a good long while, but it's only now I think I can really put it behind me, now I've said goodbye to 'im properly.'

Jess smiled. 'Good for you. That's why we came. John'll be glad too.'

Polly nodded. 'I'm flaming lucky really, ain't I? And eh – what would we've done without Mr Stevenson?' Polly could never get used to calling him Peter, however many times he asked her to. 'I think the man must be an angel.' She looked closely at Jess. 'You know 'e's done all this for you, don't yer?'

'Don't talk daft – it's for John – and you.'

Polly laughed, head on one side. 'Oh Jess – how

449

much longer are yer going to keep the poor bloke hanging on?'

'Has he said anything to yer?'

'No,' Polly stood up, stretching. Through a yawn she said, ''E don't need to.'

They ate downstairs at a long table of dark, polished wood lit by candles. As it was late, Madame Fournier did not join them to eat. She greeted them with many nods and '*bonsoir*'s, and fed them with omelettes, bread and crisp lettuce leaves on thick white plates, and with it they drank red wine. The meal was served by a solemn-faced girl who looked, Jess thought, about thirteen years old. Since she had been in France she seemed to have seen only the old and the very young.

They were all very hungry and the food was delicious.

'How does she make an omelette as tasty as this?' Peter said, wiping his plate with a chunk of the bread. 'Even the lettuce tastes nicer than anything at home.'

'Well – it's straight from the garden,' Isobel said. 'At the back of here she has quite a little smallholding – vegetables, fruit trees, chickens. The French do like their food very fresh.'

Jess sipped the wine, feeling the alcohol going almost instantly to her head. 'You speak French ever so well,' she said. Isobel was sitting next to her.

'I was lucky enough to spend a year here, before the war. In fact Madame Fournier is an old friend of mine. One of her daughters is my age – she lives in Paris now and has a family of her own. When I started this work we had to find accommodation for people on these pilgrimages, and I thought of Madame Fournier here in

450

this big house. She did take in other lodgers sometimes, and she said that if I thought the folk I was bringing were suitable, she'd provide a bed and food for them. She lost a son at Verdun. She is very *sympathique*, as the French say.'

'Very good of 'er,' John said through a mouthful of bread.

'And are you glad you came?' Isobel asked him.

John nodded, wiping the back of his hand over his moustache. 'Oh ar – very glad. Yes. Thanks very much.'

'And you, Polly?'

Polly smiled. 'Yes thank you, Miss Baxter—'

'Isobel – please.'

'Isobel. I'm all in now though.'

'You must be tired yerself,' Jess said to Isobel. 'Driving all that way while we slept.'

'Ah well – that's all right. I shall sleep tonight.'

Jess understood by the way she said it that sleep did not come easily to her. She was reminded for a moment of Iris: something in Isobel's stoic acceptance of the suffering and loss in her life. I'll go and see Iris when I get home, she thought. I've been selfish, neglecting her while I was all wrapped up in my own feelings. I must look after her better.

While Isobel was advising them all to get a decent night's sleep as they needed a good early start to reach Boulogne in time, Jess looked cautiously across at Peter. She had spent so long avoiding his gaze, that she felt very self-conscious and vulnerable doing so. But tonight was special. This would be their one night in France, and it was thanks to him that they were here. Today she had allowed herself to admit how deeply she cared for him, and if she did not find courage to risk showing him, she might never know if he still felt anything for

451

her. After tomorrow they would be home, with everything back to normal, and she might hardly ever see him. The wine made her feel mellow and more relaxed, and she dared herself to look unwaveringly at him. He was listening to Isobel, but after a moment he seemed to sense her watching him and looked back at her. The expression in his eyes was so full of affection and tenderness towards her that she felt her limbs turn weak and had to look away. After a second though, she looked back and smiled.

He came over to her as they left the table, all still talking sleepily, making arrangements for the morning. Sensing him beside her, Jess looked round.

'I'll need to help John get to bed.'

Jess clasped her hands tightly together to try and stop them shaking. 'Yes. Course you will.' This time she didn't look away, knowing he wanted to say more.

'Jess, I was wondering . . .' He hesitated, watching her face, ready at any second to draw back if she showed signs of rejecting him. 'Afterwards – I know it's been a long day, but would you like to come outside – for a walk round? There's the garden . . .'

'Are yer coming, Peter?' John was waiting in the wheelchair near the stairs. 'Sorry, pal – only my bladder's fit to bust, I can tell yer!'

'John!' Polly ticked him off. 'The whole world don't need to know!'

'Yes,' Jess said softly. All sleepiness left her in an instant. 'I'll meet yer down here.'

'What're you two whispering about?' John demanded.

Peter gave a bashful grin. 'Give me half an hour,' he said to her quietly.

Upstairs, while Polly was pulling her clothes off and

yawning in great gusts, Jess unlatched the shutters and pulled one of them back. There was a half moon in the sky, silvering the tops of the fruit trees, though she could not see far down the garden. Standing still by the window, she could feel the blood pumping round her body. The muzziness she had felt from drinking wine had left her, and she was wide awake, with a strange, enhanced alertness. She felt as if she could go on without sleep forever.

'What yer doing?' Polly had stripped to the waist and was splashing water from the pitcher over her face and shoulders.

'Looking at the garden.' She turned round. ''E's asked me to meet him – tonight.'

Polly stared, water dripping from her chin. 'Who – Peter?'

'No, Kaiser Bill – who d'yer think?' Jess retorted.

'Ooh—' Polly beamed at her. 'Well about time.'

Peter helped John Bullivant out of his clothes and into bed. He tried to pay attention to the things John was saying to him, when he was trembling with anticipation and all he could think of was Jess ... Jess. He had waited long and patiently for her, knowing that she was grieving over Ned as he had also to do over Sylvia. He was not an arrogant man, did not assume himself to be irresistible in her eyes. But he knew that he loved and desired her with great, protective tenderness. Tonight, when she looked at him, fear and love in equal measure in her face, he knew that at last his quiet waiting might be rewarded. His body was so taut with urgency to get outside and see her and talk to her in case she changed her mind, that he thought John must feel it. But John was exhausted. He lay back on the wide bed and closed his eyes immediately.

'Thanks, pal,' he murmured.

'Sleep tight.'

Peter blew out the candle. He stood in the darkness for a few moments trying to compose himself.

Jess closed the heavy door behind her and stepped out into the garden, breathing in the warm, sweet-smelling night air. A tinny church bell was striking somewhere nearby, and as she stood still, letting her eyes get used to the darkness, she heard crickets in the grass and the muffled clucking of chickens from some distance down the garden. Jess knew that chickens were usually quiet once they had been cooped up for the night, but these sounded terrified, as if alarmed by something. Stepping carefully, she followed a rough path of stone slabs along the side of the grass and fruit trees. The garden was a good width, and extended over a hundred feet. The bottom third was screened off from the rest by a row of tall conifers and behind them, Jess found the whole area given over to a cottage garden. She smiled with pleasure, making out in the moonlight the rows of healthy look-ing plants. Madame Fournier obviously knew a great deal about growing vegetables. The chickens were squawking just as hysterically, and she was afraid the noise would bring someone out of the house to investi-gate. She could make out the wooden coop up against the end wall, and as she moved closer she saw a moving streak of shadow slink off and melt into the deeper darkness of the bushes at the edge of the garden.

I've just saved your bacon, you chickens, she

thought, waiting to see if there was any more sign of movement. But there was none. The predator had been scared off. She listened to hear if anyone had been disturbed, but there was no sound of anyone coming.

Able to see much better now, she went back nearer the house and stood under one of the trees, looking up into the branches. The sight of the leaves above her, burnished with moonlight, the fragrance of garden flowers and the fact that she was waiting for him to come to her, brought her emotions fully to the surface. I love him, she said to herself over and over. All that time I had eyes for no one but Ned, and this was here waiting for me. This love, beside me all the time. She knew this with burning certainty now. Knew she felt truly sure with Peter in a way she never had in those years with Ned, always hanging on for him, putting her life off until he came back, forever insecure and worried. She longed for Peter to come, to be able to tell him how much she felt for him. Looking up at the windows she wondered if she might see his shadow moving about in one of the rooms, helping John, but there was no sign of anyone. Their window must face out from the front, overlooking the street.

Eventually she heard the door open, then close again quietly and saw him standing outside, a long, lean shape, letting his eyes adjust in the darkness. She enjoyed watching him, knowing he couldn't yet see her. He took a few paces back and forth and she heard him quietly clear his throat.

After a moment she walked out from under the cherry tree and he came towards her.

'Jess?'

She loved the sound of his voice saying her name.

'Yes – it's beautiful out 'ere.' She was very nervous suddenly, looking for something to get them over the awkwardness of meeting. 'Come and see.'

He followed her as she walked down to the dark screen of trees, and they stood looking back at the house. One of the casement windows was slightly open, but there was no light behind it.

'I think that's our window,' Jess whispered. 'I must've left it like that. I'm surprised Polly ain't having a good nose out at us!'

'She wouldn't be able to see much,' Peter said.

'There're chickens down 'ere – no wonder her eggs tasted so nice.' She led him to the far end of the garden. They stood listening, but the chickens had calmed down and were quiet now. Jess felt she could sense, rather than hear their breathing and the close cluster of warm feathers.

'I scared a fox away when I came down before. The hens were making a hell of a racket, poor things. They must've been frightened half to death.'

'How d'you know it was a fox?'

'Well I saw it, sort of. I just know it was a fox!'

'And they could tell it was out here?'

'Oh yes. Smell it a mile off – and it was trying to get in, I s'pect.'

Jess thought, I want to say I love you, and I'm going on about chickens. She knew she was chattering out of nervousness, and told herself to shut up. In the silence that followed, she gradually turned and looked up at Peter, standing like a tall shadow beside her, waiting quietly, she thought, the way he does. She was intensely aware of his body close to her, and of her own, the feel of her dress against her bare skin. Peter leaned down, closer to her. Seeing the way she looked back at him, he held his arms out and drew her into them with a cry of joy that was close to a sob. She pulled him to her and they kissed, holding, caressing each other. She felt his hand in her hair, on her back, pressing her close in his desire for her. Her body responded to his excitement with strong, fiery movements until Peter abruptly pulled away.

'We must stop. I'm sorry, Jess ... I shouldn't've behaved like that. I don't even know if you ...'

'Peter?' She touched him, making him turn to her again, and wrapped her arms round him. 'Don't say you're sorry. You're the best, kindest man I've ever met. I love yer – I loved yer touching me.'

'Do you? Love me?' He stood stiffly in her arms.

She nodded. 'Sorry it's taken me such a long time to know it. Please – put your arms round me again.'

He did, laughing with happiness. 'I can't believe this is true. Oh my lovely Jess. Can you really love a funny old stick like me?'

'That's why I love yer. Because you're a funny old stick with a great big heart inside him and I'd trust my life to yer. Oh – and you're quite handsome really an' all!'

He tickled her so that she shrieked with laughter and they both stopped, looking back nervously at the house.

'That was your fault,' she whispered. Serious again she stroked his face with her fingertips. 'I feel so much for you. As if it was all buried somewhere in me and I've found it suddenly. I've so much love in me I want to give yer.'

'Oh Jess.' Moved, he kissed the top of her head, then stroked his hands lightly down the front of her dress, resting them for a moment on her breasts, free and warm under the light cotton. 'I could do with some love

I can tell you. These've been terrible, lonely years. And I've plenty to give you in return. More than you might realize.'

Jess laid her hands over his. 'Oh, I think I do,' she said.

The next afternoon, when they sailed back to England, was one of cloudless sky, the sea a deep, glassy blue. They said their farewells to Isobel, Jess hugging her, to Isobel's evident surprise and pleasure.

'You've been marvellous to us,' Jess said, truly sorry to be parting with her. 'You take care of yourself, won't yer?'

'Oh I will – don't you worry.' She turned back to them with a fond expression as she left and waved a last time. 'God bless you – all of you.'

John and Polly spent the journey up on deck, where Jess and Peter left them sitting together contentedly in the fresh breeze, John well wrapped in a blanket, Polly with a scarf over her hair. Jess and Peter strolled back and forth, stopping to lean over the side for long spells, at all times holding on to one another, arm in arm.

'I should feel tired,' Jess said as they strolled the deck. 'But I don't.' They had stayed up all night, sitting wrapped in each other's arms in Mme Fournier's garden, oblivious of the dew, the time, or anything but each other. They talked, caressed, kissed, until the sun tinged the roof and the leaves of the cherry trees with pink and they looked up, overjoyed by the sight.

'We can soon catch up on a bit of sleep,' Peter said. He looked at her, couldn't stop looking at her, full of wonder. 'You're so lovely. I just hope I'm not asleep now.'

'You're not.' She kissed his cheek, then leaned her head on his shoulder. 'There, you can feel I'm really 'ere.'

When Dover with its chalky cliffs was still just a haze in the distance, they were still standing, gazing out over the sea, Peter with his arm round Jess's shoulders, each too happy for words. But as the land drew nearer and nearer, Peter spoke at last. He removed his arm from her shoulder and turned to her, taking her hands in his.

'I've got to say this now – I just don't want it to wait any longer. I never want to be with anyone except you, Jess. Would you agree to be my wife?'

There was no hesitation. 'Yes!' Jess cried into the wind. 'Oh yes, yes!'

Laughing, he held her close. 'Aren't you s'posed to be a bit more reluctant when someone asks you? You know – think it over a bit?'

Jess grinned up at him. 'Why waste time?'

They found Polly and John on the sunny, port side of the ship, cups of tea on the table beside them, steam whisking away in the wind. Both of them were smiling, their hands clasped in each other's.

'Come on over 'ere, we've got summat to tell yer!' Polly waved at them as soon as they appeared.

Jess tightened her hold on Peter's arm, her joyful eyes meeting first his, then Polly's. 'Yes – so've we.'

Forty-Seven

11 November 1921

'Come on, Mom – we'll be late else!'

Jess looked up smiling as Davey's face, pink with exertion, appeared round the bedroom door.

'Nearly done, pet. Just getting 'er into a nice clean napkin.'

'Will it last long enough while we're out?'

Jess laughed. David, now seven years old, was growing up into a quaint little fellow. He had little memory of his own mother, and Jess was flattered and relieved by the way he had taken her so affectionately to his heart. She had grown very fond of him.

'Oh yes. Don't you worry.'

'Our dad's waiting . . .'

'Awright. You go and tell him I'm coming. I'll be down in a minute or two.'

His scurrying footsteps receded along the landing and downstairs.

Jess turned back to her baby daughter whose arms and legs were waving about with the sheer pleasure of movement. She stuffed a fist into her mouth, clamping her gums over it.

'You're cutting some teeth, madam,' Jess said. She bent and kissed the child's soft tummy. 'Come on, Alice. Yer Dad's waiting for us. Time we was going.'

*

'It's a pretty name,' she told Olive, who had come to see her, dewy-eyed with happiness, after the little girl was born. She kissed her aunt as Olive held the baby in her plump arms, her face softened by the sight of an infant. 'And between us we'll make Alice into a lucky name.'

Olive smiled, eyes still on the child. 'I s'pect you will, bab. Knowing you.'

She had been overjoyed when the four of them came back from the Somme, first of all to see Polly looking so relaxed and cheerful, and then to hear from them all that there was to be a double wedding. Jess could tell how highly she thought of Peter. He seemed to be the one to replace Ned in her affections.

'Louisa would've been so proud of yer,' she said to Jess.

'Well you're the one that's done me proud, Auntie. Taking me in and looking after me the way yer have. You've been a mom to me. You always will be.'

Before the wedding, which they fixed for the September, Jess said to Peter that there was one thing she felt she must do.

'I left my dad swearing I'd never go back there again,' she told him sadly. 'I regret it now, even though he daint seem pleased to see me. He is my father though. I ought to tell him I'm getting married, let him meet my intended and that.'

The day she and Peter sat on the train out to Leamington reminded her acutely of the same journey with Ned. The same smoky, grimy smell of the compartment, the city folding away, fields spreading golden around them. This time it was August, blue sky with piles of puffy clouds. She sat close to Peter, drowsy in the heat. Every so often she turned, found him watching her tenderly and reached up to kiss him.

461

She delighted in showing him some of the village, but when they reached Forge Cottage it looked very run down. The windows were filthy and the front garden had been allowed to run riot. Jess was filled with misgiving as she approached it.

'Oh dear,' she said to Peter. 'Oh look – this is where I grew up, but what a mess! My mom kept it lovely, and my stepmother. There must be summat wrong. Sarah must be ill – she'd never let the place get in such a state. She was a worker, whatever else you might say about her.'

'It's very nice,' Peter said looking down the farm track, clumps of nettles blowing about on the verge. 'I bet you ran wild here.' For a second she expected him to add 'my country wench'. But it was Ned who would have said that.

She smiled, though still looking anxious. 'I did a bit.'

The door was opened by a woman in her mid-thirties with a wide mouth and wide hips encased in blue and white gingham.

'Is—' Jess hesitated. 'Is Sarah Hart in please?' She felt as she spoke that they were not there, that everything had changed beyond her imagining.

'Ooh no. Sarah's been gone from 'ere a while now. Living back over the shop, 'er is, if yer want 'er. Who're you then?'

Jess's thoughts began to race. Had Sarah given up waiting for William to learn to love her and left him? What other reason could there be – what had happened?

'I'm Jess – Hart. Is my father still 'ere then?'

'Your father? William Hart?' The woman looked deeply shocked. 'Don't you know?' She looked back over her shoulder as if hoping there was someone else there who could impart the news. ''E was killed in

Flanders, duck. Back in the war. 'Ow is it you daint know that then? Your own father?'

'In *Flanders*? But 'e was . . .' She was going to say 'too old'. But she knew suddenly that he was not, though he had always seemed so to her. He would have been in his fifties, a fine strong man. Probably told them he was ten years younger and got away with it. The very young, the older men, they had needed them all by the end. But she could scarcely take it in.

'Sorry to give yer such bad news,' the woman said importantly. 'Only I'd've expected 'is daughter to know. Listen – my 'usband knew 'im well. Worked together for years, they did. I'll call 'im for yer, shall I? Philip! Phi—'

'NO!' Jess interrupted abruptly, starting to back away. 'No – thank you. There's no need for that. You've been very kind. Thank you for telling me. We'll be going now.'

Mrs Gill shrugged as if to say 'please yourself' and stood in her doorway as they disappeared down the road.

'Well,' Jess said numbly. 'That settles that. I've no one 'ere now.'

He took her hand as they walked. 'Aren't you going to see your stepmother?'

'Oh no. She won't want me turning up. We never got on. I'd like to see my mom's grave again, make sure it's tidy. And then we'll go. I know the place where I really belong now, and that's with you.'

That November morning the four of them hurried from their little house, Alice cuddled up in Jess's arms, and took a tram through the misty streets into town to join all the others gathering round the Town Hall. Polly had said she and John and Grace would try and meet them at the top of New Street, and as they drew closer, Jess saw them waiting in the spot where they said they'd be. Polly was heavily pregnant, and needed help with John's chair, so John's brother Lol had come along and taken over pushing it. Olive was there in a black hat, holding Grace's hand. She raised her arm straight up, swirling it around, the way she always waved.

'You look nice, Auntie,' Jess greeted her. 'Ever so smart. Awright, Poll? 'Ow yer feeling?'

'Oh, I'm awright,' Polly smiled. 'Considering.'

Dotted about the square, a number of collectors stood with trays on strings round their necks, a little sign on the front saying, 'Field Marshal Haig's Appeal'. The trays contained poppies made out of delicate red cloth and wired paper stalks.

'Poppies in the corn,' John said, when he saw them.

'They make these ones in France apparently,' Polly said. 'To keep the memory of the lads who died and 'elp the ones who make 'em to 'ave a living – injured blokes they are. P'raps they'll do it next year an' all.'

They bought a poppy each, helping each other to pin them on their lapels.

It was almost eleven o'clock, three years to the hour since the war was declared finished, and a large crowd was gathering in Victoria Square under the thick clouds. Along the imposing grey flank of the Town Hall was a platform draped with tapestries of red, gold and purple on which people had begun to lay their tributes of flowers and wreaths, and over to one side of the square, the Police Band were assembled, waiting.

A few minutes before eleven, as they all stood in the now tightly packed crowd, there came a loud, booming explosion as a maroon was fired off, then another and another, and the crowd fell absolutely silent. People began removing their hats and others followed until every head was bare and bowed, waiting. Jess handed her hat to Peter. It was so quiet that she became aware of the faint sound of pigeons scuffling and murmuring high on ledges of the buildings and they heard a train let off a head of steam. Alice moved restlessly in Jess's arms and she rocked gently from side to side to pacify her, not wanting her to disturb the tense, emotional silence. None of them looked at each other, each standing lost in their own thoughts.

After two minutes the Last Post sounded mournfully across the square, and then the Police Band began to play 'Oh God our Help in Ages Past' and gradually people began to sing, the sound of voices swelling around them. Many were in tears, women sobbing uncontrollably. Polly wept quietly, a handkerchief pressed to her face, and as the slow, emotional hymn went on, the raw feelings, still so recent, the overwhelming, immense sadness of it all welled up in Jess. She held Alice clasped tight to her, kissing her cheek, wetting the child's face with her tears as they sang the final verse. There was Alice's new, innocent existence, set against the memory of slaughter of so many young lives, and even greater than that, an overwhelming sense of the nature of humankind, of the way we are, good and bad, so closely woven together. She felt Peter's hand rest for a moment on her back, and looking up at him, saw that he was also wiping his eyes.

The crowd slowly began to disperse, and they were moving towards the platform to look at the tributes when Jess caught sight of him. She saw Mary first, a little ahead of them in the stream of people, holding a baby in her arms and guiding little Ruth in front of her. Jess found herself seeking desperately to see Ned, like a bad habit she still couldn't break. She stood on tip-toe and found him moving along just in front of Mary. When he reached the platform he leaned over and laid something on it, then turned and spoke into Mary's ear, his head close to hers. Seeing him with Mary touched an old nerve, just for an instant. He looked pale, less tall than she remembered, still much the same, yet somehow he had faded into ordinariness. The sight of him affected her, made her stomach flutter with nerves, just for those few seconds. But then she felt within herself a deep calm. They had not spoken to each other in three years and she had not missed him. He was nothing to her now, except a memory which could be folded away. Her heart had moved on. In a moment it was their turn to look at the floral tributes. The British Legion had contributed a plain wooden cross surrounded by poppies and framed with laurel leaves. On it were the words,

'To those who fought and fell, from those who are fighting on.'

There were offerings from public departments and societies, and from individuals. Moved, Jess's eyes swept over them. She found herself looking at the spot where she was sure Ned had laid his tribute. It was his handwriting that made it stand out for her. Instead of a bunch of flowers she saw a single sprig of heather, and a little note attached to it, 'Jem – Rest in Peace'.

She stood looking for a few moments, then turned, and Peter said, 'Ready to go?'

Jess nodded. She knew Ned would be moving away through the crowd, that she might not see him again, might never, but she did not look back. She was filled with a great surge of joy in the present. What she had now was truly built upon rock. She smiled up at Peter over Alice's head and he was moved at the sudden radiance of her face. You are my love, her eyes said. Love is what I always wanted, and it is you I have given my heart to. She knew that he, in turn, had given his.

He put his arm round her shoulders, holding David's hand the other side, and they edged through the remaining crowd who were all decked out in the poppies, a flowering of remembrance pinned close to the hearts of the living.

In the middle of the throng of people, David pulled on Peter's hand to get his attention. Peter stopped and bent down close to him.

'Will I have to fight in a war, Daddy?' He looked up, steadily, into Peter's eyes.

'I hope not, son.' Peter smiled and ruffled his hair. 'I hope not.'

BIRMINGHAM ROSE

For John

ACKNOWLEDGEMENTS

With special thanks to: Carl Chinn, Tom Golding, Barbara Martin, Pat Oakes, Betty O'Brien, A. M. O'Meara, George and Jackie Summers and Eric Taylor.

PART ONE

BIRMINGHAM
1931–1940

CHAPTER 1

JUNE 1931

'Look at this Ronald!'

Catherine leaned closer to the window. Water was streaming off the glass outside. It was the height of the storm, the heaviest Birmingham had seen for twenty years.

'How dreadful – we must do something for her!'

There was silence from the other side of the room. The only noise came from the rain, a constant solid sound as if there were not individual drops but a torrent poured from some great vat in the sky.

Catherine, still holding the spoon she had been using for the tea, tapped it against the window. Ronald, who had been sighing over the latest unemployment figures in *The Times*, finally flung down his newspaper in irritation.

'*Look*,' she insisted. 'That poor little girl.'

Across the street a tiny figure huddled low against the garden wall of a house. Petals of mock orange and yellow roses lay in a sodden covering over the ground. She was squatting sideways, pressed hard against the bricks as if blown there helplessly like a moth by the strength of the wind and beating rain. The arm closest to the wall was stretched out straight as if to stop her from toppling over; her left arm clutched something white close to her body.

'Poor little mite,' Catherine said. 'She can only be about six. Well, she can't stay out there in this. I'm going to fetch her.' Without stopping for a coat or hat she ran through the darkened hall and unlocked the front door.

'Do you think you should?' Her husband followed her. 'You could catch a chill. And the wind's quite dreadful.'

3

'Don't be ridiculous Ronald. What is the matter with you?'

The door she was opening was flung out of her hand as she spoke and she had to push all her weight on it to clip it shut. She ran down the short path, steadying herself against the wind. In seconds her white blouse was soaked and clinging, her pink flesh showing through.

From the sitting-room window Ronald Harper-Watt watched with a mixture of pride and exasperation as his impetuous wife ran down the path. Oh Catherine, he thought. Here I am always sitting thinking about doing things and you just get on and do them.

Out in the road the only sounds were the uneven roar of the wind, the swish of the rain and water gurgling along the cobbled gutters. Catherine saw a chimney pot hurled down from one of the nearby houses.

Heavens, she thought, there'll be roofs off next.

She expected to find the girl tearful and distressed. Not wanting to spend time comforting her and getting even more drenched, she lifted her up by the waist and twisted her round into her arms.

'Come on – I'll look after you little one,' she said. 'Let's go and get into the dry, shall we?'

While she was mainly concentrating on getting back into the house, and taking in as she went the fact that the guttering at one end of the vicarage was wobbling precariously, Catherine was conscious that two dark and quite tearless eyes were watching her face intently. She bent forward, holding the skinny child close to her, and reached the shelter of the front hall gasping. Her light brown hair with blond lights in it had been teased out of its pins by the exhilarating wind and rain and was uncoiling down her back.

Her straight green skirt and the girl's thin cotton dress and bloomers dripped on to the patterned tiles in the hall. Catherine stood smiling at the little girl who had, it seemed, been blown to their door. The child stood staring back with a penetrating, solemn gaze.

'Ronald?' Catherine called out.

4

To her amazement he was already half-way down the stairs with large white towels. 'The guttering's coming down,' she told him.

Catherine took the girl's free hand as she was still holding tightly on to the white thing with the other. 'Come on, let's get those clothes off you and get you dry. One of my girls is a bit older than you so I'll find you something you can wear. Now, what's that you've got under your arm?'

The child held out the object which turned out to be an enamel dish. Her brown eyes were taking in everything hungrily from under her sodden black fringe. Her hair seemed to be cropped in a rough pudding-basin shape round her head.

'What's your name, my dear?' Catherine asked her as they climbed the stairs.

'Rose – ma'am,' she added. She was looking at the deep red staircarpet in wonder.

'And where do you live, Rose?'

'Number five, court eleven, Catherine Street,' she gabbled out.

'Catherine? Well, you won't have any problem remembering my name – it's the same as your street.' She called over the banisters to her husband: 'Catherine Street. That's a way from here isn't it?'

'The only Catherine Street I can think of is about two or three miles away. It's in the Birch Street area. Not this parish, certainly. Probably St Joseph's.' One of the slum parishes, he thought. I wonder why she's strayed away from home – a runaway perhaps? Again he felt a sense of hopelessness overcome him. Recently it seemed that Catherine had a far greater instinct for dealing with people than he did, he who had once felt this was his gift.

As they crossed the landing upstairs the sound of children's voices could be heard chanting loudly in one of the bedrooms: 'Rain, rain, go away, come again another day!'

'Now Rose, what are you doing this far from home?' Catherine asked as she knelt rubbing the little body with

5

her towel. The child's skin, spotted with bug bites, seemed to cover only jutting bones. Rose reminded her of a tiny kitten or a newborn foal, all bony knees and staring eyes.

'Been to me sister's,' Rose said. 'She's expecting, so Mom gave me the custard and raspberry leaves to take over. It's our Marj's first babby you see.'

'I see,' Catherine said doubtfully. 'So your sister – Marj – does she live here in Moseley?'

'Oh no! She lives up Sparkbrook with her husband Fred. Mom says the babby's coming in November. And she says if she takes the raspberry tea it'll stop her coming on so bad with the pains.'

Catherine smiled at this grown-up knowledge, thinking of the patched, infantile dress lying on the floor beside them.

'So you're going to be a little aunt then?'

'Yes. And Marj wants me to sleep over her place sometimes after the babby's born. I'm not sure I want to though, 'cos it'll be blarting half the night and our Marj is bad tempered enough as it is.'

Struck by the amount of talking this little person suddenly seemed capable of, Catherine asked her how old she was.

'Nine. Ten next January,' she replied promptly.

'You're nine?' Catherine managed to prevent herself from speaking the rest of her astonishment – how small you are, you poor child, how undernourished – and just said, 'Gracious, you're the same age as my Diana.'

She pulled one of her daughter's old dresses over Rose's dark head, wondering whether the child had lice, though she couldn't see any obvious signs of them. The frock hung limply on her, well down below her knees.

'Will that do you?'

Rose nodded solemnly.

'Now, you just stay there a minute and you can meet my children.'

Rose was left standing in the high-ceilinged room.

6

Without moving her feet she looked up and round, twisting her body to see the soft, comfortable-looking bed with its eiderdown well plumped up, the black and white wooden rocking horse in one corner, the shelf full of books on the top of which stood small china ornaments, hedgehogs, squirrels and cats. What caught Rose's eye particularly in all this splendour was a large black elephant, the top of its head and ears decorated with tiny pieces of mirror glass and beads. She was still staring at it when she heard Catherine say, 'Rose? This is Diana, and these two are William and Judith.'

A girl with light brown curls bouncing round her cheeks ran into the room and then stopped and stared at her. Outside the door, held back by their mother, Rose had a brief glimpse of an older boy who had the same broad face and grey eyes as his father, and a little girl with dark brown hair down her back who was trying hard to see into the room.

For a moment Diana stood staring at Rose, and Rose gazed back at her, looking at the pretty cotton print dress and white cardigan the girl had on. Then Diana said, 'You're not really nine are you? You're too small.'

'I am,' Rose said. 'And me brother Sam's ten, and me sister Grace is eight, and me brother—'

'Goodness, how many brothers and sisters have you got?' Diana wanted to know.

'Er . . .' Rose thought for a moment. 'There's Albert and Marj – but they're off married so they don't live at me mom's any more. And then there's Sam, and me and Grace and George. And me mom's expecting. So's me sister Marj.'

'Gosh,' Diana said. 'Well I suppose you can't help being small. Come on, I'll show you my room.'

'Where d'you get that elephant?' Rose asked, going over to it. She thought it was one of the loveliest things she'd ever seen.

'Daddy brought it back from India,' Diana said. 'Here . . .' She pulled out some books from the shelves. 'Come and sit on the bed and I'll show you these.' Rose

7

obediently sat down, one hand stroking the soft bed-covers. 'Now, let's have a look at these. I'm going to be a teacher when I grow up. What are you going to be?'

'I dunno.' Rose had never once thought about it. 'Where's India?'

'It's . . .' Diana ran to the bookshelf again and came back holding a tiny globe on a stand, which swivelled around when she touched it. 'There. And England's here. Daddy's a vicar, in case you didn't know. He worked with a missionary in Madras, before he met Mummy. India's part of the British Empire.'

Rose wasn't sure what a missionary was. 'Do they have elephants like that then?'

'They have real elephants and tigers and snakes. Daddy brought back lots of things. Here, if you want an elephant, I've got a little one.' She jumped off the bed, opened a couple of drawers, rummaged around and came back with a smaller elephant, about two inches high.

'I'm afraid some of the bits of glass have got lost. But you can have it – there.'

Rose looked at her, her eyes stretched wide in amazement. 'Won't your dad belt you for giving it away? You could pawn that.'

Diana laughed. 'We don't go to the pawn shop. That's only for poor people. Are you very poor?'

This was another thing Rose had not thought about before. Most people in Catherine Street seemed to live like her mom and dad. She knew there were houses where rich people lived because her mom used to go charring for them. Otherwise the only people everyone talked about were the king and queen. Grace was forever on about them.

'I dunno,' she said again. 'Are you very rich?'

'Not very, I don't think. But Mummy's daddy has a lot of money. Daddy gets a bit cross about it sometimes but I don't know why because it means we can have a lot more things. Anyway, they won't mind about the elephant. You keep it.'

Catherine called them down for tea a few minutes later

and as they went Rose said, 'What's your other name? Isn't your mom called Mrs Something?'

'It's Harper-Watt. But just call her Catherine – she'll laugh otherwise. She's like that.'

Rose sat in the big front sitting room with the family, drinking tea and eating sponge cake with strawberry jam inside and gazing round her. On either side of the fireplace, where there was a vase of dried flowers standing in the grate because it was summer, were rows and rows of books. They were arranged on shelves reaching almost to the ceiling and they had grey, red and brown spines with faded gold lettering. There were never any books in Rose's house. Everyone thought reading anything except the *Gazette* or the *Sports Argus* was a bit barmy unless you had to do it. But Rose liked reading at school and her favourite teacher, Miss Whiteley, said she was coming on a treat.

Catherine poured tea out of the silver teapot and Rose saw that all the cups matched. At home there were never enough to go round and none of them had the same pattern. Little Judith stared at her so much that she kept missing her mouth with the cake and dropping lots of crumbs. Catherine told her to watch what she was doing. William pretended to ignore her, but kept staring at her when he thought she was looking somewhere else. Rose wanted to make a face at him but she thought she'd better not.

'So, Rose,' the great big vicar said to her gently. 'Did you get lost on the way home from your sister's? Moseley isn't really on the way to Catherine Street, is it?'

'No, I wasn't lost. I just wanted a walk round. Sometimes,' she announced, 'I like to have a bit of peace.'

The two adults smiled at each other, both hearing the echo of Rose's mother who presumably often needed to make the same claim.

'Well, I'm not sure if you've had that exactly,' said Mr Vicar, as Rose called him to herself. 'But we shall have to get you home soon, or your poor mother will be worried stiff. I'll walk that way with you myself. The rain is easing off now.' Partly he wanted to make up for his lack of initiative earlier.

By the time they had finished tea, the sun had come out and the heaviest clouds seemed pushed away by its warm arms. The air grew hot and heavy with moisture.

'You can keep the dress,' Catherine said and, seeing Rose's eyes full of happiness at the thought, continued, 'and please come and see us again if you're out for a bit of peace, won't you?'

'*Can* she?' Diana asked, jumping up and down. 'I like Rose. Go on, say you will, Rose.'

Diana demanded to be allowed to walk home with Rose too. The gutters were still running with water and there were puddles all over the pavement. As they walked, trying to keep their feet from getting too soaked, they saw broken tiles, glass and pieces of branch and twigs with leaves on. At one point a large tree had been torn up and was lying across the pavement.

'I do hope people haven't been injured,' Ronald said. 'Thank heavens it didn't happen yesterday when the shops were open.'

As he spoke, he noticed that Diana had taken Rose's hand. He smiled, moved by the sight. All her mother's warmth, he thought. And once more he felt his own inadequacy.

His despondency deepened as they walked towards the middle of the city, the seething, smoking core which circled the Bull Ring, the market at its heart. The houses here were smaller and meaner, crammed back to back in street after grimy street, with factories and mills and small workshops. Those living in their two or three bug-ridden rooms lacked space and light, and their children lived – and often died – in squalid shadowy courts covered with refuse and filth, knowing little of any other street, any other life or possibility of improvement. At least this was his impression that day of this part of the city of which he in fact, to his shame, knew little.

And what about Rose, this curious little person who had suddenly been flung to their door? He watched her as she walked in front of him with his daughter, the two of them chattering as if they had known each other for months. She was hungry for something, knew there was more than her own life was showing her. Surely, he thought, I can learn from this child. He found this more cheering than all his sterile prayers of recent weeks.

Catherine Street was a row of three-storey houses, crushed together, their bricks darkened by the sooty air. The street stood on a rise above the great belly of the city. Walking down it you could see the reddish grey roofs, closely packed, and the church spires and factory chimneys poking up above them. For miles around you could make out the long, pointed spire of St Martin's Church in the Bull Ring.

'I'll go now, ta,' Rose said suddenly, and she started to run off down the slanting road.

'But I was going to explain to your mother!' Ronald's voice boomed along the street so people turned to look.

Diana ran after her. 'Are we going to be friends or not?' she demanded.

'If you want,' Rose said. 'I mean yes – please. You'd best not come to our house though. Better go now.'

Diana went back to her father and they watched Rose's small form skipping down the street, the long dress flapping round her legs.

Ronald noticed that the sky was beginning to darken again. He steered Diana round to walk home, taking a last glance back at Rose.

'Extraordinary child,' he said.

11

CHAPTER 2

Carrying her old dress and enamel dish, Rose ran down Catherine Street. She thought she might go off pop, her head was so full of all the things she had seen that afternoon: the dress and the elephant in her pocket and Diana. But going off pop was just what she wasn't going to do.

I'm not telling no one about what's happened, she said to herself. Not Geraldine, not even our Grace. I'm going to keep it all to myself. She watched the cotton dress with its tiny pink roses flying up and down in front of her as her feet took her fast along the familiar blue bricks of the pavement.

I bet when Diana got this it was *new*, Rose thought. She began to skip so that the roses lifted even higher.

Then she saw her father. As she reached the entrance to their court she thought he must have seen her – the smile, the running and skipping and the new dress. She stopped abruptly and began to walk, holding the enamel dish against her stomach as if it was a teddy bear, her old dress rolled up and hidden inside it. She hoped he wouldn't ask any questions.

Ever since she was a tiny child Rose had had secrets. They were often very small ones, and quite unnoticeable to anyone else: a rounded pebble hidden under a leaf by the wall of the brewhouse or a word of praise at school from Miss Whiteley. It might be what she had seen on one of her walks – often not far, but alone – to neighbouring streets. She felt as if she, Rose Lucas, was the first person in the world ever to see them.

At the sight of her father, though, she felt as if everything she had been thinking must be clear from her face, every detail of it. But as he dragged his large frame towards her, his laborious gait managed on one leg and one rough wooden crutch, his eyes watching the path in front of him, she realized he had not even looked up. When he did notice her he said gruffly, 'All right Gracie?'

'I'm *Rose*,' she said angrily, and instead of walking in with him she left him to struggle home by himself and ran ahead into the yard. Couldn't he even get her name right?

The sky was half covered by piled grey clouds. A peculiar harsh light was shining down catching one side of the court, the wet bricks and the small windows on which soot and grime accumulated again as fast as they were washed down. The other side, the wall where the tap for the yard was fixed, lay in deep shadow.

Her brother George, who was three, was standing dressed only in a grubby vest, chewing on a hard finger of bread crust mingled with snot from his nose and stamping his bare feet in the puddles. His bottom was naked and his little peter wiggled about with each stamp. Freddie and Daisy Pye from number six were standing with him on their bandy legs. All the family except Mr Pye had rickets.

When George saw Rose he beamed all over his grubby face and ran towards her with his arms out, saying, 'Rose. Pick me up! Nurse me, Rose!'

Rose got a bit fed up with George's endless hunger to be picked up. No one had the time, that was the trouble.

'Look at the state of you!' she said. 'I can't pick you up now. You'll have to wait.' The little boy went back to his puddles, wiping his nose with the back of his hand. Rose disappeared into the house. She shot across the downstairs room where her mother stood slicing bread and went dashing up the stairs.

'Rose!' Her mother stood at the foot of the stairs, bread knife in hand. 'Where've you been?'

Rose paused for a second to make up her mind whether her mother was really angry. She decided things didn't sound too serious and carried on climbing the bare boards of the stairs, remembering the banisters at the vicarage, the pedestal at the bottom shaped into a huge shiny acorn.

'Got caught out in the rain, didn't I?' she called back. 'Down in a mo.'

'You haven't been at Marj's all this time – I know you,' her mother shouted. 'And where the hell did you get that dress?'

Rose climbed up to the room at the top of the house where she and Grace shared one single bed and Sam and George shared the other. She wanted to hide the elephant before anyone else saw it. She'd have to think up an explanation for the dress, but they needn't find out about all that had happened that afternoon. Not yet anyway.

She had tried hiding things up there before, but it wasn't much good. There was only the black iron rim of the bedstead under the mattress and you could hardly fit anything in there. And if she put it under the blanket Grace was bound to find it.

The Lucases' furniture had dwindled over the years. This was all part of the change, the decline from 'before' when Sid and Dora lived in a house with two proper rooms downstairs, where they had their first two children. Before, when Sid had been a promising apprentice engineer, until he had come home in 1917 without one leg and the lower part of his left arm, and also missing some less tangible part of himself, perished in the scarred pastures of Flanders. All, in fact, before Rose was born. Albert, the oldest child, could just remember his father before the war. As a six-year-old he had taken weeks to accept that the maimed and haunted figure who appeared one day in a greatcoat at their door was the same man.

Rose moved the chest of drawers a fraction from the

14

wall and hid the elephant behind it. That would do for now. She's find somewhere better later.

Downstairs, her mother had disappeared and her father was easing himself awkwardly on to one of the family's two easy chairs. He propped the crutch against the wall beside him. Grace was sitting bent over a steaming bowl of water, her head covered by a strip of sacking. She was wheezing heavily. Rose realized she was trying to stave off one of her asthma attacks. We're in for a bad night then, Rose thought, not feeling very amiable about it. She felt irritable being back here with pee in a bucket in the bedroom after the new things she'd seen in the afternoon.

'Get me some tea,' Sid demanded, pushing the muddy shoe off his one foot and putting it against the fender to dry. Rose went to the hob and found there was freshly brewed tea in the pot. A tin of condensed milk was waiting with the bread on the table. She sugared the tea and passed it over without speaking. Sid gave a grunt of thanks.

'Where's Mom gone?' she asked.

'The lav – sick,' Grace gasped tetchily from under the sacking, as if she'd already answered the question once. She pointed in the direction of the four toilets at the end of the yard, shared by the six houses. 'Rose,' she whispered. 'I need a drink.'

'What did your last slave die of?' Rose snapped and then, realizing how unkind she was being, poured out more tea and placed it on the floor by her sister.

Grace peered up through her wispy fringe. 'Ta.'

'You bad again?'

'S'getting better now.' She looked up with a pink, damp face and tried to smile. She took in a deep breath so that her shoulders pulled back and her lungs whispered the air in.

Rose looked at her and then moved her gaze to their father, raising her eyebrows at Grace as she tried to gauge what mood he was in. Sid was sitting silently with his copy

15

of the *Gazette*. There often seemed to be some intense emotion caged up in him which couldn't find a way out. When it did, they were terrified of him. Their mother took the worst of it: the lashings with his tongue and the force of his fist. Sometimes he left the house abruptly, saying nothing, and went off pulling himself round the streets for an hour or two, trying to repress the violence inside him which he so loathed. Sometimes he came back easier in himself. Other times the mood had deepened so the children hardly dared open their mouths.

It was hard to read his mood now, but Grace pulled down the corners of her mouth and rolled her eyes as if to say, 'Better watch our step.'

Through the window Rose saw her mother's thin figure walking across the yard, in her faded brown and white dress. Her arms were folded and pressed into her middle and she was holding herself rather bent forward as she did when she felt ill. Rain was falling again, and hurriedly she went to the tap across from the house and swallowed a few mouthfuls of water before coming inside.

Rose waited for her mother to start on her but Dora sat down at the table as if drained of any strength. She was working four nights a week and in the second month of another pregnancy. She felt constantly faint and sick.

'Get me a cup of tea, Rose,' she said weakly. 'I want you carding tonight. Sam's at the Pyes and Grace ain't up to it, but you can get on with some of it or we'll never get them back.'

Rose groaned inside at the thought of another evening of work. To make ends meet they took in work from local factories. Rose had spent many evenings of her childhood sewing pearl buttons on to cards in the precise stitches expected by the factory until her eyes stung and watered under the gaslight. This time it was safety pins – fixing them on to cards for the shops. They'd get tuppence ha'penny a gross, and that, as Dora was forever pointing out, was worth a bag of sugar.

'Why can't Sam come back from the Pyes and do some too?' Rose asked. 'He always gets out of it.'

She saw her father's dark eyes swivel away from his paper. 'Don't give your mother lip like that,' he said. 'That's no work for a lad anyhow.'

Dora, sipping the tea with dry lips, waved her other hand at Rose to shut her up. 'Any road, they're feeding him, so that's one less of us. Aaah – that's better.' The colour was coming back into her cheeks. She sat nibbling half-heartedly at a piece of bread. She was already a slim woman, and every pregnancy, each baby carried and suckled shrank her thinner and made her look more gaunt and bony. In the overcast light of the evening her cheekbones were emphasized by the shadows beneath them and the skin under her eyes showed blue half-moons of exhaustion.

'Was Marj all right then?' she asked. 'Did you make sure she's taking the raspberry leaf? Which reminds me . . .' Dora got up and went to the kettle to prepare her own dose of the brew. Rose thought it smelt horrible, all sour. But Dora had an almost religious faith in herbs and drank it through every pregnancy.

She didn't tell Dora that Marj had said in her most petulant voice, 'She needn't think I'm drinking this muck,' and had thrown the leaves out straight away.

'She's showing a lot,' Rose said. 'She says she's already sick of carrying that belly around.'

'Huh,' Dora said. 'She's only just bloomin' started. Wait till she's at it with a crowd of other babbies running round her. Then she'll find out what it's all about.'

As soon as they'd eaten their bread with a scraping of jam and Sid had shuffled off across the yard to the Catherine Arms, Dora rounded on Rose. 'Right,' she said, emptying the pile of tiny silver safety pins on to the worn American cloth. 'Where've you been all afternoon? Where d'you get that dress from? And where's my bowl?'

'It's upstairs.' In her hurry she'd left it on the bed with her dress. 'I'll get it.' She stood up to go to the stairs.

'Oh no you don't.' Dora grabbed her arm. 'Sit down. Come on, let's hear it. You go off with a bowl of custard and come swanning back in a new dress. What's been going on?'

Rose sat down again. 'I had a soaking,' she explained. 'Right to the skin. And the wind was so strong I nearly went flat on my face. You saw what it were like! This lady saw me from her house and took me in to dry out. She put the dress on me and she said I could keep it.'

'What lady? Where've you been wandering off to this time?' Dora tapped her finger hard on the table. 'Where was this house? Up Sparkbrook?'

'It might've been Sparkbrook,' Rose said, reluctant to give away even the vaguest details. 'Or it might've been a bit further out.'

'And you don't know where of course?'

'I was ever so wet,' Rose said, staring hard at the pins on the table.

Dora couldn't help smiling at her daughter, knowing she wasn't going to get the full story. 'You're the bleedin' end sometimes Rose, you really are,' she said. 'Come on – get cracking on these or we'll be here all night.'

They sat pushing the thin wire of the pins through their cards. Dora was still feeling sick, even having eaten the small amount of food. She looked across at Rose's dark hair, the same wavy black as her father's, bent over the pile of pins next to Grace, whose hair was a lighter brown, more like Dora's own.

Her pregnancy with Rose had been the third after the war. First there had been the twins – remembering now sent a sharp twisting pain through her. They were born too early. The little mites, only the size of kittens, had barely snuffled their way into life before dying within hours of each other: two boys, Sid and Percy. Next there'd been Sam, a huge, healthy baby who she'd thought would split her right apart as his head forced out of her.

And then Rose. All her babies had been born at home except Rose. Always was a wanderer, Dora thought.

She had been working in that big house in Sparkhill.

Albert and Marjorie were ten and eight then and at school so she had to leave Sam with a neighbour.

That morning as she set out to walk to work the sky was low and grey over the rooftops and the ground coated with frost. It looked as if it was going to snow and Dora pulled her coat round her belly as well as she could. She'd felt very down in the mouth that morning, which made her think the baby wouldn't come for a few days yet. Usually, right at the end she felt a mysterious surge of energy and well-being, even when she was quite run down in herself.

Maybe I just can't feel lively any more, she thought. Too many things have happened to us. P'raps I'm just too old.

At twenty-eight sometimes she felt aged and slow, as if everything had been torn and sucked out of her. Today the lower part of her body felt taut and heavy as she walked.

She went down the Ladypool Road, where the smell of fresh bread mingled with the usual road smell of horse manure. People were just coming out on to the streets to walk to work or give shop windows a polish. A delivery boy from the baker's shop whisked past on his bicycle, pushing down hard with his legs on the pedals.

Even now, five years after Sid had come home, she could feel tears suddenly in her eyes at the sight of a young man doing so carelessly all the things her husband was no longer capable of. It reminded her with a deep ache of the whole young man, full of dreams of what he was going to achieve, whom she had kissed goodbye and cried for early in 1915.

Sid had not come back to the home he left before the war. Instead he had returned to find his wife living in one of the courts of back-to-back houses which sprawled in a ring round the centre of Birmingham. He came back to a woman who had struggled to keep herself and her children on whatever the shortages of the war would allow, who had worked in factories churning out munitions to fuel the war and who had, with hardly a break, been

19

working in factories ever since. He had watched her age, get thinner, lose her teeth. She snapped more and swore more and her laughter – once loud, generous laughter – came harder now and more rarely.

That change of address on Dora's letters had not prepared Sid Lucas for the losses he had to face on every side when he came home – of not only his limbs, but his livelihood, his dignity and of the way he and Dora had been together before. Before.

Sometimes, when she was at her lowest, when Sid had been silent for days or sweated and sobbed in her arms at night, she wondered if it wouldn't have been better if the mud and water of Passchendaele hadn't buried him completely instead of leaving her with half a person.

Work that morning turned out to be even heavier than usual. Dora did all the routine dusting and polishing with Mrs Stubbs, the elderly woman who worked mornings there.

Then Mrs Stubbs said, 'Right, I'd best go and do that silver she's on about in the pantry. You can go out and shake the rugs.'

Dora looked at Mrs Stubbs' plain, rather stupid face and wondered whether she was being spiteful. She decided she was just thoughtless, but the advanced state of Dora's pregnancy should have been obvious to anyone.

'Couldn't we do them together?' she suggested.

'I'll come and give you a hand if it gets too much for you,' Mrs Stubbs said serenely and limped off to polish the silver.

Dora dragged the two large rugs through the hall to the bricked area out behind the house which faced on to a large garden. It was beautiful in the summer. The brewhouse was tucked in at right angles to one end of the building and she and Mrs Stubbs heated the water for the wash there each Monday. The bread oven was in there too, so it was often a warm place to be. Dora was glad that the small building jutting out protected her from the main stab of the cold wind.

She picked up one end of the first rug, unrolled it and

20

started to shake so it rippled heavily along the blue bricks of the terrace, giving off great wafts of dust. Dora's arms immediately felt exhausted, as if the carpet was made of lead. She rested between the vigorous shakes, her heart thumping harder and harder. She grew hot and faint.

The pains began suddenly and very strongly. After the first couple of harsh, breathtaking contractions she stood bending forward, her hands pressing on her knees, taking in gasps of air.

My God, she thought. How'm I ever going to get back? I've got to get home!

It felt so urgent, so far advanced, that she knew already that she'd never make it back – not on foot.

She waited for a lull and then stepped over to the brewhouse. It was a bit warmer inside and rather dark. There was nothing to sit on except the scrubbed quarry tiles. Dora squatted down with her back to the stone sink. It was very quiet apart from the faint scratch of winter jasmine and rose thorns against the window. Dora knew she should get help, that she needed a midwife, but between the contractions she had no strength and couldn't raise the energy to move again.

'Please God,' she prayed. 'Don't let anything be wrong with this babby – not with me all on my own. Just help me – please, please!'

She loosened her clothes and took off her bloomers. They were wet like her legs and the back of her dress, where the warm force of her waters breaking had soaked her. A couple of times she had to pull herself up to vomit into the greyish yellow basin. Her face was shiny with sweat.

'God,' she cried, the words coming out hoarsely. 'Oh God, God!'

She knew the baby was not long from being born. As she sobbed and panted through the next contraction she heard Mrs Stubbs' voice outside, 'Dora? Dora? Where are you? I thought you was getting started out here at least.'

In a moment her head poked round the brewhouse

21

door and she saw Dora kneeling, her eyes stretched wide with pain.

'Gorblimey – Dora!' she shrieked. 'You can't have a babby in here. This is where we bake the bread!'

And then, seeing Dora's wet face, her hair hanging in lank brown strings and her clothes all undone, she came closer and said, 'You poor little sod. There ain't time to get a midwife now. It's all right, I'll help you. I've had a few myself in my time.'

She went to the door saying, 'It's all right, I'm not going to leave you. Back in a tick.' A moment later she reappeared with a ball of string, the big kitchen scissors and a towel. She knelt down and pulled one of Dora's arms over her shoulder. 'Go on – you're all right, you're all right,' she kept saying as the young woman writhed and screamed beside her. And then: 'Sssh – keep it down a bit for God's sake.'

Soon the little girl's head bulbed out from her body as Dora cried out for the last time. The pink slithery body followed, and Mrs Stubbs tied the cord and they wrapped her in the old strip of clean towel. Finally, Mrs Stubbs went off to fetch help.

'I'm going to call her Rose,' Dora said when the midwife arrived. 'I mean, if I'd been any further outside I'd've been in the blooming garden, wouldn't I!'

As they sat carding the pins in the unsteady light, Dora suddenly said, 'You're a funny kid you know. Go on – get off to bed. That's enough for tonight.'

Grace was already asleep when Rose lay down beside her in bed that night, listening to the soft rain against the windows. Something scuttled across the floor in the corner of the room.

She thought about Diana and her house and of how one day she wanted to have carpets and comfortable beds and shelves and shelves of books.

During the night she half woke, hearing sounds from the bedroom below, the painful, incoherent cries that her father made sometimes in his sleep. The shouts grew louder, until she heard him cry out, 'No. NO – over here!' and some more words she couldn't hear. Then her mother's voice over his, comforting him until his sounds stopped with hers and they could all sleep.

CHAPTER 3

Her first thought when she woke the next morning was Diana. How soon could she go back there? After all, they had asked her – twice. Rose was just resolving to go as soon as possible when she realized she must have woken extra early in her excitement.

Usually on school days Mom called up the stairs, 'Come on – get yourselves down here. No messing about. You'll be eating your breakfast on the way, else!' But even George was still half asleep. Rose could hear voices outside and she pushed the blanket back and went to the window, pushing it open a crack.

The sun was shining, lighting up one corner of the yard, and the ground was still very wet. Smells of sodden dirt and rotting vegetable peelings wafted through the window, though they didn't overcome the stink of the pee bucket. Rose had a quick peep behind the chest of drawers to check that yes, the elephant was still there and she hadn't dreamed it.

It was wash day. When Rose and the others got downstairs, Dora was hurriedly bundling up all her washing, though she looked pale and was bent over with nausea. She pointed at the table with her free arm. 'There's tea and you'll have to take your slice with you.'

Rose, Sam and Grace hurriedly drank down some stewed tea and left the house. George was standing rather forlornly by the washhouse with his slice, watching Gladys Pye rocking on to each of her bowed legs in turn as she pulled out the heavy mangle. Rose, feeling suddenly sorry for George, went and gave him a cuddle. The little boy's face shone with delight.

They called for Geraldine Donaghue and her brother Jo and the five of them set out, walking to the church school along the sunny street still littered with the debris of the storm.

'Our dad says the roof's gone off Woodgates,' Jo said.

Rose wasn't listening. She was picturing herself one day walking to the school as a teacher who'd stand up grandly in front of the class. She'd wear clothes just like Miss Whiteley's, a straight grey skirt and a white blouse with a frill down the front, and a little fob watch like hers pinned on to it. She'd be very calm, she'd know ever such a lot and all the children would love her.

'What are you going to be when you grow up?' she asked Geraldine, trying to sound like Diana.

Geraldine peered at her, bemused. 'You all right?' she asked. 'What's the big idea?'

'What are you going to be when you grow up?' Sam mimicked her. 'Getting big ideas, Rose? It'll be the factory or the big house for us. What else is there?' Sam scuffed his already well-worn shoes along the pavement. 'We're not exactly going to be King and Queen of England are we?'

'I want to be a teacher,' Rose said.

Sam snorted with laughter and Geraldine looked horrified.

'You don't want to be like Miss Smart, do you?' she asked. Miss Smart was a sour woman, given to almost savage outbursts of temper. It was whispered that she'd been jilted on the eve of her wedding a few years before.

'No,' Rose said. 'But Miss Whiteley's nice, isn't she? And she knows about ever such a lot of things.'

Geraldine looked puzzled. 'What d'you want to do that for? I'd never do that. I'd like to be a singer or one of them dancers they have on at the Hip.' She preened and posed in her skimpy dress along the pavement as if it was the stage of the Hippodrome.

'Geraldine!' her brother said. 'Everyone's looking.'

'You're both daft,' Sam said. 'Dream away. I'm going to be Rudolph Valentino. But it's only dreams. People like us don't ever do anything different, do we?'

This dampened Rose's enthusiasm straight away.

'Who d'you know who's ever been anything special then?' Sam continued.

'Mom says Dad was doing all right before he went to the war,' Rose said.

'It was still the factory though. And nothing's the same now, is it? That's what Albert says.' Sam always looked to his older brother, whom they scarcely ever saw, as the source of all information and authority. 'Anyhow, you have to stay on at school to be anything special, and there's fat chance of that.'

Rose felt very down in the dumps after that. Was Diana going to stay on at school? No one she knew in the court had carried on after they were fourteen. She'd never questioned it before, how you couldn't do anything much with your life unless you had money.

Rose knew that some time during the morning her mom would bundle up Sid's Sunday suit and shoes and they'd be down to the pawnbroker's at the end of the street until Friday when she got her money from the factory. Sid joked grimly sometimes that they ought to get 2d extra for the shoes because he only ever wore the one. Rose wondered if her mother was going to pawn her new dress.

That day she stared adoringly at Miss Whiteley as she stood in front of them next to the blackboard, the portrait of the king behind her head. She imagined Diana standing there with her curls tied back, telling them all about rivers and jungles and the kings and queens in history books. And then she tried to put herself in the same position, as she had on her walk to school before all the things Sam had said. All she could think of now were the thick darns on the elbows of her cardigan and her faded old clothes and the way she spoke, which was different from Diana.

I could never be like Diana, she thought.

As she turned from chalking up some names on the

blackboard, Sarah Whiteley noticed Rose at her wooden desk wiping her eyes with the back of her hand and sniffing.

'Are you feeling unwell, Rose?' she asked kindly.

'No, Miss Whiteley,' the girl said quietly, and she blushed such an embarrassed pink that the teacher decided not to pursue it just then.

When school finished Miss Whiteley said to her, 'Rose, would you come here a minute?'

Geraldine whispered to her, 'You're for it now. I'll wait for you outside.'

'No, you go home,' Rose replied. 'And take Grace with you or Mom'll be on at me.'

She stood solemnly by her teacher's desk when all the others had made their way noisily out of the room. She could hear them laughing and yelling as they trailed off down the street.

'Are you all right, my dear?' Miss Whiteley asked, sitting behind her big table at the end of the classroom. 'It's all right, don't look so worried, you're not here to be punished. I saw you crying earlier. Is everything all right at home?'

'Yes, Miss Whiteley,' Rose said.

The teacher looked at the serious brown eyes which were gazing apprehensively at her and she smiled suddenly. She had a soft spot for Rose.

'Are you happy at school?' She was sensitive enough to realize that something was going on inside Rose, and she also knew that whatever her disadvantages in life, this was a child with potential.

Rose just said yes again. She liked Miss Whiteley and trusted her, but standing alone in front of her she felt small and shy. She kept her eyes on the scuffed wooden boards of the classroom floor and her even more scuffed boots.

Sarah Whiteley decided to try once more. She came out from behind the desk and brought her chair up to sit next to the child.

Rose looked into Miss Whiteley's lovely plain face with

27

her round pink cheeks, quite unlike Miss Smart's angular, rather pretty face, which was so often full of spite and irritation. Miss Whiteley seemed to give off comfort, like someone handing out buns.

'What if I wanted to be a teacher?' Rose blurted out. ''Cos Sam says people like us don't do things like that and it's daft of me to think of it. Only my friend Diana's going to be a teacher.' And without expecting to she found she was telling Miss Whiteley all about the storm and Diana and how different her family were from Rose's own.

Sarah Whiteley was startled. This was not what she had expected at all. She'd thought perhaps things were especially difficult for Rose's family, as they so often were in the homes of the children she taught. She had met Dora Lucas a number of times and had taken a liking to her. She'd found her brisk, with the kind of hardness of someone who has no energy left to spare for niceties. But she isn't rough, Sarah thought. Just worn down. And again, Sarah had perceived intelligence. She hadn't met Rose's father, but she knew he had been injured in the war and could not get work.

With these thoughts in mind she struggled for words to answer Rose's eager questions. She wanted to be positive and realistic at the same time and the combination was not easy.

'Whether you could be a teacher is not an easy question to answer. I think you're a clever girl and you do well in your lessons. But I expect you'll have to leave school to go to work soon, won't you?'

Rose nodded miserably.

'But perhaps what you can aim to do is get the best work you can. If you do well at school we might be able to find you something in an office, and you never know what opportunities might come your way. And there are such things as evening classes where you can further your education if you have the means when you're older. But you'll have to be very determined. Do you think you're very determined?'

'I dunno,' Rose said. 'But I don't want to be like my mom, always sick with having babbies.'

Sarah Whiteley felt tears slide into her own eyes at the thought of women like Dora Lucas with their relentless lives of childbirth and worry.

Rose noticed her emotion and was alarmed. Blimey, what had she done to upset her?

But all her teacher said, quietly, as if to herself, was, 'Well, I suppose if you want to do anything else with your life it doesn't really do to have children.' Then she smiled and looked at Rose. 'Cheer up. You don't need to worry about it yet, do you? And you never know what might happen.'

She stood up and said, 'Come along, your mother will be getting worried. Shall I walk a little of the way with you?'

Delighted, Rose felt her dark little hand being taken by Miss Whiteley's soft pink one. The woman strolled along beside her, pointing out things on the way – a police car, a magpie, white clouds all piled up to one side of the sky – until they reached Catherine Street. Miss Whiteley leaned down and, to Rose's astonishment, kissed her cheek before she said goodbye. Rose couldn't remember the last time anyone had given her a kiss. The walk had made the afternoon feel very warm and special.

But when she got home her mother was tense and furious and snapping at everyone in sight. She'd hung her sheets across the yard as usual and the younger Pye and Donaghue children had been running muddy hands all through them and flicking water up from the puddles. She'd had to rinse and mangle the lot again, and as a result was behindhand with everything else.

'Don't tread on the floor!' she shouted unreasonably as Rose stepped into the house. 'Where the hell have you been? No – don't tell me. Just get scraping these.' She pointed to a pile of carrots. Grace, confined to a sheet of newspaper on the damp floor, had already started on the potatoes.

Dora bustled about rearranging washing on the backs

29

of chairs and over the frames of the mirror and their two pictures: one of Sid's mom and dad and one of the king and queen.

'I'll make sure those little bleeders don't get at it this time,' she said. 'Come on, set to it Rose, and stop dreaming.'

Rose picked up the peeling knife in silence and mulled over what Miss Whiteley had said. All I can do, she thought, is try as hard as I can. Try and try and try.

That night, when she and Grace and the boys were in bed, Rose heard sounds coming from down in her mom and dad's room. It wasn't the strange, rhythmic noise she sometimes heard, with her mother gasping, and at the end of it a cry from her father as if he'd stubbed his toe on the leg of the bed. This time she knew it would end differently, because he'd been down the Catherine after raising a few coppers selling kindling.

Sid turned to look at his wife as he undressed in their room on the middle floor. She was lying on her back, her face grey with fatigue. He could see clearly the lines that had appeared and deepened between her brows and round her mouth and he felt a moment of tenderness watching her there. Now she was able to rest she looked a little more like the lovely girl he'd courted and married, with her sheet of chestnut brown hair, thicker then and glossy, which he'd smoothed over his face during their lovemaking like a silk scarf.

Remembering this, he wanted her. She'd be out working the next four nights and he'd have to sleep alone. He always felt sorry for himself when she was away at night. It seemed to reinforce his sense of helplessness.

'Dora?' He pulled himself over to her on the bed and leaned on his good arm. Suddenly he felt nervous, and then angry because of it. She was his wife, wasn't she? He shouldn't have to beg any favours.

'Come on,' he said. He put his mouth to hers, feeling

how rough and dry her lips were. He felt himself harden gradually. In the old days he had only to look at her. This was the one thing he had left – that he could make her produce children.

When she felt him moving against her, a wave of despair came over Dora. How could he do this when he knew she'd be up all the next night? But she always felt guilty when she refused him. It was the only thing which made him happy for a short time.

'I need some sleep,' she said without opening her eyes. 'I'm on again tomorrow night. Some of us have to work, you know,' she finished, rather spitefully.

He always took rebuffs badly. 'That's right – and I'm no bloody good for nothing, am I?' he shouted, sitting up again. 'Your bleeding cripple of a husband. That's what everyone says about me, ain't it?'

'I didn't say that – just don't keep on. Get into bed and let me sleep.'

'Open your eyes.' His voice was still loud and full of hurt and anger. 'At least open your bloody eyes, woman!'

Dora dragged her eyes open and half sat up. She pulled back the covers and patted the bed. 'Just come and lie down Sid, please.'

Sid could feel the great dark surge which sometimes forced its way through him, a violence of anger and despair which he could not put into words. He ached to spend himself in his wife, to feel her body moving under him.

'Dora, please. Do it for me tonight.'

'NO!' Dora shouted.

Then Rose heard her mother's screams as he hit her twice, three times, giving her the bruised cheek and cut lip which would be there for all to see in the morning.

'You selfish bitch!' she heard.

Rose screwed up her eyes tight and pushed her fingers into her ears. But she could still hear the next part – what always came next. The worst part. Her father's remorse, the sobs which burst from his body alongside her mother's

31

own crying, and eventually Dora's voice trying to calm his anguish.

Rose slipped out of bed and fetched the little elephant from its hiding place. She lay stroking it in the dark.

'Try,' she said to herself. 'Try and try and try.'

CHAPTER 4

JANUARY 1935

Dora Lucas was sitting at her table with a cup of mint tea in front of her. Often now, when she had a spare moment she sat, her eyes not fixed on anything, her limbs slack and her mind numb.

She was forty-one and exhausted, like an old woman, yet she was soon to give birth again. Her belly already felt tight and heavy with the child which nudged insistently under her ribcage so that she had to keep straightening her spine to ease the discomfort.

Beside her, three-year-old Violet was clattering pebbles on the tiled floor, involved in her game and singing quite tunefully.

'Do it a bit quieter, can't you?' Dora snapped at her, without really having intended to. Weariness and irritation seemed to be all she could manage.

The others would soon be home from school. And Sam – bless him – from work. After the four grimmest and most despairing years of Dora's life they at last had a regular wage coming into the house. How she would have got by without the neighbours she'd never know – Theresa and Gladys especially. The final humiliation had come when they had been forced to go on the Parish. First there was the gruelling session in front of the board. Dora's innards turned just thinking about it. She'd remember the cold, gimlet-eyed woman there till her dying day. The board, which executed the Means Test, decided whether she was worthy of their meagre allowance of food and coal.

Sam, Rose and Grace had become familiar, sad little figures outside factories as far away as Cheapside and Moseley Street, greeting the men who came off shift with persistent cries of 'Have you got a piece for us?' They'd run after the men until they handed over any leftover portions of bread from their lunches.

On Saturday nights they would hang about in Smithfield and the Market Hall until the stallholders were packing up, and then walk home exhausted, carrying a piece of knockdown meat and bags of bruised fruit and veg. Rose would fall asleep with her head full of visions of pyramids of apples and oranges lit by the the naphtha flares which hissed next to the stalls.

The shame and desperation of those years had nearly finished Dora. When Violet was born she had haemorrhaged so badly that she'd been ill for weeks and had had to give up her night job in the metal stamping factory. They'd had Sickness Benefit, and by the time that finished she was pregnant again, but she miscarried in the third month. Again she was left weak and drained.

Dora had been desperate not to get pregnant again. She tried to fight Sid in bed, and kick him off. But even with only one arm he was stronger. He begged her and then slapped her about, and most often now pushed into her with a force which frightened her and left her sore, sometimes bleeding, and with an overwhelming sense of shame as if she had done something wrong. When she had the strength, she crept out in the dark afterwards and fetched a pail of cold water to wash herself with.

As soon as she realized she was carrying this child, for the first time in her life she tried to abort it. She had tried castor oil and Penny Royal syrup and even water which she'd boiled pennies in. She had trembled at the sin she was committing – however ineffective it proved – but even more at the thought of what Sid would do to her if he ever found out. His one remaining source of power was his and Dora's fertility.

'Think yourself lucky,' he said to her one night in an ugly mood. He was lying on the bed naked from the waist down, his member lolling to one side on its nest of dark hair. 'I saw a fella in the army with it all blown away. Where would that leave you, eh?'

She had been brought too low to feel anything for Sid now. Even pity had been drained out of her. Now when his dreams drove him to cry out in the night she turned away and pushed her fingers into her ears. She had pity now only for her children, and admiration for their pluck and spirit.

She leaned back into her chair, folding her arms over her swollen stomach and thinking of her kids one by one.

There was Albert, over in Erdington, whom she hardly ever saw, and Marj, rather smug with her two kids in Sparkbrook. She realized that these two, who could just remember the life before the war, despised what their parents had become. If that was their attitude they could keep away.

As for Sam, he was a good solid lad. She knew he'd stick by her and look after her. Sticking by people was one of the codes by which Dora lived. Disloyalty figured high on her list of human failures, along with thieving and cruelty to children. She felt Sam had inherited that loyalty from her.

'Don't worry, Mom,' he'd kept saying, while he was waiting out his last year at school. 'I'll get myself a job soon. I'll look after you.' It was a promise he'd kept. He was bringing in ten bob a week which was a start and they made up the rest with odds and sods.

Then there were the two girls. Dora smiled at the thought of Grace. She was so transparent and shared things with her mother. She used to climb on Dora's knee and show her the latest picture she'd found of her great passion – the royal family. She was straightforward somehow. Like herself, Dora thought.

But Rose was more of a mystery. Dora had never worked out why that posh vicar's daughter Diana wanted to be so friendly with her. She must have had pals with knobs on up at her public school, but she and Rose were still as thick as anything. And she didn't even seem to mind coming and slumming it down Catherine Street now and then. It was the neighbours who acted suspicious and said, 'What's she doing down here again?'

Dora couldn't help liking Diana, even if she hadn't been sure at first what she was after. Her mother's family were something titled, it was said, and she'd married beneath her. But Diana didn't put on airs. She always said 'Mrs Lucas' so politely. And she was such a pretty lass with all that curly hair round her face. But Rose went up to the vicarage more often than Diana came down here. Rose didn't want the neighbours gossiping about her or Geraldine Donaghue deliberately messing up Diana's dress out of envy.

Rose worried Dora though. She knew her daughter's contact with the Harper-Watts had shown her a kind of life that would never be within her grasp.

'Don't get big ideas, will you?' she warned sometimes.

Sid put it more brutally. 'You needn't bring her round here and get all toffee-nosed. You was born a slum kid and you'll die a slum kid so you needn't go expecting any different.'

It was already getting quite dark. The lamplighter would soon be out on the streets. Dora was about to stir herself when she heard the girls outside, and George came crashing into the house shouting, 'Rose's had the cane! Rose's had the cane!'

As was her way, she didn't ask questions immediately but pulled herself to her feet and lit the lamp. Then she turned to her daughters. Rose was still the taller of the two and bone thin, with long black hair down her back. Her face was puffed up from crying and her cheeks streaked and red. Grace, who was wheezing heavily, also looked tearful. Instinctively, Dora moved across to boil some water for her.

'What's been going on?' she demanded.

'It's that Miss Smart,' Rose burst out, her voice high

with tears and anger. 'She's a wicked, horrible bitch, she is.'

'Rose!' Dora started. But then, seeing how distressed she was, said, 'Turn round.'

Rose turned, and very tentatively pulled her ripped bloomers down to show her bare bottom. It was raw and red with stripes of blood and vivid purple welts, so many that they had all merged together in a hot, angry mass.

'God Almighty,' Dora gasped. 'What the hell has she done? What brought all that on?'

It had been the last lesson, Rose explained. They'd been sitting in the classroom, and she was next to the heavy green curtain that separated her class from Grace's. She knew Grace wasn't feeling too good that day. The weather was damp and cold which always brought on the asthma. She'd been struggling to get her breath even on the way to school. A day in the building, heated by the one feeble stove, had not helped.

As Rose sat through her arithmetic lesson, Miss Smart was teaching Grace in the next section of the room. Suddenly she became aware of Miss Smart's usually abrupt and tetchy voice saying quite clearly, 'Pull yourself together! I've had quite enough of your malingering.'

'I can't help it, Miss Smart,' she heard Grace trying to protest. 'It's me chest. I've got—'

'Be quiet,' Miss Smart shouted. 'You make that horrible noise once more and you'll feel the cane across your behind. I'm not putting up with any more of your excuses.'

Through the curtain Rose could hear Grace's wheezing becoming louder and more agitated. She could picture Miss Smart's angry, spiteful face as she stood over her sister, and suddenly she felt all restraint leave her.

She glanced up at Miss Phipps to check she wasn't looking. Then she lifted up the bottom of the heavy curtain, pushed her way underneath it and ran to Grace, flinging an arm round her frightened sister's shoulders.

'You cruel bitch!' she shouted at Miss Smart. Her voice

sounded surprisingly strong. 'Why don't you pick on someone your own size? Just because you can't keep a bloke for five minutes doesn't mean you have to take it out on my sister. She's got a bad chest, as you ought to know bleeding well by now!'

Grace's face almost mirrored her teacher's in its look of horror. Miss Smart grabbed Rose by the wrist and hauled her through the classroom with astonishing strength, bashing Rose's legs and hips against the desks.

'Come here you uppity little scum,' she hissed, her teeth locked together as though she was trying to hold back some of her rage. 'You'll be out of this school as soon as breathe after what you've just said to me.' The woman's body was quivering all over. 'But now I'm going to give you something you should have been given a long time ago.'

Grace watched, terrified, as Miss Smart grabbed Rose again by the shoulders and forced her round so she was facing the window. She pulled Rose's skirt up and yanked on her bloomers so that the entire class heard them tear.

'Bend over and empty the wastepaper basket,' Miss Smart shouted, only just able to get the words out.

Rose knew the drill. She turned the basket over, tipping out scraps of paper and some balls of fluff, and leaned down on the dusty weave of the base.

Miss Smart thrashed her with the cane as no child in the school had ever been thrashed before. She lost all control as her voice screamed out her frustration and loathing. 'D'you think I like standing here day after day looking at your ugly – ignorant – faces? I hate it. I hate it – do you hear? You stupid – scummy little – slum kids . . . You'll never – do anything – or be anything. I could be married and out of this cesspit by now, but I'm stuck here for ever. Stuck – stuck – stuck!'

Rose's whimpering broke into screams as Miss Smart brought the thin cane down and broke the skin. The lashes shot through her, making her feel weak in the legs and dizzy. She was aware only of the pain and of the saliva gathering in her mouth.

'Helena! Helena Smart – what in God's name are you doing?' It was a deep voice, from the large body of Miss Phipps, who had been teaching arithmetic next door. The beating stopped abruptly as Miss Phipps grabbed the younger teacher's arms and took the bloodstained cane from her trembling hand.

Rose slowly turned the waste basket over and retched miserably into it. She heard Grace's loud breathing beside her.

'Rose? Rose – are you all right?' Grace was crying. A thin trickle of vomit began to ooze out through the wicker and across the floor.

Miss Phipps was holding Miss Smart by one of her wrists. The younger woman was sobbing uncontrollably. 'I'll see you later,' Miss Phipps said in a low voice. 'For now I think you'd be wisest to get out of my sight.'

They all watched Miss Smart, her head sunk down and her shoulders heaving as she left the room.

Miss Phipps came over to Rose. 'Go home and get your mother to dress those cuts,' she said gently. 'Grace, you go with her.'

Rose tried to straighten up. Her behind and the lower part of her back were a tight wall of pain.

Miss Phipps guessed what was painting the worried expression on the girl's face even through her obvious distress. 'It's all right,' she assured her kindly. 'You'll be coming back to school again.'

As Rose was finishing off her story, Sid lurched into the house on his crutch, slamming the door as he always did. Dora tensed.

He looked round the room. Grace was sitting at the table with George, breathing noisily over a bowl while Dora held her hair back. Rose was standing holding a cup with a face as long as Livery Street and not a sign of his tea on the go.

'What's going on?' His voice was ugly.

'Rose got caned down at the school for sticking up for our Grace,' Dora said. 'Her behind's red raw with it.'

Sid looked at Rose's tearstained face. It was rare for

39

him to see Rose crying. She was a proud cow, in front of him anyway. Strong, independent Rose. Rose, who had all the aspirations he had had and probably even more, going about with that kid from up the vicarage. He felt a moment of identity with her, but he pushed it aside. For once she wasn't giving him that serious, knowing look of hers, that seemed to say, 'Sod you, Dad. I'm going to get out of here and do something with my life.'

He began to enjoy her humiliation. 'I s'pose you asked for it,' he said. 'You're a cheeky little bugger.'

'I didn't ask for it!' Rose shouted. She felt like someone with nothing to lose. 'She was carrying on at our Grace and I stuck up for her. Like Mom could do with someone to stick up for her when you're down there knocking her about of a night. I've listened to you since I were a babby with your bullying and your carrying on, and your – *crying*.' Rose spat the word out with all the contempt she felt. 'You're disgusting, Dad. So don't go telling me I asked for it.'

She stood unflinching as Sid lurched over and hit her round the head with both sides of his thick hand again and again.

'Stop it!' Dora screamed. Grace and George sat quite still as if paralysed with fright. 'Don't you dare hit her! Don't you ever hit my kids.' Her voice dropped to a snarl. 'I've put up with you knocking me about, but don't you ever lay a finger on my kids again or I swear I'll lay you out for good.' She was looking round wildly for something to use as a weapon when Rose simply took a step backwards and Sid lost his balance, falling to the floor heavily, on his side.

With all the dignity she could summon Rose stood over him. 'I shouldn't bother getting up, Dad.' She left Grace and George gawping and went to her room.

Rose lay with her stomach flat against the bed in the dusk light of the attic.

Dora was bathing the sores on her daughter's behind

with warm water and dabbing iodine on the cuts. One side of Rose's face was swollen and shiny and beginning to darken into bruises. Sid's outburst, as much as the treatment she had had from Miss Smart, had created a bond between the mother and daughter stronger than any that had existed before.

'I hate him,' Rose said, banging her fists on the thin mattress, and wincing whenever Dora touched her. 'I hate, hate, *hate* him. He ought to want better than he's had for his kids. He's never cared about us.'

Dora sighed. Rose became aware that her mother was stroking her hair with a new gentleness that she was unused to. She kept very still in case any movement made Dora stop.

'If it were a few year ago I'd've said that's not the truth.' Dora paused for a moment, breathless with the baby pushing up her lungs. 'Now I just don't know. He's turned sour on everything and there's no getting near him. And you can't blame him when you stop to think about it. But that don't make it any easier for the rest of us. There've been times . . .' She stopped.

As if reading her mind, Rose said, 'You'd have been just as well off without him, wouldn't you?'

'No,' Dora said briskly. 'That's not my way. You make your bed and you lie on it, and that's that, whatever happens after.'

Rose turned her head to look at her mother. In the poor light from the window she could see the outline of her scrawny neck and her thinning hair which looked lanker and more faded every year. Her skin was pasty and tired looking. She thought of Catherine Harper-Watt's rosy complexion and her thick, healthy hair. She started to cry again because her mother's life seemed so sad, such a waste.

Dora, not knowing the real reason for Rose's sobs, stroked her back in a way that surprised both of them. 'Ssssh,' she said. 'You'll feel better soon, don't you worry. Hang on a minute – I'll go and get you another nice cup of tea.'

CHAPTER 5

A month later Rose and Diana were walking to the Bull Ring. As soon as Diana had called in for her at Catherine Street Rose grabbed her coat and was off.

'Better get her out of here before she catches anything, hadn't you?' Geraldine called out spitefully as the two of them sped out of the court. They were followed a short distance by George, who was becoming a right tearaway, and Violet, lisping, 'Thweets, Diana – bring us back some thweets!'

The two girls soon left them behind. Rose was never comfortable when Diana came to her house and it didn't happen very often. She couldn't help feeling ashamed of the cramped, filthy conditions they lived in. Whenever Diana came the smells drifting from the toilets in the yard always came over stronger than usual.

Diana was always very polite. Rose had never seen her bat an eyelid at the newspaper instead of a cloth on the table or the cockroaches scuttling busily about on the floor and walls, their antennae twitching. She'd only once jumped and squeaked when one landed clumsily on a slice of bread she was eating. Dora had nearly turned herself inside out apologizing.

'Don't you hate coming to our house?' Rose asked her. 'Why would you want to with us being so rough and ready?' She felt humbled by Diana's tolerance, whereas if her friend had been haughty or critical Rose would have leapt like a wildcat to defend her family and how they were forced to live.

'Come on,' Rose said as they scurried towards town. 'It isn't half a relief to get out, I can tell you. My mom's been on at me all morning: "Rose – blacklead the grate; Rose – Violet's gone and wet the floor, get down and wipe it up will you, Rose; Rose – go and get us some fish and chips for our lunch!" Anyone'd think there was no one else in the house 'cept me.'

It always took the two girls a while to get used to being together.

'We could go on the tram,' Diana suggested breathlessly as they rushed along.

'You mad?' Rose looked shocked. 'What d'you want to go wasting money on that for? It's not much of a walk.'

'All right.' Diana smiled. 'I'll treat you to a cup of tea then.'

'You don't know you're born, you don't.' But Rose was delighted. It was a huge treat to go to Charlie Miles' in the Market Hall or one of the places in the Bull Ring market and sit drinking tea like two grown-up ladies.

'Eh, I haven't told you,' Rose said as they turned into Bradford Street. 'Mrs Smith from number three – you know, Mrs Cut Above – they had to take her to the hospital a couple of days ago. They found her swigging back a bottle of bleach at her kitchen table. Her sons walked in and saved her, before she could take' – Rose struggled to remember the right words – 'the whole lethal dose. That's what everyone said. She had to go and have her stomach pumped out. They put a great thick rubber tube in your mouth and pour water into it till you bring it all back. Mrs Pye told us 'cos it happened the once to her brother.'

'Gosh, how horrible!' Diana said. 'Is she all right?'

'She's home now. She had a bit of a go at Geraldine's mom this morning. Called her an Irish trollop, so I think she's back to her usual.'

Diana stored up this information to tell her father, who waited for the latest instalment of life in Catherine Street with great interest and shook his head in a concerned sort of way whenever she told him anything.

The long street swept them downhill towards the bustling heart of Brum. On either side of them loomed the tall, soot-coated sides of factories from which came all kinds of sounds of hammering and drilling, and the churning of machinery and shouting filled the air round them.

'Let's see if we can spot Sam,' Rose said.

They stopped by the grating over the basement factory where Sam had found his first job. The firm produced galvanized buckets and baths, and all day the sounds of banging and clanging went on as if they were fastening on manacles in hell.

'It's so noisy!' Diana exclaimed.

'Hell of a row, isn't it?' Rose peered down, trying to spot her brother's brown hair and pale, stolid face, but she couldn't see him.

'C'mon Di,' she said, straightening up again. 'Let's get to Jamaica Row for the cag-mag and then we can go over to the Market Hall.'

Bradford Street was crowded with horses and carts and motor vehicles, some stopping for pick-ups or deliveries outside the factories or moving to and from Smithfield, the main meat market at the lower end of the street. You could see the sides of meat hanging up there as you went past. In the road, piles of horse manure steamed in the cold.

Carrying the bag of cag-mag, the cheapest off-cuts of meat, the girls gradually pushed their way through the chaos of the Saturday afternoon crowds into Spiceal Street, past the slim spire of St Martin's and into the Bull Ring.

Diana took hold of Rose's sleeve. 'Better not lose you,' she said. 'Go on – you lead the way.'

Rose felt the usual excitement that welled up once she was inside the market. There was so much to look at. She could hear a band playing, and the delicious smell of roasting meat wafted from the eating houses across from the stalls. Their windows were lit and the glass all steamed up, so you could only see hazy figures moving about inside or sitting at the tables. Outside one a sign said, 'Beef & 2 veg. 11d.'

The market was packed with people swarming around the stalls heaped with fruit, vegetables and flowers. The vendors were competing to see who could shout the loudest to sell their wares.

'Only a penny the cabbage!'

'Get your oranges here – fresh juicy oranges!'

They got tangled up in a knot of people all standing round some attraction. It was the strong man. He had been tied up tightly in his chains and a sack dropped over his head. They could see him struggling inside like an animal in a snare.

'He always gets out, you know,' some know-it-all in the crowd was saying.

'There's got to be a trick in it somewhere. I don't believe in all this rigmarole,' another voice said.

But mostly people stood gasping with admiration watching the man emerge, panting and red in the face as he tore the sack off his head, his face and bare arms shining with sweat.

When Rose looked at Diana she saw that her friend's cheeks had turned quite white and she was taking in fast, shallow breaths.

'I could never do that, never. I can't bear anything over my head. It makes me want to scream and kick.'

'Come on. Forget it,' Rose said, pulling her away. 'Let's go and find something a bit more cheerful for you.'

Round the statue of Nelson in the middle of the market was the place where people always arranged to meet. Probably because they knew this, the Sally Army had set up with their brass band and tambourines. In the background somewhere a man's voice was shouting, 'He who is without sin – he, and only he – shall cast the first stone!'

From the other side of the statue Rose heard the music which she always enjoyed most in the market.

'Come on.' She took Diana's arm. 'If this don't cheer you up then nothing will.'

It was the accordion players. There were two of them,

trying hard to compete with the Sally Army, and by the look of things succeeding. The men had a certain snappiness of style even in their old black trousers and jackets, and their black hair shone with oil even in the grey winter light. One of them had a moustache. As they played they both tapped their feet and the one with the moustache sang to some of the numbers.

'Can you hear what he's saying?' Rose shouted in Diana's ear.

'No,' she shouted back. 'It's Italian. They're from Italy.'

'You know bloomin' everything, don't you?' Rose bawled back at her with a grin.

The two girls stood for quite a time watching the players. Rose thought nothing could ever make her feel so happy as the sound of those dancing tunes. They stood there so long that in the end the one with the moustache danced over to them, inclining first one shoulder and then the other as his fingers carried on playing with astonishing ease and speed. Rose saw the hairs of his moustache, and his shining brown eyes. He sang a long note on some word that sounded like 'mar-ee'. Rose and Diana put their hands up to their mouths and moved away giggling.

They were carried along by the crowd, smelling potatoes baking on a cart and crushed cabbage leaves under their feet and cigarette smoke which seemed stronger on the cold air. There were hundreds of stalls in the Market Hall, selling everything under the sun. They liked to go and see the great crabs and lobsters, bright and astonishing in their shells, and all the piles of toffee and peanut brittle.

'Oh look,' Diana said. She pointed to a big banner. 'It's a hundred this week!'

'Market Hall Centenary Celebrations', the sign read. 'February 11–18', and on each side in bigger print, '1835–1935'.

But it was Diana's turn to see her friend turn pale and serious. At the foot of the steps, leaning against the brick banister, was a man. His face was dark with several days of stubble, and round his neck, hanging from a length of cord, hung a cut-out tray made of cardboard. On it lay a few boxes of Swan Vesta matches. Rose stared at his face, tears stinging her eyes at the despair she saw written in every sag of his rough cheeks. His clothes hung limply, one sleeve of his greatcoat pinned away at the back. Many a night that coat had provided an extra cover on Rose and Grace's bed. The rough, familiar crutch stood against the wall beside him.

Rose stood watching her father, the tears running slowly down her cheeks. Bruises from the beating round the head that he had given her were only just fading. But now, seeing him here away from home, she pitied him for what he so obviously was – a wreck of a man. Her pity was partly for the squalor, the monotony of his life, but mostly it was for the way he had been broken by things too terrible to tell of, that only spoke themselves night after night in his dreams.

'Rose, what's the matter?'

'Nothing.' Rose turned away quickly, realizing he might see them.

'Come on. You were grinning like a Cheshire cat just a minute ago. What's up?'

'I'm not going to turn round again in case he sees,' Rose said sniffing. 'But look, by the steps. It's my dad.'

Diana turned her head and saw Sid's desolate figure. Then she took Rose's hand, and her friend felt a coin being pressed into it.

'Let's go and get the poor old sod a cup of tea.' The two girls smiled at each other, Rose more in surprise at Diana's unaccustomed language than because she thought it was a particularly good idea.

She approached him with the tea, feeling nervous and awkward, and handed it to him saying, 'Here y'are, Dad. You must be cold.'

Sid roused himself, looked at her without any apparent surprise and said, 'Aar. Thanks Gracie.'

'I'm ROSE,' she yelled at him. 'You silly old sod.' And she pulled Diana away, the moment of pity swept away by her anger.

Diana followed her as she stamped her way across the Bull Ring in her worn-out boots. 'Hey, Rose,' she said, running behind to catch up. 'You didn't have to go and tell him what I said about him to his face!'

Rose turned, for a moment still annoyed, and then burst out laughing. The two of them linked arms and moments later Rose was crying with laughter instead of vexation.

'Well, that's the last time I try and do anything for him,' she said defiantly. 'Now, how about that cup of tea we was going to have ourselves?'

CHAPTER 6

Dora's labour pains began in the middle of a cold night in March.

She called up the stairs, 'Sam, Sam! Go and fetch Old Joan – the babby's coming!' Sam shot out of bed and down to the outside door.

Rose scurried around. Her heart seemed more awake than her head and it was beating noisily. As she threw slack on the fire, which had almost gone out, Grace and the other children trooped in and Grace started to get them all organized.

'You come and sit here George, and Vi can sit on my lap. You can see all my pictures. Now, this one's Queen Mary in the royal box at Ascot . . .'

'Oh, not again,' George groaned.

Sid was still asleep and Dora said she couldn't see much use in waking him. She and Rose prepared Rose and Grace's bed in the attic together. They stripped off the bedclothes so the sheets wouldn't spoil, tucked the crackly newspaper round the mattress and spread sheets of it out on the floor.

'This one's a boy,' Dora said as she finally pulled herself up on to the bed. She looked exhausted already.

'How d'you know?'

'I just do,' she said, leaning her head back against the wall so the tendons stood out in her scrawny neck. 'I always know, by the end.'

Rose suddenly felt shy, helping her mother with something so intimate. Before, she'd always been whisked off

49

out of the way like the younger ones, and Old Lady Gooch or Gladys Pye called in to help.

Dora watched her daughter's brisk, practical movements and her serious face as she tucked the paper in neatly round the mattress. She knew Rose had recently started to come on of a month and had therefore become a woman.

'D'you want to stay and help with this one?' she asked. 'I think you're old enough. And Mrs Freeman'll need someone to give her a hand.'

Rose nodded. 'All right then.'

The labour progressed swiftly. Old Joan, who was not in fact very old but enormously fat, puffed and panted around almost as much as Dora. She pushed Sam off downstairs saying, 'This ain't no place for a lad. Go and make us all a cuppa tea, eh?'

'Just help yourself, won't you?' Dora said sarcastically. She knew she needed this woman, and she didn't want to fork out for the doctor as well. But the midwife was notorious for being lazy and sponging off people. She also laid out the dead on occasion and it was rumoured that things had gone missing from the rooms where the bodies were lying.

Rose at first found the sound of her mother's cries frightening. She started to sweat and she felt sick. She had only heard this from at least one floor away before. But between each bout of grunting and moaning Dora got back to normal and said, 'It's all right Rose. The babby'll not be long now.'

Rose ran up and down with water and cloths and alternated between her horrified fascination with the shadowy glimpses she kept getting of her mother's private parts and with the great coils of fat embedded round Joan Freeman's neck and arms and waist. Every inch of her looked as if she was padded with lard.

Joan seemed completely unmoved by what Dora was going through. She sat down on the edge of the boys' bed, her huge lap spreading across much of it. She drew her knitting out of her bag and sat in the candlelight with her head resting on her chins, pulling the brown wool round her stubby fingers.

'Ain't you got any more light than this?' she said to Rose. 'I can hardly see what I'm doing.'

Rose swallowed down her retort that she wasn't being paid to sit and do her knitting and went downstairs to find the small paraffin lamp that they hardly ever used.

'How's she getting on?' Grace whispered. She was very pale with circles under her eyes. Violet had fallen asleep on her lap.

'All right,' Rose said, feeling a bit superior. 'Shouldn't be long now.'

When she was half-way up to the attic she wished more than ever that she could retreat back down again. She heard her mother's cries, louder and more anguished than they had been so far. She had to force herself to climb the rest of the stairs.

'Please don't let me ever, ever have to do that,' she whispered to herself. 'I'll work as hard as I can, I'll get the best job I can. But don't let me have to have babbies!'

When she reached the top the light showed her Dora kneeling now on the bed on all fours like a dog. Her head was hanging down between her shoulders and she was panting and gasping. When she heard Rose she lifted her head. Her face was soaked with sweat. Joan was still knitting complacently on the other bed.

'There's something wrong,' Dora moaned.

Rose hung the lamp on a hook on the wall and went to bathe Dora's face, her hands trembling. Her mother's nightshirt had ridden right up at the back so her behind and legs were on view and she could see her great swollen belly and her breasts dangling beneath her as she knelt on the bed. Rose felt sweat break out all over her again as well.

'The babby – should be – coming down, but he's not – budging,' Dora panted, starting to cry in desperation, moving her body restlessly on the bed. Rose made helpless movements with her hands.

'You'll be all right,' Joan said, switching needles to begin on a new row. 'Just give him a good push.'

Dora heaved again. 'Help me – oh God, help me!'

Unable to do anything to help, Rose felt like crying herself. In the end she went to stand in front of Joan.

'Look, you old cow,' she shouted as Dora writhed on the bed beside them. 'You're s'posed to be here to help, not knit jumpers for the whole British bleeding army.'

The midwife waddled over to Dora in the shadowy light and said, 'You'll have to watch this one, Dora. She's got too much of a gob on her.'

'And you've got too big an arse on you,' Rose retorted. She was suddenly feeling exhausted.

'It's stuck,' Dora screamed. 'It won't come. Get it out, for God's sake. It's killing me.'

'You ought to get a doctor,' Rose hissed at Joan. 'You're not up to this.'

'Cheeky little sod,' Joan said. 'I've done hundreds of these.'

She bent down behind Dora, breathing heavily. Rose watched, horrified, as she pushed two of her thick, lardy fingers into her mother. Dora groaned, and Rose saw frothy saliva dripping from her mouth on to the crumpled newspaper. She was making whimpering animal sounds that turned Rose's stomach.

'The babby's ready all right,' Joan said. 'Must have an arm caught awkward.' And with no warning she forced her entire hand up inside Dora and began to manipulate the baby inside her, trying to free it. Dora's screams rose to a single high-pitched shriek like a creature caught in the iron teeth of a trap. Joan pulled her hand out, slimy with blood, and Rose squeezed her eyes tight and pushed her fingers into her ears, unable to stand it any longer.

When she opened her eyes a moment later, Dora was still screaming, but now it was more of a yell.

'Now you've woken up you can come here and give me a hand,' Joan said.

Still sick and dizzy, Rose just managed to peer under her mother, who was squatting again. Bulging out from her she could see the top of a little head covered in dark, wet hair.

'I can't – I CAN'T!' Dora shrieked.

'Just push,' Joan shouted down her ear. 'One more'll do it.'

With an almighty cry, Dora pushed the child's head out and Rose saw the blood spurt from her ragged vagina. Another push and the little body slithered out covered in blood and a white pasty substance. Dora collapsed forwards on to the bed.

'What is it?' Rose said, all her faintness of a moment before quite forgotten.

Joan's meaty hands picked up the little body and turned it to tie the cord.

'It's a boy, Mom!' Rose said, as Joan wrapped him in an old white cloth. 'You were right.'

'Told you,' Dora said faintly. 'Give him here.' She held out her arms, the palms of her hands grey with newspaper print, and took the little boy to her. 'Go on,' she said. 'You can go and tell your dad he's got another son. And Rose,' she said, as the girl headed for the stairs, 'thanks, our kid.'

Rose wasn't at home when it happened.

George ran across the court in his bare feet as if his breeches were on fire.

'Mom, Mom! Come quick!'

'What?' Dora's heart started pounding as she pulled off her apron. '*What?* Tell me.'

'It's our Violet,' George panted. 'She's gone under a horse.'

Dora was out of the court in front of him and into the street. At the top of Catherine Street by the main road she could see a small crowd of people and she tore along the pavement towards them.

Silently they let her through as if she were royalty. She heard someone say, 'It's the child's mother, the poor cow.'

53

A man was standing in front of his cart holding the bridle of a heavy black horse. Dora always remembered from that day the smell of the sweating animal, its damp heaving flanks in the sunlight and the stunned expression on the man's ill-shaven face.

At his feet lay the shape of her child. Even in the few moments since it had happened someone had run into their house and brought out an old torn net curtain and laid it over Violet, covering her completely.

Dora saw the ghostly features of her little girl's face through the two layers of net and the blood soaking into the slippery material. 'What d'you go and cover her face for?' she shouted.

She knelt down quickly and pulled back the soft curtain. Her face was expressionless as a stone as she saw the deep wound in Violet's skull and the shards of bone sticking out at grotesque angles. She was dead. Clearly, from the second the horse's hoof had smashed into the right side of her head she had had no chance of being anything else.

The man with the cart was distraught. 'I hadn't a chance, Missis. She was just there, under the horse. I never even saw her till it were too late.'

Dora nodded at him numbly. She felt no anger towards him. At this moment she felt nothing. She had no idea why Violet had been there when she should have been in the yard. Gladys Pye appeared and led her home. Someone else carried the child's body back to the house.

When Sid came home he stood looking down at her as she sat unmoving at the table. He put his face close up to hers, his breath stinking of beer.

'Can't even look out for your own kid now, can you?'

Three days later Rose was banging hard on the door of the vicarage.

When Catherine opened the door and saw the girl's pinched face and the look of desperation in her eyes she immediately led her inside and sat down with her. Ronald arrived as well, back from conducting a baptism service.

'It's me mom,' Rose said, starting to cry as the words

54

came out of her mouth. All the anguish of the past days started to pour out of her. 'Our Violet was killed by a horse on Wednesday.'

Catherine and Ronald looked at each other, appalled, but something stopped Catherine from following her instinct to put her arms round the girl. Rose was a warm person, but there was still a self-contained, dignified core to her that they'd seen in the small child they had carried in from the rain.

'I'm so sorry,' Ronald said. He knelt down beside her. Catherine watched, fascinated. For once she couldn't think what to do and Ronald, gentle and sympathetic, knew instinctively.

'But it's my mom,' Rose repeated. 'She hasn't said a word since Wednesday when it happened. She just sits there as if something's gone – you know – in her head. My dad's blamed her for Violet going. She ran out of the court when she wasn't s'posed to, on some prank or other. Dad says her getting killed's all Mom's fault. But she won't say nothing. She'll hardly move or eat or anything.'

She cried harsh, frightened tears.

Ronald suddenly stood up as if something had been decided. 'I'll come down and see her,' he said.

'*You?*' Rose and Catherine spoke exactly together.

'Yes, I,' he said and smiled wryly at their astonishment. 'After all, I'm supposed to be a messenger of the Good News, remember. And I presume you came to us for some sort of help, Rose? Well, this is the best I can do.'

Rose, who was suddenly terrified that Sid might be in when they got home, had no idea how much inner turmoil the vicar was experiencing as once again they walked together along the road towards town and Catherine Street. Rose's head reached above his elbow now, but she still had to make little skips to keep up with his long strides.

Ronald knew this was going to be a decisive morning in his life. He had realized gradually over the past years that he was in the wrong place. That his work in his present parish was not where his heart lay. He had encouraged Rose to tell him more and more about her life in the courtyards, of the conditions they lived in. Now he was going to visit the kind of place which drew him. Of course he could have chosen to walk round the Birch Street area at any time, but something had inhibited him. He would have been merely a voyeur. Now he had a real reason to go.

When George opened the door, Dora saw Rose standing outside with an enormous man, his dark clothes topped by a dog collar. She knew at once who he must be. At any other time she would have felt like giving Rose a good hiding for bringing him at all, let alone with no chance to get the place spick and span first. But at this moment she couldn't have cared less.

Dora stood up silently. She looked more gaunt and pale than ever. Ronald saw just how small were the houses in which so many large families had to live, how mean and cramped.

'Mom,' Rose said. 'This is the Reverend, Diana's dad. I told him about our Violet and he wanted to come and see you himself.'

Dora looked at this stranger whose head nearly touched the ceiling, and uttered her first words for days. 'You'd better make a cuppa tea, Rose,' she said. 'Kettle's boiled.' And then to Ronald: 'Have a seat.'

Ronald sat down on a wooden chair at the table, carefully avoiding a blob of congealed porridge on the side of it. 'I don't want to intrude.'

He felt foolish as he spoke, knowing that apart from death itself and the Means Testers from the Parish he was the greatest intrusion they'd had for years. He could hear the baby crying upstairs.

Dora folded her arms across herself as if to hide her breasts. 'Go and get him, Rose. I'll have to feed the babby, if you'll excuse me,' she said to Ronald in a flat, lifeless voice.

Rose carried Harry down. He was a bonny four-month-

56

old who looked as if he'd taken all the nourishment from his mother. He was beginning to look rather like Sam.

'Now,' Dora said decisively to Rose. 'You can take this lot outside and leave us.'

She sat down with Harry on her lap, covering herself modestly with an old cardigan as she fed him. Rose, bemused, shoved Grace and George out of the door.

When the children had closed the door behind them Ronald said, 'I'm so sorry to hear about little Violet, Mrs Lucas.'

The moment he spoke he saw her eyes fill with tears. 'All I can think of is how all her life I've been that worried by everything I've hardly had a kind word to spare for her.'

She felt very shy, sitting feeding her child and blarting in front of this huge, educated stranger. But she could also feel an enormous sympathy emanating from Ronald Harper-Watt. And he had two things that she needed: distance from her own situation, so she could talk to him, and time. His job allowed him the opportunity to sit and listen.

'You're a good mother, Mrs Lucas,' Ronald said gently. 'You mustn't think otherwise. Rose often talks about you – fondly.' He'd noticed that more and more recently. 'And it's easy to tell you always do the best you can for your children. I know things haven't been easy for you. I'm sure Violet knew you cared for her very much.'

Dora looked up at him, at his wide, handsome face, the brown hair swept back from his face and his kind, grey eyes. He was the first truly gentle man she could remember meeting.

She began to talk. She had sat in her house for three days feeling she was losing her mind. She had been afraid to speak for fear of what might come out – mad, raving gibberish so that she'd have to be locked away and never let out again.

57

For about twenty minutes Ronald didn't speak at all. He sat listening attentively, watching Dora as she talked while the baby sucked and sucked at her breast.

She told him everything, from the early, happy days of her marriage to the present, how her once loving husband forced himself on her several times every month and she had almost no feeling left for him in her heart. She spared nothing, talking entirely out of her own need as if it was her last chance.

Finally she stopped and prepared more tea, lying Harry down on a chair. He had fallen asleep with a streak of milk still wet on one plump cheek.

'So that's my life, Mr Harper-Watt,' Dora said, pouring more water into the pot. 'Not much to show for it is there? Sorry you had to listen to it all, but it's been a relief to have a talk.'

'No.' Ronald sat forward to emphasize what he wanted to say. 'You don't realize. It's been a privilege.'

She noticed suddenly that his large hands were trembling, and she felt disarmed by it.

'In fact,' he went on, 'you've probably helped me more than I could ever help you. You see, I've been feeling very – out of place, shall we say? – in my work. I'm thinking of moving to work in a parish such as your own – like St Joseph's.'

Dora stared at him. 'You're coming to St Joseph's?'

'Well, no. But I'd like a parish near the middle of the – a – city. In places which aren't quite so . . .' He was lost for tactful words.

'In the slums, you mean. Well, if you're asking me, I'd say do it. I'll be frank with you, Mr Harper-Watt. I'm not a churchgoer myself, but I've been to more than the odd wedding and funeral at St Joseph's and that Reverend Gasbag, or whatever he calls himself, he ain't living in the same world as the rest of us. We could do with someone a bit more human like you.'

Ronald sat back, feeling he'd received a great compliment.

'And by the way.' Now Dora had found her tongue

again she couldn't seem to stop using it. 'I've never thanked you and your wife for all your kindness to my Rose. You've done a lot for her. And your Diana's a good kid. I thought it wasn't on at first, them two being pals, but now I'm glad it's happened.' And she almost smiled.

'We think Rose is a marvellous girl,' Ronald said, sipping his cup of extremely sweet tea, and to his surprise enjoying it. 'We're all very fond of her. She's a bright child, you know. Given the right opportunities she could go far.'

Even as he spoke, Ronald realized that he was talking out of a different world. Opportunities were not things that had arisen much in Dora's life. She just nodded at him.

When he got up to leave they shook hands, warmly.

'Thank you for talking to me,' he said. 'And for the advice.'

'It were good of you to come,' Dora said bravely. 'I know I can't sit moping here for ever. Life has to go on, and I've got my young genius to look out for!'

In silence Rose watched his tall figure walk across the court. Just before disappearing through the entry he turned and waved to her. At that moment she really thought he must be an angel.

CHAPTER 7

JULY 1936

'I've got a job!'

They were Rose's first words as soon as Diana opened the door.

'Jolly well done.' Diana beamed at her. 'I'm so glad.'

Catherine came into the hall to add her congratulations, looking as stately as ever. She was wearing a cool, cream dress that flattered her curves and her thick hair was pinned up in a fashionable style round her head.

'Come and have a glass of home-made lemon,' she said to Rose. 'We were just sitting outside.'

They went out to the back of the house where there was a blue-brick terrace facing the old walled garden. Tendrils of wisteria hung down from the house and the garden felt warm and languid as bees buzzed round the hollyhocks and tiny yellow roses climbing the garden wall.

Judith looked up from the book she was reading on her lap. She was quite unlike Diana and William, with a smaller frame and dark hair and eyes. 'Hello Rose,' she said. 'I suppose you're all going to talk now.' She slipped off the chair and went to lie with it on her stomach on the grass.

'Come on, tell us about the job,' Diana said as she sat down. 'Was it the first one?'

'Yes,' Rose said proudly. 'My first interview. It's at Lazenby's Butcher's Remnants Company near the market. They deal with all the bits of the animals that people don't want to eat. The whole name of the firm is

Lazenby's Butcher's Remnants Co. and then in brackets, Skin, Hide, Fat, Wool etc.,' she recited proudly.

'Goodness, that sounds a bit gruesome,' Catherine said. She was afraid Rose had jumped impulsively into the first job that would employ her simply because she was so anxious not to go into service or on to the factory floor. Which was in fact not far from the truth.

'It does stink round there a bit,' Rose admitted. 'But I'm their new office girl. I start on Monday. And the offices are ever so nice. They're upstairs above the yard.' She was all puffed up with pride.

'So what did you have to do?' Diana asked, dipping shortbread into her glass. She saw Catherine frown at her.

'There was two lads up for the job as well,' Rose said, starting to enjoy herself. 'And Mr Lazenby – that's the gaffer of course – he said we had to show him how we could read and write. So I said to him, "I bet I can read and write better than either of them two." And he made us write a few things down, addresses and that. And then we had to read him a bit out of a book.'

Rose had stood and read as well as she possibly could, remembering not to drop her aitches, which she could do when she thought about it, and trying to put expression in her voice.

'And when I'd finished,' she giggled, 'Mr Lazenby said to me, "It's all right, we're not here to put on a Shakespeare play, you know. We just want a kid for round the office."'

But one of the boys had scarcely been able to read and write at all and the other, who seemed to be terrified of Rose, had read slowly, stumbling over the words. And Rose knew she had left school with an excellent reference from Miss Whiteley.

'So he said the job was mine!' she said. She didn't tell them the last part, that Mr Lazenby had said, 'Right. You can start Monday. You'll be getting eight and six a week.'

'Excuse me,' Rose said politely. 'But I thought it was ten shillings you was offering.'

'Oh yes.' Mr Lazenby stretched his jowly face into a smile. 'But you're a lass. We've only ever taken on boys before.'

Rose was a bit put out, but eight and six seemed a good amount to be taking home. Besides, she was proud to be the first girl that Lazenby's had ever employed.

'And I was thinking,' she chattered on, not noticing in her excitement that the others were very subdued. 'Just because I've left school doesn't mean I can't go on learning. You can teach me about all the things you're learning at school, can't you?' At this moment, Rose felt she could do anything.

Diana was looking lovely in a pale blue dress, her wavy hair tied up in a bouncy ponytail. Her skin was tanned from playing tennis and sitting out in the garden. But Rose suddenly noticed her miserable expression. Emerging from her own preoccupations she looked across at Catherine and saw she too had a solemn face.

'What's the matter?' She tried joking: 'If I ever saw two people looking as if they've lost tuppence and found a farthing, you're the ones!'

'Rose,' Catherine said, smiling kindly at her. She held her glass on the wood of the tabletop and slowly circled it round. 'Don't think we're not delighted that you've found a job – and so quickly. It's marvellous news. It's just that we have some news as well, and we're not sure yet whether it's good news or not.'

'You may not be sure,' Diana said, scowling. 'But I am.'

'Well go on – what is it?' Rose spread her long dark fingers on top of the table as if preparing herself for a shock.

Gently Catherine explained that Ronald had been looking for a new kind of job, and that as the diocese had not been able to place him in Birmingham he had accepted a post in Manchester.

'Manchester?' Rose was completely knocked for six. It might as well have been Australia. She wasn't even precisely sure where Manchester was. 'But what about your school, Di? And your pals? I'll never see you again if you all go up there.'

Rose's eyes filled with tears, and Diana was already crying.

'It's really rotten,' she sobbed angrily. 'Daddy decides he wants a different job and the rest of us have to change everything.'

'Look darling,' Catherine said to her outraged daughter. 'I know you think it's not what you want, but you won't know until you've gone and tried it. And when you've settled in, I'm quite sure you'll make friends every bit as good as you've got here.'

She wasn't aware of the appalling tactlessness of her last remark and its effect on their visitor.

But Diana said, 'It'll be beastly. And I'll never find another friend like Rose. How can you even think it?' She got up and put her slim arm round Rose's shoulders. Rose's lips were trembling with the effort of not crying.

'Oh, goodness, Rose,' Catherine corrected herself, horrified. 'I didn't mean – oh my poor child, I'm so sorry. How awfully rude of me. But Diana will be able to come down on the train in the holidays and visit.'

'What, and sleep at our house?' Rose asked, her voice heavy with sarcasm.

Catherine chose to ignore the girl's tone, knowing she was upset. 'Not necessarily. There are other friends of ours whom she could stay with.'

Rose stared into her lap. A tight, mutinous feeling was rising up inside her. She wanted to scream and throw all the glasses off the table. Horrible things were happening again that she couldn't do anything about, just as she thought she was beginning to get somewhere. Her joy at having found her job was for the moment completely wiped away.

'Listen girls,' Catherine said, looking at the two sullen and tearful faces in front of her. She leaned one of her plump elbows on the table. 'I know it's bad news and none of us is pleased about it. Judith and William are upset as well. But we've all got to make the best of it.

And it's not happening for a couple of months yet, so let's all be brave and enjoy the time we have got here together, shall we?'

Catherine changed the subject, talking about the civil war that was breaking out in Spain, and how she felt that Mr Stanley Baldwin was not doing any better than the Labour Prime Minister Ramsay Macdonald had at tackling the problem of people out of work. Both the girls realized she was trying to say how small their problem was compared to some of the big things going on in the world. But of course that didn't make them feel any better. Already it felt as if things were not the same. And Rose had a feeling that now they never would be.

It took the employees at Lazenby's a few weeks to get used to having a girl in the office. There was Miss Peters of course, but she was old enough to be most people's mother, if not grandmother.

Rose became a familiar figure, running errands to and from the traders on the balcony of the huge meat market, delivering statements and cheques and invoices. At first they ribbed her because she was a girl, but after a few weeks she often heard, 'Hello Rose! All right Rose!' from the lads as she made her way round between the office and the trading area.

One part of the job she didn't like was running messages down to the yard at the back of Lazenby's. She found she was surprisingly squeamish about what went on down there. She'd already seen the slaughter yard at Camp Hill. Groups of kids often gathered there to watch when they did the killing early in the morning and she'd been dragged along once by Sam. The dogs chivvied the cows or sheep a dozen at a time into the pen which was open for all to see behind a fence of palings. The slaughterers caught the animals one by one as they shrieked, sweating in terror and running at the fence trying to escape. They drove a sharp stick like a poker into their heads through whichever orifice they could reach to penetrate the brain of the flailing, screaming animal. In through the eyes or ears until the damage inflicted on them reached their whole bodies and they writhed and twitched and finally lay still.

In the yard of Lazenby's they dealt with everything leftover that could be sold. When Rose went down there the first time the stench turned her stomach. Slightly sweet and putrid, it was a smell she never got used to. The brick floor of the yard was covered with piles of cow hides which had to be examined to see if they had been holed by warble fly. Then they were rubbed over with salt and stacked in piles graded according to size. Sheep fleeces were dealt with in the same way.

Each time she went down there she had to contain her revulsion for the place and put up with the constant gibing of the yard men. The first time she stepped out into the yard they all straightened up from what they were doing and stood staring at her in their rubber boots and aprons, giving each other mischievous grins and making smart alec comments. One of them was hideously disfigured. His head and neck ran into each other and a goitre was slung like a squashed pig's bladder right round to the back. A cluster of bristles sprouted out of his nose.

'What're you doing here then?' one of them called to her. 'Come to do a turn for us have you?'

'I've got a note for Mr Freeman actually,' Rose said timidly. They were gawping like idiots as she stood in the navy skirt and soft pink blouse that Catherine and Diana had bought for her – new! – as a present for starting work.

'Ew – ectually!' they mimicked.

Rose slowly walked across the yard where there were small pieces of gristle and fat and furry bits stuck on to and in between the bricks. She slipped and nearly fell on a lump of something yellow and greasy.

'Watch your step,' they sniggered.

'This is where we keep some of the, er – accessories of the job,' the goitre man said mockingly.

The smells and the fatty lumps on the ground and the

great mauve bulge on the man's neck were already getting all mixed up in her mind. He took her forearm with his huge hairy hand and led her towards a row of bunkers at one side of the yard. Inside two of them she could see roughly picked bones piled all together, and in the other, glutinous mounds of fat. Shiny green flies were buzzing round greedily.

'And this one's where we keep the salt for the hides.'

Rose could hear the goitre man's heavy breathing as he stood beside her. She looked into the end bunker at the off-white heap of salt. Immediately she became aware that the pile was moving. It was a mass of maggots rubbing ceaselessly against each other's bodies and between the large granules of salt.

Rose knew what the man wanted. She wouldn't give him the satisfaction of looking squeamish, even though the sight sickened her. 'Well, thanks for the guided tour,' she said pertly, keeping her face quite calm. 'Now, which of you gentlemen is Mr Freeman?'

The man pointed his thick arm, letting go of Rose with the other. 'Him over there.'

As Rose made to walk off he said, 'Oi, just a minute. What part of town d'you come from then?'

'Birch Street, near by there,' Rose said.

'So you are one of us then. You look a bit poshed up in them clothes, that's all.'

In the office, though, it was different altogether. There were three main rooms where they worked. Mr Lazenby's office was up at the far end, shut off from the main workroom. You didn't go into Mr Lazenby's without permission and he sat with the door shut.

Rose sometimes knocked and crept in with messages. But she found Mr Lazenby disconcerting, although he was always polite to her, and even seemed to take an interest in her. He sat at his desk with its scratched leather top, all his things arranged on it extremely neatly: the blotter, penholder and account books or whatever he was dealing with. He was in his early fifties with a balding crown and soft, loose-looking cheeks. Rose expected them to slither down off his face at any moment. He had watery blue eyes and a rounded shiny nose. His manner was always quiet and courteous and he often asked how she was settling in with the firm and whether there were any problems.

Once, when she had come in with a message from the meat market, he thanked her and then said, 'Now, you just come round here a minute. I'll show you a picture of my kids. My youngest daughter is about your age.'

Rose walked obediently round the desk and leaned forward a little to look at the photograph. She suddenly felt Mr Lazenby's breath close to her ear and jumped back abruptly.

'It's all right,' he said. 'Don't be nervous, my dear.' And he put his arm round her waist for a moment in a fatherly sort of way to reassure her.

The photograph was another of the items placed neatly on his desk.

'There, you see,' he said. 'My two sons and my little girl.'

Three faces smiled rather stiffly out of the grey photograph. They all looked very well dressed and one of the boys closely resembled Mr Lazenby.

'Thank you,' said Rose, blushing. Mr Lazenby was staring at her and she didn't like being this close to him. He always smelt rather stale and sweaty. 'It's very nice of you to show me.'

'You're a good lass,' he said as she escaped out of the door, her feet sounding too loud on the lino floor.

At the other end of the long office space there was a storeroom for stationery, next to the stairs, and the office in between was where Rose spent most of her time. She dealt with the post and record cards and the stencilling machine. In the same office Miss Peters did the main secretarial work, and Michael Gillespie, the clerk, kept the books.

Michael was seventeen. He towered over Rose, his black hair slicked back very smartly and his blue eyes full of warmth and fun. To Rose, Michael might have been a whole generation older than herself. He seemed so grown up and knowing about the world, and he was already learning a proper skill which he could take on to other firms.

'I don't want to be stuck as an office dogsbody for the rest of my life,' he told her. Rose could hear the very slight Irish intonation in his voice even though he'd been born and brought up in Birmingham. 'There's all the world waiting out there . . .' He moved one of his strong fingers along the frayed edge of a ledger with a grin on his face, pretending it was a plane taking off. 'Lazenby's is just my runway to greater things.'

'What greater things?' Rose asked curiously, franking a pile of letters that Miss Peters had completed.

'Well now, little Rosie, let me see.' Michael sat back in the chair with the air of a tycoon surveying his latest acquisition. 'There's all sorts of things. One of these days I'm going to be running my own business. With a big office. And I'll be able to sit at my desk and send someone running for cups of tea. And I'll tell you what: you and Miss Peters can come and work for me!' He sat forward again, laughing loudly. 'What do you say, Miss Peters?'

'I can hardly wait,' Miss Peters said, looking across at him over her round, black-rimmed spectacles. 'Rose, are those letters going out this week – this month even?'

Rose smiled wryly at Michael, who jumped up and went to lean impishly over the back of Miss Peters' black Remington typewriter.

'You know what a wonderful woman you are, don't you?' He smiled appealingly, bending his head down towards her. 'So efficient, so correct, such a sense of humour. You're an example to us all.' He sensed that Miss Peters was coming round to his charm in her prickly way. 'Sure,' he said, bouncing back to his desk. 'I'd have you to work for me any time!'

Miss Peters made noises of exasperation and gestured at Rose to get off to the post. She ran down the stairs, laughing.

Rose was happy. She treasured the thought of Dora's

proud face as she set off, all dressed up on her first morning, and then when Rose had brought home her first wages. Even the pain of saying goodbye to Diana the week before seemed lightened by the fun she had in the office.

She had been at work on the day they actually left, so they said their goodbyes on the Sunday before. Ronald and Catherine had both embraced Rose as well as Diana, and even William shook her by the hand, rather stiffly, and said, 'I hope we shall see you again, Rose.'

'You'd blooming better,' Rose said, being all joky so she didn't start crying. 'I'll expect you down here to see me as soon as you can, Di.'

'Oh, I shall come, I shall. But you must write to me very, very often. I shall miss you so much.'

They'd given each other a long big hug. They didn't want to let go, and promised each other all kinds of things: above all, letters. And Rose had waved goodbye as she started for home, choked with sadness. When she reached her house she cried and cried.

Later she told Geraldine Donaghue that Diana had left. The girl's face lit up maliciously. The two had spent a lot of time together at school, but Geraldine had always remained jealous of Diana, knowing that she and Rose shared something very special.

'Going to lower yourself to speak to the rest of us now are you?' Geraldine said.

'I've always spoken to you,' Rose said impatiently. 'You know that very well. And if you hadn't always been so green round the gills about Diana we could've been better friends all the time.'

'Hark at her,' Geraldine said. 'Miss High and Mighty.'

Rose knew Geraldine was sore because she hated her boring factory job, and her dad had been laid off again. She knew the Donaghues were struggling, and none of it did much to improve Theresa Donaghue's temper.

But Rose was not very bothered about Geraldine. She had only to be in Michael's cheeky, vivacious company for a few minutes and she felt renewed and lively herself.

She had been attracted to him from the first day there, though she was not thinking about courting. She knew Michael was a regular on the Stratford Road monkey-run and had had a succession of dates. She was very childlike and innocent still about relations between men and women, although she knew that sometimes she was flirting with him. Mainly he provided a figure for her to look up to, who had an infectious kind of drive and wanted to put a lot into his life and get a lot out of it. He made her feel more alive.

'You're a funny kid,' he said to her one day as they were working together. Miss Peters, despite her crustiness, was very tolerant of their conversation so long as she knew the work would be done.

Michael looked appraisingly at Rose. 'You come down here from Birch Street all dressed up in nice clothes that would set anyone back a bit. And sometimes you talk common like the rest of us, and other times you can turn it on and put on your aitches and sound quite posh. What's your secret, eh, little Rosie?' He grinned at her. 'Are you a foundling from Buckingham Palace or something?'

'That'd be telling, wouldn't it?' she said rather pertly, and she knew once again that there was a mild flirtation going on between them.

She had come to Lazenby's with enormous hopes, to learn, as a way of getting experience for better things and eventually moving on.

But not yet, she thought. I'll stay and enjoy it while it lasts.

CHAPTER 8

The summer ended. Rose walked to work on fine days in the rich slanting light of autumn. When it grew colder she put on Diana's coat – one of a number of pieces of clothing that the family had left for her – and walked more briskly.

Though still small and thin Rose was not as painfully bony as she had been during the poorest days of her childhood. She was of a different build from Dora, more rounded, and her breasts had begun to fill out. With her dark wavy hair cut to the level of her chin and softly brushed back from her face and wearing Diana's well-cut clothes she looked surprisingly elegant for someone so young. Her brown eyes shone with vigour and intelligence.

Twice every day she passed builders working on a nearby warehouse whose scaffold extended out across the pavement so she had to skirt round piles of bricks and a cement mixer. The lads working on the site, their boots dusted grey, gave appreciative whistles as she walked by.

It didn't take her long to notice that one of the young brickies had taken quite a shine to her. As the days passed he seemed to be waiting for her, watching quietly. He wasn't one of the whistlers. He was a thin, pale lad with spiky brown hair that looked as if no amount of Bryl or any other creem would force it to lie flat.

Then he began to smile at her and say hello whenever she walked by. Once, when she had almost passed them, she heard the others egging him on, 'Go on – go and ask her name!'

Suddenly the nervous boy was beside her. 'Er . . .' The words stumbled out clumsily. 'I just wondered – I mean – what's your name?'

'Rose,' she replied, amused. 'And what's yours?'

'Alfie,' he said. 'That is – Alfred – Meredith.'

'Oh,' Rose said. 'Hello then, Alfie.'

Alfie seemed to be quite struck dumb and as Rose was still hurrying on down the road he said, 'Tara then.'

'Tara,' Rose said smiling, attaching no real importance to the meeting.

She was still smiling when she reached Lazenby's and walked into the office. Michael was already sitting behind his desk and he looked up and grinned when he saw her. 'All right, little Rosie?' he said. 'Don't you look a picture this morning? Had some good news or what?'

'Yes I have.' She took her camel coat off and hung it up. 'A letter from Diana.'

Rose had gradually told Michael about Diana and her own hopes to get on and do something with her life. She was rather afraid at first that he'd laugh at her and tell her she'd not got a hope. Sometimes she couldn't make Michael out. He could be as kind and generous as anyone she'd ever met – even Diana – and innocent as she was, she realized that the hunger for life they both shared resulted in an electric kind of attraction between them. But there was also a wild streak in him. She knew he was already beginning to drink heavily, and he had come into the office a number of times with his face cut and bruised from fights.

When she told him her greatest ambition was to become a teacher of young children he looked at her and gave a low whistle.

'Well,' he said. 'You're quite a girl, aren't you? Can't quite see you as one of them blue-stocking women though – let alone how you're going to get there. But good luck to you all the same.'

She knew it was not an ambition he could really

understand, but she was grateful to him for not making fun of her.

And hearing from Diana was always encouraging.

'I can't wait until Christmas when I come down to see you,' Diana wrote.

> I miss you and Birmingham so much. My school is all right I suppose, but I haven't really made any friends properly yet. The school is rather a long way from where we live, as we knew it would be. So William, Judith and I all have to go to school on the bus every day. Mummy says it's good for us! But I don't like Manchester as much as Birmingham.

She told Rose that her father was enjoying his new job and Catherine was getting stuck into things as ever.

> Missing you ever such a lot. With love from your good friend,
> Diana. xxx

Things were looking less cheerful for Dora. She was pregnant again. At nearly forty-three she'd hoped this kind of sickness was something she'd seen the back of. And this time it came with an intensity and violence that she recognized from nearly twenty years earlier. It could mean only one thing.

'It's twins, I'm sure of it,' she wailed to Rose and Grace as they helped her back up the stairs to bed. 'I've only been sick this bad with babbies once before and that was with Sid and Percy. What the hell am I going to do? Twins at my age!'

'It might not be twins, Mom,' Grace tried to reassure her as they helped her on to the bed, so weak from the incessant retching that she could barely stand. 'It might just be your age making it worse.'

'Ooh,' Dora groaned. 'I feel as if someone's trampled all over me ribcage.'

'Look Mom,' Rose said. 'There's no need to worry.

You don't have to do anything. The money's coming in from me and Sam and our Grace'll be out at work next year when the babby's born. We'll do everything round the house. You just take care of yourself for a change.'

'What about Sid's dinner today? You know how he carries on . . .'

'Let him get it his bloody self for once,' Rose snapped, exasperated that her father's needs were as usual the thing that overrode everything else.

Grace shushed her. 'It's all right, Mom,' she said to Dora. 'I've got a few minutes before I go to school. I'll sort out something to keep him quiet. You just have a sleep and you'll feel better. Rose – you'd better get off to work or you'll be late.'

Rose could feel her sister's stoical calmness beginning to pervade the room. She realized it would be better if she went. She left Grace methodically tidying her father's things in the bedroom and tucking the covers round Dora so that only her grey face, creased in discomfort, was visible.

It was the first time Dora had been able to take to bed during a pregnancy. The sickness left her weak and wretched, and it was several weeks before she was able to be up once the worst was over.

The day had begun well. It was a frosty November morning. The builders on Rose's walk to Lazenby's had almost finished their work, and this fact had stirred Alfie Meredith to new realms of courage. He thought Rose was the best-looking girl he'd ever seen. He longed to ask her out and spent almost all his time rehearsing what he might say. Rose, though she smiled and waved at him, never gave him a thought the rest of the time.

When Alfie approached her that morning, Rose turned to him with her usual smile and said, 'All right, Alfie? Job's about done, isn't it? I s'pose you'll be moving on soon?'

'Yes,' he said, walking alongside her. 'That's it – yes. Er, Rose. Just stop a tick will you?'

She stopped and waited, looking at him.

'I wanted to ask you . . .' He ran his sandy hand through the already wayward hair and it stuck up even more. 'Would you think of coming out with me – on a date like?'

Rose decided in a split second what approach to take to this. She wasn't keen on the idea of walking out with Alfie, though flattered by the question. She decided to let him down gently by keeping up a joking banter. She started to walk on again slowly.

'Well – I'm not sure about that,' she said. 'I'd have to think about it, wouldn't I?'

Alfie immediately took this as a refusal. He ran after her awkwardly in his cement-caked trousers. 'Well tell me your address then – or I might not see you again. We finish here today, see.'

'Court eleven, Catherine Street,' Rose called over her shoulder to him. 'Got to go or I'll be late. Tara, Alfie.'

It was a tiring day. She ran back and forth to the markets with messages amid the seething activity in the echoing building hung with the skinned sides of animals. There were so many invoices and bills to be sorted out that she was not much in the office until the afternoon. When she finally came back the short distance up Bradford Street and along the side street to Lazenby's she saw that the lights were on and the place looked quite warm and inviting.

Upstairs Mr Lazenby was standing in the main office with Jo Perks from the meat market. Miss Peters had already left, her desk cleared and immaculate. Michael still seemed to be concentrating at his desk.

'Hello stranger,' he said, looking up. 'They've certainly kept you on the go today haven't they?' He closed the ledger and tidied a few sheets of paper. 'Well – that's me done. I'm off to the Adam and Eve for a quick one.' Rose smiled as he smoothed back his shiny black hair and put his jacket on. She knew it would be more than a quick one. 'Tara. See you in the morning, kid!'

'Bye,' Rose said, smiling after him. She watched him walk jauntily to the top of the stairs. Just before he disappeared down them he turned and raised his thumb to her with a smile, and she grinned and waved at him.

Jo Perks and Mr Lazenby were standing sorting through a pile of slinks – the hides of unborn calves which Lazenby's also purchased from the markets. They went to make fancy wallets and purses.

Rose looked at her table to see if there were any jobs that needed doing, and then began to get ready to leave. Her feet were very chilled and tired and she thought longingly of soaking them in a pail of hot water when she got home.

But as she made to go Mr Lazenby called over to her. 'Rose – if you wouldn't mind hanging on a minute till I've finished with Mr Perks. I've got a couple of things need sorting out.'

Rose nodded and waited as Mr Lazenby showed out the dapper figure of Jo Perks, carrying a couple of the rolled up slinks that hadn't come up to scratch.

'Come here a minute, Rose,' Mr Lazenby said in his polite but brisk business voice.

He stood back to let her into his office, where the light was already on, making it look completely dark outside. He closed the door behind them.

With rather odd enthusiasm he said, 'I tell you what. Since we're out of hours, you sit in the boss's seat. Go on, for a bit of a joke like. Yes, that's right my dear. Go along and sit yourself down!'

Rose walked round to the big chair behind Mr Lazenby's desk. It had wooden arms and a shiny leather seat. She looked uncertainly at Mr Lazenby, who stood the other side of the desk. His worn black jacket was unbuttoned and as he leaned down to rest his weight on his hands on the desk, the flaps of the jacket swung outwards making him look enormously wide.

Rose began to wonder if he'd been drinking. She'd

never seen Mr Lazenby looking so animated. But he was normally a very abstemious man – known for it in fact. His soft cheeks had more colour in them than usual and he kept tapping his fingers restlessly on the top of the desk.

'There are a couple of invoices I'll need first thing,' he said once Rose was seated on the slippery chair, which smelt rather sweaty, like Mr Lazenby. 'Since you're so good at writing, you can write these ones out yourself. How about that?' he said.

He opened one of the desk drawers and produced a wodge of forms, then handed Rose a pen. 'This one's for Clark's, so write in the name up there – you know how to do it,' he said, pointing with a grubby finger. He gave her details of the address and Rose slowly wrote them on the invoice sheet in her very neatest handwriting. Mr Lazenby watched over her shoulder.

'Very good,' he said, and Rose jumped because the voice sounded so close to her.

'Now – the next bit,' he said.

Rose sat with her heart beating fast. She was beginning to sweat under her arms. She didn't know what Mr Lazenby was up to but he was making her most uneasy. She just wanted to get the job done and go home.

As she was listing the items on the form she suddenly felt Mr Lazenby's hands moving round her and cupping her breasts. She gasped out of shock and discomfort because he was pressing her quite hard. She sat quite still, completely unable to think what to do. What on earth had come over him? This was a mistake – a terrible mistake. Mr Lazenby must realize it in a minute and stop touching her. She thought her heart was going to burst it was beating so loud, and her hands had gone clammy.

'Stand up,' Mr Lazenby ordered. His voice sounded polite still, but had a hard, unfamiliar edge to it. He pulled her up by moving his hands under her arms and he steered her away from the chair. Rose obeyed, bewildered. She was very afraid, but she couldn't think what else to do. The building around them had gone quiet.

After that, quite silently except for his breathing, which sounded loud and fast, he pulled her against him. She was still facing the desk, the impassive blotter, the penholder and the set, smiling faces of his children. He moved up and down against her buttocks, fitting himself close to her.

He began grabbing at her clothes, the green cardigan and soft white blouse. He lost patience with the buttons and she heard the blouse tear apart at the front. The image of Miss Smart's face as she had ripped Rose's bloomers that day filled her mind for a second. At least then she had understood what was happening.

'Stop it, Mr Lazenby – please,' she begged, her voice turning high like a little girl's. 'I don't like this. Please stop and let me go home.'

She turned her head and felt a plunging sensation of revulsion at the sight of him behind her. He didn't look like Mr Lazenby any more. His eyes were half closed and seemed to be rolled up into the lids so he looked all peculiar, as if he were in a trance. And his tongue was sticking stiffly out of his mouth towards her ear.

'What are you doing?' she shouted. 'Help me some-body – please. Please!'

She tried to get his hands off her, but as if prompted by her cries, Mr Lazenby shoved her to the floor, cold against her breasts and stomach as she writhed and kicked. She felt his knee in her back pinning her to the floor, and twisting round she saw he had unbuttoned his trousers and was rubbing himself with his hand, fast up and down. He pulled off her underwear and stockings, pausing to caress himself with one hand as he did so. She knew she didn't have the strength to get away from him. She put her arms flat on the floor and laid her head down so she didn't have to see his face with its self-absorbed expression or his horrifying, swollen member.

He pushed her skirt up and made her move her legs apart. She had never taken her clothes off in front of a man before, not even a doctor. She pressed her eyes shut at the shame of it. Tears squeezed from her lids on to the floor. She thought at least she hadn't got her monthly to add to the humiliation. She knew that what Mr Lazenby was doing must be what she had heard her father do so often to her mother, but it didn't prepare her any better for what happened next.

He gradually forced one of his fingers up inside her so that she squirmed and cried out in shock and pain.

'Oh . . .' Mr Lazenby gave a low groan. 'Young, tight.'

They were the only words he spoke until he'd finished. Quickly he climbed on her and forced hard up into her from behind and she screamed and then whimpered at his repeated movements. Each time he pushed into her she felt a terrible stab of pain somewhere deep in her guts. Her hipbones and ribs were grinding hard against the floor with the weight of him on top of her and she was finding it hard to breathe. She lifted her head, sobbing and trying to take in gasps of air so her mouth dried out. It took some time before he managed to finish, and he came at last with a loud, relieved cry.

When he had stumbled off her he buttoned himself up again and watched as she slowly pulled herself off the floor and found her clothes. The wet ran down her legs as she stood up and her tears wouldn't stop coming. She didn't look at Mr Lazenby when she was clothed again. She began to walk mechanically to the door.

Mr Lazenby gave a little cough. 'Er – Rose, just a minute,' he said.

She forced herself to look round and saw he was bringing his wallet out of his jacket.

'I've been thinking. You've done you best since you've been here,' he said in his normal courteous voice. 'But I'm not sure this is really a job for a lass. I've decided to let you go and get a lad in like we've always had. It'll be for the best I think.'

He was holding out a pound note to her.

'Here – take a couple of weeks' pay. And if you need a decent reference you can rely on me, you know that.'

He came a little closer, holding the money out as if he was trying to tempt a dangerous animal. Rose quickly snatched the note, backing away from him again.

He unlocked the door and she went slowly down the stairs and out into the freezing evening, holding in her hand a larger sum of money than she'd ever earned at once before.

CHAPTER 9

12 MAY 1937

Coronation day. All over the nation there were excited
preparations to celebrate the crowning of a new king –
George VI. Red, white and blue bunting rippled and
flapped along Catherine Street in the bright spring morning. Union Jacks billowed out from the sills of some of
the houses, and as it was a day off work for everyone, the
road was more full of people than usual. Already the
inhabitants of the street were setting up trestle tables
along the pavements, to be laid later with white cloths
and heaped with plates of food for the street's celebration
party. George and his little band of followers were tearing
in and out of the courts in their draggle-arsed shorts,
pretending to be aeroplanes with a lot of roaring sound
effects and getting under everybody's feet.

In Court 11 most of the women were inside hastily
icing platefuls of tiny sponge cakes and slicing bread for
the little triangular sandwiches which would grace the
tables later on. Old Lady Gooch declared, breathing
heavily as she went to inspect what was happening in each
house, that she'd made a 'rich fruit Dundee – one of me
best'. Her large bloodshot eyes ran over every contribution to make sure everyone was doing their whack and
that there'd be enough to go round in the afternoon. She
was still wearing her working clothes. The dressing up
would come later and the pawn shops had been rifled for
suitable clothes, some of which had not seen the light of
day for months or longer.

The happiest person in the court that day was Grace

Lucas. Not only was she to leave school that summer, but she was ecstatic that there was another coronation so soon after the last. Now she'd got over her grief at the death of her beloved King George V and the startling abdication of his successor Edward VIII, she was ready to throw herself wholeheartedly into the occasion. She had trimmed the edges of her frock by hand with strips of red, white and blue, and decorated a straw hat in the same colours with elaborate ribbons and bows. With it pulled on over her straggly brown hair, her pale, sweet face was almost pretty. Even Sid had noticed and commented that he'd never seen her looking such a 'fine lass' before.

'Rose – you can't miss coming this afternoon,' Grace entreated her sister, who was scraping the last hardening crust of white icing out of a mixing bowl. 'It wouldn't be the same without you. You're not thinking of the neighbours are you?'

'Bit late for that isn't it?' Rose said sourly. 'I'm just not in the mood, that's all, and I need a rest. I cleaned that blooming pub from top to bottom yesterday and I could do with a lie down. I don't feel right.'

Grace's and Dora's eyes met and Grace shrugged. She couldn't get close to Rose any more. She felt like crying when she looked at her older sister standing by the table. She was wearing an old dress of Dora's which they'd shortened together and tucked up at its wide, loose waist. Her belly was straining forward with the unmistakable curve of pregnancy. She was having to lean more than usual towards the table to accommodate the shape of the child. Her hair was hanging limply down her back and around her face. Grace couldn't help thinking – with the realization of how aware Rose must be of it too – that she looked just like a miniature, black-haired version of her mother.

'Leave her,' Dora said rather irritably. She was tired, being now seven months pregnant herself, as well as having had to deal with all the goings on over Rose.

'I'm going to go and see how they're getting on

outside,' Grace said a bit huffily. Her mother and sister had an understanding nowadays that she definitely was not part of.

She went out into the street to look up and down at all the busy preparations. She saw someone coming towards her along the street and for a few seconds she couldn't place who it was. Then she was back across the court to the house as fast as she could move.

'Rose!' she shrieked. 'He's here again!'

Rose looked up lifelessly. 'Who?'

'That bloke – Alfie – the one who come before. He's got flowers this time.'

'Oh no,' Rose said. Dora and Grace could both hear the panic in her voice. 'Don't let him see me, for God's sake.' She was wiping her hands so hurriedly that she fumbled and dropped the cloth. 'Go and tell him I'm not here again. Tell him I've gone away or something.' And she was off upstairs.

Grace managed to reach Alfie as he was coming into the court. 'You looking for Rose again?' she asked, thinking what kind eyes he had and how funny his hair looked all sticking up like that.

'Is she here?' Grace could hear the combined hope and nervousness in his voice. 'I'd really like to see her – if she'll let me.'

At that moment young Harry waddled up and stood staring at this strange man who had appeared. He had wide blue eyes and a fat tummy. And he had nits and was forever scratching busily at his head.

'E-yo,' he said to Alfie.

'Hello.' Alfie smiled down at him. 'Doing all right, are you?'

'That's our Harry,' Grace told him.

'Nice kid,' Alfie said. 'Anyway, is Rose in today?'

'Rose . . .' Harry said, turning towards the house, and Grace could tell he was about to point at it. Hurriedly she grabbed his hands and picked him up, wishing someone would pursue her with flowers and obvious admiration, because she'd make better use of it than Rose.

'Rose ain't here,' she told him. 'She's gone away for a bit – to stay with Mom's sister down Alcester way. She won't be around for . . . well, we don't know how long really.' She didn't like lying to him, but she felt it would save both his feelings and Rose's.

'Oh,' Alfie said despondently. 'Only I was hoping – you know, as it's a holiday today . . .'

'Well I'll let her know you 've been round – when I, er, write,' Grace said. 'It was nice of you to call.'

'Here,' Alfie said, holding out the bunch of pink and white flowers to her. 'You might as well take these anyway. You have them, or give them to your mom.'

As he turned to go he pointed at number five. 'That your house then, is it?'

'Yes,' Grace said shyly. 'That's us – number five.'

'Tara then.'

Glancing up at the dark windows, Alfie felt sure he caught a glimpse of a pale face edged with black hair, before it ducked down below the sill.

He walked away angrily. What's got into her? he thought. I s'pose she thinks I'm not good enough for her or something.

There had been a number of changes in Court 11 during the past six months.

First, Rose had been faced with telling Dora she had lost her job. When her daughter walked in that November evening, Dora had only to look at her to realize something had happened. Normally she came in from work tired, but quite animated, and often full of stories of things that had happened during the day. But that night she was quite silent, as if something had been tied up tight inside her.

'Had a bad day?' Sam casually asked Rose as he polished his boots. 'Aren't you going to tell us what wonder boy's been up to today?' Sam got a bit browned off with Rose's adoration of Michael Gillespie.

Rose didn't answer him. She took off her coat and hung it up behind the door and then went to go upstairs.

'Grub's ready so don't go disappearing again,' Grace said. 'You're late enough as it is.'

Rose ignored her.

'Did you hear your sister?' Sid shouted after her, throwing the newspaper down. 'We've all been waiting for you as it is. You ought to be thankful our Grace lets you off so much of the work around here, you uppity little cow.'

Dora and the others held their breath as they waited for the explosion from Rose which would set off another of the increasingly bitter fights between them. Grace had had to intervene to pacify Sid on a number of occasions when Dora wasn't up to it.

But Rose just said, 'I'm not hungry,' and went to her room.

.She sat painfully on the bed, feeling the damp still on her clothes. Her mouth twisted for a moment with revulsion. Then she lay down, curling herself on the mattress like an unborn child. The pain throbbed inside her. She pressed her hand on her bruised private parts, and clamped her legs tight together with her hand still between them, trying to dull the ache of it. What she wanted overwhelmingly was to wash every part of her over and over, but she knew there was no chance of that with all the family sitting round down there. She screwed her eyes tight shut and wished she could fall down, down somewhere very dark and safe where she could be held and comforted. No tears came to begin washing away the shame and despair she felt.

And as she lay there she was overcome with loathing for herself. All the smells of Lazenby's seemed to seep out from her clothes and her body. She smelt the foul stink of the hides, the bunkers of bones and rancid fat in the yard. She saw the maggots squirming among the grains of salt, the frantic greed of the flies; she saw the discoloured bulging shape of the goitre man's neck and the soft, floppy cheeks of Mr Lazenby. She could see him kneeling with that horrible, trance-like expression on his face, his trousers unbuttoned and his hand busy on his penis.

She rushed over to the bucket in the corner of the room and retched over it, feeling the muscles in her bruised stomach heave painfully. She didn't hear Grace coming up the stairs.

'Are you bad, Rose?' she asked sympathetically. 'You should've said instead of just going off. I could've brought you a cuppa tea. Dad just thought you was being awkward.'

'I'll be all right,' Rose said weakly, and she sounded so wretched that Grace said, 'I'll get our mom.'

Dora slowly climbed the stairs holding a candle stuck on to a saucer. She wasn't feeling too good herself.

'What's up with you then, miss?' she demanded roughly, sitting down on the bed, panting from the climb.

Rose had only intended to break the news that she'd lost her job, but when she began talking the tears started pouring down her cheeks again. She had to tell Dora what had happend. She couldn't hold back.

The second she heard what Rose had to say, Dora was on her feet. With more energy than she'd summoned for weeks she slapped Rose hard on each cheek.

'What did you do?' Dora shouted at her, before remembering that on no account must Sid or the neighbours overhear this conversation. 'You must've encouraged him,' she hissed at Rose. She stood with her hands clamped to her waist, her elbows at sharp, hostile angles. Her shadow in the candlelight looked huge and menacing. 'Going off to a place like that in all them clothes of Diana's. You must've given him ideas, you silly little cow.'

'I didn't!' Rose wailed. 'I didn't know what to give him ideas about, did I? He just went for me – held me down on the floor!'

Dora stood over her, her mind trying to take in the implications of what had happened. Then, as if bracing herself, she said in a matter-of-fact voice, 'We'll just have to wait and see if you're having a babby. If not, then there's no harm done. You can go and find another job.'

'A babby?' Rose sat up, horrified. The thought hadn't occurred to her.

'If you didn't know where they come from before, you do now,' Dora said drily. 'God help you if your dad finds out. I'll tell you one thing though. Whatever he says I'll stick by you. You'll not be sent out on the streets like some. But you'd better start praying hard, Rose, that there ain't no babby come out of this. Because you're going to need all the help you can get.'

She gave Rose's quivering body a rough pat. 'When your dad's off to the Catherine again I'll send Grace up with a pail of water for you. We'll just tell her you're a bit feverish. It'll have to be cold though – I can't spare the slack for the fire this time of night. But if you want to wash a man off you that bad you won't be bothered how cold the water is.'

'So you're nothing but a bloody little tart after all!' Sid's harsh voice ran through the house. 'Even that Geraldine Donaghue ain't poking out at the front and she's been working down the factory. But you've been nothing but cowing trouble ever since you learned to open your gob.'

Rose noticed again the perverse triumph that came over him when he saw her put down. But she rode her father's attacks more easily than anyone's. She was used to them. And as she had promised, Dora stood like an immovable wall between him and Rose as he ranted at both of them. But even his insults felt as if they were true, she was in such an emotional state.

It was telling Grace and Sam that came hardest. One afternoon they went with George and Harry to Calthorpe Park. The two young boys ran on ahead as soon as they were released into the green space, little Harry trying to keep up with his nine-year-old brother. Sam, Rose and Grace walked behind, keeping them both in sight.

'How could you, Rose?' Sam demanded, rigid with indignation. He immediately fell into what Rose was beginning to recognize as his role of responsible citizen. His shoulders were pulled back and he clasped his hands behind his back, walking along with a rather ponderous stride. For a split second Rose wanted to giggle hysterically. She had only got as far as telling him that in five months' time she'd be having a baby.

'How could you lower yourself like that?' Sam lectured. Beside her, Rose sensed, Grace had gone rigid with distress, but would not of course be judging her. Not Grace.

'I've always had my suspicions about that Michael Gillespie bloke,' Sam went on. 'Always sounded like trouble to me. You shouldn't be taken in by things that glitter, Rose. All that glitters is not gold, you know. And where is he now you're carrying his child? That's what I'd like to know.'

'It wasn't Michael!' Rose cried, bursting into tears. She was completely horrified that that should be Sam's first thought. Sobbing, she told him who the child's father was.

'You must've given him some encouragement,' Sam said. 'That Mr Lazenby sounded like a respectable feller. You said yourself he lives in a road in Edgbaston, not a street like the likes of us round the Birch. You should be ashamed of yourself.'

'Of course I'm ashamed of myself,' Rose sobbed brokenly beside him. 'D'you think I've felt anything but ashamed since the day it happened?'

'Sssh, for goodness sake,' Sam urged her. 'People're staring at you.'

Grace put her arm round Rose's shoulder and with the other pointed across the park to the two boys. 'Go and get them, Sam,' she said icily to her brother. 'And take your time.'

The two sisters sat down on one of the benches. Rose, beyond caring that she had chosen to tell them in such a public place, leaned on Grace's skinny shoulder and cried and cried. From the evening she had left Lazenby's she had felt only a leaden depression so that some days she could hardly drag herself around. But now the pain released itself from the deepest part of her. The tears wouldn't stop coming, and Grace stroked her hair gently. Sitting there so close, as Rose finally grew quieter, her body still shuddering from the sobs, she could hear the pull of her sister's lungs.

'Why didn't you tell me sis?' Grace asked her. 'I'd never've blamed you, you know. This is the worst thing that could happen to anyone and I know you're not the type to go looking for it.'

'I couldn't.' Rose gulped. 'I mean, I had to tell Mom – about why I'd lost my job at Lazenby's and everything. But telling the rest of you – it made it real somehow. And I didn't know about the babby at first. If there'd been no babby I could've tried to put it out of my mind and just got on with it. But now . . .' She began to cry again, weakly. 'I can't do anything ever again, can I, except be like Mom and have kids trailing after me. Oh Grace – sometimes I could just finish myself, I really could.'

'You mustn't think that!' Grace gripped Rose's shoulders with surprising strength. 'Don't you ever think anything of the sort.' She was crying herself now, and the two of them sat there frozen on the bench on that icy March day as Sam stood in the distance with his back to them, staring across the park.

Little Harry toddled up and stood there gazing worriedly at them, so the two girls picked him up and cuddled him to reassure him.

'Can you feel the babby?' Grace asked timidly.

'I think so. Just a bit of a bubbly feeling at the moment, like wind!' Rose said. She was grateful to Grace for being so matter of fact and kind. She only wished Sam could find it in himself to overcome his principles and be good to her.

'Are you afraid it'll look like him?'

Rose thought about it for a moment. 'It's a funny thing – it doesn't seem to be anything to do with him somehow.

89

As if the two things don't tie up. It's my babby.' Suddenly she was speaking in a surprised, wondering tone. 'Mine. I'm the one stuck with it inside me. As for him, I hope he falls under a bleeding bus. This babby's nothing to do with him.'

They sat in silence for a while. A touch of warmth from the sun came and went as small clouds passed over its face. They watched families out walking in the park, some of the mothers pushing heavy black prams. It was as if Rose's fate was being paraded in front of them.

Finally Sam headed towards them with George in tow and fell self-consciously into step next to Rose.

'I've been thinking,' he announced as they walked to the edge of the park. 'I won't say anything else, but I'll say this. I may not like what's happened or how you've behaved.' Suddenly he sounded rather bashful. 'But you're my sister and I'll stand by you. The neighbours'll no doubt have their say and none of us'll like it. But you can count on me, Rose.'

'I'm glad you said that,' Grace said, and Rose was surprised to hear the strong edge of anger in her voice. 'You've been a right preaching old gasbag lately and we're all getting blooming weary of it. If you hadn't said you'd stand by our Rose, I'm not sure as I'd've had much to say to you again, whether you're my brother or not.'

Rather stiffly, Sam linked his arm through Rose's, and they walked home close together along the cold streets.

The gossip threaded round Court 11 in a matter of an hour or so. There were two events competing for attention. Number two, otherwise known as Moonstruck House, was again standing empty. Like so many of the former tenants in that house, the Donaghues had vanished, lock, stock and barrel in the night and no one knew where to. Things had been bad for a while, but whether they'd sit it out or do a moonlight to dodge the landlord was anybody's guess. Now the front door was swinging open and there were still a few things left inside from the hurry in which they'd had to load up the cart.

But even this piece of gossip paled when Gladys Pye put it around that Dora Lucas had told her Rose was expecting. Dora made a shrewd choice in telling Gladys first. While Dora knew Gladys would tell everyone the news as fast as breathe, she was also Dora's friend. They had helped each other at the birth of their children and shared their worries day after day. Gladys, while full of twittering speculation with the other women in the court, would in the end come down on Dora's side.

'So who's the father?' Gladys whispered. The two women were standing in the brewhouse.

'I'd rather not say,' Dora hissed back. 'It were a case of him forcing himself on her. There ain't no airy-fairy feelings on her side, you know. She's been bad ever since.'

Gladys saw Dora's eyes fill with tears, and she made sympathetic noises. 'And Sid . . .?' Gladys looked the picture of concern. She was a tiny woman, made even smaller by the bent bones in her legs.

Dora shrugged in reply to the question. 'I stick by my own,' she said. 'He can moan and mither as much as he likes, but Rose is staying home and we've got to make the best of it. But I've hardly had a decent night since it happened, I can tell you.'

Gladys tut-tutted, saying, 'As if there ain't enough to worry about. I saw you was looking anyhow lately, but I thought it was just the babby.'

'Babbies,' Dora corrected her.

Gladys gasped. 'No! You Sure?'

'Sure as I've ever been,' Dora said. 'And I can feel them both now. But I always know, and I'm just as sure our Rose is carrying a lad.'

When Old Lady Gooch heard the news from Gladys she said, 'Well I never. That'll take the little madam down a peg. Strutting about here with her airs and graces. Now she'll find out a thing or two. I should send her off to the Church Army. She'd soon find out what happens to girls who ain't careful with themselves.'

On the afternoon of the coronation, Rose lay on her back in the bedroom, seeing little white clouds move across the pale blue sky outside the window. She could hear the excited hubbub from the street as the party got into full swing. All the kids would be sitting along the tables with the grown ups standing round, everyone in little hats and all enjoying the food and the rare day's holiday. She knew this was a day of all days for Grace, who would be almost counting the minutes until the evening paper came out carrying the pictures. And then tuppence for the *Weekly Illustrated* on Saturday. A breeze blew through the open window and she heard snatches of a band playing somewhere.

Wish I was like you, Grace, she thought. Grace, who could live off other people's exciting lives and not expect to have much excitement in her own.

Rose lay, not wanting to sleep but feeling tired and muzzy. The further the pregnancy progressed the more remote she felt from her life as it had been. Even her sense of despair, which had been most acute when she first knew she was to have a child, had dulled. She felt she was living in a kind of trance which would only end with the birth.

How could she have had dreams of becoming a teacher, of being a friend, let alone equal to someone like Diana? How could she keep in contact with her now? She wasn't even equal to Geraldine who had, after all, held down her job. And when she thought of Michael Gillespie, sometimes she wept with shame. What would he say if he knew what state she was in?

She put her hand on her belly and felt the light twitching of the child inside her. She had no bad feelings towards it. It just seemed unreal and, as she'd told Grace, not part of Mr Lazenby at all. But its presence, its inexorable growth in there, and the certainty that one day she must experience what her mother had gone through, frightened her. She felt so helpless.

'You were a stupid little fool,' she said to herself. 'Thought you could do great things with your life, didn't you? Do better than your mom?'

She listened bitterly as a loud cheer rose from the street, and another and another.

CHAPTER 10

There was a moment of complete silence as the three women waited. Then a snuffle and a cough, and finally the baby let out its first anxious cry.

'He's all right!' Gladys cried. She was tying the cord as the baby lay between Rose's legs. 'You may've got here a bit too soon, my lad, but you're going to be all right!'

Dora was sitting next to the head of the bed, suckling one of the twins. The other lay asleep in a drawer on the floor. They had been born only three weeks earlier and Dora's face sagged with exhaustion.

'Well – you've done it,' she said to her daughter, suddenly feeling choked with emotion. 'So now you know.'

Rose lay back, hot and worn out. The labour had come on early and had been painful but not too prolonged.

'Reckon you didn't have it too bad,' Gladys said. 'Specially for a first. No need to've had old Joan in after all, was there?'

Despite Dora's pleas, Rose had flatly refused to have 'that old cow' anywhere near her.

She lay looking at her tiny son lying curled in her arms. His hair was very pale, even though still damp from the dunking Gladys had given him. He turned his wrinkled little face and began to snuffle at Rose's body.

'He knows what he wants, anyroad,' Dora said. 'Give him a bit of titty, Rose.'

Rose was startled by the force with which the tiny baby

sucked at her, and the pain which gripped her innards as he did so.

She looked down at his face. His eyes were tightly closed and he was already completely absorbed in feeding. 'I'm going to call him Joseph,' she said. 'He looks like a Joseph.'

It took several days before she began to feel much for the child. He was very small, with the tiniest limbs Dora said she'd ever seen on a baby. Rose gradually understood just how much her life was tied to him, so that his slightest sound would set her heart pounding and wake her from sleep or make her leave whatever she was doing to attend to him. It was his fair hair and skin that at first had made him seem such a stranger. She had never seen a baby with such fair hair in the family, and it took some getting used to. But by the end of the first week she could look at him and find tears running down her cheeks at the realization of how beautiful he was, how small and helpless.

'Let me nurse him,' Grace would say, when she was home. 'He's a lovely babby, Rose.' And sometimes Rose felt reluctant to hand him over, but Grace would take him and cuddle him close, singing softly to him until he cried to go back to his mother.

With three babies in the house, Dora and Rose were both sleeping downstairs on makeshift beds on the floor. One night as they were getting settled down, Sid came in and lurched awkwardly over to Rose. She looked up warily at him.

'It's all right, I'm not going to bite you,' he said roughly. And then out of his pocket he pulled a small wooden object. 'I made this for the kid,' he said. 'Here. Come on – take it.'

Rose found she was holding a little wooden horse, rather rough and misshapen, but still obviously a horse, with a little spot of black paint on each side for its eyes.

'Here Joseph, this is for you,' she said to him. His blue eyes were open, staring over at the gaslight on the wall.

'Your grandad's made you a little horse. Are you going to say ta?' It was a relief having Joseph between her and Sid, to use the child as a way of communicating with him. Since Joseph was born he had been gentler with her, as if he could cope with her now she was doing what a woman was intended to do.

'Thanks Dad,' Rose said, feeling unexpected tears fill her eyes.

'No need to make a fuss,' Sid said awkwardly, going to the stairs.

Mother and daughter spent most of the night up and down feeding the babies. If it wasn't one it was another.

'I've had enough of this,' Dora said one night. It was well into the small hours and she was sick with fatigue. 'These two babbies are going to have to do everything at the same time or they're going to finish me.'

The boy, Billy, was yelling loudly for food. Dora woke the little girl, Susan, and latched the two of them on, stuffing a couple of pillows under her arms for support.

'Pour me a drop of milk, will you Rose?' she said. 'I could do with something on my stomach.'

Joseph was asleep, so Rose got up and handed her mother a cup of milk in the candlelight. 'I hope he's all right,' Rose said, frowning down at Joseph where he lay tucked up on the floor. One of his hands was clenched in a tiny fist next to his cheek. 'He's not feeding as well as he was.'

'Can't say the same of these two,' Dora said wearily.

'Here,' Rose went over to her. 'Give one over here. Joseph's not interested yet and I've got enough spare.'

She took Susan off her mother and held the unfamiliar body of the little girl. Even being a twin she felt rounder and heavier than Joseph. Having been able to rest more than she had during any other pregnancy, Dora had carried the two of them almost to term. They were good-sized babies. Rose sighed and looked over at her little son.

'Be right as rain in the morning,' Dora said. 'He's just tired I s'pect.'

By the end of the night they managed to get some sleep. Rose lay down next to Joseph with her nose against his soft scalp, hearing his quick little breaths. Now her life before him seemed even more like a dream. The days and nights felt almost indistinguishable with the round of feeding and changing his napkins and waiting for him to sleep. Joseph had happened to her, and he was not just a part of her life – everything she did was connected inextricably with this tiny person next to her.

Rose was dreaming. Dreams came rarely with all the broken nights, but this one burst in on her, vivid and clear.

She was with Diana on the tram which ran south along the Bristol Road out as far as the Lickey Hills. They had done that ride together a few times, Diana treating her at weekends. The tram lurched along the tracks down the middle of the road with the hedges separating them from the traffic on either side. When they had travelled that way in reality the tram had been crowded full of people, but in her dream it was empty. She and Diana had seats right at the back, looking down the deserted carriage. When they swayed through Bournbrook the tram passed the red bricks of the university, its pointed clock tower standing tall and elegant above the buildings around it.

'I'm going to go there,' Rose said. And then suddenly she was chanting,

> Pussy cat, pussy cat, where have you been?
> I've been up to London to visit the Queen . . .

And Diana sat beside her, her pink cheeks streaming with tears. 'I don't want you to go, Rose,' she begged. 'Stay and be my friend, Rose. Please stay.'

And then they were both crying and holding on to each other and the tram rolled downhill, down and down, and they didn't know or care where it was going any more.

Rose woke, tears wet on her cheeks. Diana had felt so close to her again, and she knew with a physical ache how

97

much she missed her and how ashamed she felt. All the letters Diana had sent, full of hurt, begging Rose to write and not to forget her, were upstairs, lying unanswered in a cardboard box beside the little wooden elephant which had put the seal on their friendship. How could she reply to those letters now?

As she lay wretched in the grey dawn light, one of the twins started stirring and began to cry. she saw Dora pull herself up off the floor, still stunned by tiredness.

Perhaps Joseph would eat a little better this morning? During his first week he had thrived, but over the last fortnight he had sucked at her breast for a time and then given up to lie listlessly, as if the effort was too much.

She turned to him to enjoy lying with him while he was still asleep, trying to forget the memory of Diana's distraught face in her dream. Very gently she stroked Joseph's soft baby head with one of her dark fingers. His skin was so much paler than hers! He felt cold and anxiously she searched out his hands. They were chilled.

'Come here,' she whispered, and turned him to cuddle and warm him.

His tiny body was stiff. Looking at his face, she saw his lips were still and blue.

Rose jumped up as if she'd been bitten, her lungs constricting so she could hardly breathe. 'Mom!' she gasped. 'Something's wrong with him. Quick – come here!'

Dora hastily put Billy down and rushed over. She picked Joseph up and Rose saw her face tighten. She listened to his chest and rubbed him vigorously. Then she put her mouth over his tiny one, breathing into him again and again to rouse him. Finally, with her head down, she laid him on Rose's bed, instinctively drawing the covers over him. Very slowly she turned to her daughter, who was standing still as a rock beside her.

'There's nothing else I can do, Rose,' she told her. 'He's gone.'

*

A man had died in a neighbouring court and Dora arranged for Joseph to be carried on the hearse the next day. When the horse clattered to a standstill outside, Rose was still holding the little body to her as if her arms would be fixed for ever in that position, even after he was taken away from her.

'For God's sake get him off her,' Sid said to Dora upstairs as they readied themselves for the funeral. 'I can't stand to see it any longer.'

'D'you think I'm enjoying it?' Dora snapped. 'She's just parting with the child in her own time.' She remembered how her own dead children – the twins, Violet – had been snatched speedily away from her by everyone around, who thought it for the best.

Downstairs, Marj had arrived from Sparkbrook, dolled up in a smart black dress with a full skirt and a hat with a wide sloping brim. 'Make us a cuppa tea, Grace,' she said, sitting herself down with exaggerated relief. 'I'm worn out already after carting all the way over here.'

Sam turned his head in surprise as Grace replied, 'There might be a drop left in the pot, and if there is you can get it yourself.'

Marj pulled herself to her feet, murmuring huffily about what a welcome she got in her own home nowadays.

'You've not been so keen to look on us as your family when it didn't suit you,' Grace replied.

'Now, now,' Sam said. 'That's enough of that.' He looked at Rose. She didn't seem to be listening to the conversation at all. She sat with her eyes fixed on her little son, as if she was intensely afraid that she would forget what he looked like.

Grace went up to her timidly. 'They're here, Rose,' she said. 'The undertaker wants to know if he can take him.'

For the last time Rose slowly kissed the boy's cold cheek. She ran her finger along the line of the tiny nose and soft lips.

'I'll take him,' she said, and the others moved back to let her through.

She walked outside and handed him over to be laid in a small box that Sam had nailed together for him. The undertaker placed it on the step of the hearse, close by his feet.

A crowd was gathering in the street. The coffin lying on the hearse was draped with a Union Jack; the dead man had served in the war. As the horse began to move off, Sid solemnly saluted it, standing as straight and upright as he could manage.

The children started spitting on the ground and chanting,

> Catch your collar, never swaller
> In case you catch a fever;
> Not for you, not for me,
> And not for any of my family.

Rose stood tearless and in silence. She thought of all the times as a child that she had joined in the superstitious rhyming. And what good had it done her? Every step the horse took seemed to tear her further apart.

Suddenly she heard Marj's voice in her ear. 'It's all for the best you know, Rose,' she said in a knowing whisper, as if imparting a morsel of gossip. 'You'll get over it soon enough. And who really wants a babby at your age? Now you can get back on with your life, can't you?'

Marj would not easily forget the look of bitter hatred that her young sister turned on her that morning, or the adult hardness that she suddenly saw in her brown eyes.

A very thin, subdued Rose Lucas went back to her charring job at the Dog and Partridge. She could easily fit back into all her old clothes, although she felt like an impostor wearing them.

She started work at nine in the morning, walking into the smell of stale beer and smoke. When she got home she helped Dora, handing over all her meagre wages. She shopped and cooked, gave a hand with George and Harry and, as she had continued to do since Joseph died, she helped to feed the twins. They were the main comfort in her life. Her body was still poised to do all the things for which nature had prepared it. At least she could sleep next to Billy or Susan, cuddling up to them, and hold and feed them.

'She's lost her spirit, Mom,' Grace said one day. 'She could get herself a better job again now. She don't want to be charring all her life. I mean I knew I was going into service, but our Rose always had her eye on something better, didn't she?'

Dora sighed. 'It's early days yet,' she said. 'Give her time.'

Grace tried getting through to Rose, but never felt she got very far.

'I'm earning a wage, aren't I?' Rose would say woodenly. 'What more's anyone s'posed to want? What's the use of having dreams of doing something else? It'll only bring trouble.'

And in her head a voice kept saying: I'm not worth it. I'm cheap and dirty. I'm a slum kid with a dead bastard baby.

Grace looked at her reproachfully. 'You're still cleverer than me,' she said. 'You could do better for yourself.'

Rose just shrugged.

As autumn came round again, Alfie appeared once more in Catherine Street. He'd tried going out with other girls, but none of them could erase the image in his mind of the dark, vivacious girl he'd seen the autumn before walking to work. He had to speak with her, and he decided to give her the benefit of the doubt. Maybe she had another sister and it was her he thought he'd glimpsed looking out of the upper window that day?

He came on a grey Saturday afternoon, with rusty leaves whirling along the pavement.

This time it was George who saw him and came

101

running into the house as Alfie approached, slamming the door behind him. 'It's that Alfie again – the bloke that's after Rose.'

Rose automatically fled to the stairs.

'Mom,' Grace said. 'Ask him in. He seems a good bloke, I reckon. I'll go up and talk her round.'

She found Rose sitting nervously on the bed. 'What're you doing hiding up here?' Grace demanded.

'Well, I can't let him see me, can I?' Rose replied with nervous irritation.

'Why not? You're not expecting any more are you? If you straighten yourself out a bit and put a decent frock on you'd look a picture again. He's all right that Alfie. So why keep yourself hidden away? If I had him following me around I'd jump at the chance. You could do a lot worse.'

Rose sat thinking for a moment. Grace's last words had hit home. What was she really hiding for now? Waiting for a prince to come along? Grace was right. She could do worse, and she wasn't likely to do any better.

'Tell him I'll be down in a minute.'

Grace gave a little skip and ran smiling downstairs. She found Dora handing Alfie a cup of tea. He was talking rather bashfully to her.

A few moments passed before Alfie finally saw the thin, beautiful girl he remembered emerging slowly, almost reluctantly, from the stairs. She'd brushed out her hair and pinned it back loosely so that it waved softly round her face, and she had on a cream dress of Diana's with a pattern of navy dots on it and a swinging skirt.

She came towards him and gave him a rather stiff smile. 'Hello Alfie,' she said.

CHAPTER 11

1 SEPTEMBER 1939

The long line of children standing in pairs snaked along from the gates of the railway station and curved around the wall outside. They stood in almost eerie silence as the teachers counted and recounted them to make sure there was no one missing. In one hand they each clutched a bag of the most basic belongings; round every neck was tied a piece of string to which a large luggage label had been tied bearing its owner's name. The children waited to be loaded on to the carriages which would take them to places which few of them had even dreamed of. Many of them had scarcely travelled any distance from the streets where they had grown up.

Rose stood near George, anxiously watching his tight-lipped, mutinous face. She was glad that Alfie stood reassuringly beside her. He was seeing off his younger brother and sister, Tom and Bessie, both still at school.

'Some of them think it's just a spree,' he said. 'Look at their faces.'

'Not George,' Rose said. 'He's played hell over being sent off. It's a good job they only announced it yesterday.'

The van had come round the day before, the big rectangular loudspeakers like wide, merciless mouths crackling out the announcement. All children of school age were to be evacuated to places of safety, away from the centres most likely to be bombed, when – and it now seemed to be when and not just if – war broke out.

Immediately the mothers in the court banded together

for mutual advice and support, on what would ordinarily have been a beautiful late summer day.

'Not the kids!' Dora cried. 'They can't split up families like that. How do we know where they're sending them? We'll never have a wink of sleep worrying.'

'What if Adolf Hitler starts throwing bombs down on us?' Mabel demanded grimly, leaning her meaty arm up against the brewhouse wall. 'Then you'd be bad with worrying about them all being killed in their beds. It's for the best, you know.'

'There's not going to be bombs, surely?' Gladys asked, puckering up her face in concern.

'Don't kid yourself,' Mabel said. 'What about Czechoslovakia last year?'

'And now they're after Poland,' Mabel went on. 'Things ain't going to get any better I don't reckon, so you might just as well get used to the idea.'

The rest of that day the families could think of nothing else. For the first time in years Dora turned to her husband for advice when he came in. 'What're we going to do?'

'Asking me are you, all of a sudden?' he said sourly, swinging his good arm back and forth to relieve the muscles after supporting himself on the crutch. 'If they say send them, then do it. They're best well out of it.' He sat down heavily. 'We should've finished them off properly the first time round, when we had the bloody chance.'

'I'm NOT GOING!' George shouted.

Sid took off his cap and flung it over on to the table. 'If we say you're going then you'll go!'

'What about Harry?' Dora said. She turned to put the kettle on, trying to steady herself. 'I can't send him away – or the twins. Not that young.'

'Couldn't Edna have Harry for a bit?' Rose suggested. 'After all, most of hers are grown up and gone now. We'll club together for some money for the fare.'

Dora's sister in Alcester seemed, out of the few choices, the most reassuring one. Dora got Rose to write to her straight away.

'But the twins stay with me,' Dora said. 'And that's that.'

They'd got George ready the next morning. He soon realized there was no point in arguing. Dora tidied him up to go down to the school, tugging his collar straight and giving his face a wipe.

'Go on,' she said to him, rather roughly, to stop herself blarting there on the step. 'Don't give anyone any lip and make sure you write and tell us how you're getting on.'

As soon as he was out of the court, walking with bravado beside Rose, Dora sank down at the table, laid her head on it and wept.

Now George stood at the station in front of the two Meredith kids, all with their little paper parcels of 'iron rations': a small can of corned beef, a packet of biscuits, a pound of sugar, a tin of evaporated milk, a quarter of tea and – George's eyes had lit up for the only time that day – a half-pound block of Cadbury's chocolate.

'Still warm from the factory,' one of the teachers joked.

As the kids piled into the railway carriages, Rose tried to give George a goodbye hug, but he pushed her away with his wiry arms. 'Don't go getting all soppy, Rose.'

And Rose, like her mom, held back her tears until they'd waved goodbye to the children, all crowded up by the windows of the train, some looking excited, others forlorn and bewildered. The train gave a loud shriek and puffed out of the station, the smoke and smuts rising in clouds to the wide arching roof. Rose waved her hanky at the little dot she thought was George until the train was out of sight, and then used it to wipe her eyes.

'They'll be well looked after, you be sure,' Alfie said. 'And he's got Tom and Bessie for company. He's a tough lad your George. He'll be all right.'

'It's so horrible not knowing what's going to happen,' Rose said as they walked out of New Street Station. 'I know it's an awful thing to say, but if there's going to be a war, I wish they'd just get on and get it over.'

'Some of the lads got their call-up papers today,' Alfie said.

Rose went quiet. Alfie and Sam were both nineteen and had not yet been called, but the shadow of war, of families being split up even further, hung over all of them.

'Come on,' Alfie said. 'It's no use getting all down in the mouth. I'll take you for a cuppa. Lyons or the Kardomah?'

'Whatever you like,' Rose said. She always let Alfie make the decisions.

'The Kardomah then.'

He took her arm and led her along New Street. It was as busy as ever with trams and buses and people shopping or standing at bus stops. But there was a different atmosphere. The news from Europe was on everyone's lips. Everything felt precious, Rose thought. As if the threat from Germany had made the things they had always known sparkle and shine.

Along the street they could see preparations going on in the offices and shops for blacking out the windows – assistants trying the large black rectangles for size against the panes of glass. And already groups of people were filling sandbags and stacking them against the sides of buildings. They heard the raucous newsvendors' voices shouting, 'Germans overrun Poland! Get your *Mail* here!'

'Blimey,' Alfie said. 'He really means it, doesn't he?'

Rose felt her stomach tighten with a mixture of dread and excitement.

'I should get back to work,' she said, as she and Alfie found a table in the Kardomah amid the comforting smells of roasted coffee and warm rolls.

'They gave you the morning to send off the kids, didn't they?' Alfie said. 'Come on – have a cuppa tea and calm down. The Co-op'll survive for half a day without you!' He grinned and, leaning across the table, chucked her lightly under the chin. 'That's my girl.'

Rose smiled back dutifully and sipped the tea he'd bought for her.

Alfie sat back in his seat, looking at her. As usual he felt pleased with himself for just being with Rose. Even though he'd been walking out with her for almost two years now he still couldn't believe his luck, that this beautiful girl wanted to be with him. He'd heard some gossip about her of course, but that was all in the past and he preferred not to know about it. He was going to believe the best of her. And she seemed to have quietened down since he'd first seen her, which was no bad thing. Who wanted a loud mouth on a woman? She was his girl and he was dead chuffed with her.

Alfie himself had filled out over the past two years. His hair was just as unruly above his pale face, but he looked less lanky and more substantial. His shoulders had grown broader and stronger from his heavy work. And the fact that he'd been luckier than many in the trade and had been in work more than out of it had done wonders for his sense of himself. His blue eyes looked directly at people now and he was much less hesitant when he spoke – especially with Rose on his arm. What a picture she was in that red frock she had on! Soon, when he'd maybe managed to save a bit, he planned to make her his wife.

Alfred and Rose Meredith, he thought. That sounded truly grand.

Rose stood preparing butter in the Co-op that afternoon dipping the wooden pats in the jug of cold water and teasing the yellowish lumps into shape. She was partly mesmerized by the movement of her hands and by the rhythmic click and whirr as the money cup shot along its overhead wire to the little cash office at the back of the shop.

'Come on Rose, wake up! We need three pound of sugar over here!' the woman in charge of her called over. 'I dunno what's got into that girl today.'

Without speaking, Rose moved over and began to shovel out the sugar into the blue paper bags. Then she went back to sort out the butter and bacon again.

What had got into her was that she had, for the first time since Joseph's death, begun to allow herself to think properly. It was not something she decided to do; the thoughts just seemed to come upon her, long-buried feelings nudging for her attention.

She had been grateful in one way for the problems in Europe, for the looming war. Since they had waited tensely through the last threat, the crisis in Czechoslovakia the year before, it had all helped to take her mind off her own sorrows. And, she thought, it's brought me closer to Alfie – hasn't it?

They had things in common to talk about now, important things. Before he had talked about football or the latest murder trial.

'Have you heard about the one they're doing at the Old Bailey this week?' would have been the conversation before. Then he'd give her a long and gruesome description of the crime.

They'd shared a lot of experiences over the past months: the flicks and walks and family meals. Changing jobs. But had they shared the experience of falling in love? The question wouldn't leave her alone that afternoon, try as she might to put it out of her mind. Was what she felt for Alfie what people would call love?

From that day when he had turned up again in Catherine Street, she had tried to close her mind to everything that had gone before – to Joseph, Diana, Michael and everything about Lazenby's. To her dreams. She tried to be someone with no past. From now on she was going to be sensible and down to earth and take whatever came along.

He's made me feel better, there's no doubt, she thought. He's kind and generous and he loves me. What more could I want from anyone? I've already got more than me mom.

When she first went out with him she had felt relieved and grateful. Here was someone who wanted her and thought highly of her – she who at fifteen felt so old and soiled and washed up. And she was especially grateful to him for not probing into her past. He was prepared to accept her just as she was.

Those feelings she had had for Michael, the electric excitement in his presence – that was all airy-fairy nonsense, not real life. What she had with Alfie was real, like married people had if they were lucky.

She knew one day he'd ask her to marry him. That was another thing she'd tried not to think about. As long as they stayed as they were she didn't have to decide or face up to things. But the threat of war was overturning everything. For a moment she had an overwhelming feeling of panic. All her life – forever – spent with Alfie. Nothing else? Then she pushed the feelings away.

What's got into me? she thought. He'd make a good husband and he wouldn't knock me about. That's what matters.

Of course it made sense to marry Alfie, she said to herself. Perfect sense.

In early December the government extended the call-up age to men between the ages of nineteen and forty-one. Both Alfie and Sam received their papers almost immediately.

'At least I'm sure of a job now!' Sam joked. 'So you can keep the wireless.'

After they'd heard the soft voice of Prime Minister Neville Chamberlain crackling out of the Pyes' old wireless set, Sam had rashly gone out and bought one for their own house, with its battery and accumulator. Now, at almost every news bulletin, some member of the family was listening in.

When the broadcast finished that Sunday morning, the distant voice informing them that 'consequently we are now at war with Germany', Sid had pulled himself up abruptly and left the house.

Grace watched him out of the window. 'What's got into him?' she said.

'Leave him,' Dora said.

Out in the brewhouse, Sid Lucas stood propped on his crutch next to the old stone sink, his whole body trembling. The build-up to another war had set his fragile nerves on edge. Breathing in shuddering gulps of air, he tried to steady the emotions aroused by memories of the last war that suddenly sprawled out in front of him like fresh corpses. After the war to end all wars, here it was beginning all over again.

Dora looked out and saw the shadow of her husband's hunched figure. She could guess what was going on in his mind, but she had her children to think of now, their survival and their future. That was what mattered.

It was Grace who slipped outside and went to him. As she walked quietly into the brewhouse she knew immediately that her father was weeping. All through her childhood she had heard this sound through the floorboards from her parents' room, but she had never seen him with tears on his face before.

'Dad . . .?' She went and put her work-roughened hand on his heaving shoulder. He didn't throw it off. He didn't move or turn to her.

'I'll be all right, Gracie.'

'It's the war, isn't it?'

He nodded. After a moment, he said, 'I'm fit for nothing. The last war saw to that.'

'Don't say that,' Grace said. She took his arm. 'Come on. I'll leave you if that's what you want, but it's best you come in. We've all got to stick together now there's a war on, haven't we?'

Sid took out his grubby handkerchief and wiped his eyes in a way that made Grace's own fill with tears. At that moment he looked so much like a child.

'Come on now, Dad. Come in and have a cuppa tea.'

The evening before Alfie was due to leave, he and Rose walked slowly back from town in the blackout darkness that had overtaken the city. They had been to the flicks at the Scala and then Alfie had treated them to a hot pork sandwich from the Market Hall, so despite the freezing evening they felt quite warm and well fed.

Now and then people loomed up out of the cold, foggy darkness, close enough to touch almost before you could see them. A few were carrying small torches so you could make out little lines of light moving towards you.

'I can't get used to the dark,' Rose said. 'If it wasn't for this mist you could see the stars.'

'I s'pose it's a bit daft making you walk instead of catching the tram,' Alfie said. 'But then we'd have got there too quick. I wanted to spend all the time I could with you.'

Rose felt her stomach plunge at the thought that Alfie would be gone the next afternoon. She kept forgetting, and then something reminded her again, like the muffled lights on the few cars that passed them, which gave you a tiny glimpse of something before the darkness fell back over everything again.

'It feels like the end of the world,' Rose said.

Alfie grinned in the darkness. His Rose said the queerest things at times.

'Nah,' he said. 'We'll show that Adolf Hitler feller in no time. They'll get us all trained up and it'll be time to go home again. The lights'll be back on and we'll be right as rain, you'll see.'

Rose said nothing, wondering how much Alfie believed of what he was saying.

He peered at her, trying to make out her expression. 'You're not scared, are you? Here, stop a tick.'

Alfie pulled her arm and guided her over to the dark factory wall. He pulled her close to him. She looked up, just able to see his eyes and the outline of his angular face.

'I'll miss you,' he said. 'You know how much I love you, don't you?'

She looked guiltily up at him. 'Yes. Of course I know.'

She knew he was waiting for her to tell him the same, how she would long for him to be there, how she couldn't live without him. But the words wouldn't come. It would be stepping over a cliff if she said more than she meant tonight of all nights, when things were so serious. Once the words were spoken, she could not take them back.

Alfie leaned forwards and began to kiss her. She felt his soft, familiar lips on her mouth, and all the warmth and sincerity going into that kiss. She kissed him back, trying to summon up all her gratitude to him. She had got over his touching her reminding her every time of Mr Lazenby. Alfie had always been very gentle and never demanded anything more of her. She didn't feel revolted by him. She didn't feel – the thought came to her like a cold shock – anything. And inside, her heart was pounding with a sense of panic she could not explain even to herself.

'Rose – I wasn't going to ask you yet. I'd planned to save it. But now things are different – you know . . .' He stumbled over the words, unused to expressing his feelings. 'What I mean is, would you – will you marry me, Rose? We could have a wedding when I come home next. There's bound to be some leave in a few weeks around Christmas, and it'd give you time to get sorted out a bit . . .' he babbled on nervously.

Rose felt an almost unbearable sense of tension inside her, as all the feelings she'd been keeping at bay for the past months flooded into her in conflict and confusion. Should she be content, accept what was being offered by a good, kind man whom she could at least like? Or should she listen to that part of her which as a young girl had clamoured for fulfilment?

In utter vexation with herself she dissolved into tears.

'Hey, Rose,' Alfie said tenderly, holding her again. 'There . . . don't upset yourself. I know I'm asking a bit sudden like, what with going away in the morning. But I've put a lot of thought into our future, you know.'

'I know,' Rose said sobbing. 'You're so good to me. I don't deserve it.'

Alfie stroked the soft, dark head that was pressed against his chest.

'What d'you mean? How can you say that? My God,

you're the most fantastic girl I've ever seen in my life, and it was a miracle when you said you'd come out with me. And now you're saying you don't deserve me?' He laughed. 'You're a case, Rose Lucas, you really are.'

Rose calmed herself and stood sniffing and wiping her face. After a few moments she said with unexpected resolve, 'We'll have to ask my dad.'

'Right,' Alfie said, and she could hear the jubilation in his voice, so at odds with the flat sense of inevitability she was feeling herself. 'It's not too late. I'll come and ask him now.'

'No. You can't.'

Rose and Alfie looked at each other, dumbfounded.

'But—' Alfie said.

'But nothing. You heard what I said.'

'What the hell's got into you, Sid?' Dora gasped. 'You've always said Alfie were a good lad!'

'And we're promised to one another,' Alfie said, his voice starting to tremble.

'You can promise what you like,' Sid shouted, slamming his newspaper down on the table and standing up. 'But you're not marrying my daughter one day and going off to get yourself blown to buggery the next.'

'But—' Alfie said again.

'Look at me!' Sid's voice rang round the walls of the small room. 'D'you want to give your wife a husband in a state like this, who can't keep his family and's no bloody good to anyone? Do you? I'm not making one of my kids a war widow or marrying her off to a wreck like me, so you can forget it.'

Rose and Dora stared at him, both rooted to the spot. Sid seemed bigger and broader than they'd ever seen him. And Rose was aware, while feeling sorry and angry on Alfie's behalf, of a warm sense of relief spreading through her.

'Get married after the war's over if you come back in one piece,' Sid was saying more quietly. 'But don't ruin her life by rushing into things 'cos you think you're going to be a hero. There ain't no heroes in a war, lad – only blokes getting killed all around you.'

There seemed no more to be said. Alfie whispered to Rose, 'I'll come round and say goodbye tomorrow if I can.'

And she watched him walk, crestfallen, out into the darkness.

There was silence except for the clock ticking on the mantelpiece and Dora's coughing. Rose was still standing where she had been since they started talking, and Sid sank down into the chair again.

'Anyroad,' he said, looking up at her with defiant eyes. 'You didn't really want to marry him, did you?'

CHAPTER 12

MAY 1940

Rose sat, bleary-eyed, drinking a very welcome mug of tea as Winston Churchill's gruff voice growled at them out of the wireless.

'I speak to you for the first time as Prime Minister in a solemn hour for the life of our country, of our Empire, of our Allies, and above all, of the cause of freedom . . .'

'Well – he sounds as if he might know what he's on about. Not like the last one,' Jean said, stirring sugar into her tea.

Rose was sitting in her brother Albert's house in Erdington with her sister-in-law Jean, a plump, rather plaintive woman who Rose was quite glad she only saw for limited parts of the day. Jean was about to give her full opinion of Neville Chamberlain, but Rose raised her hand to quieten her.

'Ssh. Let's hear the end of it.'

'Today is Trinity Sunday,' the voice was saying. 'Centuries ago, words were written to be a call and a spur to the faithful servants of truth and justice: "Arm yourselves and be ye men of valour, and be in readiness for the conflict, for it is better to perish in battle than to look upon the outrage of our nation and our altar."'

'Ah,' Jean said, shifting her wide hips on the chair. 'Ain't that nice? He can string together a good lot of words, can't he?'

Rose had felt a thrill, a sensation which raised goose-pimples on her flesh on hearing the commanding speech. With all the grimness, the increasingly terrible news which

115

greeted them daily from Europe, she had been unprepared for the exhilaration she felt at the challenges with which war had presented her.

At least I'm doing something, she thought. She felt free for the first time in years. She pitied Jean, and all the other women left to fend for themselves with nothing changed in their lives except for more struggles to feed their families, and more worries to carry in their minds about their loved ones. Rose smiled across at Jean. Her sister-in-law, with her long blond hair tumbling untidily over the crumpled blouse she was wearing, smiled back, rather startled.

'You heard from Teddy?' Rose asked her, reminding herself that Jean, like Dora, was going through the hell of being separated from one of her children. Teddy, who was seven, had been evacuated out of the city.

'I just can't stop fretting about him,' Jean said. 'He says he's all right, but I don't know if it's true, do I? And after what happened to your George I can't sleep nights thinking about it.'

'Oh, I s'pect he's all right,' Rose said, laying one of her slim hands over Jean's plump one. 'Not much chance of the same thing happening to both of them, is there?'

January had been one of the coldest anyone could remember, the city clogged up with deep snow so the traffic could barely pass along the streets. It was a strange time. It felt as if everything had frozen up: the arteries of the city, the food supplies, which began to be officially rationed, and even the war itself. It had not begun to affect Britain with the intensity anyone had expected. The strange blanket of quietness brought to the streets by the snow, and the houses muffled at night by the white blanket outside and the blackout coverings inside, all added to the air of peculiar unreality.

Rose stayed at home through the winter. She saw Alfie briefly at Christmas. He had long got over the shock of Sid's outburst and was all for looking on the bright side.

'We're engaged anyroad, aren't we?' he said.

He chatted on about army life and the pals he'd made, and while Rose enjoyed his company and was glad to see him looking so full of it all, she felt even more distanced from him.

Sometimes she popped over to Small Heath to see Mrs Meredith, who always gave a gasp of delight when she opened the door, crying, 'Rose, come on in, bab! I was just making a little cake, so you can take a few slices back with you!' She always tried to feed Rose up like a turkey cock on whatever she had to hand, and always seemed to remain astonishingly cheerful.

The same was not true of Dora. Rose had been worried about her all winter. When the weather hardened against them, Dora's chest became infected and her lungs ached agonizingly as she coughed, bringing up terrible amounts of green phlegm. Rose and Grace nursed her as best they could, though Grace wasn't at her best either during the cold, with her asthma.

Christmas had been difficult. Edna managed to get over from Alcester with Harry. They put up a little tree and did their best to make it a jolly day, especially for the little boy's sake and for the twins. Dora burst into tears at the sight of him when they arrived and wouldn't let him out of her sight, holding and stroking his plump, healthy looking limbs in a way which Rose never remembered seeing her do with any of them before.

'I can't let you take him again,' she said to Edna. 'I know you've looked after him as if he were your own, but I'll not part with him again. Not unless things start to get bad.'

Edna nodded, understanding how she felt.

But the worst was that they hadn't heard from George at all since the middle of October. He'd written three sentences saying he was with a family in Wales and he was all right. Then they'd had an equally brief note from a Mrs Beamish saying that George had moved from her care to work on a farm near by. Dora looked lined and tattered with worry.

'He's probably living the life of Riley,' Grace said, without much conviction. 'He said he was all right, didn't he?' They all tried to blame his silence on the bad weather.

As usual it was the neighbourliness in the court which helped them all pull through. They compared the best ways to make the food rations go as far as possible. Mabel's corned beef hash was voted one of the best dishes.

'I fried the potatoes,' she told everyone darkly. Though quite what in she wasn't prepared to say.

When the snow came, everyone who was around came out into the court and built a snowman for the little kids who were left and Gladys and Mabel built a fire outside from an old door out of Moonstruck House, which was now in bad repair and boarded up. Everyone chipped in a lump of coal and they managed to bake a few potatoes for the kiddies. The twins, Billy and Susan, both stood wide-eyed and pink-nosed by the fire, cramming the warm potatoes into their mouths. Rose had dressed them up in so many clothes to come out that they looked quite rotund.

'All right, you two?' she said, smiling at them. She leaned down and gave them each a kiss on their round, cold cheeks. They both nodded, mouths full. Rose looked wistfully at their lovely trusting little faces, and stood with a hand on each of their shoulders, wishing she could hold them for ever and protect them from all harm.

Afterwards they all had a snowball fight. It was a memory Rose knew she would treasure for ever. She remembered Dora's face smiling at the window, still not recovered enough to be out in it, but cheered by the sight. And Old Lady Gooch trotting with her swaying gait across the yard in pursuit of Gladys Pye, gleeful as a twelve-year-old, with a huge ball of snow ready in one hand. Soon Gladys was flat on her back on the snow, helpless with laughter.

'I can't get up!' she shouted, trying to get her bandy legs in a position so she could stand up. 'God Almighty, look at the state of me – I'm caked in it!' And she collapsed into more helpless giggles.

As darkness fell, everyone was getting cold, and they all went in for a hot drink feeling more cheerful than they had for months.

By the time spring came and the snow turned grey and slushy in the streets and gradually disappeared, Hitler had progressed across Europe. Czechoslovakia, Poland, and now Norway and Denmark had fallen, and the forces of evil and destruction were pushing up against France, the Netherlands and onwards as if this was their destiny.

One evening in April, Rose and Grace sat in their bedroom talking. It was a rare moment of leisure shared together, and they were taking it in turns to brush each other's hair as they had when they were little girls. Through the window Grace saw Sid come shuffling in across the yard.

'Dad's back.'

Rose began to sing softly: 'The day thou gavest Lord is ended,' and both of them fell back giggling on the bed. It was a relief to get rid of some of the tension they all felt.

'You are terrible,' Grace said, wiping her eyes.

'Well,' Rose started to unpin Grace's brown hair. 'He always seems to be on at me.'

'You always answer back.'

'I can't help it. I know he's got some good in him really, and a lot of what's happened hasn't been his fault, but I just wish we'd had the chance to see him before and know what he was like.'

'I think you're quite alike. He was stubborn and determined to get on in them days. Like you are.'

'Like I *was*,' Rose corrected her. She stopped brushing and sighed. 'I don't know what's happened to me,' she said, hesitating to say what she was thinking.

'You mean you don't want to do all them things you used to talk about when we was at school?'

'Yes. Well, no. It's just . . .' She sat down next to Grace and spoke very seriously. 'When Alfie was here and we were together and everything, I felt as if I was in a kind of dream all the time. I didn't have to think for myself, and after all that happened with Joseph and Lazenby's I was glad not to have to. You know what blokes are like – they always think they have to do all the thinking for you. So I just let him. It was easy. Nice in a way. Like having a rest.' She smiled rather wistfully at Grace who watched her sister's brown, troubled eyes, rather puzzled at what she was getting at.

'You miss him, don't you?' she said, thinking this was the right response.

'I miss his company,' Rose said carefully. 'And I want the best for him of course, for him to be safe wherever he is. But now he's gone – I don't know.' She looked at her sister.

Grace saw that her eyes had the life back in them that always made Rose so striking as a child.

'I feel as if I've just woken up or something,' Rose said. 'Now that I can't just lean on him. I know it's an awful thing to say with the war and everything but I suddenly feel happier than I have in years.'

'But you do love him, don't you?' Grace asked, bewildered. She longed to have a young man of her own to walk out with.

Rose looked away, down at the floorboards. 'I like him of course. But I can't honestly say I know whether I love him or not.'

Grace made tut-tutting noises. 'You don't half get yourself into some messes, you do.'

Rose was silent, trying to think of some way in which she could express the overwhelming sense of restlessness she had felt since Alfie left. The past, before Joseph, had welled up, and she found herself thinking about Diana and the Harper-Watts with an aching sorrow for what she had lost.

Suddenly she said, 'You know those women we saw in town today?'

'The recruitment lot you mean?'

As they'd walked along Colmore Row, a long line of women had marched past, many of them carrying placards which urged: 'We have the Work – We want the Women!'

They were employed by many of the industries round the city. Some of them were wearing dresses and skirts, but a large number of them had on baggy dungarees in dark, heavy materials. Rose had been startled at the sight of them, but also warmed and excited. How strong and capable they looked! She had always known women who worked in factories, of course – Dora had for years. But she could never remember seeing them marching together like this, looking as if they really belonged in the world.

'I want to do something for the war effort, something really useful. I've been thinking about it all day. There's that new place they're recruiting for – the Nuffield over near Albert's place. They need a lot more workers. I thought what with Albert being away and Jean on her own with the kids, she'd be glad of a bit of company. And I could do war work in the factory.'

'I'll miss you,' Grace said.

Rose laughed. 'I was only talking. I haven't done anything about it yet!'

'No – but I know you when you've decided on something. And Mom was only saying the other day how sorry she feels for Jean. She'll let you go as long as you come home now and then.'

'Course I will,' Rose said. She began to feel excited.

Suddenly they heard a shriek from down below, then Dora's voice yelling up the stairs, 'Rose! Grace! Get down here quick! Quick!'

'What's got into her?' Grace said as they clattered down the stairs into the dusk light of the kitchen. They found Sid and Dora both standing by the Morrison shelter, the top of which was laid up for tea.

Warming his hands by the stove was George.

Both the girls fell on him, trying to hug and kiss him.

'George! Where've you been?'

'How on earth did you get here?'

Their delight soon wavered and turned to concern. George pushed them off roughly. As they looked at him properly they started to take in the state he was in. He'd always been a skinny kid, but now he looked gaunt and hollow round the eyes. His legs, poking out of a filthy, torn pair of shorts that they'd never seen before, were stick thin, making his knees look pathetically bony. His skin was grey and shadowy with deeply ingrained grime and his hair, dull with filth, was sticking out in tufts all round his head. But the worst was his eyes. The expression in them was blank and hard, making him seem a person quite strange and alien to them.

As she stood looking at him, Dora burst into tears.

'What's happened to you?' She went to him and squatted down, putting her hands on his shoulders.

George pushed her away as if she were some kind of monster. 'I want some grub,' he said. 'NOW.'

'Don't talk to your mother . . .' Sid started to say, but Dora gestured at him impatiently to be quiet. Sid himself looked shocked at the sight of his son.

'I'll get you some broth. And here's some bread to be going on with,' Dora said gently, slicing a huge chunk off the loaf. 'And you can tell us in your own time.'

'Fat lot you care,' George snarled. 'You'd have left me there to rot – the whole effing lot of you.'

'George!' Dora cried, her cheeks still wet. 'Oh George, that's not true. It wasn't like that. They told us you had to go. Because of the bombs. And we was told you were all having a marvellous time. I didn't want you to go.'

George gave her a look of complete contempt and then started on the soup. He ate like a starved animal. He flung chunks of bread into the bowl and pulled them out soaked in soup, cramming them into his mouth apparently quite unbothered by how hot they were. The family were silenced by the sight. Rose felt her insides tighten with anger and sorrow. George only paused to scratch his head every now and then with soupy fingers. They could see the nits moving between his clogged hairs.

When he'd finished he pushed back his chair and said, 'Now I need some kip.'

'Leave him for now,' Dora said as he went upstairs. In the short time since George had returned, her face seemed to have fallen into even heavier, darker lines. 'I s'pect he'll talk to us after he's had a sleep.' And her face crumpled in distress again, her lips pulled back as she cried, showing the dark gaps between her remaining teeth. 'I only wanted to do the best for him!' she cried. 'I knew it was wrong to send kids away to strangers.'

When she crept up later to look at her own little stranger of a son, he had thrown himself just as he was on his old bed and pulled the blanket over him. In the candlelight she watched him for a few moments as he slept. His frail body was never still. His eyes and his arms twitched about and he kept moving his head, painful whimpering noises breaking out of him.

What his life had been over the past seven months emerged only gradually as he began to adjust slowly to being at home again.

So far as they could gather, the first month hadn't been too bad. The Beamish family who had picked him out originally had been quite decent. They lived in a village near Llanelli in South Wales and regarded taking in evacuees as their contribution to the war effort. Unfortunately, in their enthusiasm they had taken in three at once, including George. As they already had four children of their own, they quickly realized that introducing into the family three city kids with their strange ways was too much. The children of the house had rebelled and turned against the newcomers, and in particular they disliked George, the only boy of the three.

Eventually George was told that they were going to pass him on to a Mr Evans who owned a farm some distance away from the village, who wanted a boy old enough to lend a hand on the farm.

George had not felt at ease in the first house, but at least there had been company and, as he said, 'They gave you as much grub as they could spare.' Now his problems really began. Mr Evans was a short, burly man with a gingery-coloured beard who lived alone on the farm. He had no idea about children and no ambition to learn. George had spent most of the past six months almost entirely alone, except for the surly, religious-minded Mr Evans, a few chickens, a dog and fields full of sheep.

He had not been allowed in the house except for his meals which Mr Evans supplied when he remembered – at best once a day. In the evening he usually brought him into the cold, stone-flagged kitchen for some kind of soup or stew. The rest of the day he went without. In the beginning, as it was the end of September, George had found a few blackberries. As the winter drew in there was nothing. He slept in the barn where Mr Evans had supplied him with one filthy blanket stinking of dogs. During the day he had to help on the farm – herding and feeding sheep when there was work to be done, and being sent round with the dog to catch rats.

George woke in the morning often before it was light, to a hard prod from the farmer's boot and a gruff 'Get up now', which was often Mr Evans' longest utterance of the day. He communicated more readily with a cuff or a kick, as if George was just another of the sheep or dogs from the farm.

Once the snow came, George lived wrapped permanently in the stinking blanket and an old pair of boots of Mr Evans' that he wore over his own shoes. The snow cut the farm off from everywhere, so there were no letters, there was no one to talk to, not a word of kindness or of even the most basic communication. He lived like the animals: waking, sleeping, eating only when given the chance.

Some time after the thaw came he walked away from the farm one night and reached Llanelli by the morning. From there he jumped trains to Birmingham. He hid his wiry, emaciated body in any cranny necessary to escape the guards on the train, sometimes ducking and dodging as they moved along between carriages. And a couple of

124

days later he was home. They may have abandoned him, but where else did he have to go?

His one remaining, overriding emotion was that of anger towards his family. They had sent him away to this place. left him for months now without a word of contact, as if they didn't care whether he was dead or alive. And for that he would never forgive them.

CHAPTER 13

Rose moved to Erdington at the end of April and was taken on the night shift at the new 'shadow' factory, as the extra factories built to extend wartime production were called, at Castle Bromwich, right on Birmingham's northern edge. They taught her to use a rivet gun for attaching the metal plates which made up the wings of the Spitfires.

When she first walked through the gates of the huge works she felt so frightened that she nearly turned back and went home again. The rows of long production sheds where they turned out the Spitfires and Lancasters stretched further than she could see. There were people walking about briskly in overalls, all looking as if they knew exactly where they were going.

Workers were needed from any possible source, and Rose found herself working among a wider mix of people than she'd ever been with in her life before. Alongside her stood a girl called Maureen from Londonderry. They worked just far enough apart for there to be little opportunity to chat, but the two of them often sat together in the canteen at break times and became quite friendly. Maureen came from the Catholic side of Derry, and like Rose was from a large family.

'I'd most likely have come to England anyways, even without the war,' Maureen told her. 'But now they're giving out jobs like First Communion cards, I thought I'd take the chance while it was offered.'

Maureen was a thin, anaemic-looking girl with terrible

spots. She was kind and soft spoken and Rose found her easy enough company. She was also very homesick, and spoke with special affection for the baby of the family, her four-year-old sister Josie.

'It's not the same without little ones about,' Maureen said. 'I'd give anything to see her.'

One day when she was sitting under the bright lights of the canteen with Maureen, Rose noticed the man with one arm.

'Hang on a tick,' she said. 'I'm going to have a word with him.'

The man was older than many of the employees, and when she got up close to him, Rose saw that on one side of his face the skin was shiny and puckered up as if from a severe burn.

'Excuse me,' she said. 'I hope you won't think me rude for asking . . .'

The man turned and smiled with the half of his face that worked. He had one vivacious blue eye; the other was missing. The injured side of his face remained still, as if dead.

'What's up love?' he asked.

'It's just when I saw you I thought of my dad. He's without one arm and a leg from the last war and he hasn't been in work for years.'

'Well now's his chance,' the man said chirpily. 'Doesn't he know they'll take anyone on nowadays? They've found me a little job I can do with one arm – with the petrol tanks. If your dad asks, you can bet they'll find him something – even if they turn him upside down and sweep the floor with his head!' He gave a long chesty laugh and Rose couldn't help joining in.

Within a week Sid was taken on by the Birmingham Small Arms Company, which in peacetime manufactured bicycles and motorcycles. It had reverted to turning out bombs, rockets and guns and all the ammunition needed to feed them. They found him a job packing bullets.

The day he left the house in dungarees to catch a bus to a proper job for the first time in over twenty years, Dora watched him as he pulled himself on his crutch out of Court 11. She reflected with some pride and more bitterness on the irony that her husband who had been so shattered by the last war, might only begin to feel useful to anyone again now there was a second one in progress.

At the end of May, France fell to the Germans, and a huge flotilla of British boats evacuated all the troops they could transport from the French coast at Dunkerque.

On 2 July, Hitler ordered the invasion of Britain.

'The Battle of France is over. I expect that the Battle of Britain is about to begin,' Churchill told the House of Commons. 'The whole fury and might of the enemy must very soon be turned on us.'

And the country waited, as if holding its breath for a long descent into deep, dark water.

One night, at the beginning of August, the first bombs to fall on Birmingham dropped on Erdington, in the streets around Albert and Jean's house.

When she came in from work the next morning, Rose found Jean in a proper state. She was sitting on the old sofa in her dressing gown, with a tearstained face, and clutching Amy and Mary close to her as if she'd never let them go.

'Thank God you're all right,' Rose said, putting her bag down and running to her sister-in-law. 'You poor things, you must have had an awful night. We heard them come down. We were all in the shelters as well.'

Jean sat and sobbed helplessly. The Anderson shelter down the garden had a puddle right along the middle and it had grown even damper with the condensation from their breath. It had been horrible sitting there all night, cold and scared stiff.

'I wish Albert was here,' she cried. 'He'd know what to do. I hate being here without him. I can't stand it. And he might never come back!'

'Look,' Rose said firmly, wishing Albert had married someone with a bit more to her. 'You should try and keep things normal for the kids' sake. Get them dressed and send them out to play.'

'No!' Jean protested. 'I'm not letting them out of my sight – either of them. Them planes could come back any time!' Her face was getting puffed up with tears.

Rose sighed. 'Look. Get the kids dressed. Then you give me the ration books and I'll take them down the shops. That'll give you a bit of time to pull yourself together and get some things done, won't it?'

On the streets and in the shops everyone was saying 'Wasn't it awful?'

'We're not going to stand for that,' Rose heard a woman say as they queued in the butcher's. 'Coming over here and knocking people's houses down. Who does he think he is?'

They were comments that would recur many times as the bombing intensified. The raids became so much heavier and more frequent that the journey to work in the evening was often hazardous. And then in the morning Rose travelled home, her stomach churning with worry that Jean's house might not be still standing, and wondering about Dora and the others in Catherine Street.

Every time she got the chance, Rose caught a bus over there. One afternoon in late August Dora's first words were, 'Have you heard – the Market Hall's gone up?'

'What?' Rose said, stunned. It seemed impossible that a building she'd known and loved all her life should have been hit.

'The middle of town's a right mess,' Dora said, brewing up tea for Rose. She was delighted to see her, though less likely to show it. 'Didn't you see it when you came across? I took the kids in this morning. The Market Hall's a shell. The roof's gone – the lot. And what a stink! All burnt and musty. And there was flaming rabbits and guinea pigs running about all over the place.' She sat down, laughing slightly hysterically. 'I know I shouldn't laugh, but I saw this great fat bloke chasing his rabbits all round the churchyard . . .' She sobered up suddenly. 'And there was Union Jacks all stuck in the mess – that's the British for you.'

Rose could see Dora was in a state and trying not to show it. 'How's everyone?'

'All right.'

Rose looked at the worn face in front of her. Dora didn't look well. She had never really thrown off her cough from last winter and the strain showed in every line of her face.

'I hope you're looking after yourself,' Rose said.

'I'll do.' There was a pause. 'Could do without spending the night in this thing though.' She patted the Morrison shelter.

'What about Dad?'

'Oh, he's all right. Better than the rest of us as a matter of fact. He's palled up with some bloke from the BSA who's got an allotment over that way. Your dad helps out how he can. Digging for Victory and that.' Dora smiled, reluctantly. 'Gives me a bit of peace anyroad. I even heard him whistling the other evening. No, he's not the problem . . .'

Rose saw her mother's face cloud over again. 'George?'

'He's started thieving. I found him with a clock this morning and he wouldn't say where he got it. Next thing is he's sold it and put the money in his pocket. I reckon it came from one of the houses that got it last night. I'm ashamed of him – I really am. But it don't seem no good saying anything.'

'I wish I could do more to help,' Rose said.

'You're doing what you can. And it can't be a picnic for Jean over there either.'

As Autumn came, Dora was taken ill again. Grace gave up work to be with her and take care of the family. The bombing began in real earnest in November. On the fourteenth the centre of Coventry was burnt to the ground, and it seemed only a matter of time before the attention of the German Luftwaffe would be turned more fully on Birmingham.

A few days later it began. Night after night the waves of bombers came over, dark, malevolent shadows in the sky. All night searchlights criss-crossed the darkened buildings and the ack-ack guns rattled out their fire.

Across the city fires burned and the water supply was disrupted. In the quiet mornings, after the all clear had sounded, exhausted people emerged blinking and sick with nerves out of the shelters or from under their staircases to the smell of damp, charred masonry, wet plaster and the sour smell of the incendiaries.

One morning, after another heavy raid, Grace arrived just as Rose was about to go to bed.

'What's happened?' Rose shouted down the stairs, seeing Jean letting Grace in. She was down in an instant. 'What're you doing here? What's wrong?'

'It's Mom,' Grace said. She looked pale and exhausted. 'She's been taken very bad. We had to get the doctor in after the all clear. He says it's pneumonia.'

'Oh my God,' Rose said. She just stared at Grace, stupid with tiredness.

'I can look after her,' Grace assured her hurriedly. 'Only she's fretting about the kids. It was so bad last night she wants Harry and the twins over at Edna's till it's all over. She's sure Edna'll have them.'

Rose felt a momentary pang at the thought of Billy and Susan being sent away, but she knew it was for the best. 'What about George?'

Grace gave her a look which implied how stupid the question was. 'I need you to come and stay over a night at Mom's while I take them over. It'll be too much to do it in a day.'

Rose thought for a second. 'I can get Maureen to swap with me for tomorrow. She'll do anything for kids. I'll get over early. Do me a favour and don't go till I've had a chance to see them.'

Grace nodded, knowing Rose felt they were almost her own. 'Make sure you're over sharpish though.'

*

As Rose made her way home the next day she was horrified at the extent of the damage wreaked on the city. She sat in her old grey coat, looking out of the window of the bus. Some of the solid edges that had outlined her existence were gone. It was shocking, impossible, as if the very foundations of life were shuddering underneath her.

Two of the houses at the end of Catherine Street were down. The house next to them had been shattered in half, some of it still intact, with a chest of drawers with clothes spilling out and a picture still untouched on the inside wall. It seemed indecent: the details of the private parts of people's lives hanging there on display.

Grace hadn't told her how bad it was. She must have wanted to avoid worrying her any more.

She gave the little ones as cheerful a send off as she could. Dora was upstairs in bed and had already said her goodbyes.

'Why do we have to go?' Susan raised her dark eyes to Rose with a puzzled frown.

'Well, it's because of all the big bangs you keep hearing in the night,' Rose told her.

'We don't like the bangs,' Billy whispered.

'No. Well, it'll be quieter at Auntie Edna's. And there's a lot more space to run about. And Harry'll look after you – won't you?'

Harry nodded, holding on to a very old rag doll that had been Violet's.

'I tell you what,' Rose said. 'I've got something for you two to look after for me.'

She ran upstairs, and when she came down after a few minutes she put into Susan's hand a small wooden elephant and into Billy's the roughly carved little wooden horse. Both of them beamed with delight.

'I'll put him in bed when we get there, 'cos he'll be tired,' Susan said solemnly.

'That's right. You look after them for me until I see you – all right?'

Rose found Dora in a bad state. She was very weak

132

and her breathing through her one good lung was laboured and noisy. She had a high fever and was drifting in and out of consciousness. Rose sat beside her most of the day, offering her sips of water, bathing the hot, sallow skin of her face and rubbing camphorated oil on her chest. When Rose became so tired she could no longer stay upright, she lay and slept beside her.

In the early evening, when Dora opened her eyes and seemed fully conscious for the first time, Rose said, 'They've gone off all right.'

Her mother nodded and whispered, 'Best out of it.' Then she said, 'Grace is a good girl.'

Rose smiled.

'And so are you,' Dora went on in her rasping voice.

'Don't talk if it hurts, Mom.'

'No – I wanted to say—' Dora went on, and then started coughing, her body curling in pain as she held her side tightly. It was some time before she had enough breath to speak again.

'You've had some bad things happen to you – before you should have—'

'Don't, Mom—'

'No . . .' She stopped to get her breath again. 'It's as rough as it gets losing a babby. And your friend – Diana . . .' She saw Rose look at the floor. It was the first time anyone else had mentioned Diana, and hearing her name suddenly was more painful than she expected. 'All I was going to say was – I'm proud of you – how you've come through it. Alfie'll make you a good husband. And you can have some more of your own kiddies then.'

For a moment Rose couldn't think of anything to say, she was so moved by the fact that her mother understood how bad she still felt about Diana. And at the same time she realized with a wave of guilt how seldom she worried about Alfie.

She just said, 'Thanks Mom. Shall I get you some camomile tea now?'

As she was preparing the hot drink, George came back into the house carrying a bag of trinkets which he'd rifled out of another of the houses bombed the night before. He laid them out quite brazenly on top of the shelter.

'You ought to be ashamed of yourself,' Rose said.

'Oh yeah? How's that?' he said, insolently. His little pinched face was hard and bitter.

'Look,' Rose said, infuriated, her hands on her hips. Small as she was, she looked forbidding in her anger, her slim curving figure outlined by the red dress. 'I know you think you're a special case and everyone's got to apologize to you for the rest of your life. But you're not. Mom sent you away because she wanted the best for you, and there's no excuse for you acting like a thieving litle urchin and taking advantage of other people.'

'Aw, sod off,' George said.

Rose marched up to him and gave his face a sharp slap. She turned, shaking with anger, to begin preparing their rations of food for the evening meal.

'You're a selfish little bugger,' she shouted after him as he went out of the door.

He left the door swinging open so that the forbidden light streamed into the yard. Rose went and slammed it shut.

'We'll have the ARP lot round carrying on next,' she muttered to herself. Despite her anger she saw in her mind George as a tiny child forever running to her to be picked up. She felt sorry for being so hard on him. But all their nerves were on edge and he'd become so distant and infuriating.

Soon Sid came in with a cabbage and a handful of carrots in a bag dangling from his crutch. 'You can throw these in the pot,' he said proudly. 'How's your mother?'

'She's just had some tea,' Rose told him. 'She's about the same, I think.' She took the cabbage and started to clean it up. 'How's it at the BSA?'

'Hell of a mess up there,' Sid said, easing his coat off. 'The whole of the new building went up. Awful lot of blokes went with it. We're carrying on the best we can.'

While she finished preparing the meal, Sid went round the house and checked it was properly blacked out. She heard his voice upstairs as he said a few words to her mother. It was odd getting used to seeing him differently. Now he was someone with things to do, with a role. Like a proper dad, she thought.

When he came down, she said, 'How do we get Mom into the shelter?'

'She won't come,' Sid said flatly.

'Is that what she said?'

'She didn't need to say. She hasn't been in there since she was taken bad.'

Rose gaped at him. 'You mean . . .? Well, who's looked after her?'

'Our Grace has stayed up with her. Your mother told her to go down and leave her, but Grace wouldn't hear of it.'

'Grace? You mean all these nights they've been bombing the guts out of us those two have both been . . .' She pointed towards the ceiling. Sid nodded. 'Why didn't you make them come down?'

'Don't you think I've tried?' His voice was loud with guilt and worry. 'She just won't hear of it.'

'Good God,' Rose said. 'Our Grace is tougher than you'd think. Well' – she looked defiantly at Sid – 'if she can put up with it, so can I.'

Sid shook his head. 'I thought you might've been the one that'd talk her down. I just wish there was something I—'

'It's all right. Save your breath,' Rose said irritably, and then added more gently, 'It only takes one to see to her, doesn't it?'

Her father sat down, quiet for a moment. Then he said, 'Grace is very like your mother used to be. She was always one for looking after people.'

'Good job really, wasn't it?' Rose retorted. She was finding being alone with her father for the first time in years strange and uncomfortable. She suddenly realized that Dora had always stood between them so they had seldom talked to one another without someone else to mediate.

135

'You can be a hard bitch, you can,' Sid said matter-of-factly. He stared at the plates Rose was laying on top of the shelter as he spoke. 'Whatever you think, I do love that woman up there.'

Rose turned away, knowing that whatever tender feelings she'd ever had towards her father, or might have now, she was damned if she'd ever be able to show him.

The raids began early that night. Rose spent part of those long hours lying in Sid's place in the bed beside Dora's restless, feverish body. The rest of the time she sat up or stood by the window, frozen in spite of the blanket wrapped round her.

The seemingly endless groups of planes droned past overhead, ack-ack defences hammered at them, and finally there came the crump of bombs landing at a distance or a much louder explosion if they were nearer. Then the planes roared away again. She peeped out from behind the blackout curtains and saw the searchlights moving over the city and the sky orange from the reflected light of the burning buildings. She thought she could smell smoke, but wasn't certain if it was her imagination.

She thought of Jo Pye out there helping to put out the fires, and Gladys and the kids all crushed into their shelter.

I should have volunteered for the ARP or something like that, she thought. Where I could have been out helping people.

Suddenly there was a huge explosion, so close that the house shook and the windows rattled. Rose found that she was lying flat on the floorboards without having thought about it.

Dora stirred. 'Grace . . .?'

Rose crawled shakily over to the bed. 'It's me – Rose.'

'Oh. What was that?' Dora sounded very drowsy.

'Don't know. Wasn't us, anyway!' It could only have been a street or two away though, she thought. Astonishing that the glass was still in the window. Good job they'd taped it across. If she hadn't had her mother to look after she felt she would have panicked, her nerves were stretched so taut.

'D'you want a drink?' she whispered.

Dora accepted a few sips of water, with Rose supporting her arm. She was so frail, her face and limbs pared right down to the bones. Feeling the ghostliness of her mother's body, Rose knew that she didn't have much time left to her.

'D'you remember those nights we spent together up with the babbies?' she asked Dora.

Her mother nodded her head very slightly. 'It weren't right – you losing yours like that.'

'I miss him still – terrible sometimes.'

'Course you do – mine too – it never goes.' The coughing took her over again, and the attack seemed to go on for a long time. Rose was quite oblivious now to what was going on outside. Dora seemed to doze off again when the coughing eased up, but suddenly she said, 'You'll always have Billy and Susan.'

Rose knew she was saying, look after them, keep an eye on them for me. She reached out and took her mother's hand gently in her own.

'Sod them out there,' she said. 'I'm coming in to lie down.'

When she returned wearily to work the following night she noticed that the space beside her where Maureen usually worked had been filled by another girl, whom she'd never seen before.

'You done a swap have you?' she said, puzzled. 'What's happened to Maureen?'

The girl said she didn't know because she'd been asked to move over from another block. Rose saw Madge, an older woman who worked in a position near by, moving quickly over to her.

'You'll have to know, Rose,' she said. 'Maureen was killed last night on the way to work. One came down

137

when she was going for the bus. House came down on her. She never stood a chance.'

Hurriedly someone fetched a chair for Rose, who had turned a sick-looking white in the face.

'You all right love?' Madge asked. 'I never meant to give you such a shock. Only I didn't think you two that close.'

Rose sat under the remorseless lights of the vast factory, her mind a collage of confused thoughts. Maureen walking out for her bus from her lonely digs, the bomb coming down like a great slug in the darkness, and a small Irish girl called Josie, little Josie whom Maureen adored and whose heart would break.

A fortnight later, on a frozen, gusty December afternoon, Rose, looking pale and exhausted, stood between her father and sister at Dora's funeral. They walked back from the graveside under an iron sky, between the leafless trees, Sid, Rose, Grace and George. They hadn't called the little ones back. With Sam away, this, for now, was the family.

But as the wind murmured in between the skinny branches of the trees that bleak afternoon, Rose glanced back to the spot from where they had walked. And she knew that the centre of the family, the person who had kept them together, now lay buried beneath the fast-freezing ground.

PART TWO

ITALY

1943–1945

CHAPTER 14

MARCH 1941, BERKSHIRE

The truck swayed along the narrow country lanes, its huge khaki bulk looking out of place between hawthorn hedges and elms. From the half-open back of the truck women's faces looked out at the early spring countryside and they waved at people they passed. They all held on to anything they could to keep from falling on top of one another. Deeper inside the truck, where it was almost too dark to see, someone was singing 'My Bonny Lies Over the Ocean' in a loud, tuneless voice.

'So this is the British army,' a voice piped up over towards the daylight end. 'You can see why they call them cattle trucks, can't you! I say – you've got your foot on my case. Move it, would you? There's a dear. Mustn't have my things crushed before we've even started.

'You won't be needing crêpe de Chine where we're going!' someone shouted over the growling engine, and the others round her tittered. The voice had come from a large woman with peroxide blond hair. 'And stop that bleedin' racket, will you?' she yelled down at the singer. 'Me head's thumping something awful already.'

Rose, who was standing near her towards the back, silently agreed. As the afternoon had worn on a tight band of pain had stretched between her temples so she felt almost unable to think, exhausted as she was from all the newness and strain of the journey further away from home than she'd ever been before. She could hardly feel her feet in her old down-at-heel shoes and she was hungry. The few sandwiches Grace had packed for her were long gone. The day seemed to be going on for ever.

'Here . . .' She realized the blonde was speaking to her through the gloom of the truck. 'You deaf or something? I said pass us me bag will you? Yeah. That one.'

Rose bent down unsteadily and got hold of the heavy carpet bag. She pushed it to the other woman along the floor of the truck.

'Ta. Where'd you come from then?'

'Birmingham.'

'Ooh ar!' the blonde squawked. 'Yow'm a Brummoy then – orroight are yer!' she mocked.

'That's all right with you is it?' Rose snapped at her. She couldn't place the woman's own accent.

'Now girls,' a voice called from the light end. 'No point in being cattish. We've all got to get along and live together. There's a war on, remember.'

The blonde said, 'Oooh, yes. I'd almost forgot!' and rolled her eyes round in such a comical way that Rose couldn't help grinning.

'What's your name then?'

'Rose. What's yours?'

'Gloria. From Deptford. That's London to you. This is a lark innit?' Gloria stood with her solid legs braced apart as far as space would allow. 'Could do without the old school tie brigade though.'

While they had waited for their transport at Didcot Station surrounded by piles of army supplies, the women had gathered instinctively into two groups. The old school tie group, as Gloria called them, looked much better dressed and cared for, and one of them even had a fur collar on her coat. From the loud conversations in their posh accents, Rose gathered that several of them were bound eventually for the élite Intelligence Corps. There was a rather mousy, timid-looking girl with reddish brown hair who Rose noticed because she seemed to be constantly on the point of bursting into tears. She didn't seem to be sure which group she belonged in, and hung around the posher ones as if hoping to be taken under their wing.

The second group, which Rose and Gloria had fallen into, looked scruffier, mostly togged up in second- or third-hand clothes and lumpish old coats. Gloria seemed the most brashly confident. A couple of them looked pale and unhealthy and terrified. One clearly had nits, so everyone shrank back from her.

The journey from the station to the camp was roughly four miles.

'I say – I think we're here!' someone soon called out. Others pushed towards the back end to get their first sight of the camp where they were to spend their first three weeks of initial training. Rose could see nothing at all.

'Golly, sentry boxes,' one of the posh girls said. 'Those chaps look jolly cold, don't they?'

'Look at all that barbed wire. Makes it look frightfully serious, doesn't it?'

'Let's hope they'll let us have a cup of tea now. I'm quite parched.'

The truck stopped abruptly at the reception hut and they scrambled out with their bags, those from the dark inside screwing up their eyes as they reached the daylight. The March afternoon had turned damp and windy. They all looked round at the camp which extended along the edge of the Berkshire Downs. There were row upon row of Nissen huts with corrugated-iron roofs, and round the camp stretched the spiky border of the barbed wire. It was a bleak scene, with no trees and few bushes between the huts, and the rounded greyish hills curving away beyond. Rose experienced the same feeling as on her first day at Castle Bromwich, an urge to turn round and run home. But home was much further away now, and there wasn't much to run back there for.

After they had filed into the reception hut they were each given a printed postcard to fill in saying they had arrived safely and where they were. Rose addressed hers to Grace.

A brisk officer with an Eton crop introduced herself to them as Lieutenant Waters. 'I'd like to welcome you to the Auxiliary Territorial Service. I know everything must seem very new and strange to you now, and I'm sure you're all rather tired and cold. But you will get used to us and our ways here and, before long, our ways will of course become your ways.'

She went on to say that they were part of Platoon 4, and that later that day they would be issued with ATS uniform, of which, she assured them, they would become very proud after a few weeks. Rose listened rather blankly, sitting on a hard wooden bench beside the girl with nits, who kept fiddling with her head.

Then a plump woman in uniform came in and announced herself their corporal.

'Right!' she shouted at them. 'Outside in threes!'

Carrying their cases, they slouched and stumbled out of the hut into the cold and stood in rough lines, three abreast.

'Let's see you begin on some marching,' the corporal yelled. 'When I say march you lead with your left foot. Ready? Right – march! Left, right, left, right, left . . . left . . . left . . .'

And the line of women, tall and short, plump and skinny, in as great a variety of clothes, tried to discipline their tired legs and march, heavy cases swaying in hands, to their huts. Rose heard Gloria give a snort of laughter at the sight.

Hut J, into which Rose was ordered, housed twelve women in beds with black iron frames, six down each side. Along the middle of the floor ran a very shiny strip of brown lino, and in the centre of the hut stood a stove, its rather rusty pipe angling up and out through the roof. It was not lit at the moment and the hut, with its drab greenish walls, felt cold and cheerless.

Rose sat down, slipped her shoes off and rubbed her slim, icy feet. She closed her eyes for a moment, wishing she could lie down on the bed and sleep straight away. She opened them again at the sound of a voice next to her.

'Gawd! This is the first time I've ever had a whole bed to meself.'

144

A skinny girl with a pale, rather rat-like face, her lank greasy hair held back by a couple of kirby grips, was unpacking her things on the next bed. 'How about you?' she asked Rose.

'Me too,' Rose said wearily. She was tired and didn't feel like talking. The girl had an accent rather like Gloria's. Her name was Tilly and she came from Canning Town. Rose realized she meant London as well. Between all her actions Tilly kept biting furiously at her rough nails.

Rose got up slowly from the bed and started to open her case. As she glanced down the long room she saw that Gloria was up the far end, and she recognized the mousy girl who'd been hovering round the posh group at the station.

Standing by the bed on the other side of her was a girl with wavy brown hair and round, healthy-looking cheeks. For a second Rose was startled by how much she reminded her of Diana.

The girl smiled at her. 'You look done in,' she said. 'Come a long way?'

'From Birmingham,' Rose replied. 'It's felt like a hell of a long day.'

'Yes, I'm lucky. My people only live over near Oxford, so it hasn't been too much of a chore for me. My name's Muriel, by the way.'

Rose warmed to Muriel. She was well spoken, but without a trace of the stand-offishness she'd sensed in some of the others.

'We'll be able to help each other out, won't we?' Muriel said. 'Did you know that these funny mattress things are called biscuits? Odd, isn't it?'

Rose saw that the mattress on the iron frame was made up of three thin sections: – the 'biscuits'. They also had two sheets each and four blankets.

Suddenly there was a to-do at the other end of the hut. The mouse was in tears.

'What's up with her?' Tilly asked, with more curiosity than concern. 'Can't see there's much to have a crying match about. S'like a boarding house here I reckon!'

The mouse, whose name turned out to be Gwen, had promised to write to her mother the instant she set foot in the camp and had just realized she had lost her writing paper.

'Oh for heaven's sake, wrap up,' Gloria said to her. 'Someone'll give you a bit of paper. And you've already sent her one of them cards, so what're you fussing about?'

'But the card didn't *say* anything,' Gwen sniffed. 'And Mummy worries so. She's a widow, you see.'

Rose thought for a moment of Sid, and of Grace left to look after them all. She thanked her stars Sid had the BSA job to keep him occupied. And Grace had told her that in a few weeks when she had reached eighteen she was going to volunteer at a first aid post. 'That way I can stay home with Dad and George and still do something useful,' she'd said stoically.

Now Rose wished overwhelmingly that her sister was there with her. It would be so good to see a familiar face.

Muriel found Gwen a sheet of paper and an envelope, but the moment she sat down to write they were all ordered out again. The rest of the afternoon and evening was spent rushing from one thing to the next: getting fitted into their stiff khaki uniforms and peaked caps, pulling at skirts and tunics to make them fit over hips and busts, and collecting a huge mound of kit: steel helmet, greatcoat, groundsheet, respirator . . . And clothes and more clothes, the shirts and slacks and gloves and every-thing you could think of except, for some reason, hand-kerchiefs. There were shrieks of laughter at the sight of the heavy underwear and thick khaki stockings.

'Cor – look at them passion killers!' Gloria cackled, waving a pair of stockings round her head.

Then there was bed making and a quick meal of poached egg on toast in the Naafi canteen and, finally, bed.

*

Rose lay under the sheet and heavy army blankets. A couple of girls were crying. It was very dark in the hut, but Rose guessed from the direction of the sound that one was Gwen. She wondered if she ought to get out and try to comfort her, but she couldn't think of anything to say and wasn't sure Gwen would want her.

The hot cup of tea she'd drunk earlier had begun to ease her headache, but she could still feel her heart thumping too fast. Unable to sleep in this strange new place, she thought over the peculiar day she'd had and back to one event in particular.

That morning when she had left Catherine Street, she told Grace she'd rather say her goodbyes at number five. 'I'd sooner think of you here when I'm gone,' she said. 'And you've got enough on your plate without traipsing into town with me.'

Grace had fussed around her like their mother would have done, and Rose couldn't help thinking how much her sister looked like Dora now that her face had become thinner. The two of them packed up Rose's few things in a small, decrepit suitcase.

'I'll miss you like anything,' Grace said shyly, with tears in her eyes.

'D'you think I'm deserting you?' Rose asked. She had felt many pangs of guilt at going off and leaving Grace at home.

'We'll be all right,' Grace said. 'I've got used to you being over at Jean's, and if you was here with Dad the pair of you'd do nothing but fall out anyhow. It's best this way – specially with Alfie being stuck out there and everything.' Grace still persisted in her fantasy that Rose was pining dreadfully for Alfie.

Sid had said a gruff goodbye to Rose before he left in the morning. 'I don't s'pose they let you lasses get anywhere near the action like the blokes. Just make sure you don't give 'em lip and you'll be all right.'

George just said, 'Tara,' as if Rose was off down the shops for the morning.

'You'll let me know how Billy and Susan are, won't

147

you?' Rose begged Grace. 'And Harry of course,' she added quickly. 'It's going to be the worst thing, not having any kids around.'

The sisters embraced. The strong grip of their arms round each other said everything. Neither was the sort to make a fuss. Rose walked away from Court 11, past the bomb rubble at the end of Catherine Street.

Sitting on the bus into town, she began to feel this was actually real. She was really going to leave Birmingham for the first time. Her stomach churned with nerves and excitement. It was a bright, blustery morning and she stared hard out of the window as if trying to remember every stone of her city: the dark factories, Smithfield, St Martin's, and all the other less obvious places that were so much part of her. She couldn't imagine anywhere different. Leaving it all was terrifying now she was actually facing it. But this was what she had always wanted, wasn't it? To see something of what was outside? The war had at least given her that chance. She sat hugging the small, battered weekend case on her knees, the one familiar object in a world that was shifting all around her.

New Street Station was seething with people, many of them service personnel in their blue or khaki uniforms. Rose wondered if there were others going to the same place as her. Trains were constantly moving in and out with a great clamour of engines and whistles blowing. The air was full of sharp smells of soot and cinders and acrid whorls of smoke from cigarettes.

Rose picked her way along the crowded platform, saying 'excuse me' and 'sorry' until she was somewhere near the middle. According to the long fingers of the clock there were still twenty minutes until her train to Oxford was due to leave. She wondered whether to go back and try to get a quick cup of tea.

A train slid slowly into the station from Rose's right. She stood on tiptoe to watch. It was a grand sight as it hissed finally to a halt, steam clouding up to the steel beams of the roof. The doors opened and people clambered out on to the already packed platform. Rose, like everyone else, shuffled back to give them room.

She was standing like that, deciding against the tea, when she heard the voice: a strong, well-spoken woman's voice but containing a waver of uncertainty.

'It is, surely – is it? Rose? Rose Lucas?'

Rose turned and found herself face to face with a smartly turned out WAAF officer, her fair, wavy hair fastened back stylishly under the grey-blue cap. Her vivacious face wore an apprehensive smile. In the five years since she had seen her, Diana had matured into a beautiful, poised young woman.

'It is you, isn't it?' Diana exclaimed.

The two of them eased further back into the crowd to let the other passengers past and someone behind said, 'Here – watch who you're pushing, will you?'

Diana made a helpless gesture as if unsure where to begin the conversation. 'Well. Where are you off to?'

'The army. ATS,' Rose managed to gasp out. Her heart was beating breathtakingly fast. She was amazed how Diana could begin chatting as if they'd only seen each other the week before. But then that was her upbringing – politeness, social graces.

'Good for you,' Diana said. 'I'm a WAAF – well, as you can see . . .' And she giggled, looking down at her uniform. For the first time Rose realized that Diana was as nervous as herself. 'I'm just off home on leave. Mummy and Daddy will be thrilled I've seen you!'

Rose found herself unable to speak. Lying remembering it now she thought of all the things she should have said. She should have asked after Catherine and Ronald, said how pleased she was, *something* at least. But she had felt so scruffy and ignorant and overpoweringly awkward, and those feelings were made worse by the memory of how much the two of them had shared and of the way she had cut Diana off so abruptly.

Diana quietened suddenly and looked serious. 'Listen. I'm going to have to be off shortly – train to catch. But Rose, I . . .' She struggled for the right words. 'What happened to you? We were all so worried about you and it made me so unhappy. I couldn't understand why you didn't answer my letters.'

Seeing the tears in her old friend's eyes Rose realized that she was, beneath all the jolliness of her class and of service life, still the same, kind girl she had known.

'I couldn't . . .' Rose's face felt hot and red and she knew that if she tried to explain here she would be unable to stop crying. 'I wanted to tell you,' she stumbled on. 'But you'd have hated me if you'd known . . .'

The sight of Diana's blue eyes so full of concern made Rose feel even more emotional. 'Look. You'll miss your train. Give me your address. I'll write. There's no time now and I'd just make a fool of myself. But I'd like to tell you . . .'

Diana handed her a slip of paper with her WAAF address on it. They reached out and awkwardly gripped each other's hands. And then she was gone, vanished among the other drably clad bodies. Rose was left feeling weak-kneed and suspecting it had all been a daydream.

She tossed and fidgeted on the hard bed. What am I going to say to her when I write? she wondered. More than ever, Diana had seemed to come from a different world. But the only thing to do was to tell her everything, truthfully. She owed Diana that. To finish things off. But as she drifted off to sleep, she couldn't help wondering whether this might also be the beginning of something new in a friendship that had never truly died.

CHAPTER 15

'Oh, these confounded blisters!' Muriel groaned, gingerly trying to squeeze her feet into her slippers.

They were all in Hut J because it was domestic night. Each Wednesday of the three weeks in camp they were expected to scrub the hut and catch up on any cleaning or mending chores. Some of the girls were crowded round the stove, which was lit only in the evenings.

Squatting in front of the glowing coals with her legs apart in a silky confection of a nightie was Gloria. She was holding out a large pair of scissors on which was stabbed a slice of bread she was toasting. Rose, Tilly and a couple of others were sitting round in stiff blue and white striped army pyjamas. Muriel was wearing her own floral cotton nightie, and Gwen sat swamped by a pair of pale pink winceyette pyjamas. Both she and Tilly were dabbing at their feet with blobs of cotton wool.

'Our feet'll be in ribbons by the end of this,' Gwen moaned.

All of them had sore feet but they also had pink, healthier-looking cheeks than when they'd arrived, after the new experience of half an hour's vigorous PT every morning. They tucked into the toast with increased appetites from all the fresh air.

In between the gripes about blisters and arms throbbing from the inoculations they'd had, Gloria was regaling them with tales of her men. She apparently had several in tow at once. To prove the point she'd pinned four photos on the wall behind her bed, and went through a half-

151

joking ritual of kissing them all at length before she settled down to sleep.

'That one's Bob,' she told them, pointing out a dark, moustachioed figure. 'He's my favourite really. It was him who give me this.' She flounced round in front of them in the shimmering, peach-coloured folds of cloth.

'Under the counter stuff,' Tilly said knowingly. 'Has to be. How'd he get it otherwise with rationing on?'

Gloria stood magnificently above her, curling a lock of her pale hair round a finger. 'I'll have you know,' she said disdainfully, 'that my Bob actually owns the factory where they used to make these here gowns.'

Gloria turned to Rose, who was sitting with her army jacket in her lap, lighting matches to burn off the pinkish film which covered the buttons. It was something they all did to make the jackets look more presentable.

You're a looker,' Gloria said. 'Why ain't we seen any pictures of your bloke? Or ain't you interested in fellers?'

'I'm – sort of engaged to someone,' Rose told them hesitantly, still not feeling sure it was really true.

Muriel and Gwen both said, 'Ah, how lovely.'

'Where is he then?' Tilly asked. 'He in the army too?'

'Yes, but he's in Germany.'

There were noises of horror from the others.

'Picked him up, did they?' Gloria asked, more gently. 'Is he in a Kraut prison camp?'

Rose nodded. 'I just had one of them cards, a couple of months ago. You know, name, in good health and all that. The camp's called Felsig. I think they picked him up in France.'

The others sat silent for a moment.

'That must be terrible,' Muriel said.

'Yeah,' Gloria joined in, trying to cheer things up. 'But at least you know where he is and that he's alive. Eh,' she nudged Rose playfully with her elbow, 'he won't be getting up to much mischief in one of them camps!' She gave her loud laugh. 'So in the meantime you can have some fun, can't you? I mean being engaged ain't the same as being married, is it?' She laughed again. 'I'll tell you one thing. I'll give this army lark a chance, and if I don't like it I'll be over the men's quarters right quick, getting meself a Paragraph 11!'

Paragraph 11, in army regulations, provided a let-out clause for women who were having babies. The others laughed, rather uneasily, at the thought of Gloria going brazenly over to the men's side of the camp to help herself to a pregnancy.

'That's awful,' Gwen said, blushing.

'Oh, ta very much.' Gloria was unruffled. 'I can't see any point in not having a good time when you can – specially with a war on. And I don't know why you're looking so bug-eyed about it. You only joined up to get away from that bleedin' mother of yours, didn't you?'

Gwen leapt to her feet, her face instantly a hot red. 'That's not true!' she cried. 'How could you say something so awful?' And she ran sobbing over to her bed and lay down on it, curled up tight.

Rose put her jacket down. 'I thought I had a gob on me till I met you,' she said matter-of-factly to Gloria, and went to sit on Gwen's bed. The other girl wouldn't say anything, but gripped Rose's hand.

'Time for bed, methinks,' Muriel said, with all the authority of a boarding school prefect, which until a few months before was what she had been.

Gloria grinned, making a thumbs up sign at Muriel and winking at the others. 'Definitely officer material there!' she said.

Every morning they were up at six-thirty and ready for PT by seven. This was made even more of an agony for the first few days by pain in their arms from the injections. Rose felt as if the scab was lifting up and down every time she swung her arm in the freezing air.

Compulsory inoculations had only been one part of the medical when they'd first arrived. They had also had to go through the dreaded 'free from infection' inspection.

'Oh my Gawd,' Gloria had said as they queued up.

She seemed genuinely rattled by it. 'It's the bugs, babies and scabies job isn't it? Do we really have to take our bits off in front of that lot?'

They all stood in line outside the chilly medical hut. Weak sunshine lit the grey camp buildings and a damp wind swept across the downs. Their grumpy corporal kept shouting 'NO TALKING!' and refused to answer any questions.

All of them were anxious. Most had never taken off their clothes even in front of their closest family before. When they had filed inside and Rose was stripped down to her vest and pants, she found herself trembling, and not just with cold. The stale, sweaty smell of some of the girls reminded her sickeningly of Mr Lazenby. She saw with enormous relief that the medical officer was a woman.

She listened to Rose's heart, poked about in her hair and felt along her spine. She pulled out the elastic of her knickers to have a quick, impassive glance down them, and then it was over and Rose was pronounced nit free and fit for duty.

'It's nothing much,' Rose whispered to Gwen, who was standing outside looking pale with fright.

Every day there came another trial: kit inspection. Beds had to be 'barracked' – arranged with the sheets and blankets folded in a very particular way – and then all of the kit had to be laid out in precise order and immaculately folded. Woe betide you if any of it was missing and could not be excused as being in the laundry.

And then drill. They stood in lines, an extraordinarily unformed-looking bunch in the first few days, as one of the male NCOs bawled relentlessly at them.

'Right, you lousy shower. Let's see some discipline around here! You've got to learn in three weeks what we normally take three months of army life to pick up, and I'm damned if any of you are going to let me down! Right. Chests foward, shoulders back, bottoms in. Atten-*shun!*'

Gradually, as the days of marching and saluting and manoeuvring back and forth went by, their bodies creaked and cranked into familiarity with it. They began to look as if they might belong in the army.

After lunch, for which they lined up in the canteen, men and women bantering together, they sat down for a bewildering assortment of lectures and films. One talk on army regiments or history might be closely followed by a luridly educational film about VD or how a baby is born. This was a mixed camp in a mixed army and they were expected to take all this in their stride, but there was many a green, shocked face after they'd seen the festering genitals in the VD film.

And then came the fatigues or camp chores; scrubbing floors, washing dishes or spud bashing.

One afternoon Rose was standing in the canteen hut with Gloria. They both had their khaki sleeves rolled up so they could dip their hands into the freezing, muddy water.

'You know, gypsy Rose,' Gloria teased. 'I can never make you out. What d'you really make of the army?'

Rose was silent for a moment, working on the cold, earthy skin of a potato. She turned her strong gaze on Gloria.

'I don't like being pushed around, except when I can really see the point of it. I mean I'll do what they say if it's right – for the war effort like. And I've always wanted to get away, see a bit more of life than just Brum. I miss home of course, but my mom's died anyhow and I can't stick living with my dad.'

Gloria seemed in an unusually solemn mood. 'Seems like everyone's running away from something when you come down to it, doesn't it?' She grinned. 'Quiet here though, isn't it? We hardly had a wink of sleep back in Deptford. They was bombing the balls off of us.'

Rose pulled back a wavy strand of hair with cold, wet fingers. 'Is that why you joined up then?'

'Not just,' Gloria said briskly. 'They got me brother. He was a rear gunner in the RAF. Went through all the Battle of Britain, right till the end. Then he went out one day and they lost him over the Channel. We was close, me and Jo. It was only me he told how scared he was – brown trousers, the lot – you know. When he went I thought, I'm not going to just sit here with them dropping this bloody lot on us night after night. I'm going to get the buggers.'

Rose still found Gloria an unlikely addition to the army with her peroxide hair, her curl papers and slinky nighties. 'D'you think you'll stick it?'

'Oh, I'll stick it,' Gloria said grimly. 'I'll stick it if it kills me.'

'So all that you said about Paragraph 11 – you was joking?'

Gloria gaped at her in astonishment. 'Course I was bleeding joking! What d'you take me for?' With a broad grin on her pink face she picked up a wet potato and lobbed it over in Rose's direction. 'The very idea, you cheeky bugger!'

It was two weeks before Rose found an opportunity to write to Diana. She sat under the stark light in the hut with her pillow propped against the black iron bedhead. She wanted the letter to be warm and friendly. It was easier to write than she'd feared. Away in this place that was so different from home and Birmingham life, she felt almost as if those terrible years had happened to someone else. She wrote about Lazenby's and, as clearly but briefly as she could, about what Mr Lazenby had done to her.

Yet when she described Joseph's short, fragile life, tears began to pour down her face and on to the paper. It brought back vividly what she tried to keep from her mind: the feel of his soft, downy head, and the tiny frozen hands she'd found that terrible morning. She knew with renewed clarity that that day would be the worst of her life – far worse than the day Mr Lazenby assaulted her and worse than anything she might face in the future.

'I wish now I'd told you, Diana,' she wrote.

Now I think back I know you'd have understood – and your mom and dad. But at the time I wasn't thinking straight. I just felt dirty and ashamed all the time and I couldn't see how you'd want to be friends with me again. I hope you can forgive me. I know you'd never get yourself in a mess like that – much too clever, you are! And I want you to know I never stopped thinking about you and wondering how you was getting on. And your family too. They were all so kind to me. Please remember me to them.

I'd like to see you again some time. Maybe in more cheerful days after this war's over?

She signed the letter,

With kind thoughts from your friend,
Rose.

After that, when she'd wiped her face, she dashed off a quick note home. She usually found herself talking in her mind to Grace as she wrote.

'I miss you ever such a lot,' she finished off. 'When I come home next I want to see you in your nurse's uniform!

'Love to all – Rose. xxxx'

She heard the door open, and glanced up to see Gwen come in looking wet, dishevelled and flustered. She sat down miserably on the edge of her bed without even taking her coat off. After a moment Rose realized she was crying. She put her writing things down and went rather timidly to sit beside her.

'What's up with you?' she asked.

Gwen looked up, startled and rather uneasy. She hadn't even noticed Rose when she came into the hut, and she wished that if anyone had to be there, it had been Muriel.

'You'll think I'm so stupid.'

'Why should I?' Rose asked, genuinely surprised.

'You give the impression of being, well, not exactly worldly, but of knowing a lot about life.'

157

'Me?' Rose couldn't help bursting into laughter. 'Gwen, you do know this is the first time I've ever set foot out of Birmingham, don't you? Come on – out with it.' She patted Gwen's shoulder.

Gwen mopped her eyes with a delicate lacy handkerchief. 'I went to the Naafi tonight. And one of the chaps – it doesn't matter who – kept making up to me all evening. He seemed quite nice, but then he asked me to go outside with him. It's raining, so it wasn't very pleasant, but he didn't seem to care. He pushed me up against the ablutions hut and started . . .' She paused, her head down, ashamed. 'He kept pawing at me. And then he grabbed hold of me and started sticking his horrible tobaccoey tongue in my mouth. It was disgusting. So I just pushed him off.' Her voice had gone high and plaintive with emotion again. 'I mean it was all wrong! D'you think there's something the matter with him, Rose? Or with me?'

Having so recently revived the memory in her letter to Diana of how she'd had to find out about sex herself, Rose felt her heart go out to Gwen. 'Look,' she said gently. 'I know it seems a bit funny if you've not done it before, but that's just a way of kissing.'

'*Kissing!*' Gwen squeaked. 'That's not kissing. It's . . . it's – insanitary!'

Rose looked at Gwen's distraught face in silence for a moment, trying to work out how to phrase what she knew she had to say next.

'You know that film we saw last week, about the babby being born?' she said. Gwen nodded, eyes wide. 'You don't know how it got in there in the first place, do you?'

'Well, Mummy said they just get sort of planted there . . .' Gwen trailed off. 'No, I don't. She told me I didn't need to know anything about 'that' until I'm married. And she said even then I'd be luckier not to find out. She's very protective.'

Rose sighed, and then, as carefully and clearly as she could, so that Gwen could be left in no doubt what she was talking about, she explained. She watched Gwen's expression change from astonishment to disbelief and horror, and then to a stunned gratitude.

'So when they call us ATS 'officers' groundsheets', that's what they . . .?'

Rose nodded.

'And that's what Gloria meant about Paragraph 11,' she said slowly, her horrified expression returning. 'That she'd actually . . .?'

'It's all right,' Rose reassured her with a wry smile. 'From what I hear in this place she wouldn't be the first to try that way out. But I'm sure she was only joking – honest.'

By the end of the final week of basic training, they had been drilled and barracked and bumpered into something that not only resembled army discipline, but was also becoming second nature. Now it was time to be assigned a trade. They all sat through aptitude tests and interviews designed to help the army allot each of them a suitable job. Rose found most of the tests less formidable than she'd feared.

During the interview with Lieutenant Waters, the question Rose remembered despite her nerves was when the woman, sitting behind her desk, asked in a crisp voice, 'You're from Birmingham, aren't you, Private Lucas? What was your father's occupation before the war?'

'Well, he was an engineer—' Rose began to tell her.

'Ah,' the officer said, jotting something down. 'At last, some mechanical potential.'

Rose didn't have the heart or opportunity to tell her that Sid hadn't worked as an engineer since before the last war.

When she came out of the interview she met Muriel outside.

'So – what was the verdict?' Muriel asked her.

A broad smile spread across Rose's face. 'Driver. I'm off to start at Camberley next week.'

She felt not only pleased and excited but flattered too.

She, little Rose Lucas, being able to drive Jeeps and trucks about!

She walked to lunch with Muriel in the moist April wind, across the open area where they did their square bashing, saluting a male officer they passed on the way.

'Gloria's furious,' Muriel said. 'They've told her she's got to be a cook!'

'Gloria?' Rose exploded into laughter. 'Oh my God, heaven help the poor sods who have to eat her cooking! What's yours then?'she asked Muriel.

'Oh, admin. Predictable, I suppose. I've done a certain amount of helping out in my father's firm. Gwen's doing something similar – or is it wireless operations? And Tilly'll be on the telephones I think.'

So the five of them from Hut J who had been thrown so incongruously together were now to be scattered again.

At the end of the three weeks they waited with all the others for their transport back to Didcot to begin on their new careers. They looked a very different collection of women from those who had arrived, all setting off to equip themselves with skills that a few weeks ago they would scarcely have dreamed of. Except for Gloria, who was vowing furiously that every meal she cooked would be sabotaged until they let her do something else.

'Burnt sodding porridge – that's what they'll get!' she yelled out of the back of the truck.

They parted with more emotion than they would ever have thought possible for such a mixed group of strangers within the space of three weeks.

CHAPTER 16

NOVEMBER 1943, AT SEA

The merchant ship *Donata Castle* slid slowly away from Southampton in a grey choppy sea and under a heavy winter sky.

Those who stood at the quayside saw that the decks were lined from bow to stern with the drab khaki colours of army personnel. Among them, for the moment cordoned off in their own separate section, were three hundred women of the British ATS.

It was a solemn hour for all those on the ship. They knew neither when they would be returning home, nor where the *Donata Castle* was bound. The land receded behind the stern, becoming less distinct until it shrank to a soft line on the horizon like a land in a dream. Then it was gone.

As if released, everyone began to move away from the rails of the ship. They had really left England now, so it was time to look forward instead of back. They needed some immediate purpose, and most made their way towards cabins and berths to sort out the rest of their belongings.

A slim, pale young woman with reddish brown hair and a rather perturbed expression was one of the last to turn away from the rail. As she did so, her eye was caught by another of the khaki-clad figures walking away from her on the gently swaying deck. A short young woman, dark hair curled round her ATS cap, a neat but somehow intensely purposeful walk . . .

'I say – Rose!'

The young woman turned, brown eyes searching out the voice. Then her serious face was suddenly smiling broadly. 'Gwen!'

They gave each other a strong hug, something unthinkable in their early army days.

'I didn't see you when we came on board,' Gwen exclaimed.

'I was late.' Rose was looking Gwen up and down. 'Well – you're a sight more pleased with yourself than when I last saw you!' She laughed. 'I thought there wasn't anyone I knew on board here. I *am* pleased to see you.'

'Oh, me too,' Gwen assured her. 'And I can't get over the sight of you. You look marvellous!'

It was true. The reliable army food and plentiful amounts of fresh air that Rose had had access to for the past two and a half years had improved her looks no end. She had gained weight, so that her cheeks were no longer gaunt, and her complexion a healthy pink. Her petite figure was now curvaceous instead of skinny, her rounded breasts and hips filling her uniform.

'Fancy you signing up for abroad!' Rose said, remembering the anxious girl she had first known at the Berkshire training camp. 'What about your mom? She must've had a fit.'

Gwen's expression suddenly turned stiff and obstinate. She glared back at Rose with blue eyes that held a new conviction. 'Mummy is having to fend for herself,' she said abruptly. For a second she wavered and looked appealingly at Rose. 'You must think me terribly hardhearted, but it's taken the war to make me see just how much my mother ruled my life.' She smiled. 'Come on. Let's go and get a cup of tea and have a good old chat. I want to know all about where you've been.'

They climbed down to the makeshift canteen and sat together with mugs of tea next to a porthole where the dark slant of the sea kept appearing as the ship rocked back and forth.

For a couple of minutes neither of them knew where

to begin. It was less painful to look to the future, with all its uncertainties, than to look back on the past couple of years of the war.

They had been two of the grimmest years anyone could remember. At home there had been the separation and uncertainty over loved ones, the privations of shorter and shorter rations, bitterly cold winters, and of course the bombing, things precious and familiar being destroyed all around. Across the world, what Churchill had in 1940 called 'the foulest and most soul-destroying tyranny' had swept on relentlessly. Those years had brought defeats on the eastern front in Russia, the Japanese advance through Malaya into Singapore, and the failed invasion of the Allied forces at Dieppe as they tried to get a foothold in occupied Europe.

Then, when things could not have looked bleaker, there was at last one overwhelmingly hopeful piece of news. General Montgomery and the Eighth Army had fought against German commander Rommel's forces in the deserts of North Africa. And they had triumphed at El Alamein in northern Egypt. There was a sense that the tide had turned. British and American forces had landed first in Sicily, then Italy. The balance of the war had shifted, but many of the memories Rose and Gwen looked back on now were associated with the darkest days of 1941 and 1942.

'Do you really drive those fearful trucks?' Gwen giggled. 'Silly question, I know. Girls do it all the time. But it looks so difficult.'

'You just learn it like any of the jobs,' Rose replied. 'But it was hard at first, I can tell you. When we got to Camberley, at the start I'd be at it day and night. When I wasn't driving I was dreaming about it. I'd wake up with the sheets all tied up round my legs with trying to double-declutch in my sleep!'

At first she had been astonished at the responsibilities that the army seemed willing to entrust to her. She had learned to drive anything: army pick-up trucks, fifteen hundredweight Bedford wagons, and the huge canvas-covered three-ton trucks. It seemed absolutely normal now that she should.

'So where were your postings?' Gwen wanted to know.

'Oh, all over – all HAA Batteries. First it was Lancashire, Widnes. I was driving the supplies, messages. At one place I even had to empty the lavs, oh my God! You needed to be patriotic to put up with Lancashire that winter. It were enough to freeze the balls off a brass monkey! In the March I went down near Winchester for a few months. And then it was Essex for the rest of the time. Tillingham Marshes, another ack-ack battery, trying to get the planes before they got to London.

'Then they asked me if I wanted my name down for abroad, so I thought, what the heck? I'm not at home anyway and I feel like a cuckoo in the nest when I'm back there. So I might just as well be even further away.'

'My feelings exactly,' Gwen agreed.

She told Rose that she had been sent to Sussex originally to do clerical work. But she had found it very tedious and had proved lucky in applying for a change.

'Once I'd managed to break away from home I thought I might as well go the whole hog! So I applied to train in Signals and as they were short at the time they agreed to let me go. I'm Royal Corps of Signals now.'

'By the way,' Gwen said, after Rose had fetched more of the warming tea. 'I heard news of a couple of the others we were with. Tilly got pregnant fairly early on and was released after the six months. And Gloria didn't last long as a cook – surprise, surprise. She served up such unspeakable food that they let her change after a couple of weeks. She's on a predictor at one of the ack-ack batteries somewhere round London.'

Rose grinned. 'Good for her. So she's getting the buggers after all.'

When Rose went back to her four-berth cabin, she found to her relief that she was alone. Wearily she sat down on her lower berth, leaning well forward so as not to bang her head on the one above. She rested her elbows on her khaki skirt and rubbed her eyes. The journey to Southampton after a couple of days of leave in Birmingham had been a strain. There had been several delays and she had wondered if she was going to miss embarkation.

The two days she had spent in Catherine Street had not been easy. She felt so changed, so enlarged by her experiences. The army had become her life for the time being. It was closer, more immediate and exciting, and in many ways easier.

She had been greeted like a hero by the neighbours, and she'd managed a reasonably cheery visit to Mrs Meredith, who was as delighted as if she was a physical extension of Alfie himself. Even Sid had seemed openly proud of her. Grace cooked the best meals she could manage on the rations, and the great treat for Rose was that they managed to get Edna over for twenty-four hours with Harry and the twins.

Billy and Susan had grown into robustly healthy-looking six-year-olds who were faring well on fresh eggs, country air and Edna's kindness. Rose hadn't seen them for two years, and she knew they could scarcely remember who she was. She couldn't help crying when they left, especially when Susan, forgetting Rose was her sister, said, 'Bye bye, Auntie Rose – it were ever so nice to meet you!'

'I wish I wasn't missing them growing up,' Rose said wistfully to Grace afterwards. 'They'll be so used to Edna when the war's over that they won't want to come home!'

Grace frowned. 'That's the best thing really, isn't it? No good having people swanning in and out of their lives. They want someone who's always about.'

Rose swallowed the reproach in silence, hurt but knowing she was right.

Grace was also growing in confidence. She had trained as a nursing auxiliary and worked several nights a week at the first aid post in the local baths. Rose knew without seeing her working how good she'd be at it. She was outwardly just as kind and warm a person as she'd always been, but Rose knew there was a new distance between them. They could not at present share the kind of closeness achieved by living with each other and sharing the same concerns.

George was still causing them worry, going off for several days at a time, although he always came back, and Grace told Rose she'd learned to live with it.

Being back in Catherine Street also brought back sharply Rose's grief at Dora's death and the huge gap it had left in her life. She could sense her father's loneliness even though he seldom spoke. Away in the army the loss felt less real.

With all the shadows of the pre-war years crouching round the house, and her feeling of being an outsider in her own family, she was glad to leave again, even with the sadness of not knowing when she would be back.

She sighed, sitting there in the half-light of the cabin. Other reminders of the past were tucked into her kit-bag. She drew out two more of the standard cards which she had received from Alfie. He was still in Felsig POW camp, apparently in good health. There were no other details. Rose stared for a long time at the two cards. They seemed to bear no relation at all to the Alfie she had known four years ago in Birmingham. She tried to picture his pale face, his kind expression, which she could only remember rather sketchily. She wondered in what ways the war would have changed him, as it had changed her. And suddenly she wished, for the first time in months, that she could see him. At least then maybe she could make up her mind how she felt about him. She still told people she was engaged. Partly because strictly speaking she was, and also because it was useful to avoid getting involved with all the forces men from whom she was constantly receiving attention and offers. Little of it was welcome. After Mr Lazenby she still found it hard to trust men, or even like most of them.

She had trusted Alfie. Memories of the good times

they had had together filled her mind. It was not easy, after all that had happened since, to remember the passive, dependent state she had fallen into when she was with him. She felt anything but passive and dependent now.

She put the cards aside and took out the other envelope that she was still carrying with her. Inside there was one letter on thin, wafer-like blue paper, and the beginning of another on a thicker, cream-coloured sheet. Rose lay down on her side, resting on one arm, and read them both again.

The blue paper letter gave only the central WAAF mailing address and the date: 2 September 1941.

Dear Rose Lucas,

I hope you won't mind my writing to you, but I felt it right that I should, and am sorry not to have done so sooner.

I'm afraid that what I have to tell you will come as a terrible shock. I am writing as a friend of Diana Harper-Watt. We were fellow WAAFs and mostly recently I have been posted with her. Diana was killed last month when she was travelling up to London from our base. The train received a direct hit before it pulled into Waterloo and only about half the passengers aboard survived.

Diana's mother has requested that as a close friend I look through her things down here to see if there was anything that needed tying up. In the course of doing so I found your letter dated 30 March this year, and also the enclosed letter that Diana had obviously started to write in reply. Knowing that you were also a friend, may I send my condolences for the sorrow we all share at her death? She was a marvellous person. I'm sure I don't need to tell you.

With my kindest regards to you and apologies for bearing such ill news,
Celia Ravenscroft.

Diana's own letter consisted of only a few lines.

My dear Rose,

Thank you so much for writing to me. I shall truly
treasure that letter. My apologies that I've taken so long
to reply – WAAF life is so hectically busy. I'm sure you
know from your own service life. Your letter made me
feel so, so sad, I can't tell you

It broke off there as if she had been called away. And
that was all. It was so tantalizing, this minute taste of
her thoughts. If she had finished the letter, at least
Rose would have had a fuller picture of her, of the
person she had become. The letter and their brief meeting
gave her just enough to know that things could heal. 'My
dear Rose', she read over and over again. 'My dear
Rose'. She had long ago written a brief note of condol-
ence to Ronald and Catherine and had received a brief,
though warm letter in reply. She knew her own letter
explaining herself would have reached them among
Diana's possessions.

She read the letters again, and then climbed back up
to the deck with them in her hand. The ship was travelling
at a steady speed now, and she stood looking out over the
water with the rush of the cold wind against her cheeks.
Standing by the rail, she thought of the first time she had
seen Diana in her bedroom at the vicarage. Her beautiful,
curly-haired, generous friend who had accepted her
immediately and without hesitation. And of that last
time, her blue eyes hurt and questioning, on New Street
Station. And she remembered for a moment Diana's face
that day when she saw the strong man in his chains
struggling to loose himself inside the heavy sack. She
closed her eyes against the pain of it, hoping fervently
that Diana's death had been instant, that she had not
lingered there, trapped and suffocating in the railway
carriage.

She wanted to open her mouth and scream and scream
into the wind. Instead she tore the letters into tiny cream
and blue pieces. When she opened her hands the wind

whisked the light fragments away instantly towards the stern of the ship.

'They've taken the ropes down between the quarters,' an excited voice announced at the door of Rose's cabin. 'Now we'll see some fun!'

They were a week into the voyage and until this point the male and female troops had been kept firmly apart. The ropes across the passages separating the two were guarded at night, and fraternizing was strictly forbidden.

Now everything suddenly became more relaxed. The sky was a pale, clear blue and, though not hot, the sun was shining and it was a great deal warmer than it had been in England. The sea had turned a rich green-blue, its surface ruffled by a strong breeze. Conditions for the voyage so far had been perfect. Now they were allowed the run of the ship, and romances started to blossom in every nook and cranny. Promises were made, weddings planned, and it all felt like a fantastic holiday reprieve after the dark winter of war they had left behind.

But of course the war was never far away.

'I wonder where we're going,' Gwen kept saying as she and Rose paced restlessly up and down that morning. They spent most of their time on the ship together.

'I think it's Australia,' Rose said. 'I mean they've given us all that lightweight uniform, haven't they? Must be somewhere hot, wherever it is.'

'It could be quite a number of places, couldn't it?' Gwen said, staring rather absently out over the endless water. 'But it's awfully unsettling not knowing.'

They were to find out sooner than they realized. Just as Gwen, screwing up her blue eyes, had said to Rose, 'I say – it's not my imagination, is it? That is land over there?' an order came that they were all to assemble on the deck where Rose and Gwen were already standing.

When the three hundred women were standing smartly

169

to attention in the bright sunlight, their new Company Sergeant Major Marjorie Keaton told them she had an important announcement to make. She was a tall, thin, pleasant-faced woman with large teeth that made her look as if she was permanently on the verge of smiling.

'Some of you may already have noticed that we're sailing pretty close to land,' she shouted, trying to make her voice carry as far as possible. 'I am now authorized to tell you where we are to be posted. Later today we shall pass through the Straits of Gibraltar – between the coast of Spain and the north coast of Africa,' she explained carefully to those whose geography was not what it might be. Three hundred pairs of eyes gazed at her intently.

'We shall then enter the Mediterranean. From there, if conditions stay as they are, it will take us approximately six days to reach our destination. The ship will dock at Naples. The orders for our company are that we staff the new Allied Forces Headquarters which have been transferred to Caserta, seventeen miles to the north of Naples.' They all saw her smile. 'Evidently our work is to be housed in a royal palace. That'll make a change for some of us, won't it?'

A wave of appreciative murmurs and laughs passed through the crowd.

Then CSM Keaton's face grew solemn again. 'Enjoy the rest of the voyage,' she said. 'There will be a great deal of work to do when we arrive. Every effort will be needed in order to help the progress of our forces northwards.'

The women's assembly broke up, all chattering excitedly as they moved off to different parts of the ship.

'So much for Australia!' Gwen teased.

'Italy?' Rose seemed completely bemused by the news. 'We're really going to be living in Italy? I hardly know a thing about the place. Doesn't seem real, does it?'

That afternoon, the ship slowly negotiated the Straits of Gibraltar. People lined the rails of the decks pointing out the famous Rock, monkeys and all. And there were constant cat-calls from the men to the ATS on board: 'Come over here!' 'Give us a kiss girls!' 'Go on – get your knees brown!'

As soon as they were through the straits they all noticed a number of small boats peeling off from the Spanish coast and homing in on the *Donata Castle* before she had a chance to pick up speed again. As they drew in closer everyone leaned over the rails to watch, and started cheering and whistling when they realized what was going on. In the painted boats dark Spanish men stood up unsteadily, their legs braced against the sea's movement.

'Stockings!' they shouted up in accents which sounded strange to English ears. 'You buy stockings – silk, nylon – very good?'

Silver coins, half-crowns and shillings, started to rain down from the *Donata Castle*. The Spaniards passed up the stockings on long thin poles. There were squeals of excitement from some of the ATS on board as the goods were examined for their colour, length and lack of holes.

'Here – let me treat you to a pair, may I?'

Rose and Gwen turned to find out who the rather smarmy voice belonged to. A strongly built, red-haired fellow was standing behind them smiling. Openly he looked the two of them over and targeted Rose as the more obvious looker of the two with those sultry dark eyes.

'Let me buy you some of the merchandise they're offering?'

Rose returned his stare quite indifferently and said abruptly, 'No thanks.' She turned back to watch the noisy, hectic scene on the water below.

The man smiled knowingly at Gwen and winked at her. 'Well, what about you?'

Gwen, flattered by the attention and rather embarrassed by Rose's lack of grace, nodded, smiling and blushing.

'My name's Brian by the way,' the young man said. He pushed between them and called out, 'I say – over here!'

One of the vivid blue and red boats sped over on the bright water, the boatman rowing eagerly.

Brian tossed a half-crown down and the boatman reached up, trying to snatch it from the air. When he'd passed the nylons up on the pole he made off again at high speed.

'Well, that is kind of you,' Gwen said, beaming at him.

She held up the stockings to admire them, and Rose turned to watch. She saw Gwen's smile drop into an expression of horror and embarrassment. The stockings only had one foot between them.

Brian grabbed hold of the one and a half nylon legs he had just bought, shouting, 'Of all the damned cheek! Come back here, you thieving, cheating . . .'

He disappeared along the deck yelling helplessly down at the boatmen between everyone else's shoulders. If he had been listening, he would have heard Rose's unrestrained cackles of laughter.

Gwen, one hand clapped over her mouth, started to giggle too.

'Oh – his face!' Rose cried, straightening up and wiping her eyes. 'I'll never forget it as long as I live!'

When they had stopped laughing, Gwen said to Rose, 'You don't like men very much, do you?'

'Oh – some of them are all right.' Rose's black eyebrows pulled into a slight frown. 'I just can't stand the ones who think they can buy a favour before they even know your flaming name.'

Rose sensed they were approaching land even before she was out of bed. It was only five-thirty in the morning, but she found she was completely awake, her heart pounding, and she knew she would get no more sleep.

When she'd dressed, very quietly so as not to disturb the other three in the cabin, she went outside into the bright, chilly morning.

There it was, nearer even than she had expected. The

curve of the bay was blurred as yet, so that she could not make out any clear details. She could only form an impression of the brightness of it, the buildings near the top of the slice of land must be dazzling white. She stared, quite mesmerized, as the *Donata Castle* inched nearer and nearer.

There were only a couple of other people out on the deck at that hour. She noticed a young private standing not far away, staring with fascinated attention in the same direction as herself. She was struck by the concentrated look of interest on his face as he gazed towards the land, unaware of her watching him. She saw that his short hair, just showing round the edges of his army beret, was very light brown, almost blond. He was slim, not especially muscular in build, and he stood gracefully resting his weight on one foot as he leaned on the rail.

He turned suddenly and saw Rose watching him. Without smiling or changing his expression, he walked slowly along the deck and stood beside her.

'Incredibly beautiful, isn't it?' he said. He had a soft voice, his accent southern, she thought, and quite well spoken.

'I've never seen anything like it,' Rose said. She spoke quietly and rather correctly, affected by his serious presence.

He turned and pointed back to one of the open arms of the bay. 'That's Vesuvius,' he told her, indicating the grey, cone-shaped mountain rising up from the sea. 'The volcano. Quite spectacular. I hadn't realized just how near it would be.'

'How did you know about that?' she asked.

'I've done a bit of reading, that's all. I've always been fascinated by volcanoes. I didn't know we'd end up here of course.'

For the next hour the two of them stood side by side, almost entirely in silence, watching the lines of Naples slowly grow clearer. The city seemed to tumble down to the sea in layers, made up of a hotch-potch of terraces, with houses and trees stepped at different levels down the cliff. The vivid blue sea lapped at its feet and, above, a few puffs of white cloud were the only marks on the sky.

The white brilliance gradually turned to more ambiguous greys and yellows. They could see trees, and roads like nail scratches zig-zagging down the steep cliff. Gradually, drawing into the port, the briny sea smell became obscured by the stench of sewage. Any illusion that they were entering a shining, pearl-like city melted away rapidly as the *Donata Castle* nosed towards the remnants of the heavily bombed port area of Naples.

CHAPTER 17

'Blimey – what a pong!'

'See Naples and die, smell Naples and you *will* die. Not far wrong!'

'What the hell must it be like in August?'

Kit-bags slung on shoulders, they all made their way down the plank walkway from the *Donata Castle*, a long stream of khaki-coloured movement in the warm air of what was now almost midday in Naples. They walked briskly away from the sea to the trucks which were waiting to transport them to their new billets. Everyone was glad to be back on land.

Around them the stench suggested a city festering like a corpse left for days in the sun. The Allied bombing of the port area, before the Germans had finally given up the city in September, had wrecked the sewers and cut off the mains water supply. The two hundred thousand already impoverished Neapolitans the bombing had left without homes were camping out where they could among the rubble of bricks and unrecovered bodies. It was a city stinking not only of charred wood and sewage, but also of disease, starvation and death.

It was early enough in the day for the transport to take them straight to Caserta.

'You ought to be driving us,' Gwen teased Rose as they climbed up into one of the trucks. Rose didn't reply.

'By the way, who was that feller I saw you with this morning?' Gwen chatted on in the back of the truck. 'He looked awfully nice, I thought.'

For a moment Rose stared blankly at her. 'Oh – you mean when we were coming in? I never asked his name.'

'You're hopeless,' Gwen told her.

Rose wasn't in the mood for talking. She had made sure they had been almost the last to get into the truck so as to be near the back. She didn't want to miss a single opportunity to take in this new place.

As the trucks rumbled further into the city, Rose saw people in the streets, some shouting and waving, standing in front of the rubble or the dusty husks of houses. Some were hawking a selection of their posses. ions on the pavements. Dark-eyed, scrawny children, wearing only the filthiest remnants of clothes, ran after them for a few yards yelling things they couldn't hear. Faces looked pinched and pallid even under the dark skin. In contrast, the Allied servicemen on the streets, who came from many different countries, looked well fed and full of muscular energy.

There was little traffic. The Neapolitans had been starved of petrol along with everything else, and the trucks passed only some bony mules pulling carts and a couple of very decrepit old cars with patches riveted on to the tyres.

There was a lot to take in at once, but one detail which didn't escape anyone's notice was that across the entrance to each side street off the main road was strung a wire bearing a bold army sign: 'OFF LIMITS – OUT OF BOUNDS. VD AREA'.

'That inspires no end of confidence, doesn't it?' someone said.

Most of the comments were adverse.

'Of course, they don't live, in places like this,' a voice said close to Rose. 'They merely exist.'

Rose turned and saw a fair, milky-skinned face, freckled and healthy looking. She shouted over the noise of the truck, 'What part are you from then?'

'Me? Oh – Buckinghamshire,' the young woman shrilled.

'And you know all about being poor, obviously,' Rose

bawled back at her. Even under those conditions the sarcasm communicated itself quite clearly.

The young woman looked very taken aback. Rose felt Gwen nudge her hard with her elbow. 'D'you have to be so damn prickly all the time?' she yelled in Rose's ear.

Her touchiness was part of a more complicated emotion. Almost from the moment she had caught sight of the Italian coastline, and with increasing force since they had docked, she had felt drawn to the place. As she looked out at the old, splendid buildings of central Naples and saw at the same time the plight of its people, a powerful sense of kinship came over her. These hungry, downcast Neapolitans seemed, astonishingly, part of her. She didn't even know yet whether she liked the place. All she could be sure of, instinctively, was that she was meant to be here.

As they reached the northern edge of the city Rose caught sight of a huge cemetery which overlooked the Bay of Naples, containing some graves the size of small stone houses. Then they were away on the road north to Caserta. They passed small villages with crumbling tile roofs, fields showing a down of tiny green growth surrounded by fig trees and vines which had fingered across and clung on to the trunks.

It was slow going. There had been rain in recent days and the road suface was covered with a slippery layer of mud. The journey took over an hour and a half, and on the way they saw several Jeeps overturned in the ditches by the side of the road.

'Goodness, someone needs driving lessons!' Gwen shouted when they'd passed the third Jeep.

'They're all American ones!' Rose called back with a grin. Now out of the city, she was exhilarated by the new countryside, which even in winter looked so much lusher than England, with the dark shape of Vesuvius behind them pushing steam clouds into the sky.

Caserta was a small town of faded red roofs and cream and yellow paint peeling from the fronts of old buildings. Rose took in the wooden shutters on the windows, the tiny wrought-iron balconies, the slim square tower of a church. But the town itself seemed completely dwarfed in size and significance when they caught sight of the palace. There were gasps of astonishment from those who could see out.

'Is that where we're going to live?' Rose asked.

'I don't think so,' Gwen said. 'That's the headquarters, I think, where we'll work. We're going to our billets now.'

It was during their first viewing of the inside of the eighteenth-century palace the next day that they were to discover the full extent of its majesty. The vast central block of rooms was the royal apartments. It was possible to walk through those for a long time without finding a room that looked in the least commonplace. Every floor and doorway was a work of art in different colours and textures of Carrara marble; the ceilings soared above, resplendent with gold and rich-coloured oil paintings and intricate designs of paintwork and stucco. Each room was different, and each magnificently designed. At first the sight was impressive and awe-inspiring. But after walking round for any length of time it cloyed and overwhelmed.

'It's like hogging a whole plate of cream cakes all at once, isn't it?' Gwen commented wearily. 'Rather indecent really.'

'Out the back's the best bit,' Rose agreed. 'Now that is beautiful.'

From the back entrance to the palace an enormous landscaped garden extended as far as the eye could make out any detail. A narrow road ran straight through it, thinning to a pencil width as it climbed the tree-covered mountain in the far distance.

The real glory of the garden lay in the fact that from a far point up the mountain water rushed in cascades over the rocks. The water was channelled into a long line of stone tanks, from where it fell splashing into a green pool. Watching over this stood a semicircle of stone statues. As a recreation ground for the huge number of forces people

178

who were to be living in the area it could not have looked better.

Their billet, a mile from the palace, had previously been a hospital. It was a stark white building, housing groups of sixteen of them in blocks which each extended off a long central corridor. Rose and Gwen made sure they took beds in the same block, along with the young freckled blonde Rose'd had words with in the truck.

She latched on to them straight away. 'My name's Wilhelmina,' she announced.

Rose grimaced and said, 'Oh my God,' flinging her kit-bag on the bed.

'Is she always so rude?' Wilhelmina asked Gwen.

Rose grinned repentantly. 'Only when there's an R in the month. But for heaven's sake, we can't carry on calling you Wilhel— whatever it is. What in God's name did they call you that for?'

'Most people call me Willy,' the girl said apologetically.

'And what's your name?' Gwen asked the solidly built young woman who had taken the bed on the other side of her. She had dark brown, rather greasy hair, cut in an abrupt bob round the bottom of her ears.

'I'm Madge,' she said gruffly. 'And before you ask, I'm a driver, and I come from Leeds.'

'Rose is a driver.' Gwen pointed her out.

Madge put her hands on her broad waistline and stared at Rose. 'Where you from, then?'

When Rose told her, she said, 'You look all right. At least you're not from down south – well, not quite, anyway.'

'Glad I qualify for the human race,' Rose quipped. She took to Madge straight away with her straight talking. Eyeing her up and down she asked, 'Do they use you to jack up the trucks when a wheel needs changing? You could do it with one hand I should think!'

Gwen and Willy looked anxiously at Madge to see how she'd take this. She gave a great snort of laughter. 'They

179

just call me in when the blokes can't get their nuts undone!'

Everyone else joined in the shrieks of laughter.

After they had returned to their unpacking there was a sudden squeak from Willy. 'This is blood here – look!'

They went over to where she was kneeling by the bed, peering anxiously at some reddish brown stains on the wall. 'Doesn't that look like blood to you?'

'It does rather,' Gwen said. 'Goodness, what a thought!'

'Well, what do you expect in a hospital?' Madge said. 'That's why the beds still feel warm.' She gave her great bellow of laughter again. 'Don't worry. I think some American WACs have stayed here already. You won't catch anything!'

Life soon began to settle into a routine. Rose was assigned a three-ton truck and was soon occupied in taking people from their billets to the palace for work and back, bringing in the loads of rations from the Divisional Headquarters and transporting the laundry and all the other requirements of the huge community they lived in. It was often her job to carry the German prisoners from the POW camp near by to the compound where they worked. And there were nurses to transport to the hospital, lifts to be given to officers in pick-up trucks, and messages to be relayed. All day she was in and out of some vehicle or other, refuelling them, sometimes repairing them, but, more often than not, on the move.

She wouldn't have changed her job with anyone in the service. At the beginning of the day she climbed up on to the hard bench seat of her truck to handle the big steering wheel, with a load of passengers in the canvas-covered area behind. The seats in the trucks were high, but she still needed to add a firm cushion to give her a good view out. Even though most of the journeys were fairly short, she was exhilarated seeing this new place, the villages around Caserta strung together by muddy tracks, the ragged *contadini* working the fields, mules pulling carts and hens bustling in consternation across the road in front of the truck.

Though it was winter the weather was better by far than it would be at home. The cool, often sunny days were more like an English spring, so there was not the struggle to wield a spanner with hands she could barely move for the cold. She felt no envy at all of Gwen, who spent her shifts on duty receiving the coded messages from her wireless set deep in the cavernous basement area of the palace.

'It's odd, isn't it,' Willy said to Rose and Madge one day, 'how whenever we go out anywhere for fun we have to be chaperoned to the hilt, yet you two go driving off all over the place on your own.'

'Typical army logic I'd say,' Gwen commented.

At Christmas they did the best they could to brighten up their sleeping block. They hung home-made coloured paper streamers across the bare white walls and brought in cuttings of greenery from outside to decorate the corners and windows. Some of the German POWs had also made little wooden Christmas trees which they put on the windowsills. The place still looked pretty bleak, but the decorations did something to soften the hard angles of the room.

'I think it's going to be a good Christmas,' Gwen said the day before Christmas Eve as they were all getting ready for bed. She sat down on her bed beside Rose's. 'In fact, I have to admit I much prefer Christmas in the army to being at home.'

'It's not the same without the kids around,' Rose said sadly. 'That's what I really miss. But they're not even at home any more.'

Gwen reached over and took Rose's hand. 'Come on – let's try and be cheerful,' she said. 'I know it's not the New Year yet, but let's talk about resolutions. What great things are you going to do in 1944?'

Rose, her chin set in her determined way, and just waiting for Willy's look of bewilderment, said, 'I'm going to learn to speak Italian.'

CHAPTER 18

By the beginning of January 1944 the Germans had established a defensive line across the shin of Italy known as the Gustav Line. At its central point was the Benedictine monastery set in craggy isolation on the peak of a high mountain called Monte Cassino. The Allied troops, made up of British, American and many other nationalities, found themselves unable to progress further north. They were enduring a gruelling winter camped out among the sharp ridges and muddy gullies of the Abruzzi Mountains.

In the middle of the month the Allies, convinced that the Germans had taken possession of the monastery as an observation post, began to bombard Monte Cassino. It was the beginning of a long, mainly futile and mutually destructive battle. And on 22 January, Allied forces landed on the coast at Anzio, a point north of the Gustav Line, as a way of trying to break the stalemate. However, instead of moving immediately north from there, they delayed, became trapped by German forces, and were once again unable to make progress. The destruction of Monte Cassino continued.

In Caserta, in the Allied-occupied south, things remained relatively peaceful. It was possible to work each day at the royal palace and almost forget that there was a war going on.

One morning in late January, a REME engineer, Tony Schaffer, was walking across the open area at the front of the palace, enjoying the feel of the sun through his cotton shirt. He noticed a three-ton army truck pull up in front of the building. The small figure of Rose Lucas jumped from the cab. Tony smiled and headed over to her. She flexed her legs, stiff after sitting for several hours, and reached up into the cab for her canvas bag.

'Hello Rose,' Tony said. 'Buzzing about as usual?'

She turned to look at him and a smile transformed her thoughtful face. 'Hello Tony. Yes, I've been trying to keep the army fed again.'

Since she had been in Caserta she had a number of times run into this young man with whom she'd had her first sight of Naples on the *Donata Castle*.

'I'm just off for a cuppa,' she said. 'You got time for one?'

The more Rose saw of Tony, the more she liked him. Her automatic caution in relating to men had been allayed by his own obvious shyness. He wasn't one of those cocky sods, she thought. He didn't put any pressure on you. He wasn't like some of the other blokes who wanted to kiss you the minute they'd said hello, if not before. He seemed to want friendship, and he was interesting to talk to.

They strolled down the curving path to the palace which ran along the front of one of the stable buildings. Rose was telling Tony about where she'd been. He liked the directness of her conversation, the spontaneity which had not been curbed by too much education, but which made her seem to him somehow vulnerable. He felt very protective towards Rose, unlike a number of other chaps around who were put off by the sharpness of her tongue.

'You really enjoy your job, don't you?' he said. 'It's good to hear someone who's not constantly full of complaints. That's the trouble with institutional life – the way it leads to this constant carping about everything.'

'I do like it,' Rose agreed, thinking suddenly what a solid person Tony was. He reminded her with a pang of Sam, though he was less stodgy. 'I never thought I'd do something like this,' she went on. 'I mean what other job gives you the chance to—?'

She stopped talking abruptly, with a gasp that made Tony look round, concerned that she was in pain.

'What's the matter?' he asked. She didn't answer.

In front of them, a tall figure had turned out of one of the stable doorways close to the palace and was walking towards them. He was dark haired, with wide, muscular shoulders which looked constrained by the khaki tunic top. Rose noticed he was walking with a slight limp as he came forward whistling 'Run Rabbit Run' with extra flourishes and patting his breast pocket as if in search of cigarettes. Despite the limp, she would have recognized the jaunty, slightly bow-legged gait anywhere.

As he reached them he nodded, interrupting the whistling to say 'Morning', and was clearly going to carry on past.

'Michael?'

He stopped and turned, clearly not having any idea who she was.

'Michael Gillespie.' It was not even a question. She knew it was him.

He stared at her. 'You sound like another Brummy but who the—?'

Rose said just one word: 'Lazenby's.'

She saw Michael register the word. Then he slowly pointed a finger at her, still unable to believe it. 'Jesus – if it's not little Rosie!'

And to her astonishment he came forward and picked her up easily by the waist, swinging her round and laughing, and Rose laughed with him, completely delighted to see him.

'Oh, Michael,' she said breathlessly as he finally put her down. 'You always were a mad sod!'

Suddenly she remembered Tony and introduced him. The two men nodded at each other. Tony muttered, 'Pleased to meet you,' and Michael said, 'All right Tony?' and they all stood together in the bright morning sunlight.

'Well,' Michael laughed. 'Lazenby's. That's real old times now, isn't it?' His memories gradually began to come back to him. 'You did a bunk from Lazenby's,

184

didn't you? What got into you? Old Lazenby came in blinding away one morning, saying you'd gone off without a please or a thank you and he'd have to get someone else.'

'Did he?' Rose said drily. 'Well it wasn't quite like that. Let's just say me number came up. Anyhow – what on earth are you doing here? Got time for a cuppa?'

'No – 'fraid not. I'm late already. I'm after having a bath – the first in a long while I can tell you. And now I'm clean and fit, and this is sound again' – he stamped his left foot – 'I've got to rejoin my unit pronto. I've had sick leave. Smashed me ankle up jumping off a wagon soon after we got here. Not much of a war wound eh?'

'What division are you?' Tony asked him.

'Infantry,' Michael said. 'One of the poor buggers who goes up front and cops all the shit – 'scuse me, Rosie. These bust-up bones down here have got me out of quite a bit of it so far. There's no putting it off now though.'

'You're not going to Cassino are you?' Rose asked, horrified.

'Not Cassino, no. Further east along the front some-where. Dodging the mines.'

Rose's eyes showed her dismay, so that Michael bent down and kissed her on the cheek. 'You're a sight for sore eyes,' he said. 'Look at you in that uniform – you're a picture. I've got to go now, but don't you worry, Rosie. I'll see you in Corporation Street when it's all over!'

And he backed away, clowning around and singing 'We'll meet again, don't know where, don't know when!' with a flourish of his arm, and then he was gone.

'Mad sod,' Rose said again, and realized suddenly that she had tears in her eyes.

'Are you all right?' Tony asked. 'You look a bit shaky. I take it Michael is an old flame of yours?'

'Oh.' Rose was startled. 'No. No – not really. I worked with him. It's just – things keep happening like that. Bits of the past and bits of home blowing in when you're somewhere else and not expecting it.'

As they sat drinking a cup of tea Rose found herself

telling Tony about Lazenby's and Michael and the sort of work she had done there. She didn't explain why she'd left. Tony sat listening, his grey eyes attentive, his large hands curved round his mug.

'Sorry,' she said after a while. 'I'm running on again.'

Tony smiled. Rose liked the way his wide mouth with its generous lips made his smile look completely wholehearted.

'That's all right,' he said. 'I was enjoying hearing about it. Your life's been so different from mine.'

Tony had already told her that he came from a village in Sussex and that his father had died when he was five. He and his brother and sister had been brought up by their mother. Tony had been an apprentice engineer when the war started.

'You've had a decent education, haven't you?' she asked him.

'Well – we had a good local school,' he agreed. 'I think I educated myself really. I was the sort of child who sat reading *Encyclopaedia Britannica* and filled my mind up with a whole collection of apparently useless snippets of information. It's surprising how often they come in handy though.'

'We never had books in our house, except a few a friend lent me now and then. I remember reading *Treasure Island* out in the lav to get a bit of peace. Someone always came knocking on the door sooner or later though. I thought I was going to surprise them all and become a teacher. Some hope.'

'But just because you haven't had all the chances doesn't mean . . .' Tony saw Rose was watching him very seriously as if hungering to be given assurance. 'I mean intelligence just shines out of you. Look – there are a lot of well-educated ATS here, but how many of them are taking the trouble to try and learn Italian like you?'

Rose shook her head. 'I dunno. I don't understand a lot of the people here. We've been given the chance of a lifetime really, haven't we? To come and live in this country, which is fascinating – to me anyway. And all most of them can think about is the next social and what bloke they can get hold of . . . It's not the only thing is it? They all live as if they're still in England. I mean, what the hell's the point of that? We'll be back there sooner or later and none of them'll be any the wiser.'

'Oh, I agree – although my goodness, it can be a harsh place.' Into his mind flashed the uncomfortable image of a warehouse in Naples where a misguided friend had taken him a couple of weeks before. All around inside, women waited impassively to give their bodies there and then to any man, in return for tins of army rations. The men had queued awkwardly at the door. Ashamed and revolted, Tony had put down some food and left. He didn't feel he could tell Rose about this so he just said, 'You need to be careful.'

'Yes, but I want to see a lot more,' she said. 'More of Naples for a start. Get to know people. I've found someone to help with the Italian already.'

She told Tony she had got to know an old woman across the other side of Caserta who did tailoring.

'She's called Signora Mandetta. She's making me a skirt at the moment – you know, she's only got that black stuff like the old ladies wear. Anyway, she said she'd help with my Italian. I think she likes the company, so I pop down whenever I get the chance.' Rose sighed as they stepped out into the sunshine. 'Touble is, to get anywhere much there's all this ruddy chaperone lark.'

'Well . . .' Tony looked at her shyly. 'Would I do?'

Suddenly Rose felt full of confusion. She had seen Tony as a friend. Was he now asking her on a date? What did he expect from her?

'I . . .' she stumbled over the words and then decided to cope with anything that happened when the time came. 'Thank you. That'd be very nice.'

'Right,' Tony told her. 'If you want to see Naples, there's going to be transport over on Friday evening. Let's go, shall we?'

Rose nodded, excited, noticing with relief that unlike most people he didn't refer to the leisure transport as 'passion wagons'.

It took them just over an hour to reach Naples. The sun was setting over the bay as they wound through the evening clamour of the city's streets. The uncertain light, and the familiar stench, to which was added a smokiness as evening fires were lit among the rubble, made them hurry towards the familiarity of the Naafi to spend the evening drinking and dancing.

Even over that short distance they were surrounded by a gaggle of children, their hair caked in filth, most wearing the meagrest of rags. The boys gave out gruff adult cries, 'Ey – ey!' they shouted, bony hands prodding at the well-fed foreigners, fingers snapping for attention. They wanted food, cigarettes, anything that was on offer.

'You come!' one of them shouted at Tony. 'My sister pretty! *Mia sorella molto bella* – ey, jig a jig!'

Some members of the party, in slight panic, threw cigarettes and coins. The children scrambled for them like wrangling birds.

'My God – they're starving!' Rose said, horrified, once they had entered the relative comfort of the club. She had been moved almost to tears by the sight of them.

One curly-haired boy who could only have been two or three had stood silently, his huge brown eyes staring, his small hand stretched out to them. He had been covered from head to foot in filth. 'Oh, I wish I could've taken that little one back with me and looked after him!' she said.

Tony smiled at her. 'There must be thousands out there like him,' he told her. 'You can't feed them all. Let's just try and enjoy the evening, shall we?'

Rose was beginning to look disgruntled. 'We're not going to see a lot of Naples sat in here, are we? Home from bleeding home again.'

Couples sat round the tables laughing and drinking. A

band was playing songs of home: 'The Lambeth Walk', 'There'll Be Bluebirds Over' and, as ever, 'In the Mood'.

As Rose sat beside Tony they were joined by another fair-haired lad who Tony introduced as Alex. He was a fellow engineer and the two of them were soon chatting beside her. Opposite them, a chap called Stan from Huddersfield was trying to entertain everyone by telling jokes. The ATS girl with him kept snuggling up like a kitten, resting her head on his shoulder, giggling. After a quarter of an hour of this Rose could have happily socked the pair of them.

Lightly she nudged Tony, who turned a little apologetically from his conversation with Alex.

'I'm just going to find the Ladies,' she murmured.

She walked towards the front entrance where there was a small reception desk, as if to enquire. Then, casually glancing back towards the table to check none of them was watching her, she walked to the door. A moment later she was standing alone out on the street.

CHAPTER 19

She knew she needed to move fast. Her eyes adjusted quickly to the dark of the unlit city. Now that the Germans had moved out of Naples it was their turn to bomb it, so the inhabitants were still constrained by a curfew and blackout. When she reached the end of the street the Piazza Municipio opened out in front of her. In the gloom a huge building loomed up, round, dark turrets at its corners, and she remembered having driven past it. It was the Castel Nuovo.

She made the mistake of stopping for a moment to get her bearings. The sea was a whisper to her left. From somewhere else she could hear a wheezing, squeaking sound as if someone was playing a very old and asthmatic concertina. She heard carts go by, creaking to the exhausted clop-clop of the mules' hoofs, and a number of shadowy figures passed her in the darkness, some of them in uniform.

And then she felt a hand grip her. She jumped, giving a loud gasp, feeling bony fingers clasping her lower arm. She turned to see a minute old lady standing beside her whose body was bent forward so that her shoulders were rounded into a grotesque hump and she had to twist her head round to look up. Her mouth appeared like a terrible empty hole in the darkness and Rose could make no sense of the cracked whimpering noises she was making. In revulsion and panic of which she was immediately ashamed, she jerked her arm down to rid herself of the goblin-like figure beside her and walked away very fast. She began to hear other voices calling out to her from people she could barely see.

Rose knew she had no definite way of finding her way back once she left the main square. But she had been taken over by her old drive to press on and explore, and it would not let her turn away. She turned her back on the sea, her stomach churning with fear and exhilaration, and walked quickly towards the dark, mouth-like openings of the side streets. She could just make out a pale OFF LIMITS sign over her head, suspended in the smoky air. She felt as if she was watching herself from the outside and not really responsible for what she was doing: an ignorant, reckless foreign woman heading into the blackness of the slum streets; and thought, I must be off my head.

And then she was inside, or that was how it seemed: that these streets were the real heart of the city. It was even darker here, the sides of the buildings looming on either side of her very close together, so that looking up she could just make out a ribbon of sky above her head between them. There were a couple of stars showing their minute clear light. Around her the shadows were thick and menacing. She had no idea whether anyone was watching her, but ahead she could see a faint flickering light which must have come from a candle burning in one of the *bassi*. Further along the street she became aware of an orange glow playing on the outlines of the buildings. She could hear voices, women shouting, and somewhere a man was singing.

There was no chance of walking very fast. There was too little light and the thick paving slabs underfoot were littered with rubble from the destruction wrought by the bombing and such rubbish as the Neapolitans could spare lay rotting and urine soaked on the street. Among the stones and chunks of wood, Rose felt her foot slide on something rounded and yielding and nearly cried out in revulsion.

As she moved along, now and then she felt hands clutching at her. She held her bag clutched tightly to her chest, cursing herself for bringing it. She pushed people away with a roughness born of fear and panic. She was beginning to realize just how foolish she had been to come.

I'll just go a bit further and then I'll get myself out of here, she said to herself. She was breathless with fright.

As she drew nearer the glow of the fire she saw that it was burning in the shell of what had once been a tall building like the rest around them. Some lower sections of the outer wall were still standing. Inside was a chaos of stone and timber with beams jutting across at odd angles to the floor and heaps of rubble. In a space among the obviously dangerous ruin, what looked like two or three families were clustered round the darting flames. The stench of drains was even worse here. She watched the circle of people crowded round the fire over which a large cooking pot was balanced on a makeshift support.

She stopped for a few seconds, only to find herself surrounded by clamouring children. The shadows of the fire wavered over their faces, and Rose felt herself unable to move from fear and helplessness.

'I haven't got anything for you,' she shouted. 'Go away – leave me alone. *Va te!*' Adults, attracted by the noise, were joining the children. She was crowded in by stinking bodies, all shouting and groping at her, moving in like vultures.

'Leave me alone,' she cried again. 'Let me go!'

Only once before had she felt such fear: that November evening in Mr Lazenby's office. But here she was also aware that she could disappear and never be seen again in this dark, fetid warren. An image pressed on her mind of the crowd carving her up and roasting pieces of her on sticks by the fire.

She tried to back away from them, hitting out in panic at the grabbing fingers. Someone wrenched her bag out of her hands and made off fast into the darkness. She found herself pressed up against the crumbling stones of the building opposite the fire. In despair she clamped her arms across her chest and shut her eyes tight.

She sensed a ripple of movement and the clamour around her quietened. She opened her eyes just as strong, male fingers gripped one of her upper arms and another hand reached roughly round her back and wrapped tightly over her mouth so that she had no chance to make a sound. The man shouted a few rough words to the people around who stepped back to let them through. Without loosening his hold on her, the man half dragged her along the street and round a corner.

They stopped, and still gripped by one arm, she heard him opening a lock. In the dim light she could make out a huge wooden gateway. Then a small door set into it swung open and she was pushed over the step and inside. She heard the dull slam of the door behind her and his key turning again in the lock.

He released her slowly, and she could hear him breathing heavily beside her. He stood in silence for a moment, and then uttered one angry word: '*Pazza!*'

Madwoman.

From then on it was like a dream. Rose realized they were standing in the entrance to an inner courtyard. There was a scratching sound as the man lit a match. He handed her a thick, white candle.

'Follow me.' Bending down to pick up a bundle wrapped in newspaper which had been lying by the outer door, he walked across the courtyard.

They came to a doorway which led to a flight of stone stairs. At each level the side of the building that looked over the courtyard was partly open to the air through high, rounded arches like huge windows without glass, with a low protective rail to stop anyone walking off the edge. In some of the arches Rose saw the wilted shapes of plants in heavy pots.

On each floor, doors opened off the stairway. She followed the young man's legs in their dark trousers, bewildered, but sensing that he meant her no harm. They climbed three floors and then he turned off and walked to one of the doors. As she held the fat candle near the wall, Rose saw that on the greyish green of the plaster were painted in rough white letters the words *IL RIFUGIO*. The man knocked briskly three times on the door.

'Where are we?' Rose asked timidly, praying that her Italian might be good enough to understand at least some of the answer.

The man turned and she saw his face properly for the first time, a smooth, surprisingly aristocratic face with a long aquiline nose and thin lips. His curly hair was clipped neatly round his head and he had large eyes which he kept directed at the door as if he was listening.

'Don't worry,' she thought he said to her, rather absently. 'I'll take you back.'

Then they heard a woman's voice calling softly through the door. 'Francesco?'

Impatiently he replied '*Si, si,*' and they heard the door being unlocked inside. A young woman with a round, gentle face and black hair curling over her shoulders was looking out at them with anxious eyes. 'Thank God,' she said. And then, 'Who's this?'

As they went inside Rose heard Francesco explaining how he had found her in the next street. He unwrapped the parcel he was carrying and showed the young woman what was inside, though Rose couldn't see what it was. The two of them conversed in the sort of quiet voices Dora had used when there was a baby asleep near by. She noticed that Francesco had seemed more relaxed the moment he was inside the place.

Rose looked round her as they talked. They were standing in a sizeable square hallway off which led four doors. On three of the walls there was nothing but bare, crumbling paintwork. Against the fourth stood a small shrine where a tiny candle burned in front of a statue of the Madonna, casting shadows over her gaudy face and robes. Around it hung carefully placed strands of flowers and leaves.

The young woman moved closer to Rose. 'Who are you?' she asked cautiously. 'Are you American?'

'No,' Rose said. '*Un'inglese.* English. A soldier.' She

194

tried to explain that she had been lost, and the young woman smiled suddenly.

'You have learned Italian?'

Rose nodded. 'A little.'

One of the doors in front of them opened and Rose found to her further confusion that she was suddenly face to face with a short, plump nun, her heavy black clothes reaching to the floor. Cradled in her arms was a young child. The nun smiled, a rather odd gnome-like smile as she had a bad squint in one eye, and her expression suggested someone without all their mental faculties.

'She needs water, Margherita,' she said in a high, lisping voice.

The younger woman disappeared, returning a few seconds later with a small china cup and put it to the child's lips.

Rose felt herself drawn towards them. She could see the child's black curls resting on the nun's arm. She reached out and stroked the dark mop of hair. It felt stringy with dirt. She knew all their eyes were on her.

'You like children?' Margherita asked her softly.

Rose nodded. Margherita looked questioningly for a second at Francesco, who gave a slight nod.

'Then come.' She beckoned Rose forward. 'I will show you.'

Still holding the candle, Rose followed her to the door from where she had seen the nun appear. She came with them now, the scrawny child in her arms. They walked through the dark doorway into a long room which must have extended along the back of the building. There was one other candle in the room. Beside this other fragile light a second nun was sitting on the floor, her face in shadow.

After a moment, Rose took in that the little bundles of rags of varying sizes in rows along the floor were the bodies of children. There must have been twenty or thirty of them. She became aware of the sound of their breathing as they lay in exhausted sleep. Despite the size of the room she could smell the dirt on their bodies, and realized that the pungent stench of excrement was coming from a tin pail which stood near the door.

Looking first at the others for permission, Rose walked slowly along between the sleeping children. Some of them lay on mattresses which appeared to be stuffed with something coarse like straw. Others had only an arm crooked under their heads for a pillow. A few of them twitched and stirred in their sleep. They reminded Rose of George, how he had slept without really resting when he came back from his months in Wales.

Her mind was alive with questions about these people. As she drew near the seated nun, she saw that she was watching over a young girl. The nun's face was pale and thin, with prominent cheekbones, and she looked up at Rose through thick black-rimmed spectacles.

Seeing the tenderness in Rose's eyes as she looked at the girl she said in a whisper, 'This is Maria Grazia.'

Rose smiled and nodded, looking at the little girl lying asleep on her side, her face half hidden by long, straight hair. She had to struggle to understand the next part of what the woman said.

'*E gravida*,' she said sorrowfully. '*E ha solo dodici anni.*'

Rose frowned. The girl was only twelve. She had understood that. The nun made a graceful gesture, a curving movement out from her stomach.

Rose gasped, pointing at the girl's belly. '*Un bambino?*'

The nun nodded, watching the horrified pity spread over the stranger's face. 'Her father is dead,' she explained. The woman spoke so fast that Rose could understand only snatches of what she said. She gathered that the girl's mother had also recently died and that to survive she had 'pleased' the soldiers. 'All these children,' the nun went on, 'they have seen terrible things. Some of their families are so poor they even try to sell them.' Gesturing round the room she indicated that though they could only take in a few, they tried to create a home for them.

Rose was aware as she listened that Francesco and Margherita were watching her and discussing something in low, urgent voices. They beckoned her to come out of the room with them. Rose noticed that Margherita looked almost excited, as if in anticipation.

Now she spoke slowly and carefully. 'What is your work in the army?'

Rose couldn't think of the word and mimed turning a steering wheel and changing gear. She saw the two of them exchange glances.

'I see by the way you look at the children that you have a special feeling for them. We have decided to ask you if you can help us.'

The dreamlike peculiarity of Rose's evening was increasing even further. 'I don't understand.'

Francesco made as if to answer, but Margherita gestured at him to be quiet.

'We need help here from wherever we can find it,' she said, still speaking slowly. 'Our refuge is linked with the Church, but it's not official.' Seeing Rose frown she said, 'Francesco and I were members of Catholic Action when we were students. We are also anti-Fascists. The Fascists banned Catholic Action, a long time ago, from any sort of involvement which was not Church related. We stayed in Catholic Action but we carried on our other activities outside. You understand?'

Rose nodded. She had picked up most of it.

'Now that Mussolini has gone things have become a little easier.' Margherita continued. 'But our bishop has confused feelings about us. We are loyal Catholics, but we are also seen as troublemakers . . .'

'You mean the Church supported Mussolini?'

Margherita sighed. 'At first, no. Later – yes. Mussolini did deals with the Church, offered bribes . . . presents for them,' she explained. 'Anyway, because of who we are we cannot get official support from the Church for

197

our orphanage. Not in the form of money. This building belongs to the Church. We do not have to pay rent. And the sisters, Magdalena and Assunta, help us with the work. And candles.' Her mouth curved into a wry smile. 'A lot of candles! But we have to feed the children from the black market like everyone else. There is hardly any water. Sometimes it is dangerous because people try to steal from us. They are hungry too, of course.'

Rose was struggling to keep up with her. 'I'd like to help,' she said, cursing her slowness in the language. 'I like children. What do you want?'

'Anything you can bring,' Margherita told her. 'Food, soap, blankets, clothes. We can use anything or we can sell it. I know you cannot come here often. But you come how and when you can. We cannot give you anything in return.'

'Yes,' Rose smiled, 'I think you can. A refuge, perhaps.'

And the two women laughed for the first time. Rose had taken to Margherita straight away. She felt that they could be friends.

'I will come,' Rose said. 'I promise. But you must show me the way back. My friends will be worried.'

'What were you looking for here?' Margherita asked.

'I wanted to see Naples,' Rose said. 'Even at night!'

Francesco indicated that he was ready to leave and Rose went out with him. 'You were very foolish to walk here alone. It is dangerous for us, but even more so for you.'

As they walked down the stairs again they heard hasty footsteps coming towards them and a man appeared, with something stuffed under his jacket. He looked startled as he saw them.

'Evening Enrico,' Francesco said. 'What's that? Bread? Rosa, this is Enrico – he is a magician. He finds bread from the stones.'

The man was staring with wide eyes at Rose and she saw sweat on his pallid skin even though it was a cool night. He had brown hair and a thin, stubbly face.

'This is Rosa,' Francesco said. 'An English soldier. She is going to help us.'

The man gave her a long, intense stare, fearful or hostile she was not sure, and then ran on up the stairs.

'He does not speak,' Francesco explained to her. 'We know almost nothing about him except that he has shown he can be trusted. We think perhaps he is a little—' Francesco tapped a finger against his head. 'But he has connections and from somewhere he brings us food.'

He walked with her, back to the edge of the dark square, from where she said she could find her way.

'When you come again, you will remember,' he said. 'We are in the street next to Via degli Spagnoli. You will help us?' For the first time he smiled, rather appealingly.

'Oh yes,' Rose said. 'I will.'

'Good. Then you will need this. It's for the outer gate.' She felt a large key being pressed into her hand.

Then he turned to go, saying '*Arrivederla.*' And disappeared into the darkness.

'Where the hell have you been?'

Tony was standing outside the club, rigid with anxiety and anger. 'God knows what might have happened to you!'

'Why?' Rose asked stupidly. She had just returned as if from another existence and didn't have her wits about her. She'd only just remembered that she was without her bag. Fortunately there had not been much in it.

'Why?' Tony shouted, and then lowered his voice to an infuriated whisper, not wanting anyone else to her. There was no one standing near them. 'You walk out and disappear for almost an hour and a half and you ask me why I'm worried! For God's sake, I thought you had a brain, woman. And besides,' he added rather petulantly, 'you've made me look a proper fool.'

Rose was astonished at the strength of his anger. He was usually so gentle and soft spoken. She looked at his thin face and felt sorry she had let him down so badly.

'I'm terribly sorry,' she said, reaching out to touch his arm. Instantly he pulled away from her. 'I just wanted to have a look round the place. It was so boring in there and—'

'Oh – I apologize for being boring. I was under the impression you liked my company until now.'

'I do, Tony. But you were talking to Alex and that Stan was carrying on and getting on my nerves. I never meant to stay out for so long – honestly I didn't. I don't know what came over me.'

She was very surprised to find it was now only ten-twenty. It felt as if she had been away for hours, and she realized that it had not even crossed her mind to worry about being stranded here if they'd left without her. The passion wagons were due to start back for Caserta at eleven.

The two of them walked a short distance down the slightly misty street.

'Look,' she appealed to him again, glancing at his dejected face. 'It was stupid of me. I'm sorry. But I'm all right – see?' She did a mock curtsey to try and make him laugh. 'I just didn't think you'd be that bothered.'

'Well you were wrong then, weren't you?' he said grimly. Rose realized to her consternation that the young man beside her was not far from tears. 'Just because I don't—' he stopped abruptly.

Rose stepped closer and went to touch him on the shoulder, moved by the emotion she seemed to have aroused.

'Don't,' he said savagely. He turned to her, his white face looking strained, the lick of fair hair falling down over his forehead. 'It'll be wrong. We'll just get each other all wrong.' He stood in silence for a moment, hands thrust down hard into his trouser pockets, looking away from her. A few people passed – the shadowy figures of other servicemen, some with women on their arms, laughing and necking together after an evening's drinking.

In the end he said almost formally, 'I just want you to know I do have feelings for you, Rose. That's all.'

'Well, I'm fond of you too,' she said helplessly, thinking how strange he was.

'Come on,' he said impatiently, as if unsatisfied by what had been said. 'Let's go and have a last drink before it's time to go back.'

CHAPTER 20

MARCH 1944

By the third week in March, Rose had only managed one brief visit to Il Rifugio. She felt she had failed them badly. The first time she had tried to go back, in February, she had only managed to get together a few bars of army soap, some cigarettes and a few tins of food. She had a lot to learn. Naïvely, as she realized afterwards, she had packed the supplies into her army bag, which was instantly recognizable even though she was dressed in mufti herself.

After the truck from Caserta had dropped them off and she and Tony had parted, Rose walked quickly into Via degli Spagnoli looking around her anxiously. She had just begun to take in the full destitution of the place in daylight when she felt a hand hard on her shoulder. Thinking it was someone begging for food she tried to shake the grasping fingers off.

'And where do you think you're off to?' an English voice said sternly.

She turned to find herself staring into the mocking eyes of a Red Cap, the Military Police. She couldn't think of anything to say.

'Open the bag,' he ordered from under a little ginger moustache.

'You from the Midlands?' Rose appealed to him as she unfastened the bag. She thought she heard a familiar ring to his accent.

'Coventry,' he snapped. 'Though I hardly see that's

any concern of yours.' He took a notebook from his breast pocket and bent over to look into the bag.

'What have we here? Army soap, army rations – cigarettes. Hmm. I see. Got your legs under the table in one of the *bassi* have you? My God – I thought it was only the chaps who played at that sort of game. You want to watch you're not rounded up with all the other prostitutes in the VD wagons.'

'I beg your pardon!' Rose shouted at him, absolutely livid. 'Don't be so bloody rude! Who d'you think you are talking to me like that? You and your poxy little notebook.'

The young man glared at her, infuriated.

'And a fishwife to boot,' he said. 'Now, let's see: being found in an area designated out of bounds to service personnel, unauthorized use of army property . . .'

'But that's all *my* stuff,' Rose argued. 'It's none of your business what I do with it!' She was wild with frustration.

'. . . and insubordination to a senior officer.'

'You're only a ruddy corporal!'

'Which makes me senior to you, doesn't it, *Private* Lucas?'

As a result her leave was cancelled, she was ordered to return to Caserta immediately, and spent a substantial part of the day waiting for transport. As well as that, she was confined strictly to the limits of her working area for a fortnight.

'Well, what were you doing in Naples?' Madge asked, standing by her bed and attempting to squeeze her large waistline into a non-uniform skirt. 'I should've thought you'd have had more sense. Anything for a quiet life, I say.'

'Oh, I was just nosing around.' Rose bent to undo the laces of her heavy black shoes, evading Madge's curious eyes. If that was army rules, she thought, then they were made to be broken.

As soon as the fortnight was up, Rose went to Signora

Mandetta in Caserta, who had made her a skirt. The widow sat at her old sewing table, her gnarled hands working on the intricate seams of a wedding dress.

'I need to look like an Italian,' Rose said.

Signora Mandetta smiled indulgently at her. She was a woman of about sixty with faded hair and a large wart on her left cheek. But her eyes were like those of a seventeen-year-old – a little watery, but still dancing with life.

'Rosa . . .' She held out her hands, palms up, and shrugged as if to underline Rose's eccentricity. 'You already look like an Italian – your hair, your eyes . . . Tell me the truth. Your father – he is really a Neapolitan?'

Rose laughed, enjoying the signora's teasing. 'Not wearing these clothes I don't,' she said, pointing at the khaki. 'I need to look really Italian. I want black clothes made of old material.' Her Italian was coming more easily now through use at every possible opportunity.

The signora narrowed her eyes with shrewd curiosity. 'You have a boyfriend? An Italian *amante*?'

'No.' Rose wondered how she could possibly explain. It might be easier if Signora Mandetta thought she was disguising herself to meet a lover. She giggled with as much coyness as she could manage. 'Well . . . it's a secret. You'll make me the clothes?'

'Of course. Whtever you want.'

'Marvellous. *Grazie*. Now look what I've brought.'

She often brought a cake or two from the Naafi with her and shared a snack with the signora. This time it was a couple of rock cakes. Signora Mandetta chewed on hers thoughtfully, pouring out tiny tumblers of rough red wine.

'Better if they leave them for the rocks next time,' she commented.

Rose grinned. 'Next time I'll bring doughnuts.'

Within a few days the signora had produced a black outfit for Rose, cobbled together out of some other old clothes. To top it off she offered her a threadbare cardigan and some worn black mules of her own for which Rose paid as well.

'These look just right,' Rose told her as she tried them on.

Signora Mandetta cackled unrestrainedly when she saw Rose in her 'new' clothes. 'Now you just need a fat belly on you to look like a true Italian signora with at least four children!' she cried, wiping her eyes. 'Holy Mother, what a transformation. I only hope he doesn't go off you, *mia cara*!'

When the leave day finally came round Rose brushed a drop of olive oil through her hair. She also bought herself a couple of string bags in which she carried the objects, well wrapped, that she was going to take into Il Rifugio. She changed in the Ladies at one of the Naafi clubs, slipped out the back entrance and walked briskly across the square towards the Via Toledo.

The black market was flourishing on almost every street corner, and she identified with some amusement the array of army goods laid out to be sold on the streets. The food, cigarettes, soap and many other objects which were spirited away from the docks with the collusion, quite often, of army officials and sold openly to the locals. Rose approached one of the little makeshift stalls and bought another handful of packets of cigarettes so that Francesco or Margherita could sell them and buy something they really needed.

Then she made her way through the filth of the Via degli Spagnoli, startling fat green flies with her feet as she walked. She let herself quickly into Il Rifugio. Francesco and Margherita greeted her with admiring hilarity.

'You should have been a spy,' Margherita cried, kissing her with real warmth. 'Oh, look at this! Soap, Francesco, and meat. When can you come again?'

'Soon,' she told them. 'At the beginning of April I get two days. Can I stay here and help you? I will try to bring more things with me.'

'Come when you can. Stay as long as you like,' Francesco said with a shrug. Then he grinned at her. 'You're welcome – *pazza*!'

205

She spent a few hours there that day, talking with Francesco and Margherita and playing with some of the children. The oldest of them, Margherita told her, was fifteen and the youngest only just over a year old. The routine seemed surprisingly relaxed, and they sat outside in the late afternoon after feeding the children and giving a few of them as much of a wash as was possible with the limited supplies of water which had to be fetched from a pipe outside. Some of the children played out in the courtyard, watched by a couple of the elderly tenants occupying lower rooms in the building. Sometimes they sat out and talked to the children, but mostly they kept to themselves.

Rose picked out the figure of Maria Grazia trailing round the courtyard, her pregnant belly protruding from her pitiful, stick-thin body. She had long straggling hair, and deep-set, myopic-looking eyes which held a sad, dreamy expression. She and another little girl were playing with a filthy cloth doll.

'What will happen to her?' Rose asked Margherita, who had sat down wearily on a stool beside her in the courtyard.

'She will stay here. We can help her care for the baby.'

'But after . . .?'

Margherita shrugged. 'What will happen to any of them? We shall have to see what God intends for them.'

Rose was silenced by this. Her practical upbringing had not accustomed her to leaving things up to God to decide.

After a while Francesco came out, stretching and yawning from a long siesta. He sat beside them on the ground in the pale afternoon light, his arms round his legs.

Margherita smiled and rumpled his curly hair with her hand. 'My husband would sleep all day if there was not work to be done,' she said affectionately.

'Husband?' Rose said, wondering if she had heard right. 'I didn't know you were . . .'

Both of them laughed, so much that Rose wondered

whether she had said something hilarious in Italian by mistake. They laughed even more at her astonished face.

'You are not a Catholic, are you?' Margherita gasped out eventually. 'You think the Church would even give us candles for this place if we weren't married? Can you imagine the bishop, Francesco!'

That afternoon Rose learned as much as she could about everyone at Il Rifugio. Margherita told her that Francesco came from a wealthy Neapolitan family who had a large house at Vomero, the affluent suburb high up on the cliff overlooking the bay. He was evidently something of a rebel. When Italy entered the war he had been completing his studies in political history at Naples University. His family knew where he was but left him to follow what they saw as his bizarre inclinations.

'He calls you mad,' she said, 'but the family think he is truly . . .' She tapped her head with one finger. 'For them, madness is to live here and to identify with the poor. To make their troubles one's own.'

Francesco silently shook his head as if what he was hearing made him sound too heroic. 'But,' he said, jumping up suddenly, 'I have not given away all my possessions to the poor. Let's have some music.'

In a moment he was back with an old wind-up gramophone which he set down on the pale paving slabs. He wound the small machine and fed it with his thick records, songs in Italian and French, most of which were strange to Rose.

'The soul must have music,' Francesco pronounced, in the solemn manner which made Rose unsure whether he was taking the micky out of himself. 'I will sell my body to feed the poor, but not my gramophone.' He saw Rose looking at him rather quizzically and laughed. 'She takes me very seriously this Englishwoman.'

While the tinny sound of the music played cross the courtyard, Rose asked Margherita whether the two of them had married as students.

'No, only when we came here,' she said. She told Rose that her family came from a village near Torre del Greco,

207

and that she had met Francesco while studying literature. 'My family are much poorer than his,' she said. 'We got married very quietly.'

'But you're happy, I can see that.' Rose was impressed by the pair of them, by the degree of freedom they seemed to have with each other along with a respect and commitment matched only by their devotion to Il Rifugio.

The two nuns, Assunta and Magdalena, had also made her very welcome during the visit. Magdalena, for all her soulful appearance, proved to be a very down-to-earth woman in her thirties, who could always be relied upon to get things done.

Assunta, who tended the shrine in the hallway as lovingly as if it were another of the children, spent her life waiting for miracles to happen. All her conversation that day while they were preparing food for the community was of the flying monk at Pomigliano. He was said not only to have demonstrated the stigmata, bleeding from hands and feet, but also to have left the ground and soared up to rescue an Italian pilot from a burning plane. Assunta was completely convinced of the truth of this. But for Rose, who nodded politely as she listened, hearing these bizarre claims from Assunta's pallid, cross-eyed face made them seem only more barmy than they would have done otherwise. The children, however, seemed to adore her, and whenever she was not busy with some task she sat cradling one of the younger ones in her plump arms.

The only discomforting presence was the brooding Enrico, who stood at the edge of rooms, silent, always watching. Then he would disappear without even indicating to anyone that he was going. Rose could not quite make out what was odd about him but he made her feel very ill at ease.

The day passed far too quickly, but seeing the children, getting to recognize some of them and realizing at the mealtimes just how little food they had to live on was a spur to her to think up more ways in which she could help.

'You see the problems?' Margherita had said to her while they were eating, all sitting round on the floor of the long room where Rose had first seen them asleep. 'We can manage to feed them – just. But it means we spend so much time finding food. We have so little time to give them any teaching or the love they need.'

Rose looked round at all the dark faces, wolfing down the tiny portions of sloppy army meat and vegetables that she had brought in tins, mixed with macaroni. She would have liked to put her arms round every one of them, dirty and ragged as they were. She felt as if she had found herself a family in Italy. And she was damned if she was going to let them go hungry.

As spring progressed the temperatures grew quite hot. The country was at its most beautiful, with oranges and lemons hanging heavy on the trees. During off-duty periods the men and women stationed at Caserta spent more of their time outside in the grounds of the palace. The last long tank into which the cascades fell was large enough to land a light aircraft on. It was certainly big enough for a swimming pool and already people were making use of it.

One evening Rose and Tony were strolling towards the cascades in the uncertain light of dusk.

'I always forget what a long way it is,' Tony said. 'It must be a couple of miles I suppose.'

Rose just said, 'Umm.'

Tony turned to look at her. Her thoughts were obviously elsewhere. For a moment he enjoyed looking at her face, the soft line of the cheeks and her dark, pensive eyes.

'Sorry,' she said suddenly. 'I was just wondering if there's going to be any more bombing tonight.'

A couple of nights ago they had heard heavy raids on Naples and, knowing that most of the raids were concentrated on the port area and Il Rifugio was not very far from the sea, Rose was concerned. Her mind was constantly occupied with thoughts of how she could help them further. It had ocurred to her that Bill, Gwen's young man who worked in supplies, might be prepared to help. Most likely not. He seemed a bit of a stuffed shirt. Because what was she really thinking of? Stealing from the army? On a large scale? The thought frightened her. Of course odd things were going missing all the time – but more than that . . .

'That Virgin parade in the town,' she said to Tony suddenly. 'Those costumes the girls were wearing. A lot of that was army mozzie nets wasn't it?'

'Certainly looked like it,' Tony said, bemused.

Rose snorted with laughter at the memory. 'Virgin parade!' she said with her deep chuckle. 'God Almighty, have you ever seen anything like it?'

The young women in the town's parade had been wearing an astonishing collection of clothes, many trimmed with netting dyed in dazzling colours. They marched through the streets of Caserta to display their chaste beauty.

But as these 'virgins' passed, voices of Allied soldiers had piped up in the crowd, 'Eh – that's Rita (or Theresa or Maria); I was with her last night!' which caused raucous outbursts of laughter all round.

Seeing Tony look rather embarrassed at her forthrightness she asked, 'D'you think it's wrong to steal from the army?'

'I suppose it's wrong to steal from anywhere really. But you can't help thinking when you see some of the poverty around this place that we probably wouldn't miss a bit. Why – thinking of joining the black market?'

Rose laughed rather nervously. 'When d'you think I'm going to find time to do that?'

They passed the rows of tanks until they were at the bottom of the cascades, where white water rushed down over the stones. It was possible to scramble up the rocks alongside the water, but on the hillside round behind the cascades, pathways had been cut on both sides, zig-zagging up steeply until they rejoined at the top. Up there, where the water gushed out of the ground, the spring was covered by a great rock, carved round and hollow inside like a shell, so that it made a small cave.

Rose suddenly felt full of energy and mischief. 'Tell you what, I'll race you to the top. You go that way and I'll go up here. Go on, I dare you!'

'Are you joking?' he asked. Clearly, this time it was his mind that had been elsewhere.

'No, course not. Come on.'

Tony roused himself. 'All right then. You're on.'

They set off, each taking a path on opposite sides of the cascades. Immediately she lost sight of him and stared up the path, Rose began to feel frightened. There was a gate behind the cascades which opened on to the rest of the mountainside. There was no knowing who might be wandering about up there, and the darkness was falling fast. But she enjoyed the sense of danger, scrambling up in the half-light smelling the sweet scents of herbs and plants by the path. All her senses were alert and her body felt strong and capable.

She reached the top a fraction later than Tony, her lungs heaving, and stopped beside him panting and laughing.

'Oh, thank God!' she gasped. 'I thought I was going to get caught by bandits down there and never make it to the top!'

Tony laughed, leaning over to get his breath back. She could see the sheen on his honey-coloured hair in the last of the light.

There was something about the scented warmth of the air, the loneliness of the place, that allowed feelings to come to the surface. Rose knew she was not in love with Tony. She had not come out of herself as far as that yet. But she was aware from the evening they went to Naples together, as well as from many small acts of kindness and affection, that Tony cared for her. And she felt that, given time, she could love him. His very reticence had broken through her fear and mistrust. But there was never more from him. Never a touch, any other sign, except for his quivering emotion when she had disappeared in Naples. What was it? Was he afraid of her? She felt very strongly that she needed to understand.

Tony straightened up and saw her dark eyes watching him. It was a look he had never seen on her face before. Whether serious or full of fun, he knew that Rose had strong defences, usually showed you herself only at one remove from what she was feeling. Now her expression was disarmingly naked. Even in the half-light he could read bewilderment, sadness and a kind of hunger. It was a moment he had feared would come.

'Shall we go up on top?' he asked softly. A short flight of steps led up to the flat top of the rock, which gave a marvellous view of the palace, the town and over to Naples and Vesuvius. Tony let her climb up first and they stood together in the light breeze looking at the gleaming ribbon of water below, and the sky still rimmed with light. Over the volcano the light deepened to a pink incandescence.

The pressure for one of them to speak increased every moment. Rose struggled to find words that would not sound complaining or critical.

'Tony, can I ask you something?'

'Of course.' He didn't turn to look at her. 'I think I can guess.'

'Can you?' This confused her even further. 'I just feel muddled up about . . . well, how to feel about you. I feel a lot for you, as a friend, but—' She broke off, feeling that each of her words sounded more clumsy and unfortunate than the last. 'When we're together we're not like – well, like a man and a woman can be. Oh dear. I can't say this properly. I'm sorry. You must think I'm ever so forward.'

'You mean I don't hold you or try to kiss you?'

'Well I don't mean you should,' Rose said hastily. 'I mean I don't want . . . mostly I don't want men touching me.' She could feel her cheeks burning with shame and embarrassment in talking like this, but she knew Tony well enough to be certain she could confide in him.

'Because you're supposed to be engaged?'

'No. Not really. That's what I tell people. I mean I *am* – supposed to be. But it's not that.'

Taking a deep breath she told him quickly about Mr Lazenby and Joseph. When she'd finished she saw he had turned and was watching her, his sensitive face full of emotion.

'My poor Rose.' He stepped close to her and took one of her hands in his and stroked it. His hand was very warm and reassuring and surprisingly soft.

'You really pick your men,' he said, and she was startled by what sounded like anger in his voice.

'What's the matter?' she asked, her own voice turning high and tearful. 'I just don't understand you.' She felt tears running down her cheeks. 'I don't know how to feel about you!'

And then to her distress she realized that he too was weeping.

'Tony,' she cried. 'What is it?' She moved forward to comfort him. To her surprise he accepted, and for the first time they held each other. She felt his slight body in her arms, smelt the familiar salty smell of him, and she could feel his heart beating against her.

'Please tell me what's the matter.'

'I'm afraid to.'

He was silent again and she reached up and stroked his face with her hand. He removed her arms until he had hold of her hand again and wiped his eyes. He led her to the low parapet which ringed the rock and they sat down, leaning against it.

'Rose – I want you to know that I feel a great deal for you. Much more than I ever believed I could—' He broke off abruptly. 'You're a marvellous person, so bright, so full of life. I can't express very well what you mean to me. But I can't . . .' He stopped again as if he simply could not bring the words out of him.

'You can't love me?'

'I do love you. That's what I'm trying to say.' His voice grew louder with frustration. 'But not . . . You have to understand. I can't love women. Not like a man is supposed to love a woman.'

He loosed her hand and lowered his head nearer his bent up knees as if to shelter from a blow.

'You mean . . .?'

'I mean that, sexually, I love other men. Only men.' He spoke very deliberately and slowly. 'Ever since I can remember, Rose.' He paused. 'I'm sorry.'

She was silent. Eventually he looked up, interpreting her silence as disgust or disapproval.

'You won't tell anyone. Please?' She shook her head. 'Rose, I'm so sorry if you feel I've been deceiving you. I do love you, in a way which is very important. But I can't make love to you. It's not in my nature.'

'It's all right.' She looked up at him and he saw how powerful her gaze was even in the poor light. 'I'm just trying to think about it. It's the first time I've ever known anyone . . .'

'Homosexual?'

'Yes.' She could feel herself, like a sea anemone that had begun to reach out slowly and tentatively towards love, touched by something unexpected and shrinking back. But her thoughts were more objective. Those very occasional knowing looks when she was young, hushed talk of 'queers'. How different it was when it was real. When it was someone you . . . liked.

'I'm glad you told me. I wanted to understand, and now I do. You got me confused, and the reason I liked you to start with was that you left me alone – you know – like that. But now I know where we stand I won't do anything stupid. We can be friends without spoiling it, can't we?'

Tony watched her. 'I don't disgust you?'

Rose considered this for a moment.

'The father of my son disgusted me. What he did to me had nothing to do with love or kindness or anything good. I know you better than that. No – you don't disgust me.'

The conversation stopped and started with patches of thoughtful silence.

'D'you have anyone. A bloke, I mean?' she asked after a while.

'I think perhaps, yes. It looks like it. You don't know him. He's an American. His name is Lewis.'

'And you care about him too?'

'I don't know him as well as you. But we have certain things in common.'

'Like both going for other blokes.' Rose cursed herself immediately for her sarcasm.

'You're right to be angry.'

'I'm not angry. I'm sorry. Anyway . . .' She hesitated. 'I've just thought. You can help me out.'

'Me? Of course. How?'

Suddenly excited, she confided to him her discovery of Il Rifugio. 'It's perfect,' she said. 'If you don't want people to know about you and Lewis, you can carry on letting them think you're going about with me. If you're my chaperone to Naples on leave weekends, you can meet Lewis and that way I'll get left alone as well and I can go and help with these kids!'

Tony burst out laughing in pure astonishment. 'My God, Rose Lucas, you're one of the most extraordinary people I've ever met! You mean to say you've been wandering about in the slums of Naples dressed up as an Italian because you've fallen in love with an orphanage?'

She nodded happily. 'That's where I was, that night I went off. I'm sorry I didn't tell you before, but it all seemed like a dream at the time. And I hadn't realized I was going to get so involved. But you should see the kids, Tony. They're poor little mites who've been left on the streets by their families. Some of their moms and dads are dead, but not all. Some of them were even sold into prostitution. I want to find ways of getting more food for them. We've got more than enough here and there must be some way . . .'

'So that's what that was all about. Now wait a minute.

Just wait a minute. Are you talking about diverting army supplies? Because if you are, you could get yourself into one hell of a lot of trouble.'

Rose looked down at the ground, away from him. 'I don't know what I'm talking about really. I haven't thought it through enough. But it's not right that they're hungry and that Margherita and Francesco have such a struggle. It's not the kids' fault there's a war.' She was becoming quite emotional, trying to convince him.

Tony sighed. 'You're right, of course. Relative morals, I suppose. You can count on me to help – I think. And yes, the Naples weekends are a grand idea.' He touched her shoulder gently. 'You must believe that I wish with all my heart I could marry you Rose, if things were different.'

She reached up and stroked the hand on her shoulder and they sat in comfortable silence.

As they did so they became aware of a strange sound, a distant roaring as if a massive beast was roaming somewhere in the sky behind them.

'What the hell . . .?' Rose said.

Tony was on his feet instantly, looking back towards Naples. 'Good Lord!' he cried. 'Look! She's going up!'

The sky round the volcano had turned blood red, and from the top of the crater they could see what looked like great clumps of fire being hurled into the air, with giant orange sparks, as Vesuvius spat fury and venom out into the night sky. From lower down the sides trickled bright streams of lava, bleeding down the volcano's flanks from points like giant stab wounds.

There was nothing they could do except stand watching in petrified silence. A massive belly of cloud had gathered over the volcano, the eruption a low, growling roar beneath it. Every now and then they heard a louder sound, like a great hoarse voice, and a pillar of fire shot up from inside the cone, hurling itself up towards the cloud and the terrible sky.

They watched for a long time as the night air around them grew colder. It reminded Rose of the nights of the

Birmingham blitz: such complete helplessness when faced with destruction all around.

'Will Naples be all right?' she asked, and Tony knew immediately whom she was most afraid for.

'It's quite a way round the bay, so it should be. But God help all those towns and villages underneath it.'

After a while he said, 'It's enough to make you want to pray, isn't it?'

And Rose nodded. Prayer did not come naturally to her, but she was praying with her whole heart tonight.

CHAPTER 21

By the time she returned to Il Rifugio in April – this time for a whole precious weekend – the force of the eruption had abated. While it was going at full strength, the sky had stayed grey and soupy for days, and soft grey ash fell to a depth of at least half an inch for miles around. Walking through the streets of Naples, Rose saw that even the graffiti of the multitude of political parties, and the large black letters proclaiming 'DUCE! DUCE' (now often crossed out with blacker paint), were dusted over by a layer of ash which clung to the crevices in the walls.

Naples, now convalescing from its days and nights of fear and prayer, had been spared the full destruction of the volcano. Many of the population were convinced this was due to the beneficence of their patron San Gennaro, who had watched over them for fourteen centuries since his martyrdom in Pozzuoli, just along the coast. His protection had, however, been of no help whatever to the inhabitants of the towns and villages strung along the fringe of coast between Vesuvius and the sea, many of which had been engulfed once more by the lava.

Francesco opened the door to her, and she saw at once the strain and exhaustion plain in every line of his face.

'Are you all right?' she asked anxiously. 'You look terrible.'

'It has been a terrible time.'

Rose searched around with her eyes. 'Where's Margherita?'

Francesco pulled one of his hands through his unruly

curls. 'She's gone to visit her father. He had found a place to stay. He was away from home when the eruption started. Her mother and sister – both gone.' He made a wiping motion with his right hand, his face full of pain and bewilderment. 'The house was destroyed.'

'You're saying that . . .?'

'Now she has only her father and one sister. She has two older brothers who are in the army.'

In English, Rose said, 'My God. How terrible.'

She wanted to comfort Francesco somehow, but felt shy of him. After all she barely knew him. If Margherita herself had been there it might have come more naturally.

They were still standing in the gloom of the hall, Rose holding her two parcels of rations. From the big room, where Magdalena and Assunta were keeping the children occupied, came the sound of singing.

Francesco seemed to rouse himself. 'There is something else I need to tell you. Another person has come to live here. A friend of ours called Paulo Falcone. We were at the university together. He is a bit older because he was a medical student. He arrived two days ago from Rome – God knows how, across the lines. He says he has been with a group in the resistance, but he will not talk to me any more about it. Perhaps if Margherita were here . . .' His expression seemed to sink further into tiredness and pain. 'I am telling you to warn you that he is not easy to be with at the moment.' He pointed to the small room to the left of the big room, where they stored and prepared food for the community. 'He is sleeping in there now, but we can go in. He won't wake.'

Francesco suddenly reached out and touched her hand in an unexpected gesture of gratitude. 'I'm glad that you have come, Rosa.'

She smiled sadly at him, picking up the parcels which she had put down while he was speaking. 'I hope I can relieve you all a little. You must be so tired.'

They carried the food parcels to the storeroom. Rose felt how small and inadequate they were. How could she do better?

She could hear the man's deep breathing from where he lay in shadow under the window on two poor straw mattresses laid end to end. He was lying very straight as if sleep were a duty rather than a relief. She went and looked down at him, intrigued to encounter another of their educated friends. The young man was sleeping with a slight frown on his face. He looked well built, though thin, but his naturally rounded jawline had prevented his face from turning gaunt. The closed eyes were fringed by long dark lashes, and his black wavy hair had grown untidily down to his shoulders. The lower part of his face was shadowed by several days of stubble. It was hard to picture him as a doctor, reassuring and authoritative, perhaps smartly dressed. He lay vulnerable as a child battered by the hurts of the day before. Rose surprised herself with an impulse to reach down and stroke his brow, to smooth the perturbed expression off his face, but she held back.

'Come,' Francesco whispered, surprised by her attention to the stranger. 'Let's go.'

She went and joined Magdalena and Assunta, who greeted her with delighted though tired smiles. On seeing her arrive, one of the boys, a three-year-old waif called Emilio, ran to Rose crying, '*Bacio! Bacio!*'

She knelt down to take his small form in her arms, giving him the kiss he wanted so badly. She sat with him on one knee, and on the other a younger girl who sidled up to her shyly. She pressed her face against Emilio's, and against the plumper cheeks of the little girl, enjoying the feel of cuddling children again. Emilio turned and put his skinny arms round her neck.

Magdalena finished off the session by saying the Angelus with the children, and then it was time to prepare something to eat.

'Let me help tonight,' Rose offered. 'You should all sleep. I do little enough here. I'll sit up to watch the children.' They took it in turns to perform this vigil, partly to comfort any children who woke up disturbed in the night, and also to make quite sure no one else found their way into the building.

220

Magdalena nodded in response to Rose. 'It is good that *il dottore* Falcone has come,' she said. 'He can help us with Maria Grazia. That child needs every help we can give her.'

It was not until they were settling the children down for the night that the doctor woke up. He stumbled out from the small room carrying a cup of water in one hand, his expression entirely bewildered, as if he had woken to find himself in another country. The eyes which looked round at them were large, dark, fringed by the long lashes Rose had noticed as he slept. She saw his gaze settle curiously on her and linger there for a moment.

'So Falcone – you feel better?' Francesco called to him.

Falcone nodded absently. Now he was standing, Rose could see he was a powerfully built man, though, like almost all Neapolitans she had seen, too thin for his build. His dark grey trousers and green shirt were dirty and extremely worn. The shirt had only two or three buttons remaining near the bottom, so that it fell open in a V, showing the dark, curly hair of his chest. He stood watching them all from the doorway as they settled the children, covering them with a strange array of old curtains, army blankets, tablecloths – anything they had managed to get hold of.

Some of them wanted comforting before they could sleep, and when they were all settled Assunta stayed in the room for a while, sitting in a ring of candlelight with her rosary beads held between her fingers.

The others went quietly into the room opposite the kitchen storeroom, where there was a thin rug on the floor and an assortment of old chairs.

'Rosa has brought some English tea,' Francesco announced, perking up for a moment. 'The life-blood of the British army.'

'I'd better make it then, hadn't I?' she laughed. 'Goodness knows what you might do to it!'

As she stood in the dim light of the kitchen, waiting

for the flame from the gas cylinder to heat the water, she heard knocking on the outside door. She realized Francesco was letting Enrico in and she felt immediately uneasy. He sloped in behind her, laying a number of wrapped loaves of bread on the table. She jumped slightly when she turned and found him watching her, his pointed features accentuated by the candlelight.

'Good evening,' she said coolly.

Enrico nodded, still staring hard at her, and for a moment she thought he was about to speak. But he turned and went out of the room again.

The place seemed strange and empty without Margherita. Rose sat drinking the black tea with the strange assortment of people who were left: Magdalena and Francesco both seemed stunned by exhaustion, Enrico, whose eyes carefully watched everyone else, and the troubled figure of Falcone, who despite Francesco's attempts to rouse him was often wrapped in his own thoughts.

'Should I take Assunta some tea?' Rose asked.

'No, leave her. She is saying her rosary every night. For the liquefaction,' Magdalena said, yawning, her eyes straining to keep open behind her spectacles.

'The what?'

Francesco explained. 'It is a miracle which shows us that there will be good fortune for our city. The blood of San Gennaro which is kept in a phial in the Duomo liquifies. Assunta is very worried that too many bad things are happening. The war, the eruption. She's frightened that there will be no liquefaction this May, so she's saying a special rosary every evening.'

Rose nodded solemnly, glad that she had managed to bite back the words, 'Thank God for that – I thought it might be something really important.'

After a moment Magdalena said, 'What are we going to do about Maria Grazia? Margherita thinks she should be taken to the cemetery before the child is born and I think she is right. She should be able to see her mother's grave. Her mind has nothing to settle on.'

'But when?' Francesco asked wearily. 'We have so little time and transport is impossible. It would take us all day to walk up there. I don't even know when Margherita is going to come back.'

At the thought of Margherita they fell silent again, so Rose took her opportunity. 'I've been thinking,' she started timidly, gathering courage when she saw they were all paying attention. 'I don't come here very often, and when I do I bring very little with me. You asked me for help, and I think I have disappointed you. I should be able to do more. After all, I'm a driver. I could transport almost anything, except I don't know how to get hold of it. I can't think who to ask.'

Francesco nodded. 'It's always a question of making the right connections.'

Suddenly, to everyone's amazement, a voice said, 'Why the bleeding hell didn't you say you was a driver before?'

Everyone looked round for the owner of this English voice. Enrico.

'If you've got a truck,' he went on, addressing Rose, 'then that's all I need. I can get the rest of the gear. Blimey – I've been trying to get hold of a driver who can shift the stuff free for months but no one'd cough.'

'What did he say?' Magdalena pulled on Rose's sleeve impatiently. 'He's English too? Who is he?'

Falcone and Francesco were both looking astonished. Especially when Rose burst out laughing.

'So that's why you've been giving me those queer looks every time I've seen you! You're a deserter, aren't you? D'you think I was going to blow the whistle on you or something?' She laughed again. 'We all thought you had a screw loose!' The others watched, totally bemused. 'Enrico, my foot,' she said. 'What's your real name then – Fred?'

'No. Henry,' he said, looking rather sheepish. 'I'm from Bromley. Couldn't stick the army. When they moved on through here I just stayed. There's quite a few of us in Naples you know. Scared the arse off me – all

223

them mines every time you moved a foot forward. I can fight a better war helping to feed these kids than anything I could ever do with that lot. But I couldn't work you out at first. I had to size you up and make sure you wasn't trouble.'

'So – come on, then. How d'you get hold of the food?'

'Easy. The depot. When they've taken the stuff in from the docks it all goes into the warehouse. I've got a couple of mates there. They can make a packet selling the stuff, but they'll give me the odd load free – in a good cause.' Henry winked at her. 'Anyhow, I've managed to get hold of a bit of petrol, which makes a good price, so they don't do it all out of love. Problem is, I've never had proper transport. If you can get yourself over here a night or two in the month, we can get these kids fed up like turkey cocks.'

'Excuse me.' Magdalena gripped Rose's arm, no longer able to contain herself. 'Please – what is he saying?'

Rose explained. 'Don't you speak Italian?' she asked Henry.

'Nope. But I can tell what they're going on about as long as it ain't too involved.'

Rose could feel her breathing going shallow from excitement and anxiety. In Italian she asked, 'D'you think it's right that I take my truck and steal for you from the army?'

There was silence for a moment, and then Francesco said, 'Of course. Already we eat their food, their bread. You know, even the fish in the city's aquarium have been eaten by now. What choice do we have?'

Suddenly they were all startled by Falcone's voice, low, but full of conviction. 'We have to do what is good for the children,' he said. 'What use are the laws of peace during a war? Our Lord tells us to feed the hungry, so that is what we must do, even if we have to take a little from the rich.'

'You sound like another Lupo,' Francesco teased, referring to the Robin Hood figure of Domenico Lupo who travelled in the south with a small gang of bandits, raiding the army and the black market to feed the poor of his people. 'You'll have us holding up trains next.'

Falcone said nothing, but sat staring at the ground between his knees.

Henry pressed Rose further. 'We'll have to be on the spot about times and meeting places. No hanging about. It's a risky business. So – d'you think you're up to it?'

Rose took in a deep, fearful breath. 'I'll have to find a way, won't I?' she said.

CHAPTER 22

It was a night Rose would remember all her life. The sisters and Francesco gratefully accepted the chance of rest and soon all of them were fast asleep. She sat up watching the children with Falcone.

At first it looked like being a long, hard night. Rose was very unsure of this silent, scruffy man who sat leaning against one side of the doorframe smoking cheap cigarettes. For a while she busied herself by walking round the room with a candle to check on each of the sleeping children. As she turned at the far end of the long room and her huge shadow leapt up the wall behind her, she realized that he was watching her. When their eyes met he moved his solemn gaze to the wall opposite him.

When she had exhausted all the activity she could think of, Rose offered to make tea. She sat tensely on the floor at the other side of the door, drinking the watery brew, unsure whether to try to talk to him.

Eventually she said, 'You are an old friend of Francesco and Margherita?'

He pulled the cigarette out from between his lips and said, not ungraciously, 'Yes. We studied together.' Then he added, 'That seems a very long time ago.'

After another silence he said, 'You are English. You do not look English. Why are you here?'

'I wanted to help.'

Suddenly he turned his whole head to examine her fully. Shyly, she turned also and looked into his large brown eyes with a hint of challenge in her own. But in his she read sorrow and vulnerability. Francesco had hinted that Falcone was holding back a weight of feeling that he could not communicate and in that moment she knew it was so. That exchange of glances between them after such brief conversation seemed to carry an intimacy which went a great deal further than their words.

But they could not find any more to say, and Rose began to resign herself to the fact that the rest of the night would be like this.

After about half an hour they heard the sound of planes overhead, followed by a number of bangs. Rose saw Falcone jump, shocked out of his thoughts. Several of the children began to cry. Glad of some diversion to keep her mind off the bombing, Rose went round whispering comforting words to the little ones who, only half awake, were only too happy to sink back into sleep again.

There was another wave of explosions from outside, evidently from the port, as the Germans sought out Allied supply ships. As she sat holding her breath it brought back vividly to Rose the night she had spent watching over her mother while the blitz raged outside.

She heard another shrill voice calling 'Rosa! Rosa!' It was Emilio. She went to sit beside him. To lull him to sleep she sang 'Golden Slumbers' in English because she didn't know any lullabies in Italian.

There was one more wave of bombing and then it seemed to go quiet. A brief raid, thank heaven. Rose stayed by Emilio, humming to him and rocking her slender body in time with the tune until she began to feel quite sleepy herself and closed her eyes.

A shadow moved in front of the candle. When she opened her eyes, Falcone was squatting down opposite her looking at Emilio. Curious, she watched him. As he gazed into the child's face she saw in his expression an extraordinary sympathy and tenderness. Emilio, barely awake, smiled up at both of them and she saw Falcone smile for the first time, lighting up the dark eyes with a warm, mischievous light. Emotions she could barely identify stirred in her.

He said softly to her, 'You must love children very much. You could be resting in comfort away from all this.'

As she looked up at him she too felt trusting as a child, and spoke without hesitation. 'My own little son died when he was three weeks old. I never saw him at this age. If he was alive now he would be seven this year.'

Falcone looked a little puzzled. 'You have a husband?'

She shook her head. 'I was raped. By the man who employed me.'

How strange that she should make this confession to this stranger whom she had sat with for only a couple of hours. That she should feel able to trust him as much as anyone in her life before.

Falcone said sadly, 'That is a terrible thing. And to suffer the death of your child as well. Now I understand why you long to be with children.'

'I don't usually tell people,' she said. 'I felt you wouldn't judge me.'

He let out a sharp rush of breath as if she had said something outrageous. 'I am not fit to judge anyone.'

Suddenly he sat down facing her and scanned her face. 'You do not look English,' he said again. 'Perhaps your face does not look quite Italian, but your colouring, the clothes – one could almost think . . . You are very beautiful.'

Rose smiled, looking away from him to deflect the compliment. 'Your name – does it mean, like the bird? Is it the same?' she asked.

'Yes, *falcone*, the bird with the sharp, vicious beak. I hoped that I wasn't like this bird but I'm not sure what my nature is any more.' His face took on the sad, troubled expression it had worn for most of the evening.

'Why are you here?' she asked gently.

He replied slowly, as if he had not spoken the words before but had been thinking for a long time how to say them. 'I'm here to wait for the end of the war. Until it's finished I have to be like someone without a real home. A wandering soul.' Seeing Rose frown at this rather abstract notion he went on, 'As soon as the war's over I

228

shall enter the seminary of San Domenico Maggiore. I'm going to be a priest.'

'A priest?' Rose cried, then lowered her voice again, looking round to see if she had disturbed any of the children. 'But you can't do that. You're a doctor.'

'I was a doctor.' His voice was bitter. 'Actually I only practised for a short time after I qualified. I don't have a lot of experience.'

'But being a doctor is one of the most important things you could do,' Rose argued. 'Honestly, you people with an education don't know you're born. All that work to become a doctor and you want to give it up and be a priest? You must be mad.'

Falcone didn't rise to her anger. 'You didn't have an education?'

'Not much, no. It was what I wanted, badly. To be a teacher. But . . .' She shrugged. 'Dreams.'

'I would've thought you were educated. You're a very intelligent woman. And you speak my language well.'

'Thanks.'

'You're right though. It's a great privilege to have an education. But you see, to be a doctor – a doctor is supposed to have reverence for life, to cherish and preserve life.' Falcone cupped his hands as if holding up a large and delicate egg shell. 'And I'm tainted. This war has given me a feeling of guilt, of loathing. Whatever I try to do for the best, I'm pursued by death, by destruction. You see?'

He saw that Rose's eyes were full of sympathy and interest. He knew she would not condemn him, that he could lay on her the weight that was pulling his mind down, sometimes it seemed, towards madness.

Rose indicated that they should move back to the door so as not to disturb the children. She fetched them each half a cup of water, and they sat each side of the door again, surrounded by their shadows and the sleeping children.

'When Italy became involved in the war I was still finishing my studies,' he began. 'I felt it right to stay

229

because I was doing something dedicated to giving life instead of working to destroy it.'

'Didn't you have to join up?' Rose asked. She had wondered the same thing about Francesco.

Falcone smiled wryly. 'The Italian army does not even have enough socks to go round. We steal them from the dead when they have finished with them. No – not everyone joined the army.

'When I finished it was 1941. By then we were occupied by Germany. Things were very hard. Naples was growing hungrier by the day. I went home to my family in Cellina, north of Caivano and Acerra, not all that far from Caserta. My father was the town's doctor. Perhaps I would've simply taken over his role. Who knows? For about eighteen months I helped him in the practice. It wasn't difficult work. I enjoyed it, using the skills I had been trained in. Even under occupation a job like that brings a lot of satisfaction.

'Then everything changed. It was December forty-two. I had been out on a late call and I was still in bed. That was why my father was the one to open the door. The body of a German soldier had been found in a side street off the main square. He'd been stabbed in the night and bled to death there. Naturally no one would admit to such a crime. When the Germans found out they had to have their revenge. To teach us Italians a lesson. They are a people who carry out vengeance with mathematical precision. For each German, the life of ten Italians. The ten most prominent men in the town. The mayor, Signor Pacelli, the postmaster – and of course they came to the house of the doctor. They took my father.

'The same morning, they made them stand—' Falcone made a slow pointing gesture with his finger. 'A line of them against the wall of the post office. They made sure there was a big crowd to watch the spectacle. They didn't even blindfold them. I stood there in the piazza as they shot my father. One moment he stood, looking so old suddenly, so frail. He was looking for me, I could tell. But his eyes did not find me among the crowd before the guns went off. And then they were all on the ground. The wall of the post office is broken open with holes. We were allowed to take them for burial.'

Falcone paused for a moment to light another cigarette. Rose sat very still, not wanting to interrupt now that his story had begun to flow out of him.

'For a time I stayed at home alone. My mother died when I was a small boy, and my sisters and brother are all married and live elsewhere. I tried to keep the practice going, and for some time I succeeded. But all the time I was corrupted inside by anger and guilt. If it had been me who opened the door that morning my father wouldn't have died. It would have been me. For the first time in my life I experienced the power of real hatred. I'd felt it touch me when our country was invaded. I'd known disgust and loathing against the Fascists. But nothing which approached this bitter need for action, as if I was possessed. It lay inside my intestines like a poisonous snake. I wanted to join the resistance, to fight back, but there was no organized resistance in the south. Nothing that I could find.

'It was when they threw out Mussolini in July last year. The army was taken over by General Badoglio. All through the winter before there had been signs that Fascism was collapsing. There were even strikes, up in the north – Milano, FIAT at Torino, many other factories. This was unheard of under Mussolini – people like that speaking with their own voice. Such signs gave me hope that it was possible to achieve changes by direct, personal action. So I left Cellina and went to Rome.

'At first I suppose I was filled with an enormous kind of joy, of euphoria at being able to join the resistance at last. I made contact with the Gappisti – GAP is Gruppi di Azione Patriottica. The groups work in many cities to subvert German and Fascist operations. They – we – planted bombs. We attacked columns of soldiers on the move. Assassinated prominent German officers. We attacked the prison, Regina Coeli, the opera house when it was full of German soldiers . . . One of the first actions

I was involved in was to plant a bomb in a petrol depot for German trucks. Everything went up – the drums on the trucks, the storage depot itself. What a feeling that was! We destroyed more than two thousand gallons of their gasoline that afternoon.

'The life we lived was very hard. For those of us without many contacts there was nowhere to sleep except in stone cellars with their cold, hard floors. Often we shared them with prisoners who were trying to escape, English, Canadians, Poles. And we became sick living like this. But the extraordinary thing was that the atmosphere among the people was such as I had never met before. The unity of feeling against the Germans. I was brought up in my faith to believe that people are unified by the love of God. But I discovered there how strongly people are brought together by hatred.

'I lived this life of destruction for eight months. Then, only a few weeks ago, I was ordered to be involved in an ambush against a column of German forces. They weren't just an arbitrary collection of soldiers. We'd heard they were training on the streets of Rome specifically to search out and destroy partisan cells both in and around the city. Our attack was to show that we were not prepared to be intimidated. It was really just a statement, of course. Already they had executed more than half the partisans in Rome.

'The plan was to ambush the column as they passed down the Via Rasella. It's a narrow street with a tunnel at the end. It would be hard for them to turn back or escape. I wasn't one of the key operators. There were members of GAP with much greater nerve and skill. But I was involved as surely as one brick holds up the others in a wall. My job was to watch the column approaching along the route and to signal to Pietro, the next in the chain along the way. In the Via Rasella, one of our women was waiting to give the signal to a man called Bentivegna who was disguised as a rubbish collector. His cart was loaded with explosives. Others were ready to throw mortar bombs.

'We all waited. How can I tell you how it felt that day? It was as if my body was pumped full of electricity. One touch and I would explode. The Germans were over an hour late. We were wondering whether to give up the attempt, all terrified that the police would search Bentivegna's cart. Then they came at last, marching perfectly – beautifully, though it is horrible to say it – the way German soldiers do. The attack went according to plan. The mortar bombs went off, Bentivegna lit the fuse, and we all began to run towards the Via Nazionale.'

Falcone stopped talking for a few seconds. Rose looked at him and saw him take several deep breaths.

'The whole place was in chaos. The bombs blew thirty-three of them to pieces and wounded a great many others. The Germans were there within minutes and we heard gunfire in the streets. While we were escaping, scuttling like rats to our cellars where we hid, the SS were rounding up civilians, door to door, dragging out anyone they could find and loading them on to their trucks.

'The mathematics was the same. That night they took at least three hundred and thirty people – from the gaols, ones they had pulled out of their homes – almost anyone to make up the numbers. Ten Romans for every German soldier.'

His breathing became shallow as he talked, and he was having difficulty taking the air in.

'The orders came direct from the Führer. They drove them to the catacombs, the Ardeatine caves. You must have heard of them. The German soldiers who took them had been drinking. They were blind with drink, taking it like an anaesthetic. Blind enough to lead the prisoners inside, five at a time. They had lit torches so that the shadows shuddered in the caves. Then they made the people kneel and shot them in the back of the neck. It went on until dawn. The last ones had to climb over the dead to be shot. Then they sealed up the cave and blew it up inside.'

Falcone's shoulders were heaving so violently that Rose thought he might vomit. His strong frame was shaking with the horror of those memories. Through chattering teeth he said, 'It was inaccurate. The German commander was very angry. They shot five too many.'

Rose fetched a blanket and wrapped it around his shoulders. He trembled under it as if he had a fever. She handed him some water, and when his hands were shaking too much to take the cup from her, she raised it to his lips herself, so moved she could not speak.

When he was a little calmer he said, 'I haven't talked about it before. It's made it come alive again.'

'Could you not tell Francesco?'

Falcone shook his head. 'Francesco was part of my life when I was a different person. I did not know what destruction I was capable of. I can't bring myself to speak of it to him, or Margherita, though she is so kind, so well meaning. Although they work in this place and it's hard, their lives have been smooth until now. They haven't even known the suffering that you've known. I find I can talk to you.'

'I think Margherita is suffering now.'

'Of course,' Falcone corrected himself.

Their eyes met again with the peculiar tenderness which communicated itself between them, the more so after their shared confidences.

'I knew I should have to tell someone, or such memories would corrupt me even more.'

Though it was the small hours of the morning they continued to talk for the rest of the night. When Falcone had recovered he seemed eager to listen. In those hours Rose talked more than she had ever done, disclosed more about herself than she ever had to anyone in her life. She found herself telling him about her family, about Diana, about Lazenby's, and finally about Alfie. And Falcone talked more about his father, of his rather distant respect for him, and of the little he could remember of his mother. He tried to explain his motives for entering the priesthood, a point on which they could not even begin to agree.

'To be a priest is the highest service you can give to

234

God,' he told her. 'If you were a Catholic you would understand.'

'Just because I'm not a Catholic doesn't mean I'm stupid,' Rose replied heatedly. 'I just can't see the good of you wasting all you've learned by going off and saying prayers all day.'

'I feel strongly that my life has become corrupted. As a priest I can dedicate my life to the truth. To repentance. Perhaps even to holiness.'

'But why not as a doctor?'

'This is my calling now,' he told her. 'I feel sure of it.'

After they had talked and argued through the night, the light gradually seeped over the city as dawn broke. They saw daylight round the edges of the shutters, and after a time, Magdalena appeared looking surprisingly fresh and rested.

'I will sit until they wake,' she said. 'You go and sleep.'

Falcone thanked her. 'But first I want to go out and see what damage they did last night.' He looked at Rose. 'Do you want to come?'

Early morning light washed over the weary, battered city. Already, as they set out through the smoky air towards the sea, people were coming in the opposite direction carrying pails of shellfish which they could try to sell for a few lire. Voices echoed through the streets and children squatted to relieve themselves among the refuse. They crossed the Via Speranzella and headed for the square. One of the narrow side streets behind the Via Toledo was completely blocked by rubble where buildings had collapsed, making it impossible to pass or even see much light along it. People were digging frantically among the rubble looking for loved ones. Somewhere a dog was howling.

The dead were already being laid in rows away from the rubble, to be loaded on to carts. Among them were several children, and into their cold arms the survivors had thrust huge, pink plastic dolls, their gaudy splendour probably far superior to any toy the children had possessed when alive.

Falcone gently steered Rose by the elbow back in the direction of Il Rifugio. 'It was a mistake to come,' he said. 'There's only so much any of us can do, and the authorities are doing their work. We should sleep.'

'I don't want to sleep,' Rose protested. 'I haven't come here to sleep.'

'Sleep!' Falcone commanded as they climbed the stairs. 'We don't want any martyrs here. You must sleep!'

CHAPTER 23

'Who d'you think you are, Gracie Fields?' Madge demanded, astonished.

Rose had walked into the dormitory singing. All the ATS girls were getting ready for an Easter dance to be held in the ballroom at the palace. The contrast of all this colourful gaiety with the doleful Italian Holy Week was striking.

'She's in lo-ove!' Willy sang as she rubbed cream into her already perfect skin. 'I never thought I'd see you looking this half soaked over a man, Rose!'

'That Tony's obviously doing something for you that no one else can,' Madge teased.

Gwen, looking up from flattening out the skirt of her floral dress, said with a bright smile, 'Are you two really getting serious? I'm so happy for you. I've never felt so good in my life as I have since I met Bill. It's marvellous, isn't it?'

Rose just smiled and unfastened her uniform belt.

'Oh heavens, why are you always so flipping secretive?' Willy asked, frustrated.

Rose looked round at them all, bewildered. Was it so obvious? Had she changed so much that they could read it in her face? 'There's not a lot to say really,' she told her inquisitive room mates. 'Tony and I are just very good pals that's all.'

She knew she had changed. She also knew that she was in love with Paulo Falcone. It was as if the feelings that Tony had stirred in her had found their completion in him. She did not think what this might mean for the future. Falcone determined to become a priest and herself engaged to Alfie. It made no sense. While the war, the agonizing crawl of the Allies towards Rome continued, it was not possible to contemplate the future. For the moment the newness of her experience of passion – of her excitement at the thought of seeing him, of the way they could confide in each other, and the expression in his eyes when they rested on her – these were enough. She was also rather enjoying the way Gwen, Madge and Willy were all jumping to the wrong conclusions.

The dance was already warming up when they arrived at the palace ballroom. Rose walked in beside Willy, who was wearing a shimmering emerald green strapless evening dress, her blond hair fastened immaculately on her head. Willy always looked very pure, freshly washed, every line neat and crisp. Beside her Rose felt dark and rather gypsyish. Willy was immediately surrounded and taken off by a circle of admirers.

Tony was waiting by the door for Rose. 'I say – what a stunning dress,' he told her. 'Is that one of the signora's creations?'

Rose nodded, smiling, and Tony was startled by the ecstatic glow of her face. The plain, close-fitting black dress she was wearing was not cut from expensive cloth, but Signora Mandetta had tailored it perfectly to the shape of Rose's curving figure. She had brushed her hair up into a simple knot at the back, and the smooth, unfussy style emphasized her large brown eyes and the fine shape of her face.

She danced with Tony for as much of the evening as she could, though other partners frequently tried to cut in and split them up. Rose's radiant looks and Tony's admiring, affectionate expression gave all the impression of two people who were strongly attracted and perhaps falling deeply in love.

The ballroom was huge, its beautiful floor inlaid with brown and white Carrara marble, the walls and ceiling encrusted with rich gold ornamentation, and warmly lit by lamps suspended from wall brackets and crystal chandeliers which hung on long chains from the ceiling. The centre of the ceiling was covered by a vast mural of what looked like courtiers, dressed in rich reds, blues and greens. At one end of the room was a low, red-carpeted dais on which a low gold throne upholstered in maroon cloth usually stood. Tonight it had been shifted to one side to make room for the band.

'You're not really the impoverished little child you've told me about, are you?' Tony teased Rose as they danced, holding each other lightly. 'You're really an Italian contessa in disguise.'

'Oh, if only!' Rose laughed. 'You don't reckon I'd be driving for the British army if I was do you?' Her eyes wore a mischievous expression. 'How's Lewis?'

'For heaven's sake keep your voice down. He's fine, thank you, since you ask. And we're all right too – together I mean – if that was your next question. We haven't fallen out or anything.'

'Good,' Rose replied, rather taken aback by his flustered response.

During the next dance she could not resist murmuring to him in a low voice, 'It's tonight, by the way.'

'What is?'

'The first drop.'

Tony nearly stopped dancing altogether on hearing this. 'You're going to Naples – tonight?'

She nodded serenely back at him, as if they were talking about a day's pleasure trip to Sorrento or Capri.

'I'm driving the midnight shift over. Then I'm off. Sorry to desert you.'

'But what about the truck? You'll be so late back.'

'Oh, I've got it OK'd – special delivery. They don't ask too many questions as long as it's back for work the next morning.'

'I'm coming with you,' he said heatedly. 'You can't go wandering round the countryside at night on your own. Let alone in Naples. God knows what might happen.'

'No you're not, Tony,' Rose said, still smiling, and

239

rather enjoying the sense of danger inherent in discussing her plans while surrounded by all these people. 'Henry and his mates are meeting me. And then Francesco, or someone else from the refuge.'

To his puzzlement, Tony was sure he noticed a blush seep across her cheeks.

'They'll carry the stuff in. I've got to do this on my own.'

At half past eleven Rose said goodbye to him and slipped out of the ballroom to go and change. Twenty minutes later she had signed the truck out of the compound for the shift drive and was on her way to the palace again carrying a group of signallers and other administrators.

'Thanks Rose!' they called as they jumped out. 'Sorry you're missing the dance.'

She backed the truck up and then drove along the sweeping curve at the front of the palace. Turning into Caserta, she took the road for Naples.

Henry had briefed her that afternoon a fortnight ago at Il Rifugio. He had given her details for 'the drop' as he insisted on calling it. He gave her a plan of where to find the supply depot in Naples.

As she sat in the cab her mind ran over the instructions again. From the yard behind the depot to the Via Toledo and as near as she could get to the Via degli Spagnoli. Her mind kept leaping forward to delivering what she had picked up. Who would come to help fetch it in? And what if the truck was raided while they were doing it? Who would come to help? Would Falcone come? Would she see him? She forced her thoughts back to concentrate on the driving.

She left the sleeping town of Caserta and headed out across country. It was a dark night with no moon, and the lights of the truck were half muffled by blackout shields throwing the light down on to the road. It was fairly warm, and she was not chilled by the air rushing past the

240

open sides of the cab. She drew a couple of squares of chocolate out of her bag and sat chewing them. Cadbury's, all the way from Birmingham. It was so dark that the truck created its own little world of light and she could not see anything other than the road immediately ahead.

During the journey to Naples she passed only a couple of *contadini* who were trudging wearily along at the side of the road, another with a mule and cart and, at one terrifying moment, an army Jeep coming towards her. But as it rushed past she realized it was an American one. They pipped their horn briefly and sped on towards Caserta.

Approaching the outskirts of Naples, she pulled up for a moment to study the map again. Following the northern road from Caserta into the city she memorized the main junctions of the first part of the journey. It was not too complicated, though it was an area she was not familiar with. She looked at her watch. A little after one o'clock. She had got there even faster than she expected. So long as she didn't get lost she should arrive just about on time. Suddenly aware of all the darkness around her now she was not moving, she hurriedly pushed down on the clutch and pulled the long gear lever into first.

The road came into the city from the north-east, and she found herself muttering the directions out loud as she went along, very nervous now, every fibre of her body awake and alert. She could already smell the city, that fetid, urine-soaked smell. Supposing she got lost and let them all down?

'Turn into the Via don Bosco,' she told herself. And then she kept saying 'don Bosco, don Bosco' until she had found the turning and was looking out for the next one. She had to take a turn off to the left, which seemed an impossible task in a strange street with no lights. A church on the corner, Henry had said. Not a big one – need to keep your eyes peeled. Once along that road she should find herself eventually in the Piazza Nazionale. After driving in frustration down several streets which might or might not have been a continuation of the same one, she saw the square open out in front of her. It was already one-fifteen. A few more turnings and she would be there.

Finally, after ten minutes, she had located the depot, and drove quickly round into the street behind. At once the doors of the yard swung open and she reversed inside.

'Get your engine off quick,' Henry hissed at her as she slowly negotiated the space between the high gates. He flashed a torch into the cab. 'There could be trouble. We've had wire cutters out here. I've only just managed to get shot of them.'

'Wire cutters?' Rose turned off the engine as they swung the gates shut behind her, and in the darkness and sudden quiet she realized how hard her heart was pounding. She sat taking long, deep breaths.

'They nick the telephone lines to sell the copper wire. Anyway – you all right?' Henry suddenly appeared beside her with the torch. 'Any problems?'

'No, not really. It was a hell of a lot harder than I thought in this pitch black though.'

'Better get cracking then. Open up will you? Johnny's started bringing the stuff through. Best not to use the torch unless you really have to.'

By the time Rose had got out and unfastened the tarpaulin at the back, Henry was already on his way over with the first load from the gate at the back of the yard.

'What's in there?' Rose asked.

'Christ alone knows,' Henry said, grunting as he hauled it up into the truck. 'They'll have to sort that out when we get it there. Imagine Margherita's face when she sees this lot though, eh?'

For half an hour the two men ran back and forth with boxes, and threw in a few extras like blankets and mattresses for good measure. Rose found herself smiling at each new item that was brought across. How good all this would be for the children – for everyone at Il Rifugio!

When the floor of the truck was covered inside and part of it stacked up at the sides as well, Henry told her to close up again. He called Johnny to come and lock the gates behind them, and jumped into the cab beside her.

'Let's go then.'

As soon as they reached the arranged place on the Via Toledo, where they could not take the truck any further into the narrow streets, Francesco melted out of the shadows and came towards them.

'Any trouble?' he asked anxiously.

Rose and Henry reassured him.

'Now we've got to be quick,' Henry said. 'You stay with the truck, Rose, and we'll make sure there's always someone else here too. Take this.' She found a rifle being thrust into her hands. 'Chances are most people are asleep, but you never know. I'll take a few bits over and bring Falcone and Magdalena back with me. The others are staying with the kids.'

'How's Margherita?' Rose asked Francesco.

'Back with us at least. What else can we do but carry on?'

Rose nodded, and they stood in silence until the others came back. As they emerged from the complete darkness of the side street Rose could feel her heart beating faster. First she saw Magdalena. Falcone was behind her. When he came up close to the truck she saw that his hair was shorter, clipped round into his neck.

Dark though it was, she easily caught his smile and it lifted her, filling her with happiness. He looked slightly amused to see her wearing army trousers and tunic but with her hair still arranged as it had been for the dance.

'*Buona sera,*' he said softly, and she smiled back and said good evening to him and Magdalena.

After that, one of them always stayed while the other three carried the supplies back to the courtyard at Il Rifugio.

Only once, briefly, were she and Falcone left together.

'Are things going well for you?' Rose asked.

'Il Rifugio is a very peaceful place to live – even with all the children. You understand what I mean? It's one of the few places to make something good out of this war.'

'Yes, I suppose that's true. In England I felt I was doing something. Everywhere was under threat, you see. But when I came here, at first the army seemed so peaceful – such an unreal life. I suppose I'm fighting the war through the children.'

'You've done well tonight. It will make Margherita very happy.'

'We've done it together. I'm surprised. I thought there would be trouble of some kind.'

Falcone smiled in the darkness. 'So perhaps God is on our side after all. When are you coming next?'

'I have a weekend. May the sixth and seventh.'

'You know the sixth is the day of the liquefaction, at the Duomo?'

'That business Assunta was on about?'

'The blood of San Gennaro. Why don't you come with me? You'll learn a lot about Naples. Make sure you dress like an Italian.'

Rose agreed happily as the others came into view from across the road.

'Rosa?' Francesco approached her. 'Margherita sends her love and says thank you a thousand times for all this. But she has another request. We need help to take Maria Grazia to the cemetery. Since Margherita has lost her own mother she feels . . .' He didn't need to finish the sentence.

'Of course,' Rose said. 'But it might have to be at night.'

'OK, if it has to be. The child will be born in June, so we have some time.'

'We'll arrange it,' Rose said. 'I'd better go. See you all in a fortnight.'

Magdalena gave her a kiss before she climbed up into the cab, and Falcone took her hand for a second.

She started up the great growling engine, which sounded horribly loud in the street, and waved as she moved off.

'*Ciao!*' she called through the window. She could just see them all waving.

During the drive back along the deserted road she was fully awake and elated. It had worked! She had really managed to bring in something they needed. It made her feel more a part of the place. And he had been proud of her – that was what seemed to matter most of all. She shivered, half with cold, half with excitement.

Soon after four-thirty she was undressed and in bed.

CHAPTER 24

As usual they were discussing and arguing almost from the moment they were together. Rose drove the truck through the darkened city on the way to the cemetery. Beside her in the cab, Falcone sat with Maria Grazia on his lap. And in the back was Henry, who had volunteered to stay and guard the truck.

'But how can you say that?' Rose demanded, her hands tight on the wheel. 'Which way now?'

'Left,' Falcone instructed. 'And it's not me that says it. The Church teaches that it's wrong ever to destroy life.'

Rose snorted. Sod the Church, she found herself thinking, but fortunately could not have said it in Italian even if she'd wanted to. Maria Grazia, about whom the conversation had started, sat holding a bunch of flowers and looking dreamily out at the shrouded streets. Occasionally she stared wonderingly up into Falcone's face. He had been looking after the health of all the children in Il Rifugio, and hers in particular. She seemed to have formed a strong bond with him.

'But what have they done to stop all this destruction?' Rose asked. 'What about Cellina? What about what happened in Rome?'

'You don't have to remind me,' Falcone said bitterly.

'OK, but apart from the war, how many women have you seen die from having too many children? You're a doctor. You know what happens. My mother's life was destroyed by having too many kids.'

'But it is against nature to prevent it. Against God.'

246

Rose was growing ever more exasperated. 'If your God says you should spend your life miserable, and exhausted and sick even if you can do something about it, then I don't think much of him.'

Falcone was silent.

'After all, it's not the effing Pope who has all the babies, is it?' Rose muttered in English. She often felt frustrated in Italian because she spoke more slowly and correctly. It didn't feel natural.

'What did you say?'

'I just mean, what have all these rules to do with real people?'

'It's an ideal we're supposed to try to live up to, however miserably we fail because we are human.'

'You're so sure about it, aren't you?'

Falcone gave her a surprised look. 'It's all I have left. I don't really know if I'm sure about anything any more.'

It had been the same when she went with him to the liquefaction. She had come to Naples with Tony that morning.

Summer had truly begun. The fields were full of ripening plants with chaotic vines twining along the edges. In Naples blinds were being pulled down over windows, and the street hawkers stood with newspapers draped over their heads.

'You sure you'll be all right?' Tony asked. He was going to meet Lewis.

'Perfectly, ta. Once I've changed out of this garb anyway. Go on. Have a good weekend.' They kissed each other on the cheek.

By the time Rose and Falcone arrived at the cathedral in the muggy late afternoon, there was a tense, hysterical atmosphere and Rose noticed the Military Police were gathering at the edge of the crowd.

'Do I look Italian enough?' she murmured, half joking, to Falcone.

'Everyone will think we are husband and wife,' he

replied mischievously and, to her embarrassment, Rose blushed.

'But you won't be allowed a wife if you're going to be a priest.'

'True. So you see, priests don't have everything their way.'

They stood among the garlic-fed, sweating throng, Rose sickened by the stench of unwashed bodies. A few yards away, an old woman collapsed and Rose watched, helpless, as she disappeared under the feet of the over-wrought crowd.

'She'll be killed!' she shouted to Falcone, pointing to where the woman had fallen.

They tried to elbow their way towards her. They had nearly reached her, when two men lifted out her body, the face still and dry as parchment.

'*Morte! Morte!*' they yelled. Most of the faces did not even turn to look, their eyes fixed in rapt expectation on the Duomo.

'Perhaps she died as she fell,' Falcone said.

'This crowd's enough to finish anyone off,' Rose called back. She felt shaky at the way death was taken so lightly.

At the edge of the crowd someone had started smashing shop windows and the police moved in, arms swimming through the bodies. Several people seemed to be in a trance-like state, rushing here and there where space permitted and shouting out in strange, high voices. Rose saw a crinkled old man shrieking in a shrill, unearthly tone. A yellowish froth spewed from his mouth.

She indicated to Falcone that she had something to say and he bent his ear close to her mouth. For a second she longed to kiss his dark, stubbly cheek.

'This is horrible!' she said. 'Why do people believe in this?'

'In what?'

'In this saint who's supposed to stop the lava flowing and keep everyone safe.' He hadn't saved them from the bombs after all, she thought. 'And all these great big churches. Why don't they use the money to help poor people?'

Falcone bent close to her and said, 'If there weren't any churches there'd be nowhere better for the poor to go. People need somewhere to shelter their dreams, their hopes. These people have been through so much. First the Germans, now the British and Americans. At least the Church is something constant for them to hold on to.'

'I can see that,' she yelled back. 'But why not give them something better to believe in than a little bottle of blood?'

'Sssh!' Falcone said urgently. 'Not here of all places. You'll get us lynched. This is the Neapolitan way. Just watch and see, OK?'

She heard the defensive note in his voice and was ashamed of sounding so critical. After all, she loved the place, but she also wanted to understand.

It was impossible to see any of the ritual. Only the earliest and most privileged had a place inside the Duomo. The crowds in the streets could do nothing but wait for the news.

Bursts of shouting could be heard near the doors of the cathedral. Sometimes a surge ran through the crowd, a powerful ripple forcing them towards the building, crushing the people in front. Sharp elbows dug into Rose. With each terrifying sweep forward she was afraid she too would trip and be swept underfoot. Then everyone would fall into a doom-filled silence again. The liquefaction was a long time coming.

Soon after eight a cry went up. The miracle had taken place! Slowly, reluctantly, as they heard later. But it had happened. A collective sigh almost like a breeze passed through the crowd before voices all around them, cracked and hoarse from thirst and tension, were raised in jubilation and relief.

Rose turned, smiling, to Falcone, and saw to her surprise that he was standing with his eyes closed. She bit back what she was going to say, not wanting to intrude.

The rejoicing of the crowd was in the end fairly muted, and soon everyone began to move away.

'Let me take your arm,' Falcone said rather formally as they set off. 'Otherwise you may get lost.'

Rose linked her arm through his dark-skinned one, intensely conscious of every contact of her flesh with his. She looked up at his thoughtful face, which wore an expression of slight puzzlement.

'So are we safe for another year?' she asked as they walked slowly down the Via Tribunali.

'Only until September,' he replied, looking down at her with smiling eyes. 'The liquefaction happens twice every year.'

'Oh, blimey,' Rose said. In English.

'Don't fall asleep for God's sake,' she hissed at Henry as they climbed out at the cemetery gates. 'It's more than my life's worth.'

'Trust me. Anyway, you're not going to be that long, are you?'

It was a clear night, with a few wisps of cloud covering the stars. The thin slice of moon gave little light. Crickets were loud in the scrubby vegetation as the three of them slipped away from the truck which Rose had parked in the dense shadows outside the main cemetery entrance. Maria Grazia walked between them, holding tightly on to Falcone with one hand, and on to her flowers with the other, her back very straight to balance the weight of her pregnancy. The main iron gates were chained and padlocked, but to one side of them a stiff-hinged wooden door in the wall was left open for late visitors.

Inside the cemetery, Rose became aware of huge shapes around them, the towering old mausoleums of the wealthy with their roofs and doors and plaques. For a few seconds Falcone switched on the torch Henry had given them, and shadows leapt and shuddered up their walls. Rose saw that many of the graves were decorated with pictures of the dead and bright sprays of red and white gladioli.

'Better switch it off,' she suggested. 'The shadows are horrible.'

'Don't be afraid,' he said, extinguishing the torch. 'We'll be all right. We need to go down.'

'Is it far?' Maria Grazia asked in a trembling voice. 'I don't like it here.'

'No, not far, *piccola*,' Falcone said tenderly. 'Come on – you're safe.'

They headed down the hillside, along the terraces lined with graves and vaults. Rose's heart was pounding in her chest. She was trying to keep her thoughts away from ghosts and the stories she had heard about Italian burial traditions. Sometimes bodies were unearthed after being buried for a year. The bones were scraped, then laid in much smaller boxes which were stacked in a chancel house.

She had asked Falcone about it, horrified. 'They don't really do they?'

'It does happen here, but more further south. You have to understand – this isn't a big country and there are a lot of people. In many parts the ground is made of solid rock, so it's difficult to find places for burial. You have to find a way to deal with it. You see?'

She had been amazed by his acceptance of such macabre practices.

'That's why many cemeteries have wall graves, built above ground. It's all to save space.'

Rose had seen them, the coffins inserted into slots in a stone structure like a giant chest of drawers.

She sensed Maria Grazia shivering beside her, so she took off her jacket and wrapped it around the child. They walked on slowly, the sound of their feet crunching on dry earth.

Suddenly they all stopped. There was a strange, unearthly sound in front of them, a high moaning, growing louder, making the hairs rise on the back of their necks.

'My God,' Rose said. She wondered for a second if it was a cat, but the sound was too loud and full. Maria Grazia turned to Falcone and buried her head against him.

Then they heard another noise, a low grunting, rhythmic and urgent. After a few seconds both cries began to die down together. Rose's eyes met Falcone's as the intimacy of what was happening so close by dawned on them both.

Falcone looked away quickly and bent to cuddle Maria Grazia in the darkness. 'It's all right,' he soothed. 'It's nothing to be afraid of.'

Without looking at Rose, he said, 'Lovers meet here during the day. I had not expected them to be here at night too.'

As they continued down the path in silence, Rose was seized by an overwhelming desire to giggle. Tight bubbles of hysterical laughter were welling up inside. She could see herself from the outside, a stranger in a foreign cemetery at two o'clock in the morning, with a prospective priest and a pregnant twelve-year-old, listening to the coupling of complete strangers in the dark. Who would believe her if she told them? A loud snort of laughter escaped and Falcone turned in bewilderment.

'Are you all right?'

Rose began laughing then, and couldn't stop. Maria Grazia, quite unused to people roaring with laughter around her, started to giggle at the sight, and eventually, completely astonished, Falcone joined in as well.

Gradually they got themselves back under control. Falcone reached out and put his arm lightly round Rose's shoulders. 'You crazy woman. Do you English always act like this when things are horrible? I haven't laughed so much since – well, I can't remember.' Quickly he removed his arm. 'Come on – we must go.'

Further on the path became much rougher and more stony under foot. Small pebbles rolled away as they walked.

'This must be the oldest part of the place,' Falcone said. 'I'm lost.'

He switched on the torch and shone it in front of them. The sight that met their eyes instantly wiped away any last traces of laughter. At this side of the cemetery some of the oldest wall graves had been built against the rocky side of the hill. With age and erosion, and perhaps from earth tremors in this turbulent area, most of the graves had collapsed. Among the rubble they could clearly make out the broken shapes of coffins. From some, the shrunken bodies had slid out, white, petrified figures, tossed carelessly about among the ruins. Rose would take away the memory of perfectly preserved fingerbones at the end of an arm, pointing up from behind a slab of stone, the hand bent forward at the wrist as if the person behind was relaxing in a bath.

Maria Grazia screamed and rushed in to Falcone's arms. She had seen the dead before many times, but never in these conditions.

'D'you still want to find your mother's resting place?' Falcone asked her gently. 'Or would you like to go home?'

'I want to see it,' she said, sniffing. 'I want to know where my mother is lying.'

'It must be that way,' Falcone said, pointing.

Once they reached the lowest level it was not difficult to find. All signs of attempts at individual Christian burials came to an end, and in front of them, as Falcone flashed the torch around, was a large area where the ground had been disturbed and refilled to cover one of a number of mass graves. The bombing, the typhus epidemic, the general ill health of the population meant that death carts trawled the streets as if in a medieval plague, and none but the wealthy could hope for a gravestone above their heads. Maria Grazia's mother had been poor. It was a bleak, sad sight. Flowers and trinkets had been scattered among the stones on the rough soil. Otherwise the graves lay unmarked and indistinguishable from each other.

Maria Grazia stood staring at the place. Falcone laid the torch down on the ground.

'Find a spot for your flowers,' he said, putting an arm round her shoulders. 'You can make it hers. You are very near her.'

The child walked miserably forward, a skinny, pathetic sight with her bulging belly, and her half-crushed blossoms.

She found a place where there were no other flowers, and knelt on the dry earth to place them. After a few moments she threw herself forward on to the ground, weeping. Then she sat back on her knees, rocking slowly in what seemed to be prayer.

Rose moved as if to go and comfort her but Falcone stopped her. 'Leave her,' he said. 'It's good for her to do this.'

They stood watching her, and Rose felt tears come to her eyes at the thought of her own mother, and the freezing day on which they had buried her. How long ago it all seemed: England, her family, everything, as if it had happened in another life.

She knew that Falcone's eyes were on her, and she turned to look at him as they stood in the shadow behind the torchlight. He moved awkwardly towards her. Then his arms were round her, drawing her to him, and they embraced, his lips seeking out hers. All the tenderness and longing they had seen in each other's eyes were expressed in that kiss. Falcone stroked Rose's hair, and then her face, with wonder, and she leaned against him, filled by emotions she had never known before. For the first time she knew what it was to respond to a kiss, to long for the other person.

She did not know how long they stood in each other's arms. It was only when Maria Grazia finally stood up and walked slowly away from the grave that they parted. Falcone picked up the torch and they went to meet her. Supporting her between them, they began the climb back to the gate.

'Thank Christ for that!' Henry exclaimed as soon as he saw them. 'You've been gone blooming ages. What the hell've you been doing?'

'It took us a bit of time to find her,' Rose told him vaguely. She had a strange, dreamy sensation of complete happiness, as if nothing mattered, neither the truck, nor geting back to Caserta, nor being exhausted the next day. Everything she needed was here.

They drove back to the city in silence, except for Falcone's directions. She wondered whether he was thinking, as she was, of the night's strange, conflicting moods. He sat beside her, his hand laid on the head of the young mother who had fallen asleep across his lap.

CHAPTER 25

On 4 June, two days before the D-Day landings on the coast of France, General Mark Clark led the tanks and trucks of the Allied Forces along the sweeping, majestic roads into Rome. For many of the troops there was an awesome sense that they were moving along the paths of history. But when they reached Rome there was no decisive battle to determine which occupying force should control the fate of Italy. The Germans immediately shifted north to consolidate another line straddling the country's knee. It felt as if the slow crawl up this long, spiny country would never come to an end.

A week after that, another small but momentous event took place at Il Rifugio. Maria Grazia gave birth to a son, a tiny, fragile creature with only enough strength to snuffle into life. The birth was hard and Falcone was forced to call upon another doctor for help to be sure of saving the child. But enter life he did, and he clung to it. Maria Grazia called him Mauro.

Rose first saw him when he was ten days old, and was entranced by his crinkly perfection.

'He's so beautiful,' she said, smiling tearfully down at Maria Grazia as she let her hold him. 'Isn't it an amazing thing?'

The young girl stared blankly at her. She was very pale, and now she no longer carried the weight of the child it was clear how thin she was. Every effort was being made by Margherita, Falcone and the others to feed her up so she could nourish the child with her barely formed breasts.

Thanks to Rose and Henry's monthly 'drops', which had so far gone miraculously well, the children were all thriving, except for two boys who had fallen ill and been removed to the hospital for fear of infecting the others.

If it had not been for Falcone distancing himself from her, Rose would have spent the summer in a haze of happiness. How many times during those weeks did she regret that kiss! Such a small thing, that moment of intimacy, but it changed everything. It had brought into the open the powerful current between her and Falcone which, once acknowledged, could not be ignored.

But wasn't she committed, at least verbally, to Alfie Meredith? It would soon be five years since she had, in a backhand sort of way, agreed to become his wife, a man from a different life, imprisoned in a country she had never seen.

She had tried to abide by her promise, but her feelings for Falcone overpowered everything else. Who was that person who had bound herself to Alfie back in Birmingham? A sad, fragile girl who had no idea of what she was capable. How could she have foreseen meeting Falcone, or the feelings aroused in her by his presence, of wanting to reach out and touch him each time they found themselves close, to stroke his thick black hair or smooth the back of her fingers down his cheek?

She remembered the kiss with longing, but also with a poignant sense of loss. Her own confusion was simple compared with the tension her presence appeared to have set up inside Falcone. He had been so sure where his future lay! Now when she was at Il Rifugio, they were almost never alone, nor did Falcone create opportunities for them to be so as he had before.

They still talked and argued about things, but usually in the presence of Francesco and Margherita, once the children were all asleep. Often they talked about Italian politics. What should happen once the war was over, now that Fascism seemed to be defeated? Magdalena would join in in her deep, animated voice. When Rose and Falcone were alone she found it possible to express her

257

thoughts in a direct way, but she was intimidated by this gathering of educated Italians. She felt truly at home only when they were dealing with the children. Yet she needed more now from Il Rifugio than her work with the children. She needed Falcone. To talk with him, be alone with him, to understand why he was withdrawing from her, shutting her out.

In every other way her life felt charmed. The country came into bloom. Caserta flowered with red and pink geraniums hanging from almost every window and bright blooms of bougainvillea stained every wall across the town. In the countryside oranges and lemons hung ripe on the trees and the vines were heavy with grapes. The heat of the sun softened the road surface, giving it a spongy feel, and the air blowing in at the sides of the trucks was warm and caressing.

Behind the palace the long sweep of grass turned brown and wiry, and the tanks below the cascades gave off a slightly stagnant smell. The ATS pulled up their light cotton frocks on the grass to sun themselves during their hours off duty. Rose found that she had formed an easy, if not intimate camaraderie with Willy, Madge and, of course, Gwen.

As the temperature rose, Naples steamed and came alive with fat green flies which shimmered in dark clouds and settled on anything damp, heading for the face, mouth and armpits.

'It's beyond me why you spend your weekends over there when you could get out to Amalfi or Capri,' Tony said to Rose. 'God, the stink of the place! Lewis and I get out as fast as we can. Anyway, I thought you were mad keen to see the country round here?'

'But you've never been to Il Rifugio,' Rose retorted indignantly. 'And it's much cleaner there than you'd think. The two nuns spend half their lives cleaning up.' But he did have a point. There were so many places she still hadn't seen.

*

One Sunday afternoon, Rose was sitting in the courtyard with Mauro in her lap while Maria Grazia slept. The baby's tiny hand gripped her little finger as he lay half asleep. Rose smiled down at him. She'd found a spot in the shade on the warm stone flags, her back against the wall, and she could smell the pungent leaves of a geranium plant growing in a pot near by.

She looked up, to see Falcone watching her. He was standing, his hands in the pockets of his blue dungarees, leaning against one of the pillars of the arched entrance to the staircase. He had been talking with Francesco. Now he stared at her in silence, and she saw in his face such a depth of longing and bewilderment that she had to turn her face back towards Mauro.

Falcone pushed himself away from the pillar and turned to walk inside.

'What's eating him?' Francesco asked.

'He's in love with Rosa,' Margherita said without looking up from her sewing at Rose, who started, but kept her eyes on Mauro.

'He's *what*?' Francesco exploded. 'He can't be! He's going to the seminary.'

Magdalena snorted, pushing her veil back over her shoulders. 'Can't be? What nonsense you do talk.'

'Of course he's in love. It stands out a mile,' Margherita told him.

'I haven't noticed anything,' Francesco said rather petulantly.

'What do you expect?' Magdalena was scornful. 'You're a man.'

'Rosa?' Francesco leaned down to see her expression. 'Is this true?'

Slowly she raised her head, her cheeks burning red. There was no need for her to reply.

'And you love him?'

'Of course she does,' Margherita said, biting off a piece of thread. 'It's obvious.'

'So what's going on?' Francesco had the air of someone who has had a fast one pulled on him in a card game.

'You don't speak to each other any more. Falcone is like a mule with a sore bottom. What is the matter with you both?'

'Falcone is trying to decide his vocation,' Magdalena explained, in the kind of patient tone she usually reserved for Assunta and the children. 'Not everyone gets a visit from an angel to tell them which way to go.'

'Do you think he will be a priest?' Rose asked. 'It's all very strange to me.'

'Only God can tell us that,' Magdalena said, smiling at her.

'He's no priest,' Margherita said firmly. 'Two heads on the pillow. That's his vocation, and deep down he knows it really.'

'He won't even speak to me,' Rose said. It was a relief to confide in the others. 'I don't understand him. I never even see him alone any more.'

'Go now,' Margherita told her. 'Assunta is asleep. He's alone up there.'

Rose stood up and laid Mauro in Magdalena's arms.

The others watched as Rose and Falcone crossed the courtyard together and unlocked the gate. Out in the baking streets the stalls were closed down and the usual clamour was muted by the routine of the Sunday siesta.

Not speaking, they walked down to the small strip of parched parkland which edged the Mediterranean at Santa Lucia. Scrubby pine trees offered a meagre shade, and they chose a spot to sit away from the sea, where there were no bodies snoring in the heat. Through the trees they could see the white glare of light on the water, and make out the hazy, grey shape of Vesuvius, quiet now, in the distance across the bay.

Falcone said, 'It's my fault. I'm sorry. When you're not here I begin to believe that I know what I'm supposed to do with my life. As soon as I see you again, I'm thrown into confusion.'

'Sometimes, the way you look at me,' Rose said

haltingly, 'I begin to think you hate me, that I'm nothing but trouble in your life.'

'You know I don't hate you.'

'But it would be better for you if I did not come here – to Il Rifugio?'

Falcone sat leaning his elbows on his raised knees, his head between his tanned hands, staring out to sea.

He shook his head. 'No. That's not true either. You know as well as I do that you're far more help to them than I can ever be.' He picked up a small, dry twig and threw it hard towards the sea. 'I couldn't even manage to deliver Maria Grazia's baby safely on my own. I'm no great asset to them. It's not you that's at fault, Rosa. It's me. I told you: everywhere I go I bring hurt and destruction. I thought things were clear. God's call felt . . . strong, pure. I don't know if you can understand that. And sometimes I can feel it. But when I am near you I don't know which is the right path for me. In the meantime I just bring you pain.'

In the silence that followed, Rose found herself crying. They were mostly tears of frustration, at not knowing how to console him since she was the source of his conflict. She wanted to take him in her arms and hold him, but she knew that for him it would be like being embraced by a thorn bush.

'Rosa?' Falcone said in distress. 'Please. Please don't.' He made helpless gestures with his arms and laid one of them briefly round her shoulders before withdrawing it again. 'Please don't cry, dearest Rosa. It's better for you if you're not near me – I'm so confused, I only hurt you. That night in the cemetery, I allowed my feelings for you to – to sweep me along. I shouldn't have. It was wrong.'

His words only made Rose weep even more. Why was it wrong? Why?

He stood up suddenly. 'When the war's over you'll go back to England and marry your English husband. Think only of that and forget me. Please.'

He turned from her, aghast at himself, and walked away from Santa Lucia and back towards the Via Toledo.

When he crossed the courtyard of Il Rifugio alone, only half an hour after they had left, the others exchanged sad, puzzled glances.

Rose sat for a long time under the dry, bleached pine trees, crying for both his anguish and her own.

She tried to bring down her protective shutters as she had done in the past, to stop any expression of her feelings for him, even to herself. As the autumn came and began to turn to winter, and the fields faded to blander colours once more, she carried on with the drops. She spent her leave weekends at Il Rifugio, but as far as possible she avoided contact with Falcone. It wasn't difficult. They were polite to each other when they had to work together. Rose talked to him briskly and brightly, almost as if he was a new arrival in the place whom she barely knew.

'Could you go and fetch a bucket of water please?' she might ask, or, 'Margherita says she needs you to look at one of the children upstairs.' And Falcone would nod respectfully as if she were in charge and do as she asked.

She stayed just as committed to the place, but her mind began to hunger to see more of the country around. She mentioned the fact to Margherita and Francesco, and they encouraged her to go.

'Perhaps Falcone could take you?' Francesco suggested.

Margherita looked at him as if he were a half-wit.

'I can easily find a chaperone from the army, thank you,' Rose said rather bitterly.

'I'll take a weekend to go some time,' she said to Margherita later on. 'But I'd like to come here for Christmas. Is that all right?'

Margherita gave her tired smile. 'You know you don't have to ask. Just come when you can.'

*

As it turned out, she did not spend Christmas at Il Rifugio. One evening in November Gwen came rushing into the dormitory as most of them were preparing for bed. She looked as if she was about to explode with excitement. 'Bill's just asked me to marry him.'

'And . . .?' Rose said.

'I've said I will.'

'Course you have!' Madge dashed up to supply one of her bear hugs. 'As if you'd have turned him down. We'd've all lynched you after the amount we've heard about your Bill this year!'

All of them went to add their congratulations. Willy had tears in her eyes. 'Oh, it's so romantic,' she cried. 'Are you going to get married at the palace?'

'Yes,' Gwen told them. 'We've fixed it for Christmas Eve. We thought it would be an awfully nice time, when everyone's feeling festive anyway. Goodness knows if we'll be ready by then though.'

'What's the problem?' Madge asked. 'All you need is a bloke and a dress, isn't it?'

Gwen laughed, looking really pretty. 'Yes, I suppose you're right. But where shall I get a dress from?'

'Ah – I can help you there,' Rose said. She knew Signora Mandetta would be pleased to have the work, though she would have been more delighted had it been Rose's own wedding dress.

When the fuss had died down, Gwen came and sat on Rose's bed.

'I'm so happy for you,' Rose told her. 'Bill seems a good bloke.'

'Thank you,' Gwen said, smiling again. 'He is, really.' She was watching Rose, her auburn hair curling round her face. 'I wanted to ask if you'd be my bridesmaid. I'd be ever so pleased if you would.'

'Of course,' Rose said. 'I'd be honoured.' She leaned over and gave Gwen a hug. 'I'm really chuffed.'

'I'm not going to tell Mummy,' Gwen told her, looking serious suddenly. 'Not until it's all over and settled.'

'Oh, blimey,' Rose said. 'Don't you think you

should? She could hold it against you for the rest of your life.'

'She'll do that whether I tell her now or later.'

Gwen became Mrs William Charles Crowther in the little blue-walled chapel in the palace, with her ATS friends standing round. They had gone to great lengths to get hold of flowers to decorate the place, which already had its share of marble and ornate white inlay against the blue ceiling.

Signora Mandetta had made Gwen a beautiful satin dress which hung in soft folds round her hips and swept the floor behind her, decorated with tiny mother-of-pearl seeds. For Rose she had chosen a dress in a pale blue material, and both of them held simple bunches of white lilies.

'It's funny, isn't it?' Rose said to her, before they set off to the palace in a specially decorated army Jeep. 'I can't help thinking about the first time I saw you, at Didcot Station that day when we'd joined up. I'd never have dreamed I'd be doing this with you.'

Gwen looked solemn for a moment. 'Sometimes it makes me go cold thinking about how my life would have turned out if I hadn't joined up.' Suddenly she stepped forward and put her arms round Rose. 'I'm so happy,' she said. 'And you've been a real brick the way you've helped with everything.' She looked into Rose's face. 'Maybe it'll be you and Tony next. Maybe our wedding'll give him a push in the right direction.'

Rose smiled back, impishly. 'Stranger things have happened, I s'pose.'

Standing with Gwen as she and Bill made their vows, Rose was glad of Tony's solid presence behind her. Everything went smoothly, and when she danced with Tony at the little celebration afterwards, Rose realized she felt almost light-hearted, glad of a break from Il Rifugio and from Naples.

'I was thinking of going to see Capri on my next leave weekend,' she told Tony. 'Any chance of you sparing some time to show me around?'

CHAPTER 26

APRIL 1945

The letter from Grace arrived two days before Rose's weekend leave. It was the second that fortnight, which was unusual for Grace who never wrote more often than every month or so, and only a brief note when she did. In the first letter she had announced her engagement to a GI called Joe Landers. He had just been posted and she was missing him. Just like Grace not even to mention him until she really had something to say.

The second letter was only a couple of sentences: 'We had a telegram today. Sam's been killed. Thought you'd want to know straight away. Love, Grace.'

Rose re-read the skeleton of a letter, trying to take in the reality of it. She knew its brevity stemmed from Grace's shock and grief, and also from the fact she didn't know any more than that. After all, what else was there to say? But Rose longed for detail. Where was he? How had he died? Suddenly the reality of home poured in on her, of life back in the greyness of England, stuck there, waiting for news. In Italy it had all receded from her mind as if Catherine Street was an old film she had seen years ago and half forgotten. Home. The place she would go back to when this was all over, with no Dora, no Sam. No reliable, pedantic Sam.

Over the next two days she thought more about her elder brother than she had in the whole of the war. Memories of their childhood kept forcing themselves into her mind: of playing marbles with him out in the yard; of Sam rescuing her little cloth doll when one of the Pye children threw it over the wall into the next court. Sam going out to start his first job; his stiff loyalty when he found out she was pregnant.

The next weekend she had planned to go to Sorrento with Gwen and Bill and a friend of Bill's. They'd made up a foursome on the previous leave to see Positano and Amalfi. Tony had taken her to Capri for one weekend, and she had revelled in the rich blue of the sea, the sparkling beauty of the island with its bright white villas and cobbled squares where people lingered and drank and talked, even in winter, as if there was no war anywhere in the world.

Rose had only been to Naples for the weekend once since November. She could not face spending her days so close to Falcone while they were so remote from each other. Now she felt a strong need to talk to Margherita, who she saw as her closest friend in Italy. Several times Margherita had confided in her, breaking down and pouring out her worries about her father, living in a new place surrounded by strangers. Rose knew Margherita was the one person she could allow to see her feelings.

Without mentioning Sam, she told Gwen she would be going off with Tony for the weekend after all. Gwen smiled knowingly at her.

'What is it?' Margherita asked as soon as Rose set foot through the door. She was sitting pounding at some piece of cloth in a bucket of water, her eyes ringed with tiredness. A circle of children stood watching.

Rose burst into tears for the first time. She started to shake and sob. 'My brother is dead.'

Margherita stood up and led her into the little sitting room, indicating to the children that they should not follow. She put her arms round Rose and let her cry for as long as she needed to, as Rose had done for her a number of times in the past. She stroked Rose's hair as she sat beside her, her kind eyes solemnly watching her friend's face.

Then Rose, still shaking, but quieter, was able to tell the little she knew. 'I don't even know where he was –

what country,' she said. 'I know we'll find out in the end. But it seems terrible to die so far from home.'

Margherita nodded, understanding.

'I feel so guilty,' Rose said, starting to cry again. 'I've hardly given my family a thought since coming out here. I've been so wrapped up in the army and this place – you've all been like my family. It's suddenly come home to me all they've been through, and I've been no help at all.'

Margherita sighed sadly. 'I know,' she said. 'Believe me, I have those feelings too. When the eruption came and I lost my mother, that was when I realized I had hardly seen them since the war began. The children had taken all my time. Francesco and I were always so busy, so involved with each other and this place. My family only lived across the bay, and still I did nothing for them. Now I shall never see my mother again. Every day my heart aches when I think of it.'

Holding Margherita around her waist, Rose felt how thin she had become. When they let each other go, she realized they were not alone. Falcone was standing in the doorway, his face full of concern and at the same time surprise at seeing Rose there at all.

'What's happened?'

'Rosa's brother has been killed,' Margherita told him. 'Somewhere,' she added. '*Qualche parte.*' The words hung woefully in the air.

'I'm so sorry, Rosa,' Falcone began.

'You need some time,' Margherita interrupted. 'You shouldn't be working here this weekend, Rosa.'

Rose started to argue, but Margherita silenced her.

'You must go somewhere else, somewhere more peaceful and pleasant. Falcone – you take her.'

'But . . . I—' Falcone started to say.

'You are the person we can spare most easily,' Margherita continued ruthlessly. 'Take her. Look after her.' She sighed, tilting her head on one side with a certain impatience. 'Forget your own struggles for a bit, eh?'

'No!' Rose cried immediately. 'No. I'll stay here. It

will do me good to be working.' A few months ago nothing would have filled her with greater delight than the idea of two days alone with Falcone, but now, the thought of him being forced to take her away for a weekend against his will filled her with panic. 'If I'm busy I won't have to think,' she protested.

'Go,' Margherita said. It was an order. 'You need to think.'

Rose had never heard her so steely and commanding before. It seemed as if she and Falcone would be thrown out bodily if they refused to go. They looked at each other warily for a moment. It was the first time their eyes had met for a very long time. Rose went and picked up her bag.

'Where are we going?' she asked as they stepped out into the warm spring air of the streets. The hawkers were in full throat on the pavements.

'I know a peaceful place I can take you. I used to go with my father. We had holidays there when he needed a rest. You'll like it.'

'I'm sorry you have to do this.'

'You don't have to be sorry,' he said stiffly. 'Margherita's right. I've been too wrapped up in myself. I need to do my duty by other people.'

Quelled by the coldness of the word 'duty', Rose fell silent again. They walked along the majestic Corso Umberto and into the Piazza Garibaldi where they could catch a train. Rose felt her spirits plummeting. The easy friendship, the fire of discussion between them, the tenderness – all this had vanished. Now they were like wooden puppets with each other. She felt despairing at the thought of the cold, awkward weekend ahead.

They took a train for Sorrento. Falcone had money and they each paid for their own ticket. He also bought a newspaper. They sat opposite one another, and throughout the entire journey Falcone read the newspaper. Rose often glanced across at his solemn face, the brown eyes

269

moving in concentration across the print. A stranger's face, she thought. Had she loved him? Who was he? Where was the vulnerable, complex man she had given her heart to?

Determinedly she looked away from him out of the window. She wanted to see more of Italy, didn't she? But she could have been seeing this same place so much more cheerfully with Gwen. She stared out at the louring shape of Vesuvius. The lava fields from the eruption lay greyish mauve, spongy looking, and cool now. Villages, orange groves and vineyards pushed defiantly right to the edges of them. On her side of the train she caught glimpses of the sea, the morning sunlight wrinkling in its deep blue surface. How these sights would have exhilarated her had her mood not been so sad.

The train climbed high along the verdant cliffside, and Rose smelt the pine trees. For a time they looked right across the sea, and then gradually rolled down into Sorrento.

Everyone climbed out at the small station. Immediately the place felt different from Naples. Quieter, with almost a holiday feel. Rose was terrified of meeting any service people who might recognize her, and she was relieved to get away from the station. Walking with Falcone and dressed in her black clothes she was certainly not conspicuously British.

'We have a way to go,' Falcone told her. 'I hope you're not too tired? My friends live on the hillside outside the town.'

'I'm all right,' Rose said, though in truth she felt dragged down and exhausted.

Falcone led her along the cobbled streets, usually walking slightly ahead of her, though she was unsure whether this was through impatience to get there or because her presence was unbearable. As they left the town and toiled uphill, past rough cottages with flowers bright at the windows, the stones burning hot under their feet, she became convinced it was because he could not stand to be near her. That long walk in the heat, bothered

270

by flies, seeing his back in front of her, was the lowest point she could remember since being in Italy. With her head aching and her hand sweaty on the handle of her bag, she could only think about what she had lost and this terrible silence that had grown up between them.

For the first time she found herself thinking, 'I wish I could just go home. Get away and forget it all.' Hot tears stung her eyes and she wiped them away crossly. She was not going to let him, an alien creature, as she thought of Falcone now, see her cry again. At that moment she hated him.

Falcone stopped finally at what seemed to be the end of the road, at a large house, its front covered in pink, crumbling plaster and shaded by two eucalyptus trees. As he went to knock at the door they heard a dog give a moaning bark somewhere behind the house, and two white geese waddled out from among the weeds and stood muttering at them.

Rose put her bag down and wiped the sweat from her forehead. There was a slight breeze up there and, suddenly refreshed, she looked around her. Not far from the house, where the road petered out, a stepped path built from huge, pale stones wound upwards between the trees which covered the higher slopes of the mountain. She longed to walk there and lose herself among the trees, to escape from Falcone and these people she now had to meet.

The door opened and a voice cried, 'Paulo! Is it you, really? How marvellous. Welcome, welcome . . .'

An elderly man, with steely grey hair and a stubbly little moustache, opened his arms wide in greeting. His face was deeply lined and tanned the colour of strong tea.

'Who's this?'

'This is Rosa, Signore Finzi,' Falcone said loudly. 'Rose Lucas. She is English.'

'*Un'inglese?*' Signore Finzi looked puzzled, staring at Rose, who suddenly found herself blushing at the thought of all the questions that must be going through the old man's mind.

271

Falcone explained briefly what they were doing there, and their host offered condolences while leading them inside to a large cool kitchen.

'Clara, Clara! Look who's come to visit us!'

No sooner had Clara Finzi set eyes on Falcone than he was clasped tightly in her plump arms amid loud expressions of delight, and wasn't he thin and where had he been all this time and, finally, tears, which she mopped from her round, soft-looking cheeks. His father, his father. It would seem like the old days young Paulo being here – but holy Mother, how it made her think of Doctor Falcone . . . What a terrible, terrible thing . . .'

As soon as Rose was introduced as a friend she also found herself crushed against the signora's bosom, and kisses landing on her cheeks from lips with a hint of moustache above them.

'Fetch wine, Angelo – and water,' the signora commanded at the top of her voice. Rose had quickly grasped that Signore Finzi's hearing had almost gone. They sat down at the scrubbed wooden table. On a side table the signora had been cutting long strips of tagliatelle. Her husband sat down with them having brought the drinks and the signora talked and talked while she carried on preparing the food.

'You have come right in time for a meal!' she exclaimed. 'It's so long since anyone has been to stay here. We have the rooms ready, but not even the soldiers come. They don't know we are here, of course, and they want the sea, the bars, the shops. Nothing is like it was in the old days. And we make no money.' She stopped to take a swig of the wine. 'But now I have someone to cook for,' she added, almost like a threat.

'We must drink to your father,' she said to Falcone. Looking at Rose she added, 'Ah – *il dottore* Falcone. What a gentleman. What a doctor!' Her tears started to flow again. 'Of all the places he could have stayed, he came again and again to our poor house. Every year, with his children. From when this one was a small boy. Look – I have a photograph.'

Rose glanced nervously at Falcone, but saw nothing but affection and amusement in his eyes. He had relaxed suddenly, and looked younger, as if revisiting this place of his childhood had stripped some of the troubled lines from his face.

The signora swung herself back to the table after taking a small photograph from a shelf of the dresser.

'There. You remember?'

She held out the picture between Rose and Falcone. Rose saw a tall, thin man with a serious but gentle face, standing rather formally beside two boys. Behind them was the Finzis' house. The three of them were dressed in dark trousers and jackets. The taller of the two boys next to him closely resembled his father, the face thin and hair lighter than his younger brother's. Clearly the smaller of the two was Falcone, even if Rose had not known he was the youngest. Darker and stockier than his brother, he stared out of the photograph with the mischievous expression she recognized and those long-lashed eyes.

Without thinking she turned and smiled at him. 'You've hardly changed at all.'

'It's true, he hasn't,' Angelo Finzi said. 'He was always like his mother, God rest her.'

To Rose's surprise Falcone returned her smile, the warmth suddenly back in his eyes. The Finzis exchanged glances.

Signora Finzi put in front of them bowls of delicious tagliatelle with *pomodoro al sugo* and an egg on top, which they both ate hungrily. All the while the signora talked and reminisced and lamented the war, and the tragic murder of *il dottore*, so that neither Angelo Finzi, who sat nodding at what he could hear, nor Rose and Falcone were required to say anything at all. They sat eating beside each other in what now felt a more comfortable silence.

'You need to rest now,' Clara Finzi instructed them.

She led them upstairs and into a small passageway at the top from which led several doors. The first she opened was for Rose. It was a simple, white room, very cool, in the middle of which a huge wooden-framed bed took up most of the space. Wooden shutters were closed at the windows, and when she pushed them open, letting in warmer air and languid flies, she realized the room looked over the back of the house. The Finzis had a small plot of land which stretched out to the point where the trees took over. They cultivated it intensively, and among all the rows of growing vegetables and tomato plants, chickens and geese ran here and there. Rose could still hear the dog, but it was not in sight.

She breathed in the warm air, her headache easing off a little now they were out of the direct heat, and turned to the whitewashed room behind her. Over the bed hung a small wooden crucifix. There was a chair and a rough chest of drawers with a deep porcelain bowl resting on top. That was all.

Well fed and tired enough now for all thoughts to be blocked out, she lay down gratefully on the firm, white bed.

CHAPTER 27

When she awoke, the only sound was the clucking of chickens below the window. She had left the shutters open and the light had grown softer, with the gentle, pinkish tinge of late afternoon. Her watch said four-thirty. Slowly she drank the cup of water by her bed and stood up, stretching her limbs.

There were no signs of life in the rest of the house when she left the room, so she let herself out of the front door. She would walk. It would be good to be alone, really alone for a time. Army life meant always being with other people.

The air outside was caressingly warm, full of the scents of herbs and gorse, and from somewhere the smell of frying onions. Rose turned towards the path which led up the hillside and began to climb, still feeling rather muzzy from her sleep. Every few yards along the sloping path there was a deep step, and she could feel the muscles in her legs pulling hard as she climbed between the greyish olive trees, with salamanders scuttling away from the path and the loud, abrasive rhythm of the crickets and cicadas.

She soon realized this was more than a convenient path up the side of the hill. In fact there were no other houses up there that she could see, nowhere for the path to lead. But at every other bend in the route as she made her way up was a little brick shrine, about waist height. Bending to look inside she found that set into each brick column was a roughly painted picture, each bearing a number. The pictures were the same as she had seen on the walls of the austere Naples churches, the fourteen Stations of the Cross. Jesus receives the Cross, Veronica wipes Jesus' face, Jesus is nailed to the Cross. On the sills of some of the shrines she saw the remains of candle stubs and wilted flowers, perhaps left over from the Easter procession.

It felt appropriate that she should have come walking here to think about Sam. Sam, who had had his own beliefs, in his way, even if he would have staunchly disapproved of the colourful Catholic imagery in this thread of shared belief she was following up between the trees. She tried to concentrate on Sam, to talk to him.

She sat down on one of the cold steps, suddenly overcome by a great welling up of feeling. Hot tears ran down her cheeks.

'I'll miss you. I'll miss you so much.'

Putting her hands over her face she wept for a few minutes, picturing the old, hard life in Birmingham, the way it had all been swept away by the war, changing and displacing all of them. Killing them, one way or another. None of it would ever be the same again. This thought was reinforced by the sight of the worn black skirt pulled tight over her strong tanned legs. It seemed such an alien thing. Who was she now? Who was Rose Lucas? Alone in a far-away country, dressed in strange, foreign clothes, giving her heart to a man who could not love her back. She remembered the smile Falcone had given her as they looked at the photograph together, and it made her cry again. It felt so cruel, that glimpse of how things could have been.

Angrily she stood up and walked on up the hill, trying to work the pain out of herself by physical exertion. She passed the final three stages of the pilgrimage without stopping to look at them, her legs aching.

At the top there was a small stone chapel. Outside stood a pale, bland-faced statue of Mary. The path led on upwards behind the chapel, but it looked less well tended.

She pushed open the door of the chapel quietly. It was gloomy inside, but her attention was drawn straight away to a raised altar where stood a Madonna quite different from the lifeless image depicted outside. She was dressed in heavy blue velvet, and at her breast was pinned a large metal heart, pierced through with a bristling collection of pins, large and thick like nails. One of her arms was outstretched, and her mouth was open as if she was constantly crying out, her grey eyes staring across the chapel in anguish. This was no serene plaster statue, but a woman who had watched her son die a most terrible death and had been powerless to stop it.

In front of her lay all kinds of tributes: garlands of flowers and sacred hearts, offerings of money and rosary beads. And more personal objects: the army cap of someone else's son, a ring and some bracelets, a pair of thick black-rimmed spectacles. Had she been able to save the kin of others when she had failed so completely with her own?

Rose stood staring at her for several minutes. As if sharing the grief of the woman in front of her, she thought of all the people she had lost, Falcone among them. Try as she might to think of anyone but him, he was rarely out of her mind. She remembered that first night when they had talked all through the hours of darkness with the children sleeping round them, how there had been that new sense of herself moving out to him from her very centre, which she later recognized as love.

She turned to look at the rest of the chapel, and jumped violently. As if her thoughts had spirited him to the place, there he was, kneeling at the back of the rows of chairs, looking across at her.

'I'm sorry,' he said gently, standing up. 'Didn't you know I was here?'

'No. I thought I was on my own. Have you been here all the time?'

'I've been here nearly an hour,' he said, walking towards her. 'It's a very peaceful place, isn't it? My father used to come here often and sometimes I came with him.'

He stood beside her, looking up at the statue.

'You know she shares in all our sorrows?' he said. 'When I came and prayed here as a boy I used to remember all my father's patients, those who were suffering great pain, and the ones who had died. It was as if I could commit them all to her.'

'And now?'

Falcone shook his head sadly. 'Now I wonder if even she can comfort all the suffering in the world.'

As they walked out into the early evening light he said, 'The path doesn't end here. Come, I'll show you, it's lovely. No one comes up here except on feast days. There's just an old man who looks after the olive groves.'

Rose climbed beside him. The stones here were further apart, with tufts of wiry grass and weeds poking up between them. Falcone did not rush on ahead as he had earlier, but walked beside her, quite unlike his harsh self at midday.

'Were you thinking about your brother?' Rose noticed with bewilderment that he sounded rather nervous.

'Yes. I was thinking about all my family. How the war has changed everyone. Taken away so much of what was there before. And the way everyone has become someone else.'

'Do you think the people we were are still somewhere inside us?' he asked, in that way she remembered, as if he really needed her opinion. 'That one day we can be reunited with ourselves again?'

'Not the same,' she insisted. 'I know I'll never be the same after being here.' After you, she added in her thoughts.

When they had climbed a little higher the path forked, one branch continuing upwards, obscured by the vegetation around it. The other, which Falcone took, led into a clearing. There was a flat area like a ledge that had been cut into the hill to make a semicircular space, the long, straight side of it against the body of the hill. In the middle of that line stood one more statue, this time of the risen Christ, its stone stained by green lichen. Through the trees he looked out over the town, his arm raised in benediction.

'It's beautiful.' Rose walked to the edge of the clearing.

The air was hazy, but the faded terracotta roofs of the town were easily visible below. She stood trying to absorb herself in the sight, but she was acutely aware that Falcone was watching her. Her body tingled under his gaze. Her heart was beating hard. She knew that something had changed, that the charged atmosphere which had existed between them before had returned, but she did not know how to react, or what to do with the turmoil of feelings inside her.

When she realized that he had come to stand just behind her she said. 'You were very angry with me this morning, weren't you?'

She heard him make a low sound, as if in pain, and turned round quickly to look at him. She was moved by the look of sorrow and desire she recognized in his eyes.

'If you knew,' he said. He looked down at the ground, unable to face her.

'Every step of the way up here as you walked behind me, all I could think of was that you were there, as if your shape was burning into my back, and I couldn't look at you. The train was torture, pretending to read that newspaper when I could only think that you were there, a few feet away from me. I knew if I was alone with you again it would be like this. If I'd looked at you or touched you I would have—' He shrugged helplessly. 'I want you so much. I can't help it.'

Each could feel the other trembling as they moved into each other's arms. They kissed again and again, faces, lips, necks, in a great hurry as if at any second the experience might be snatched away. Rose made little whimpering sounds, almost of distress, at the strength of the emotions he aroused in her.

It did not occur to her to hold back from him. They clung together, exploring each other's bodies with their hands. Slowly, Falcone unbuttoned the black blouse Rose was wearing, uncovering her breasts, cupped in a black cotton bra. His hands were trembling so much as he tried to undo it that she reached round and unfastened the hooks herself. She pulled the little garment out through one sleeve, freeing her breasts with their dark, generous nipples, already peaking at his slight touch.

'You're so, so beautiful,' he said. As his hands moved over her breasts, stroking her, he heard her give a sharp intake of breath at the intense pleasure of it. Never had she been touched like this before. Alfie had not had the imagination to give her more than a clumsy squeeze through her clothes. But this, this stroking, his taking her nipple between finger and thumb sent waves of desire through her body such as she had never even begun to experience before. Her legs were trembling, and the lower part of her body had come alive. She felt a sharp, warm sensation of need rising in her.

'Don't stop,' she said. 'I couldn't bear it if you stopped touching me.'

Quickly they looked round for the softest part of the dry, stony ground. There was not one patch which appeared better than any other, so they knelt down together anyway, unfastening clothes, and they were in each other's arms again, with Falcone's shirt spread out beneath them.

It was awkward, their lovemaking that first time, their unfamiliarity with each other's bodies, the hard ground, but they barely noticed the discomforts of it. At the height of it she called out some words in English and burst into tears at the release. He held her tenderly until both of them quietened, stroking her wet face. He stayed inside her for a long time afterwards.

'I love you,' she whispered into the silence. 'I love you so much.'

She heard his voice, felt his warm breath on her neck. 'And I love you.'

He came to her that night, after they had eaten with the Finzis and talked long into the evening over fish and bread and glasses of wine until the old man fell asleep in his chair, snoring softly, his whiskery mouth hanging open.

As she let Falcone into her dark room, their lips were on each other before either of them had even spoken, their bodies already tight with wanting each other.

'I can't see you,' Falcone whispered. 'I want to see you naked – every part of you. Is there a candle in here?'

'I'll open the shutters,' Rose replied, shivering slightly. 'There's a moon tonight.'

Laughing as quietly as they could manage, they released the shutters, both saying 'Ssshh' with childlike exaggeration as one of the slatted wooden blinds banged too loudly against the frame.

'Well *he* won't hear us anyway,' Rose whispered.

'No. But the signora, she's always had ears like a cat.'

To Falcone's amusement Rose was still wearing her striped army issue pyjamas, not having bothered to get any others. Smiling down at her he unbuttoned the jacket. The solemn, concentrated expression in his eyes made her want to take him to her straight away, but she stood still. He pulled the top away from her breasts and pushed it off down her arms. He slid his hands gently inside the top of her trousers and eased them down over her hips until she could step out of them. She stood naked in front of him, her black hair falling in soft waves over her shoulders, her eyes wide and vulnerable, looking up at him.

For a moment he didn't move to touch her, but stood gazing at her, the moonlight casting deep shadows on her small, curving body, the strong hips and slight curve of her stomach, her full breasts. How many times he had tried to imagine her like this, unclothed, ready for him.

He moved towards her but she raised a hand. 'Wait a minute.'

He had changed into a very worn cotton shirt and frayed shorts. She pulled the shirt off and ran her hands through the black curling hair on his chest, feeling the powerful beating of his heart, aware of his wide brown eyes watching her, a little shy at her taking control. His body was slim but muscular, and she stroked him tenderly across his shoulders, down over his chest and belly. She brought her hands slowly along the soft hair of his thighs, feeling him shudder and flex his legs slightly in anticipation. When he was naked, hard and ready for her, she took him between her hands, caressing him until he gasped and moved to stop her.

'No – wait. Not yet, please.'

And then he was touching her all over, his lips kissing her mouth, her breasts and limbs and then, laying her on the bed, exploring between her legs until she was whimpering with amazed desire, aching to have him inside her. At last she pulled him close, guiding him into her. They both cried out with relief and pleasure and both came almost instantly, first he, then she, and she began to make such a noise that Falcone lovingly laid one hand over her mouth until they both lay back laughing, quietly but slightly hysterically, in each other's arms.

They stayed like that for a time, talking drowsily, sleeping at last on the hard bed. Later in the night Rose woke to feel Falcone's hands moving over her body. The moon had moved and it was darker, but they made love under the covers, more slowly this time, with less urgency, an experience more of touch than sight, both taking longer to climax, but still moved to tears by each other's pleasure.

When she awoke, Rose expected to find him gone. But as the lemon morning light bathed the room through the open shutters, she realized he was beside her still. His face and hair looked very dark against the coarse white linen of the pillow. He was lying with his head resting on his bent arm and she saw his smiling, long-lashed eyes watching her.

Rose half sat up, startled. 'You shouldn't be here! What if they—?'

'They get up very early. I can hear them outside. Don't worry.'

He stroked her hair and kissed her. Then, as they embraced, he pulled her over on top of him, moving against her. The feel of her immediately hardened him, and he lifted her until he could enter her. She sat, both of them moving together gently, his hands stroking her breasts.

'You are a miracle,' he said, rising under her like water until she felt herself come alive again with the tingling at her breasts and his reaching deep into her.

'It feels very good, like this,' she told him. 'I can feel you so far inside me.'

He smiled. 'Good,' he said, 'good.'

She saw his eyes half close as the power of the sensations overcame him, and once more they moved together until they were lost in each other, and every other thought or feeling was taken from them.

CHAPTER 28

MAY 1945

It was over!

On 2 May the German forces in Italy made their official surrender, and the fortunes of Europe had fallen to the Allies. After the long stalemate in the Italian campaign, events had suddenly speeded up during April in a landslide of activity. The Allied Forces finally crossed the enormous span of the River Po, which had long proved such an obstacle, and pushed across the northern plains to the French border. It was a time of sudden reversals, of power overthrown. Mussolini and his mistress, Claretta Petacci, were seized by a colonel in the partisan army in a farmhouse at Dongo on Lake Como to which they had retreated in hiding. The two of them were shot and hung ignominiously by the feet for all to see outside a garage in the Piazzale Loreto in Milan. And on 30 April Hitler and his mistress Eva Braun committed suicide.

The Victory in Europe celebrations were set for 8 May. Caserta was taken over by an air of fiesta and celebration, although the work of administering the army still had to go on. The war was over! They would be going home! Sooner or later they would be back in Blighty with familiar people and places around them. Home, far away and long unseen, was enhanced in the memory and seemed the very sweetest place to be.

But among all the dances, the hugs and kisses and drinking and singing, there were deeply mixed feelings. Some ugly scenes broke out when British soldiers exulted

284

in their victory by taunting the local Italians, whom they saw as defeated. Fights broke out, and at least one Italian in the area was stabbed to death. As it began to sink in that returning home was not just a dream which might be realized some time in the future, memories grew sharper, less softened by nostalgia.

'I'm longing to set up a home with Bill,' Gwen confided to Rose as they walked round the palace grounds. 'Make a real cosy nest, have lots of children. But in some ways I dread going so much. I'll have to face Mummy, and she's going to expect us to live as close to her as possible and I know she'll never leave us alone.'

'Go and live near Bill's family then,' Rose suggested. 'His Dad's not too well, is he? That's a good enough reason I'd've said.'

'Not good enough for Mummy,' Gwen said grimly. 'If I go and live in Bromley she'll never speak to me again. Are you looking forward to going back?'

'No,' Rose said bleakly.

Earlier in the war she had longed to see Grace and the twins and Harry – even George. But so much time had passed that although she did want to see them they felt like strangers. How could she leave Italy now, when the person she loved most in all the world was here? Her mind was already working on how she could arrange to stay. The thought of making her life here with Falcone was the only future she could imagine.

'You and Tony haven't . . . I mean – is there any chance?'

Rose looked at her, frowning for a moment as if puzzled. Then she registered what Gwen was saying. 'Tony? You mean us getting married? No. Tony and me have never been anything but good pals. That's all.'

Gwen sighed sympathetically. 'I'll miss you such a lot, you know, Rose. You've been ever so good for me. Don't know what I'll do without you in fact.'

Rose smiled, her dark eyes warm and suddenly amused. 'We've all been good for each other, when you think of it. Look at that toffee-nosed Willy for a start.

She's almost human nowadays!' They laughed together. 'Anyway, come on. We're not leaving yet. Knowing the army it'll take them months to get round to demobbing us.'

Rose went to Naples a week later. The truck carrying them there could not move fast enough for her. She was almost frantic with anticipation at seeing Falcone, of feeling him close to her again. In her mind a plan had been forming over the past days. It was exciting, frightening, but right. She knew it was what she must do. This was home, the place she wanted to give her life to. When her number came up for demobilization she would not leave. She was going to stay on. Whatever else mattered in her life, there was nothing so important as being here with Falcone.

As they reached the city and rumbled over the cobbles, the usual stench hitting them, she felt like putting out her hand to stroke the faces of the dusty, weary-looking buildings. They had become familiar to her and she knew she was meant to remain here among them.

Napoli, she said in her mind. Napoli, Napoli. My home, God help me. And she smiled so broadly that the barrel-chested corporal opposite her in the truck might have mistaken it for a come on had her mind not been so obviously elsewhere.

She half walked, half ran to Il Rifugio through the squalor of the back streets. She had not bothered to put on her old black clothes this time, and she had gathered quite a bunch of poking, nudging children around her by the time she reached the rough wooden entrance. She opened the gate with her key and locked them all out behind her. She ran up the stone stairs, her heart pounding, and hammered on the door. Next to her on the wall, more faded now, were the rough letters she had first seen: IL RIFUGIO.

Margherita opened the door. Rose saw her look of pleased recognition tighten into one of sorrow, fear

286

almost. Without speaking she took Rose's hand and led her inside, not even kissing her, and she shooed away the children with unusual sharpness. Rose felt her insides turn with dread.

'What?' she gasped. 'What is it? Where is everyone? Where is he?'

'Rosa,' Margherita said gently. She led her to a chair in the little side room and made her sit down.

She went over to the old table and opened the drawer. For a second she hesitated before turning to Rose with an envelope in her hand. Rose saw that she had tears in her eyes.

'He left this,' Margherita said. 'Rosa, I've never seen him more distressed, more frightened of himself.'

Numb, not understanding, Rose took the army issue envelope and opened it, her hands beginning to shake. She realized as she read the short letter, written in bold, black ink, that she had never seen his handwriting before.

'*Mia carissima Rosa*,' it began. 'My dearest Rose,

What can I write to you that will ever make you understand what I have done? In my mind I can see your eyes filled with nothing but pain and I know that I, and only I, am the cause of it.

As you read this you'll know I am thinking of you, as I begin life in the seminary of San Domenico Maggiore, because I can think of nothing else until I can be sure you have left Naples and I know there is no chance of us meeting again.

Now that the war is over, I know that you will go back to your country, my beautiful English friend, for your life is there. I know that this is what you have to do, that our days together here during the war have been a time like no other that we shall never have again. I have asked myself a thousand times if we could make a life together, but I know that your home is really in England, and that my certainty that I must try this vocation would stand between us. Please know that you take my heart with you. I am following God's call, but believe me, it's a road of thorns.

I don't have the words to ask you to forgive or to understand. I know only one thing. That I love no other human being as I love you.

Please accept this ring as a bond, a memory of a time like no other. Forgive me. Go well, my love.

Paulo Falcone.

Slowly Rose tipped the envelope and shook it, and into her hand fell a slim, silver-coloured ring. She recognized it as one of the many hammered out and sold as souvenirs in the area after the eruption. Into its rim was engraved 'NAPLES '44'.

For a few seconds she sat staring dumbly at the letter, at the ring, both of which seemed to bear no relation to him, to the man she loved. Then, leaping up, she exclaimed wildly to Margherita, 'Where is he? Where is San Domenico Maggiore? It's on the way to the Duomo, isn't it? I remember. I can walk. I must go.'

Solemnly Margherita held her back, taking her firmly by the shoulders, almost shaking her to make her stand still.

She looked hard into Rose's distraught face, willing her to accept, to understand. 'No,' she said. 'It's no good, Rosa. Even if you go they'll never let you see him when he's just entered. It's the rule.'

She watched her friend's face, so alight with love and anticipation when she arrived, as it crumpled finally into shock and grief. For a long time she held Rose in her arms that afternoon as her heartbreaking sobs filled the room, the sound of a woman beyond hope and beyond comfort.

PART THREE

HOME
1947–1957

CHAPTER 29

MAY 1947

Gradually she came to, feeling sick and muzzy, and opened her eyes, becoming aware of the white room. She saw the edge of a long blue and white curtain hanging beside her, and, above, a light with a white institutional shade over it like a stiff little hat. Wherever was she? She tried to move, and felt a sharp, tearing pain across her stomach which made her sink back on to the bed again.

After a moment a face appeared, smiling down at her. A young woman with blond hair pinned back under a starched white cap.

'What happened?' Rose demanded. 'What's wrong?'

'Wrong? Nothing at all,' the nurse said soothingly. 'You've got a lovely little daughter, Mrs Meredith. Just over seven pounds. You needed a bit of help with her, that's all. Anyway, now you're awake I'll bring her to you. Your husband's waiting outside.'

Soon Alfie walked into the ward following the nurse who was carrying their tiny child wrapped in a white cellular blanket. Alfie was grinning broadly. Rose felt the blanket bundle in her arms and saw the baby's small squashed face, her eyes closed and a shadow of brown hair on her head.

'There,' Alfie said, as if he'd given birth to the child all by himself. 'Meet Hilda Grace. Our firstborn. Ain't she grand, eh?'

Hilda. Rose tried to smile back at him. So he had named her already, before she, Rose, had even come round. They had argued for months about the name.

Rose had wanted Diana if it was a girl ('That's a toff's name,' Alfie had said), or Dora, or Margaret. Hilda was Alfie's mother's name. Though she was fond of Mrs Meredith, Rose thoroughly disliked the name. But it had been said. Once a new baby had been greeted by its name it seemed too late to go back on it.

She looked down at this child, whose birth she could not remember and whose name she had not spoken, with a strong sense of unreality. She was lovely, it was true, healthy and wholesome. But even at a few hours old, so obviously Alfie's child – his colouring, his narrow eyes. What connection did she have with her mother?

Alfie's face wore a delighted, triumphant grin as he watched Rose suckling their daughter, oblivious to the hard, angry expression on her face.

'Ah, Mrs Meredith. You're back with us I see.' A doctor with dark, bushy hair was striding towards the bed, white coat gusting out behind him. 'Feeling all right? Your baby was breech I'm afraid. Feet first, in other words, and very awkwardly positioned. So we had to whip her out by Caesarean section. All's looking good now though, as I can see.' He spoke very fast.

'Just have a quick glance at you.' He pulled the curtain across briskly on one side and gestured at Alfie to move out.

When he'd checked her wound and opened the curtains again, the doctor suddenly turned with a smile. 'By the way, do you speak Spanish by any chance? Or Italian?'

Bewildered, Rose said, 'Italian. Well I did. In the war.'

'I've been hearing about you from my staff,' the doctor told her with an amused grin. 'Believe me, you haven't lost your touch. You caused quite a stir – chatting away nineteen to the dozen in Italian as you came round from the anaesthetic.'

'Oh my God!' Rose was suddenly delighted, and smiled back at him. Then she saw Alfie scowling beside her. He didn't like hearing anything about Italy, about her war. He was jealous of it in ways he didn't really seem able to explain.

Cautiously she asked, 'What did I say?'

'No idea,' the doctor said. 'Afraid none of us speak the lingo. I was out east myself. Picked up a smattering of Hindustani. You must have worked hard at it. Apparently it was quite impressive.'

When Rose was finally left alone and Hilda had been taken back to the nursery, she lay drowsily in bed, trying to take in the existence of her daughter. It all seemed very new and strange. Her body, having recovered sensation, felt battered and sore from the operation, and her breasts tingled with the forgotten pains of feeding. She had not yet experienced much in the way of any stirring of love for her child. But those feelings would come, she hoped with all her heart. That little girl had to be the centre of her life, for what else was there? A baby. A child. Was it not, if she was honest, mainly so that she could have children that she had agreed to change her name from Lucas to Meredith?

Hilda was crying. Again. All afternoon, on and off, she had screamed and cried until Rose, after trying to work out what it was that was distressing her, had now reached the point where she could scarcely bring herself to care. The sound set all her nerves on edge again. Tutting with infuriation, she picked the baby up and started suckling her in the hope that it would put her back to sleep.

As she was gently lying the child in her wooden cot, she heard the slam of the back door.

'Got the dinner ready?' Alfie shouted. Holding her breath, she heard him drop his heavy boots on to the floor one by one. Then she heard him rattling the lid of the big stewpot, the contents of which had been simmering for over an hour, the smell of gravy and vegetables filling the little prefab house.

'Smells a bit of all right,' he called out.

Hilda stirred in her cot and let cut a loud, cracked-sounding wail.

Alfie padded through in his dusty socks, daubs of

greyish cement stuck round the ankles. 'Hello. All right, love?'

'You've woken her up again!' Rose snapped at him. 'D'you have to shout about the place every time you come in?'

She had meant it to be different. She was going to try much harder today: smile at him when he came in; make life sweeter between them.

Alfie shrugged. 'Can't have your whole life ruled by a babby. They have to fit in with everyone else. That's family, ain't it?'

He came over to try and cajole her, putting his arm round her shoulders as she picked up Hilda, who was showing no sign of wanting to go back to sleep. Rose flinched at his touch.

'Can't you get changed first? You're filthy dirty.'

'Oh, a dirty frock won't hurt. Not when you hear what I've got to tell you. Got some news. I've got a new job. Bigger firm – not just houses like MacMahon's is, so we shouldn't get buggered about so much. All that on, off, on, off with the government. Don't know if you're coming or going. And it's fifteen bob a week more. How about that?'

'Oh, good,' Rose said, trying to sound enthusiastic.

Alfie kissed her. 'I knew you'd be pleased,' he said. He unfastened his trousers and slipped them down as he sat on the bed. 'You'll see,' he said. 'Half this blooming city needs rebuilding. I'll have me own little firm one day.'

She tried to arrange her face into a tired smile. 'I 'spect you will.'

His shoulders flexed back allowing his work shirt to slide off and revealing his very white, though quite muscular torso. Fishy white, Rose thought, staring at his back. Alfie turned to look at her, deliberately, she suspected, not putting his clean shirt on straight away. Did he really imagine the sight of him would excite her, with a restless baby in her arms?

'We're going places, you and me, Rosie,' Alfie said,

his grey eyes showing his habitual optimism. 'We're going to give our kiddies the best you can get.'

Hilda was now looking up at Rose with eyes that were the image of her father's, and though her face was flushed she was quiet, as if listening to them both. Rose stepped over the pile of filthy clothes her husband had left lying carelessly on the floor and went towards the kitchen.

'Spuds should be ready by now.'

She laid her wakeful four-month-old down to kick on a blanket in the little living room next to the kitchen. Then she went through and strained the potatoes and mashed them without any milk. After all, there was gravy. Something was always in short supply it seemed, and at the moment it was milk. As she pushed the masher through the potatoes, Hilda began to cry again.

Rose stood still, closing her eyes. The cries grew louder and more agitated until Hilda sounded as if the whole universe must be collapsing around her. Rose slammed the lid on the potatoes and marched into the living room.

'What d'you want?' she demanded roughly, Hilda was already in such a state that sweat glistened on her pink skin. Sometimes she screamed for so long and so vigorously that her fine brown hair became drenched and stringy.

Rose picked her up.

'Why can't you just be quiet?' she shouted. 'For God's sake stop this sodding racket. There's nothing to scream about.'

'Don't talk to her like that.' Alfie came in behind her, still smoothing Brylcreem into his wayward hair. 'Here – give her to me. That's no way to talk to a babby.'

'Well, *you*'d soon yell at her if you had it all day!' Rose screeched at him. 'You can't even stand five minutes of it when it's your precious sleep she's breaking into!'

It was true. Alfie would mumble drowsily, 'Can't you do something with her?' as Rose hurried out of bed in the night. She felt permanently tired and foggy in the head. The days seemed to swim around her, shapeless, busy, but tedious. She had no spare energy to do anything but care for Hilda's needs, and for Alfie's, and to take a quick nap in the odd half-hours that Hilda slept during the day.

Mrs Meredith, on her occasional visits from Small Heath to see her granddaughter, was kind and fussing and full of unwanted advice.

'If you have a happy mother, you get a happy child,' she told Rose one day, her plump little frame perched on one of their two old chairs. Rose, hollow-eyed, sat staring at her, hardly listening.

'Your job is to pull yourself together and look a bit more cheerful,' she said. 'Then the babby'll soon perk up, you'll see if she don't.'

Rose did feel everything was all her fault. She had selfishly had a child by a man she didn't really love and everyone was suffering.

Now Alfie was walking round the little square of garden in the late afternoon sun, with Hilda in his arms. Rose sat down and burst into tears. She cried a lot nowadays, and Alfie, at first sympathetic, was growing rather impatient.

'What's up with you?' he'd ask. 'You've got a nice home, and a bonny babby. What more can I give you?'

Then he'd assume that protective, fatherly air which made her want to scream with frustration. But she could not break through it without saying things which would have been far crueller than he deserved.

After a while he came in with Hilda dozing in his arms, went through and laid her in her cot. He kissed Rose on the cheek. 'Come on Rosie, that's me girl. Let's see a smile out of you, eh?'

Rose turned her mouth up into a guilty smile.

'That's more like it,' Alfie said. 'Now – how about some of that stew?'

The stew had cooked too long and the carrots were mushy, but Alfie shovelled the food down without comment. Rose watched him gratefully. He was as uncritical over her cooking as he was over housework, not seeming to notice whether she'd done much or not.

'So,' she said. 'How did you get this job then?'

Alfie looked at her with a rather sheepish expression on his pale face. 'It was just – well, a bloke Eddie knows.'

Rose rolled her eyes upwards. 'Might've known he must've had something to do with it.'

'Look, he's all right. I keep telling you.' Alfie forked his last mouthful of potato into his mouth. 'He's on the level, honest he is. He just has the contacts, that's all.'

'Alfie,' Rose said emphatically, 'Eddie is as on the level as Dr Crippen. He's a horrible bloke. Why did you have to pal up with him of all people?'

Alfie looked across the table at his wife's thin, tired face. A little frown line was beginning to form between her dark eyebrows. He loved Rose, proudly and loyally, and knew that he always would. But he couldn't hide from himself the fact that she'd changed, that his affection for her was stronger than hers for him. He could live with that, provided she was there for him. What was harder was this sharpness, the way she was so critical of people. She hadn't been like that before the war. Tart as an acid drop now.

'If I get this job, money and all, I don't s'pose you'll want to moan about that, will you?' he said, sarcastically.

Rose looked at him in silence, refusing to be drawn. 'If you want the job, then you'll do it. Not up to me, is it?'

'No,' Alfie agreed. 'It isn't.'

As she was pouring the boiling water into the teapot after their meal, Rose heard a hasty tap on the glass of the back door. She opened it into the dusk, the air still warm.

Grace was standing on the step, her hand still raised to knock. 'There's trouble,' she said grimly. 'It's George. He's been arrested.'

Rose gasped. 'What the hell for?'

'There was a big job last week. One of the warehouses over Bordesley way. They had parts in there for one of the bigger firms. I don't know if it was the Austin or what. But it was done over. They shifted a whole load of stuff and one of the blokes had a gun on him. George was in on it.'

'No!' Rose protested. 'He wouldn't. Even George wouldn't go that far, surely.'

'Oh wake up, Rose,' Grace snapped. 'George is as crooked as a bent half-crown – has been for years. I always hoped the army'd straighten him out, but he's come back even worse. Since he's been with that spiv Ronnie Grables he's turned professional. He'll have been in on it, no two ways.'

Rose banged the teapot down hard on the wooden surface. 'Silly little sod,' she said. 'What the bloody hell's the matter with him?'

As they carried the tea through she said to Alfie, 'I suppose you heard all that?'

'All right, Gracie? Yes, I heard. It don't surprise me. He's been heading that way for a long time I reckon.'

'Did they come round to the house to pick him up?' Rose asked as they all sat in front of their cups.

Grace shook her head. 'No, thank God. They found him with Ronnie somewhere.' She was silent for a moment. 'Anyway, it'll be the magistrates next week, and then we'll see, won't we?'

Rose sighed. 'He was such a nice little kid.'

Grace shrugged. 'Weren't we all?'

The war had changed Grace in a number of ways. Though still only twenty-four, the skin stretched over her bony face looked aged, with the kind of lifeless greyness Rose had noticed in most of the people who had stayed in the city during the war. The sweetness which had marked her out in her teens had turned sour. Perhaps we'll just be bitter now, Rose thought, for the rest of our lives, over what we've lost. And as for George, his own bitterness, his damage, had begun even earlier in the war.

Alfie pushed back his chair. 'I'll just go and have a walk in the garden before the light's all gone.'

Rose smiled gratefully at him, knowing he was leaving them alone for a talk.

The two sisters sat on despondently at the table.

'If he goes to prison,' Rose said, 'we'll have lost him, sort of, won't we?'

Grace looked dispassionately at her. 'We lost him years ago.'

'But he's our brother. We can't just turn away from him for all he's done. We've got to stand by him.'

'No,' Grace said. 'He ain't our brother. Say what you like, but it's his choosing. We've all done our best. I stood by him for years while you were off in the army and I've had enough of it. He's made his choice in life and he can go to hell his own way.'

Rose was startled. Was this Grace, idealistic, sweet Grace? 'Well what choices are *you* going to make then?' she challenged her.

'I'm going to train to be a nurse if they'll have me. A proper one. If I'm going to have to work for the rest of my life then I might as well do a job worth doing.'

'Does that mean you'll be living in, at the hospital?'

'How else am I going to get out? Dad can take care of himself when he needs to. You got out – everyone else has, one way or another. Why shouldn't I?'

'No—' Rose held her hands up as if to protect herself from this onslaught of resentment. 'You've got me wrong. I'm not getting at you. I think you're right. I've always felt bad that you've been the one left taking all the flak. I think it's just the right thing for you. In fact I . . .' Suddenly all the frustration of her own life bubbled up. 'I wish I could get a job. I wish I could get out and do anything except being stuck here all day long. Hilda just screams and I can't get anything else done. And Alfie—' She bit back the words. She could not let the truth out, even if they both knew it. Alfie bores me. I have no feelings for him. I should never have married someone so dull and calm, so kind, so limited . . .

Grace watched her sister with anger and disgust written plain on her face, as if she had sucked all the angry, guilty thoughts out of Rose's mind.

'You're a silly cow, d'you know that? Never satisfied, are you? Always have to be off wanting something else than what you've got. D'you know what I'd give to have a kind husband and a home of my own and a babby daughter? You can't see yourself for looking, Rose, and if you don't pull yourself together and act a bit more like a proper wife you're going to lose what you have got!'

CHAPTER 30

Grace had not heard that Joe was dead until weeks after the war ended. A letter arrived one morning on thin, crackly blue air mail paper from a neighbour in Peoria, Illinois, who had been drafted at the same time as Joe. Only then, once he was back in mid-western America late in the summer of 1945, had he thought to write. Grace's hopes of a reunion with the only man she had ever given her heart to were cut to nothing.

It had happened only shortly before Rose arrived home to find what was left of her family still in Catherine Street, shrunken by loss and grief. She felt that she added nothing to it except her own restlessness, her own loss and mourning.

Since she had been one of the first group, with Gwen, to be posted at Caserta, she was also among the first batch to be sent home. Those final three months, before they began their journey across Europe, should have been the sweetest in Italy. The atmosphere had become more relaxed, and there was more opportunity for 'jangling off' on excursions all round the area. For Rose and many others there was a poignant sense of making the most of the warmth and the languorous beauty of the country before the goodbyes began and they all had to head back into new, possibly more difficult lives.

When Rose went for the last time to Il Rifugio, steeling herself to say goodbye to Margherita and Francesco, she found the place depleted. Apart from the one great absence in the house which made it so painful to her,

301

Henry was gone too. He had hot-footed it out of Naples as soon as the war was over.

'I'm sorry our home has come to be such a sad place for you,' Margherita told her. 'Please don't forget us. You have been a very good friend – to me especially.'

On the very few occasions that she had seen them since May, Rose could never hold herself back from asking, 'Have you heard from him? Have you seen him?'

'Not a word,' Francesco told her each time. 'Truly. If we had I would tell you straight away. You must understand. They have to adjust to a new way, their lives are so disciplined . . .'

She had still been unable to believe it completely; to accept that he would not change his mind as he had done so often before; that he could transfer such feelings of passion into a way of life that she could not begin to understand. Some time before she left, she still hoped he would come back to her.

'I wish I could be angry with Falcone,' she said to Margherita.

'It's true he treated you badly,' her friend said. 'Though he did not mean harm, I'm sure.' Margherita always tried to be fair on the motives of others. 'But no one could blame you for being angry.'

'I'm not, though,' Rose said flatly. 'I just feel . . .' She searched round for the right word and settled for the simplest: '*Triste.*' Sad. A deep, deep sadness which never seemed to leave her, which Gwen and the others attributed to her 'failed' relationship with Tony.

'What will you do, Margherita?' Rose asked. 'Will you stay here?'

'Of course.' Margherita looked as calm and steady as ever. 'And perhaps now the war is over we can persuade the Church to give us some proper backing. After all, there is no British army for us to live off now.'

'Well, God help you,' Rose said, without irony.

The two women stood with their arms round each other for a long time before Rose left. Magdalena and Assunta and Francesco all came and embraced her,

Assunta with tears running down her kindly, cock-eyed face. When Rose handed back her key and heard the wooden door slam behind her for the last time, she held in her hands a beautiful, poignant present from Francesco: the copy of his favourite French song that they had listened to so often, '*J'attendrai – le jour et la nuit j'attendrai toujours* – I will wait . . .'

The journey to England took them several days on trains with hard, slatted wooden seats. Rose and Gwen travelled together, exclaiming when at last they saw the Channel and the white cliffs of Dover, which they seemed to have left a whole lifetime ago, and at how lush and neat and altogether more cosy the English landscape looked than anything they had seen during their years away.

'I say – it all looks bigger, doesn't it?' Gwen exclaimed as they gazed out at the Kentish orchards, and the elder and hawthorn along the railway tracks. 'I suppose we did leave in the middle of winter, but even so, everything seems to have shot up.'

Rose nodded silently. She felt disorientated and strange, as if returning to another foreign country, not her own. The feeling took quite some time to wear off.

Once she and Gwen had been to the army clearing house and were released from the ATS, they said their farewells in central London before catching trains for their different parts of the country.

'You'd better write!' Gwen said.

Rose nodded. 'Of course.' She had already made Tony the same promise.

On her journey out of Euston in a hot, smoke-filled railway carriage bound for the Midlands, she pulled from her bag the letter each of them had been given from the Senior Controller of the ATS.

'As you say goodbye to service life,' it began, 'I am writing to thank you in the name of the Auxiliary Territorial Service for the loyal and devoted service you have given to your King and Country.'

Rose looked up for a moment, glancing at the drab outskirts of north London which were beginning to give way to countryside. The man in the seat next to her glanced curiously at her letter.

'You will be called upon,' she read, 'to make further efforts in the service of your country, and I know that you will make them with the same generosity which has always marked the work of the ATS. Goodbye and the best of luck.'

The train was crowded and a number of those on board were men and women obviously as freshly demobbed as she was. But even amid the hum of conversation and jokes and scraping of matches to light cigarettes, she felt a kind of solitude descend upon her. The letter made the army seem official and impersonal again. There was a sense of it all falling away from her, the experiences of the past four years beginning to recede, dream-like. Now she needed to reshape herself, though how, as yet, she didn't know. She thought of Gwen heading towards her mother's home to wait until Bill was released. What would her reception be? And her own? How would it feel to walk into Court 11, Catherine Street, again?

Birmingham came as a shock to her. Although she had been there during the worst of the bombing, the city had somehow reformed itself in her mind while she was away. She had tended to remember it still complete, with the Market Hall standing and the rows of terraced houses undamaged. But now she saw afresh the jagged gaps which the war had left in the city: the bombsites between the houses, a few levelled off, but many still with rubble in place. Young lads took them over as playgrounds, still plundering shrapnel, and thistles and purple fireweed pushed up between the timbers and bricks.

As she stepped in her solid service shoes across the dirty blue bricks of Court 11, she was struck for the first time by just how small were the houses in which thousands like her had spent their years growing up. She put her hand up automatically to knock at the door, forgetting for a moment that this was where she now belonged. This was life now and she had nothing else. She was home.

Only Sid was in. He was sitting at the old table, a paper open in front of him. He looked up as she opened the door, seeing for a moment a beautiful, neatly dressed stranger in khaki, her hair still arranged carefully under the ATS cap as if she was afraid to take it off.

He looked blankly at her for a moment.

'Rose?'

He pulled himself up, then waited at a loss as she closed the door and came in to stand the other side of the table, putting her bag down on its newspaper surface.

'All right are you?' he said eventually.

Rose could tell he was finding it difficult to think of anything to say, and she was faced with the same problem. She felt tears slide into her eyes. Nothing had changed, although everything had. Sid's face looked thinner, haggard and unshaven.

'You still at the BSA, Dad?' she asked finally, looking for a point of contact.

He shook his head, and she saw how many grey hairs there were among the black. He was fifty-four and he looked an old man.

'They let me go,' he said. 'Back to making bikes now the war's over.'

'Oh. I'm sorry,' she said.

Sid shrugged and then frowned, his pallid skin wrinkling as if he was trying to remember something. 'Where've you come from then?'

'Italy. Near Naples.'

Sid nodded slowly, bemused. 'Have a good journey then, did you?'

Rose knew at that moment that it would be quite pointless trying to talk to anyone at home about her years out of England. It was too far away, too removed from their own experience.

She nodded. 'Got cheap tickets on the train – cut rate if you've just been demobbed.'

She looked around. So far as she could remember, the room was exactly the same as when she had left, almost eerily so.

'Where's Grace?' she asked.

'Up Willett's. She's got a job. On the bedsteads like.'

After a moment he said, 'Fancy making us a cuppa tea?'

And that was that. His sole interest in her war.

The distance was there with Grace too, though the two of them embraced and laughed and looked at each other with tearful eyes when she came in from work. Rose was shocked by Grace's thin, careworn appearance. She felt there ought to be years' worth of things to say, that they should be making up for lost time, yet no one could think what to say.

'How are the twins?' Rose asked eagerly when the two of them were peeling and cutting up vegetables together late that afternoon. 'Have you seen them?'

'Oh, they're full of the joys,' Grace said. 'And Harry. All at school near Edna's. To tell you the truth, she can't bear the thought of parting with them. I asked her if she wanted to send them back here now it's all over. But as she says, they've been there nearly all their lives.'

'I'll have to go over,' Rose said. More people, she felt, who would be lost to her.

As the days and weeks passed after her homecoming, Rose fast began to resent the narrowness of the life she had been thrown back into, and her own lack of independence. How restless she felt! How could she ever settle down to this drab existence of rationing and dreariness after her time in Italy?

It was 'Where've you been? Make sure you're in by ten. Who've you been with?' From Sid, from Grace. Not that she went out much anyway. But Grace had got into the habit of questioning her as if she was her mother. She had completely taken over the role of woman of the house.

Everything seemed shrunken and oppressive. Even the

clothes Rose had left behind when she joined up no longer fitted her new, rounder figure. Number five was like a doll's house, while Rose felt like a giant who had been out striding across the world. Why couldn't they realize that after these four years she was now an adult who could run her life without being questioned all the time?

Once more, when there were important considerations like the family's mourning for Sam and Grace's personal grief over Joe, Rose found herself cast in the role of the restless, selfish one, always looking over the wall for fresher, greener grass.

After a month at home she found herself a job as a delivery driver for Snell's grocery store in Balsall Heath. Of course it had none of the excitement of her Italian driving, but at least it got her out and about and brought another wage into the house.

She would never forget her sister's face that day. Usually when Rose reached the house after Grace she found her sister's skinny form bustling round, tidying, handwashing, the evening meal already in hand.

Opening the door, Rose thought for a few seconds that there was no one in. She put down the few groceries she had bought on the way home – Typhoo and milk and Rinso. A ray of late afternoon autumn sunshine had managed to reach its way through the normally dark court windows and lay in a bright slanting shape on the table-top. Rose was already adjusting her mind to doing the evening meal herself when she saw her sister sitting there, to her right, the horsehair chair swivelled towards the window which looked over the court.

Grace didn't turn to look at her. Rose watched for a couple of seconds, seeing her cheeks drained of any colour, and the tight compression of her lips. She was taking in quick, shallow breaths.

'Are you all right?' Rose asked anxiously. 'Got an attack coming on?'

She stepped closer. Still Grace didn't move. Then Rose saw the letter in her lap, the thin blue paper.

'What's happened?' she asked gently, kneeling down by the arm of the chair, her heart thudding.

Without turning her head, Grace said, 'It's from Joe's mom.'

Rose frowned. Grace knew he was dead. What more could be wrong? 'Poor woman – she must be in a right state.'

'No.' Grace's head whipped round suddenly. 'She ain't in a state. She's got nothing to be in a state about.' Her voice suddenly rose to a piercing shriek. 'Because he's not dead! He's not bloody dead! And he's getting married next month!'

She got up suddenly and moved agitatedly round the room, as if she couldn't think what to do with her body. She picked up the bread knife.

'I could stick this in me!' she screamed at Rose. 'He's stuck enough knives in me to make me feel as if I'm bleeding to death!'

And then the sobs broke out of her. Rose took the knife from her, and drew her shaking sister into her arms.

'I don't understand,' she said softly, after she had let Grace have a good cry.

'That bloke who wrote to me,' Grace gasped out, her head pressed hard against Rose's shoulder. 'He must've known Joe was still alive. They were pals. They live in the same town. Joe must've told him to say he was dead – just to get rid of me.'

'Oh my God.' Rose suddenly saw it as clearly as Grace had done. 'What a bastard.'

'All he's put me through,' Grace went on in her distraught voice. 'Thinking he'd been killed, when all the time . . . He could've had the guts to write and say we was finished.'

'Men have a queer way of going about things,' Rose said drily.

She led Grace back to the chair to sit down, and

knelt beside her, holding her and letting her cry, as Margherita had done for her only a few months ago. For days and weeks afterwards she comforted her sister through the shock of this betrayal and, perhaps Grace's most hurtful realization, that at least if he had been truly dead, she could still have carried on believing that he loved her.

During her first weeks at home, Rose had to try to adjust to all the details of living back in an England freshly recovering from war.

Closest to home were the changes which had taken place in the court. The only familiar faces left were the Pye family and Mabel Gooch's household. The two sisters from number four had both died during the war, one quickly succeeding the other, and the house was now occupied by an old couple. Moonstruck House still had occasional tenants, who never stayed long, probably more because of its atrocious state of repair than any other kind of blight on the place. And there was a new family at number three.

Apart from learning the names of the new neighbours, she found she had to carry an identity card, use a ration book and clothing coupons still and register with the grocer and the butcher. There was the damp, drizzly weather and the worn, grey people around her, many of whom – with some justification she soon realized – gibed at her for being 'well out of it' down there in Italy.

The elections that year also shocked many people by removing Winston Churchill as prime minister and replacing him with Clement Attlee.

'How could they do it to him?' Grace demanded. 'After all he's seen us through. They'll be throwing the king out next.'

Rose, who had looked round at her country with new eyes on her return, had heard all the voices clamouring for change and decided to join them. Things had to be moved on, to be improved after the war, otherwise what was the point of it all? She didn't tell Grace, but her vote had gone to Attlee, and she rather suspected Sid's had as well.

There was talk of all kinds of changes, of visions almost unheard of before the war. Of a 'Welfare State' – better support for the out of work, for big families – even for getting looked after when you were sick. Who would not vote for that?

During all this time when change seemed to be constantly in the air and Rose struggled to endure this regressive state, as it felt to her, of living back at home, she had one more adjustment to make – really the biggest of them all.

When she walked in from work one afternoon, Alfie was waiting for her.

'Look who's here!' Grace said as Rose pushed open the door. There was a note of warning in her voice, Rose realized. 'Don't waste this opportunity,' she was saying. 'Make the most of him. You don't know how lucky you are.'

'Alfie!' Rose cried, more startled than pleased. She had known he must come home soon if he had survived the war, and no one had heard that he hadn't. But she had kept pushing the thought from her mind.

There he was, in his slightly too big demob suit, thin and pale, his hair cropped so short there was not enough of it to stick up in its unruly spikes. He looked older, Rose realized. His jaw was stronger as if his whole face had broadened a little.

'How are you?' she asked, full of confusion. So strange him being there, looking much the same, yet with these small changes which were all that signified nearly six years' absence.

'I'm all right.' Bashful and nervous, his eyes lingered over her wonderingly. How her figure had filled out! His eyes moved hungrily down over her breasts, her curving sides. She was wearing a tight-fitting jumper of moss green, and a straight tweedy skirt cut with all the meagreness of war garments, which she had managed to alter so it fitted her.

'You look a treat,' he said.

Rose blushed. She wasn't ready for this, this direct-ness, this talking as if the war had passed in only a few days and nothing had changed.

'Have a cuppa tea,' Grace said firmly, pouring hastily from the brown teapot. 'He wouldn't have one till you got here, Rose. Come on, sit down both of you.' She handed Sid a cup and then sat at the table with Rose and Alfie. Rose watched her smile at him – about the warmest smile she had seen on Grace's face since she'd arrived home.

'I'm sorry to hear about Sam,' Alfie began awkwardly. 'He were a good bloke.'

Rose and Grace both nodded. 'Thanks,' Rose said. 'Yes, he was.'

'Where was it? Out east somewhere?'

'Burma,' Grace told him.

Again they all nodded sadly, lost for words. They didn't talk about the losses of the war much; everyone bore them privately.

'Grace tells me you was in Italy?' Alfie said. 'What the hell were you doing there?'

'ATS. I was a driver,' Rose said, feeling suddenly prickly. His voice held a slight mockery, as if he didn't believe it. 'Was through most of the war.'

'You mean they let you loose on them trucks!' Alfie chuckled, looking at Grace as if expecting her to confirm the joke. 'God Almighty, what a thought!'

Rose gave him a hard, defiant look. 'So where've you been all the war then? Found a better hole to go to, did you?'

She saw her words had hit home. Alfie turned red and looked down at his tea cup.

'It weren't my fault,' he said. 'That's how it was, going into France. If you'd been there you'd have seen.'

Prisoner of war through the whole thing. It was a hard homecoming. Not much to brag about.

311

'Sorry,' Rose relented. 'It must have been grim for you.'

'Thought at times we'd be there for the rest of our lives,' he said. 'It was only hearing from people . . .' He turned to look at her with a hurt expression in his eyes. 'You could've written more.'

'I did!' Rose exclaimed guiltily. She knew that her communication with him, especially once she had reached Italy, had been the bare minimum. 'I'm sorry. We were very busy.'

It was hard for her even to look at him. Had his feelings stood still during the war? What else did you have to change them when you were locked up in a prisoner of war camp?

'It was such a long time,' she said wearily.

'Come out with me tonight,' Alfie said suddenly. He wanted to be with her away from the others. Kiss her. Get back on their old footing. After all, she was the girl who had promised to be his wife.

Walks, the flicks, evenings spent at her house or his, with Mrs Meredith fussing adoringly round them both. It was more peaceful at Alfie's. To make ends meet, Mrs Meredith had taken in a lodger, a widow in her fifties, but she kept herself to herself most of the time.

Rose found Alfie easy undemanding company. Gradually she remembered that he had made her laugh sometimes, that he was kind and generous. That he adored her, and being adored was warming in itself, even though the feeling was not mutual and she knew it. During the winter of 1945–6 they met almost daily. Alfie soon found work amidst all the rebuilding of the city. When both had finished for the day they met up, already washed and changed, and spent the evening together. Anything to get out of Catherine Street, with Sid morose, often half drunk, and Grace sad, quiet and dutiful.

'When w 're married,' Alfie said one evening, 'you

312

won't have to work any more. Not having my wife working.'

Rose looked round at him startled. It was growing dark and they were walking away from Catherine Street after he'd come to pick her up.

'Oh – and what d'you reckon I'm going to do all day long then?' she said indignantly. He had not even asked her to marry him again yet.

'You'll be looking after the babbies, won't you?' he said, as if it was obvious.

He had voiced something that she had not realized yet in herself. Was this not the one thing left that she really wanted? Babies – children? Passion, locked deep in her as a part of the past, did not seem accessible now. Perhaps it was something you could only have for a short time, a dream time, not part of real life. She didn't see much passion in the tired, struggling people around her.

But babies. Something in her surfaced and said yes. Please. If she could have nothing else out of life now, she could have children. That was what Alfie was offering.

In April 1946, in St Joseph's Church, Birch Street, Rose became Mrs Alfred Meredith.

CHAPTER 31

MOSELEY, BIRMINGHAM, 1949

'Rose? Coo-eee. Rose!'

Rose's neighbour Joan walked down the side of the little prefab house, pulling her eighteen-month-old son Freddie by the hand. She found Rose pegging washing on the line. As she called out again she saw Rose start violently. She turned, the peg-bag in one hand and the other laid over her heart.

'Oh, Joan. I was miles away. You didn't half make me jump.'

'Well, who did you think it might be – Jack the Ripper?' Joan moved over to the line. 'Here, let's give you a hand with the rest of this lot.'

She was a sturdy woman in her early thirties with heavy arms and legs and long, thick brown hair. She soon had the rest of the washing pegged out. Then the two of them turned to watch Freddie and Hilda, who were both bent over something that had caught their attention at the other end of the garden. Hilda was growing up to look the image of her father, though her hair was more manageable than Alfie's and hung in wispy strands round her head.

'Mom!' Hilda shouted imperiously. 'Come here – look!'

'You'll have to watch her,' Joan said. 'She's turning into a right little madam.' It was said inoffensively and Rose knew it to be true.

'I know. Sometimes I don't know how to deal with

314

her. Mind you,' she laughed, 'that's what they all said about me!'

After a moment Joan said, 'Actually the reason I came over was, I was wondering if you could have Freddie for a bit of today. Dave's off sick like, and he can't stand his noise . . .'

'And you need a break,' Rose finished for her. 'Yes, course I can have him. If you bring a bit of something over for his dinner he can stay all day. Be good for Hilda – she's better when there's company.'

Joan's fleshy face broke into a broad smile. 'Are you sure? Thanks Rose. Oh, what a difference it makes to have good neighbours, eh? Now, if there's anything I can do for you – bits of washing or anything you just bring it right over.'

'Right,' Rose said. She loathed housework. 'You're on.'

As Joan left, full of gratitude, Rose watched her with an amused expression. She wasn't at all sure she believed the story about Dave being poorly, but it didn't matter. The fact was, Freddie was a good kid but Joan couldn't stand to have him round her. Not day in day out. Any excuse and she brought him over to Rose. And she wasn't the only one. 'Oh, I 'spect Rose'll have him' was a common refrain among her neighbours with small children.

One way or another, most days the house was full of them, sometimes with their mothers, but more often without. In fine weather there were often five or six, with Hilda playing Queen Bee at the centre of it all, bossy, perverse, but generally easier to handle when there were other kids about.

'I don't know how you manage it,' the other women would say gratefully as she ran her unofficial little nursery. 'You're a godsend!' And they repaid her with admiration, company and small offerings they could spare out of their rations. They took in her washing and ironing, and sometimes even offered to clean her house – all of which seemed less fraught than spending their time in the company of their offspring.

This was how Rose filled her days. Alfie wouldn't allow her to work, so she managed in her own way to do what she loved best, caring for small children.

Rose used everything she could get her hands on for those kids. Alfie didn't mind how she occupied them, so long as the mess was all cleared up by the time he came home. Often the mothers didn't come to collect their children until the afternoon, and they'd stop and have a cuppa, sometimes bringing their own tea. They sat round as their little ones told them in shrill, excited voices all they had done during the morning.

'We helped Rose in the kitchen!'

'She gave us a apple and toffees!'

'I sat on the potty!'

And Rose smiled delightedly at them all, at their enjoyment of coming to her house.

'When you going to have another then?' Joan asked when she came round later that afternoon. 'Hilda's two now, ain't she? Don't want to have too big a gap.'

'When it comes, I 'spose,' Rose called through from the kitchen. She was mopping Hilda's cotton dress where she'd spilled her drink down it. 'Can't have one any sooner than that, can I?'

'You do remember what you have to do, don't you?' another of the women teased. 'They don't just grow inside by magic after the first one, you know!'

'You try telling my old man that!' Rose quipped back, going back to join them in the living room.

It was partly a joke. But after the women had left, Rose's emotions were stirred up by this conversation, leaving her unsettled and sad. There was much less lovemaking between her and Alfie than there had been in their early days of marriage and it was nearly always at his demand. Although she wasn't sorry he left her alone more nowadays, she did wonder why it was taking her so long to conceive another child. Was there something wrong? She had taken the risk with Falcone but

316

there had been no baby then either. Often she wished there had been. Perhaps she wasn't able to bear many children?

She thought she had put behind her all those painful feelings of longing and restlessness which had plagued her after the war. She had even managed to quell her frustration at being married to Alfie, burying her desire for a wider, more challenging life by putting all her energy into her most lasting and satisfying love – small children. If this was her life, then she must make the best of it. Look at George, locked away for what might be as much as five years. And Grace, who had been denied the opportunity to achieve even her modest aspirations. She had not been accepted for training by any of the local hospitals, and was still at home, still taking jobs in factories and keeping house for Sid. Wasn't she, Rose, lucky? She should strive to return Alfie's kindness and affection and build a life which was good for both of them and for Hilda.

She had made an enormous effort to create this new life, like a person who has had a couple of limbs amputated and must adjust to new ways of living.

'It's good to see you looking happier,' Alfie had said to her recently. 'All that looking back to the war – don't do anyone any good, you know.'

She knew he resented her war, even though she had told him only the barest details of her life in the ATS. His own had been so limited, so unheroic. She tried for her own peace of mind to block out her memories. It was another country, another time. Over.

She submitted dutifully to Alfie whenever he turned to her in bed. She had almost forgotten the feelings her body was capable of. Alfie was quickly aroused and very soon satisfied. Invariably he mounted her almost immediately after a kiss and a quick feel of her breasts and he would enter her, almost unable to wait until he was inside, and then it was over. Rose patiently held his slim, pale shoulders time after time as he murmured 'Oh, Rosie, Rosie' into her left ear, feeling nothing except his moist, softening member withdrawing from her. He expected nothing more, and seemed never to notice that she got as much excitement from peeling potatoes as from his lovemaking. He was content. He had a good, pretty wife who other men envied him for. She never complained, so she must be all right. He was not aware there could be anything more and Rose had shut out any expectation that there might be.

But if she could not even have more children . . . She began to shake, her body letting out the tension that her mind had been keeping so tightly under control. She sat in the little living room as Hilda sat watching her with wide, frightened eyes. Finally, the tears came and Hilda began to cry too.

Rose picked her up and cuddled her. 'It's all right love, don't you worry. Mommy's just feeling a bit poorly, that's all.' She felt steadied by the child's warm body.

Could there ever really be love between a man and a woman? Mr Lazenby, Alfie – both used her in their way. And what about Tony? That was unreasonable, she knew, but in her state such terrible thoughts came. Worst of all, the one she tried to keep furthest from her mind persisted. What about Falcone? Had his words, his confusion, the looks of tenderness and desire that she had from him all been his way of using her? Of getting what he wanted and then dropping her for a 'higher calling'? Had she been deluded even when she responded to a man with every fibre of herself? All these doubts stabbed into her mind.

Though she had tried to avoid thinking of Italy, and especially of Il Rifugio, she knew that what sustained her and kept her feeling worth something was the knowledge that she could truly love and be loved in return. If no one else ever showed her that, then Falcone had done so. Try as she might to forget Italy and him, the thoughts still came to her from time to time.

Sometimes she dreamed of him, seeing his dark, serious eyes close to hers. In some of the dreams he was telling her how much he loved her. She saw herself back in the Finzis' house with the moon slanting through the windows on to their naked bodies. Or in Il Rifugio, making love with him on the thin straw pallets where she had first seen him sleeping. In other dreams he kept telling her over and over again that he had to leave her. He was cold and distant, cruel even. She would repeat the feeling of desolation of returning to Il Rifugio to find him gone. Sometimes she would wake crying, finding Alfie stirring next to her. The depth of her disappointment that he was not Falcone made her weep even more – harsh, quiet tears that she could never share with him.

A few weeks earlier she had had a letter from Gwen. She and Bill had compromised between their two sets of parents and settled in a small village in Berkshire. Bill was working in a bank in the nearby town.

'We're not very far from where we all started out together!' Gwen had told her. She already had a son and a daughter, Edward and Elizabeth, and was expecting her third child.

'I must say, I'm awfully happy,' Gwen wrote. 'Bill is a good husband and father and provides wonderful protection against Mummy when necessary! I should so love you to see E and E and to meet Alfie and your little Hilda. Perhaps we shall all be able to meet up one day?'

Gwen had apparently found a settled, serene sort of happiness with someone she loved. It was possible. But Rose knew she did not love Alfie.

As she sat that afternoon, holding a now rather drowsy Hilda and looking blankly over the child's shoulder, she knew starkly that though she had settled for what she could get, for filling her life with children, it was not and never could be enough.

She had to believe in her love for Falcone and his for her, even knowing she would never see him again. Without that life seemed worth nothing.

CHAPTER 32

Rose was hanging decorations on a little Christmas tree when she heard the banging on the door. With her were Hilda and Freddie and another little girl, all squabbling eagerly over the few baubles and the home-made foil stars.

'Hey! Anyone in?' a voice shouted.

She went to the door. Outside stood two men, struggling to support Alfie between them, his arms pinned over their shoulders and his body sagging between.

'About time,' one of the men said. 'He's a dead weight.'

Rose looked at them all, dumbfounded. Alfie's head was lolling to the right and his eyes rolling strangely from side to side like those of an idiot.

'Move out the road,' the older of the two men grunted at her. 'Let's get him on the bed. Silly bugger's got himself properly tanked up. Been a right game getting him over here on the bus, I can tell you.'

They hoisted Alfie into the bedroom and half laid, half threw him on to the pink-candlewick-covered bed. His eyes rolled upwards and then he closed them.

'He looks terrible,' Rose said. The sight of him really disturbed her. She stood close to the door holding back the three curious children. 'What's got into him? He's not a big drinker.'

'Oh, he'll be right as rain by tomorrow. Must've been putting it away while no one was looking. He'll have one hell of a head on him in the morning!' The younger man laughed knowingly.

The other, more serious, said to Rose, 'You'd better tell him, though, one more do like this and he'll be out of a job. He's lucky they're not putting the boot behind him today like. He'll have to watch himself.'

Still startled, Rose watched them go as they called out cheerfully, 'Tara, Alfie. See you in the morning.'

'Save it till Christmas next time, mate!'

Rose sat the children down in the next room with a beaker of rosehip syrup and a biscuit each, and came back in to her husband. He was lying with his eyes closed, but when he felt her unfastening his boots and pulling them off, he opened them.

'Rose?' he murmured indistinctly. 'I feel terrible.'

'Well, what were you thinking of?' she asked him. She knelt down by the head of the bed. 'No wonder. You're not used to more than the odd pint.'

'No.' Alfie's voice sounded thick and strange; out of his control. 'I told them – I kept saying . . . I haven't had a drop. Nothing.'

Rose frowned. 'What d'you mean? Look, you don't have to make a big secret of it. Was it something the others gave you? Whisky?'

'No,' he slurred back. 'I told you . . . nothing. I don't know. I'm scared, Rose.'

Suddenly very alarmed, she bent close to him and smelt his breath. There was not a trace of alcohol on it. She stood up quickly. 'I'll get a doctor.'

By that evening Alfie was in Selly Oak Hospital. Rose left Hilda with Joan and went in to see him. She found him lying in a long ward with rows of beds along each side, his face almost as white as the stiff pillow case and his eyes closed. Rose stood for a moment looking down at him. His hair was sticking up on top of his head and still looked greyed from the dust at work. His neck was bent rather awkwardly to one side as if he had a crick in it, and the shape of his body underneath the thin covers looked slight suddenly, and vulnerable.

'Alfie?' she said softly. On the floor by the bed she put the little bag of his possessions she'd brought in: pyjamas, shaving brush and razor, and the day's paper, thinking he'd have been feeling better.

His eyes opened slowly, trying to focus. He also seemed to be trying to smile.

'How you feeling?'

'Bad,' he said. 'Never . . . had anything . . . like this . . . before.'

She reached under the covers suddenly, surprising them both by taking his hand, feeling compassionate and protective towards him as she would have done towards a child.

'They'll look after you,' she told him. 'Soon see you better.'

Alfie nodded slowly and his eyes closed again. 'Sleepy,' he managed to say.

Rose sat by him until he was deeply asleep and then went to speak to the matron, a tall, well-spoken woman with a sheaf of papers in her hand. She had a brisk, forbidding air which suggested she might be kind so long as you submitted to her totally.

'My husband, Alfred Meredith,' Rose said, rather timidly. 'Do you know what's wrong with him?'

'Mr Meredith,' the woman said, her grey eyes scanning the ward for inspiration. 'Ah yes, the *ataxia* – new admission. No. Too early to say I'm afraid. Could be something quite simple but you never know. Might be a few days before we're sure.' She made as if to walk off.

'But how long will he be here – please?' Rose called after her. The woman seemed more intimidating than any officers she had come across in the ATS.

'Oh, I couldn't possibly say,' Matron replied. She noted something down on one of the papers she was holding. 'Let's wait and see what they say in the morning, shall we?'

Rose walked desolately out of the echoing hospital building to catch the bus home. Seeing Alfie lying there had come as a terrible shock to her. He looked so broken and helpless. Though she did not love him with anything approaching passion, she knew that it mattered to her a great deal what happened to him. She relied on him, on him being there with her, on his bland optimism and steady kindness. She had simply grown used to him. And he was Hilda's father. She was really frightened.

Before she reached the bus stop she changed her mind. Hilda would be asleep by now at Joan's. It was already dark. Instead, she made her way to Catherine Street. She felt completely churned up inside and she needed to see them, to tell them what had happened. Grace may have hardened herself to many of the problems of others, but she could always summon up sympathy for anyone who was sick.

Rose knocked on the door of number five. Outwardly the house looked much better than it had in the old days. The back-to-back terraces in Catherine Street were among a number that had been 'soled and heeled' by the council, who could not keep up with the demand to build new houses and had decided to patch up some of the ones they already had. New roofs, windows and doors had made the whole place look smarter. The front door was painted a cheerful sky blue.

'What you doing here?' Grace asked when she opened the door.

Rose walked in amid the smell of meat cooking and the gaslight which seemed so much dimmer than the electric they had out in the prefabs. She noticed there were no signs of Christmas about the house.

'Where's Hilda?' Grace demanded anxiously.

As Rose sat down, Grace stood by the table, hands on hips. She was dressed in a drab brown skirt and fawn blouse, on top a flowery apron which Rose realized with a pang had been cut down from an old dress of Dora's. Grace's hair was fastened up in an old scarf, the end tucked in at the front, to keep her hair out of the way while she was working.

'Hilda's with Joan,' Rose said. 'I've been with Alfie. He's in Selly Oak. Been taken bad.'

Grace automatically reached out and poured Rose a cup of tea. 'In hospital? What's up with him?'

'They don't know.' Rose began to cry at last, the worry and shock of the afternoon finally released.

Grace leaned close to her sister's dark head and put an arm round her shoulder. Rose got a whiff of the sweaty smell from under her arms, sharp, but somehow comforting.

'They brought him home at dinnertime. Looked as though he'd had a skinful. He was all over the place – eyes rolling, could hardly get a word out of his mouth, the lot. And he hadn't touched a drop.'

Grace looked quizzically at her. 'You sure he's not just having you on? After all, what with Christmas coming up – you know what they're like.'

'No,' Rose sobbed. 'He hardly drinks ever. He'd never lead us on and make us think he was bad when he wasn't.' She looked into Grace's concerned eyes. 'When you were nursing, d'you remember seeing anyone like that – like Alfie is now?'

Grace shook her head. 'I've seen blokes in a proper state – shocked and that. But not like you said. Never heard of that.' She patted Rose's arm with sudden kindness and Rose could hear the wartime nurse coming out in her. 'Anyhow, the doctors do all they can, so there's no point in fretting all night about it. You should get back to Hilda before she thinks she's lost both of you.'

As she spoke, the door opened and Sid pulled himself into the room. His hair, so dark when he was a young man, was now a powdery grey.

'Dinner ready?' he asked Grace, and she got up to spoon out the meat and vegetables.

'Alfie's in Selly Oak Hospital,' Rose told him, and tried to explain what was wrong. She wished overwhelmingly that Dora was there for her to turn to.

'Oh ar,' Sid said. Then through a mouthful of swede he commented dispassionately, 'Blooming shame. I always thought he looked a weak little runt though.'

Rose stood up abruptly. 'Time I was going,' she said bitterly. She put her coat on. 'Tara Dad. I see you're much as usual.'

Sid raised one hand as a goodbye, but Grace followed Rose out into the yard.

'It's no good expecting anything from him,' she said, with more gentleness than Rose had heard from her for a long time. 'He lives in his own little world now and the rest of us might just as well not be here.' She touched Rose awkwardly on the shoulder. 'If you need anything, come to me, all right?'

Rose smiled at her. 'Still here, aren't you – after all this time. Running about after everyone.'

Grace shrugged rather evasively. 'Looks like that's what I'm good for, don't it? Now remember what I said. Just ask for help if you need it.'

Humbled, Rose kissed her quickly on her rough cheek. 'That's nice of you,' she said. 'Ta.'

Alfie spent Christmas 1949 in hospital. Hilda kept saying, 'Where's my Dad?' Rose brought her in to be with Alfie for a short time, walking into the warm ward from the icy air outside. When Hilda saw him she ran to him, dressed in her little red coat and black boots, her hair tied up in two pigtails.

'Hello little monkey,' Alfie said as Hilda hurled herself at him. He was propped up on several thick pillows. His voice sounded stronger now and his words were easier to understand.

'Not on the bed, please,' a nurse said as she walked past. 'I know it's Christmas, but we still have to keep the rules.'

'She's a real daddy's girl,' Rose told her apologetically. 'Been missing him like anything.' She lifted Hilda down on to her lap. The nurse walked off in her heavy black shoes, smiling.

'How are you?' Rose asked. 'You look a bit better today.'

'I feel better,' Alfie said. He was even wearing one of the coloured hats they'd all been given to jolly things along for Christmas, and the soft orange tissue paper kept slipping off his clumps of hair. 'It's wearing off a bit. My hands felt all queer, sort of numb. Scared me, I can tell you.'

His pale face suddenly lit up with an adoring smile. 'It's lovely to see you, Rosie. Give us a kiss, will you?'

She stood up and leaned forwards to kiss him. Affectionately she straightened the orange crown. 'I'll have to bring some Brylcreem in,' she joked.

But Alfie was staring at her with a seriousness which silenced her. 'I love you,' he said. 'You know that, don't you? I should tell you more often. Only when you're always about I forget . . . But, if anything was to happen . . .?'

'I know,' Rose said. She couldn't look at him straight, and felt her cheeks turning red. Hilda was pulling at her skirt, impatient at this conversation which took the attention away from her.

'You'll be home soon though, won't you?' Rose said brightly.

They didn't tell her then. It was a couple of days later. A condition affecting the nerves, the doctor with the grey hair and distant eyes said. Very hard to predict how it would progress. Some patients lived normal lives for years. Attacks and remissions, that was the pattern. Sometimes he'd be perfectly all right, sometimes not.

'Does he know?' Rose asked. Her eyes rested on the doctor's dark blue tie.

Looking out of the window beyond her, he said, 'He's known for a little while. He's had the chance to think about it. Said he'd rather I told his, er, family myself.'

'What about work?' Rose asked. 'Will he be able to carry on?'

'Your husband's a builder I see.' The doctor made a sharp, regretful intake of breath. 'Very difficult. Building's not a good job to be in with his condition. Any work off the ground, on scaffolding for instance, could cost him his life if he had another of these attacks. You must impress that upon him strongly, Mrs Meredith. He can't afford to be careless with himself.'

'Course I'm going back to work!' Alfie said. It was January, snowy, and thick fog covered the city, so dense that the traffic was having trouble passing along the streets. 'I feel fine. Don't s'pose they'll be doing a lot today anyway, but I've told them I'll show me face and see what's cooking. Don't you worry, Rosie,' he said, seeing her anxious expression. She was standing at the door with Hilda in her arms. 'I'll keep me feet on the ground. After all, someone's got to be the breadwinner round here!'

After he'd kissed them both they watched him, Hilda waving as he walked away, fast disappearing into the fog.

Two months later Alfie collapsed again. This time he was at home, and the attack seemed even more severe. Rose was terrified by the fear and distress on his ashen face. A pattern emerged. Hospital, a recovery period, a time when he felt weaker perhaps, but more or less normal, and then another attack. By the late summer of 1950 he was barely recovering between each one. His legs, from which he was gradually losing all sensation, finally became paralysed. He could do very little without help. Alfie had become a permanent invalid.

CHAPTER 33

CATHERINE STREET, BIRMINGHAM, JANUARY 1951

'This house is all pongy!'

Little Hilda, only a few months off her fourth birthday, sniffed distastefully as she eyed up the place that was to be her new home. She had grown into a pale, rather scrawny child, her brown hair scraped back into a high ponytail, the end of which did not even reach as far down as the back of her neck.

'Moonstruck House.' Mabel Gooch's gruff voice came from the edge of the room, where her barrel-shaped body was leaning up against the doorframe. Mabel, still the matriarch of Court 11, had aged from a woman with a strong, handsome face into one who looked almost masculine, with a hint of a moustache gathering on her top lip. 'Bet you never thought you'd end up here, eh, Rose?' There was a strong hint of satisfaction in her voice. But then she added, 'Still, it's good to know there's someone decent living here for a change. God knows, we've had some rum'uns in here, I can tell you.'

'It'll have to do us,' Rose replied flatly. 'I can't keep up the rent where we are.'

Like number five, Moonstruck House had been soled and heeled. All the windows were in, the doorframes had been replaced and the roof fixed. But on the inside it was a different matter. The smell of damp was unmistakable and there was mould growing all along the walls under the windows. In the downstairs room there was still some paper on the walls – a yellowish colour with clusters of dull pink flowers and a border of green cheese-plant leaves a few inches from the ceiling. A few sections of it near the floor had been ripped off upwards, and in other places the corners were curling back.

Upstairs, both rooms showed the barest traces of paper. Otherwise it was bare plaster, some of which had fallen or been gouged out in places where through the holes you could see the bare brick. In the second-floor room the floorboards opened up suddenly to the stairwell which plunged down in a corner. It was bleaker than number five had ever been.

'Never had anyone in long enough to take a pride in it. But you could soon cheer it up, give it a lick of distemper.'

Rose nodded absently. Mabel noticed how painfully thin she had become again. Even her pre-war clothes hung on her now and her eyes seemed more prominent in her face.

'He'll have to have a bed downstairs,' Rose was saying. She was grateful to Mabel for sticking around to talk things through. 'I can't get him up the stairs of a night. And anyway,' she added resignedly, 'it's hard to get him out of bed in the first place nowadays.'

'Like that is it?' Mabel shook her head sympathetically. She felt suddenly rather maternal towards Rose. 'Well, you'll have to make it as easy on you as you can. You working and night school and that. Don't worry' – she patted Rose's shoulder with her thick hand – 'we'll see you through. Your mother would've done the same for any of us.'

There were tears of gratitude in Rose's eyes as she turned to her old neighbour. 'Yes,' she said. 'I know she would.'

They did fix Alfie up with a bed downstairs, along the wall away from the front window. Rose put up some net to stop people gawping in. The Pyes lent her a hand one weekend in filling in the worst holes in the walls and giving the place a couple of coats of whitewash upstairs.

Rose scrubbed down all the floorboards with disinfectant and laid down what she had in the way of old peg rugs and little off-cuts of carpet they had acquired in Moseley.

Alfie half sat, half lay watching her one Sunday morning as she attempted energetically to carry on turning the place into somewhere they could call a home. It was cold and she had built a fire and was sweeping up the scullery.

'You should get out of bed,' she told him patiently. 'You know what the nurse said about you getting sore if you lie about all day.'

Alfie looked up at her languidly. 'It's so cold,' he protested, in the strange, slurred voice he spoke in now. 'And you've got too much to do already, Rosie.'

'I can do that later,' Rose said, growing impatient. 'Come on – let's get you up.'

Hilda appeared from upstairs as Rose was preparing a bowl of warm water to wash her husband. 'What can I do?' she whined.

'D'you want to come and help me give your dad a wash?' Hilda had grown very used to seeing her father's body since he had been ill. His place at the centre of all that was going on made his a very public illness.

'No,' Hilda said, sitting on the bottom step of the stairs and kicking at the wood with her heels. 'S'boring. And smelly.'

'Well go out and play then,' Rose said, trying the temperature of the water in the bowl.

'Don't want to.' Hilda's face twisted into the expression of stubborn sulkiness she often wore nowadays. 'You're just trying to get rid of me.'

'Yes,' Rose snapped. 'I am. Sitting around moaning at me. Now do as you're told and get out there with the others.'

'Me dad'd never be so horrible to me,' she said snidely as she pulled her old coat on.

Silently Rose began soaping Alfie's scrawny white arms. He had lost all the muscle tone that his building work had given him, and the translucent skin seemed to cover bone and little else. His arms had become stiff and awkward, and she had to lean on them to bend them. She washed under his arms, the light brown wiry hair turning white with soap. She'd tucked a towel under his shoulders so as not to wet the sheets. Gently she wiped his face, and then slid her hands flat under him to turn him so that she could wash his back. The nurses had showed her how – the lifting and bed baths. How to position a little container between his legs to catch the urine which dribbled from him beyond his control.

When she had turned him back over and was washing his chest she realized he was watching her, and that tears were rolling down his cheeks. She stopped what she was doing and stroked his hair which was rather greasy and needed cutting.

'What's the matter?' she asked softly.

'I'm sorry, Rose.' The sobs shook his body, his thin, gentle face growing pink and streaked with the tears. 'You shouldn't be having to do all this.'

'Ssshh,' she said, trying to soothe him, tears of sorrow and pity filling her own eyes. 'Don't say that. I've told you. I'm your wife, aren't I? Who else should be looking after you?'

'But living back here.' Alfie's voice came out horribly slurred from the disease and his distress. 'It was the last thing you wanted. I was going to do so much for you, Rosie, give you so much. I'm sorry . . .'

In the early days, when she had first begun caring for him, he had wept like this often, full of remorse, frustration and fear as to what was going to happen to the family. He had worried how they would live on sickness benefit alone. About how Rose would manage, and what would happen to Hilda. And in sheer horror at what was happening to his body. Worst of all had been the times when, at first, he had still wanted to make love to her.

'Rosie, come here,' he'd beg, wanting things to be all right, for at least that to be possible between them. She would lie in his arms as he took her breasts in his hands, touching her, kissing her desperately, trying to force some sensation into the limp lower half of his body. Sometimes he would say, as he had never done when he was well, 'Will you help me? Will you touch me?'

Pityingly she had taken him in her hands, trying to kindle him, caressing the soft, small part of him which could feel nothing, and trying, more for his sake than for her own, to arouse him. He would lie watching her with a fixed expression of concentration on his face, longing, willing himself, and it was that desperation she saw in him which made her cry, and his failure and shame which brought on his own tears, so that they would end up lying in distress in each other's arms, in a strange way closer than they had ever been before he was ill.

They no longer attempted lovemaking now. Rose cared for him and he, most of the time, just accepted that this was how it had to be. Seeing him in this broken state she grew to realize how grateful she was to him, and that she did indeed care for him, not as a lover – which she never had and never could – but as a kind, familiar friend, and the way she would care for a child or any sick, fragile creature.

As she dried his tears that cold morning, he appealed to her in a whisper, 'Give us a kiss, will you?'

She bent and kissed his lips, smelling the rather stale, sour smell of him despite the wash. When they had kissed she smiled kindly at him. 'I'll change your sheets again. Come on – let's get you into a chair.'

'I'm sorry,' he said again.

'It's not your fault,' she told him, touching his bony shoulder. 'Look – it's all right.'

In a way it was. Her feelings at that time were so mixed, so mercurial that at times she could barely make up her mind what she felt about anything.

Moving back into Catherine Street had symbolized for her the end of any aspirations of her own. The circle had closed. Now she was back just where she began and could hope for nothing better. But in another way it had been a relief to see the familiar old faces and know she could always rely on them for help. At that moment that was her greatest need.

At other times she was overcome by an extraordinary exhilaration, even through all the tiredness. It was like a resurgence in her of someone entirely forgotten. There was the thrill of risk, and the challenging sense that she was in charge. She could no longer be dependent and passive. She began to experience some of the zest for life she had felt in the army. Now at last she could do something.

'I'm going to have to earn more than the odd bob or two,' she had said to Grace. 'I'll have to learn how to do something. I'm only fit for the factory floor or a shop.'

So she had started the evening classes. She signed on for three evenings a week at Sparkhill Commercial School over on the Stratford Road. English, typing and shorthand, she decided, would stand her in the best stead for the future. Meantime, whatever job she got they would have to make the best of it until she was trained to do something better.

She applied for a job working in the offices of a firm in Burton Street, only a couple of streets away from home: Turner's Metal Smallware.

Since it was so near at hand she was able to run home in the lunch hour and give Alfie a few moments' company as well as hastily making Hilda something to eat. The rest of the day either Mabel or Gladys Pye saw to her and she played with the other kids in the court who were too young for school.

Her duties at Turner's ranged from seeing to the outgoing post, of which there was a great deal to be sealed and stamped on the cranky old franking machine, to helping actually to pack the goods: shining piles of hairgrips and hairpins and metal coathangers and straight pins, which were boxed up and sent out to shops all over the country.

Though the work was often tedious and she felt guilty leaving Alfie and Hilda, the fact was she had no choice in

333

the matter if they were all to eat. As her mother had done before her, she was going to keep her family, though at the moment the money was never enough. Mrs Meredith helped them out a little when she could, but it was the kindness of the neighbours which really kept them going: Gladys popping in saying, 'Look – we've a couple of portions of stew left over. You have it, Rose. It'll go bad else'; or Mabel coming by with a loaf or a cake or a pat of margarine. Even the neighbours who she had not known all her life pitched in. Rose sometimes wept at their unquestioning generosity.

Often in the evening, when she had walked the couple of miles to Sparkhill after a hasty bite to eat, she would sit for two hours learning the intricacies of Pitman shorthand, her whole body throbbing with tiredness. Despite that she was one of the best in the class. She practised at every opportunity. Whenever she had to write something down she would think how to do it in shorthand.

'Some people have a natural bent for shorthand,' the tutor told her, smiling. 'And you're certainly one of them.'

Rose beamed with delight at learning something new and being praised for it.

One evening, when she had been going to Sparkhill for a few months, she walked down the front steps of the school with some of the other girls from the class. They were chatting, groaning over their typing speeds on the heavy Underwood machines. It was a warm evening, still light, and the air was soft and still, scented with fading laburnum and lilac. Occasionally a car passed by on the Stratford Road.

'I'm tired,' Rose sighed as they reached the pavement. 'I've a good mind to get on the bus and to hell with it.'

'Money down the drain,' her friends reminded her cheerfully. 'Bus or bread.'

Rose smiled. 'It's a good job you're here to keep me in line. Anyway, by the time I've been into town and out it'll take me just as long. And at least it's still light.'

They said their goodbyes and set out in different directions.

Rose turned, still smiling from the friendly company, to walk towards the side street where she would turn off towards home. She caught a whiff of roses from the gardens and breathed in the scent, so different from the usual smoky smells of the city.

Just before she turned off the Stratford Road, wondering whether Hilda had played Grace up about going to bed, she felt a hand settle firmly on her shoulder. Startled, she turned with a gasp, and behind her she found a handsome, and suddenly familiar face grinning at her.

It was Michael Gillespie.

CHAPTER 34

MARCH 1952

Again she woke from a vivid dream, those dreams which came only occasionally now. She realized her face was wet with tears. It had been so vivid.

They were in Il Rifugio, alone in the storeroom where she had first seen Falcone on the maize-straw mattresses. The others may have been around somewhere but the two of them were alone, and knew they would not be disturbed. She did not recall any particular words, or that they had spoken at all. What was most overpowering was the atmosphere of tenderness and passion as they loved one another. She remembered his body, slim and strong and dark, in every detail, as if they had only truly been together the night before. And the look on his face, his delight in her and care for her and her own sense of giving herself unreservedly and with joy.

For a moment she lay wiping her eyes, still completely taken up in the mood of the dream. Then other thoughts forced themselves into her mind, thoughts which filled her with excitement, but at the same time with strong pangs of guilt. Michael. She had agreed to meet Michael tonight. Though her conscience and common sense cried out not to do it, she knew that she would go.

She had seen Michael a number of times, at first only occasionally and seemingly by chance, after their first meeting. Seeing him there had truly delighted her.

'Michael!' she'd cried in wonder. 'You're alive. All this time you've been alive!'

He'd laughed at this, bending his strong body down to

give her a kiss on the cheek. 'Oh, I'm alive all right. Even survived the River Po and that's saying something, I can tell you. Sea of corpses it was when we crossed.' His expression lost its exuberance at the memory. 'But that's long in the past, and we both came through it, eh?'

'I was never in much danger down there,' Rose said. 'Hell of a lot quieter than it was here really.' She stood staring at him, amazed at the thought that the last time she had seen him had been outside the stables at Caserta. And it was so precious, that memory, that link with the war. Just those few minutes when they had stood together with Tony. Someone else who would remember him, remember the place.

'You living round here?' Michael asked.

'No. Been to school.' She outlined briefly what she was doing, told him about Alfie and Hilda.

Michael let out a whistle of sympathy. 'That's really rough. You poor kid. I thought you wasn't looking as bonny as when I saw you in Italy. But you always did have guts, I'll say that for you, Rose. Can't see my wife getting out earning a living.'

'You're married then?' They were still standing where he had caught up with her, Michael pressing one of his shiny black shoes up against the wall facing him as they talked. A tram made its way noisily along the road.

'Oh, yes. The wife and I live on down there a way. Edge of Hall Green.' He pointed down the Stratford Road. 'Mary her name is. Good Irish girl. I've a lad too – Joseph. He's two.'

Rose felt a pang at the name Joseph. For a second she calculated how old her own Joseph would have been now. Fourteen this year. A grown lad, perhaps just starting out on a job.

'I've got the bookies down the road,' Michael was saying proudly. 'My own little outfit. Gillespie over the door. Doing well. You know how it is with a growing family. We've another on the way – due in October.'

'I'm glad. It's really good to see you.'

'Listen – come for a drink with me,' Michael urged.

He went to put an arm round her shoulders and usher her along. 'Jesus, you're skinny! We can have a quick one in the Mermaid.'

'I can't,' Rose told him regretfully. 'Sorry Michael, I just can't. I've left my husband and kid all day.'

'OK,' Michael said easily, removing his muscular arm from her shoulders. 'Then let me walk you home.'

'Well . . .' Rose hesitated. 'That'd be nice. But what about your wife? Weren't you on your way home?'

Michael made a quick, dismissive gesture. 'Oh – she'll be off to bed any minute. She gets tired, what with the babbies and that. Anyroad, I'm out most nights to tell you the truth. She never kicks up a fuss.'

All the way back to Catherine Street they chatted and reminisced. Michael told her he had met Mary, his wife, three years ago.

'It was one of these Irish dos. Lots of booze and the music going and all the couples dancing and all the old'uns getting sick for the home country. She was fresh over here and she stood out. Really pretty face she had – well, she still has, except she's got a bit of fat on her after having Joseph, of course. But she's a good lass. Looks after me all right.'

'Bet that takes some doing,' Rose teased him. She realized, as ever with Michael, that she had began to flirt with him. 'Not sure I'd fancy the job myself!'

'Would you not?' Michael sounded mock wounded. 'I'd've said we'd have made a pretty fine team, you and me, Rosie.'

Rose realized he was not entirely joking, and she blushed in the dusk. Guiltily, she knew she had not felt so alive, so stimulated by anyone's sheer presence, in months and months. She steered the conversation on to less personal things.

When they said goodnight at the end of Catherine Street, Michael gave her another kiss on the cheek.

'Come for a drink another time,' he called, turning back towards Sparkhill.

Inside, to her surprise, she found Sid dozing in the

chair beside Alfie, who was also asleep. She crept in, and Sid roused himself as she closed the door.

''Bout time,' he said, looking up at her with the bleary eyes of an old man. 'Our Grace has gone home to bed.'

Rose looked at the clock. She had taken half an hour longer than usual to get home. Had she and Michael really spent so much time talking? It had seemed to pass in seconds.

She saw Sid out, giving herself a ticking off when she remembered how much help they were giving her.

She and Michael met for a brief drink some weeks later, but then it was months before she saw him again. There was no English class on the Thursday evening before Christmas, and they arranged to meet then. Rose knew she was deceiving Grace, who would spend the evening with Alfie. But sometimes she thought Grace would be lost now without her role in Rose's house. It had become part of her life. And Rose hungered for company, for interest and someone to have a good talk with.

As she sat opposite Michael in the busy Mermaid pub, she found all her doubts disappearing, and relaxed back into enjoying his company. They made an attractive pair, Michael in what looked like a new dark blue suit, his hair cut perfectly and greased back, and Rose with her long hair curling down prettily over her shoulders. She looked beautiful, especially when animated by her conversation with Michael.

They started talking about general things: Michael's business, the way money was so tight still, and of Michael's satisfaction that Winston Churchill had been re-elected to office in October.

'Now things'll get back to rights again,' he told her, with the almost superstitious regard in which some people still held Churchill. 'All that Labour lot messing about. What we need is a proper government – someone who knows what they're doing. Been like rats from a sinking ship, all these people looking to go abroad to work. What good's that to our country?' He pushed back his stool. 'Another?'

Rose watched him going to the bar. He still walked with the trace of a limp which had stayed with him from his injury in Italy. He was a fine-looking man with strong features and those direct blue eyes, always a hint of mischief in them.

He's a bit of a chancer, she thought. Bet he gives that poor wife of his the runaround. But she couldn't resist being with him this evening. He was a connection with the past, and being able to go out and meet him made her feel she could laugh and be her age again, for a short time at least, instead of driven, worried and over-worked.

'I was just thinking,' he said, sitting down with their drinks, a pint for him and port and lemon for her. 'If you're out working all day, who looks after your husband?'

'Neighbours. I moved back to the Birch Street area again when Alfie was taken bad. They all help mind Hilda, my little girl, too. Me and Grace do the shopping between us – I mean, who's got the time to stand in a queue for hours on end? Anyroad, that's all that's left of the family now. My brother George is . . .' Blushing, she looked down at the table. 'He's in Winson Green.'

'Jesus! What for?'

'Burglary. He went bad on us during the war. I was away of course, so I hardly saw it coming. But Grace had him all through. She's done with with him. She don't even go and visit.'

'But you do?'

'When I can. Only every month or two, and he's due out soon anyroad. He's my brother. I always had a soft spot for him as a kid. I s'pose it was after the evacuation – he ran away, and he was never the same after he came back. It's as if—' She looked up at Michael, and he saw that tears had filled her brown eyes. Gently he leaned over and laid one of his large hands over hers, which were clasped tensely together on the table.

'It's as if he went off like a pint of milk. You can't get through to him any more. When I go over there' – she grimaced at the thought of the dark stone walls and towers of the prison – 'he sits there, all pinched in the face. All hard looking. I don't know who he is any more.' Slowly she pulled her hands away.

'I'm sure you're doing the right thing,' Michael told her. 'Though God knows, with all you've got on your plate no one'd think bad of you if you didn't go.' Then he asked gently, 'And your husband – Alfie, isn't it? How much can he do?'

'Nothing.' Rose sounded very matter of fact. 'It's got to him very hard and very fast. He doesn't move out of bed. Can't do anything for himself at all. Someone has to be about all the time.'

She took in Michael's appalled expression, realized that he was reaching for her hands again, but she kept them under the table. At that moment she felt that if he touched her she might just turn into his arms and cry out all the worry and tiredness and frustration of the past months. She longed for such comfort, to be able to lean on someone as solid and kind and reviving as Michael.

'Oh, Rosie,' he said. 'You poor, brave kid.'

She could think of nothing else to say to him, and was relieved when after a few moments he started talking. As she wiped her eyes she realized that her telling him about her own life and worries had released him and he was now able to disclose to her his own.

'When I met Mary, I thought I'd found the best woman ever,' he told her. 'She was pretty and sweet. She looked up to me and I loved her. I really thought the world of her, Rosie . . .' He hesitated, and as she looked across at him she saw confusion in his face.

'But . . .?' she prompted.

'I don't know if it's having the babbies that's done it. Joseph's a great kid, and now we've got little Geraldine and she's a bonny babby. But Mary, she's got time for nothing else. What with feeding Geraldine at night and both of them on all day. And she frowns all the time.

341

You may smile, Rosie, but before I'd hardly seen her crease her face in that way. She was the sweetest girl . . . But now she's got a line, as if someone's taken a pencil right down.' He pointed to the little bridge of flesh between his eyebrows. 'She never had that before.'

Rose leaned across the table and pointed at her own face, so that a man at the next door table watched with a puzzled expression. 'Look – I've got one too. They ought to call it the mother's mark!'

'But I don't get it . . .' Michael trailed off, frowning. 'You've got more worries than she has. She's not got a care in the world. All women have kiddies, but they don't go all mardy on you like Mary. She ain't got time for me, not in any department.'

He sat in gloomy silence for a moment, his deep blue eyes staring unfocusing across the bar. Around them people were laughing and two old men had started singing 'Roll out the Barrel'.

He brought himself up with a jerk. 'Sorry, Rosie. Didn't mean to bring you here and pour out all my troubles. You won't want to come again?'

She knew it was an invitation.

'But don't you think sometimes, looking back to when we was kids at Lazenby's, we were full of all we were going to do. What was it you went on about? Teaching kids, wasn't it? And I was going to run the world, have a big business . . .' He chuckled bitterly. 'And now look at us.'

'But you're doing all right?'

'All right. That's about the sum of it. But I wanted more, much more than that. Maybe that's where I went wrong.'

They talked a little while longer before Rose told him she really had to go in order to get home at the normal time. They walked back together, further into the darkened city, where the points of greatest light and noise were the pubs on corners and down side streets.

'Meet me again, won't you?' he asked as they parted, and she nodded. She knew that this meeting, and the way they had found they could confide in each other, had sealed their need to see each other.

Before she could stop him, he took her in his arms briefly and kissed her hungrily on the lips.

As she walked into Court 11 she tried to push from her mind what had just happened. It was a mistake, the result of an evening of resuming old friendship and sharing emotion. She wouldn't let it happen again.

Quietly she released the catch on the door and pushed it open. For a few seconds she stood startled in the doorway, watching unnoticed before Grace turned, conscious of the draught from the doorway.

Alfie was lying as usual, on one side in the bed. They had to turn him every couple of hours to relieve the pressure on his bedridden body, which opened up his skin into deep sores. Grace was sitting beside him, tenderly holding one of his hands in her own.

Unsettled, and feeling strangely guilty at the apparent intimacy of the scene, Rose moved in briskly, pretending not to have noticed. Alfie's eyes opened and his face lit up as far as it was able into his lopsided smile.

'Everything all right?' she asked. 'Hilda asleep?'

'She's well gone,' Grace told her.

Rose poured some tea for all of them.

'These sores, Rose.' Grace pointed at Alfie. 'They're not getting any better, are they?'

Rose sighed, sipping the warm tea. 'It's a losing battle. I don't know what else we can do.'

The two of them gently turned back Alfie's bedclothes, and he stirred slightly, his eyes closed again. A rank smell emanated from him, a mixture of sweat and urine and the discharge from the sores.

'We'll turn him,' Rose said. 'I'm glad you waited. It's a job on your own.'

They slid their arms under Alfie's inert body, pulling him gently across the bed, and rolled him over on to his other side.

Grace tutted. 'Sheet's wet again. We'll have to change it.'

Manoeuvring Alfie's body from side to side, they pulled out the bottom sheet and smoothed over another one. Washing and more washing. Rose carefully wrapped his reddened heels and elbows in soft cloths to help protect them against the bed's chafing.

They eased Alfie out of his pyjamas. His limbs kept stiffening into muscular spasms, so that for minutes at a time they could not straighten his arms enough to slide on a fresh pyjama jacket.

Before they replaced the trousers, Rose turned her attention to the worst sores at the bottom of his back. On the right side, the top part of his buttock was beginning to break up, the skin all red and cracked, and they were doing all they could to prevent it getting as bad as the other side. On the left a full-blown sore had developed into a discoloured, oozing hole large enough to hold a golf ball. It looked appalling, though Alfie said he was not aware of much pain from it.

Rose carefully pulled off the lint dressing and grimaced. From inside oozed a yellowish grey, foul-smelling liquid. 'We'll have to dress it again,' she said.

The nurse had recommended packing the wound with lint and a concoction of whipped egg whites, something which Rose had a decreasing amount of faith in as a remedy. When they had finished they tucked a bottle between his legs to try and keep the urine off the sheets, and covered him up again.

'D'you want your tea now, Alfie?' Grace asked him gently. Almost imperceptibly he nodded his head.

Rose met Michael on other occasions after that. What was the harm in meeting a friend, she reasoned. Except – and the thoughts hovered around and were pushed to the back of her mind – she couldn't bring herself to tell Grace.

Michael was like a lifeline. How could she give that up when the rest of life, the drab, everyday routine of illness and Turner's and rationing and struggle offered so little?

As she got out of bed that March morning, the dream of Falcone gradually sliding from her mind, she tried to quell her excitement at the thought of meeting Michael in the evening. After all, they were both married people with families meeting for a chinwag. So why should her feelings be so stirred?

CHAPTER 35

'I needn't go tonight,' she told Grace, her guilt making her wish that her sister would demand her presence. 'I'll stay if you think you'll need me.'

Alfie had a bad cold which had gone to his chest, and she had been helping Grace to prop him up so that he could cough and clear his lungs.

'No, you're all right. You go,' Grace said, seating herself on the wooden chair beside Alfie's head. 'I can always fetch Gladys in.'

Rose wondered if she was imagining that Grace really preferred it when she was out of the way. Or did she suspect that Rose was not going to a class at all?

'Well, all right,' she agreed. 'I'll get back as early as I can.'

'No need.' Grace pulled some knitting out of an old cloth bag. 'We'll get on fine – won't we, Alfie?'

As she walked into the cosy light of the Mermaid she saw Michael raise an arm to her. He was as usual dressed immaculately. She had never seen him wear anything the least bit worn or shabby. He had on a dark blue suit which emphasized the already powerful outline of his body.

'Sorry I'm late, Michael,' she gasped, sitting down at last with relief on the bench opposite him.

'Oh, no need to apologize.' He got up as she unbuttoned her coat. 'What'll you have?'

Clearly he'd managed to fit in a couple of drinks

already. When he came back to their table with the glasses and sat down, Rose immediately sensed a tension between them, something which made her self-conscious, and she found it hard to look him in the eyes.

She chatted to him nervously. They must keep things normal and conversational. Within bounds. She must not let him touch her hands across the table as he had done before. Otherwise she could not carry on persuading herself that she was justified in meeting him.

'Your family all right?' she asked. 'How's Mary? And the babby?'

'Mary's getting more sleep nowadays,' Michael told her. He was sitting with a generous tumbler of Scotch in front of him. 'They're all OK. They're doing fine.'

He sounded evasive, as if he didn't want to go into how things were between him and Mary. Rose had begun to realize that Michael only found it possible to confide in her if she first disclosed something about herself or showed emotion in front of him, and she was deliberately keeping that at bay.

Suddenly Michael said, 'I've been meaning to ask you something. About your . . . about Alfie.' Rose waited. 'Well, how is he?'

Rose was puzzled. 'Well, he's not too good. He never is of course. But he's got a chill at the moment.'

'I meant . . .' Michael looked down at the floor between his legs. 'Is he never going to get right again?'

'No. There's nothing anyone can do for him. No cure. Michael, you know that. I've told you endless times.'

He shook his head sadly. 'I thought – I was just making sure.'

'Anyroad,' Rose went on. 'The next thing is George is coming out, next week some time. God knows I've wished him out of there often enough, but now he's really coming I don't know what the hell we're going to do with him. I'm scared at the thought, Michael, to tell you the truth.'

'Where's he going to live?'

Rose shrugged again. 'I s'pose he'll have to come

home. I mean where else? Grace hasn't said a word about it and Dad might as well have forgotten who he is. We'll just have to see if he can hold down a job.'

'Can he do anything?'

'Thieving. He's good at that.'

Michael laughed, pulling out his cigarettes. Rose felt as if his blue eyes were piercing right through her. 'You only see your family as they are, don't you, Rosie? Not like me. Always wanting to put Mary on a pedestal like a plaster statue.'

'Well, how else?' Rose joined in his laughter and accepted a cigarette. 'Bit late to go making up fairy stories about them, isn't it?'

'Not for me. It's just the way I like to dream about people.' And again the sadness crept back in to his eyes. 'Trouble with statues on pedestals is that one way or another they keep getting knocked off.'

Then he asked, with the kind of intensity she had started to dread from him, 'What about you, Rosie?' He asked the question as if he wanted something from her: some pronouncement or decision. 'What are you going to do?'

'I'm going to look for a new job,' she told him. 'I should be able to get better money now, so I'll be looking around. I've got one place in mind, but really I'm being a bit cheeky. It's in town, with a solicitor. But I might as well have a try.'

Michael was draining his glass as she spoke. He put the glass down excitedly. 'Maybe I could find you something. I'm sure I could.'

Rose decided to treat this as a joke. 'Let me try out my wings first before you rush in to rescue me. But thanks for the offer. Now, let me get the next one in.'

But Michael stubbed out his cigarette with sudden resolve and picked up his coat. 'Come on, Rosie. It's not cold out. I'll take you to see my place. It's only a walk along the road.'

'Your house?' Rose asked, astonished.

'Jesus, no. I'll show you the business.' Seeing her hesitate, he urged her, 'Come on, what's the harm? I'd be proud for you to see it. You'll be home with time to spare.' He took her arm.

It was a cloudy night and mild, with a threat of drizzle. The shop was only a few streets away, and they walked in silence, well apart, as if they were afraid even of their hands touching by accident. It was an apprehensive, embarrassed silence. Rose knew why he was taking her there, and he knew that she knew. It all seemed inevitable after their meetings, but suddenly so very uneasy. Not at all a comfortable progression from confiding friendship to possible lovemaking, but driven, and somehow at odds.

He stopped outside a quite smart-looking shop front and, looking up, she saw 'GILLESPIE'S' in bold dark letters above the window. He didn't go into the darkened betting shop. Instead he led her up a narrow staircase, between walls covered with brown, chipped paint and smelling of stale cigarette smoke and general dirtiness.

'Not too nice, that bit,' he apologized when they reached the top. 'Come on in here. This is my office.'

He produced another key, and she stood waiting behind him, looking at the weave of his suit, depressed by the smelly seediness of the staircase and wondering what to expect from the room on the other side of the door.

'People have to knock to come in here,' he told her proudly.

Once he had pushed the door open and switched on the light she looked round in real surprise.

In contrast to the staircase, the room was freshly decorated in cream paint, and she found her feet suddenly cushioned by what looked like brand new carpet with a crimson background patterned with fashionable skater's trail curves in black and white. All the furniture was brand new as well: a sideboard, its wooden veneer still gleaming with the sheen of newness, and two easy chairs covered in a vivid green woven fabric. In the middle of the room stood an enormous desk behind which Michael evidently presided from a chair covered in bright red and black material.

'Blimey, Michael!' Rose said, laughing. 'This furniture's a bit bright, isn't it?'

Proudly he joined in her laughter. 'Right up to the minute that,' he told her. 'Makes a change from all that blooming depressing brown stuff, doesn't it? Makes me think of nothing but the war that does. Mary still likes it though. So I thought, well, if I have to put up with all that old fashioned look at home, then I'll have my own little place here where I can do just what I want!'

Although the room did not seem all that warm, Michael took off his coat and hung his jacket over the back of the red chair. Rose watched his broad, muscular frame with some curiosity as he went over to the sideboard and squatted down to open one of the low cupboards. He was really such a stranger to her.

'I'll get us another drink,' he said. 'Will you be having a nip of Scotch? Haven't got much else.'

'Oh – no ta,' Rose replied quickly. She already felt light-headed from the pace he had set drinking in the Mermaid. 'If I have any more I'll get bad.'

Unbuttoning her coat, she walked round Michael's very tidy desk. From one of the frames facing his chair Mary smiled sweetly back at her. Face like an angel, Rose thought. Poor cow. Her wavy hair looked as if it must be a middling brown, and the camera had caught her glancing up, as if it had taken some persuasion to make her look in that direction at all. Round her neck you could just see a small crucifix gleaming at the bottom of the picture.

She's lovely, Michael, Rose wanted to say. She's beautiful. But she couldn't bring herself to speak. To say such things would be to bring Mary into the room between them.

There was a second photograph, evidently more recent, of Mary holding the baby Geraldine, with Joseph leaning into the picture beside her. The little boy's expression was solemn. Geraldine had that startled kind of baby face, all eyes. Michael's eyes. Mary was smiling. Did being married to Michael make her happy, Rose wondered?

She realized Michael was watching her. She glanced up at him. His eyes looked slightly glassy: at once sad and lustful. She pitied him, but with a sense of panic. Everything about this was wrong.

'Come away from the window,' he said. She didn't resist when he took her by the hand and led her to a corner of the room. She wanted, needed him to hold her, to allow herself to feel excited by him. She wanted that dreamlike, swimming feeling which would allow her to make love with him, give herself up to the swell of it and forget everything else.

As soon as he moved against her and they began to kiss, she felt her body come alive with all the sensations she had not known for so long. His hands reached insistently inside her clothing to touch her skin, to close over her breasts, and her eyes closed as she gave way to the pleasure of it.

Michael released her slightly, his eyes half closed. 'God. It's been so long since she's let me.'

Something like icy water sluiced through her mind and she was out of the dream, eyes wide open and seeing herself and Michael with clinical clarity as if from a distance. She was in a room above a betting shop, with a man's body pressed to hers, his black hair close to her cheek. Black hair which could almost have been Falcone's but wasn't. A man who aroused her, filled her with sexual desire, but whom she did not love. She thought of the last time she was forced to the floor by a man in an office where photographs of his family looked on from the desk, and she knew that whatever it was she'd desired of these few minutes, she could only ever see them as cheap afterwards. Soiled and cheap.

Michael felt her stiffen and straighten up, withdrawing from him. She pulled on her blouse, buttoning it over her breasts.

Michael's eyes opened and he made a despairing sound. 'Oh God, Rosie,' he implored her. 'Don't pull out on me now. Please.'

She removed his arms from round her and moved away, rearranging herself. 'It's not that I don't want you. You know that. But I can't do it. I feel as if everyone's here watching us – Mary and Alfie and everyone. I'm sorry, Michael.'

He turned from her abruptly and went to pick up his glass, draining the last gulp from it. He lit a cigarette and sat down on one of the green chairs in silence. She knew he was not going to try to force her.

'I don't go with women, you know,' he said finally. 'That's not the way I was brought up. It's just – you're different Rosie, I can talk to you, and we go back a long way. There was always something there between us, wasn't there?'

'There was. And there is, in a way. But I can't do this. We'd be doing wrong to so many other people.'

There was an awkward silence before Michael spoke. 'What you said, about your husband, him being bad and that. I mean you and him, you don't . . .?'

'Not any more, no.'

'Then why?'

'He's still my husband. He's had enough bad luck without his wife going bad on him. And there's Mary. I looked at that picture and I thought I'd like her if I met her. That's daft I know, because what difference does it make? But I couldn't do it to her either. Or to myself.'

'But they'd never know. I don't want to hurt anyone either. It's between you and me, Rosie. Even if it's only the once, it's just for us.' His blue eyes suddenly looked very young in their appeal.

'I'm not going to come here any more, Michael.'

'Not come?' He made to stand up and she turned away from him. 'What? Not even for a drink now and then?'

'I can't. If I keep coming it'll always come to this, won't it? Because it's always there between us. Sooner or later I'd give in to you and I'd hate myself for it. And you wouldn't be happy either. Not in the end.'

Michael shook his head. 'You always were more grown up than me, Rosie. I can't help admiring you for it. Come here, will you? Just for a moment?'

She went to him and they held each other again briefly.

'Go and give Mary some of your time,' she told him as they released each other. 'And your kids. They're what matters. If you stick with them I bet things'll work out.

Michael kissed her. 'I hope you get that job of yours. I'll miss you.'

She told him she would walk back alone and he let her out of the office and the door on to the street.

She was late home again. Grace was sitting in her usual position by Alfie's bed. The fire had burned down to a glow in the grate, and beside Grace lay a long skein of knitting which she had abandoned out of sleepiness.

She said nothing when Rose came in through the door, but her whole manner spoke of reproach. She bundled her things into the cloth bag and placed it pointedly beside the door. Still in silence the two of them settled Alfie down for the night. Usually they talked and made tea while Alfie dozed, but tonight he lay watching them as they went about their tasks, their eyes not meeting each other's nor a word passing between them.

They re-dressed his sores, though this time the sheets had stayed dry and did not need to be changed. When he started coughing again they supported him between them by his skeletal shoulders and dosed him with linctus, waiting until he was calm again.

Eventually Rose asked Grace, 'D'you want a cuppa?'

'No ta.' Grace took her apron off. 'I'll be glad to get home to my bed. And not before time either.' Rose could hear the anger pressed into her voice.

'By the way. I'm stopping the classes. I'm ready to go for a better job now.'

Normally Grace would have looked pleased for her and asked questions about where and how much. 'That'll be a relief for everyone, won't it?'

Rose sighed. 'I can be home evenings.'

Grace continued to look huffy, busying herself with her bag. 'Well – we'll see about that, won't we?'

Then she was gone.

Rose boiled some water on the gas and made tea. She poured for herself and Alfie and helped him, spooning the sweet liquid into his mouth. Often when she came in he was sleepy and hardly seemed to notice she was there. But tonight he was wide awake, partly perhaps because of his troubled breathing. She knew he was watching her as she moved round, tidying away the cups and getting the room ready for the morning because it was always such a rush.

She went over to him. 'Would you like me to turn you again? Would it help you to breathe better?'

'No. I'm OK.' He carried on staring up at her. His gaze seemed to hold a knowing sort of wisdom which made her feel ashamed. In the end she could bear it no longer.

'What? What Alfie?'

In his stumbling, slurred way he brought out the words, 'Wanted . . . something . . . more than . . . half alive . . . did you?'

She knelt and laid her head down on the bed next to the thin curve of his body. 'I'm sorry,' she whispered. 'I'm so sorry.'

For a moment he managed to stroke her hair before his arm went into spasm again.

'You deserve . . . better,' he said. When she looked up at him she saw he was crying too.

'I'm going to be here now,' she told him. 'Evenings and all. I'm going to get a better job and work hard – for all of us. I'll make things better if I can.'

She took one of his stiff hands in her own. 'Grace makes you a better wife than I do, doesn't she?'

She looked into Alfie's wet face, and reached across to wipe away his tears.

'But you're . . . the wife . . . I want. Always. You know. I love . . . you.'

CHAPTER 36

George Lucas stood outside the entrance to Winson Green Prison for the first time in over four years and heard the heavy gate shudder behind him. He stood for a moment or two in the overcast March morning, turning his pinched face this way and that, trying to take in the fact that after all these months he could make choices about his own movements. He appeared weighed down by the responsibility of it.

He looked even thinner after his time inside, giving the impression that he had grown taller, like a plant that has bolted up in poor light, and his skin had a yellowish, waxy look. Under his arm he carried a small bundle of the few possessions he had with him when he went into prison, and these he carried wrapped in a strip of white towelling. With his old, threadbare jacket pulled close round him and a crushed-looking brown felt hat pulled over his cropped hair, he began to walk slowly away from the prison in the direction of Birch Street.

The same morning Rose made her way into the middle of Birmingham. She stopped at the entrance to some narrow offices squeezed in near the bottom end of Temple Street. Screwed to the wall beside the heavy wooden door was a brass plaque which read, 'LAURENCE ABEL AND MATTHEW WATERS: SOLICITORS'.

Rose checked there were no stray bits of fluff on the full navy blue skirt she was wearing, and adjusted the collar of her white blouse, relieved they wouldn't be able to see the mend in the right sleeve under her thick navy cardigan. On her head she wore a little felt hat with a narrow brim in a royal blue which looked striking against her jackdaw hair and, to finish off the outfit, some high-heeled black shoes. She wished the shoes had been navy as well, but the neighbours had rallied round to help her out and lend her clothes for her interview and she had had to take what she could get. She peered at her faint reflection in the window of the corridor leading to the office. Nothing seemed to be amiss, so she patted the hat gently and said in a whisper, 'Come on, Rose Meredith. Get yourself in there.'

She was precisely on time. When the door opened she found she was facing a tall blonde woman of about forty with an immaculately made-up face, who looked at her appraisingly and then held out her hand with what Rose could only feel was disdain.

'Good morning. Mrs Meredith?' The 'Mrs' was definitely unenthusiastic. 'I'm Miss Crosby.'

Miss Crosby had a small outer area to work in off which led the two offices of Mr Waters and Mr Abel. Each had a slim wooden sign on his door. Miss Crosby sat down behind her heavy black Olivetti with an affected caress of the back of her skirt. Every hair on her head sat in precisely the right place.

Brassy cow, Rose found herself thinking.

'You have a very satisfactory recommendation from Sparkhill Commercial School,' Miss Crosby said. 'Your shorthand and typing speeds are well within our requirements. Have you kept them up?' she asked suspiciously.

'I've only just left the school.'

The woman's stony blue eyes watched her coldly. 'You've been employed as an invoice typist in the pool of a small firm. Do you really imagine you're capable of taking a job as a personal assistant to a professional solicitor?' She spoke the words 'personal assistant' as if the position was second only to membership of the royal family.

'I think I can do the job,' Rose told her. 'I've got good speeds, I'm well organized and I'm a very good worker.'

'Perhaps I should make it clear what is required here. I have been secretary to Mr Waters, the senior partner, for several years. It is only in the past month that he has gone into partnership with Mr Abel, who has come to join us from Manchester. Mr Waters will be retiring in a couple of years – that's why Mr Abel is now named first in the practice.'

Rose had the definite impression that Miss Crosby's nose had been put out of joint by all these changes.

'Mr Abel needs his own personal assistant, since I am fully occupied with all Mr Water's affairs. If we were to take you on – and I have my doubts as to whether you'd be up to it, quite honestly, Mrs Meredith – you would be working under me. Is that clear?'

Rose nodded. 'Do I have to be seen by Mr Abel?'

'Oh, that won't be necessary,' Miss Crosby told her briskly. 'Mr Waters and Mr Abel leave all that sort of thing to me.'

Miss Crosby seemed on the point of pronouncing one way or another as to Rose's prospects with Abel and Waters when one of the inner doors opened and an energetic figure bounded out of the office. Rose saw a man with a round, cheerful face wearing a suit which looked good quality but was somehow comically ill-fitting on him, who bustled across the room, a newspaper tucked loosely under one arm.

'No, no, don't get up,' he said. 'I'm Laurence Abel. So, Miss Crosby, is this my new secretary or do you have a whole line of others waiting breathlessly outside?'

'I was just discussing with Mrs Meredith whether she is really suitably qualified for the position.'

Just then their interviewee, who had been looking anxiously up at Mr Abel, let out a loud gasp. Rose's hand rose automatically to her mouth to apologize for the sound.

'What's the matter, Mrs Meredith?' Laurence Abel joked. 'Is my presence too much for you?'

'I'm sorry. It's just – you'll think I'm very odd, but I noticed your newspaper.'

Laurence Abel frowned as if he had forgotten he was carrying the thing. He pulled it out and spread it out on the desk. It was a copy of *Corriera della Sera*.

'It's Italian,' Rose explained unnecessarily.

Miss Crosby was looking at her as if she thought Rose had lost her mind. But she had Laurence Abel's avid attention.

'I used to speak it.' Rose glanced anxiously at Miss Crosby. 'I was there for nearly two years. In the war.'

'Good Lord!' Mr Abel cried. Rose was almost sure his feet left the ground in his enthusiasm. 'How marvellous! You mean you really speak it? Can you remember it?'

Suddenly he launched into a list of questions, mostly in energetic Italian, but with the odd English word thrown in when he got stuck. Having heard Rose's replies he said, 'You're obviously a darn sight better at it than I am. Come on into my office for a minute.'

He led her into what seemed a surprisingly orderly room for so chaotic-looking a character: the walls lined with shelves of all his files and reference books with gold lettering on the spines.

'You know, I really should be working,' Mr Abel said, leaning back at his desk, his podgy stomach pushing out the front of his shirt. 'But I can't throw up an opportunity like this.'

Rose found herself telling him about the ATS and a little about Il Rifugio and her feeling that she belonged in the country.

'I know what you mean about the sense of belonging,' Mr Abel agreed eagerly. 'I had exactly the same feeling. I go back as often as I can. Couldn't do without it.'

'You go back?' Rose was amazed. She never imagined such a thing. Italy was part of the war, not accessible at any other time.

'About once a year. Managed a quick visit before moving down here. It's not quite the other side of the world you know.'

'It is when you've got no money.'

Laurence Abel looked at her in silence for a moment. 'If you came to work here, would you agree on a condition that when we're not actually dictating letters, we'll speak in Italian?'

Rose grinned at this bizarre request. 'That'd be lovely.'

She almost danced into number five that evening to tell Grace the news.

'I've got the job!' she cried before she was even properly through the door.

And then stopped abruptly. Grace was standing by the table wearing her apron and a grimmer, angrier expression than Rose could ever remember seeing on her face before. Sid was sitting on the other side of the room by the fire, but was for once intent on what was going on. And at the table sat George, his hat lying in front of him, a cigarette in his mouth, his defiant eyes staring down at the table.

'Oh my God,' Rose said. 'I'd forgotten it was today.'

'That's obvious,' George said bitterly. He pulled the cigarette out of his mouth, wincing as if it tasted bad and held it in one hand, tapping his fingers on the table.

'Well – what's going on?' Rose asked. The atmosphere was pure acid.

'He thinks,' Grace's voice grated out, 'that he's going to come swanning back in here to live as if nothing had happened – and have me waiting on him hand and foot again no doubt. And then' – she leaned down and shouted into George's face – 'I s'pose you'll just be off thieving and getting into more trouble and expecting the rest of us to carry the can for you! No. I'm not having it. I'm not having you back here. You can go where you like, go to hell for all I care, as long as you're not coming in and out of here.'

George sat in silence. He had walked most of the day, with no money for food as he made his way home, putting off going to the old house where he had grown up, skirting round it time and again, until by the afternoon he was so hungry and weary from the unaccustomed exercise that he had finally slunk into the court.

Sid had opened the door and when it dawned on him who had arrived, he said, 'You'd better come in, but I don't know what your sister'll say.' He'd let him have tea and bread and jam and a slice off a leathery bit of leftover beef.

Rose could tell that, for all his toughness, George was upset. She was horrified at what she was hearing from Grace. Grace hadn't been to see him once in prison and was turning him out now as if he was a stranger who meant nothing to her at all.

No one had spoken after Grace, but she leapt to her own defence as if they had, her hands clamped to her waist. 'Say what you like. You come in here and I go – simple as that. You can go rot for all I care.'

George looked over at Sid for some sign of authority, of contradiction, but saw only his father's watery eyes staring defeatedly back at him.

Sid shrugged tiredly. 'You'd better do as she says.' He couldn't have Grace walking out on him, after all.

'George.' Rose spoke more gently and he was struck even at that moment by the difference between his sisters: Rose's animated beauty despite her thinness, compared with Grace's haggard, bitter face.

Rose laid her hand on the back of his chair. 'What are you going to do, George? Find a job and get yourself straightened out or what? You can't go on the way you've been. You don't want to end up back in there, do you?' She looked with pity at the side of her brother's face with his shorn brown hair. He was a sad sight.

'I dunno,' he said. 'What can I do?'

'Never done a straight day's work in your life.' Grace's voice drilled on into him. 'Come as too much of a shock to you, wouldn't it?'

Rose frowned at her to shut her up. 'Look,' she went on. 'If you'll say you're going to try and find a job, I'll help you. There's a few going round here – and if you

361

promise you're not going to go fooling about looking up all your old pals who're no good for you, I'll have you to live with us. Hilda can move down to sleep with me. You can pay me a bit of rent and I can always do with someone else about to help with Alfie and that. But just you watch yourself.' She wagged a warning finger in front of George's face. 'Any sign of trouble, of anything, and you're out. Right?'

George nodded in silence.

'You'd better get your lodger off home Rose,' Grace told her. 'I'm late with the tea already and what there is is only enough for two.'

George picked up his meagre bundle of possessions and slunk out with Rose across the yard to Moonstruck House. They were both well aware that other eyes were on them from the windows.

'Never thought you'd end up here, Rose,' George said as they went through the door. 'Thought you had ideas well above this place.'

'When did having ideas ever do anyone any good?' She felt completely deflated after her euphoric mood earlier. She turned to Alfie, ignoring George's horrified expression as he set eyes on him.

'You remember my brother George? He's coming to lodge with us for as long as he can keep his nose clean.' Then more kindly she said to George. 'I s'pose you're hungry. I'll get something on in a minute.'

Hilda, who was sitting near her father, gazed at George with interested eyes. She liked men: they picked her up and paid her attention and played games with her. 'Is he a real brother?'

'My brother. Your uncle.'

'This is your kid?' George asked astonished. Though Rose had told him what Hilda was getting up to on her visits, the child had never progressed further than baby-hood in his mind.

'This is Hilda.'

Hilda was standing in her little flowery frock, lips pursed ready to give George a kiss. Rose watched her

362

brother's confusion. Any such display of affection was something unusual enough in their family, and to George was a part of life long forgotten. Kissing a child was something he could barely imagine how to do. Slowly he bent down until he was level with Hilda, who popped a kiss on his cheek. As he stood up she rubbed her lips. 'You've got prickly cheeks, like Grandad,' she said. 'But I'm glad you're coming to live with us, Uncle George.'

CHAPTER 37

JULY 1952

'What're you doing here?'

The moment Rose opened the door of Moonstruck House she felt herself tense up, infuriated. George was supposed to be out at work, at yet another of the jobs she had found for him. Instead, he was just sitting there, smoking.

'I asked you a question.'

'Oh, don't go on. You get to sound like her over there.' He nodded in the direction of number five.

Rose was almost afraid to hear his reasons for being at home at this time. Had she wasted yet more time and energy helping him to find a job which he had either just walked out of or got the sack from for idleness and bad timekeeping?

In the end he said, 'Couldn't stand that bloody place. Got on me nerves. I thought bugger it and came home.'

'Got on your nerves!' Rose flared up at him. 'You're an idle little sod, that's what you are!'

She strode over to him furiously and snatched the cigarette from between his fingers. 'And you can put that bloody fag out and all. This is my house, and if you're living here you do as I say.'

'Leave me alone, can't you?' George snapped back.

Rose went to the window and flung it open, throwing the stub of cigarette, still burning, out on to the ground.

'Uncle George is going to buy me a bicycle,' Hilda chimed in from by the fireplace.

Rose swung round. 'And pigs might fly.'

After George had slammed out of the house, Rose went up to her bedroom. She felt despair wash through her, as strong as any she had experienced since her first days back at home after the war. The summer afternoon air drifted in through the window, and she could hear children shouting and laughing in the courts around them. The long, lonely evening stretched ahead of her.

Tears began to slide down her face. She lay face down on her bed and let them come on like a child. For so long she had been so busy, so driven by all the necessities in her life that there had been no time to think about anything. She found herself remembering her first meeting with Diana, and the dress with the pink sprigs of roses. How much hope she had had in those days!

Even lately she had persisted in believing that if she tried hard enough things would come right in the end. God knows, she had made enough effort with George. She had goaded him on day after day to look for work. And when she could manage to find the time, she walked the streets herself on his behalf, even in her own dinner breaks. Finding him a job was not especially easy, though there was plenty of work to be had. She saw vacancies for toolmakers, die-sinkers, stampers, rivet-makers and a whole host of other skills. But George had no skills.

The only jobs he was able to get were of the most menial; the unskilled, heavy work of stacking and loading and cleaning up after those doing the better-paid jobs. The money was never up to much and George had neither the application nor the staying power to stick to the work. Rose knew, and feared, that he could make easier and quicker money elsewhere.

'Why can't you give it a bit more time?' she'd implore him when feeling more patient. 'Can't you try a bit more than you do?'

Usually he'd just shrug off her questions, her encouragement. Once he turned to her and said, 'Give it a rest will you, Rosie? I'm no good for anything, so just don't keep on.' And she'd seen a wooden, beaten expression in his eyes.

But she had still believed, naïvely, that given a few more chances, a bit of help, he could go back to being someone more like the old, sparky George she had known as a child.

She heard the door downstairs open and voices. It was Grace. Since she had spent so much time looking after Alfie, she still kept up a slightly proprietorial air over his care and was always popping in to check things were being done properly.

'Where's your mother got to?' Rose heard her say to Hilda, before shouting up the stairs.

'Be down in a mo,' Rose called back, trying to make her voice sound normal and not weepy.

Grace stood leaning up against the sink in the little scullery that was still filled with gloom despite the bright sunlight and echoing summer sounds from outside. She had her hair wrapped up in a scarf as usual and wore her shabby brown skirt and flat, sloppy shoes. She looked as if she might be well on in years compared with Rose, who was still smartly dressed from work in her floral skirt and pink blouse, although she had taken off her heels to lie down.

'Coming round to my way of thinking, are you?'

Rose nodded miserably in reply.

'I warned you. You could've saved yourself the bother. You know who's sniffing round here again, don't you? Ronnie Grables.'

Silently Rose got on with peeling potatoes.

'Did you hear me?'

'He wouldn't. Not after all this.' Her secret fears about George seemed to be being confirmed one by one.

Grace let out a harsh, cynical laugh. 'None so blind as them as won't see,' she said. 'How do you know what he'd do? You don't know where he is now or what he's doing, do you?'

That evening she sat down with a new copy of *Corriera della Sera*. Alfie was asleep. Rose looked across at him. His face was moist with perspiration. It seemed so strange, him lying there and her in a tussle with this language she might never have any proper chance to speak again.

Why she carried on with it she wasn't even sure. After her initial enthusiasm at Mr Abel's offer, she had had to ask herself, who she was kidding?

At first she found the reading a terrible struggle. And she felt triumphant when she managed to make sense of short sentences, then longer ones, and gradually whole paragraphs. But tonight she was finding it hard to concentrate. She was very unsettled and anxious. It was partly because of George, of course. He had not come back for the evening meal and was still out somewhere. Doing what? Who with? Her mind followed him anxiously out into the streets.

And there had been an incident at work which had in a strange way brought her a little closer to her odd colleague Ella Crosby, and yet at the same time she felt depressed because of it.

It had dawned on Rose only gradually that Ella Crosby was in love with Mr Waters. At first she thought she was reading the signs wrong. Of course a secretary looked up at her boss with attentiveness when he came in to give her some work. But surely not always with the gaze of hungry pain that Miss Crosby directed at Mr Waters? Say something to me, it seemed to say. Just one extra thing which is not on the subject of work and which shows me you even notice me! But the longer she worked there, Rose found the situation at first unbelievable, then pitiful. She began to warm to Miss Crosby for that, if for no other reason.

That morning the two of them had been working hard at their typewriters with a stack of papers in front of them when Mr Waters' door opened. Miss Crosby and Rose both looked up.

Mr Waters was very tall, almost unhealthily thin looking, with such sallow, papery skin that when Rose first saw him she had thought immediately of the cemetery at

Naples. He was carrying a sheaf of papers in his left hand, and Rose saw Miss Crosby's cheeks turn a deeper red under all the powder as he laid them down rather impatiently in front of her.

'I'm sorry, Miss Crosby,' he said. As always he was polite, but there was a tetchy edge to his voice. 'I'm afraid we really can't send them out like this. They'll all have to be done from scratch. Rather a waste of time, of course. Still, I'll leave them with you. I know you'll do your best.' Without another word, he drifted back into his office again.

And to her horror, Rose saw Miss Crosby bring her hands convulsively up to her face, and she realized the woman was trying to hide approaching tears. She could feel her pain and embarrassment across the room. Rose wondered what to do. She decided to carry on typing for a while to give the woman time to recover.

Eventually, when she could see that Miss Crosby had regained some of her control, she stood up and said carefully, 'Never blooming satisfied, are they? D'you fancy a cup of tea?'

Miss Crosby nodded.

Rose was saddened by this. Did no one ever love the right person, she wondered? Were so many people really doomed to spend their lives longing and wishing and never happy?

She got up to check on Alfie and Hilda and brewed herself a last cup of tea for the night. She felt so tired that she was tempted to stop reading. But if she did stop, then what? On this night in particular she would start thinking and brooding. As she had been reading Italian she would find Falcone insistent in her mind and she did not want her emotions disturbed again.

She was settled in bed beside Hilda's warm body and already drifting off to sleep that night when she was aware of George coming back into the house, his loud, thoughtless tread on the stairs up to the attic. It had not long struck eleven o'clock. Rose closed her eyes and turned to lie with her back against Hilda. Where he had been and what he had been doing were not things she wanted to think about now either.

As the months went by things did not improve. George gave up any pretence that he was going to try and hold down any sort of job and yet Rose could not bring herself to throw him out. He came and went, back to his old pattern of disappearing for days at a time, paying her odds and sods of rent but nothing regular. She never knew where he was and she worried and Hilda sulked and was unsettled. But there was no trouble as such, no police round, nothing that she could actually hold up in front of him. Only the constant anxiety and suspicion which left her feeling worn down and angry.

Alfie's health was an increasing strain. Grace came and helped them often again now, apparently glad to be back in her role as nurse. Alfie went through chest infection after chest infection, his weakened body wracked by terrible coughing. Time and again she got for him the new wonder medicine – antibiotics, which fought off the infection for a time before it returned again, apparently stronger and more tenacious than before. She was mystified by his strength, how he managed to keep going after all these months. For what, she often wondered guiltily. What reason does he have to live any more?

As the autumn wore on and the days closed in, dark, and often foggy and wet, she was finding it hard to hide her strain and exhaustion at work. Her face looked pale and sunken and she was bone thin. Both Laurence Abel and Ella Crosby noticed.

'Is there something worrying you?' Miss Crosby asked one afternoon when Rose was yawning over her typewriter and struggling to keep her head clear. 'You don't seem quite yourself.' She blushed slightly, unaccustomed to trying to extract confidences from others.

It was a relief to tell her.

'It's my husband. He's very bad. I've been up a lot nights.'

'Oh, I'm sorry,' Miss Crosby said rather stiffly. She suddenly felt rather moved by the pale, lovely young woman in front of her. 'If there's anything I can do . . .'

'I don't think so.' Matter-of-factly, Rose added, 'We don't reckon he's got long left. There's not much anyone can do.'

'I didn't realize . . .' Miss Crosby looked genuinely sorry. 'I had no idea it was as bad as that.'

A kind of numbness overcame Rose, as if she could bear feeling no more. She was waiting for Alfie to die. Not because she willed it, but because she knew it must come. It was plain in his face. The nurse who came in tutted and said so in hushed tones as well. And now life was strung between these nights of waiting, watching his struggle with his weak, helpless body.

One December evening when she had finished work, she walked home from the bus stop in a wet dusk. The wheels of cars and buses hissed through the puddles, and she could hear the soft, rhythmic sound of windscreen wipers even over the engines. The red lights of the cars seemed to glow more warmly in the rain.

Inside the house she was slowly peeling off her wet coat when there was a tap on the door, and to her surprise she saw Sid standing there with his cap on, the raindrops shining on his dark, stubbly cheeks.

'Someone to see you,' he said. 'Over at our place. She's been waiting.'

He turned his back and went on his crutch back across the court. Frowning with irritation at him, Rose slid her coat back on again. He could at least have told her who it was.

'Stay with your dad a minute,' she said to Hilda.

She followed Sid across the wet bricks and stepped into number five. She saw someone stand up immediately and move towards her. The face had aged, of course, and looked tighter somehow, but was instantly recognizable.

'Rose – my dear!'

A moment later she was being drawn into the arms of Catherine Harper-Watt.

CHAPTER 38

Rose could hardly take in Catherine's sudden appearance. Here she was, thinner but still beautiful, her thick hair arranged in an elegant chignon and wearing an obviously expensive suit tailored in slate blue and black checks and all nipped in nicely at the waist. She sat on the old wooden chair by the table in Grace's poor kitchen looking quite at ease as she might anywhere, so accustomed was she to mixing with anyone and everyone. Sid and Grace had taken their meal over to eat with Alfie.

Rose began to chop off florets of cauliflower for cauliflower cheese, waiting for the pan of water to boil.

'I know this'll sound rude,' she said. 'I'm ever so pleased to see you. But why are you here tonight suddenly?'

'No, it's a good question.' Catherine remembered that even as a child Rose had always gone straight to the heart of things, no messing about. 'The practical truth is that I'm here in Birmingham because I was sent down to a meeting in the Town Hall. More of my organizing and interfering with other people's lives.' She smiled.

'I have to admit this isn't by any means the first time I've been back, and I've thought of calling in on you. I came this evening to see if anyone could tell me your address, and to my astonishment I find the person I'm talking to is your father! But I'm sorry not to have warned you, Rose dear. I had fully intended to write you a better letter after you wrote to us so kindly during the war. And to have come and looked you up much sooner. But I just

371

– even now it's . . .' She laid the palms of her hands flat on the table in front of her. 'I just couldn't do it.'

Rose put down her colander, realizing with consternation that Catherine's voice was breaking up with tearfulness. She reached out to provide the family comforter. 'Let me get you a cup of tea while we're waiting.'

'I knew I must at some point,' Catherine told her, accepting the cup of strong tea. 'When we moved to Manchester and got settled in, Diana made a lot of friends, of course. She was always that kind of girl – you remember how open and friendly she was. But you know, despite all the differences between you two, I don't think there was ever anyone she cared for as much as she did for you. Perhaps we make very few real friendships in our lifetime. When I think of Diana's childhood now, that's the first thing that comes to my mind – you and her.'

There was a moment of silence. The two women looked at each other across the poorly lit kitchen and Catherine saw that Rose's brown eyes were full of tears.

'It's ten years since she died, and it's taken me all this time. Only . . . I know I've got William and Judith, and they're a great support to me and both doing so well. But losing Diana, losing any child is just . . .'

'I know,' Rose said gently.

'You poor girl, what a time of it you've had. Here am I, carrying on. Of course you know how it feels.'

'You know I met Diana. At New Street Station?'

'She told us. She was so delighted. You see she thought she'd done something terribly wrong when she didn't hear from you. After she got your letter I remember her saying to me, "If only Rose had told us. Why d'you think she felt she couldn't? I wanted to be her friend whatever." It's all right' – Catherine stood up and took Rose by the shoulders, seeing her really beginning to cry on hearing this – 'she understood. You poor child. You were young and afraid, and so . . .'

'Ignorant,' Rose finished for her, sniffing.

'Well, yes, you were in a way. But so very bright and

lively with it.' She embraced Rose briefly, and then the two of them carried the food to the table.

'I haven't talked about Diana,' Rose said as they ate. 'Not for years. There's been no one I could tell. No one round here would want to know anyway.'

'I should have done this years ago!' Catherine said later as she laid down her knife and fork. 'What a chump I've been, thinking it would all be terrible and gloomy. You won't be able to keep me away now, Rose. But for tonight' – she looked at her slender wristwatch – 'before I have to go I want to hear a lot more about you.'

Their shared memories allowed Rose to open up and relax in a way she had not done for years. The Harper-Watts' talent for helping others to confide and Catherine's motherly concern for her made her feel she could say anything.

She told her about Dora's death, about her war and Sam and Grace and Grace's fiancé; about the factory at Castle Bromwich and about the ATS. And to her own relief, pleasure in fact, she told her about Italy and Il Rifugio and the drops, and quite straightforwardly she told her about Falcone. She explained too how things had been since the war, with Alfie and Hilda and her work, and Alfie's illness.

'So at least I've got myself a more decent job,' she finished, 'which means we're doing a bit better now. But Alfie's very bad. No one thinks he's got long, to be honest with you. To tell you the truth, Mrs Harper-Watt—'

'Call me Catherine, please.'

'Well, Catherine then. The one place I always hoped I'd get away from was Catherine Street. I had all these ideas. And here I am. Square one.'

Catherine smiled sadly. 'You had so many dreams, both of you, when you were children.' She watched Rose's face carefully as she asked the next question. 'And this man, this priest. He was something very special to you?'

Rose paused. 'He wasn't a priest then. But yes. Like no one else, ever.'

'Oh Rose!' Rose saw the sympathy in her eyes.

Catherine suddenly started and looked at her watch again. 'Heavens, I shall have to go.' She got up and put on a soft grey wool coat, belting it round the waist. 'The time has gone so quickly,' she said. 'Now listen, my dear. Thank you for feeding me at such short notice. And please thank your family for putting up with this disruption. It was most kind of them all.'

As they stood at the door, she said, 'I'm so glad I came.'

Rose nodded with pleasure, not sure what to say, and Catherine kissed her quickly on the cheek. Smiling, and suddenly elated, Rose watched her smart figure disappear quickly out of the court.

Two days later when she arrived back from work she found a long white envelope waiting, addressed in black ink in Catherine's beautiful italic script. Under their Manchester address on the thick, white paper she read,

My dear Rose,

I hope you will not take this amiss. I am not at all sure whether I conveyed to you when we parted on Tuesday just how much our meeting meant to me. You and Diana were so special – but then I think I *have* said all that.

I should be most grateful if you will accept the enclosed. It is not meant to be seen as charity or anything you need take offence at. You'll know I have always had means of my own, and I should love you to think of yourself as something of a daughter who need not feel ashamed of accepting a gift from me. I should like to think that as soon as circumstances allow, you, who were such a dreamer as a child and whose dreams have been so consistently pushed aside by events, might be able to put this little offering towards fulfilling those dreams in some way, whatever that may be. I would gladly give you more if you were not too proud to ask. I can't do anything for Diana, but I have at least found you.

I told Ronald about my visit to you and he was overjoyed (a very Ronald word!) and sends much love to you, as do William and Judith.

I do hope to see you again before long, if you don't mind.

With much gratitude and affection from us both,
Catherine H-W.

Folded in the sheet Rose found ten £10 notes. The moment she had read through the letter and had re-read it in wonder, she pushed both it and the money hurriedly back inside the envelope. Pulling out one of the loose bricks from round the fireplace she arranged the envelope neatly behind and replaced the brick. No one else need see that money just now.

But she thought about it endlessly as she got on with the evening's chores. Dreams? What dreams did she have left that were not buried almost deep enough to have been forgotten? She had no clear idea what she might do with such a sum of money. Except for one thing.

'I'll do something special for Grace,' she thought. Grace, whose life had been so lacking in excitement, who had always stood by her and helped out when she was needed, even if she did have a good moan about it. She'd think of some way, however small, to pay Grace back. She deserved it.

'He ought to be in hospital,' the nurse kept saying, tutting over Alfie. 'He's in a terrible state! Look at those sores, and hark at his chest!'

'We've done the best we can,' Rose told her exhaustedly. 'And he doesn't want to go.' Even Alfie himself had tried to impress this on the nurse in his more lucid moments.

The new doctor who had started coming supported Alfie's wishes, rather to Rose's surprise. 'You know that your husband has not much time left?' she told her gently.

'So everyone keeps saying. To be honest with you we've all wondered how he's kept going this long with what he's been through.'

As Sid had put it only yesterday, 'You'd never have thought that weak little runt'd have held out like this, would you?'

The past weeks had, of course, prepared Rose. Several times she had walked warily over to Alfie, her own breath stilled in her throat, thinking he'd stopped breathing altogether. But each time there had been a pause and then his loud, laboured breathing had started up again. They could talk very little now. Mostly his eyes were closed, so he did not take in what she or Hilda were doing. But paradoxically her life revolved round him more and more: on his washing and feeding routines, or simply being there as much as possible, even though the nurses were spending more time there during the day, and one neighbour or another was constantly with him.

For the first time she had seriously begun to think how she would feel after he died, and again to her surprise, the thoughts which came filled her with apprehension verging on panic. For what was her life now without Alfie to care for?

Hilda had begun to say to her at night, 'Will Dad still be here in the morning?' The mother of one of her classmates had recently killed herself and it was always on Hilda's mind. And people kept saying Alfie hadn't long.

'I hope so,' Rose would tell her, with decreasing certainty. 'Don't get all worked up about it. Just go and give your dad a kiss, love.'

The night he died, Grace was there as usual. They took it in turns, each sleeping half the night in Rose's bed, and sitting for the remainder downstairs with Alfie. It was agonizing and exhausting. Each of his breaths seemed to demand from him such effort. And his poor, contorted body looked so corrupted by the illness.

Occasionally Rose allowed herself to think of him as he was when she had first met him before the war, and she would weep at the sight of him now. He had become such a strange thing in the room, his unconsciousness a mysterious barrier against them all. Was it simply sleep, or had he already begun to leave her behind?

Grace ran up the stairs and pulled on Rose's shoulder, rousing her from a light, confused sleep.

'What? WHAT?' She sat up at once.

'It's just – he's changed. I can't tell you. You'd best come and see.'

The two sisters skimmed down the cold stairs again in their nighties.

Alfie's breathing had grown even louder and more irregular. Watching him from the bottom of the stairs, Rose felt he might rise bodily off the bed in his attempt to capture his next vital lungful. His chest rose and fell, rose and fell, the rasping breaths hauled in and out. Then they stopped.

Hypnotized by the rhythm, for a moment both women carried on staring at him. The silence continued. They looked at each other, unable to move.

Then Rose rushed over to the bed. She took Alfie's emaciated wrist and felt for a pulse. For a few seconds the tips of her fingers felt for the delicate blood vessel. Nothing.

'He's gone,' she said solemnly.

It was Grace who fell to her knees by the bed wailing 'Oh Alfie!' and laid her head down on the covers beside him.

The burial took place in the cemetery where they had laid Dora. Unlike the overcast day in 1940 when Rose had stood beside Grace and Sid at that graveside, the day was a crisp, bright one in February, with the old rusty leaves of autumn crackling underfoot. The beauty and calm of the cemetery with its mature trees and sloping green areas dotted with the silent stones moved Rose. Alfie's death and all the suffering of his life weighed heavily on her. She had lost a friend, and the focus of years of care and energy. The future lay blank in front of her. But what felt worst was the knowledge of how little of herself she had really given to him. Everyone kept telling her how marvellous she'd been, what a staunch wife. And it was true that she had served him and cared for him in his physical need. But no more.

After the ceremony, Rose held Hilda's cold little hand in hers, with Grace supporting her on the other side, as they followed the slow progress of Sid and Mrs Meredith along the curving path. George had not made an appearance. Grace's face was as drawn with misery as Hilda's and Rose's own.

'A couple of days more,' she said softly to Rose, 'and he'd have died exactly a year after the old king.' She seemed to find this comforting.

Rose nodded, squeezing her arm. A little further on she said, 'Grace, if he'd asked you – back in the early days – would you have married him?'

Grace kept her eyes down, looking at the dry twigs and pine needles along the path. 'You know I would. And not just then either. Any time. Right up to the end.'

Then she looked round at Rose with a most wistful smile on her thin face. 'But it was only you he had eyes for. Ever. You know that, Rose.'

And then she stroked her sister's arm as Rose finally began to break into sobs beside her.

CHAPTER 39

AUGUST 1953

For months after Alfie's death Rose felt tired to the very core. It seemed a huge task just to get to work in the morning. Through the end of the winter and the lightening days of spring she dragged herself around feeling only half alive, as if Alfie had taken a part of her with him, her own youth seeping away gradually through his illness.

She missed him more than she had ever imagined possible. One thing had been certain, ever since she moved to Moonstruck House: that Alfie would always be there. Whenever she came down in the morning or in from a class or work, there he was, almost as she had left him. Wakeful and watching her, providing as much conversation as he could manage, or dozing, semi-conscious – but there. Now, just as certainly, the room was empty of him.

But like a gift, from somewhere within her, her vitality and zest were returning. She had other things to think about. George for a start. And, with a certainty which increased with each summer day, she knew what she was going to do with her money from Catherine Harper-Watt. One of the things that she had thought most unattainable, that Laurence Abel had talked of yet still sounded like a fantasy, was now within her grasp. Italy. She would go back, and she probably even had enough money to take Hilda.

'It's a barmy thing to do,' she thought to herself, almost giggling with excitement. It was a baking hot Saturday. On the sunny side of Court 11, near the brewhouse, Rose was standing bent over an enamel bucket, swilling through some of Hilda's clothes. A few children were listlessly playing marbles in the shade. 'I could do up the house, move out even. I could buy us all new clothes or furniture, or just put it away for a rainy day. But I'm damned if I'm going to!'

Italy was her dream now, and Catherine had prescribed the money for a dream. She could go and visit Margherita and Francesco. She still received cards from them at Easter and whenever they had had another child, always with entreaties to visit. It was clear to her that this was what she must do. Just as her idea of what she could do for Grace had come to her with equal force a couple of months earlier.

As June approached, coronation fever had struck the court, the city, the entire country and, of course, Grace, who showed the kind of excitement that only a royal occasion ever brought out in her.

'A queen!' she cried. 'Oh, isn't it going to be lovely to have a queen for a change! Elizabeth the Second. Doris at work says it's going to change everything. Things'll never be the same again. Oooh, what I'd give to live down London!'

For weeks beforehand the talk and activity all centred round bunting and flags and plans for street parties and big celebrations with brass bands and fireworks.

'What if you could go?' Rose said to Grace one day in May. 'You know, go down and really see it, in London?'

'I'd give my right arm,' Grace replied. 'But we'll hear it all. And we might get a sight of one of them televisions somewhere. And all the pictures'll be in the papers.'

'No,' Rose told her. 'You're to go. Down to London, on the train. It'll be my treat.' She blushed at sounding like Lady Bountiful with her sister. 'Look – you've done nothing but help me over the past few years. I'd like to pay you back a bit. One way I can think of anyway.'

Grace's face had gone pink with excitement. 'But – you can't afford that, can you? It'd mean the price of the train and . . . and new stockings, and . . .'

Rose grinned. 'That's all right. Listen. No one else need know about this, but when Mrs Harper-Watt came she gave me a bit of money. It doesn't matter how much, but take my word for it, it's enough for you to have a new frock and your rail ticket. And I'll stand you taking Doris as well if you like.'

Grace was flabbergasted. 'But why don't *you* come? If you've got enough money for the two of us?'

'I'm not that keen really, you know that. Go on – go with Doris and get into the spirit of it. You'll have much more fun with her.'

So Grace went, feverishly excited and wearing a new peach-coloured frock. She and Doris sat out all night in the Mall with a flask of tea and their sandwiches with all the other thousands of people breathless to catch a glimpse of the new monarch. And she came back brimming full of it all: the procession and the flags and trombones and all the aeroplanes flying over, and how the woman next to them had shared her ham sandwiches with them because they'd run out, and how everyone cheered and cheered when she came out of Westminster Abbey and stood there for hours with their little flags despite all the showers.

So it went on for days and weeks after. Rose was never in any doubt as to whether she'd made the right choice.

Things with George, though, were getting worse and worse, and Grace's excursion brought things to a head.

'So who paid for that, then?' he demanded.

'I did, if you must know.'

'Where d'you get the money from?' he asked in his usual sneering tone.

'Some of us do a job of work if you remember.'

She watched her brother with loathing that day as he sat smoking, as usual. Fag after fag, flicking the ash towards the fireplace and missing half the time. All the sympathy she had mustered for him had evaporated over the past few months. God knows she had tried. But he had given her no respite, and not an ounce of help or sympathy. He sickened her. He couldn't even be bothered to come to her husband's funeral. Things she had hoped never to say tumbled out of her mouth.

'I used to think it might be worth helping you out,' she spat at him as he sat staring indifferently at the floor. 'But you're a useless sod if ever there was one. Other people have problems and get on with their lives, but not you. Poor old George. You sit on your arse and wait for everyone to run round you. And then you turn round and go back to thieving and wasting your stupid, useless life away.'

George's head whipped round savagely. 'Who says I'm thieving?'

'Well, aren't you? You're up to something. Out all hours and mixing in with God alone knows who. Anyone out at the time of night you come in is up to no good. And you're not stony broke are you? So where's it all coming from if you're not nicking it?'

'Leave me alone, you silly cow!' George yelled at her. 'Stupid nagging bitch. You're all the bloody same!'

Rose watched her brother's face, its expression of pure malice. His grey eyes were the coldest she had seen for a long time. Shuddering, she thought of Mr Lazenby.

'I tried with you,' she said more quietly. 'I'm the only person who's even tried.'

'Only so everyone could tell you how bloody marvellous you are. You thought I'd come in here and be your dogsbody, looking after that cripple of a husband of yours, and your stupid kid. But now people can start doing the running for me for a change.'

'What d'you mean?'

George sat down again, nipping his cigarette nervously between his lips. 'Never you mind – sis,' he said contemptuously. 'You just go on being a good little girl and working for your nice law man. I s'pose he's giving you one, is he?'

'Get out. Take your things and get out of my house.'

George turned to her with mock casualness. 'Going to make me?'

Thinking back over this now as she wrung out the

clothes, Rose could feel the rage rising in her again. Things had settled down for the moment it was true, but sooner or later she was going to have to face up to it. She pegged out the clothes and flung the water down the drain. She had to do something about George. She simply could not stand the sight of him.

In September everything changed at work. She reached town rather late that morning, trying to hurry in her tall slim heels through the usual sounds of thumping and drilling and all the dust and mess that signified the resurrection of the city. She hoped Ella Crosby would not notice she was late.

Climbing the stairs up to the Abel and Waters offices, she became aware of more crashing about and shouting from inside. What the hell's going on? she thought, hurrying even more. It sounded as though the offices were being ransacked.

She cautiously pushed the door open and was greeted by an incredible sight. Near his closed office door, as if trying to take refuge from it all, stood Mr Abel.

'No – please!' he cried as if that was the last straw. 'Not the typewriter, please! They're so expensive! Ah Rose – Mrs Meredith. Thank goodness you're here!'

Across the room was strewn what looked like the entire contents of Miss Crosby's desk. There were short-hand pads open and spread over the floor, files and typed letters and crumpled sheets of carbon paper, wodges of new stationery with sheaves of envelopes fanning out across the carpet, and against the wastepaper basket the blotter stood tipped up at an angle. A typewriter ribbon lay unravelled in black coils across the layers of paper.

Ella Crosby still seemed to be searching for things to throw, a snarl of fury trapped for the time being in her throat.

'What's happened?' Rose asked. 'What on earth's going on?'

'It's . . .' Mr Abel tried to explain.

'The stupid, selfish, miserable old—' Ella Crosby finished the sentence with a screech of fury. She thumped her fist down on the desk and the sight was so melodramatic that Rose wondered for a second whether she was putting it all on.

'What the heck have you done?' she demanded of Mr Abel.

'Not me!' Laurence Abel squeaked. 'God in heaven, not me! It's Mr Waters.'

'He's only gone and died, hasn't he?' Ella shouted. 'He's gone and damn well died on us!'

'It was a heart attack,' Laurence Abel explained. Last night. Someone found him this morning lying on the floor downstairs.'

Rose walked cautiously over to Ella Crosby, who had sunk down on her chair and was sitting sobbing at the desk.

'Miss Crosby,' she said gently. Somehow she did not dare touch the woman. 'You've had a shock. Why don't you go home and have a bit of a rest? Take the day off?'

Ella Crosby looked round at her slowly, rather stunned. 'But I've made such a terrible mess. I'm so sorry. I should clear it all up at least before I go.'

'No. You're all right, I'll do it,' Rose told her. 'Go on. We'll see you in the morning.'

Slowly Miss Crosby picked herself up, wiping her face with a handkerchief, and went out of the door.

Ella Crosby applied for another job. Laurence Abel was left with the sole running of the practice, and Rose stayed on with him. It took several weeks before things began to settle down.

'I'll be able to pay you a bit more now,' he told her. 'You'll be doing more work for a start.'

'Well, I'm not going to complain about that,' she told him.

'But,' he went on, 'come hell or high water I'm going to take the time off that I'd planned. Complete folly of course in the circumstances, but I can get someone to stand in for me and do at least the basics for a fortnight.'

Rose smiled at him without the sense of wistfulness that she had always felt before whenever he mentioned his trips to Italy. It was her secret. She was going to go as well! It didn't matter how soon, but she was going.

She realized that Laurence Abel was looking at her with unusual intentness.

'I'd have thought you must be in need of a holiday too,' he said. She noticed that his cheeks were turning pinker as he spoke. 'You could – er – come with me. I mean, don't get me wrong, Rose. I know how much it'd mean to you to go. I'd be happy to pay for you.' He laughed nervously.

Rose was so startled she could for a moment think of nothing to say. What was it he was actually asking her? He had been extremely kind and understanding to her during the last weeks of Alfie's life. But now she was back to being a single woman, was he trying to push things further? She wanted to believe the best of him, but she found her old mistrust flaring up again.

She sat staring down at her typewriter, her cheeks burning. She could feel his own discomfort even though she was not looking at him.

'I'm sorry. Don't take that the wrong way, will you? I wasn't expecting . . . anything of you. I'd just enjoy the company.'

She wanted to believe him. She looked up shyly at him. 'Thanks. But I couldn't just go, anyway. I've my daughter to think of.'

When Laurence Abel returned from his trip in November, it sharpened even more her own longing to go.

'Hilda,' she couldn't resist saying one night as she pulled the bedclothes up round the little girl, 'how would you fancy coming away on a little trip with me?'

'To Weston?' Hilda asked eagerly, half sitting up.

'No, not Weston. But we might see the sea.'

'Ooh yes!' Hilda said, and wriggled with excitement. Then she wrinkled up her nose. 'Would Uncle George have to come with us?'

Her uncle had been losing his glamour as the months passed and all his promises failed to come true. Since Alfie died, she had clung increasingly to Rose, the one really reliable person she had left, and they had grown much closer.

'No, not Uncle George,' Rose said. 'We don't want him along with us, do we? It'd just be you and me.' With a sudden rush of affection she leaned over and kissed Hilda's warm cheek. 'Now you go to sleep and dream all about it, eh?'

As she made herself a cup of tea she resolved that before she and Hilda went anywhere, she had to get George out. She sat down, kicking off her shoes and stirring sugar into her tea.

She hadn't seen him for two days. Perhaps she could threaten him with the police? Call his bluff? She had absolutely no proof that he was doing anything, but she knew him too well and he had to be up to something. She couldn't just throw him out. She had tried that. She began to think of something that would work. Money. She could bribe him. She put her cup and saucer down. Give him some cash for a clean pair of heels? Perhaps she could spare some of Catherine's money. That would mean she would have to delay her plans a little, but it would be worth it. She could save the rest up gradually.

She went over to the fireplace and jiggled the loosened brick out of the wall to recount the money.

Her fingernails scratched against the brickwork. For a moment she scrabbled around, not believing it. Where was the envelope? Growing frantic, she slid her hand all round the inside of the cavity. Nothing.

A horrible suspicion filled her mind. Heart thumping hard, she ran up to the attic, to George's room, where she had not ventured for weeks.

The stench of stale cigarette smoke hit her immediately. With trembling hands she held the candle high and looked around. The bed was unmade and the old cupboard door was hanging open. Beside the bed lay the only remains of George to be seen in the room: a white saucer brimming over with cigarette stubs.

A week later a letter arrived from Catherine Harper-Watt. They kept up a regular correspondence, but this letter was different and short. Rose read it through several times, the full implications of it taking time to sink in. Finally she laid it down, shaking with anger and embarrassment.

My dear Rose,

Just a quick note to let you know that all is well and I am most happy to have been able to help. The fact that you felt able to send your brother here when he needed assistance is most gratifying to me, and he seemed such an interesting and purposeful young man.

I was able to let him have £50 to help him on his way, and we left him at Piccadilly heading north to his new life feeling we had truly done someone a service. Perhaps this removes a burden from you, and of course of that I am also glad.

We are all well. Judith has announced that she is at last to be married to her teacher friend Robert. How old that makes me feel!

I shall write again, but I just wanted to set your mind at rest.

Loving greetings,
Catherine Harper-Watt.

The winter months passed very slowly. Rose felt as frozen inside as the weather outside. Even work seemed less enjoyable. To her surprise she missed Ella Crosby, and it was lonely sitting in the outer office on her own.

She could not bring herself to write and tell Catherine the truth. For a start it might sound as if she was asking for more money. She had not even told Grace what had happened. Now she did not have Catherine's money as a back up, she felt compelled to save as much as she could of her wages, scrimping along as a matter of habit.

Laurence Abel was keener than ever to speak Italian whenever possible, and although she went along with it, it only rubbed in the fact that she never seemed to get anywhere in her life.

What she needed to do now, she told herself, was to forget all this foolish hankering for something that was past, and build the best future she could for herself and her daughter. Hilda, after all, was the future.

The bus drew up with its brakes shrieking. Climbing inside Rose realized she had the chance of a seat and squeezed across to sit next to the window. It was a surprisingly warm spring day and the bus felt hot inside. She was on her way home from work, tired and stuffy in the head.

On her lap with her bag was her last newspaper from Laurence Abel, a December copy of *Corriera della Sera*. She knew she was feeling too inert to make any sense out of it at that time in the afternoon, but she opened it up, taking care not to wave it in the face of the man next to her.

The words seemed to shout at her, from a small news item in the middle of the second page. She blinked hard and tried to make sense of it.

'Vatican makes example of rebel priests', was the headline above the words that had drawn her eyes: Paulo Augustino Falcone. Father Paulo Falcone.

Many of the words in the article were unfamiliar to her as she seldom bothered to read stories connected with the Church.

She tore home, the paper not even properly folded in her hands. Once she was sitting down at the table with her dictionary she began to make more sense of it.

Three priests were referred to in the story. All of them

had preached or taught on issues of faith or morals in a manner which had come to the displeasured attention of the Sacred Congregation for the Doctrine of the Faith. Rose had no idea what that was so she skipped over it. The story said that the Vatican had decided to clamp down on these three to provide a moral example to the rest of the Catholic community. Consequently, all three had to some degree been silenced by suspension from their duties as priests.

Rose skimmed over the details about the other two.

> The most severely reprimanded of the three and also the youngest is Father Paulo Augustino Falcone, ordained three years ago in the Dominican house of San Domenico Maggiore in Naples. His radical views on issues such as poverty and contraception, and his calling to question the obligatory state of celibacy for all priests have resulted in his being banned from teaching, preaching, or celebration of the Mass.

Rose sat staring across the room, only realizing after a moment that Hilda was prodding her arm.

'I'm hungry, Mom. What's for tea?'

In a dreamlike state Rose got up and started spreading margarine on bread, the past still crashing in around her. Just reading his name like that rekindled such strong feelings.

'I said I wanted jam!' Hilda protested, swinging her legs crossly against the chair when the food arrived.

Rose stared, confused, at the slices of bread. Instead of jam she had put margarine on them twice.

He was still there: he was real. And now, after all his agonizing, all those years of training, his commitment to the priesthood was leading him into what, she recognized, devoid as she was of any real understanding of the Catholic faith, must be a good deal of pain and confusion.

'Mom! Listen to me! Can I have some jam? Is there any cake?'

Now she knew with a kind of frightening clarity that whatever it took, whatever the outcome of it, she had to go there. Finish things if necessary. She had to see Falcone again.

Standing by the table with the saucer of strawberry jam in her hand she said to Hilda, 'You know I said – ages back – that we'd be going on a journey? Well, I've been saving, and I'm going to go on saving our money until we've got enough to go – together. What d'you think of that?'

'Smashing,' Hilda said. 'Now please give me some of that jam!'

CHAPTER 40

SEPTEMBER 1954

'You really going tomorrow then?' Grace's voice held a definite tone of disapproval.

Rose was folding clothes into a decrepit old suitcase of Alfie's that had stood for years in her bedroom. 'Looks like it, doesn't it?'

'Beats me why you want to go off over there,' Grace said, shifting her weight to lean up against the doorframe. 'You could've gone anywhere for a break – a week by the sea at Rhyl for a quarter the price. I'd have thought you'd have had enough of over there in the war. They say it's ever so dirty and smelly.'

Rose smiled. 'Do they?'

'And you could've left Hilda with me and our dad. No need to go dragging her along as well.'

'I want her to come,' Rose said. 'She's seven, old enough to see it and remember. And Margherita's got kids. They can all play together.'

'You sure you've got enough money? Is that Mrs Harper-Watt paying for you to go?'

'No,' Rose said briskly, pushing a pair of shoes down into the side of the suitcase. 'She sent me some money for my birthday so I put that in the pot.' She turned to look squarely at Grace. 'The money she gave me after she came that time—'

'How much was it?' It was something Grace had always been dying to know.

'A hundred quid.'

Grace's eyes widened in astonishment. 'Blimey. She must be rolling in it!'

'When I'd taken some out for you and some other bits and bobs, there was still about eighty left. George had it off me.'

'You gave him eighty pound?' Grace screeched at her, standing absolutely upright now.

'Course I didn't. He pinched it, when he went off. And he stopped by in Manchester and conned some more out of her on the way to wherever he's gone.'

Grace stared at her, speechless for almost half a minute. 'Did you tell her?' she managed to say at last.

'No. Couldn't really, could I? It'd have sounded as if I was on the scrounge or something. What we're going away on is what I've saved, bar the ten pound she sent me.'

'He should be strung up.'

'Probably has been by now, for all we know.' Rose shut the case and struggled with the rusty fastenings. 'There – all set. Oooh.' She gave a little jump. 'I can't believe it, Grace. I'm really going – for ten whole days!'

'Nor can I,' Grace said drily, though she was smiling. 'Must be mad.'

With rhythmic, comforting sounds, the Naples train eased its way out through the suburbs of Rome. It was not very crowded and they had seats facing each other. Hilda, exhausted already from the excitement of a very long day – travelling on an aeroplane! – was dozing, her head lolling against the window. Rose felt she could not have slept even if she had been heavily drugged. She watched Hilda, her cheeks soft and lovely in the gentle light of the approaching sunset. Her perverse, self-willed but lovable daughter, here with her in Italy. Bringing these two parts of her life together seemed quite extraordinary.

She turned her attention to the regal Roman buildings outside the window. Even in the suburbs many of the tenements had a grandeur about them, with their flaking paint in yellow or terracotta or pink, and the contrasting greens and blues of the wooden shutters. Rose took in a deep, satisfied breath. This country! Whatever happened while she was here, at this moment she felt deeply content just to see it, to take in all the half-forgotten things that she loved about it. Fig trees and peeling trunks of eucalyptus softening the sides of buildings, the washing strung across narrow side streets glimpsed as the train hurried past; the baskets and buckets hanging outside windows ready to be let down to receive a delivery of bread or groceries. All the different smells that were so peculiarly Italian, the trace of drains and cigarette smoke mixed with the evening air – and she was sure she could smell the *prosciutto* between chunks of white bread that the elderly woman was tucking into on the seat across the passage.

As the light began to fade they passed through miles of fields, with small towns and villages strung along the railway line. Part of the land was fallow now that the summer was closing, and some fields held late crops of hay or spindly maize, with mules and carts still out collecting the dry cobs. On the left ran the line of the mountains, sometimes close enough to see the dark green cover of trees, sometimes smoky grey outlines in the distance, the foothills of the long spine of Italy.

When it was completely dark outside and the lights were on inside the train, Rose pulled Margherita's latest letter out of her bag. It seemed incredible that in a few hours she and Hilda would be sleeping in Francesco and Margherita's flat, and waking with the sun to meet their children.

'Carissima Rosa,' Margherita's bold writing looped across the cheap piece of paper.

We are so happy that you are coming and bringing your daughter with you. How excited we all are about seeing you – it seems now only like a dream!

I hope you will forgive our little place – it is small and cramped with all of us in it, but we can always find the space for such a welcome guest.

393

Your train will arrive in Naples at about 22.00, and Francesco will be there to meet you, we promise you faithfully. I hope you will recognize each other! Please stand in the area near the ticket office and he will come to find you.

We wait in eager anticipation of your visit – and until then, love and blessings from us all.

Margherita.

The train began passing between buildings again, some of them higher than any Rose remembered from the war. Like Birmingham, she thought. The war has given us all a new face. As they rattled past tenements and factories still dotted with lights, and junctions with roads where cars, lorries and carts waited facelessly behind the gates, she began to smell the sulphury city smell.

He's out there somewhere, she thought. His city. The train was slowing now from its hectic pace so that the buildings slid past instead of being whisked immediately from view. They were replaced by light and the concrete of railway platforms as they drew to a halt in the great yawning central railway station in Naples.

'Hilda!' She leaned across and shook her gently. 'Come on, love. We're here.'

Francesco spotted her the moment she and Hilda walked out from the railway platform. Before she had even had time to look for him he was beside her.

'Rosa!'

'Francesco! Oh, Hilda, this is Francesco.'

And their arms were round each other, laughing and exclaiming and oblivious to anyone else in the huge, echoing station.

'*Come sta?* Are you well?'

'*Bene – benissimo!*'

'I think you've got a bit fatter, you know.' Rose prodded him playfully. 'It must be married life!' She found herself speaking slowly, feeling her way into the language again.

'But not much, truly. With six children you don't get

394

fat! And you – you look lovely as ever. A little different perhaps . . .?'

'Older – but then who isn't!'

Francesco bent down and Rose watched as he smiled warmly at Hilda who glanced doubtfully at her mother before smiling back.

'Welcome, *piccola*.' He pinched one of her cheeks affectionately. Unsure, Hilda drew her face away. 'We have a lot of friends at home for you to play with.'

Rose explained this to Hilda in English.

'She'll come round,' she told Francesco. 'By tomorrow night she'll be bossing them all about even if she doesn't speak the same language. Oh – I can't wait to see them all!'

Still laughing and joking, with Francesco carrying her suitcase, they walked out to a side street near the station.

'My brother Carlo lent me his car,' he said, unlocking a shiny red Fiat. 'He works as a salesman,' he said with slight mockery. 'Impoverished school teachers like me don't have cars. In any case, if we did we'd never all fit in it.'

Rose watched him curiously as he settled Hilda on the back seat and stowed her case away. It was true he was not as painfully thin as he had been during the war, but despite her teasing he was still a slim man. And he really did look older, much older. She remembered his pointed, aristocratic face as she had known it before: that aquiline nose and the striking blue eyes. But there was something different now. He looked – she kept glancing at him as he drove them home, struggling for the right word – he looked more *ordinary*. That was it. And did she look so to him? Had she ever seemed extraordinary? Perhaps it had been the war, its romantic element of adversity and drama that had lent them all a touch of romance. Was this how everything would look now she was back? Ordinary? And if so, would that make it any less of a pleasure to be here, now they were all back to everyday life?

'Why did you move to Pozzuoli?' she asked, as Francesco steered the car rather joltingly out west away from Naples to the small town along the coast.

'My job is in Pozzuoli, the school. I try to cram some history into their unwilling heads. And my brother lives there, so we can borrow his car!' he joked. 'No – but it is smaller, and quite cheap. It's OK.'

'And you're happy there?'

'Happy enough,' Francesco said with a shrug. 'Yes, why not happy? It's not a question I often find time to ask myself.'

It was not a long drive and soon they pulled up in a side street outside a pale, four-storey building. It looked pinkish in the streetlight.

'We're on the first floor so it's not too much of a climb,' he told her.

Rose could hear dogs barking and a buzzing sound, something electric. Cats shrank in and out of the shadows.

'Margherita is on tenterhooks to see you. And with any luck all the children should be asleep by now.'

The three of them climbed a dark, rather musty-smelling stone staircase. As they got near the top they heard a door open. Margherita must have been listening for them.

'Francesco?' Rose heard her soft, so familiar voice.

'Yes. We made it,' he called to her.

And there she was, outlined in the dim light from the flat. Rose almost stopped climbing the stairs in astonishment. Was that really Margherita? The figure of the woman standing at the entrance to the flat was plump and thick limbed, her long hair draped down over her shoulders.

Before she had had time to take in fully the changed appearance of her friend she was at the top and they were embracing and kissing, both with tears of joy on their cheeks.

'At last you are here!' Margherita cried. 'I have been so longing to see you! Come in. Come and have some coffee and we will get you settled in. And you, little Hilda – I have some milk for you, *cara*'.

Francesco disappeared to take the car back to Carlo. Margherita disappeared for a moment and came back cradling a baby who had a shock of thick black hair.

'She is wakeful tonight,' she told Rose. 'This is my little one – Magdalena. She is nearly six months.'

Rose smiled wonderingly at the baby and called Hilda over to admire her too.

'She's lovely, Margherita. Quite beautiful. You have so many children already.'

Margherita smiled with the gentle wistfulness that Rose remembered. She had not really changed so much once they got talking.

'I have been blessed with so many little lives,' she said. Then with a despairing look she passed her free hand down over her waist and right hip. 'But that is why I am so fat. You would have walked past me on the street, eh, wouldn't you? With each one I seem to gain kilos and they never go again. We Italian women are fated this way. Whereas you – you look just the same!'

'Well, I've only had one, haven't I?' Rose laughed.

Margherita led them into a little kitchen with a tiled floor and pale blue walls.

'I am so happy to see you.' Margherita sat suckling the child. 'I really missed you when you left. And you left us so sadly.' She smiled quickly and then switched the conversation.

'Your little girl is lovely. Hilda, you are beautiful! She is the same age as my Marco, so they will be able to play. But of course the older ones will have school tomorrow – and Francesco too! We shall have a nice lot of time together. Come now.' She stood up, fastening her blouse. 'You can have a look at my babies.'

Suddenly extremely weary, Rose followed her along a little passage to the bedrooms. The children had all been moved in together to leave a room for her and Hilda.

As Margherita pushed open a door the light fell on some of the children, some in beds and two on the floor. Rose learned the names of the quiet, sleeping faces.

'Come. We can talk tomorrow.' Margherita leaned

over and kissed both of them again. 'Thank you for coming – you have made me so happy.'

For two days they did hardly anything but talk. Margherita did not mention Falcone and at first Rose was content to enjoy simply being there. She soon felt at home in the chaotic, ramshackle flat with its crumbling paint and old furniture, shelves and surfaces spilling over with books and papers and children's clothes and drawings and toys. And she helped Margherita with her chores as they got to know one another again.

While the three older children were at school, Hilda settled into playing with the others. Caterina, who was three, looked up to her as if she was some kind of pale English goddess, and they soon found ways of communicating. And little Giovanni followed them about and they fussed over him and chivvied him to join in their games.

Rose learned that Margherita and Francesco were, as he had put it, 'happy enough'. But they were constantly worried about money, like so many of the families around them. Though Margherita clearly had a Neapolitan adoration for all her children, Rose noticed a suppressed kind of restlessness about her.

'How many children d'you think you'll have?' Rose asked her the second evening. They had spent the day shopping for food and walking in the town and were preparing spaghetti for the evening meal.

'As many as God gives me.'

'You're not serious!'

Margherita looked round at her, and Rose saw a look of desperation in her eyes.

'What else can I do? There's no way of stopping it. The Church tells us that if we limit our relations to the time in the month when it is safe . . .' She sighed. 'For some women that works. For me, it doesn't make any difference. I couldn't easily say this to anyone else, but I wonder sometimes why I studied. Why do they allow us women to have an education if our fate remains the same

– to bear child after child and bring them up in poverty because there are too many of them?'

The tears welled up and ran down her cheeks. Rose put her arms round her.

They had barely even mentioned Il Rifugio during those two days. Rose was growing anxious and frustrated. She was eager to reminisce – one of the things she had most looked forward to about coming. In the evenings, once the mayhem of the children had died down for the night, they sat in the stuffy little flat drinking cheap wine and eating bread and late summer fruit, and talking, but they avoided the subject she most longed to discuss. If she asked a question they moved quickly on to something else. Most resolutely they did not talk about Falcone. Up to now she had not been able to bring herself to mention his name either. But to be here so near him, yet as closed off from him as she had been in Birmingham, was agonizing. She found herself constantly watching for his face among the crowded streets, even though they were not in Naples.

By the third morning she was beginning to feel that if she or someone did not mention Falcone soon she would explode. She walked with Margherita down to the little port to go to the fish markets, the stalls strung out along the front next to the sea. Hilda was fascinated by the fish. They strolled along with the vivid blue of the Mediterranean on one side, dotted with sunlight and coloured boats. And on the other, wooden tubs painted pale blue inside seethed with live eels or shellfish like piles of coloured pebbles, or small silver and orange fish flitting about in the shallow water. On the stalls behind lay heaps of prawns, and larger fish, already dead and glassy-eyed on banks of ice. Their smell was pungent on the air, and mixed with that of the sea and the drains.

'Oh look, Mom!' Hilda cried, running to bend over a row of tubs where lobsters tangled their claws together, crammed in in a brick-coloured mass. From a nearby one a number of large octopuses stared out balefully, some of their tentacles slipping experimentally out over the side and curling as they touched the ground. Caterina was chatting excitedly and Giovanni gingerly dipped his fingers in the water.

As they were occupied for the moment, Rose took Margherita's arm. Speaking loudly to be heard over the long, doleful cries of the fish hawkers, she said, 'I've heard what's happened.'

Margherita frowned. 'What?'

'To Falcone.'

Margherita's expression showed first astonishment and then apprehension. 'How did you know?'

'I read it in a newspaper. Why won't you talk about him?'

'We hoped you would think of him as a priest still. That nothing had changed. We wanted to avoid causing you pain – if that's what you would feel after ten years, of course. How could we know what you would feel? You might even have forgotten.'

Rose shook her head impatiently. 'You've seen him recently?'

'Yes, a month or so ago. We didn't tell him you were coming, by the way. He's in a lot of trouble. He began to question what the Church teaches and of course that disturbs a lot of people. He's obviously very unhappy. He loves his faith deeply, but he's so disillusioned, with the priesthood especially. And the hierarchy have come down hard on him. You'd think it might be enough to crush a person.'

Rose hesitated. 'Did he ever mention me – when you saw him after the war?'

'Of course. In the beginning.' She paused. 'I know I never thought he was cut out to be a priest, but that's for God to decide. He's had so much to bear, and whether now you should be part of this . . .'

Rose gripped Margherita's arm again with a determination that clearly communicated itself.

'I have to see him.'

CHAPTER 41

The church of San Domenico Maggiore was a forbidding building of stained, sandy-coloured stone.

Rose stood in the piazza looking at it. That Falcone had worked and studied here for so long was hard for her to imagine – a place which seemed to suggest such rigidity and conviction. She could not reconcile that with the man she had known; so tender and so confused.

Now the prospect of simply walking round the building to the seminary and knocking on the door seemed quite impossible. After all, what if he opened the door? She had been partly prepared for approaching the place by Margherita, who seemed to have decided that if Rose was going to do something of such doubtful wisdom she might as well give her as much help as she could. She had insisted that Rose leave Hilda with her for the day.

'Go to them and ask for Father Falcone,' she told Rose. 'Tell them that you want him to hear your confession. They may try to get you to accept someone else, but you can say you have something particular to ask him. If he's busy you can always go back later, can't you?'

I'll go and have a look at the church first, she said to herself. Get a feel of it.

She walked slowly over to the entrance. She was wearing a pleated skirt in a soft yellow poplin, cream court shoes, and a close-fitting navy blouse. The skirt swished luxuriously round her legs as she walked. She had felt very smart and feminine when she put them on, but now she was unsure of herself. Should she have worn something darker and more staid to come to a place like this?

The inside of the building was almost as austere as its exterior, the floor flagged in black and white marble on which her thin heels seemed to make far too much noise, and a ceiling which was plain except for frescos above the aisle, and even they were in restrained colours. There was very little else in the way of decoration.

She had evidently arrived just at the end of the Mass. As she entered people were beginning to stream out of the building. A few stayed in their places at prayer or moved to the front to light candles. Others stood round in small clusters talking. She watched those who were leaving bow to the altar and cross themselves and she made an attempt to do the same, overcome with a sudden distaste.

Bowing and scraping, she thought.

As she looked up towards the high altar, two figures caught her attention. Long white robes, with black cloaks over them which wafted out behind as they walked, seeming to glide across the floor. For a few dizzying seconds his face was superimposed on each of them. Then she focussed properly. One had white hair and was short and stocky. The other was tall and slim with black hair, but everything else about him was wrong; the nose too long, the eyes, brows, complexion all unknown to her. She stood watching. So this was his life, here, doing this.

Soon she was almost alone in the church, still standing there in the aisle. The younger priest had disappeared. She knew that if she did not act now she might never find the courage again.

She walked up towards the altar. The elderly priest was standing to one side in one of the choir stalls, leafing through a book. His thick, white eyebrows were pulled into a frown.

She wasn't even sure how to address him and when she spoke her voice sounded too loud.

'*Signore? Mi scusi!*'

The priest looked up with an irritated air. 'Yes. What is it?'

'I – I'm looking for Father Falcone.'

He stared at her for a moment, then with startling force he slammed the book closed so that dust flew up from the wooden choir stall. He stepped out and began to walk briskly away.

'Father Falcone is not here.' He spoke over his shoulder with unmistakable dislike.

Rose followed him for a few steps. 'Where is he – please?'

The priest stopped and turned round abruptly, obviously shocked. His first answer should have been enough. She was not supposed to question further.

'Father Falcone is away on retreat – again. Not, as one would expect of a priest in a position as serious as his, in a religious house of prayer, but' – he flicked his right wrist several times, dismissively – 'in some place of his own choosing. Where that may be I have no idea.'

He turned and was gone.

The impact of the old man's bitterness left her reeling and close to tears. Only as she was walking back along the black and white flagstones did she know just how consuming was her need to see Falcone. But she was no closer to finding him.

She sat down on one of the seats at the back of the church. His church, which felt so desolate now she knew he was not here. She stared up at the high altar, shrouded and mysterious at the far end of the church.

'Please. Please help me find him,' she found herself whispering. Perhaps his God would come to her aid?

She thought of him kneeling in here day after day. He was in deeper trouble than she could have imagined. He had felt the need – or been sent – to get away and think about things, and not for the first time by the sound of it. And he had even chosen to go somewhere they would not think of looking.

And then it came to her, making her catch her breath.

Of course! If Falcone needed time to think, her instinct told her, she knew the first place he would go. Not even questioning now the need that drove her on to find him, she ran out of the echoing church and across the piazza.

Less than an hour later she was on the train to Sorrento.

She might have revelled in being in Sorrento had things been different, but as it was she hardly took in the town at all. By the time she had walked up the road to the Finzis' house, having several times had to ask the way, it was one o'clock, and though no longer the height of summer it was hot enough to tire her. Her feet were sore from walking in her flimsy, high-heeled shoes.

The bubble of excitement and eagerness which had driven her on in the early part of the day had almost evaporated through weariness and thirst. She felt very nervous. All the things she had planned to say on meeting him again, the scenes she had so often visualized had vanished, and instead she could only think of flat, lifeless things. The day had gone wrong. And she was only guessing that he was here.

When she caught sight of the Finzis' house she slowed down, her heart hammering in her chest. The house had recently been painted in pale green, and the shutters in a darker shade, so that the whole place had a newer, fresher air about it.

What on earth was she doing here? If he really was here, what could she say to him? But to turn back now would be unthinkable.

Without waiting to summon up courage she knocked on the door. There was a pause before it opened and she was facing a middle-aged, heavily built man who stared at her in silence. He was chewing hard on something and clearly in the middle of a meal.

'Yes?' he said eventually.

'I'm sorry to disturb you.' Her heart was sinking. It

was all a mistake. The Finzis weren't here any more. 'I am looking for Paulo Falcone – Father Falcone.'

The man nodded. 'Yes,' he said abruptly, showing no surprise. 'Come in.' And she was stepping back into the Finzis' house.

The inside had also been painted, and as she walked through the coolness of the rooms it felt strange, less homely than she remembered. He led her immediately to the kitchen which was little changed from when she had stayed there.

Before she had time to collect her thoughts the man was saying, 'Paulo – someone to see you.'

Not their meeting as she had pictured it at all. She stood in the doorway looking into his face as their eyes met, trying to take in that it was really him. He was sitting at the table, fork in hand, dressed not in the white robes she had seen earlier, but in a shirt and trousers, both black and worn. He looked much the same as she remembered: serious, a little more careworn perhaps. Those large, long-lashed eyes stared back at her, puzzled. Whatever emotions may have been present in him, whether surprise or dismay, did not give themselves away in his face. He put down his fork and pushed the chair back.

'Rosa?' He stood in front of her, apparently unsure what to do. Then convention took over and he held out his hand. Somewhere in her mind she registered how warm it felt. She tried to smile at him, but her lips barely seemed to obey.

'Er – we were eating,' Falcone said, quickly. 'Will you join us and have some food?' He pulled out a chair for her.

'Thank you. That would be very nice.' She imagined him with the worshippers at San Domenico Maggiore, measured and courteous.

He gave her some of the tough bread and a dish of spaghetti with meat and tomatoes.

At the table Rose was shocked to recognize Clara

Finzi. She had aged greatly, her once plump cheeks sunken, her eyes watery and holding an absent expression.

'Clara.' Falcone spoke to her loudly. 'This is Rosa – from England. She stayed here once, during the war. When Angelo was still alive. Do you remember?'

He looked at her then. Rose found herself blushing. He remembered. Of course he remembered. And what else could he have said to the old woman, who just nodded, mumbling something indistinct. Clearly Clara did not recognize her.

'I'm sorry,' Falcone said with the same formal politeness. He gestured to the man who had opened the door to her. 'This is Lorenzo Finzi, the eldest son of the family. He has been living here with his mother since Signore Finzi's death.'

'I'm sorry,' she said. 'About Signore Finzi.'

Both men nodded, acknowledging the comment.

'Where are you staying?' Falcone asked her.

'With Francesco and Margherita in Pozzuoli.'

Falcone smiled for the first time. 'And all their lovely family?'

'My daughter is with them.'

He looked attentively at her. 'You're married.' It was not quite a question.

'I'm a widow.'

'Rosa . . .' He stopped. 'How did you know I was here?'

'They told me you were on a retreat somewhere, and I thought . . .'

'They? Margherita and Francesco?'

'No. A priest. At your church. He didn't seem very happy at me asking.'

'You went to San Domenico?'

She nodded, unable to work out his reaction to this. Was he angry? Had she made things even worse for him? He was shaking his head gently from side to side, whether in amazement or displeasure she could not decide. She felt terribly embarrassed and clumsy, and longed to leave.

Even her clothes felt wrong. She was overdressed, a stranger even to herself.

She looked away from Falcone's face, down at his hands, dark against the red and white checks of the tablecloth. They looked so familiar that the sight of them brought a lump to her throat. Those gentle, loving hands. Incredible that the hands of this stranger beside her had once known her so intimately. She was a fool for coming, for reviving the memories. She would go immediately. She could not even finish the food on her plate. If she and Falcone could have anything to say to one another it was quite impossible here.

'I really have to go now.' Getting up nervously she said to Clara and Lorenzo Finzi, 'Thank you both for your hospitality. I'm very grateful.'

Falcone took her to the door. She felt the lump in her throat again as he walked behind her. She could not have imagined a meeting as dreadful as this. She had visualised conversations where he reinforced to her his priestly vocation, and stood up for his decision to leave her so abruptly: perhaps rejected her all over again and with even more force. Anything seemed preferable to this unreadable formality.

'I'm sorry for disturbing you.' She was having difficulty controlling her voice. 'I should not have come here.'

She turned and began to walk away down the road so he would not see her tears.

'Wait!'

Almost angry now, she turned to him.

'I . . . You must understand how surprised I am to see you,' he said lamely, walking to stand closer to her in the dusty road. She stood dumbly in front of him, hardening her feelings. She could not speak.

'I had no idea you were coming, and . . .' He stumbled over the words. 'You look so different.'

He turned aside from her, looking up at the trees on the opposite side of the road. He was breathing in fast, shallow breaths.

'Look . . . I'm sorry. I can't . . . Every time I speak it

407

condemns me.' He gestured despairingly with his hands. 'Seeing you again . . . Could you – would you come back?'

'When?'

'Tomorrow – afternoon? I'll be walking.' He pointed up towards the mountain. 'I often do at that time of day. Lorenzo will not bother us.' He seemed to recover himself a little. 'I'm sorry you have come so far and I am unable to – that I can't be more . . . welcoming today.'

In a dignified voice Rose said, 'I'll come tomorrow, if that's what you want?'

He nodded. 'Please, Rosa.'

She turned and walked back down towards the town.

It was a warm, languorous afternoon bathed in rich autumn sunlight which touched the fading leaves with gold. Walking to the house, she saw red blooms still on the geraniums, tiny children watching her from doorways and cats curled sleeping in the sun. She was dressed differently this time, her feet comfortable in flat shoes, feeling the warmth on her arms. She felt strangely calm, as if anything that happened was now up to him. She was here, come what may.

There were no signs of life at the house and she walked past. As she began to climb the first deep step to the Stations of the Cross, the sense of recognition hit her oddly – those stones, so unchanged. At every other twist of the steep path were the stations she remembered; the crudely painted little pictures each protected by its alcove of brick, which also held their tributes of candles and flowers. She looked fondly at them, though their actual meaning was mostly lost on her.

Perhaps she had come too early? They had not agreed on any particular time. She sat down on one of the steps and looked back. The town was just becoming visible through the trees, though they had grown and thickened. She thought back to the last time she had sat up here on one of these steps. She had been thinking of Sam, still soaking in the shock of his death.

She breathed in the smells of the herbs and trees around her. There was a light scuttling sound. A salamander dashed off into the dry grass alongside the path in alarm. Startled, Rose turned her head.

Falcone was standing watching her. He had come down from the chapel where he had spent some of the early part of the afternoon, thinking perhaps to meet her. As he turned the bend in the path he had come upon the sight of that familiar little figure sitting below him. He stopped, narrowing his eyes to make it out more clearly, as if perhaps it might be another dream. She had come to him many times before, dressed in the old black blouse and skirt, her hair taken up in a coil behind her head. It was an image that had haunted him against all the power of his will for the past nine years.

As she turned, she heard his voice saying softly, as if unsure, 'Rosa?'

She stood up and slowly climbed up to join him. When she reached the step on which he was standing she looked up at him solemnly. It was impossible for either of them not to remember their last time together in this place.

Falcone looked back at her, then as if in some way defeated by the sight of her, he directed his gaze away at the ground. But in that brief moment of contact the emotions she had seen in his eyes were all she needed.

Together they turned and began to climb.

'So,' she asked softly, 'why are you here up on this mountain instead of getting on with being a priest?'

'Well.' He sighed heavily. 'I'm in a mess.'

To his amazement, Rose suddenly grinned. 'Are you always in a mess, or is it just whenever I turn up?'

Falcone burst out laughing. The sound startled her. He stopped and leaned up against the rocky wall next to the steps.

'I had almost forgotten,' he said. 'How could I forget – how you . . .? All the time I'm surrounded by earnest, righteous people telling me I'm mistaken, that I must stop speaking my mind because it will threaten the whole fabric of the Church. And then you come along and blow right through the whole thing! But in answer to your question: since I'm no longer allowed to do any of the things that are normally the framework of my priesthood, they can't think what to do with me. They keep sending me off to "reconsider my position" on various questions. To examine my conscience and so on and so forth. So here I am, trying to do just that.'

'And are you getting anywhere?'

'Oh . . .' Falcone tilted his head back for a moment, wearily, as they walked on. 'No further perhaps than I should have got if I'd taken more notice of you when we used to argue back then.'

He turned to face her. 'I don't want to go over and over it again. It's – oh, it drags you down. Rosa, I'm so sorry about yesterday. Your coming here at this time was so extraordinary that I didn't know how to react. Why did you come?'

'I had to see you.'

They'd reached the little chapel and sat down together on the top step at the entrance, soaked in warm afternoon light.

She felt bold because there was no time not to be, but also because the priest figure had gone, and they could talk as immediately, as honestly as ever.

'I saw what had happened to you in the paper,' she said. 'There's a man I work for at home who gives me Italian newspapers. When I saw your name again, real like that suddenly, I knew I had to come. I don't know if you realize how cruel it was, the way you went and never spoke to me again. Your letter. It left me all ragged at the ends. I could never settle, not really. It never ended for me you see . . .' She trailed off, her cheeks burning and suddenly wet with tears. 'I always loved you.'

Falcone was sitting with his face in his hands. She longed to touch him, but hesitated, before gently laying a hand on his shoulder and stroking him.

After a moment, trying to control his voice, he said, 'Oh, Rosa, Rosa. Would you believe me if I tell you that not a day has passed without me thinking of you? Of how I treated you? When I saw Margherita after you'd gone back to England, she let me know very clearly just what I'd done. She was so angry with me. She would never show that she despised someone but she must have despised me then. It was another guilt to add to all the others. But at the time I couldn't – really couldn't think what else to do. I wouldn't have been any good to you, not then. Margherita even told me she didn't think I had a vocation to the priesthood. It's dangerous to say such things of course. I've had to find that out for myself.'

'Without Margherita I think I would have fallen apart.'

'But you married – your English husband? I knew that. When I heard, it made things easier for me in a way. To think that you were really taken from me. That you loved someone else.'

'No,' Rose said bleakly. 'That was my mistake. And I say that more for his sake than mine. I could never give him what he really deserved from me. I had learned what love was before that and I could never forget it. However much I tried not to think of you, you took something from me that I was never able to give again, to him or anyone.'

He turned to look at her and she saw his eyes were full of pain. 'Rosa – come here.'

And they were in each others arms, he rocking her gently as she laid her wet face against his chest, his own tears falling on her hair.

'I'm so, so sorry,' he said. 'All this time you have felt so much . . . And sitting here now I feel so close to you, as if I saw you only last week.'

'I feel it too,' she said through her tears. 'Paulo – what will happen to you?'

'I think I stopped being a priest in the way they define it a long time ago. When my conscience could no longer stomach some of the teachings, but I was expected to act

411

as if I believed absolutely that they were God's laws. It's a sickening position to be in. Only I hadn't yet found the courage to let go of it. But now . . .'

She turned her face up to his and they looked into each other's eyes before they kissed, at first soft, quick touches of their lips, each still full of wonder at the other's presence.

Their hands began to rediscover each other's bodies. Rose wanted to touch every part of him: the soft curve of skin at the back of his neck, his shoulders, his warm flesh under the rough shirt, and she felt his hands moving hungrily over her hair, down her back and round to her breasts which ached for his touch.

In moments they were taken over by their desire for each other. He lifted her on to his lap and she sat astride him, her skirt riding up round her waist. She could feel his hardness pressing beneath her and his face was taut with the urgency of it.

She took his face between her palms, steadying him. 'I don't want you to regret this.'

'Never. This is not what I regret.'

When he came up into her their cheeks were wet with tears again before either of them had climaxed. Rose held Falcone tightly as he came, his body shuddering, hands gripping her back as if in pain. As she reached the height of her own pleasure she cried out, 'I can't bear it' and heard him making reassuring sounds as if to a child.

They clung to each other for a long time as their breathing slowed, her cheek pressed against his, and he still deep inside her.

Afterwards they sat very close, talking until shadows slipped over them and cooled them as the night drew in and mosquitoes whined round their heads. There was so much to share, to tell of their lives.

When it had grown almost completely dark, Rose got up, stiffly and reluctantly. 'If I don't go now I shan't even catch the last train back.'

It was not easy to move away from this place where

the communication had grown up between them again, from roots which had never been destroyed.

'Can you come again?' Falcone asked with sudden awkwardness. 'Bring your daughter so that I can see her?'

'I'll bring her tomorrow. But then you must come and see Francesco and Margherita. They'll think I've deserted them. Are you allowed to?'

Falcone shrugged. 'I suppose so. If not, then it will be just one more transgression to add to all the others.'

They stood at the top, reluctant to take the first step, as if fearful that going back down to the rest of the world might destroy what had happened there that evening.

'Look – I'll have to go.' She could see his eyes watching her, the faint remainder of evening light shining in their dark surface.

'Don't leave me again,' she said.

Falcone moved towards her. 'My love.'

And then they held each other, very gently this time, like old, fragile friends, standing together between the dark shapes of the trees in the scented night air of the mountain.

Margherita and Francesco were both waiting up for her, though it was very late by the time she let herself into the flat. She had long missed the last bus to Pozzuoli and had had to take a taxi.

They were very relieved to see her, and the glow on her face was unmistakable to both of them as she walked in, startled to find them both up. Margherita was watching Rose's face intently and Francesco handed her a glass of wine.

'Well?' he demanded. 'Come on – what happened?'

'Rosa?' Margherita said more cautiously. 'Holy Mother – what have you both got yourselves into this time?'

Rose put her glass down. 'One moment. I just need to go to my room. I'd like you to do something for me.'

She stayed long enough to kiss Hilda and return to them carrying a flat package.

'Francesco, have you still got your record player?'

She smiled when he nodded in reply. 'Play this for me then.'

And she drew out his old gift to her: the long unplayed recording of 'J'attendrai'.

CHAPTER 42

ITALY, JUNE 1957

The voice she could hear shouting somewhere in the house was unmistakable, and though it was impossible to make out a word of what was being said, she smiled to herself in amusement.

It must have been quite a house once, she thought, examining it before going right up close. Certainly more promising than she'd expected when she was travelling out here on the train. All those drab little towns north of Naples! Cellina itself was one such town: small, poor and more or less featureless, except for one redeeming sight, a little church she had caught a glimpse of, with a vivid turquoise dome. Otherwise the place seemed to consist only of that one square, the Piazza Garibaldi, streets of ill-kempt houses and a few dismal shops.

But this house, out towards the more peaceful western edge of the town, reassured her. The doctor's house. It stood detached, and behind it was an orchard, planted with a mixture of citrus and apricot trees. The place was in need of some repair, of course, but these things took time – and money.

What pleased her most about the front of the house was the tiled plaque obviously newly attached to the wall beside the front door. In dark green letters on a cream background it read, 'ORFANOTROFIO DIANA – ORPHANAGE DIANA'.

She banged on the heavy brass door knocker, and as she did so caught sight of a man, stooping under the weight of a heavy box of vegetables, hurrying round the side of the house with an annoyed expression on his face. He flung the box into his little three-wheeler truck, and started up its rough, coughing engine to rev off down the road.

As she watched, the door opened.

He looked different from how she had imagined, more gentle and approachable, and certainly more casual, in his cotton trousers and open-necked shirt. Not at all her image of an Italian doctor. Despite Rose's descriptions she had visualized someone in a suit and perhaps rather aloof. Instead – what warmth in those eyes! Although slightly startled, they already held a welcome.

'Dr Falcone? I'm Catherine Harper-Watt.'

His face creased into a delightful smile. In awkward English he said, 'Of course. We wait for you.' He beckoned in that Italian manner, almost as if shooing her away. 'Please come.'

As she stepped into the house she heard the voice again: 'Paulo – *chi e?* . . . Oh Catherine it *is* you. At last!'

Rose ran forward and the two women flung their arms round each other.

'Oh, I'm so glad you've come to see us!'

'I heard you even before I arrived,' Catherine told her teasingly. 'You seem to be familiar enough with the language to hold your own!'

Rose chuckled, translating what Catherine had said to Falcone.

He also laughed, shrugging in mock despair. 'You should tell her that now you've learned to swear in Italian as well there's no stopping you!'

Rose repeated what he said. 'It's just that bloke who comes round delivering the veg. He always tries to palm off all the old frowsty stuff on me. I'm sure it's because he thinks I'm a foreigner and I won't notice. So I gave him what for this time. Anyway, come on through and let's get you settled. I'm dying to hear all the news.'

Falcone took Catherine's bags to her room, and the three of them went through to a huge, white-tiled kitchen at the back of the house. The room was slightly clinical with its grey lino on the floor, and a huge white sink and steel range. But there was a pot simmering on the top of it which was homely, and on the windowsill above the sink stood several flowering plants.

Four children, all between the ages of two and four, were sitting at a large wooden table in the centre, tucking into thick chunks of bread. Watching them was a plump-faced young woman who was sitting with her rounded arms resting on the table. The children fell silent at the sight of Catherine, their brown eyes watching her every move as their little cheeks bulged like hamsters' with the bread.

'So these are part of the family,' Catherine said. 'I shall have to learn all their names.'

'This is Anna Lucia,' Rose said, indicating the young woman, who nodded and smiled back amiably. 'She works here now every day except Sunday. We couldn't do without her.'

Rose placed a bottle and some glasses on the table.

'There are nine children here so far – and Hilda, of course. The older ones are at school and we do the best we can with the rest. There's about room for a couple more.'

Falcone put a hand on Rose's shoulder. 'Shall we take them out for a run about when they've finished? Then you can talk.'

Catherine watched smiling as the little ones all climbed down from the table and followed Falcone and Anna Lucia out of the door.

'You seem to have got yourselves organized quite speedily,' Catherine said, accepting a glass of wine and some of the bread.

Rose looked at her gratefully. 'We couldn't have done it without your help.'

'And the help of some worthy WI women in the Manchester area,' Catherine reminded her. 'They've been quite fired up by the idea of this place. You have a little money from the town now?'

'Yes. That's something. You've come at a good time.' Rose sat down. 'We've just heard that Paulo's registered to practise again, so now he can go back to what he's meant to be doing. It's a bit of a relief too, because the money his father left is all but gone. There've been so many extras to get the place going.'

'And for your wedding.'

Rose laughed. 'That didn't set us back much. It must've been one of the quietest weddings ever to happen in Italy! Which was fine by me and it was all we could afford. And another reason was that even after the dispensation came through so we could get married it took him quite a while to get used to the idea that he wasn't a priest.

'I didn't care what we did so long as I could just get back over here with him. You'd think with all the time since the war that another couple of years wouldn't make much odds, but I've never known two years go so slowly!'

'You were very patient,' Catherine told her. She leaned forward to take off her soft fawn cardigan. 'How beautifully warm it is here! And you're looking positively marvellous, my dear!'

Rose was dressed in a frock in her favourite navy, a colour which always flattered her dark looks, and her hair was taken up in a swinging ponytail. Catherine was noticing for the first time just how beautiful Rose could look. Her face had always been attractive, arresting even, but now, the one ingredient which had been lacking before – the bloom of happiness – had transformed her.

'You must work hard with all these children, but I must say you don't look at all worn down by it.'

'Well, we've got Anna Lucia. And Paulo's been around a lot – though that'll change when he's back to being a doctor. I s'pose it is tough, but I love doing it, that's all. Doing what you like isn't too difficult is it?'

When Catherine had settled into the tiny spare bedroom, Rose showed her round. It was a spacious house, with five bedrooms and plenty of room to accommodate the growing 'family' downstairs.

'The surgery will be here,' Rose said, opening up a

room beside the front door. 'It was where Paulo's father worked, so he can soon get it all set up again.'

The room must have been much as the older Dr Falcone had left it, with shelves of books and an old wooden desk with a crucifix hanging behind it. Against the opposite wall stood a high, flat examination bed.

After their little tour she led Catherine out of the back door of the house. They sat out on a terrace where so much grass had grown up between the stones that they were almost completely hidden. Rose found some old wooden chairs on which there was still some peeling brown paint.

The scents of honeysuckle and other flowers that Catherine could not identify filled the air, and pink bougainvillea burst its colour all over the wall along one side of the garden. On the dry grass under the trees Falcone was entertaining the children by teaching them to turn somersaults, while Anna Lucia stood by giggling.

'He's very good with them.' Catherine watched Rose carefully as she looked over at her husband, happy to see the love so plain in her eyes. She had come to feel as protective towards Rose as if she were her own daughter and she was anxious to see her happy.

'He's so much freer now – laughs more than I've ever known. Hilda loves him, she really does. He's the first proper dad she's ever had. Of course her real father was special to her, but he could never play with her. And she's teaching him English! I think she's picking up Italian quicker though.' She turned to Catherine. 'Tell me how things are at home. Any news?'

'Well, most of it's reasonably good. I stopped by in Birmingham on the way. Grace sends all her love of course, and . . .' She paused. 'I asked her if she'd like to come out and see you both.'

'You mean . . .?'

Catherine held up a hand, embarrassed. 'I'd love to help. Don't say any more.'

'Oh, thank you!' Rose actually clapped her hands together with delight.

'Paulo!' She shouted across to him. 'Catherine is going to send Grace over to see us!'

He smiled and waved back, and was promptly toppled to the ground by the two four-year-olds who shrieked with laughter. Rose and Catherine laughed too.

'I can't get over how fast Birmingham is changing,' Catherine said. 'All those tall buildings going up. Real skyscrapers. Of course you'll have seen a lot of it, but the centre of the city seems to be altering almost beyond recognition. They're going to redo the Bull Ring completely you know.'

'I know.' Rose sighed. 'Sometimes I wonder if I'll know any of it if I go back. In a way I'm glad not to see it happening.'

'But the big news is that they're going to demolish Catherine Street and all the others round it.'

'What? Grace never told me.'

'She's only just heard. Apparently they've got the choice of moving out somewhere on the edge of the city or having one of the new flats close by. Grace says she's determined to stay near the same spot. She thinks the suburbs will be all kippers and curtains and your father would embarrass her by still insisting on cutting up his squares of newspaper for the lavatory. She made me laugh over it in fact. And he seems prepared to do whatever she wants. To tell you the truth, he barely said a word the whole time I was there.'

'That's Dad for you,' Rose said. 'Poor old Grace, though. He always had a soft spot for her and she's never really had a break from him. I don't s'pose he'd have lived for long with me even if I had stayed around to let him. We'd have fought like blooming alley cats.'

'Grace seemed remarkably cheerful, I thought.'

'I don't half miss her,' Rose said thoughtfully. 'Fancy the old place going, though. I knew they were going to get round to it some time, but it really will be the end of an era. Can't picture Grace in a new flat. But then I 'spect she can't picture me over here either.'

'There is one piece of bad news,' Catherine said hesitantly. 'Your brother George has been arrested. In Glasgow.'

'Glasgow?'

'That's where he went, evidently, on your money and mine. Oh yes, Grace wasn't going to let me go without putting me straight about that. For goodness sake, Rose, you should have told me. I wouldn't have been angry. Anyway, for some reason he gave the police the Birmingham address. Perhaps he hasn't got a fixed abode up there.'

'What's he done this time then?'

Catherine shifted her gaze to the ground. 'I'm not certain.'

Rose looked at her closely. 'You *do* know, don't you?'

Catherine gave a painful sigh. 'Well, all right, yes. He's been acting as a pimp. Lining his pockets quite successfully I gather.'

Rose's mouth fell open. 'A pimp? My God. All that time he was with me! To think – what did I have in my house?'

She sat silent, shocked, until Catherine thought of something else.

'A more cheerful piece of news. Grace said she'd heard from Alcester. One of the twins? Apparently she's recently had her first baby. A little boy called Jimmy.'

Rose smiled, shaking her head in wonder. 'Dear little Susan. Fancy.'

They spent an uproarious few hours when the older children arrived back from school. Hilda, a tanned and healthy ten-year-old, was thrilled to find someone else in the house who spoke English, and chatted away non-stop to Catherine.

Once they were all fed and in their beds and Anna Lucia had gone home, Rose cooked a meal for the three of them. They ate in what was still the dining room of the

421

house, with its dark, formal furniture. Rose put candles on the table. A bowl of nectarines and green grapes glistened in the light at the centre of it.

They ate tagliatelle and fried fish, with a salad of huge, succulent tomatoes by the side of it, and drank the rather harsh local red wine.

Catherine watched Rose and Falcone together. She found she liked him immensely. Though most conversation had to take place through Rose, she noticed that he listened attentively when she talked, as if eager to make out her words. Every so often he would join in a joke with them, exploding into wholehearted laughter which transformed his rather serious face. Sometimes when he laughed he would reach over and touch Rose's hand for a second, and Catherine saw her smile back at him, the shadows from the candles moving tenderly over her face.

She asked Falcone, 'How are people reacting to you now that you're back here? They must know you've been a priest?'

'There's been some disapproval, from a few. Those who did not know my family mainly. But the welcome we have had I owe entirely to my father.' He laughed softly. 'It's the reverse of what it says in the Bible – that a prophet is never welcome in his home town.'

'Also you're a doctor and you and your wife are caring for children who would otherwise be destitute?'

'I'm sure that also helps,' he agreed.

'And you have made an old woman from England very happy with your Orfanotrofio Diana,' she told them, slightly self-mocking.

'Old, my foot,' Rose interrupted.

Looking at the two of them and what they were creating here, Catherine knew she had before her a strong couple. She was longing to tell Ronald about them already. It was all so right. So improbable at first sight, but so entirely right.

'I must toast your future,' she said, raising her glass of

422

the inky red wine. 'Here's to the Orfanotrofio Diana – and to you both, with all my heart.'

They raised their glasses.

It was a time of night that Rose always loved, and on this night it was particularly special. When her husband was asleep, his hands resting softly against the curve of her back, she slipped off the huge, lumpy bed and went to sit for a while by the window. She opened the shutters a crack so that she could just see the half-moon casting its light on the trees behind the house.

She was excited and stirred up by all the news from England, and at the same time had a sense of enormous joy in her life. She was becoming certain that she would have another piece of news to tell first Paulo and then Catherine this week: that soon she would be adding another child to the household, a real brother or sister for Hilda after all this time.

She sat for some time with no clear thoughts in her head, just fragments of the day passing through. Then she went quietly out of the room and through the upper floor of the house, looking in on all the children who lived here in their care. Every bed was full tonight with Catherine sleeping at the end of the corridor.

Finally she climbed back into bed beside Falcone's warm body. Impossible as she knew it to be, she fancied as she lay down that she could feel the child moving inside her.

ANNIE MURRAY

Birmingham Friends

Pan Books £5.99

Anna Craven has grown up captivated by stories of her mother's childhood in Birmingham and of Kate's friend, Olivia. Theirs was a magical friendship and Anna has always regretted that with Olivia's tragic death during the war, she will never meet the woman her mother loved so deeply.

But when Kate dies, she leaves her daughter a final story, one that this time tells the whole truth of her life with Olivia Kemp. And as Anna reads, she is shocked to discover how little she really knows about the mother she felt so close to. With Kate's words of caution ringing in her head, she goes in search of the one woman, very much alive, who can answer the urgent questions she now has about Kate's childhood, and even her own . . .

Birmingham Friends was first published in Pan as *Kate and Olivia*.

> 'A meaty family saga with just the right mix
> of mystery and nostalgia'
> *Parents Magazine*

ANNIE MURRAY

Birmingham Blitz

Pan Books £5.99

Genie Watkins, a Birmingham kid, dreams of having a proper happy family like her Italian friend, Teresa.

But it's August 1939. Genie hasn't reckoned with the outbreak of war, her already rocky family being split up and the strangely liberating effect it all has on her mother. Narrated in the cheeky, courageous voice of Genie, the disasters that follow display her powerful capacity for survival. Under skies darkened by blackout she tries to hold her family together, keeps up her spirits with her nan and glamorous Auntie Lil, shares her fears and hopes with Teresa and amid it all discovers love . . .

Family life seems set to be destroyed as violently as the city streets around them. But from the rubble come extra-ordinary surprises, glimpses of hope – and, above all, a miraculous resilience.

'A tale of passion and empathy which
will keep you hooked'
Woman's Own

ANNIE MURRAY

Orphan of Angel Street

Pan Books £5.99

A vivid story of love and courage

Abandoned at birth, little Mercy Hanley shows a fierce
determination few others can match. Her inner fire burns
brightly, even in the harsh conditions of turn-of-the-century
Birmingham.

For behind Mercy's pale and haunting face, there is a mind
of steel, as her harsh foster mother, Mrs Gaskin, soon
discovers. Beatings, threats and poverty cannot halt Mercy's
efforts to improve herself, or to create a new life for Susan,
Mrs Gaskin's crippled daughter.

Even in the worst times, it is as if someone is watching
over Mercy. Willing her to succeed . . .

Through the dark shadow of world war, Mercy continues
her fight for survival. She will first earn her freedom and
security. Then at long last she can give her love . . .

'Full of warmth and domestic detail which inspires
the reader, Annie Murray brings her characters
and their neighbourhood vividly to life'
Denise Robertson